Y0-DMC-589

DATE DUE

PRINTED IN U.S.A.

29096

The Case Of Mrs. Wingate

AMS PRESS
NEW YORK

"Then, on our wedding night," said Mrs. Wingate after a pause, "he broke down and made a *shocking* confession!"

THE CASE OF *Mrs.* WINGATE

By
OSCAR MICHEAUX

Author of
"THE WIND FROM NOWHERE"

BOOK SUPPLY COMPANY
Publishers
40 MORNINGSIDE AVENUE
NEW YORK
1945

Library of Congress Cataloging in Publication Data

Micheaux, Oscar, 1884-
    The case of Mrs. Wingate.

    Reprint of the 6th ed. published by Book Supply Co.,
New York.
    I. Title.
PZ3.M5809Cas5   [PS3525.I1875]   813'.5'2   73-18593
ISBN 0-404-11404-0

Reprinted from an original copy in the collections
of the University of Iowa Libraries

From the edition of 1945, New York
First AMS edition published in 1975
Manufactured in the United States of America

AMS PRESS INC.
NEW YORK, N. Y. 10003

To

ALICE B.

LEADING CHARACTERS
IN THE ORDER OF APPEARANCE

HEINRICH SCHULTZ
> A Negro Nazi spy, sent by Adolf Hitler to the U.S.A. to report on American activities from the Negro sections.

KERMIT EARLY
> Assisting him from the inside. A highly educated but mysterious Negro, who is dissatisfied with the way his race are treated in America.

FLORENCE WINGATE
> Wife of a millionaire textile magnate, who becomes strangely involved with Kermit Early, and is the cause of his peculiar silence.

SIDNEY WYETH
> A Motion Picture Producer and Author, who refuses to make a "hate" picture Kermit Early has written, and around whom much of the story revolves.

MARIE COLEMAN
> His assistant.

EDRINA VINSON
> A stage-struck actress, who didn't mean Sidney Wyeth any good.

BERTHA SCHULTZ
> Heinrich's sister. Sent to America to assist her brother, who fell in love, and changed her view point.

HANS SCHILLER
> A German secret agent, in charge of subversive activities in America.

DR. GUSTAVE VON BARWIG
> A ruthless and heartless Nazi who, angered by Bertha's falling in love with an American, orders her to commit a diabolical act.

TIME: 1939 through 1944.

PLACE: AMERICA.

The Case Of Mrs. Wingate

CHAPTER I

THE EUROPA, Transatlantic Luxury Liner was three days out of New York, Bremen, Germany, bound. This was, of course, prior to September 3, 1939.

It was a beautiful morning in the late summer of a year the world was soon not to forget. The sea was both calm and smooth, as smooth as glass, hardly a ripple other than that stirred by the forward driving of the huge liner, visible on the surface of the water. Every stateroom on the liner was not only taken but filled, upper and lower, to the port holes. Passengers had been informed on arrival at the pier in New York that they would have to share their quarters with others, reasons for which became obvious a few days later.

The people of the world were in a state of apprehension. Every newspaper in America, England and the world over was blazing in conspicuous headlines that negotiations regarding the fifteen mile corridor to Danzig through Poland, had been suspended, and that Adolf Hitler was preparing to invade Poland. England and France had clarified their positions: that they were through with appeasing Hitler, and that if he invaded Poland, there would be war. His answer was to continue the preparations he was making.

Aboard the liner, Germans returning to the fatherland, said that the Jews were the cause of it, that in some strange and peculiar way, they were directly and indirectly responsible for every war that had swept Europe since before Napoleon. In the debates going on all over the ship, those of German sympathies declared that among those involved with the Jews in the threatened outbreak was no other than Franklin D. Roosevelt, president of the United States. They argued that Poland would have let Hitler have the corridor that he was demanding, if England and France hadn't urged Poland not to grant it, that they would back up and protect her, but that England and France would never have taken the stand they did if

Roosevelt had not assured them that America stood solidly behind them and not to appease Hitler any further.

But our story is not a history of the outbreak of World War number two, but about some of the circumstances that was the result of it.

Among the passengers returning to Germany aboard the liner on this final trip across the seas was one Baron Otto Von Mueller and his wife, the Baroness Ernestine. Baron Otto was an important figure and high up in the affairs of the National Socialist party in Germany. He was one of the few aristocrats of the old school, active in Hitler's set-up, who still retained his titles and estates, which were near Potsdam.

Baron Otto and his fraulein at the moment were standing by the rail of the steamer, gazing out across the sea when they were attracted by footsteps and a shadow, which crossed behind them, as a man walked up to the rail a few feet away and leaned his elbows thereon. They turned slightly and gazed across at him, then turned to each other, exchanging expressions of curiosity. As if by instinct, they turned their faces again toward the stranger, studied him a moment, then turned to each other again in curiosity.

"I wonder who that young man is," mused the Baron idly, and turned again to glance over his shoulder at him. The steamer was in high speed, doing about thirty knots an hour and the spray from below sprinkled their faces with salt water, from which they did not turn because, combined with the soft morning air, it was rather pleasant.

"A Negro, too," replied the Baroness, after another glance at him. "Yes, I've been wondering who he could be."

"He doesn't look exactly like the colored people we saw in America, yet he must be one of them," ventured the Baron.

"Maybe he's an actor or a musician. We often see them in Germany." The Baron turned and glanced at the Negro again, then shook his head.

"No. He is neither. Doesn't have that kind of appearance. And I'm not even sure if he is an American Negro." The Baron was thoughtful a moment, as if trying to recall something. Then, continued.

"Now that I remember, I heard him giving an order in the salon this morning, and in perfect German."

"Then he is not an American Negro," she said. "It's possible that he could be a German after all. We do have a few, especially in the Rhineland since the last war."

"But he couldn't be," said the Baron. "He is obviously older than any of them."

Again they surveyed the object of their curiosity, who seemed completely unconcerned and as completely oblivious of their presence as well as curiosity. Instead, he drew away on a cigarette, flecked the ashes from the end of it and gazed out over the waters. The Baron turned to his wife, his eyebrows puckered.

"The more I look at him," he said, "the more I seem to recall having seen him before somewhere. Must have been a long time ago, but there is something familiar about his face. I have a peculiar feeling, away in the back of my head, that I've seen him somewhere."

"Maybe you saw him in America after all. Maybe in Washington. We saw lots of nice looking, highly educated colored people down there. Maybe he is one of the professors of that big colored school we drove by one day, the one on the hill, above Washington. Many of them might speak German. Many—" the Baron again cut her off by a shake of his head, his eyebrows contracted.

"No. He is, I'd wager, not a professor, either. And if he was, he would have spoken German slowly, picking each word and he would have had an accent. This man spoke it as well as I do, without any hesitation whatsoever. No. It must have been in Germany and some years ago, for had it been lately, I would remember it."

"Then, if so, whereabouts in Germany?" his wife insisted.

"I can't recall, Ernestine, I can't recall."

"Well," she said, with a sort of sigh, "since we're both so curious regarding him, why not try to find out who he is? It should prove somewhat of a diversion. I've been rather bored during the whole trip. Almost nobody we know to talk to. So do some thinking and some planning and find a way to get information about this curiosity," she finished blandly.

"That's a poor way to put it, Ernestine," he said, in disapproval.

"I understand, Otto," she exclaimed apologetically. "I'm bored and I'd appreciate something to lift me out of the dumps, as they say in America. Out of the dumps," and she laughed lightly to herself.

At that moment dinner was announced and turning, they made their way across the deck toward the dining room, turning as they reached it, to see the colored man heading the same way.

It was some time before they were seated at a table and their order taken. Then, and what to them seemed an unusual coincidence, when they looked up from the menu, it was right into the face of the colored stranger. All started, exchanged glances, then turned to him and bowed respectfully. He returned the bow and they had a chance in that glance to study him more closely.

He was obviously handsome. He possessed a strong chin, eyes full set but determined. Closer to him, they could see that he was German all right. He possessed all the characteristics, even though one of his parents was obviously a Negro. He wore his hair, which was curly, in an attractive pompadour. He was obviously tall, though they could not tell how tall he was since he was seated.

It was not until they were leaving the dining salon and had bumped into him as they were coming through the door, that the Baron got his opportunity to speak to him without just "butting" in.

"Oh, pardon me, please," cried the Baron, smiling.

"As much my fault as yours, Baron. I accept your apology, and in turn, offer you mine," said the Negro. The Baron started, then smiled relieved. The Baroness smiled too.

"Oh, you know me?" said the Baron in surprise, drawing his wife to one side to be out of the way of people, going in and out of the salon.

"Yes, I know you, Baron Von Mueller," he said, easily, and smiled. "I can see that you've forgotten me, however."

"Indeed, but this is a pleasure." He paused to turn to the Baroness. "He knows me, Ernestine. Now I'm sure that I've seen him before."

"He's been insisting that he had," she said.

"Oh, pardon me again, my fellow," cried the Baron hastily. "This is my wife, the Baroness Ernestine Von Mueller, Mr. or is it Herr?"

"Just plain Heinrich Schultz, Baron Otto, of Berlin, thank you," he said. Turning to the Baroness, he removed his hat and acknowledged the introduction. The Baroness extended her hand.

"Now let us find seats," cried the Baron, "before they're all taken.

A frightful crowd aboard this liner. I've never been surrounded by so many people in all the trips I have made on it."

"Lots of people," said Schultz. They started across the deck, the Baron leading, but nervously glancing at the Negro.

"I'm anxious to get seated somewhere and comfortably and hear you tell where it was you met me. Now—"

"By the way, Baron," suggested Schultz, "we can perhaps find seats at the lower end of the ship. It's shaded down there at this hour and might be more comfortable."

"A brilliant idea, my good fellow," cried the Baron, gratefully, "A brilliant idea indeed!"

They turned now and a few minutes later were seated comfortably at the rear of the liner, where they could see the water as it was being churned by the propellers, driving the great ship forward, homeward bound to Germany.

"Now," said the Baron, removing his hat and relaxing. "I want to tell you at the outset that the Baroness and I were very curious about you."

"We've been wondering who you were ever since leaving New York. So now if you won't mind telling us, we'll be very pleased," said the Baroness, anxious to get into the conversation.

"Now, Herr Schultz, where did you know me and how long ago was it?"

"And how do you, a—colored man," interjected the Baroness, before Schultz could answer, "happen to speak such perfect German?"

"Well," said Schultz. "I should. I was born in Germany."

The Baron and his lady started, exchanged expressions, then looked again at Schultz.

"You—were—born in—Germany?" exclaimed the Baron, a bit incredulously. Turned to look at the Baroness, then turned his eyes back to Schultz.

"I was born in Germany," Schultz nodded. "My mother is living there now, also some sisters and brothers."

"And was it there—in Germany, I mean," said the Baron, "that you—knew me?"

Schultz nodded and smiled.

"Born in Germany," mused the Baroness, as if to herself. "You, a colored man, born in Germany?"

"Oh, there are quite a number of colored people in the Reich who were born there, especially since a portion of the Rhineland was garrisoned by colored troops after the last war," said Schultz.

"So you got started after the occupation," said the Baron.

"No, I was born shortly after the war started. The occupation was after it was over."

"Naturally," said the Baron hastily.

"Now as regards to where I knew you," said Schultz. "Do you remember a colored boy who used to shine your shoes in the lobby of the foreign office in Berlin? They called him Henry?"

Gazing quickly at him, the Baron's eyes flashed in recognition.

"Little Henry! Well—" he exclaimed. "Do you mean to tell me that you are—that lad?"

"That lad grown up, Baron. I am little Henry."

"Well, I declare!" the Baron exclaimed and reaching out, grasped Schultz's hand and holding it tightly, looked across at the Baroness.

"Do you remember, Ernestine that I used to tell you about the little colored boy who shined my shoes, who seemed so ambitious and always on the job? Well," he said, relaxing but still holding onto Schultz's hand, "This is that little boy, grown into a fine, big man!"

"Hold on, Otto," the Baroness spoke up quickly, her eyes flashing somewhat triumphantly. "I happen to have known him also when he was still that active little shoe-shine boy, as you call him." The Baron turned to her in surprise.

"You?" he repeated.

"Yes Otto. The times I met you at the foreign office I noticed him shining shoes and on several occasions I had him shine mine, too."

"This is indeed a pleasure," said the Baron, finally relaxing his grip on Schultz's hand. "A pleasure that is most interesting." He turned again, more calm now, to look Schultz up and down. "Grown into a fine, tall, handsome young man."

"And is he handsome!" cried the Baroness, admiringly. Both paused to look at Schultz anew. They seemed to admire him.

"Well, tell me, my lad," said the Baron. "What has been happening since? You seemed to have gone places. In fact, you *must have* gone places, returning to Germany—like this," and the Baron pointed at him.

"I'm returning to Germany, Baron. It is still my home, although I've been in America on—on business for the past few months."

"Indeed! Do you mind telling us something about yourself? We are interested."

"We are *very* interested," added the Baroness.

"Shipboard, you understand, Herr Schultz, is a good place to make acquaintances; it is a still better one to resume old ones," and the Baron and his wife laughed lightly.

The Baron paused and glanced skyward. The sun was now shining straight down on them.

"The sun," said he, glancing up at it with a frown, "seems to have caught up with us, and it is a bit warm."

"Very warm," added the Baroness. "It is uncomfortable."

"Why can't we retire to our stateroom? It will be pleasant down there now with a port hole open," suggested the Baron.

"Why not?" said the Baroness, rising to her feet. The others followed. The Baron took Schultz's arm, bowing somewhat astutely. "Do you mind going with us?"

"I don't mind."

"Just a minute, Otto," said Baroness Ernestine, as they started away. "Perhaps the young man has some one—"

"I'm all alone, Baroness Ernestine," said Schultz quickly.

"So we continue as we started," said the Baron, as they proceeded to their cabin.

A few minutes later they were seated comfortably in the Baron's stateroom, where they resumed their conversation.

"Now, my good fellow, time is on our hands and we're in the mood to hear your story."

"I'm sure it must be interesting," smiled the Baroness.

"It's got to be interesting. From a shoe shine boy to a—what?"

"Not so fast, Baron Otto," laughed Schultz. "Not so fast. It might be From shoe-shine boy to a gangster, and, since I'm traveling as you see me, to a 'big-time gangster.' 'Big shots,' they call them in America."

Both paused uncertainly and glanced at each other. Schultz quickly patted the Baron on the arm as if to reassure him, which caused the Baron to smile again.

"Nothing like that, I assure you."

"Start with when you left your job in the foreign office lobby." suggested the Baron.

"No, Otto. I want to hear the story of his birth; about his father and mother, and how he happened to be—in Germany."

"Sure," cried the Baron, enthusiastically. "That's the place to start."

"Who was your mother, your father. Which one was colored," inquired the Baroness. "Start from the beginning—tell us your whole story."

"There's nothing so interesting about it as all that, I assure you," smiled Schultz, modestly. "But since you insist, I'll try to tell it. When you've been bored enough, I'll try to understand and finish before you begin to sigh." And then he laughed deprecatingly.

"We will not sigh, because we will not be bored."

"Just like going to an exciting motion picture and listening to interesting dialogue. That never bores anybody," assured the Baroness.

"My mother was, or is, for she is still living, and as I think I remarked, in Germany."

"'See,' said the Baron, thoughtfully. "Then—it is your father who is colored?"

"My father was colored; an American Negro who got into Germany shortly before the last war. He was a cook."

"Pardon me for again interrupting," said the Baroness, leaning forward. "But in reference to your father. You say *'was'?*"

"*Was*, because—he is dead. But before he died, he took up residence in Germany—just stayed there. Meanwhile, he met my mother who was a waitress in the hotel, where he cooked, they soon learned to like each other. She taught him to speak German and in due time, married him. A year later, I made my appearance," he paused now to smile at the humor of it, in which they joined.

"And still two years later a sister came. They had two children, then, a boy and a girl and were very happy. Then the war broke out! The call of the sea got into my father's blood again and he finally shipped out aboard the Emden."

"The Emden!" the others exclaimed, awed.

"The famous raider!" echoed the Baron, ominously. They were beginning to understand now why Schultz's father *was* dead. They looked at Schultz, whose head was bowed. He reached over and patted his wrist kindly, and shook his head sadly.

"The greatest Raider the world ever knew," said the Baron, reminiscently. "The Emden did her part for the Fatherland."

"As you perhaps recall, Baron," Schultz was saying. "The British finally caught up with her."

"Yes, I remember all about it, my boy. Caught up with her and sent her to the bottom off the coast of South America."

"Well," said Schultz, sighing. "That was the end of the Emden, and —"

"—all of those aboard her. Both my wife and I recall the whole, tragic story."

"We never saw him again," said Schultz.

"War is a terrible thing. And we are on the verge of another. If I had my way, which is not as the Fuehrer sees it, there wouldn't be any. We should wait—at least a year, as I see it, before invading Poland. But—" and the Baron shrugged his shoulders, helplessly, throwing out his hands as he did so.

"Let Herr Schultz go ahead with his story, Otto. We won't get into another war, at least until the Feuhrer invades Poland."

"When the war was over, my mother took my sister and moved down into the Rhineland. Maybe you recall that they had stationed some colored soldiers from America there?"

"We remember all about it, my lad," said the Baron.

"She met another colored man down there. A very fine fellow. They started going together and later he married her. When the troops were withdrawn and returned to America, my mother went with him and took us children.

"We had started grade school before leaving Germany, so we continued after reaching America. My mother spoke English very well and had taught us as best she could, but our stepfather was well-educated and in America, where we heard nothing but English, except from our mother at home, we went right through grade school and entered High School in the fall when our step-father died. As quickly as my mother could adjust matters, she moved back to Germany. Her husband had left some $10,000 worth of compensation insurance, which was sent to my mother in installments by the United States Government and that was a great help to her in sending us through school back in Germany. That was during the time I shined shoes to help out, and when I used to see you at the foreign office."

"Now we are up to when you left your work in the lobby of the foreign office."

"I left there to go to college."

"To college?" said the Baroness. "That was nice. Where?"

"Heidelberg."

"Oh," cried the Baron. "To Heidelberg? Great school!"

"After we finished Heidelberg, our mother wanted us to know French. I wanted to take a course in diplomacy. My sister refused to let me go alone. So she sent us both to the Sorbonne in Paris."

"Now we're getting somewheres," said the Baroness. "After the Sorbonne, what?"

"A job back in the foreign office."

"But not shining shoes any longer," she said and they all smiled.

"No," said Schultz. "In an office. I was interested in America from the German standpoint. I felt I could be of service to the Reich by returning to America to study the conditions, treatment and reactions regarding the Negro there."

"Being of Negro extraction, I can see your point," said the Baron.

"Thank you," replied Schultz. "I don't like the way America treats Negroes. They continually play them down, down, down, until most of them are in a way, discouraged and do not know it. It is deplorable that so many people, 13,000,000 of them, should be treated so."

"Yet President Roosevelt has been fomenting a war because of the way he feels we are treating the Jews," said the Baron.

"When and if war comes, we shall always blame the Jews and President Roosevelt for it," cried the Baroness, vehemently.

"What did you learn about the Jewish situation, if anything, in particular, in America?" inquired the Baron, evenly.

"They are the leading tradesmen there as elsewhere. As regards the Negro, he runs almost everything in their neighborhoods."

"And exploits them unmercifully," said the Baron.

"Unmercifully isn't half of it. In a way they enslave them," said Schultz.

"What is the Negro's reaction?"

"My people," said Schultz, after a brief pause, "seem by nature to be lackadaisical, care-free and easy-going."

"An African characteristic, descended down through hundreds of years."

"But they should be growing away from that by this time," said the Baroness. "I observed that many seemed to be very well educated."

"But education alone has failed to free them," said Schultz, seriously. "Theirs is about the most involved problem I know of. I am deeply interested in it. I have thrown myself into it and have been studying it very closely. While there, among other things, I made a very fine contact. This contact, in particular, happens to be one of the highest educated Negroes in America. He has also made the race question there, his life's study. It is such an involved situation and it cannot be solved in a hurry if ever at all. Yet, as I see it, I can be of great help to the Reich by returning there, going into it heart and soul and keep Germany informed regarding that angle."

"In the event of war, you can, as I see it," said the Baron, "be of great help in that capacity to the Reich. If war fails to result from the Fuehrer's invasion of Poland, the information you can stock in our foreign office will be indispensable and well worth your research."

"That's the way I see it," said Schultz, obviously deeply moved. "Being of Negro extraction, in case of war, I can operate almost without restriction or restraint. Having such a low opinion of the Negro, playing him down at every turn and insisting on confining him to the rôle, I might say of—clown, comedian and idiot, they won't be expecting any of them to be gathering information and reporting on what's going on."

"Man," cried the Baron. "I begin to see your angle. If war comes, they'll be watching every German in America."

"But being of Negro extraction, and living among the colored people, they won't be watching me—unless, of course, I become very careless."

"That is the finest plan I've heard for a long time," cried the Baroness, enthusiastically.

"I think this should be brought to the attention of the Fuehrer himself. You are going to meet him at Berchtesgaden soon after our return, Otto. Why—"

Laying a hand on her wrist and patting it the Baron said, "I'd decided to do so, Ernestine, and I will. Meanwhile, go on, please."

"I'm glad you see and appreciate the logic of it, Baron Otto," said

Schultz, warmly. "I am returning to Germany to take the matter up with Von Ribbentrop, whom I feel sure will agree to my returning to America soon for the purpose I've just explained."

"And you say you've developed satisfactory contact already?"

"Very satisfactory, Baron. This man knows the Negro situation from every angle. He is naturally resentful, as all sensitive and intelligent Negroes are as regards it. So he is willing to work with me. In fact, he is already working with a group of Germans in Chicago and Milwaukee who are financing his efforts thus far and they have the ground work laid in a big way to start things as quickly as we decide to begin.

"Roosevelt is too busy sponsoring the Jewish cause and trying to kick Hitler in the shins, because of having put the Jews in their place in Germany, and letting them fill him full of sympathy—for them and the way Germany is supposed to be treating them, to give much thought to the Negro situation."

"America has been so misinformed regarding the true Jewish situation in Germany, that they simply do not know what it is all about," said Baroness Ernestine, impatiently. Turning to Schultz suddenly, she added. "Do they really love the Jews that much in America?"

Schultz laughed.

"Oh, it's not that bad, Baroness Ernestine," he said, "Nobody pretends to love the Jews, and to the credit of the Jews, I'll admit that they do not want anybody saying and pretending that they do. All the Jew is interested in back there, is making money, and to do so he must cheat, at least does cheat, steal, exploit, lie and do about everything but commit murder. He is the same the world over. In a way, it is their religion, inherent and traditional, and as far as I'm concerned, I just take them as they are and try not to think so much about it."

"A sensible way to look at it, too, Herr Schultz," commented the Baron. Then, after a moment's thought, he turned to Schultz with a new thought.

"Speaking of America's disregard of what the Negro population thinks, and of the tendency to play them down, that's their English tradition. England originated it; that contemptible disregard for the thought, ambition and views of darker peoples. I observed this tendency you speak of while in America, unless they have an emotional interest in some group, like the Chinese at the moment, for instance. Being proud of your country, I presume that you, as most Germans, are given to reading a great deal, Herr Schultz?" queried the Baron.

"Yes, Baron Otto, a very great deal, some of it, current works of fiction and the more serious magazines and books."

"Then do a bit of reflecting. Although Japan is obviously one of the great nations of the earth, you rarely observed any books in America translated from the Japanese. Now did you?"

After a brief reflection, Schultz shook his head in the negative. "No, I did not."

"I know you didn't because it wasn't there. Yet, you don't have to think very hard to recall a number of books, translated from the Chinese, do you?"

"A long list of titles," said Schultz. Turning to the Baroness and nodding his head vigorously, then back to Schultz.

"Just picture how stupid! It confirms what we are talking about. Only when they are emotionally inclined, do they evidence an interest in the darker peoples."

"That's what I found right there in America, Baron. People, who were born there, been living there since the country was settled, almost. And as you say, the same thing obtains also in England, but they are more diplomatic and cunning as regards it."

"Well, for your benefit, Herr Schultz, if you don't already know it, some day America is going to awake, or be awakened to a sudden realization that they're making a serious mistake as regards Japan. Instead of meddling with the way we are supposed to be treating the poor, persecuted Jew in Germany, America had better begin to read some Japanese books and acquaint themselves with what Japan may be thinking, planning, and doing. If they do, they might get a shock," insisted the Baron, shaking his head, sagely.

"It has never crossed their minds. The rich Jewish politicians with their money and their propaganda are completely in the spotlight over there. Nobody seems to be concerned about what Japan is thinking or may be planning to do," said Schultz. "But that isn't America half as much as it is Roosevelt. In truth, the masses of Americans are resenting it. They don't care any more about the

Jews in America than we do in Germany. I found a great undercurrent of resentment and hatred back there which someday will break out suddenly."

"He has managed to hoodwink the American people for the time being, but in due time there'll come a day of reckoning."

"And when it does, watch things begin to happen," and Herr Schultz laughed ironically.

"You've been over there several months, how is he able to do it, Herr Schultz?" inquired the Baron, crossing a leg and lighting a cigarette. Passing them around, he looked at Schultz and waited for him to answer.

"It began in the election of 1932. In the throes of a great depression and impatience, they voted Hoover out, because they charged him with the country's condition, although he wasn't responsible for it any more than you or I. But they were impatient and promptly voted against him at the election in 1932. They were not at the time, voting half as much for Roosevelt, as they were against Hoover. Anybody on the democratic ticket would have been elected. It happened to be Roosevelt who was running. Elected he immediately began to spend.

"First, since there are more labor votes than there are in any other group, he led labor to feel that they would be allowed to take over industry and run it, which meant, according to their philosophy, shorter hours and more pay. They got it, with five days work a week, six days pay, forced by sit down strikes.

"The Jewish votes meant something: their money to help finance the campaign, more. To get this, he began the fight on Hitler which may plunge the whole world, indirectly into war before it's all over. He implied that if they would vote for him and help carry New York where their greatest power is concentrated, he'd kick Hitler on the shins and make him behave himself."

The Baron and his wife laughed.

"We come down now to the poor people and the Negroes, the disorganized elements, but who comprise the greatest number of votes of all. Relief checks got them. They labored under the impression that 'he was taking it away from the rich, the dirty, cruel rich people, and giving it to the poor,' which, as they put it, was the way it ought to be. So he got their votes almost in toto."

Again the Baroness and the Baron laughed heartily. Schultz himself was compelled to laugh.

"Well, it's too long a story for me to tell. I wouldn't finish by the time we reach Bremen, so I'm going to lay off now," and he took his handkerchief and dried his forehead.

"You have certaintly acquainted yourself with the conditions in America, all right, Herr Schultz," said the Baron.

"And how!" cried the Baroness, "as they say in America. You know the answers, and Baron Otto, I assure you, will talk the whole matter over with the Fuehrer when we meet him at Berchtesgaden in a fortnight."

All rose to their feet and prepared to go on deck again. It was late afternoon, and was delightful on the broad decks. Smiling, a few minutes later they were strolling together there, looking out over the sea, which was beginning to get rough. The sky had become overcast and there was a suggestion of rain that might develop into a storm before morning.

CHAPTER II

WE PROCEED now to introduce the second important character, Herr Heinrich Schultz, of Berlin, being the first, in the development of our story. So let us now meet Mr. Kermit Early, A.B. of Atlanta University, M.A. of the University of Chicago, and finally the crowning degree, Ph.D. of Harvard. Kermit Early was the contact Schultz referred to in his conversation with the Baron and Baroness Von Mueller, and was considered one of the most highly educated Negroes in America.

Tall and brown, growing a bit ponderous around the waistline with age, Kermit was not exactly what colored women referred to as a "pretty" man, but he was handsome. His hair was soft and curly, threatening at this period of his rather strange and unusual life, of growing thin just above the forehead. It was Early's eyes, however, that attracted one's attention more than anything else. He had pretty eyes, noticeable the moment one met him.

His thorough academic training was reflected in his appearance. No one could meet him the second time without concluding that he was anything but a man of great mental training. Nevertheless, Kermit Early had been embarrassed as almost every intelligent and dignified Negro has been, at one time or another, in his career by having some white man snap his finger at him and call: "hey, boy," and offer him a quarter to carry his luggage or do some other menial task.

A portion—the greater portion, in fact, of the training he had acquired had been during the past six years and since he had been graduated from high school back there in Wakefield, Georgia, where it had all begun.

Early represented a strange and peculiar position in American society. To begin with, for the past several years he seemed to have gone out of circulation, as it were. Before that time and shortly after finishing school and getting his final degree, he had been very popular, although during his entire career nobody had learned or knew very much about him. He was too highly educated to talk to and mix carelessly with the current run of Negroes, or to have much in common with them. He persisted, however, in the statement that he was a "race" man, which about every Negro claims to be, educated or otherwise.

But as we started to explain, nobody, however, knew much about Kermit Early, with all his literary training. In due time you will understand why they did not. Like a great many educated Negroes in America, Early was dissatisfied. With all his training, he had not, as most Negroes, learned much if anything about the art of making money. Early insisted that nobody in America seemed to know how to do that but Jews. So it's little wonder how and why he had become allied, with a subversive group, operating out of Chicago and Milwaukee, and had come to hate Jews as others did, blamed them and America for any adverse condition that existed anywhere and when and where it did not exist, by their conduct, debate and discussion, they built it up and made it adverse.

The pro-Germans whom he had long since been operating with as an associate, were agreeable to blaming America for the way the Negro was treated, and which, of course, was due to their contact with Kermit, who had not, we repeat, and as most Negroes, learned the art of making money. Rarely did they blame themselves for it. It was far easier to charge it up to race prejudice, on the part of the white man and to hate him as most educated Negroes do, regardless.

Since all subversive groups realized that it was unpopular to preach their philosophy from the housetops, or to talk with anybody but those known to share their views, it is clear that few if any Negroes, therefore, knew much about Kermit Early.

He didn't even fraternize with women, which so many had tried to encourage him to do. Some wondered if he cared for women, for if he didn't, he must be a *fairy*, but none ever got well enough acquainted with him, except a few years back when he had taken a part in the promotion of Negro fairs, pagentries and the like and as far as they knew, he wasn't a *fairy* or a *pie face*, nor was he charged with *going into the bushes,* various Negro terms for perversion.

Almost immediately after securing his Doctorate from Harvard,

Early became affiliated as co-editor of a so-called socialist publication, the other editor being A. Phillip Merivale. It was during this short-lived period as co-editor that Kermit Early reached his greatest popularity.

Up until the depression, Negroes placed a greater value and more importance on education than they did after, since the depression rather let them down in being just educated. It didn't buy food, pay rent or purchase clothing, so a great many, a very great many, were forced onto the WPA. Not Kermit Early. As we shall presently see, at no time in his career, was he ever in any financial danger.

The publication hook-up did not last long, although A. Phillip Merivale and Kermit Early became two of the leading and most popular Negroes in America during the time it did exist. They seemed to represent a new philosophy on Negro life.

Neither was a Republican, or a Democrat, so could not be "bought out" to often sell their race "down the river", by a good job, a scholarship or an award. Nobody knew if either was offered such, but on general principles it was considered that they must have had many offers, for they were welding great influence toward helping or inspiring the Negro to become more militant. It had long since become a custom that when anybody wanted to get rid of a troublesome Negro, who threatened with his big mouth to make matters unpleasant, the best way to shut his mouth was to give him a good job, good only from a Negro standpoint.

After that he invariably launched on a career of "keeping Negroes quiet," by going about the country making speeches and advising those who persisted in insisting that "something ought to be done," in reminding them that "the time wasn't right" for that and that and so and so. In such instances, the time *never* became right and after the first or second burst of steam on the part of the persistent Negro, the matter usually died and most soon forgot what they were "persisting about." We have, let us pause to explain, digressed so completely from the story we started out to tell, that we must apologize. We will now try to return to it, by discussing Kermit Early, and what had transpired in his life before leaving Wakefield.

It was late afternoon around the same time Heinrich Schultz and Baron Von Mueller were returning to Germany. Early entered an apartment building, crossed from the elevator, turned a corner, went a few steps, then turned into an alcove at the end of which was a door. It was one of those deluxe Apartment buildings on the south side of Chicago which Negroes had run white people out of when they invaded the section a few years before. This building was one of the finest on the south side, and accordingly, one of the most expensive.

Inserting his key, Early opened the door, glanced at several parcels of mail, mostly advertising, on the floor, including a few letters, stepped across the threshold, closed the door, stopped, picked up the letters and what nots, sorted through them as he crossed the room and entered a comfortable living room. As he did so, his eyes fell on one letter, post-marked Atlanta, and sent via air mail the day before. He smiled indulgently at it as he recognized the handwriting. He was always pleased to receive letters with that handwriting. The writer was his one great pleasure, diversion and sole interest in life. He decided to make himself comfortable before breaking the seal.

So laying everything on the table where he paused, he crossed the room, removed his coat and hat, and took a comfortable robe from a hanger, and which the writer of the letter referred to, had made him a present of the Christmas before. He then walked into his bedroom, removed his shoes, carrying the robe with him, loosened his tie, unbuttoned his collar, exchange his shoes for comfortable house slippers, left his bedroom, crossed into the bathroom where he remained a few minutes, and returned to the sitting room. There he picked up the particular letter, sat down, adjusted himself comfortably, broke the seal, withdrew the contents, spread the sheets out before him and started to read. A moment later he recoiled violently.

"*What's this,*" he cried aloud, sitting erect and gazing excitedly into its contents, which began as follows:

Atlanta, Georgia
Thursday, P. M.

My darling Kermit:

Arrived safe, a week ago, stopping over in Nashville to visit with some friends on my way home. Guess you received my wire in which I explained my delay in reaching home.

I would have written sooner, but I have delayed doing so due to a very important reason. By that, Kermit, dearest, I mean that what I have been praying for is a reality. In short, Kermit, I am pregnant; I'm going to have a baby.

It was this which brought such a shock to the quiet and unassuming Kermit Early. He rose and standing, looked again at the letter.

"*What does she mean — going to have a baby?*" he exclaimed out loud. "*Has she gone crazy? She can't have a baby, — she can't dare to!*" He strolled across the room and then turning, came back, paused, and gazed excitedly into space.

"*But Florence, you can't do this!* Don't you understand? You can't go having a baby! It will spoil everything — *everything!*" He turned and walked the floor again, trying to understand if he was awake, or asleep.

True, she had wanted a baby ever since it all started, but both understood too well why it was insane to even think about it and they had not talked about it much lately except during their moments of sexual excitement, when she always cried, "*I want a baby, I want a baby, Kermit, I want a baby!*"

He sat back down and began to read the paragraph again, hoping that he had been mistaken. But it read the same way the second time, so he went on further into it, hoping that she might be joking.

"I failed to come around again, which is the second month I've missed, so it is obvious that I am in family way, and can look forward in due time to becoming a happy mother as I have so long wanted to."

He rose again from his seat, paralyzed with excitement. "*Has she gone crazy, blind and completely insane,*" he said half to himself, and beat himself with the fist, in which he held the letter.

It is obvious by his actions that the writer was *not* Kermit Early's wife—! That would be enough under ordinary circumstance to upset a man and annoy him when he realized as Kermit Early did, that the forthcoming *blessed event* was his.

The writer was not only *not* Kermit Early's wife, she was a *white woman!* And not only a white woman, but a wealthy and aristocratic white woman, scion of one of the oldest families in the south—and the *wife* of a wealthy white man! the owner of a string of textile mills, stretching from Virginia across both Carolina's to Northern Georgia. Several times a millionaire!

All of which sounds too fantastic to even think of — until we relate how it started, and how it developed. To understand it more fully, let us go back a few years, while Kermit Early was still in high school and Florence Wingate, the writer's name, née, Adair, were both in Wakefield. If you were now back to those days and had lived in Wakefield, you would have heard Florence Adair, as beautiful as a Goddess, referred to as the "prettiest girl in Wakefield" the most shapely, and by those closest to her, but by those only, as *the most passionate!* Her parents were descended from one of those families you meet so often when you travel South, who "had been wealthy — before the civil war," when they owned anywhere from a hundred to a thousand slaves.

It seems that every white person you meet with any ancestral pride and heredity, from the South, has descended from a family who "owned many slaves," during the days of slavery. But Florence Adair's great-grand parents *had* owned many slaves and had been wealthy during that period. They had gradually lost everything until all that was left was a memory and a position of respect among the leading white people of Wakefield. Her father was cashier of one of the two banks, earning enough, by being careful, to maintain their position, to keep the younger children in school and send the girls away to a boarding school, two Negro servants at $2.00 each per week, the balance in food and old clothes. And so we meet the Adairs. Florence had spent two years at a girl's school in Virginia from where the lady dean had written her mother to "be very careful with Florence, always. A lovely girl, kind and good," and as we know, beautiful, — but *so passionate until it was difficult* for her since she was twelve to control it!

"Try to get her married off to some young man as quickly as possible," the dean went on to say in her letter to Florence's mother just before graduation. "Otherwise," she continued, "you might be sorry — and she's too nice a girl for anything sordid to happen to her."

As to Kermit Early, his father was a barber, and so was his father's father. He conducted a barbershop for white trade in Wakefield, now in the third generation of its existence and ownership, so Kermit possessed, as far as Negroes went, tradition of a kind. All his forebears had been educated. His father had shaved and knew most all of the "best white people" in and around Wakefield and had been doing so for years. They were highly respected by these white people. His brothers and sisters had all been to school in Atlanta; some had gone north. His sisters had all married and at no time had any played the role of concubine to white men. Though all were pretty, shapely and attractive, they had escaped this blight and scourge. So Kermit's mother and father, then in the afternoon of their lives, were happy and contented with no plans to go north and get away from the *mean white people* of Georgia.

Kermit finished high school at sixteen and it was around this time when Florence Adair, who knew him and started, in passing the barber shop, by hitting him lightly without letting on and would call. "Hello, Kermit," in reply to which he always smiled and replied. "How do, Miss Florence" and nobody thought anything about it.

It was shortly after Florence returned from the boarding school in Virginia when passing by the barbershop, which was located in the heart of the town's small business section, that she had paused, caught his hand for a brief and fleeting moment, squeezed it and when he looked up in surprise, stuck her tongue out at him and made a mischievous face.

Leonard Warner, his boy friend who worked at the drug store two doors away, had happened by chance, to be looking out the window and saw it. He strolled along a few minutes later, paused, leaned toward him and buzzed:

"Saw that Adair gal squeeze your hand and make a face at you awhile ago. Better be careful, Kermit, that gal's dynamite."

"What do you mean, dynamite?"

"She's as *hot* as hell. Needs a man, plenty of him, but she's too sensible to play around with white boys carelessly. Her mother watches her like a hawk. She don't want nothing to happen."

"Whew!" cried Kermit. "It wouldn't be hard to go for her—and I don't mean maybe."

"I agree with you, but we're down South. Negroes are not supposed to even know pretty white girls like her, and she's the prettiest one in town."

"You're telling me! But take it easy, boy. I ain't thinking about acting a fool."

"If you do, it won't take 'em long to have you dangling from a limb."

"And it's me that knows it. I ain't thinking about Florence Adair."

"But she is about you. I've seen her giving you the goo, goo two or three times."

"Quit your kiddin'."

"I ain't kiddin'. That gal's hot, as hot as fire and I'd be willin" to bet that she would go with a niggah if she had half a chance."

"Not *this* niggah, 'cause I ain't givin' her no chance to get me lynched."

"Every white boy in town would give half his life to just feel her, but she's got plenty sense. She ain't going to let any of them fool around and *set her up.*"

"Wonder if any has ever got next to her?" said Kermit.

The other shook his head. "I doubt it."

"Why?"

"As hot as she is she's got sense enough to realize that if she started playing around, she'd be having every white boy in town."

"That right," said Kermit. "She couldn't control herself."

"But if she could steal into a back room somewhere, she'd take a chance on some nice looking, educated colored boy like you to play with."

"Not me, nevuh." cried Kermit, and laughing, went into the barber shop.

It was around this time when short skirts became very popular for the second time in a decade. Florence shocked Wakefield by coming out in one that barely reached her knees. With beautiful, rounded and shapely calves like she possessed and slender ankles to add to it, with a wealth of heavy, golden hair, which covered her shoulders, when she went through the streets, almost everybody turned to look at her, especially her beautiful conspicuously displayed calves.

A few weeks went by and it was getting along towards the end of the summer. Kermit was looking forward to entering Atlanta University that fall, so was trying to make a little money so as to have some spare change to spend when he went up to the big city, as Atlanta was referred to in Wakefield. He had, therefore, had his shoe shine chair repainted and made more attractive; a cushion to make it more comfortable when they sat on it, and parked it on the sidewalk every day and solicited shines from every white person who came by whose shoes seemed to need it. Occasionally, a white woman got a shine, but he was careful never to speak to her unless she first spoke to him.

One day, about the middle of the afternoon when everything was quiet, he was sitting by his chair, reading a magazine and did not notice or seem to hear a pair of footsteps come up to him and stop. Conscious after a moment that some one was near, he raised his eyes, and the first thing that met his gaze was the beautiful legs of Florence Adair.

"Kermit," she said, at which he was on his feet and bowing, solicitously.

"Yes, Miss Florence. What can I do for you?"

"Can I—get a shine?" she said, evenly.

"Why, of course, Miss Florence. I'll be glad to shine your shoes, and I'll give you a good one, too, I sure will."

"Thank you, Kermit," she said and held out her hand for him to help her upon the chair. He took it and was thrilled by the softness of it. He lifted her and she seated herself in the chair, rather carefully, he thought.

"Do you mind, Kermit," she said, after she was seated and had adjusted herself, he recalled later, rather carefully, "letting me see your magazine while you shine my shoes?"

"Of course not, Miss Florence," he cried, reaching and picking it up. He was in the act of handing it to her, when his eyes, on the way up, fell on an object, where they halted, lingered a moment, during which he almost lost his balance. A fleeting second, and he recovered sufficiently to complete what he had started to do, hand her the magazine, to find her looking at him out of half-closed and subtle eyes.

His breath came short and he was so nervous that he fumbled among the polishes. He dared raise his eyes again—*and there it was,* still exposed to his gaze! Never since the day he was born had he been so tempted! So tempted to—commit suicide! After fumbling the polishes again, he dared steal another look, then breathed an unheard sigh of relief to see that she had closed her limbs, ending the agony.

He was perspiring all over: his brain was in a whirl. As explained, Kermit Early's people were the best colored folks in Wakefield. His sisters had never worked in the white folks kitchen. The family had lots of pride, had raised their children well, to control their passions, among other things, and not be common like most Negroes.

So Kermit did not *run around;* he had never been intimate with a girl and hadn't ever really thought much about it. Now the *picture* he had seen, which she had deliberately exposed to his view, had him almost insane. He managed to shine her shoes, which didn't need it at all when he looked at them. So he knew that she had come for it to purposely show him what he saw! He thought about his conversation with Leonard. Then Florence Adair *was* playing him. Florence Adair he realized now, would be willing to make a date with him if he'd let her.

Well, he didn't intend to let her do anything of the kind. He was ambitious; he had visualized a future, the first part of which was to complete his education, to go places thereafter — and he couldn't realize any of these living things by letting a *passionate and designing* white girl, get him hanged to the limb of a tree!

When she got down off the chair, she held a coin toward him and in taking it, which was a quarter, she said, softly, "keep the change" and squeezed his hand again, then turning, left him, to pause when a few steps away to smile back at him over her shoulder.

Two doors away, Leonard was standing, watching all that had happened through the window of the drug store. As soon as convenient and he could slip away, he strolled across to Kermit, who was sitting beside his shoe shine stand, still trembling as he was seeing over and over again, the picture she had brought, and posed it full into his face.

"'Lo, Kermit," said Leonard.

Kermit started, and looking up saw that it was Leonard, sighed. "Hello, yourself, Len."

"I *saw* it," he said, easily.

Kermit looked up, quickly. "You saw what?"

"Don't try to kid me, Kermit. You know what I saw."

"Yeah?"

"Yeh. That Adair gal. She's going to get you lynched yet."

"Not me."

"If she keeps on coming by here, making a play for you like she did just a while ago, some dirty old white boy who'd like to get next to her himself is going to see it and then—a dead nigger."

"It was all her. I did nothing."

"I know you didn't, but if somebody decides to start accusing you, nothing you could say about what you didn't do would mean a thing."

"I know it. I wish she'd let me alone."

"If she don't, you ain't going to live very long, I can tell you that."

"If she'll only let me alone for a few weeks, she won't have a chance to bother me thereafter. I'm going away to school in Atlanta in September."

"Better go now and be sure to keep on living."

"I wish I could. But there's a few things I've just got to do before I leave. In the meantime, don't you go telling anybody what you saw, or that this little gal is making passes at me."

"I'm too good a friend of yours and of any other niggah, to do that. But take a fool's advice, *get out of Wakefield before she gets you in trouble.*" And with that, Leonard turned and went back to the drugstore.

Kermit Early kept thinking about what he saw, and became conscious for the first time in his young life that women had something to fire a man's imagination, a man's desire — *and unhappiness!*

Almost every waking hour from that day on was a disturbing hour. He had always pictured that men and women should meet each other intimately only after they had married. Now he was conscious of a change. What Florence Adair had showed him was giving him a new slant on life. He tried to shake it off. It was annoying, yet he couldn't. Still he knew that he must; that he had to. If he was going up to Atlanta to enter college and put in four years of hard study, he had no time to go indulging in lurid dreams, fantasies and all that went with it. Yet the dreams went on and the fantasies joined in and the calm peace and boyhood he had enjoyed was all changing.

Still Kermit Early had lots of will power, and by sheer force of will he put the tempting picture out of his mind and forced himself to be again like he was before it happened. Florence Adair continued to pass the shop as she had been since he had known her; but she could never catch his eye. He was always looking elsewhere when she made an appearance. But this peace was not to continue. Florence Adair was passionate, and she was designing and impelled by her maddening passion, she planned a new way to force her attention on the colored boy she had by now begun to admire beyond just sexual desire.

The Sunday before Kermit was to leave for Atlanta, was one of his best days for shines. Cotton and tobacco were being marketed, money was in circulation, and the men were free with it and he had made nearly five dollars when he dragged his chair back into the shop from the sidewalk where he had made so many shines and so much money. He was very happy.

Inside, he was cleaning up, preparing to go home to get dressed then to go down on Railroad Avenue, the Negro Broadway, and spend his last Sunday for a long time in Wakefield, having a good time. Suddenly he heard a light knock on the front door. He was not sure so paused and listened, more closely. Presently he heard it again, this time a trifle louder. He was in the rear of the shop. He wondered who it could be. He peered through the large glass windows, with drawn blinds, and could see an outline shadow of someone. So thinking it was, perhaps, Leonard, he went forward and opened the door. Some one slipped in and by him so quickly he hardly saw who it was until he closed the door and turned — and lo and behold, it was Florence Adair! Fright seized him.

"Oh, Kermit," she cried facing him excitedly. "I—"

"Miss Florence!" he managed to gasp, and then choked before he could say more. Cold fear running down his back, he began to tremble from the effects.

"I know, I know," she cried, hurriedly and in subdued voice, laying a consoling hand on him. "But take it easy, Kermit. I'm not going to stay long."

"*Please go now, Miss Florence, quick before some white person sees you.! Please go, for God's sake, Miss Florence, please go!*" he cried, beseechingly, almost in tears. He reached to open the door but she grabbed his hand and held it tightly.

"Please, Kermit," she cried, trembling all over with amorous anxiety. "I'm lonesome, Kermit, so lonesome, I want to talk to you. I won't take long. Please listen," and she drew him closer to her. He resisted but in her excitement she seemed stronger than he, and before he knew it she had drawn him so close until her hot breath was in his face, as he cried:

"What on earth do you want to talk to me about?" He was so frightened by now that tears were running down his cheeks; his teeth chattered. She looked at him oddly.

"You — you know what you saw when I came for the shine? I—I want you to—to put your arms around me now Kermit. Put your arms around me and hug me. Squeeze me tight, Kermit." She tried to draw his hand around her waist.

"Please go, Miss Florence. I didn't see anything. *Please in heaven's name* go, leave the shop before the white poeple find out and come and lynch me. Please go, Miss Florence," he whined, pitifully. Still she persisted — more now than ever.

"Yes, you did, Kermit," she whispered. "I arranged my clothes so that you would; so you couldn't help seeing it. I saw you start, so I know you saw it. So please hug me now, Kermit. I want you to," she said, holding his right hand as in a vise. He beat his side with his free hand.

"Oh, Miss Florence, why do you want me to die. I ain't never done nothing to you; I haven't ever done anything to anybody. Please go, *now,* that's all I ask you to do, please go — *quick.*"

"Take it easy, Kermit. I'll go quickly after you do what I ask you to; as quickly as you do what I want you to." she said, holding onto his hand as for dear life and trying to force it around her waist. "I've been planning to have you do so for a long time, Kermit. I was watching from across the street and rushed over as quickly as the people all got out of sight."

He was weeping by now without restraint, like a helpless child. She tried to shake some sense into him, but failing, she became thoughtful, her eyes closed as if with a new purpose. She loosed his hand and glaring at him through half-closed eyes, she whispered:

"Listen, Kermit and be sensible. I let you see everything I had and now I want you to — do what I ask. I don't care anything about the white people in this town or anywhere else. I'm burning up with passion and I've got to have some satisfaction. I can't afford to fool with any white man, but nobody will suspect that I would with you. We're all alone here in the shop. There's a cot in the back room. I know it's there for I've seen it when I've been here to get my hair trimmed. I want you to go into the back room with me for a few minutes. I don't want to get you hurt, but you'll either go back there and do what I want you to, or I'll — open the door and scream! scream as loud as I can, do you hear?"

"Oh, Miss Florence, you want to get me lynched, you want to get me lynched! God help me and let me pray." He started to his knees, but she jerked him so hard that he had to stand erect.

"Quit the whining and come with me to the back room, do you

hear?" Again she shook him. He trembled all over and his teeth chattered. "Will you go, or shall I open the door and scream?"

"I'll — I'll go, Miss Florence. It won't do any good because I'm too scared to think, much less do what you're asking me to. Oh, God, forgive me." Without further words, she half-lead and half-dragged him towards the rear, with him still crying, tears flowing now all over him.

Back there she sat down on the cot and tried to drag him down, but he managed to stand. She tore his trousers open and—just then somebody shook the door. Both gasped. She rose quickly to her feet and glared excitedly in that direction. Again the door was shaken. She now looked around quickly. There was a back door. She rushed across to it. It was locked but the key was in the lock. She turned it, slipped out, closed the door softly and a moment later he heard her footsteps rush away toward the alley in the rear. He sighed bewilderingly. Then somebody shook the door again. He heard talking outside. Somebody else had come up. It was the mob, he was sure, gathering to lynch him.

"They've come for me," he cried to himself. Then looking down, he buttoned his trousers. Then after he had dried the tear marks, he walked toward the door, his heart in his mouth, but rubbing his eyes to pretend that he'd been asleep. Opening the door, he got another shock! There stood Dump Oakes, the town policeman. He was talking with two other white men, all three of whom turned to look at him. His eyes opened wide with fear, but Oakes smiled broadly, as he cried:

"Hello, Kermit. Don't be afraid. I'm not here to arrest you," and he laughed good-naturedly. The other men turned and walked away.

"I was asleep in the back room, Mr. Oakes. You woke me up."

"That's what I thought, Kermit. How you niggers can sleep, too!"

Kermit laughed like a "nigger." Never had he been so glad to play the good darky as he played it now.

"My wife told me to get my shoes shined before I came home to dinner. She's going to have company this afternoon, and said she didn't want me looking like a bum. But I forgot all about it all morning. Then when I came, I saw you'd moved your stand off the sidewalk. So I decided to take a chance and rattled the door. I'd decided you'd gone home, so was about to turn away when I heard you shuffling this way," and he laughed again, good naturedly.

"All right Mr. Oakes," he cried, so happy that Oakes had come in the nick of time. "I'll be glad to fix you up. I'm going to give you a shine that will make your company look at your shoes. I sure will. Get right up on the stand, Mr. Oakes, please," he said. Laughingly Oakes obeyed.

"You saved my life, boy. I sure am glad you decided to take a nap before going home." He pushed his big feet hard down against the holders so that Kermit could do a good job, took off his cap, wiped his big, red face and relaxed against the back of the chair while Kermit went after his shoes as he had never shined a pair before.

Sitting there in his apartment in Chicago, Kermit Early stirred, having lived through the first episode of his acquaintance with Florence Adair. He shifted comfortably, got up and found himself a drink of ice water, set the silver pitcher, after taking a big drink, where he could take another later, let his mind drift back again into his yesteryears.

It was near the close of his second year at Atlanta University. In Atlanta he had, out of the sight of Florence Adair, got himself under control again, and had put in two strenuous years of study and was hopeful of being able to finish and get his A.B. six months in advance of the usual four year period. While his parents paid his tuition, he tried to make his board and room rent by working after school hours at a cleaning and pressing shop.

He often thought of Florence Adair, wondered if she had gotten married and often sighed, happy in the thought that he had escaped from the worst temptation he ever experienced. He knew he would never forget the fear that he lived through in the few minutes she had tried to force him to risk his life.

All this fear had left him by now. Atlanta was large enough and cosmopolitan enough in its reactions to pay little attention to what anybody did. He had met and knew colored men since coming there who boasted freely of having white women and met them frequently at private houses, where they talked about it and nobody paid any attention to it. Colored men were frequently even caught with white women and arrested. Good lawyers invariably got them off at the most with a fine. The greatest danger, and one that couples were careful to avoid, was the police. If the officer decided to shoot a Negro, caught with a white woman, the Negro was just dead, and most times that was the end of it.

So Kermit liked Atlanta. When he finished Atlanta University, his plans were to go north to Chicago and secure his M.A. degree there. He was happy. All Negroes are happy when they can have freedom. And Atlanta was easily one of the freest towns in the South for a Negro.

He had been to deliver some clothes to a house in Peachtree Circle and was on the way to his room when he heard a squealing of brakes, and somebody vigorously blowing a horn. He kept on, not thinking it was to attract his attention, so the horn was blown again, louder and longer. He paused and looked in that direction. Somebody stepped from a fine Cadillac Coach, waved their hand and called:

"Kermit, oh, Kermit! Come here!" He looked at who was calling more closely, then smiled when he recognized Florence Adair. He crossed to where she stood, waiting for him. She was smiling all over and reached out her hand which he didn't hesitate to take, when he came up.

"Kermit Early, you," she exclaimed and seemed very pleased.

"And you, Miss Florence. I'm surprised, but glad to see you again."

"And I'm more than glad to see you, Kermit," she said, looking him up and down. "You're looking fine."

"Thank you, Miss Florence, and so are you."

"Thank you, Kermit. I feel fine. How are you anyhow?"

"Oh just fine, Miss Florence, just fine."

"You look it. How are you getting along in school?"

"I expect to graduate six months ahead of schedule."

"Wonderful," she cried and beamed. "I'm so glad to hear it."

"Thank you, Miss Florence. Meanwhile, how is Wakefield?"

She started.

"Oh, Wakefield," she repeated, a little absently. "All right, the last time I was down there."

He expressed surprise by a flash of his eyes.

"The last time you were there?"

"Yes, I'm living here now, you know."

"Oh, you're living in Atlanta?"

"Yes, Kermit. Been living here since I married."

"Since you married! And so you're married? That's fine, Mrs. — "

"—Wingate is my name now. I married a man by the name of Wingate."

"Oh, you did? Wingate?" he murmured, thoughtfully. Then raising his eyes, "He wouldn't happen to be related to the Textile Wingate, I suppose?"

"He *is* the Textile Wingate."

"Oh," cried Kermit. "A very rich man!"

Her reaction didn't seem enthusiastic. Instead, she merely shrugged her shoulders lightly.

"I've been married a little over a year," she said.

"Isn't that fine," he exclaimed. "Well, I'm not surprised. You're a very pretty lady, Mrs. Wingate. You were entitled to marry some rich man." Again she shrugged her shoulders lightly, and still failed to register any enthusiasm. Instead, she seemed at the moment more interested in him.

"What are you doing, Kermit, other than going to school?"

"I've got a little job in a pressing shop, working after school, Saturdays and holidays."

"I see. Do you like it?"

He shrugged his shoulders carelessly.

"It's just a job, Mrs. Wingate. I get almost enough to eat on and pay my room rent.

"Wouldn't you like a — better job?"

"Anything that is better than what you have is just that much better."

She was thoughtful a moment, then raised her eyes.

"Step into the car," she said, swinging the large door wide. He stepped inside. She moved over under the wheel to give him room to sit down beside her.

"How'd you like to come and work for us, Kermit? For — me?" He turned to look at her, not making reply at once for no reason that he could understand. As he caught her eyes, she lowered them momentarily. Both were thinking of what happened back in Wakefield. He pushed it away and started to reply, a reply which she seemed to be expecting, and, as we shall see, was prepared to counter even before he began to make it.

"I'm very thankful for the offer, Mrs. Wingate—"

She raised her hand before he could get the "but" out.

"Now, now. No 'buts', Kermit," she said, chidingly. She shifted, and went ahead more firmly. "The fact is, Kermit, I've been wanting to get in touch with you for sometime. I even wrote to friends back in Wakefield to advise me where I could reach you. They weren't successful and I was much disappointed. Now that coincidence has favored me, I want to at least have a long talk with you." Then to herself, I have to be careful or I'll frighten him away. Feel my way, get him interested. Meanwhile, Kermit felt he might get out of it by explaining about his school hours.

"You understand that I'm going to school, Mrs. Wingate; about to graduate from college and that requires lots of study. I don't really have so much time. I — "

"I've considered all that, Kermit. I want to see you complete your education. I admire you for your ambitions and always have. We can arrange the work you are to do at your convenience. We — I can offer you a better job, bigger pay. I know you aren't getting much where you're working now. You said almost enough to buy your meals, pay for your room. That's not enough, Kermit. You need more spending money so that you can go see a movie now and then, gad around a bit. I'll — see that you get enough to do so". She paused and sought for words. She was thinking fast, she wanted to get in her part before he made his decision. He was listening to her.

"By the way. Why not drive me out to the house where we can talk the matter over in detail? I live straight out Peachtree, in Buckhead. You know where that is, sorta out in the suburbs." He knew where it was and that only the rich and aristocratic lived there. Wingate. One of the richest men in Atlanta. He turned to look at her. He was thinking that her husband must be much older than she. It was usually the way. Rich man married to a young and pretty girl. That was white people's way. They got all the breaks. Then suddenly for no reason that he could understand, he turned and smiled his consent.

"I'm glad," she cried, happily.

"Thank you. Which way and where do you want to go?"

"I'll show you."

He got out then and went around the car and opened the door on the driver's side. She smiled at him sweetly, and moved over. He got in and took the wheel.

He was strangely relieved. She was the little girl he knew back in Wakefield again. Of a sudden the events there jumped back into his mind and paraded again before him. But they were in Atlanta now, big and free Atlanta and he wasn't afraid any longer. If Mrs. Wingate wanted to play with him, he wouldn't be afraid. Atlanta was too big and too busy for anybody to care what went on, or what somebody else wanted to do. Oh, what a feeling, just to be free, not afraid and he wasn't afraid any longer.

"Now turn at the next corner," she said, pointing her finger in that direction, "to the right into Peachtree Street and just drive straight out that street until after we go under a Railroad. That's the Southern. We live about five blocks on the other side of it."

He obeyed her and both became strangely silent and formal, like Mistress and servant. This continued all the way to the mansion she pointed out for him to turn into. He drove the car up to the steps where he stopped it and looked at her.

"Now," she said, "tell me what time you can come to see me tomorrow?"

"Classes are over at 2:30. I'll go to the shop and make my deliveries which may take until five o'clock. Then I could, if you wish me to, come directly here."

"Supposing that we make it say, at between five and six?"

"That'll be all right, Mrs. Wingate. Often there aren't so many deliveries to make and I get through earlier."

"That'll be fine, Kermit. I'll be expecting you at between five and six tomorrow." She paused and he got out quickly and ran around the car and opened the door on her side, took her hand, which was still as soft as it was back in Wakefield, and assisted her to the steps, leading up to the house, where she turned thanking him again, went inside. He went to the street where he would catch a Peachtree Street car which would drop him off at Peachtree, and Whitehall, near five points, from where he planned to go down on Auburn Avenue.

In spite of the many Negroes, the noise, and the excitement he found on Auburn avenue, he couldn't put Mrs. Wingate out of his mind. He kept seeing the picture she had pushed into his face in Wakefield over again; her visit to the shop and her effort to get him to make a fool of himself. He recalled her saying so many times, so many more than he thought necessary, during their conversation. "I want to talk to you . . . I want to have a long talk with you . . . We'll talk matters over." What could she mean by all that? She was Mrs. Wingate now, married to a rich man, no longer Florence Adair, who didn't want to fool around with any white boy and get talked, about, become disgraced. Wakefield was too small to get careless in.

He realized that there was nothing to do but wait and hear what she had to say on the morrow. She had done all the talking, and made all the movements back in Wakefield. She did most of the talking and made all the arrangements about his calling to see her that afternoon. However he felt, he knew he would let her continue to do all the talking, the next day and the next and as long as he worked for her. That was the sensible thing to do. Let white people offer to shake your hand; let white people speak first, let white people take the initiative in everything when it came to dealing with Negroes. Then you wouldn't ever get in trouble. Atlanta was big, and it was free, but it was still down South.

Then he thought about her husband, whose name was often in the papers. She was married now and she was no doubt, he conjectured, being satisfied. Maybe she had put all she tried to have him do, of what she showed him, out of her mind. She'd ought to have, but had she? Well, he'd soon see.

Until he completed his deliveries just before five the next day he had lived through a maze of imaginary events, anxiety. It seemed the time would never pass, but as time does, it always passes. During those waiting hours he thought of about everything. He even recalled how white men had colored women back in Wakefield. So common. With the exception of his sisters, the town had few pretty colored girls that white men had not had or did not at one time or other, play with. He recalled how they'd put pretty ones who let themselves get careless, drunk and finally get locked up; and while they were in the hoosegow, white deputies, constables, and arresting officers would slip into the cells and demand sexual intercourse on a bargaining basis with the poor unfortunate girls. Sometimes they were kept there several days while three or four of the officers satisfied their lust before they would let them out.

"White people can be so dirty, crackers especially," could always be heard in the Negro section. "A jig ain't got no chance." Most pretty colored girls had to go north to keep from being forced to be intimate with white men. Even when they married, they had to often submit, and very often come up with white babies when their husbands were black men. Most Negroes, therefore, had a grudge against white people, and if they were educated and sensitive, they hated them. So during the night Early began to develop a desire to get even. If he could have a pretty white woman, he could feel that he was getting even in a small way for some of the wrongs white men forced on colored women since the South began.

In a conversation with a friend on his way to his room that night, he listened with strange interest to what the other seemed anxious to talk about.

"Plenty niggahs got white gals in Atlanta," said the other.

"Really?"

"Sho."

"Whores."

"Naw. White gals from these small towns. When they get to Atlanta and up no'th, the first thing they wants is a niggah. I've heard 'um say: 'white men always layin' 'round with niggah women. I'm going to have all the niggah men I can stand up under, the first chance I get" and he laughed.

Shortly after five P. M. the next day, he knocked on the back door of the Wingate home in Buckhead, and waited. Not for long, for she had been waiting for him and opened the door.

"Kermit. You're on time. Come in."

He entered. "Why didn't you come to the front door? I was looking for you there. When I saw you going around to the back, I had to run all the way back here to let you in."

"I'm sorry, Mrs. Wingate."

Oh, it's all right, except we've got to walk all the way back to the front now to get upstairs where I've arranged to talk to you. Follow me, please," and smiling, she led the way toward the front.

Early followed her out of the kitchen, into and through a large, attractive dining room, which opened into a large, wide hallway. Out of this whirled a winding stairway to the second floor. She mounted the steps as he came up, paused to smile at him like she had back in Wakefield. He hesitated.

"Why don't you smile, Kermit," she said, looking at him. "This is Atlanta. People are too busy here to pay any attention to their neighbors or anybody else. So relax, take it easy. Be real." She smiled upon him again, sweetly.

"Now come and walk beside me, not behind me, always behind like an old cow's tail," and she laughed again. He grinned. "That's better," she said. "Now come on. You and I are going to have a long talk." She turned now and he dared walk beside her to the top of the stairway, where she paused, and affected tiredness.

"Some steps, eh, Kermit?" He looked down.

"They're pretty. The whole house is pretty."

"Yes, the house is pretty" she said with a peculiar emphasis on the house. He became conscious that in some way she was acting a bit peculiar. He wondered why.

"Now we start back to the rear again," she said, turning and reaching, took his hand and dropped it after they had started. There was a long hall up there, too, but not as wide. They passed bedrooms, all gorgeously furnished, on the way back. Then, just before reaching the end of the hall, which opened on a porch, she turned sharply to the left and bumped into him. She was closer to him now than ever, and he found himself looking straight into her eyes. He caught his breath, for in hers was the same thing he had seen when she looked at him in the barber shop that day.

"I should have told you that we would turn." The collision had brought them to a stop. She took his hand again and this time held onto it, loosening it only when they reached a door, where she paused and took some keys and unlocked it. He didn't know what to do. She opened the door, walked in, turned.

"Come in," she said, smiling. He entered. She turned and latched the door after he entered.

"This is your room, Kermit."

"*My room?*" he repeated in surprise.

"Of course. I want you to stay here."

"Oh," he echoed, and looked around the room a bit curiously.

"I'll show it to you." She walked ahead; to one side was another door which when opened, displayed a large closet.

"Your closet. Don't you think it's nice and roomy? It'll keep your clothes nice and clean."

"Sure is nice, Mrs. Wingate."

"When we're in the room alone, Kermit, call me Florence. I'll like that better."

"I could never get used to addressing you like that, Mrs. Wingate."

"Try it. You will — after a while." She led him a few steps and opened another door.

"Your bath," she said, going inside. He followed. It *was* nice. With a large tub and shower. He never thought he would ever get to live in such a room. There was a whole rack of towels, soap, everything clean, immaculate. She turned to face him and smiled again.

"Like it?"

"Yes, maam, but — "

"No buts. Now I'll show you the rest of it." She left the bathroom then, he following. There was a fine bed, with a light over it, a table on one side.

"So you can check through your studies in bed and at leizure. I fixed all this myself — after you left yesterday." He didn't know what to say, so said nothing. But he did like it.

She led the way now around the bed to the other side of the room, where she opened another door. Another closet. He looked in.

"Two closets. One for your trunk, so it won't spoil the looks of the room, by setting around in the way."

"My," he managed to say.

She smiled at him, then led the way now to a door at the rear, opened it. It led to the back porch and a few feet away a pair of stairs led downward to the floor of the porch below.

"A back entrance so you won't have to come through the house when you return to the room at night."

He smiled appreciatively. She stuck her thumb in his side playfully as she led the way back into the room, and paused over near the bed.

"Two large windows, so that you can open them and get cool air at night."

"It's too fine a room for a — servant, Mrs. Wingate."

"Not for you, Kermit. You're an educated servant. You have imagination, you need a chance to develop it. I want to help you develop yourself."

"You're very kind, Mrs. Wingate."

"You can't say 'Florence?' "

"Oh, Mrs. Wingate, no, I — "

"Oh, all right. Yet, I'm going to teach you how before it's all over."
There was a large, overstuffed chair; and an occasional one, with a small low table between.
"Sit down," she said, pointing to the overstuffed chair. He obeyed. She sat on the occasional chair, moving it a bit closer to his before doing so.
"Now we'll have that talk," she said.
About what, he thought. Why was Mrs. Wingate doing all this for him? He was to soon see. He tried to push his chair away a little.
"Oh, don't Kermit. Quit being afraid. I don't like you being afraid of me."
He grinned, sheepishly. What was all this leading up to, he wondered. It was what he'd thought he'd like a few hours before. He had dreamed and visualized such a situation. Now that it was upon him, he was plainly frightened. She looked at him and understood, so smiled reassuringly.
"Remember what I said. We're in Atlanta now, not Wakefield where it was sensible for you to be scared. Don't be that way any longer. Nobody is going to know, nor pay any attention to what you and I do up here," so saying she slid her chair closer to him again. He sighed and looked bewildered.
"I'm sorry, Mrs. Wingate," he said. She sighed, so he didn't finish what he started to say.
"I want to tell you what's on my mind and what I've been planning to do after meeting you yesterday, if you'd quit looking so frightened. Won't you just try to act like you — know me, so that I can?"
He sighed and tried to perk up.
"I'll try to, Mrs. Wingate." She moved her chair up against his now and seemed to be trying to decide just where and how to start. She reached over and unfolded his hands, took the right and laid hers on it. She stroked his hand then.
"Now remember, Kermit, anything that happens between us, you and me, understand, it's me that did it. I want you to feel comfortable and safe at all times. You'll be all right after you get that fright out of yourself. You see, you're educated. That always makes a difference. You know how far to go, and I — trust you. What you must do from now on is trust me. Let us try to be mutual. In public it is one way here in this room, it will be, I hope, as we want to make it, I want to

make it." She was *so* nice, he was thinking now.

She reached over with her free hand, placed it under his, and stroked the top of his hand with her other. He sat there completely helpless, leaving everything to her.

"But your husband, Mrs. Wingate. Your husband, so rich, so — "

She jerked her hands away and flashed her eyes, impatiently, rising to her feet. She stood over him and seemed to go through some strange transition. He looked up frightened, a fright that she did not see, for she was looking over his head into space, as if some terrible revolution was going on within her. He stood up.

"I'm sorry if I — I said something you didn't like, Mrs. Wingate."

She looked at him oddly, then relaxing, smiled, turned and sat back down and motioned for him to do likewise. He obeyed her. She took his hand again and stroked it. He looked on vaguely.

"You spoke about my husband. That's what I want to tell you about, all about, and then — perhaps you'll undestand." She dropped his hand and covered her face with hers. A moment later she lowered them and turned to him.

"It's hard to talk about it and you will be the first person that I have. I — I don't see how I can tell anybody else — not even my own mother."

Again she paused, covered her face with her hands again and wept this time. She took out a kerchief and dobbed her nose and her eyes, shook her head and turned again to him.

"You could never understand, Kermit, nobody can unless I tell them. It isn't anything that I want to advertise. But I'm going to tell you, Kermit, tell you because I know you can be trusted to keep a secret as I have done since the first night I married him."

"You mean, Miss Florence, your — wedding night?" He had a strange suspicion now and was beginning to understand.

"My wedding night!" she exclaimed, and in a moment became a wild-eyed tigress. "My wedding night! I had no wedding night — I've never had one; I never will have a wedding night." Eyes flashing fire, she gazed into space, a hopeless something. He looked hard at her, and managed to say:

"Why, Miss Florence — what — do you mean?" Again she relaxed.

She seemed so unhappy that he was almost tempted to lay a consoling hand on her. In fact, he started to, then paused, hesitated and drew it back. She raised her eyes, tears flowing down her cheeks, in time to see it. His eyes were soft with sympathy.

"Just what I said, Kermit, I've never had a wedding night; I never will," and again she fell to weeping. Face down, she sobbed the words. "Everybody envies me, thinks I married so well when they should be pitying me, pitying me," and she wept.

"Miss Florence, please. I'm so sorry to see you so — unhappy. Why, all this? You have a fine home, a husband, a rich husband. Isn't he good to you?"

Face still down, eyes hidden, she nodded her head up and down.

"Yes, Kermit, he's good to me, just as good as he can be."

"Then, why — " She sat up, proceeded to wipe her tears away.

"My husband, Kermit, is not a — *normal man.*"

He recoiled, eyes wide.

"Not a — *what!*" he cried.

She looked at him out of sad, pitiful eyes, nodding her head as she did so.

"Not a normal man, Kermit, if you know what that means."

"Oh," he echoed, and didn't know what else to say. His mind then went back to an incident, an incident that all the world had followed a few years before. A murder trial. It happened in Georgia, so she would remember it; she would know all about it.

"I'm a passionate woman, you know that, Kermit. You know as no one else does, how my passion lead me — almost to desperate measures. Still I never did cross the border. Except when I tried to make you play with me, I never made an advance to a man before or since. But all my life I'd dreamed of that night, my wedding night when I could relax into all the excitement that only wedding night can give a girl. So imagine when that night came, here in this *house* where he brought me, he broke down and made a *shocking* confession, instead. All the future, children, sweet babies that every healthy girl longs for and expects, never to be mine." She fell to weeping again at the thought of it. He stared at her and thought again about the trial of a man who was *not normal* and the terrible tragedy that was the result of it.

"But he can't help it. He was born that way. And, strange as it may seem, and as disappointed as I am, I don't hate him for it. I feel sorry for him. He is so much older than I, and I didn't want to marry him from the beginning. But my people were poor but proud, especially my mother. My father was getting old and the bank was planning to retire him. My sisters and brothers were in school. We hated to take them out — it would have been a tragedy, a calamity with my family struggling so hard to keep their chins up. So — I — consented to marry him. I felt that a sacrifice on my part would save my people — and it did. And now — I'm paying the price." She shook her head sadly, hopelessly.

"Do you mean when you say that your husband is not a normal man, that he was, perhaps, like — like Leo M. Frank?"

She sat quickly erect, eyes wide.

"Leo M. Frank!" she exclaimed. "How'd you happen to think of him?"

"They said that he — was not a normal man."

Now let us go back a few years; to the trial of Leo M. Frank.

Frank had been sent to Atlanta from Brooklyn, to manage a pencil factory. He was charged with killing Mary Phagan, a young Irish girl, employed at the factory, a few years before. He was charged with luring her to the factory where he planned to have an unnatural relation with her.

The trial was more sensational than usual because Frank was convicted on the testimony of a simple, ignorant Negro. Because of this fact, a powerful New York daily paper, came to his assistance, employed the great William J. Burns, himself, imported him into Atlanta, and with unlimited money to fight the case, succeeded in throwing everything out of gear and a governor, who later was retired from public life for a commutation he granted, changing the Jury verdict which had convicted Frank and sentenced him to be hanged.

In the Negro's testimony, he related how Frank practiced unnatural relations with certain women who satisfied him for pay. But Frank wanted nicer women, in this case a girl, who was innocent. In his passionate state, the Negro testified, that he'd act like he was crazy.

He went on to relate how Frank arranged with him to be on hand on this particular day, and that he'd fooled Mary Phagan into coming to the factory so that he could be alone with her. He proceeded then to arrange matters to fit into the scheme of things, by having the Negro take up his watch at the foot of the stair, after the girl came and went up stairs to get her pay. "So I," the Negro testified, "took up my watch at the foot of the stairs and waited." He went on to say how he overheard Frank talking to the girl; of him making an advance and of her refusing. "You see," the Negro testified Frank said, "I'm not *built like other men*." When asked what he meant by that, the Negro said that Frank *went down* on women.

The Judge at this point called a recess and when court resumed the next morning, only men were permitted in the court room to hear the testimony of the Negro who went on to explain what he meant by "going down".

He testified that when the little girl refused, Frank was so impassioned and desperate that he attempted to *make her*. This brought on a struggle. She got her fingers in his face and scratched him so until he had to strike her to make her turn him loose.

"I wanted to be with the little girl but she refused me," the Negro said he told him. "Then we got to struggling and she got her fingers in my face and scratched me something awful. I had to strike her to make her turn loose, but I guess I struck her too hard. She fell and hit her head against something and then she lay there still like she was dead."

The part that created so much excitement and made everybody, who heard the testimony, want to kill Frank, was when the Negro told that while the little girl lay on the floor, unconscious and helpless, Frank committed the unspeakable act. Examination of the girl's vagina afterward revealed that she was a virgin, had been tampered with, but there was no fluid to reveal that it had been in the natural way.

Through, his passion cooled and picturing the girl rising from the floor when she came to and staggering into the street in her condition to make Atlanta ring from end to end with what she would tell *and show* was too much for Frank. Crazed, he found a cord, tied it around her neck and strangled her to death. He then called the Negro from the stool and had him help try to dispose of the body. They took it to the basement where Frank ordered the Negro to put it in the furnace and burn it. At this the Negro balked and refused. Frank pictured then that if he could get him intoxicated, he would while in that condition, do it. So he gave the Negro money which he took and went to a boot-legging joint nearby, as prohibition was in effect in Atlanta. The Negro went there and got so drunk until he became sleepy and went home to have a nap and when he woke up, it was too late. Frank, in the meantime, wrote murder notes and put them around the body in the hope of throwing suspicion on the Negro. And since Georgia was notorious for lynching Negroes, it was Frank's hope that with suspicion cast toward the Negro, a mob would gather and lynch him so quick, that suspicion would be diverted from him. He reckoned wrong, for they did not lynch the Negro but a year or two later, when the governor was persuaded to commute his death sentence to life imprisonment, Frank was taken from the prison by twenty determined men from Marrietta, Georgia, home of the girl, who stormed the prison farm hospital where Frank was recovering from a wound a fellow prisoner had made, trying to cut his throat. They carried him 100 miles to the town where the little girl had lived and hanged him to the limb of a gum tree.

"Leo M. Frank," Florence was saying after a pause. "Yes, my husband is like Frank. So now, Kermit, you understand. Just like Frank," she repeated and looked at him helplessly. "Oh, it's too awful to think about. My life here in this big empty house, is a life — of hell!" Again she wept in self pity and again he felt sorry for her.

"Some day, and I think of it so much until I imagine at times it is about to happen, I feel I'll go crazy. Oh, I can't stand it longer, Kermit. I just can't go on putting up with it!" She rose to her feet and walked the floor. He sat there and just looked at her and felt sorry for her. Her life he could now understand, must be terribly unhappy. She had, on the one hand, everything, on the other, nothing. She returned to the chair after a time and sat down again.

"In spite of imposing myself on you back there in Wakefield the way I did, I've been a nice girl. I'm still a virgin insofar as any sexual actions are concerned, but I have to put up with so much punishment, in a way, to satisfy him until I'm worse off always than I was before. I've still got to go on being careful. I dreamed of a man, a fine young man since I was twelve years old. I wanted to be embraced, hugged and kissed, but was afraid to let any white boys do all this back there. It was then that I began to notice you. I kept looking at you; I kept thinking about you. Then I would look at you again, and I noticed that you had pretty eyes, such beautiful eyes."

She leaned over to look into his more directly. He was forced to smile. She smiled too, the first time, it seemed, for a long time.

"You *have* got pretty eyes, Kermit, beautiful eyes. Hasn't anybody ever told you that you have before?" He was forced to smile again, but said nothing.

"Have they?" she repeated.

"I don't know," he lied modestly.

"You're telling a story," she said and reached out and took his hand again. "I think you have," she said, cuddling them. "Did you think I was a—bad girl, the way I acted? I mean, in Wakefield?"

"Oh, Miss Florence," he cried. "You mustn't talk to me like that. It won't ever do, ever."

"Why won't it?" she cried, and bouncing up, sat quickly down on his lap.

"You know, Kermit," she said, with him really frightened in earnest now. "There are white girls, many white girls, who'd like to be nice to some colored man. In fact, there are many who'd like to have a colored fellow if they had a chance."

"I wish you'd get up, Miss Florence. This isn't right at all."

"It is," she pouted. "And I won't get up. I want to sit here and I want you to want me to."

"I don't want you to," he said.

"You do, but you're just scared. When are you going to get over it?"

"Never."

"Oh, Kermit. Why don't you be nice to me?"

"I have no right to. This is still down South, even if we are in Atlanta."

"If we were up North, say in Chicago, for instance, wouldn't you— like to — then?"

"We're not up north. I wish you'd get up."

"I'm trying to be nice to you but you keep on being scared, a fraidie cat." She looked at him now, deep into his eyes, and smiled, sweetly. "Such pretty eyes," and she shook her head with admiration. "Let me kiss them," and leaning forward she kissed his brow, then kissed his lips.

"Oh, my, so soft, so sweet. Do you know, Kermit?" He was silent. "I like you." She leaned over and kissed him again. "I've always liked you." and leaning forward, kissed him again. "I'm always going to like you, even if you won't kiss me back, I'm mad," she said, poutingly, and rose to her feet. Paused, and looked down at him at a sort of profile from where she was standing. She sighed deeply, took a turn around the room. She came back and sat down on the chair, then turned to him, now seriously.

"I'm interested in your education, Kermit."

"Thank you, Miss Florence."

"I like being called Miss Florence better than Mrs. Wingate, I don't feel that I am a mistress. But getting back to what I started to say. I am interested in your future. I don't want you to think that I am only interested in — but we haven't got to that. I'm interested in your getting your education, and from now on, I'm going to help you — if you'll let me."

"That's very kind of you Miss Florence."

"I'm all alone in this big old house, except for mammy, who does the cooking and I bring in another woman twice a week to do the cleaning.

"Now, you see, by you being here in this room, you'll be lots of company. You don't know how lonesome I get, so lonesome I don't know what to do. So after I met you yesterday, I came and fixed this room up so that it would be so nice and comfortable until after you've stayed in it a while, you won't want to leave."

"That is very kind of you."

"If you can have a nice place to study and prepare any writings, you can get along so much better."

"I'm terribly grateful to you for that."

"Are you, really, Kermit?"

"I would be most ungrateful if I was not."

"Thank you. That encourages me." She got up and crossing, sat down on his lap again.

"Do you like me, Kermit?"

"I don't know, Miss Florence. I'm all confused, my brain's in a whirl."

"Still scared."

He sighed.

"Well, I'll just have to be patient and give you time."

"Don't you think I ought to be going?" he said, stirring.

She glanced at her wrist watch, and with a light sigh, got up. He followed. They were close and he towered over her. She looked up at him and smiled. He was forced to smile too.

"You're tall. I like tall men. I like to look up to a man."

He smiled now, indulgently, but said nothing.

"When are you going to move in?" she said.

He crossed toward the door, thinking as he went and she followed. At the door, he paused and turned to face her.

"Whenever you say."

"How about tomorrow night?"

"Okey by me," said he.

"Then I'll look for you tomorrow night, around ten o'clock. Does that suit you?"

"Yes, maam." He turned now and placed a hand on the knob. She came closer.

"Wait a minute." She came up and looking up into his eyes, placed her arms about his neck and kissed him three times. Relaxing, she smiled up into his face. He opened the door and she called.

"Good night, Kermit."

"Good night, Miss Florence."

He went down the steps which were but a few feet away as he heard her close the door and was gone.

Kermit Early came back to himself again, sitting there in his comfortable parlor, from his reminiscences, and looked around him, down at the letter which had started him out on it. He sighed pleasantly, for in truth, he had begun to enjoy it. This strange drama of his own life and the woman whose letter to him had set him out upon it. He glanced down at it, read another paragraph, but found his reminiscence more interesting at the moment, so slumped right back to where he left off.

He hadn't acquired very many clothes, only enough to change about twice and present a neat appearance daily at class. There were many nice girls of his own race in his class, some of whom smiled at him and by doing so, invited him to be more friendly. He was friendly to them, but was too engrossed in his studies to go any further. They sighed and would look at him a bit oddly, then sigh again and usually let him alone after that.

When he got up the next morning, and before hurrying off to class, he began packing the most of what he had into two large suit cases, planning to finish doing so when he returned from making his deliveries that afternoon.

His studies at the school that day were more strenuous than usual, which served to make him forget Florence Wingate and he was relieved, for he had grown strangely anxious for that night to come, and the exacting studies that day made the time seem to go quicker.

When he got to the shop, he was given piles of suits and dresses to deliver, and the use of the side car to do so in, whereas he usually made most of his deliveries by foot. By the time he had finished, returned to his room, completed his packing, being able to get all he possessed into two suit cases, the time was drawing near. He had taken the books which he kept in the room, some volumes of reference and research to school, where he planned to carry them to Mrs. Wingate's when he was fully settled.

He went to the landlady's room when he had completed his packing, knocked on her door and paid her, telling her that he had secured a better job, but one that required him to stay on the place. She was sorry to see him go, but glad he was able to pay her in full, and not resort to the usual alibi, which always ended in never paying. She wished him God speed, promised to "pray" for him, and around nine o'clock he left with his belongings.

He had to transfer to the Peachtree car at five points, which car put him off almost in front of her home in Buckhead.

Remembering the back stairway, he went around the big house and found his way up the backstairs, and then as he set his suit cases down and started to find a key to admit him to his room, was chagrinned to realize all of a sudden that he had forgotten to ask her for it. He bit his lips in vexation, then reached out to just try the door as a matter of course, and started when it opened. He breathed a deep sigh of relief, stepped inside, felt around the wall beside the door, found a switch, turned the lights on, went back to the porch, picked up his belongings, and returning with them inside, set them in the middle of the room and going back, closed the door and paused to take a survey of his new surroundings.

He crossed the room and opened the door that led to the inside of the house and paused to listen. All was silent and he wondered if Mrs. Wingate was in or had gone out, or retired. He heard a ticking and turned and found upon looking that she had placed a handsome clock on the table near his bedside, which he could look directly into the face of while in bed. He smiled his thanks and closing the door, removed his hat and coat, rolled up his sleeves and put in the next half hour, unpacking and arranging his possessions in and about the room. Through, he sat down at the table, over which a subdued light protruded, which he switched on, got up, went back to the door and switched off the one that lit the entire room, returned to the table and checked through his studies, to come up in class the next day for another thirty minutes, at the end of which time he was conscious of a drowsiness, so got up, removed his clothing, found his pajamas, and switched on the light over the bed.

He turned the covers back after switching off the table light, pressed up and down on the middle of the bed with his hand, was relieved and pleased that it was soft and springy, then got into it and was more pleased still.

What a wonderful set-up, he thought. Never had he been even near so much complete comfort. He could surely study hard and go right on through his class until the end of the session, living in such a perfectly, delightful and comfortable environment.

Far away from noisy Negroes, where he would never be disturbed by police sirens, arresting some fool Negroes who'd got into trouble by drinking and fighting which so often ended in the police Station on Decatur street. Not even a Grady hospital siren, buzzing through the streets to haul a Negro to the hospital who'd been shot or had gotten into a stabbing fray.

Just solid comfort and peace. He sighed happily, reached up, switched off the light, and a few minutes later was entering slumberland when he heard a slight knock on the door and slowly opened his eyes. He was not sure, so listened more closely until it was repeated. He sat up in bed, turned on the bed light, and looking toward the door, called: "Yes."

Some one tried the door, and it was only then he remembered that he had forgotten to lock it and was annoyed. The door was opened softly — and he started up in great surprise, for, wearing a striking silk negligee, over which was a dark robe, with her hair down over her shoulders, stood Mrs. Wingate. He uttered some sound, and looked around. His robe was across the foot of the bed, and she had entered the room and he could not get it without exposing himself, so suddenly slid downward, drawing the covers up around his throat.

She turned and locked the door behind her this time and also latched it, then turning, came across the room to the bed and sat down on the side of it and looked at him. He was really frightened this time and she, observing it, smiled at him and reaching out, patted his cheek.

"Will you ever get over being frightened — dear," she said and leaning forward, kissed him. He closed his eyes and groaned.

"Oh, Kermit, please. Please don't act like that. I'm really not going to — hurt you." He opened his eyes and looked at her, blank like. As he did so and she smiled down upon him sweetly, he caught a faint odor of rich perfume.

"We, you and I, Kermit, are all alone here. Nobody is in this big house but us. Mr. Wingate is in New York, where he'll remain for a week or ten days longer. Got a wire from him to that effect this afternoon. So please loosen up, relax, unbend and begin to try to be nice to me." She slapped his shoulder, hard, then coming closer, kissed him again, once, twice, three times, then sitting up, looked down into his face.

"Now," she said, patting his cheek, "doesn't that show that I mean all right by you?" and she smiled down at him again, stood up, removed her robe, crossed to a clothes tree across the room, in her negligee, with him staring at her back. She hung the robe up, turned, posed as if for his benefit, then returned to the bed, stood over him to smile down at him again in her negligee, under which she had on a fine silk nightie. As she stood there he could see the outline of her body, silhouetted through both. She turned now and sat down again on the side of the bed and smiled at him. He still gazed at her blankly and said nothing.

"This is *some* affair, isn't it?" she said, and laughed lightly.

He shook his head dumbly but managed to smile, "I don't know."

"You don't know? Why, Kermit, use your imagination. You have plenty, with all the education you have. Must I make all the overtures? All the advances? Just picture now, a — a beautiful, white girl, married to an old man, an old man who has never, because nature created him in the image of Sodom or Gomorrah, I don't know which. Maybe both, but he has gotten himself married to a pretty, passionate young girl, who has been waiting practically all her life for a wedding night. Then, wedding night and all this beautiful girl's expectations. In her bedroom, dressed like she is now, waiting, waiting. Then to her he comes, falls on his knees and weeps. She's surprised, she doesn't know what about, but is afraid, listens. He confesses to her through his tears, that he is not a normal man. He should have used Leo M. Frank's words, but guess he didn't think of them. 'You see, I'm not built like other men.' The young girl was not much more than a child, a tender virgin that authors since the beginning of time have been writing about, will go on writing about. She's young but at last understands and falls weeping. Pours her whole heart into her tears. He tries to explain it away; tries to show her *his way,* which frightens her more. She had heard of such ways and knew then and there, and would keep on knowing, that she wanted none of it. He begs, he pleads, he cries, but she drives him from the room and locks the door behind him, returns and tries to die.

"But the pretty young girl does not die. She lives on to suffer and die over and over again, a living death. Then out of somewhere comes a stranger dark and handsome, with pretty eyes. He is afraid of her, speaks no words, makes no overtures. Just sits and listens to her, but listens so beautifully. This stranger happens to be a — colored boy, therefore love between him and the princess, the Southern Princess, is a forbidden thing. He knows it and she knows it. He doesn"t propose try to override this tradition, but she doesn't care. She is hungry, hungry for affection, and she likes this dark and handsome young man, even if to love him is forbidden. Maybe that makes her love for him sweeter. Anyway, she doesn't care anything about the old tradition. She has but one life to live, it is her life and she proposes to get something out of it — even if she has to impose herself upon the handsome, dark-eyed and shy young man.

"She casts aside everything, and on a night when he returns to the room she has prepared for him with her own dainty hands; a room in which she thought only of how comfortable she could make it, all for him. He likes the room. That is what he thinks as he arranges his clothes and papers and what-nots about it. Then retiring happy and contented, he falls into a peaceful sleep. But the fairy princess, who is real flesh and blood and passion was not asleep. She had been waiting and watching, knew when he arrived, for she heard his footsteps go around to the rear, come up the back stairway, pause at the door and could feel his annoyance when he realized he had forgotten to ask her for the key. Then he tries the door — and to his surprise, relief and delight, it was not locked at all and opened when he turned it. The Princess had thought of all that as she had of everything else and had arranged it.

"So the dark Lochinvar enters the room, turns on the light, looks around. Is pleased. More pleased than he had ever been regarding a place to live. He then arranges his things around the room she had prepared so thoughtfully. He finds a table where it ought to be where he could spread his studies upon; a light over the table where it ought to be. He sits a while and goes through and prepares his studies for the next day's classes. Finally, conscious of drowsiness, the fine young man of ancient extraction, rises, removes his clothing, gets into his pajamas, tries the bed with his hand and happy to find it comfortable, gets into the bed, and is more pleased still. He sighs and says to himself. 'Solid comfort, how good.' Then, after a time he drops off to sleep, to be awakened, soon by a knock on his door. He becomes frightened, suspicious that it is the princess. And it is, for she had been waiting all this while, waiting for him to finish his day's activities and retire, and then she comes in.

"And now Kermit, I am back to reality. I've told you my story. You understand that the man I'm married to is a husband in name only. You know enough about me by now, and I want you to feel sorry for me. I need your pity, I need your sympathy. I have grown so strangely fond of you until you've become a peculiar part of my life, and you will always remain so. The fact that you're afraid is no more, under the circumstances, than can be expected. So I am taking over, making all the advances, all the overtures. Now — just one more thing. Switch off the light, please."

He obeyed her. It was light enough in the room to note a shadowy movement only, but bright enough for him to see her take off her negligee, heard her kick off her slippers, and before he was aware of what she was doing, she had pulled the covers back and crawled into bed beside him!

And that was how it all started. Kermit sighed and rising to his feet in his apartment in Chicago, poured himself another drink of ice water, swallowed it, let himself enjoy its cooling effect for a moment and then strolled over by the window and looked out into South Parkway, stretching wide and busy below.

"And now she's going to have that baby she's been wanting since it all started," he sighed. "A wealthy and aristocratic woman, married to a tycoon, in family way by a Negro. What a situation!" He turned and walked back across the room, paused at the table, beat his hands thereon, and feeling helpless and unable to turn any way to try think some way out, he sat down and gave himself up again to reminiscences.

That never-to-be-forgotten night in Atlanta was how it started, or how it had gotten off to its start, but only the start of it. It had soon developed into a perfectly mutual relation. He soon began to like Mrs. Wingate, who insisted from that night on that she was in love with him and didn't care who knew it. She told him that he had brought happiness into her life when she had despaired of ever being happy. Every night, when Mr. Wingate was away, and which was often, was a wedding night for them. They never seemed to grow tired, always seemed to be new to each other. They never disagreed, got angry or quarreled. Never had two people so widely separated from a social point of view become so completely suited to each other. Yet their entire relation was based on sexual intercourse, which, as we understand had to seem clandestine. In fact it wasn't, but by the nature of it, it had to seem that way. It was mutual, nothing more, nothing less.

As we know, Kermit was poor as are most Negroes. Mrs. Wingate was rich. Under the circumstances, it was not like a woman in this condition, to let a man who meant much to her, go wanting. So she soon bought Kermit all the clothes he needed. Yet he never asked her for anything. He found it hanging there in his room when he returned.

Circumstances favored their relations. Mammy was too old to know or suspect what was going on, for at no time did Kermit Early, by nature careful and conservative, get careless. The woman who came twice a week to clean never observed anything. The Wingates had a country home and farm, mostly as a diversion, which served handsomely. Mrs. Wingate liked to go out there, and Kermit always had to drive her. And every time almost, they went out there, he had to serve her in the way she wanted to be served. It seemed to appeal to and please both. Always shortly after they arrived, and again before they left. All mutual, all agreeable, all pleasant.

"I love you, Kermit," it seemed to please her to say, and she repeated it as often as she had a chance. "As I look back on it, I guess I must have fallen in love with you back there in Wakefield. But I'm ashamed now when I recall how bold I was as regards you. I will never forget your fear, your fright, and how I had to add to it that Sunday. My darling," and she would then nestle her beautiful head on his shoulder and he would comfort her. He had long since begun calling her by her first name, which always pleased her.

In due time he graduated from the University, and together they discussed and agreed on his next move. It was to be to the University of Chicago, where he decided to major in administrative management. So Kermit went to Chicago and Mrs. Wingate followed him there a few days later. He stopped at a colored hotel on the South side, while she checked in at the Palmer house. He could go there to see her for they have always permitted Negroes to stop at the Palmer House without restriction. So there they would have dinner together, go to shows, be completely sociable in every way like two free people.

She helped him select the apartment where we met him, opened an account in his name at one of the big downtown banks with a substantial deposit and gave him the pass book and a supply of check books, large enough to last him for a full year.

"When the bank returns your cancelled vouchers at the end of each month, dear," she told him, "please send me the yellow sheet," which meant that she would see that his balance was always ample.

Kermit Early was not an extravagant man and she liked that, not because he was by disposition conservative, but it showed that he was not out to exploit her. So she was forever urging and insisting that he spend more, use more for his needs. When she came to Chicago even afterwards to visit him, she checked in at the Palmer House, but spent most of her time at the apartment on the South side.

She had always liked to cook, and he liked to do marketing, so they enjoyed life in the apartment, where she insisted on preparing the food. Even while living at her house in Atlanta, she would do this, bring it up to his room, and there eat and drink with him.

"You should, Kermit, dear," she said, during one of her many visits to the windy city, "plan to take about two more years after you get your Masters at the university here, go in for a Doctorate."

"Oh, Florence," he cried, "I think I have enough. I'm planning to quit after getting my master and find something to do, go to work."

"That's fine of you, but ten years hence, the two years you spend now, won't be missed, during which time you wouldn't go far enough for it to mean anything, anything at all."

"But I've been — on you so long, Florence. It's — "

"I understand, sweetheart," she said softly, "and I like you better for feeling as you do about it," and she paused then and kissed him twice. "But your destiny will begin more quickly if you continue your studies and get your Doctorate. I'll like it better, too, but of course you've got to do the deciding."

"We've always agreed, haven't we, dear?"

"Sure have — in everything." He had sat down now and she crossed and sat on his lap, something she'd never gotten tired of doing, and something he never got tired of having her do. He placed an arm about her waist, she an arm around his neck.

"We're so happy, aren't we, Kermit?"

"So happy, Florence. You've certainly proved a real companion. Stood shoulder to shoulder with me through thick and thin."

"Where would you like to take your Doctorate? Had you considered where?"

"No, dear, because I was planning to call it finis when I get my master. I should go to work."

"But if we finally decide that you should have a Ph.D, what school would you like to go to get it?"

"Where would you rather I go?"

"To Harvard," said she.

"Harvard! Whew!"

"I want you to get it from a school that'll give you the most prestige."

"Well, Harvard's that place."

"Then it's to Harvard you go."

"So expensive, dear."

"Not much more, if any, than the University of Chicago."

He was silent. "Let's not think about the expense. I won't be satisfied until I see that Ph.D. behind your name, and a Harvard sheepskin on the wall."

"You're so sweet, Florence and so good."

For this she kissed him again. "I won't ever, it seems, get entirely used to you."

She looked at him and frowned, pouted a bit.

"Oh, Kermit, why?"

"I don't know," he sighed thoughtfully, gazing at nothing. "Every time I kiss you, it always seems like the first time."

"Funny," she said, playing with his tie. "I feel the same way about you. Everything we do and every time we do it, always seems like the first time." For answer he drew her closer. She put her face beside his, cheek to cheek and sighed happily. "Isn't it wonderful, Kermit? I mean, just you and I? How little did we think when I used to pass and strike you playfully, back there in Wakefield, and stuck my tongue out at you, and — "

" — made mischievous faces," he cut her off to say and laughed.

" — that it was going to come to — all this."

"To all this, dear." She relaxed a bit now, was thoughtful a moment, then turning her face to him.

"If you say the word, I'll divorce Mr. Wingate, and — "

" — marry me?"

"Yes, Kermit, divorce him and marry you."

"I wish we could be married. As happy as we are, if we could only feel that we were man and wife — well, I'm sure we would both feel better about it."

"If you say the word, I'll go to Atlanta, tell him frankly that I'm in love with you and ask him to give me a divorce."

"You can't afford to do that, Florence."

"And why not?" she said, turning to face him.

"For so many reasons, I don't want to start enumerating them."

"Well, enumerate a few, for instance."

"Your people for one thing."

"That's the least to keep me from doing it."

"It would be considered an eternal disgrace by every white person you know."

"All the white people in the world don't mean half as much to me as you do, Kermit, and I mean that."

"I believe you."

"You've brought me more happiness than I thought I would ever

know, compelled to take it as we are, too, like this."
"We'll have to keep on taking it this way."
"If we were man and wife, I could have—that baby I want so badly."
"I wish you could."
"If you let me divorce him, we could start getting one, two, three— a gang, maybe," and she laughed. "Right away." He patted her cheek fondly.
"No, dear," he sighed. "We'll have to be satisfied taking our happiness this way. If your husband — died, for instance, then it — "
Turning to him playfully, yet with a sudden and strange something in her eyes. "Maybe I should kill him," she said and laughed, but there was still that peculiar look in her eyes.
"Like Ruth Snyder," he suggested, humorously, "and go to the Electric chair for your trouble."
The peculiar expression had left her eyes by now and she relaxed.
"The only reason I haven't divorced him of my own accord is because he is so good to me, and I feel sorry for him. He can't help his condition — "
"And since matters are going along as well as they are, why upset them?" said he. "Getting a divorce from him to marry a poor, struggling student, doesn't look like the sensible thing to do, even if you do love the poor struggling student, a colored man, whose future success is as indefinite as judgment day. No, darling," he went on seriously. "Let's postpone and forget the idea. I think you're very fortunate that he does not interfere with you."
"It *is* rather unusual, isn't it, but he never has. He is a very busy man, spends half his time at his New York Office, but he never has advanced one word of criticism. I have a feeling that he knows there is somebody else, and because he is — like he is, he feels that — oh, well, that's the way it is and — "
" — the way it is going to stay," said Kermit with finality and emphasis.
"But the baby, Kermit," she continued, and was again emotional. He looked at her. "If I don't have a baby before — it's too late, I'll feel that I have lived in vain."
"Well," he sighed, "I'd like one, too, but — oh, dear," and his tone was somewhat hopeless, "How can you and I go to having a baby —

under the circumstances?"

"As for me, I'm willing to forego and forget the circumstances," Florence said, "and just have it, let the future take care of itself. Once I have a baby I don't care what happens after."

Again he looked at her. And then he sighed again.

"I'm tempted so often to — leave the rubber off during the tender period. If and when I do, I'd be pregnant in thirty days," she went on, boldly. He started, and his eyes were curious as he looked at her. She returned his gaze quietly.

"But — but, dear!" he began.

"I won't for a while, until you've finished your education at least." His sigh this time was one of relief. She smiled into his face now and kissed him. He returned it profusely. She stretched her mouth open now and looked drowsy. He looked at her and smiled tenderly.

"Getting sleepy, sweetheart?"

"M-m."

"Want me to put you to bed?" She nodded and looked cute. He kissed her for it.

"I want a bath. Will you come in and scrub my back?"

"Like I always do?"

"Like you always do. I miss you so much when I'm away."

"Do you?"

"I do, so much, darling."

"I'll try to make up for that every time I massage you while you're here."

"Thanks, sweetheart."

"I'll go in now and turn on the water." He lifted her bodily, got up, set her down in a chair, turned to pat her cheek, then went to the bath and a few seconds later, she heard the water pouring into the tub. When he came out he was carrying her robe. She stood up and let him take her clothes off. She liked at such times to play helpless. Disrobed, completely, he put her robe on and she went to the bathroom, followed by him.

He tested the temperature of the water, while she removed the robe, stuck her toe in the water and pulled it back, quickly.

"Too hot, honey?"

"Too hot, darling," she said.

"I'll fix it," and he increased the flow of cold water. As she stood there waiting beside him, he glanced around at her and was reminded of a Goddess as the artists paint them. A Goddess on a September morn.

"Now try it," he said, getting up. She stuck her toe in it again and relaxing, let her foot settle to the bottom of the tub and smiled as she put the other foot in and sat down.

"Oh, my," she cried. "This feels so good."

"Glad to hear it," he said as he prepared the sponge and brushes nd leaning over, soaped her body, thoroughly, then began the massag- ig by rubbing her shoulders and back, down to her hips.

"Oh, Kermit, that sure feels good. If you knew how much I enjoy the comfort you give me, you wouldn't ever want to let me go away."

"I miss you as much, perhaps more than you do me."

"That's impossible, but we won't quarrel about it," she said, holding ıp first one arm and then the other, to let him massage them. He had once worked as a masseur, so knew something about it.

"Now stand up," he said when he had massaged her upper body completely. She did and he massaged her hips and lower limbs, which eemed to satisfy her even more. Through, he let the water out and with a heavy towel, proceeded to dry her body, while she relaxed and continued to enjoy as fully as she had the bath. Through, and after he put her robe about her, she left the bathroom and strolled back into the bedroom.

Outside, she crossed to the bed, removed the robe so that her body could air, thoroughly, and which she also enjoyed, and then sort of aired her hair with a large comb she kept beside the bed so that it dried more thoroughly. Coming out of the bath, he glanced across at her, and was reminded of the Mona Lisa painting, she looked so beautiful. He found her nightie and stood over her while she worked a bit longer at her hair, then laying the comb down, looked up at him smilingly, and he dropped it over her shoulders, helping to fit it around her, turned back the covers, adjusted the pillow, then turning, lifted her and laid her down. Adjusting the pillow beneath her head, he took the comb and spread her hair about over the pillow so that it could continue to dry, while she closed her eyes and seemed to enjoy the little things he liked to do to make her comfortable.

Through, he turned the bed light out over her head and crossing the room, sat down at a table and proceeded to work through his studies for the next day's classes.

Again Kermit Early came back from his reminiscing during which he seemed to have dropped off to sleep and when he sat up and looked around, he rather half-way expected to find her. Instead, he glanced down at the letter which was still in his hand, and sighing, started to read it again.

"It just happened this time, darling. I didn't do what I've so often threatened to, and wanted to. This time it got by me somehow and I had nothing to do with letting it. I am happier nevertheless, because it has, since I cannot, at least, feel that I've been indiscreet.

"I know this news will upset you, perhaps very much, but I am too happy to let it annoy me. I won't have to say anything about it to him for five or six months yet, during which time please leave it to me to decide how and what best to do. I think you know that I've always been able to face and deal with any situation that involves you and me and instead of being upset and frightened with the realization, I feel strangely relieved and more happy over it than upset. With our baby on the way I am forced to reckon with something that we have avoided all these years. After it has been dealt with, as I shall deal with it, have no fear, then I can come to you and we can be married and the father of my child will be my own, good, lawful husband as I have so wanted you to be all these years.

"So write me a long, sweet letter, Kermit, dear, and try to be as happy about it as I am.
Lovingly,
"FLORENCE"

Kermit Early sat there for a long time, just gazing into space. He did no further reminiscing. After graduating from the University of Chicago, he had gone on that fall to Harvard, where he entered for his final course. She joined him and together they took an apartment in Boston, where she visited him as regularly as she had while living in Chicago, provided for his needs, kept him amply supplied with funds, opening an account for him at one of the branches of the First National Bank there, and so Kermit Early finished, secured his Ph.D, which was what she wanted. He then set out in life to do things, and as we know, hadn't done so much, but his close friendship with Mrs. Wingate had continued without interruption through the years and they were as much devoted to each other at this time as they had been from the beginning.

He had returned to Chicago and made it his home again, and had for some time past refused to accept anything from her, though she watched over him and was ever ready to advance assistance. Then he met the leaders of the subversive group with whom he had become finally allied. They paid him well for his activities, and he found himself, as far as finances were concerned, quite independent.

It was through the subversive group who were plotting against America for the benefit of the Third Reich, that he met Heinrich Schultz. Being of the same race, although Schultz was a Nazi, their interest became mutual at once because both resented vigorously the way the Negro was played down and treated in America. Both being highly educated, these facts became more exaggerated with time than might have otherwise been the case. After a brief association, both had agreed to fight it to the bitter end at whatever cost. And so they had developed their interest in common, and since the white men they were allied with provided ample funds with which to back up any activities they felt inspired to propagate, Kermit had been busier than ever before, working out a plan which he had laid before them and Schultz just before he started back to Germany.

Among the people Kermit knew and had in a measure become friendly with, was one Sidney Wyeth, of New York, for years America's only Negro motion picture producer. During the summer he met and had long talks with Wyeth, who was in Chicago, writing a novel he had set up a company and published some months before. Wyeth had been forced to suspend the production of pictures for lack of funds, and they had talked about it. Wyeth told him that he was writing the novel and planning to sell it to make a living since he was a good salesman. Early had thought about it and hinted to Wyeth that he might be able to help him get back into pictures. Naturally, Wyeth was interested, but Early had formulated no plans as to how he would proceed before Wyeth finished his novel and returned to New York to publish it.

It was just before Schultz sailed for Germany that a plan became sufficiently fixed in Kermit's mind. The group he was allied with — a branch of the National Socialist party of Germany, and the leaders were very much interested in his plans. They also of course, hated

Jews and were desirous of reducing their influence wherever they could.

Actually a failure, Kermit Early was not unlike many Negroes who thought they could succeed by just getting a great amount of education and acquiring more degrees. They continued in school until many became old men, were prone to blame somebody for their failure, never admitting even to themselves that they were failures. So blaming the white man and hating him with it, per see, Kermit had included the Jew, and because the philosophy of Nazism was Anti-Semitic, his associates readily approved his suggestion when he laid it before them about going to New York, persuading Sidney Wyeth to produce a motion picture, the purpose of which would be to expose the Jew, and make Negroes hate them, by showing in the picture how the Jew was unmercifully cheating and exploiting Negroes.

"Great, Kermit! That's the best plan you could have thought of. But in the meantime, have you taken it up with this man?"

"No, because I hadn't thought it out that far when he was here."

"Then you aren't sure that he will do so?"

"Not until he consents."

"If he should refuse?"

"He needs money and wants to get back into making pictures. Every man who ever made pictures, always wants to go on making them. The Jews thought he was making a lot of money and that there was big money in making colored pictures because when they happened at a theatre where one of Wyeth's was playing there was always a crowd. If he talked with the owner of the theatre which in most cases was a Jew, also, they were told that Negroes liked colored pictures and 'gang' pictures and urged them to get into it and make some.

"The one thing he did not tell them and what neither thought of but if they did, it would have been the same, was that Wyeth wrote his own stories, directed them, and that Wyeth understood Negro philosophy and what pleased them only as a Negro could understand.

"Feeling that they knew it all, these Jews finally jumped into making colored pictures, with more money to spend on them at their command than Wyeth had or could perhaps get. They hired white scenario writers in Hollywood, those struggling ones, to do the stories. These men, of course, would try to do anything to make a little money and they were not paid much by these producers, but just to do a story that they could actually see later on the screen, fully produced, was enough to make these struggling writers do it cheap.

"So they started out to write stories about Negroes, with as much knowledge regarding the innerlife of the Negro, as they had about the inner life of Chinese in Chungking. These producers hired certain Negroes, educated ones, too, but yes-men, to advise them, who gave them the wrong kind because the ones they hired didn't know any better. Well, they jumped into making Negro pictures with a big fanfare. They had the support of the Negro Newspapers who gave them plenty of printers ink. Nobody had sense enough to realize that while Negroes might like Negro pictures and gang pictures, as advised, they did not picture the Negro as the gangster. So when they came forth with pictures showing Negroes putting other Negroes 'on the spot' and forcing them to pay off through the usual protective association the Negroes laughed at them.

"But the Jewish theatre owners were behind them — at the start. Promised bigger rentals than they'd ever divided with Wyeth on the assumption that these better made pictures from the coast would draw better, until after two or three, which not only failed to draw better, but soon drew so badly that many theatres quit playing them. Wyeth, alone, with no money and trying to get along, was forced out while the Jewish producers lost their bankrolls, went broke and the entire making of colored pictures, due to their interference, collapsed, and Wyeth had to quit and turn back to writing novels to make a livng."

"Interesting. Then — "

"As I view it," said Kermit, "if you folks will advance Wyeth some money to resume the production of some Negro pictures, of his own, I'm sure I can persuade him to make one or more, for us that will expose the Jews and the way they cheat and exploit us."

"Great! If you can just get Wyeth to do it. In the event that he will not, however, isn't there somebody else?"

Early shook his head in the negative.

"He is the only Negro in America that has ever made a motion picture. Wyeth has an uncanny insight into Negro life. If he makes the kind of picture we have in mind, it'll serve our purpose. It'll make the Negroes sensitive to the way he is being cheated and exploited and he's liable to break loose any time and anywhere and tear Jewish business in the Negro neighborhoods to pieces."

"Okey. We're behind you. As we understand it, we're to finance all the pictures, including your exposee picture, for Wyeth."

"That's it. By offering to finance his own pictures, Wyeth is to direct and produce ours, which I have already written."

"We've read it and it has our O.K. It should inspire lots of Negro riots against Jews all over the country. Now what?"

"I want to go to New York and see Wyeth, where I may remain until Schultz gets back from Germany."

So it was decided upon and agreed, and a few days later Kermit Early left for New York.

CHAPTER **III**

MARIE COLEMAN, stenographer, office girl, bookkeeper and general assistant to Sidney Wyeth, pushed open his office door on this particular morning, as she had been doing for years, and entered. Across the door of the office was written, WYETH PICTURES CORPORATION.

After removing her hat and coat and hanging them in their usual place, the first thing she did as she had been doing for years, was to pick the mail up off the floor, where it had been pushed through the door by the postman, sort through it, open, examine all letters, telegrams and etc., then get busy answering them.

During the past year or so, the picture business had been slowly dying. Their pictures had all been "played out", and Wyeth, as we already know, had been pushed out of making pictures by Jewish interests from the Pacific coast, and other Jewish interests in the east, who felt it could be made very profitable. After two or three years of making pictures, spending money and exploiting them, this was found not to be so, so as quickly almost as they had entered the limited industry, which for twenty years theatre owners in the Negro sections of the country had considered as Wyeth's because he had made the first full length all colored cast one, and so many of the ones that had been produced since until it was considered his line and nobody had sought to interfere seriously.

Everybody connected with it, including the few hundred theatre owners the country over in Colored neighborhoods understood that colored people wanted to see themselves pictured on the screen as they were, and not as white people were prone to visualize them, mostly as clowns, comedians, idiots, and as the Negroes put it, "just plain fools."

So Sidney Wyeth, called the pioneer Negro Motion Picture producer, more than twenty years before, had started making the kind of colored pictures that pleased them, starting off with one from a very popular novel he had written. It was a "silent" and had achieved immediate success. Since, he had made no end of the same kind, from the standpoint of theme. And it was some fifteen years before, when as a pretty young girl, just graduated from High School, that Marie Coleman had come to work for him and had continued to do so ever since.

So Marie sorted through the letters, amongst them this morning, being a telegram. She looked at it a moment. Neither the company nor Wyeth received many telegrams any more, for they had been dependent almost entirely for more than a year on the sale of the book that Wyeth had written, set up a company to publish and was fortunate enough to get it to going before they went entirely broke as picture producers, and the company had been able to keep Marie on in her job.

So most of her work was recording orders for books, wrapping them and mailing them. Rarely did they receive a telegram any more, whereas during their picture days it was mostly telegrams, often more, than a dozen daily and an equal amount sent out. So when her eyes fell on the telegram, she crossed to her desk with the handful of letters, found her letter opener and opening the telegram, unfolded it, looking first at the sender's name. It was a night letter, addressed to her boss. She smiled after reading it and shook her head a bit amusingly, turned, crossed into Wyeth's private office and laid it on his desk, where it would look him directly in the face when he came and sat down.

She returned to her desk in the outer office then, and with the letter opener, proceeded to open letters, take out money orders, some cash, which they advertised could be sent as a deposit on books ordered, an occasional check, all of which she would pile together, write the name and address from whom received, and was going along nicely when she heard a knock on the door, lightly, timidly. She looked up and called:

"Come in."

The door was slowly and timidly pushed open as if by a child, so she paused and looked up curiously. A dark face finally made its appearance and she looked up to see that it belonged to a man. Being dark, the man, of course, had to be a Negro. By this time he had gotten far enough to look around the office, scared-like

"Please come all the way in, Mister. It is a business office, open to anybody that has any business to attend."

After sweeping his eyes about the room, and ducking his head, slightly but which movement reminded her of a rabbit, before venturing from a hiding place. Presently he turned his eyes towards her and peered at her a moment, oddly.

"Yes?" she said.

He looked at her more closely now, and ducked his head in that pecular but amusing way again.

" 'Scuse me, Miss," he began, then paused to look around the office again as if to make sure. "But is dis de Wyeth' Pichuh Co. Office?"

"Yes, this is the Wyeth Pictures Corporation office?" Marie rose to her feet then and moved toward the door, which he had managed with caution and a measure of stealth to get through and close behind him. "Can we serve you?"

Again he looked around, ducked his head in that slight way this time to remind her of a chicken that had been frightened out of its wits to realize when it was over that he was still living and safe. Presently turning to her again, he looked her up and down. She was inclined to be impatient but as he looked her up and down as tho' she was a statue or some oddity, she showed amusement. "This Negro is funny," she thought.

"Yessum," he said. Relaxing a bit now and removing his hat which he seemed to have forgotten. "My name is Jackson, Miss."

"Thank you, Mr. Jackson," she said and bowed slightly.

"Fountain Jackson. Fountain iz my udder name."

"So I'm presuming, Mr. Jackson."

"Well, Miss, I has a story."

"You have a story?"

"I has a story."

"That's interesting," she said, looking him over now. She didn't see anything, so was wondering where it was, but he was talking again.

"It'll make a fine pitchuh, Madam. Ah knows hit will."

"Indeed!" she exclaimed, elevating her eyebrows and struggling hard to keep from bursting into laughter. Instead, she tried to be respectful, courteous and patient.

"So you have a story, a good story and feel that it will make a fine picture?" She looked him up and down for the sign of a script more seriously this time. "Well," she said, going on. "Where is it?" Then holding out her hand, "May I see it, please?"

Looking at her oddly, after again ducking his head in that funny way, he didn't seem to understand what she meant.

"I asked you," she said, "to let me see your story, don't you understand?"

He looked more puzzled now than ever and shook his head in the negative, slowly. Marie was vexed.

"I asked you," she said again now, "to let me see your story." Almost in pain from trying to understand what she meant, as simple as it was, he managed to turn, look at her, and ask:

"You — you mean?" and pointed at her a bit, helplessly.

"I mean where is your story?" she cried more emphatically, "where's the manuscript?"

"Aw," he cried, trying to show some intelligence. "You means de — de — mannerscrip?"

Helpless, she nodded her head kindly toward him.

"Yes, Mr. Jackson. That's what I mean. The script."

Whereupon he started, and she sighed, for she saw she would have to go all over it again, she couldn't guess, how many times. "Oh, our dumb people," she sighed, but not aloud, and to herself. Jackson was more helpless now than ever, so all he could do was to utter, helplessly:

"Aw."

"Oh," she said, quickly. "Oh, what?" Then seeing she was getting nowhere, she made a final try. "Haven't you a — script? You say you have a story. Then if you have a story, you must have written it out on paper in words, and that would be, then, your script. Now where is that? Let me see it please," and she reached out her hand again and made an impatient gesture with it.

"Uh, scrip," he repeated, still not understanding but trying to. "A scrip," he muttered more to himself than to her. Then looking up at her with a bold effort:

"No, maam, I ain't got no scrip. I has a story, but I ain't got no — scrip.'

"Then what are you talking about, anyhow?"

"I has a story awright, but no scrip as you call hit." She looked at him with pity in her eyes and sort of nodded to make him feel more comfortable. He went on now with more confidence, warming up.

"Yessum, I has a story awright. Hit's a story ob mah life. It'll make a lub pitchuh. Ah comes heah to tell you all about hit."

She sighed, helplessly, hopelessly.

"It stahts out lak dis." He adjusted himself to tell it to her, when she raised her hand.

"Just a minute, please." She smiled, and turning, went to a cabinet, where she found an old scenario, large and voluminous, for Sidney Wyeth when he wrote, always had a story to tell. She returned to where he was standing, walked up beside him and displayed the script under his eyes. She then opened it and went on to explain:

"Now this, my dear sir," she began, "Is a scenario, or script, as we call them to avoid long words."

"Um-m," he mumbled, glancing down at it, and up at her and bowing agreeably. "This is what we make the picture from."

He um-m'd again, then pointing, interjected, his eyes, brightening.

"Ah fugot to tell yuh, Miss, that I is a actuh, too, an' I c'n play de he-man lead in dis story. Also, I has a gal who wants to play de swee' ha't, you understans' de female lead, ah du leadin' lady." He smiled up at her now, satisfied that at last he was getting somewhere.

"Thank you," she said, "but just a moment, please, and let me explain."

"Yessum," said Fountain, respectfully.

"Before we can do any casting, or let you do any, the story must be written first, and then put into continuity form," at which his face went dark. She was obviously — anything she said — too deep for him. She handed him the script then, which he took a bit gingerly, and looked at it oddly.

"If you feel at all serious about what you've tried to tell me, then I suggest that you take this," she said, pointing to the scenario, "Set down over there in that chair," pointing to it, "examine this and try to get some idea of what it's all about, see?" He didn't, but he nodded his head, agreeably. So he obeyed her. She lead him across the room to a chair and seated him on it, with the script.

"Now when you feel that you have some idea of what this is all about, I'll be glad to talk with you again," bowing and smiling upon him sweetly, turned and went back to her work.

She didn't get to sit down again before she heard footsteps coming down the hall, familiar footsteps, which moved quickly and she knew that they belonged to Sidney Wyeth.

She turned to meet him with a smile and the usual word of welcome as he entered and closed the door. He glanced at Jackson as he passed by and went on into his office, followed by her, with the letters that came that morning in her hand. She took his hat and coat as he removed them and hung them in the proper place, and after he had become seated, laid the letters before him and picking up the telegram, began:

"Now before going into the business of the day, Mr. Wyeth, here is a telegram from our boy," and she smiled down at him as he looked up in impatient surprise. "You know who I mean, of course," and she spread out the wire before him. "He is, as you see, in Baltimore."

He glanced up at her, then taking the wire, did as she had, read the signature first, then turning to Marie,

"I didn't know he was in Baltimore."

"He left here Saturday night for Baltimore, at least, that is where he said he was going, and since the telegram is from Baltimore, it is obvious that he did go there — but read the wire and you'll understand what happened."

Wyeth read the heading without interest, and then the message aloud:

> "I fell downstairs here Sunday night and fractured my hip. Had to be carried upstairs after the accident, as I couldn't walk. Don't know how badly I am injured until they take me to the hospital for an X-ray this Monday. Will send you the details, special, after I've been examined.
> "Carter Thompson"

"And so he fell downstairs and broke his hip, eh? Too bad it wasn't his head! That old dumb, round pretty head, filled with nothing but frog eggs and rain water," said Wyeth disgustingly and impatiently.

"Why Mr. Wyeth," cried Marie, affecting a shock. "How can you be so unkind!"

He looked up at her quickly.

"Oh, excuse me, Marie. Of course I'm sorry." Then after a

moment's thought, looked back up at Marie.

"What was he doing in Baltimore, anyhow?" he cried, impatiently.

"You should know," smiled Marie.

"I should know? What do you mean, anyhow?"

"He met her at one of the schools where you were reviewing your book . . . " Marie was tantalizing that morning.

"At one of the schools where I was reviewing my book?"

"And while you were doing it, so was Carter doing his usual, too," and she laughed, amusingly.

"You mean — "

"Making love, of course."

"Oh, of course."

"And it wasn't in a hotel this time, Mr. Wyeth."

"Then where was it?"

"Can't you guess?"

"Oh, I haven't the time to think about where that crazy, good-looking Negro met any girl, for all he did and has ever done is to goo goo with first one and then the other."

"But he told me you were with him when he met *her.*"

"Me?"

"Yes, Mr. Wyeth, you. He told me you were with him when he met her; when it all started."

"Oh, fiddlesticks, Marie. Let's forget that simp and get down to business." He looked at the mail. "How was the mail this morning?"

"Monday's mail is always good," she said, picking up the letters. He smiled as he saw several checks, money orders and one dollar bills, then thinking, turned to her, jerking his finger over his shoulder. "Who's the glook outside? What does he want?"

"Oh, yes, him," said Marie, as if just remembering Fountain. The office was quiet as both listened a second. Then motioning for silence, Marie tip-toed across to the door, peeped out and smiled. She turned to Wyeth and beckoned. He got up and came over by her, peeped out.

Across the reception room, Jackson with his legs sprawled apart, was fast asleep. As they looked at him and smiled, the script on his lap fell to the floor and woke him up. He jumped to his feet quickly and Marie opened the door and crossed over to him.

"Well," she said, taking the scenario he had picked up and handed back to her. "What do you think of the idea by now, Mr. Jackson?"

"Oh, de story was fine, Miss. Yes, mam, jes' fine." He placed hat on his head and turned as she said:

"Thank you, Mr. Jackson."

"Tankey, Miss." Then, shuffling. "Well," he said, sort of saluting her. "Ah'll be seein' yuh." Finishing the salute, he turned and left the office.

Marie was smiling when she returned to Mr. Wyeth.

"So you got rid of another," said he with a laugh.

"Why, Mr. Wyeth!" exclaimed Marie.

"They come in with a big idea about a story, with themselves invariably cast in the leading role, their friends in the other ones. You show them a big script, which is about the most involved looking something you ever saw when you don't know what its all about. You set them down over in that chair, they look at it, get a headache, go to sleep and when they awaken, they've forgotten what they came to the office for," and he laughed, heartily. She joined with him and when it was over, they both turned to their work for the day.

CHAPTER IV

ADOLF HITLER sat down as the air around him resounded with thunderous applause, mixed with salutes of "Heil Hitler! Heil Hitler!" He had been speaking, his greatest and longest address since he became chancellor, the greatest chancellor since Bismark, it was freely said. He had spoken for two hours and twenty minutes. It was his last speech before invading Poland, one week later. Into that speech Adolf Hitler had put everything. He reviewed his activities since becoming chancellor, and Germany long before becoming so. As he had been doing since his rise to power, he attacked and tore to pieces the treaty of Versailles which he exhorted, sought to enslave Germany, took away territory, which incidentally he had succeeded in restoring and intimated strongly that more would be taken. Austria and Czechoslovakia as we know, and as all who heard him knew, had never been German territory. Austria, since the dismemberment of the old Dual Empire, he argued, perhaps truthfully, desired to become a part of the Reich. The people of Czechoslovakia as the world knew, however, had no desire to become any part of the Reich, and had been "sold down the river" a year before, to appease the Fuehrer, but was not enough to do so — and now Poland, which as the world knew, had declared against any further appeasement.

Every German leader from over all the Reich was present in person at Berchtesgaden to hear the Fuehrer on this Sunday, which before it was all over, was to be called a fatal day, and his speech, short waved throughout the entire world, was to be later remembered as a fatal speech. In one week, at the head of his legions, the most powerful army the world had ever seen, Adolf Hitler had planned and prepared to invade Poland, wipe this government off the map — and begin what was in the years to come, his ignoble end.

In his long speech, all can surmise that the Jew had by no means been left out. He was charged with about everything that had gone wrong with Germany during the last war, causing her of course to lose that war. "International Jewery," he argued, "will, if we are not careful, destroy Europe in due time as it was about to destroy Germany and was the greatest contribution toward our losing the last war. If war comes again, which we pray will not, it will be due to the Jew and his effort to exploit the world, culture, art and everything that has made us a great people, the master race, for profit.

"And no man has given him half as much encouragement and assistance in again disturbing the peace of the world than Franklin Delano Roosevelt, President of the United States," he declared, loudly, pointing his finger in the direction of America.

"All of you know," he went on, "that we want no quarrel with America and there is no quarrel between the people of Germany and the people of America. It is all the result of Roosevelt playing politics at the expense of the good relations existing between the two countries. This danger, and I say that it is a grave danger, is being agitated and propagated and instigated entirely by the influence of the rich Jews in America. Why was our Ambassador virtually sent home and relations between our two countries practically broken off long before all this started?" he asked. "The Jews. I stopped their exploiting Germany, drove them out of the high places where they were able to do so much damage, so much harm, but I did not, nor has Germany in any way, begun to even think of doing to them, what America is doing to 10 percent of her population, right there in America. In this I refer to the Negro population over there. Germany has never lynched a Jew and perhaps never will. Yet in America, which Roosevelt represents, lynching Negroes is a national pastime. They pay no attention to it. It has been going on since Abraham Lincoln freed the Negro, before that a slave. It has gone on and from all reports will continue unabated, while Roosevelt fumes and frets and points his finger across the ocean to Germany and cries: 'How dare you treat the Jew as you are doing? I want you to stop it, stop it now, once and for all, else I'll, kick you on the shins, Adolf Hitler.' He reminds me so much of a spoiled baby. Fretting and fuming and playing up to the lordship in England, endangering the peace of the world, all because of International Jewery, determined to go on exploiting the world and all its people for gain so that he may feel safe. As you know we have operated on and successfully cured the disease of Jewery in Germany. And never again in our time will it be allowed to develop to the proportions it had and endangered our national existence.

"I have just been given a full and complete report on America, among other things, of the treatment of the Negro there, of the failure and neglect regarding him, his views and condition. Remember, there are 13,000,000 colored people in America, constituting 10% of the entire population, against 4,000,000 Jews, or about 3%.

"Yet these four million Jews have more influence with the present administration over there than forty million Catholics who are mostly white people and the entire Negro population. Why is that? They are non-christians. They did not help to build America like the Germans did. It was the Germans who went into the middle states years ago when it was a wild prairie, a wilderness, where nothing but the buffalo, the wolves and Indians lived. It was the hardy German settlers who blazed this wilderness and turned it into the fine agricultural Empire, with beautiful and prosperous cities and communities, it is today. Did the Jew go from the shores of persecuted Europe, as he claims, and make conquest of anything? No! He waited safely here in Europe where there were plenty of people to steal from, cheat and exploit, until after 1880 when America had grown to its present proportions before he went there in any great numbers. He never did go into any wilderness and develop it for the benefit of civilization. Oh no, he found cheating and bargaining and exploiting so profitable right in New York, where almost half of them still live, that he didn't need to go and expose himself to the rigors of conquest as our hardy Germans did. Of the 50% not in New York, 90% of the balance are scattered in and around the larger cities, where now he is combined and organized and is wielding a greater influence on the foreign policy of America than all the other forces over there combined.

"If the world should ever again be plunged into war which God forbid, rest assured that it will be the Jew who will be the cause of it."

Among those present and who had closely listened, to every word Adolf Hitler said, was the Japanese Ambassador. Smiling occasionally, he would turn to a companion and whisper something in Japanese and then both would nod in agreement, turn back and listen to more.

It was when Hitler referred to America's disregard of what the Negro thought that they seemed most interested. They had been receiving reports for a long time from their spies in America, that

America had developed a disregard for Japanese culture to the point where the race was being held almost in contempt by the political administration there, all of which was resented, but nothing Japan could do, they claimed, could get America to take Japan's position, as they viewed it, seriously.

It was Hitler's criticism regarding the way America treated the Negro and his emphasis on lynching, compared with the fact that Germany had never lynched a Jew, that gave them something to justify the veiled criticism and growing dislike developing among the Japanese for America.

"Some day and not many months away," whispered the Ambassador to his companion, "we'll knock that smirk and American contempt into a cocked hat; we'll shock them and that high hat from stem to stern." He did not smile when saying these words, but his face was dark with a smoldering hatred.

While waiting for the day Hitler was to make the speech he had just finished, Baron Von Mueller had been admitted to an audience with Hitler, at which Von Ribbentrop was present.

"He is, I venture to guess, about the most informed man on American affairs in general, and most especially as regards the badly treated Negro, over there, in our service," said the Baron.

"You mean this young Schultz," said Von Ribbentrop with interest.

"Exactly who I mean." The Baron went on then to relate his meeting with Schultz aboard the Europa. Hitler showed interest, so the Baron proceeded to repeat Schultz' plan to return to America and report on conditions relating to the Negroes position there in detail.

"In the event we are ultimately forced into war with America, this man ought to be of great value to the Reich," said Hitler.

"Of uncalculable value, Adolf," said the Baron.

"The fact that America does not take the Negro seriously, and is not likely to because of tradition, Schultz would be able, living as he will be and does, among the Negroes, to gather valuable information and keep us informed as to any moves that may be of value to us," said Von Ribbentrop.

"He has all the intelligence which having been born and raised in Germany only could give him. During the years he lived in America, he learned to speak the best of English, so he fits into our scheme of things perfectly. He told me, and which interested me more than anything else," the Baron said, "that through the Negro servants sailing on ships down into the Caribbean he plans to find out, if and when war should come between America and Germany, the sailing time of most of the coast-wise vessels to the West Indies and South America, and to keep our submarine commanders informed as to when they sail . . . "

"A splendid idea!" cried Hitler, striking the table loudly with his fist as his eyes flashed. "I can see and understand this kind of leak regarding information to come from the Negro By all means send him back to America, promptly, provide him with ample funds to carry on his work and," turning to Von Ribbentrop, "keep in touch with him and let me know at intervals, just how he is succeeding."

In due time, therefore, Heinrich Schultz received a call to see Von Ribbentrop at the foreign office, where he met the Baron again, and for more than an hour he was questioned, which questions he was able to answer to their entire satisfaction. In the end he was provided with ample funds and assured full and complete support and cooperation, and a few weeks later, taking his sister Bertha, with whom we will become better acquainted in due time, Schultz again set sail for America, via Italy, since England and France had declared war on Germany and the blockade had gone into effect. So they traveled South to Genoa and set sail for America aboard the Italian Luxury Liner, Conte De Savoia.

CHAPTER V

SIDNEY WYETH sat in his office, struggling between trying to keep awake and reading a magazine, not having much success with either. Marie had left for the day, so it was after office hours and he was alone. Nodding away and fighting to keep awake, for he really couldn't sleep in comfort except when he was in bed, he was presently aroused by a knock on the outer door. Sitting erect and not feeling sure if he heard a knock, he waited and listened. It was repeated the second time and louder. The door was not locked, so rising, he crossed through his office and pausing in the doorway, called across the reception room:

"Come in." The door was pushed open and a tall, brown-skinned man with pretty eyes, which one had a way of noticing the moment he looked at the owner, stood on the threshold.

"Kermit Early—of all people!" exclaimed Wyeth, and crossed the reception room to meet him with outstretched hand, as Early stepped forward with his hand extended.

"Sidney Wyeth," cried Early, as they grasped each other's hand. "My old friend and my good friend!"

"Well, well," said Wyeth, beaming on the other, "The first time I recall seeing you in New York since you were co-editing the Socialist magazine, a long, long time ago," at which both laughed. Turning now, with a swing of the hand.

"Come in the office," said Wyeth, and closing the outside door, followed Early into his private sanctuary, pointed to a comfortable seat and crossing around and behind his desk, sat down, and turned to smile on the visitor.

"Where did you come from, anyhow? The last time I saw you was in Chicago,"

"While you were writing your book," Kermit reminded him.

"That's right. I returned to New York shortly after, published it and have been engaged in the business of selling it ever since to make a living."

"That's interesting," said Kermit, and was thoughtful a moment, presently raising his eyes to Wyeth and studying him a moment. If Wyeth was down from making pictures to selling his book to make a living, he ought to be able to interest him in what he had come to New York to get him to do.

"I came from Chicago," he said, simply, answering Wyeth's question.

"You've been around Chicago for quite a while now."

"It's home. The only one I know," explained Kermit.

"I like Chicago," said Wyeth. "Like it better than I do New York. Have always liked it, although New York is a freer city for Negroes to live in now."

"You think so?" queried Early.

"I know so. I live in New York but spend lots of time in Chicago. See you out there, so am pretty well acquainted with both towns. The Southerners are able to wield more influence in Chicago than they can here."

"Well, I don't know," said Early, not entirely convinced.

"But I do know, Kermit. And it's a strange thing how it all came about."

"What do you mean?"

"How the Negro happens to be freer here than in any other city in America, barring Boston."

"I'd like to hear how," said Kermit, relaxing, lighting a cigarette and crossing his legs, preparatory to listening.

"The Jews did it," said Wyeth.

Early started, sat straight, eyebrows contracted.

"What do you mean, the Jews did it?"

"It isn't easy to explain and is a long story," said Wyeth. "Still it is true. There's a Negro detective here, been on the force a long time, and he was the first one to explain all about it to me fifteen years ago when I met him in Atlanta, down there with Wm. J. Burns on the Frank Case."

"The Frank Case," repeated Early. "Do you know about that?"

"Down there when they tried and convicted him."

"Is that so," mused Early, his mind going back to that night with

Florence Wingate, at her home on Peachtree, a long time ago. He brushed it away, because Wyeth was talking.

"According to this detective, there was plenty of prejudice and discrimination going on in New York until the Jew began, through larger numbers, to enter and wield a greater influence in politics. They were out to set him in his place along with the Negro, but the Jew had too much power and too much money to back it up to let them get away with that. So he found that if he expected to be free, he'd have to carry the Negro and other minority groups along with him. They decided that everybody living in New York should be free, so he had to drag the Negro into the campaign, along with himself, so as to reduce discrimination to a minimum, and that's how the Negro happens to be freer in New York than in Chicago, although they'll refuse a Negro in a few places in both towns yet—at least try to when they get a chance."

"I agree with you on most you say, but I'm not convinced on all you say, especially about the Jew being the cause of this freedom."

"It wasn't because of any particular love for the Negro that the Jew did this. He's too busy making money, and finding other ways of how to make more, to think much about the Negro, but freedom for everybody in New York was the only way he could be assured of freedom for himself. We just happened to be in the way and have been benefitted because of it."

Since Kermit, as we know, was in New York to get Sidney Wyeth to direct a hate picture, purporting to expose the Jews exploitation of the Negro, and had been thinking about it and planning it for so long, it is obvious that he couldn't permit the Jew to be made a hero and not find some objection. Realizing like the educated and sensible man he was that he could get into a big argument, that might interfere with the purpose for which he was in New York, he decided, for the moment at least, to by-pass the subject and turn to something else. So lighting a new cigarette, drew away at it and blew a cloud of smoke into the air, then relaxed comfortably, and went on.

"Well, how're you making out with your book?" he inquired, laconically.

Wyeth shrugged his shoulders.

"Not bad, Early," he said, simply.

Kermit glanced around the office.

"You haven't made any pictures lately."

"Not for over two years," said Wyeth, and Early detected a sort of sigh, a regrettable sigh. "A few years ago I was saying that I was wedded to making pictures and would continue to make them until I died—or at least was forced by old age, perhaps, into retirement. And now, at middle age, still living—and haven't made a picture for over two years. I guess I may as well call it quits."

"There's no reason why you should quit," said Kermit, sympathetically. "You've developed maturity from the standpoint of characterization; you possess from long experience, that insight into human emotions so essential to the telling of a story. Why should you think about quitting or even retiring?"

Again Wyeth sighed.

"But it costs money to make motion pictures, Kermit," he said. Inwardly Kermit smiled and felt encouraged. He waited and listened while Wyeth went on to explain.

"Yes, it takes a lot of money, even to make a colored picture. I'm not sure if I ever want to fool around with it again."

"Meaning what?" asked Kermit.

"That there's hardly money enough in it to justify the cost and effort."

"You mean that the actors—"

"No, no. That is the least of the effort. It's the Unions that they put on you. Force you to hire a dozen men and pay them a lot of money for a few hours work when you don't need but six. It's not the Negro actor who gives you the headaches. They are so anxious to get into a picture and to later see themselves reflected on the screen until many, not real actors, of course, would be willing to work for nothing, which I never did let them do for me. Then, since the crowd on the coast butted in and got white boys to write Negro stories that soon died right before the Negroes' eyes, and got the owners of the 400 odd theatres that we play disgusted, they cut down so on the rentals I was getting for a picture, that it became a tragedy. That's what I mean. In short, it developed too many headaches and I got tired of it."

"These producers whom you say butted into your little set-up, what became of them? Where are they? Aren't they still making pictures?"

"Hell, naw!" exclaimed Wyeth. "They quit as quickly as I was forced to. No, they've all gone with the wind to God knows where!"

"Then you have the field again, all to yourself? I'm sure it wouldn't take long for you to get our group back to appreciating the kind of pictures you know how to make again."

"I suppose not, but I haven't that kind of money and I don't feel like taking a chance of upsetting my little book business, which I am developing very satisfactorily and in truth, getting along better in it than I ever did in pictures, where, of course, I handled more money."

"I understand," said Kermit, agreeably.

"I don't feel like going out here begging a lot of Jews to put up money to make pictures with any more. Just don't feel like it. I know, I've done it before and I could do so again, perhaps, if I had to, but, as stated I just don't feel like running the risk of spoiling the business I'm in to go out chasing somebody elses cash when I am setting here in perfect peace and making a good living in the book business."

"Yes but you're due to do bigger things, Wyeth. You're a man with vision and imagination."

"I can employ that more effectively, perhaps, writing novels, I'm sure. If I have half as much as you say I have, I can express it more effectively in telling stories on printed pages. It doesn't take much money to do that, just a lot of hard work, a lot of thinking and I like to think."

"That's where you're unlike the most of us," said Early and laughed, Wyeth laughed, too

"But the book has got to be published."

"I can do that myself, too I published the one I'm selling now."

"I mean in a bigger way."

"Publishing a book is simple a simple procedure compared with making pictures. If I make a picture it's got to be well and expensively enough made to be appreciated by at least Negroes when it reaches the screen. But regardless how well and in the case of a Negro picture, expensively made, it couldn't get beyond being shown in about 500 theatres catering almost exclusively to Negroes. The major picture business has long ago been taken over by Wall Street. It is a huge and gigantic industry and trust, operated through about a half dozen or more what you call 'major' film companies, who own or control all the best theatres not only in this country, but in Europe. especially England and South America. These big film Companies reciprocate their pictures with each other. 'I'll play your pictures, in the theatres we control' they say in effect to each other, 'If you'll play ours in those you control.' And so it goes. If I spent a million dollars to make a colored picture and if it was as good as the best picture ever made, I couldn't play it anywhere except in what they call Negro theatres, unless I could persuade one of the major companies to release it, and they're not interested that much in Negroes and what Negroes are either thinking or trying to do.

"Now, for the sake of argument," Wyeth went on. "If I write a book, or anybody else for that matter, and the book is interesting, so interesting until it absorbs and compels you to read it through to see how it comes out, there's nothing to keep me from selling it to white people, and they will read it just as quickly if a Negro wrote it as anybody else, depending on how interesting and exciting the story is, no more, no less."

"Then why aren't you doing that with regards to this book? I read it and I think it is damn good."

"That's what everybody who reads it says," agreed Wyeth. "I find that white people like it as well as Negroes and say so, for the interest is human; but I didn't know when I wrote it like I've learned since, that if I hope to interest the white people who review books for the big Metropolitan dailies, that I've got to write a shocker."

"A shocker, what do you mean?" queried Kermit.

"Just what I say," insisted Wyeth. "You see, Kermit, and this is some of the many things I've found out since writing my book, which is a novel narrative of contemporary Negro life. Currently, white reviewers are not interested in a novel of modern, intelligent, Negro life. At least they don't think they are original and as to my present book, for that reason, I don't think they read it when it was sent to them. I didn't send it to but a few and getting no response, I saved the books and sold them and didn't try to secure reviews very hard.

"Now, to begin with, most of them have a fixed idea as to how the Negro should be. First, they'd prefer him to be funny, to continue funny and stay that way until the end of the story which would make them laugh a-plenty. If anybody would or could write that kind of story, and I can write it, if I wanted to, his book would be far more popular with the reviewers than the kind I've written. I'm not going to use up my energy writing that kind, however. I'm too concerned with the mental, moral, social and economical development of this awful race of ours, to go into a seance and write a whole novel about a fool. We're fools enough, I'll admit, but our condition and our future, is too serious for me at least, to treat it in the light of plain and simple comedy.

"Happily, hardly anybody else has been able to write that kind of story to their satisfaction for so long until they've had to read something else; something about the Negro in the form of a novel that nobody happens to write, perhaps more than about once every five years. We've had one novel by a Negro author that seemed to please them for a while at least."

"*Nature's Child* is the one you refer to, I suppose," suggested Kermit.

"Yes," agreed Wyeth, "and another, and an entirely different kind, but one that leaves the Negro stranded, as usual, but which they are buying as no Negroes at least have ever bought. I've heard no reader say that they liked it, but they are buying it and reading it, and that is all that matters from the publisher's point of view—and the author happens to be a Southern white woman."

"You mean *Passion*," said Early.

"Just that."

"But both these books let the Negro down. They pick him up in the dog house, as it were, and leave him right where they found him, in the end."

"*Nature's Child* sent us to the electric chair, so in that respect, you're mistaken," and both laughed heartily. "*Passion* takes us to the graveyard of despair and hopelessness—and leaves us as you say, right there. All of which supports my contention. They have grown to look at us through distorted eyes. We're not supposed to have a contemporary life like other Americans. I don't suppose that any of them are actually aware of it, but I am. I know that if I ever write a book that the critics are going to open and read through to the end and then write reams about, I've got to develop the Negro and carry him through a peculiar maze of events, and these events must be real and as he reads them, remember that what I say is true, though seemingly fantastic. If I hope to arouse their interest at all, I've got to, in short, shock him to his vitals.

"I've been thinking how I could write such a book. Any book that I write has got to, however, treat the Negro as he is, and leave him in the end, decent and respectable. I'm sure it can be done, but it's up to me or some other Negro that knows how, to do it. If not, he will continue to be distorted all out of proportion, and played down, which seems to be the popular current way to treat him in fiction. But I have talked clear away from the subject. I don't think I finished asking you what I started out to from the beginning." Kermit smiled.

"What you've talked about, I assure you, is more interesting than whatever you started to ask me about. In the meantime, and before getting down to what I'm here to see you about, for I have come to New York, especially to see you."

"Indeed!" exclaimed Wyeth, his eyebrows raised. "This is an honor."

"Not an honor, but coldblooded, down-to-the-earth-business. But before we go into that, I'd like to ask you a few questions."

"Fire away," declared Wyeth. "I guess I can answer. I'll try to anyhow."

"They are intimate questions, direct and to the point, but questions you might feel are a bit—impertinent."

"My mind is as wide open as the Dakota prairies from where I came," laughed Wyeth. "So fire away, ask me anything you like. Get it off your chest and your mind."

"How do you feel about the Jewish situation, the Jews themselves, I mean?" inquired Early.

Wyeth paused, his smile vanished; he turned to look curiously at Kermit.

"How do I feel about the Jews?" he repeated. "Why about the Jew? Why not at the same time and as well, about the Italian, the Greek, the Chinaman—about anybody? I don't understand you."

"You're covering too much territory," said Early. "After the second generation all other nationalities, except the Chinaman and us, of course, become more or less molded into one group. White Americans. Only the Jew remains outside the realm, he never changes. He may claim to be an American if he's born here, but—"

"—he is. The same as everybody else who's born here, including us."

"I don't mean it just that way. What I meant to say is that in his dealing, association and otherwise, he remains always a Jew."

"I agree with you in that respect. And for the Jew's own benefit, that is unfortunate, for after all is said and done he *is* a white man, just as white from the standpoint of pigment, as any other white person."

"Now you're getting somewhere," said Kermit. "I suppose my asking such a question appears a bit odd, far fetched as it were, for currently we have only a passing interest in the Jew. We meet him only when we go into his store to buy something. Beyond a business transaction like the purchase of clothing, or food or otherwise, we have no interest in common with him. But I had a very good reason for asking the question I did as you will, if not presently, ultimately see and understand."

At the moment Wyeth, by his expression, did not understand.

"Now, while you were writing on your book in Chicago, you told me that the Jews were responsible for your being forced to suspend making pictures. I happen to know, personally, that you have gone along in the making of colored pictures very successfully for a number of years. Yet within two years after they combined and became a competitor, you've been forced to suspend, and after you were forced out, they folded up and disappeared as competitors, also. Why?"

"Well, regarding the statement about saying that Jews had forced me to suspend, I didn't mean it literally. I want to explain that I just have a way when I refer to certain people by emphasizing their race. If we talk long, you'll hear me say those Negroes or we Negroes or us Negroes or those Italians or that Greek and so on down. When I speak that way, due to having grown more emphatic than necessary, for I should just say those persons, or something else. Well, to cut a long story or explanation short, I didn't mean anything in particular by it."

"Still you did say the Jews had put you out of business," argued Kermit.

"Any competition in the matter of making motion pictures is Jewish competition, for the show business and the picture business, especially is greatly monopolized by them. Anyway, answering your first question, 'what do I think of the Jews'? I still don't know what you mean. But I have no particular opinion regarding them any more that I have an opinion about any other group," said Wyeth.

Kermit shrugged his shoulders.

"I simply asked how you felt about them."

"You must have had a reason. A man of your training, education and contact, wouldn't just ask such a question without a reason. Out with it?" Kermit looked at him as if he didn't care to go any further at the moment, but suddenly said:

"Then you like Jews, maybe? Is it possible that you consider him a friend of the Negro; of ours?"

"I don't consider him anything of the kind. He's as good a friend of the Negro as he is of anybody else, but being a friend of anybody's isn't exactly his forte. He's too involved in trade and commerce, cold business and profit. Why should he lose any time or thought being a friend of ours? As I said it isn't worth his time or thought."

"Well, I suppose not. But—" and then he broke off, and didn't finish what he started to say.

Wyeth was curious by now, so he made a gesture and went on:

"Now, Early. Lay your cards on the table. Why have you asked me such a question, anyhow?"

Turning to him more frankly than before, Kermit looked straight at him and replied:

"Because, Wyeth, I'm in a position to do you some good; to possibly help restore you to making pictures. Yes, that's it. To help you."

"That's very fine of you, I'm sure. I don't know just how you can help me. Meanwhile, if you *are* in such a position, and you may be. You're not a man to make such a statement unless you know whereof you speak. Still, there is, perhaps, a string tied to this help you speak of, yes or no?"

"Maybe," replied Kermit with a little shrug of the shoulders.

"Once a man has made pictures, the desire to continue is, I think, forever with him. I made almost fifty full length feature photoplays, and I would make more if I had the money. Before I quit two years ago, I had prepared three very fine stories, broke them down and had two rehearsed and ready to produce—then I was let down by somebody who had every reason to have financed the making of them; somebody who would have profited even more than I."

"Still they let you down."

"They let me down."

"Bet he was a Jew."

Wyeth looked up and smiled.

"I can get you the money, all you need, more than you've ever had to make pictures with before," said Kermit, evenly. "If you're willing to do a little—compromising."

"You're a bit vague and indefinite on the one hand, while you hold a beautiful picture up before me with the other. Just what kind of a compromise? You've got me curious now."

Kermit suddenly glanced at his watch, then looked up at Wyeth.

"It'll require quite some time to lay the plan before you in detail, and I don't care to go into it just now. In fact, I've an appointment elsewhere, and am over due now." He rose to his feet, Wyeth followed, an expression of disappointment on his face. Kermit extended his hand in a perfunctory manner, which Wyeth took.

"I'll get in touch with you maybe tomorrow, or within a very short time. We'll take our time and go to the bottom of the matter. I believe you'll come with me when you understand fully what it's all about. Meantime, so long and goodby until you hear from me."

Grasping Wyeth's hand, he shook it and turning, left the office and went to meet Mrs. Wingate, who was coming up from Atlanta to meet him.

CHAPTER VI

AFTER EARLY left, Wyeth went downstairs, ate his dinner at a small restaurant on the first floor, then returned to the office and went to work on a new book sales campaign plan. He was therefore very much interested in being alone, especially after Early ran out on giving him any more information as regards that strange, vague plan to secure him funds to resume the production of pictures.

He had been at work an hour or more and had about completed the first draft of the plan in long hand and was about to move into the outer office and type it when there was a knock on the outside door, so soft and low that he was not sure about it. With a frown of impatience on his face, he listened and presently it was repeated, a bit louder.

Getting up, he crossed to the outer door and called: "Who is it?" There was no answer and this annoyed him, so striding across the reception room, he took hold of the knob, jerked the door open impatiently—and then started, perceptibly, his mouth agape as he did so. For there before him stood a very beautiful girl, attractively dressed and smiling up into his, a moment before, very impatient face.

"Oh," he sort of breathed, and swallowed like a guilty boy. "Miss Vinson."

"Yes, Mr. Wyeth, me. I hope I'm not disturbing you. You looked so impatient when you jerked the door open, you frightened me. I'm a bit afraid now and feel that I should run away," and she started to turn, but reaching out quickly, he caught her arm and led her into the room, closing the door behind her.

"By no means, Miss Vinson. I—I—"

"—what," she said, looking up at him coquettishly.

"Well, I wasn't expecting anyone, and I thought you were some person calling to apply for work in the pictures. We are not making any just now and I was busy and—"

"Didn't want to be annoyed? Well," and she turned as if to go out the door, and again he caught her arm and went on profusely.

"Please no, I didn't mean you. Not you at all. I'm glad you came. It is a pleasant surprise and I welcome you. So let me take you right into my little private sanctuary and make you comfortable."

She made eyes at him, but permitted him to lead her into his office, close the door, and find her a comfortable seat.

He had met the girl, whose first name was Edrina less than a week before on Seventh Avenue. He was on his way to the office, while she was in company with a song writer by the name of Donald Howard, a hang-around-the-show-man, whom he had known for a long time. She impressed him very much. About 28 years of age, she was tall, but not too tall and she was slender, still not too slender. Sort of a keen looking, light brown skinned girl with beautiful dark hair, dark eyes and pretty teeth, which showed when she smiled. She looked keen and very intelligent and interested him then and there. They had talked about a star of his, whom she admired and it was during this conversation on the sidewalk that he invited her to call at his office sometime. And now before him she sat, looking as sweet, he thought, as sugar, smiling across at him.

She wore a cute little hat that permitted her beautiful dark hair to stand out conspicuously from under, with a feather on the top, reaching above it, and a little veil, that crossed her nose about halfway, that set off her appearance, and he was greatly flattered as he gazed across at her.

Howard told him that she had been on Irvin C. Mantan's show the season before, doing a turn and a couple of songs, and that she might be interested in working in pictures before the show went out again, and told her to call and see him about it.

"Well, Edrina," he started, looking at her with unrestrained admiration, "if I may call you that."

"You may, of course," she said sweetly, and smiled back at him and seemed more beautiful than ever. He was conscious that his heart was now beating faster.

"Thanks," he said, and seemed much pleased. "Since you've been so nice as to call, in response to my invitation, I want you to relax, take it easy and I hope we can become better acquainted."

"Thank you, Mr. Wyeth," she said, bowing her head a bit. She had a soft, pleasant voice.

"And, incidentally, when you get to know me better, my first name is Sidney. You won't need to be so formal. Sidney is only one word, while Mr. Wyeth requires two," and they both laughed and felt more comfortable.

"I'll start calling you Sidney now," she said, elevating her eyebrows, beautifully. "That is—if you want me to."

"I want you to, Edrina," he said seriously.

"Do you really," she said, leaning forward slightly, also anxiously.

"Yes I do, Edrina, seriously."

She relaxed against the back of the chair and seemed to sigh her next words more than just say them.

"You said that so beautifully, until I'm almost tempted to believe you; to believe that you really meant it."

"I was never more sincere in my life, Edrina," he said, leaning toward her, his face more serious than it had been for a long time. His smile was gone and he seemed deeply in earnest. "You must feel that I do mean it, Edrina," and shoving his chair forward, drew closer and laid his hand on hers. She waved at him with her free one, deprecatingly, as if to say, "go on. You're kidding." He read that in her eyes and grasping her hand a bit, cried:

"You know, Edrina, and this has been on my mind since I met you. That with a little encouragement I could become very much interested in you."

She pretended to pout and looked at him out of the corner of her eyes, then shook her head.

"Now, now, Mr. Wyeth and excuse me for being formal again, but I'm afraid you're turning out like all the rest. When I had begun to hope—even believe that—you were different."

He paused and relaxed, and then she suddenly grew anxious. She was not sure if he understood that she was only joking. He was speaking.

"I don't claim to be so different from other men, if any, even. But I do know that I have a great many responsibilities, so many until it does not interest me to jive or to try to jive a girl, as they say. I'm sure that I have more to keep me occupied than the average run of our men, I mean, colored men."

"If you're responsible at all, and obviously you must be, you're more than most colored men, I admit. Responsibility is something that few even pretend to have, or assume, at all."

"From the moment I met you last week, there was something about you that appealed to me," he now said.

"There you go again, dear Sidney. Trying to kid me," she made the usual deprecating sound with her tongue between her teeth and shook her pretty head teasingly.

"Please Edrina," he went on, holding her hand between his two. "I ask you to believe me—you must believe me," he pleaded, sincerely. He was close to her now, and she became more serious as she looked at him.

"Do you want me to, Sidney?"

"I do, Edrina, seriously." She seemed at a loss for a moment how to proceed, what to say. Lowered her eyes to think, then looked up at him: "And, if I do?"

"I will never let you down," he insisted, earnestly. Pausing, like one cornered, and not knowing where to go, for there was no escape, she presently sighed.

"Well, I don't know. I'd like to believe you Sidney—in fact, I even want to believe you. But a girl gets let down so badly and so often these days until she doesn't know whom to trust, who to believe."

He looked at her closely, thoughtfully for a moment and the grip he had on her hand was relaxed. His look at her now she thought, was a bit hard.

"Who's been fooling you?" He asked rather bluntly.

Immediately she became a show girl, in other words, a bit tough.

"Who, me?" she threw back at him coldly.

"Yes, you," he said, his expression by now was tempered with a bit of amusement, which she didn't catch and understand at once.

"I haven't let any man fool me, Sidney—and I don't intend to.—"

"—let me," he assisted, cutting her off and pointing at himself. Now he was himself again. He smiled on her, kind and tenderly, so much so until she could no longer doubt him. He squeezed her hand.

"Oh, I'm so sorry, Edrina. I didn't intend to be unkind, or to anger you."

She laid a hand on his, and looked tenderly up into his eyes.

"Keep on talking and acting like that, Sidney. I'm sorry if I hurt you. I didn't intend to; I don't want to." She smiled upon him reassuringly. Then, squeezed his arm: "I—I do like you, too—a little, and that's why I came here to see you tonight—alone." Feeling that she'd said enough, she lowered her eyes and affected sadness. After a pause, she raised them again. "Now will you—believe me?"

"I believe you, Edrina. So let's agree on that at least. Let's believe each one is interested in the other and get fully acquainted. What do you say?"

She smiled up at him now, happily, and stuck out her free hand:

"Shake, partner," she cried, enthusiastically. "It's a deal!" And they grasped hands like two pals. Then laughing, they both automatically rose to their feet.

"Now, where do we go from here, partner?" said Edrina, and waited for him to make the next move, a smile spreading over her face.

"Well," said he, cheerfully. "I'm free, single, disengaged and hungry again, although I ate only three hours ago. Do you happen to feel the same way?"

"Have you ever met a show girl in Harlem that wasn't?"

Both laughed heartily at this, and moved toward the door, paused again and faced each other.

"In that regard, Mr. Wyeth, I don't claim to be any different from the rest of us up here. We're always hungry, so hungry in fact, that we seem to stay that way to avoid getting hungry," and they laughed so much at that until they leaned against each other and felt closer as a result. They moved into the reception room now, still laughing. Pausing after a time, he turned to face her.

"I've always said that if a man made any money at all, he could hardly go bankrupt, eating. And I don't mind feeding a hungry girl at the same time. So everything is mutual. Where do you want to go?"

She reached up and adjusted his tie, which made both feel more intimate, as she replied: "It's your money that we're going to eat and drink on, Sidney, dear. You choose the place," and looked up at him.

He tickled her chin with his fingers, and she smiled as though it pleased her.

"No, no, dear Eddie. There must be some place you'd like to go better than just any place. I want to please you, understand?"

She nodded her head and found something to fix at on his coat, vest, tie or shirt. She was silent. He went on.

"So you name the place, dear girl, and it is there we will go."

She looked up into his eyes now kindly, trustingly.

"You are a nice fellow after all," she said, softly. "Frank, plain, honest and big-hearted like I'd hoped you were, and, I'm afraid," she sighed, "I'm going to learn to like you, maybe a lot, if you keep on being nice like that, before it's over." She paused to look up at him coquettishly. He could no longer resist her appeal, and then he dared. He leaned down and her eyes opened like she was a bit frightened, but wishing to please him as he'd said he wanted to please her, she met him half way, and they kissed.

Each underwent a sudden thrill. The kiss had been so tender, so soft, and so sweet until both were lifted up, by the contact, as it were, to strange and dizzy heights. Impelled by an irresistible force, which neither understood or could longer resist, he kissed her again, and then he placed an arm about her waist and kissed her again and again. Then holding her close, so close they could feel each other's heart beat, he sighed and relaxed and was forced to turn his eyes away.

"Oh, me. You—you—overwhelm me, Sidney. Overwhelm me so until I've forgotten where I am, what I'm doing. You asked me something before it started. I can't remember now what it was."

"I asked, dear Edrina," he said, looking down into her eyes, his arm still about her waist. "Where you wanted to go?"

"Oh, yes, yes, of course," she said hastily. "Pardon me for forgetting so quickly."

"I fear that I could go on forgetting in exchange for such moments as have just passed, beautiful, exhilarating, never-to-be-forgotten moments."

"Oh, Sidney. You can even be—romantic, when you try. I've always viewed you as cold, distant, and domineering."

"Great goodness," he cried, affecting fright.

She giggled.

"Well, I have," she said, protestingly. "I met you only last week, but I've known you for a long, long time."

"Really?"

"Who doesn't know Sidney Wyeth? You're the only one of our group to make pictures. I've seen your pictures, many, many of them. I liked them, too. They say you make the best of all the colored pictures, and I know they draw great crowds. They say, the theatre owners, that when they have a Wyeth picture, every day is a holiday."

"Thank you."

"You haven't made any for quite some time now. At least I haven't seen any?"

"No, I haven't."

"Why?"

"Oh, dear, that's a long story—too long for us to go into now. I'd rather talk about you—and me."

She smiled up at him sweetly, and he kissed her again, quickly. She shook her head at him and pointed an accusing finger.

"Never would I have believed anybody if they'd told me you were like this," she accused him, tantalizingly.

"Neither would I. I'm surprised at myself, but I'm sure there's a reason."

"What reason, may I ask?" He looked at her.

"I'm looking at the reason. Easily and plainly, you."

"Oh, dear, dear," she cried, and leaned on him. He squeezed her close. She relaxed and looked up. "Before I forget again, I'd like to go to the—Bamboo Inn."

"To the Bamboo Inn." He repeated after her. "Then," and drawing her close, kissed her once more.

"It's to the Bamboo Inn, we go!" laughing, happily, he turned, his arm still around her waist. He switched off the light with his free hand, turned the night lock, swung the door wide open, and relaxing his hold around her waist, waved her into the hall before him, followed, turned, closed the door, rattled it from the outside to see that it was locked, and together they left the building for the Bamboo Inn.

CHAPTER VII

WYETH AND MARIE were hard at work in their little office in Harlem the next morning when a messenger with a special delivery letter entered the office. Marie signed for the letter, looked at the postmark, smiled, knocked on Wyeth's door and entered. Wyeth looked up with a slight frown, then relaxed it when he saw her face and the smile and the letter, which she opened as she talked.

"Well, the special is here from our boy." Wyeth looked at the letter, then with an impatient wave of the hand told her.

"Go ahead and read it. I don't decipher many of his words very easily." Thompson was not related to either. Referring to him as "our boy" was a joke.

"Dear Mr. Wyeth," Marie read.

"Supplementing my telegram of recent date, I was going from the bathroom to my room at Miss Gentry's home here when I slipped and before I could regain my balance, fell to the floor, rolled down the stairway to the bottom. They had to carry me upstairs as I couldn't walk. In addition to fracturing my hip, my face was badly bruised also. Today an ambulance came and took me to a hospital where I was X-rayed three times, then brought back to Miss Gentry's.

"The Doctor told me to stay in bed for a week, then move around on crutches for two or three weeks longer. By this you can understand why I've decided to stay in Baltimore indefinitely. Besides, I've been offered three jobs already, so this is to ask you to please get my laundry and belongings from the room at Mrs. Morgan's and send them to me."

Marie paused and looked down at him.

"Well, what do you think of it?" she ventured. He looked up at her a bit absently. His mind seeming to be on something else. He shrugged his shoulders.

"What am I supposed to think," said he. "The letter speaks for itself."

"Of course," said Marie, "with your mind on your business and so much planning, you would hardly understand. But when Thompson fell downstairs at Miss Gentry's home, he did not, figuratively land on the floor at the bottom of the stair. He did in a physical sense, of course. But in spirit he landed smack dab into her arms. Get what I mean?"

"I think I do, but it couldn't be as serious as all that."

"Wait and see what happens — but I have no right to take up your time by gossiping about Thompson. I'll continue it with my mother at home tonight. There are other matters of importance to command your attention this morning."

"For instance, what?"

"I made an appointment for you to receive and talk with Mr. Early, of Chicago at eleven this morning."

"Oh, yes." He glanced at his watch.

"Yes. He said that it was very important that he see you, so he's calling promptly at eleven and asked me to be sure to keep you in the office until that time."

"That's just fifteen minutes away. I'll see him," and then as if to himself, "I wonder what he wants to talk to me about, anyhow?"

"I haven't the least idea," said Marie, and he started and looked up at her and smiled.

"I was talking to myself, Marie. I was thinking aloud to myself. Still it is just as well that you heard."

"What ever it is, it seemed most important to him, that he see you, so I wouldn't like you to forget and go out as you so often do."

"I won't forget that I won't go out." And then again he mumbled to himself.

"This Kermit Early has always been a sort of man of mystery. He isn't married; I never see him with a woman, yet I'm sure he isn't a fairy. He seems to live well, has what he wants, yet has nothing to do with anybody that I've ever seen. So what, exactly, does he do, and what has he got against the Jews? Something strange and peculiar about the whole thing." Then relaxing, and looking up at the girl. "Well, he'll be here presently, so I'll just wait and see." He called her and by the time he had dictated the letters to be answered that morning Kermit came and was shown into his private office by Marie.

"Now picking up where we left off yesterday, Wyeth. You intimated that you'd like to be financed so you can make a series of new pictures."

"I would be interested, yes."

"And I said that I was in a position to get the money for you to make them with, correct?"

"Correct, — with a string tied to it, you also implied."

"There is a condition."

"And what is that condition?"

"That you produce a certain kind of picture that we are interested in having made for our use."

"Why have you singled me out to make this certain kind of picture?"

"Because of your uncanny insight into the conditions we want this picture made around. I consider you the only man in America able to do this to our satisfaction."

"That would seem like a compliment, but before I become enthusiastic, an enthusiasm superinduced by the vision of having enough money once in my life to make some pictures. I do not wish to be worried crazy with fear: the fear of being unable to pay off before it is finished."

"You will be relieved of all financial worries if you go with us. I can assure you as to that."

"All's well enough thus far. What kind of picture is this that you want me to make for you and your associates to release?"

"A picture exposing activities of the Jew for the benefit of our group; to be shown, primarily, to our group."

"M-m. I was afraid it would be something like that. Too bad."

"Why too bad?" said Early. "You need money, don't you? You've said you'd be glad to have real money to make some pictures with once? If you had real money you could make the kind of pictures you are capable of producing, couldn't you? You've never had that kind of money, so what?"

"But I have never made a hate picture."

"But you do hate Jews, don't you? They forced you out of making pictures? Messed up the business you set in motion years and years ago?"

"But I don't hate Jews. I don't hate anybody."

"After all they did to spoil your business?"

"They didn't go into it to hurt me; to put me out of business. They went into it on the theory that they could make some money. They had a right to." Early paused before going on.

"But they put you out of business, they — "

"The Negroes didn't like their pictures, and stayed away from the theatres in such great numbers when they played them that they were forced to suspend, give it up. It was just my bad luck the way things turned out. That doesn't give me any leave to go off sulking, to start a campaign of hate."

"But consider what it can mean to you? Put you back on your feet more solidly than you have ever been!" Early insisted.

"I've considered all that, Early, but I'm simply not a Red a communist or a Nazi. I hold no brief for Jews. Many times during my fights with them to try to get a decent rental price for my pictures, I've often felt like killing them, they seemed so mercenary. But I'm too concerned with the deficiency of the Negro, and I'm too involved in trying to improve or help improve the condition of our group, to have any time to hate Jews."

"Jews are the scourge of America. They are the greatest disease in our economical and political life. Some day you're going to admit, along with everybody else that the Jews are the cause of this war, the last war, all the wars since modern civilization; wars that have destroyed millions of people in Europe."

"Maybe so, and if it is, it will continue. My going out here and producing a hate picture isn't going to change it."

"It'll help expose the dirty chiselers in the eyes of Negroes. That's worth something." Looking at him more closely.

"Who's behind all this, anyhow, Kermit? Not Negroes, of course?"

"Oh, no."

"Naturally they wouldn't have that kind of money, and if they had, it isn't something that they would be sponsoring. In short, it just isn't Negroes, is it, Early?"

"No," admitted Early.

"I thought not," said Wyeth. "Then who?"

"I'd rather not say. All you have to do is just give me your word that you'll make this picture and leave the rest to me. Only this I can say at this time. These people hate Jews and feel it is a patriotic duty to expose his methods, his exploitation, his chiseling and his cheating."

"A strange patriotic duty. Why not call it by its right name, a hate duty."

"I don't see it that way."

"Supposing for the sake of argument that I made this picture. Where would you show it, with the Jews owning most of the theatres? People can be persuaded only to go to theatres to see pictures in any large numbers."

"That is not a part of your responsibility. All you're to do is just produce the picture. The rest is our responsibility."

"I couldn't, Kermit, as much as I'd like to get the use of the money you promise for doing so. My heart wouldn't be in it, and when my heart isn't in a thing, I don't do much good at trying to do it." Turning to him seriously. "Do you know what I could do so much better than that."

"What?" asked Early.

"Make a picture exposing the Negro. His laziness, shiftlessness; his wasteful tendency and his irresponsibility — a whole lot that is so completely wrong about him; so unnecessarily so; things that he could so easily, with a little effort, correct and make right. A picture exposing the Negro for his own good. I'd like to title it, 'Go look in the mirror, you fool! That thing looking back at you, is yourself.' By this, it is meant that the Negro is made up of about everything that is contrary to his own welfare. His word is no good, and I repeat, he is irresponsible, trifling and lazy, wasteful and extravagant. We even hate each other. Heard a speaker while in Chicago writing my book say that no Negro has ever risen to power and success by the help of Negroes. Consciously and unconsciously, he hates his own kind, doesn't want another Negro to get ahead of him, and if he can, will reach up and pull him back and down and tramp on him. Education has neither changed or improved this condition. In fact, the more educated the Negro is, the more he seems to play his fellow man down, hold him in contempt, laugh at anything he attempts to do and lauds the white man at every turn. He doesn't hesitate to betray his fellow man to any white man who'll pay him.

"Does the Jew play such cheap politics? You know he doesn't. The Jew is the world's oldest and most successful merchant. He is responsible, employs hundreds of thousands of people right here in America. Do we? I know, we've been free only 80 years and haven't got that far. At the rate we are going, hating and anxious to keep each other on a level with ourselves, how far do you suppose we will have gone in another eighty years?

"No, there is so much wrong with our group and we need to be exposed for our own benefit more than anybody else, that it seems vain even to go thinking about exposing Jews."

"Well, Wyeth," said Early, rising to his feet, and smiling. "I expected you to refuse to do what we want you to do at this time. I'm here in addition to persuading you to make this picture, also to wait and meet somebody else, due here in a few days from abroad. So don't make up your mind now, just take it easy and keep thinking about it. After all, you could make the picture and use a fictitious name, not your real name. I've decided that you only can do this picture, from a story I have written, like nobody else can, and I'm going to stay on your tail until you consent to do it." He paused now to look at his watch.

"It's noon and what about going downstairs and having a bite of lunch with me?"

A few minutes later, seated in a booth with a couple of bottles of beer before them, while they waited for their order to be prepared, they couldn't help overhear a conversation between two colored women, seated in the booth behind them, that amused them.

"Dey wa'nt no tuhkey to be had, so I decided to buy a chicken instead," said one, whom the other was calling Lucy.

"None to be had up heah in Ha'lem," said Helen; "but plenty down town fo' white fo'kes. So dat's wha' I went and got mine."

"You did?" cried Lucy, amazed.

"Sho did, and I got a good one, too."

"Well, I decla'," cried Lucy, and her tone indicated her chagrin. "Well, gittin' back to what I stahted tu tell yuh."

"Sho. Go ahead. I'm interested. Meantime, why you think we couldn't get tuhkeys in Ha'lem when dare wuz plenty downtown?"

"Dey was a ceiling on'm, and dey been puttin' so many Ofays in jail fo' ovuh chargin', until dey was afraid to, and ef dey can't steal frum and cheat us niggahs, dey won't be bothered wid going regular to oblige us. So dey wouldn't put dem selves out to go an buy tuhkeys to sell to niggahs and just make a ceilin' profit."

"Well, gittin' back to what I stahted tu yell yuh. Have anudder drink," and she proceeded to pour it.

"Sho."

Early and Wyeth smiled at each other as they listened to the women.

"I goes into dis sto. The man was busy in de rear and when he seed me entuh, he motined fo' de woman to go wait on me. She was fat, lak most Ofay womens is, especially aftu dey gits mai'ed and has a kid or two." The other laughed.

"So she bustles up to me, smilin'. 'C'n I serve you, lady,' she said, gracious like."

"They knows how tu flattuh you," said the other.

"And how," cried Lucy. "Well, she smiled at me, and says: 'A chicken? Nice, fat, tender chicken,' and pointed to a pile ov'm displayed in the front window. I pointed to one I lacked, so she picks it up and throws it on the scale.

"How much?" I asked.

"She looked at it. 'Dollar ninety-eight.'"

"Seemed kinda high fo' the size. 'How much a pound?' I asked. She didn't seem to want to say. Instead she repeated, 'the chicken is a dollar ninety eight cents.' And I calls back just as loud. 'How much is the chicken, a pound, woman? You sell it by the pound, don't you?' My niggah was beginnin' tu rise now. She glanced toward the man, who shook his head, and then turning back to me she said '44 cents'. I looked at the scale. It registered 3½ pounds. I did some figurin' in my mind. 'Come on,' she calls, 'do you want it or not?' At 44 cents a pound, the chicken would total about a dollar and fifty eight cents.

"How come a 3½ pound chicken to cost a dollar and ninety eight cents,' I asked, loudly. She picked the chicken up an threw it back on the pile with the others, and turned to wait on somebody else. I stood there, glarin at heh, fightin' mad. I looked right at her cheat anudder niggah right befo' mah eyes, but he just out and paid what she asked without doing any checkin'."

"Or thinkin'," said the other.

"That's it. No thinkin', jes' let a duhty Ofay cheat his eye balls out and not know it, even."

"It's a shame."

"Hit's going on all ovuh Ha'lem. Ofays cheatin' niggahs, and niggahs not known' it even."

"I wanted to ruch ove de countah and grab dat Ofay bitch and beat heh yes, yes all ovuh dat sto. But de culud papers had been say'n so much about us niggah's fightin', ready tu fight at de drop of a hat, swearin' and black guardin'."

"De'se Ofays uz enough to make us fight."

"Ain't it so."

"Las' tanksgivin'," said Helen, "I was shoppin on eighth avenue and stopped in front of a sto wha a nice lookin' young tuhkey was displayed. De Ofay inside saw me and come out an asked me to come in and sold me the tuhkey, I taught, cheap."

"It always seems dat way," said Lucy.

"Jes' seem's dat way," admitted Helen, "But it all 'Jes seems."

Lucy laughed.

"When Xmas come, I was shoppin' Christmas mawnin' fo anudder tuhkey and stopped in front ob de same sto' again. The same Ofay come hustlin' out, recanized me and asked me in de sto' to buy annudder tuhkey. He jes' named a price lak dis woman did tu you 'bout de chicken. I keep on askin' 'how much a pound?' He finally named it, but I could see he didn't want to, and dat made me 'spicious. I paid him and when I got outside, I sorta tested de weight of dis tuhkey up and down and it seemed lighter dan it oughta be. I went into a sto' next do'. I asked de man to put dat burd on de scale, which he did. It was nearly fo' pounds sho't ob what it was supposed to be, and was I mad! I go back to dat sto' and he saw my niggah wuz up. I raised my finguh and beckoned to him. He come up and tried to be mad. I didn't caeh nuthin' bout dat. It wuz me dat was mad, sho' nuf mad. I said 'you been cheatin,' white man, and onless you gimme back du money you has cheated me out uv, I gwine 'pot you to de law."

"Dat did it, I bet," laughed Lucy.

"I'll say it did. De co'ts know dese Ofays in Ha'lem cheat, so when you haul 'em dare, dey go befo' de Jedge wid one strike against dem befo' they staht. Dey hates to be called to co't on cheatin' cha'ges. So this Ofay fo'koes ovuh a dollar rat quick, and sulks back to de rear of de sto'."

"Dey has a way of weighin' something heavy on a scale dat only weighs a few pounds, wid de reg'lar scale hid under de countuh wha he can change rat quick. So on dese sho't scales, he throws somethin' heavy and you can't tell how much it weighs. He then says, 'so much or so much' and you get cheated tu death and don't know what hit's all about."

"An talk about liahs! Dey 'cuses us niggahs ob bein' liauhs, but we is amatuehs compa'd wid dese Ha'lem sto' keepuhs."

"You heard them," said Kermit, with a smile. "Those are some of the things I want to show up."

"Oh, I'm aware that there's a lot of cheating going on. Everybody knows that the Negro is exploited in many places, shamefully, but I don't agree that your method will stop it. It'll perhaps make it worse, in a different way."

"You have a chance to do a great racial service by jumping right into making this picture — even if you wouldn't be getting a chance to have your other pictures financed, you should be racially patriotic enough to do it for the good of our folks. If a few thousand of our folks could see a picture telling the same kind of story those women have just related, can't you see what it would mean? They would start to checking up on these merchants; begin to look at the scales and ask a few questions. It might take more than one picture to open their eyes. Maybe two, three, four, maybe a series, but it ought to be done and it ought to be started right away.

"Did you ever hear the story of the snake, the rattlesnake and the Negro?" said Kermit.

"No," replied Wyeth. "What kind of a story?"

"A parallel. I take the Jew as he is, and all these women have said, is no more than I expect to hear, and we will go on hearing it until the end of time, for it is current to expect the Jew to cheat, the same as a snake is expected to bite. Now I'll tell you the story of the snake, as nearly as I can remember a fellow telling it to me, many years ago.

"A Negro, as the story goes, was coming along a dusty country road one chilly morning. He didn't have many clothes on, just a shirt and overalls, was bare-footed and shivering himself, when he met a rattlesnake in the road, and the rattlesnake was crying." Wyeth laughed.

"The rattlesnake," went on Kermit, "was crying—tears in his eyes and he appealed to the Negro as follows: 'Brother, please save me. I'm cold, almost frozen and unless you save me, I will surely die.'

" 'How c'n I save you, Mistah snake?' asked the Negro, pausing to look down at him. 'Take me, brother,' said the snake, 'put me inside your shirt next to your body where I will get warm, please do that and save me.'

"So the Negro, as the story continued, gathered the rattlesnake and put him inside his shirt next to his flesh and went on down the road. Presently he felt a movement and looked down. The snake had become warm and had stuck his head out of the shirt and was looking up at the Negro boldly, and as the Negro's eyes met the snake, he stuck his tongue out like he meant to do something. The Negro stopped and looking down at the snake, cried 'Hey, you, what does this mean?'

" 'That I'm going to bite you,' replied the snake and flashed his forked tongue at the Negro, threateningly.

" 'But, but,' cried the Negro. 'Didn't you tell me back dare when I picked you up and put you inside my shirt, dat — '

" 'Yes,' replied the snake, flashing his red and ugly tongue at the Negro again, 'but I'm a snake.'

Wyeth laughed.

"So a snake is supposed to bite, regardless how much he is befriended, or who it is that befriends him and that means that a Jew is supposed to cheat, regardless of the circumstances or who you are."

Both laughed heartily.

"Thats the inference, Early," said Wyeth, "which of course, is only an inference for, while many mercenary and perhaps, struggling and 'don't care' Jews do cheat, I have in mind a lot of Jews that have done, and are doing, a great deal for posterity, and who can not be charged with being mercenary even."

"What do you mean?" inquired Kermit.

"What about Julius Rosenwald, for instance, the father of the Negro Y.M.C.A.?"

"Oh, well, he was different."

"Isn't the example he set, along with a lot of other rich but kindly Jews and what they have done for mankind and the Negroes, especially in the case of Rosenwald, to be credited as against the activities of these Jews, whom the story compared with the snake?"

"I suppose so," said Early. His tone indicated that he would like to change the subject.

"Rosenwald paid for and caused to be erected more than 5,000 school buildings for Negroes in the south, left a revolving fund to pay part of the teachers' salaries and to maintain and keep the schools up indefinitely. This, in addition to helping to finance every Negro Y.M.C.A. and Y.W.C.A., as far as I know in the entire United States.

"I chose to consider acts of this kind when you insist that I ought to make a picture designed and conceived to make Negroes hate Jews. It wouldn't be right, Early and you know it wouldn't be."

At this point the waiter brought the food they had ordered and they fell to eating.

Late in the afternoon of this self-same day, in Berlin, Germany, Henrich Schultz and his sister Bertha, a year younger, left the foreign office where they had been in conference with Von Ribbentrop with regard to their mission to America. As we know, even Hitler himself had approved the mission, so they were enthusiastic when they left Von Ribbentrop. Germany was sending hundreds of agents to America at the time, but since war had been declared on Germany by England and France and the blockade put into effect, all ships, including the Europa, were held in German ports and Schultz and his sister, a medium sized, beautiful and affectionate girl, started for America via Italy.

Because she was so devoted to her brother, Bertha Schultz had followed him off to Heidelberg and then to the Sorbonne and had majored in the same studies that he had taken, and was therefore the best assistant he could have chosen and he had persuaded the foreign office to give her a commission, along with his, so the two, considering themselves fortunate, were happy to think they would be together in America, work together and be close to each other.

Bertha had not been to America since her mother took her and the rest of her children back to Germany many years before, so looked forward to their returning with anxious and happy anticipation.

Accordingly, therefore, in that year, late autumn, Bertha and Heinrich set out for America, journeying southward to Genoa where they had reserved passage on the Italian Luxury Liner, Conte De Savoia, scheduled to sail from there a few days later.

Bertha had been told about Heinrich's tie-up with Kermit Early, so looked forward to meeting him. Heinrich had cabled Early when they were leaving and about what day they would arrive. He had also cabled Early a sum of money with which to rent a suitable apartment in the Negro section in Harlem where they could work from and not be suspected or molested.

On the way across Bertha and Heinrich encountered many Germans, all headed for America as secret agents of the Reich. The ship seemed to fairly swarm with them, men and women, all assigned, more or less to different cities, but all over America. Some were assigned to South America, but via New York where most were to remain awhile, possibly to check up on conditions in America so that they could compare the sentiment on reaching S. A.

There was a ball every night in the huge salon of the ship, plenty of wine, beer and Schnapps. They were wined and dined daily, being singled out it seems because of their color, and the object of much curiosity. Many told them of individuals they were to meet on arrival in New York, Chicago, Milwaukee and other cities; names that later became conspicuous in Newspaper headlines for subversive activity.

They were met at the pier by Early, who shook hands with both, then ushered them into a taxi, where they were driven to the Pennsylvania Hotel, where they met Mrs. Wingate, Kermit having checked in there until Schultz would arrive, after which all planned to take apartments in the Negro section in Harlem.

When Mrs. Wingate was introduced to Bertha, young and beautiful and so highly educated, for a fleeting moment she experienced her first jealousy. In that moment she pictured Kermit, with all his super-education possibly falling in love with this beautiful and gorgeous creature. She became so jealous, that she decided to accompany them to Harlem the next morning, to examine the apartments that Kermit had leased, one for Bertha and Heinrich, the other, and in a different building, for themselves. That night she decided to talk with Kermit about her baby, due to arrive in six to seven months. She artfully maneuvered the conversation around to the subject in a roundabout way, and was relieved to have him bring it up instead of her.

"Now about the baby, Florence," said Kermit, crossing his legs and lighting a cigarette, which he passed to her, then lit one for himself.

"Have you decided just what to do about it, I mean, as regards

Mr. Wingate." She was silent a moment, then looked up.

"Yes, dear," she answered.

"I've decided to tell him the whole story, and ask him to give me a divorce."

"M-m," mused Kermit. "I suppose he will grant it?"

"I don't see why he would not. I feel sure he knows that I am friendly with some other man."

"Do you feel he might be aware that I am that man?"

"He has never intimated that he did. In fact he has never intimated that he knows that I have such a friend. Anyway, I've thought it all over very carefully, and that's why I'm glad you sent for me so that we could talk it over and agree just what I should do. So what do you think?"

"As always, Florence, ours has been a case where you have invariably taken the initiative. If you must divorce him, and I suppose, under the circumstances, there is nothing else left for you to do, I'll be happy. Since we've meant so much to each other and for so long, I'd be happy if you could ultimately marry me and we could have each other and no longer suffer the feeling that ours is a cladestine love."

She rose and crossing to him, sat down on his lap as she always liked to, and placed an arm about his neck.

"Oh, won't it be sweet, darling. You and I at last, man and wife."

"Man and wife, darling, never to part again."

"It will be just like a honeymoon, sweeter than a second one because we haven't had an unrestrained first one yet."

"Sweetheart, my darling Florence," he said, patting her. Whereupon she laid her head beside his.

"Do you still love me, Kermit" she said, a bit oddly.

He tried to look at her but their faces were too close and they were enjoying the comfort too much to disturb it.

"I shall always love you, Florence. Why did you ask me that?"

She sat up now so that she could look at him. She looked at him oddly a moment which he couldn't understand. She laughed a bit sheepishly and leaning forward, hid her face against his shoulder.

"For the first time since we've been with each other, I experienced a moment of jealousy tonight."

He turned to look hard at her now in complete surprise.

"You, jealous, Florence?"

"M-m," she mumbled and continued to hide her face.
"But why, and of whom?" She sat up again, her eyes on the floor.
"That girl you brought here, that very pretty girl."
"You mean the Schultz girl?"
"M-m."
"Well, of all people." She turned and throwing her arms about him, cried just a little. Then, drying her eyes.
"Oh, it was silly I know, and I had no reason to feel the way I did — even for the short moments that I did."
"You most surely did not. I — "
"Oh, I'm not accusing you of giving me any reason for you didn't. But it is just natural that a woman might feel that way about another, especially about one young and so beautiful as she is. Don't you think she is beautiful?"
"Well," said Kermit, after a moments thought, "come to picture her, I suppose so."
"She is. Don't misunderstand that. One of the prettiest girls I ever saw, anywhere."
"Is she really all that beautiful?"
"Why of course, Kermit. Rich color, large, beautiful, soft dark eyes. Just about everything, including the most perfect shape I ever saw a girl have."
"Couldn't be more perfect than yours."
'Oh, yes. I might have had perhaps, a pretty shape some years ago."
"You still have, darling."
She looked at him and smiled. He reached over and kissed her.
"Thank you, sweetheart," she said. "But we've been sweethearts so long. It would be very easy for me to begin to get jealous of my darling, see?"
"Let's return to the subject we started to talk about."
"Our baby. Of course, dear."
He looked down at her stomach. She followed his eyes.
"Oh, it will not begin to show for months yet."
"No?"
"Of course not, darling. Women don't usually begin to swell up until three months before their time. I won't begin to get out of shape for a long, long time yet."

"In regards to Mr. Wingate?"

"Since I've been wanting the baby for so long, I am resigned to what I have to do. He knows that I've always wanted a child and he, in addition to not being *built like other men,* is deficient otherwise, and could never become a father."

"How unfortunate."

"So, unfortunate, yet that's the case. So I'm all ready when I return to Atlanta, to take him into my room and tell him the whole story."

"I wish you didn't have to," he said sympathetically. She looked down at him.

"Thank you, darling. I wish that I didn't, but I've been happy since I married him, only because of your coming into my life. That has meant more to me than anything which could have happened. I'm still a young woman, and I'm still entitled to some happiness. Since God only can be responsible for his misfortune, to tell him the truth and have it over with and as soon as possible, is the best way out as I can see it, so that is that and I'm ready to have it all over with him and be free so that we can get married and give our child a name when it arrives.

"Now since that is settled about as much as it can be before I tell him, let's talk about something else."

"What, for instance?"

"That man Heinrich Schultz and his sister, especially, his sister."

He laughed and pinched her cheek.

"No, I'm not jealous any longer, dear."

"Then what?"

"Curious."

"Curious? I see. About what?"

"Their mission to America."

"They're German agents, which is confidential, you understand."

"Of course I understand, dear, and any talking and asking questions will be only of you and with you."

She was thoughtful a moment.

"All right, darling. What do you want to know?"

"He is the fellow you've been telling me about for some time."

"Yes. He was here during the past summer and that was when I met him."

"I see. Where, dear?"

"In Milwaukee."

"Milwaukee? That's a German City is it not?"

"Not now. The town was founded and settled in the beginning by Germans."

"Then they would be German sympathizers, pro-Germans, you'd call it?"

"I guess so, darling."

"With this country so pro-English, in time don't you think there might be some sort of — collusion?" Kermit was thoughtful.

"This country is made up of so many kinds of groups and races and elements, it is rather difficult to figure out just who is who and what is what."

"I guess that is true, but just what is your position in this whole affair, dear?"

"I represent the Negro angle. My position is to advise and direct the Negro side of the set-up."

"Now at this time, what are you supposed to do?"

"Get a colored fellow up town by the name of Sidney Wyeth to make a picture showing how the Jews cheat and exploit Negroes, and to show it to Negroes all over the country."

"Somebody should make a picture showing how they cheat and exploit white people, too. They cheat and exploit everybody, including themselves, when they can. I despise the funny-eyed creatures. They don't care anything about anybody or anything except the almighty dollar. I'm with Hitler for putting them in their places. We need a Hitler over here." Kermit was beaming. This was the first time he had talked with her in detail about what he had been doing for a long time. Now to have heard her say what she had, which was so agreeable along with his plans, that he felt he could talk more about it with her.

"I'm glad to hear you express yourself as you have, Florence."

"Most Southerners hate Jews."

"I know they do, but I wasn't sure as to how you felt about them."

"What does this man Wyeth think? How does he feel? Is he going to make the picture you and your associates have planned?"

Kermit's face fell. She noticed it and became anxious.

"He hasn't agreed to yet."

"Why not? What is he waiting for?"

"Well, he says he isn't a Red; that he doesn't hate Jews, that he's not anti-semetic, that—"

"Maybe he loves them."

"No, he doesn't particularly love them. He seems to be a sort of pacifist in spirit, doesn't hate anybody."

"Well, what are you going to do about it? Can't you get somebody else to make it?"

"He's the only one who can put the feeling that ought to go into the picture in it, in order to stir Negroes into action."

"Is that so?"

"Yes, I'm sorry to say, for unless I can succeed in persuading him to do it, we might have a big hole knocked in something I've planned very thoroughly and sold my group on the idea, one hundred percent."

"Then what do you plan to do?"

"Oh, I haven't given up hoping that in some way I can ultimately get him to do it. I've just started trying. I intend to keep on after him."

Florence was thoughtful a moment, then turned her eyes to his.

"I suppose this Schultz is interested in getting Wyeth to do it, also?"

"Oh, very much so. He thinks I've got his consent and he's under the impression that production is to start shortly."

"Now what are you going to do?"

"I haven't had time to tell him what Wyeth thinks about it yet."

"Of course not, with him just arriving this afternoon."

"That's it. I won't say anything about it, unless he asks me, until I show them to their apartment and get them settled. That'll take a week, meantime, I'll go see Wyeth again and try to get him to see these Jews as I do."

"Meanwhile, I have an idea."

"Yes?"

"This sister of Schultz, if neither you nor he can get Wyeth to do so, why not sic her onto him."

"You mean, get her to try to persuade him?"

"Of course. As pretty as she is, and so obviously intelligent, she might succeed where you fail."

"That's an idea."

"Is Wyeth married?"

"No," said Early. "He's single."

"Not married and I don't suppose she is?"

"I haven't heard, but don't think so."

"Well," she said, rising from his lap and pausing over him. "You keep that suggestion in mind and if you fail to budge Wyeth, then take it up with her and her brother with this in view."

"Smart idea, Florence, and I'll keep it in mind."

"Do you have tickets for the show, sweetheart?"

"I do. Haven't been to a floor show for some time, so it's about time we begin to dress." They dressed in evening clothes and went out to one of New York's leading downtown night clubs and saw a good floor show.

The next morning Early took Schultz and his sister, via taxi, to the apartment he had leased for them, high up on a hill in Harlem; in that section they call "Sugar Hill".

"So this is Harlem," said Bertha, looking out of the taxi window after they left 110th Street.

"Black Harlem, Miss Schultz," Kermit explained. "Here we enter the largest Negro City in all the world, a city within a city."

"It seems a bit — ordinary," she commented, looking at the crowd of Negroes, idling, playing and carrying on boistrously and loudly on the sidewalks, as the taxi spun along.

"It is ordinary, *extraordinary*," laughed Kermit "and otherwise. Within the environs of this black city within a city dwell more than 400,000 people of our group, at least, my group," said he, correcting himself, not knowing just how Bertha might regard herself.

"Include me, too, Mr. Early. I am a German first, but a Negro always. I am in sympathy with the Negro and his struggle to reach a higher plane of thought and action. I have come here to dedicate my future, as it were, first to the service of our Fuehrer, and the third Reich, at the same time to The Negro and his peculiar problems. I want to study it from the inside and ground up. Maybe in a small way I may be able to mean something before it is all over. I hope so, at least."

"Our people present a peculiar problem here. Held down so long by southern white people, they almost consider themselves failures. A long time ago I heard a great leader, called Booker T. Washington say that the hardest task in all his life had been to convince a colored man that he could be anything."

"Booker T. Washington was a great man," said Heinrich, thoughtfully. "About the first book I remember reading when we lived in America, was a story of his life, called UP FROM SLAVERY."

"I read it, too, Heinrich," said Bertha. "Don't you remember that mother bought it among other gifts at Xmas time and you and I used to struggle over who was to read it first and then mother had us draw straws."

"That's right, sis. I remember it all now."

"And who won?" inquired Early, smiling at one, then the other.

"He did," said Bertha, looking at him fondly. "My brother has always seemed to be strangely lucky."

"Really?" said Kermit.

"Really, Mr. Early. Ever since he was a child, luck seems to have followed him. Just consider his good fortune in being able to get this commission for each of us. I wouldn't have missed coming to America for anything."

"We were fortunate in that regard," said Heinrich. "Because if I don't miss my guess, if we hadn't when we did, we might not have gotten out of Germany for a long, long time, maybe not until the war was over — and it's going to be a long war, Early, longer than even the Fuehrer himself anticipates."

"You think so?" said Kermit.

"I know so. I made a careful study of conditions while in this country last spring and summer. This country is so pro-English and the Jews wield so much unnoticed power, that the whole world may be in it before it is over. The Jews want America to get into a war with Germany."

"Do you think so?" said Early.

"I'm sure of it. Through it they visualize a way, if America should win, of over-throwing Hitler, whom they hate, of course."

"How do they feel about it in Germany?"

"Too early for many to have formed a definite opinion. Currently, however, the consensus of opinion is that Hitler will tear into France next summer and take Paris before either England or France can prepare. They are dreadfully unprepared, while Germany has been getting ready almost ever since Hitler came into power. The entire

Reich is a beehive of preparation right now."

"While America sleeps and Roosevelt plays politics," suggested Kermit. By this time they had reached the building where he had leased their apartment, so pulled up at the curb. Kermit helped both to the sidewalk and a few seconds later they were speeding to the floor upon which the apartment was located. It was one of the best. Had seven rooms and two baths. He got it for a smaller rental than current because it was larger than most Negroes could afford, and the leasees prohibited many things that were permitted in other buildings in Harlem, where, if one was able to pay the rent, most anything went, including an occasional shooting and now and then a murder.

Bertha and Heinrich were well pleased with the place, checked and rechecked it from one end to the other, and arranged to go down town the next day and select their furniture.

CHAPTER **VIII**

SIDNEY WYETH was called to Washington by telegram regarding the sale of his book, so got into his car the next morning and drove down there, leaving Marie to look after matters while he was away, as she always did.

After attending to the immediate business that called him there, he went milling around the theatres as he had always done when he had pictures to book. Driving up New Jersey avenue to where it ends and U street begins, and just as he crossed Florida avenue, his eyes fell on the front of the Howard Theatre, where a show seemed to be playing. He circled a few blocks and a few minutes later parked his car on a side street and went into the lobby and was looking at the pictures when he saw that it was Irvin C. Mantan's show.

And while doing so, among the pictures who should he see but one of Edrina's. He started. He had been too busy since the night she called on him at the office and he took her to the Bamboo Inn, to think much about her, but as his eyes spied her picture, he decided then and there to look her up and renew what had started out to be, he thought, a very pleasing affair.

When the curtain rung down that night, he hurried around to the stage entrance, something that he had never done, but was excited. He wanted to see Edrina.

So parking himself after getting inside, he met the performers on the way to their dressing rooms, hoping that Edrina would pass that way to her dressing room, so that he could speak to her and let her know that he was in Washington.

Presently she came along, hurrying with her eyes down and had almost passed him when he reached out and caught her arm, whereupon she turned with a frown on her face, to have it disappear suddenly, as, on looking up her eyes fell on him, and her frown disappeared, her mouth opened.

"Why, you!" she exclaimed, happily and carried away with delight. "Sidney Wyeth, you, you, you!" Throwing her arms about him she embraced him right there, without regard to the others. With show people, such scenes invariably go unnoticed.

"Oh, oh, oh!" she exclaimed, hugging and squeezing him. "I'd kiss you if I didn't want to spoil your sweet lips for later with all this old make-up on mine." She relaxed then long enough to look up at him, her expression too happy for words, and cried:

"Where did you come from anyhow, and if you knew I was here, why didn't you wire me so that I could have been made happy, waiting and preparing for you? Why —" then breaking off and looking around, she caught his arm, and said: "But come to my dressing room. I'm *so* glad to see you." So saying she half-pulled and half-dragged him up a flight of steps and around and through a narrow hall to her dressing room, where she let him in, then closed and locked the door behind them.

She found a chair and sat him down upon it and started again, talking so fast and with so much enthusiasm and delight until he couldn't say anything. He hadn't been able to even greet her yet. "I was so frightened when I saw you, I liked to have fainted. For a moment I thought you were a ghost. Oh, dear!" She laughed then and he joined her.

"Now, darling," she said, patting his cheek, "just try to be comfortable and patient while I get out of this makeup and costume, and I'll be right with you." So saying she patted his cheek again, and disappeared behind a screen where she started to talking to him again, though neither could see the other.

"You know, Sidney," she called. "They say you never hang around back stage or run after show girls. Is that so?"

"I don't know." He didn't know what else to say.

"You don't know? Then who would? It wouldn't be because — you don't care for — women?"

"What are you doing," he called back. "Feeling me out?"

"Maybe."

"I'm not a fairy, if that's what you're trying to find out."

She laughed but seemed satisfied. "I'm back here because I'm interested in you. I wanted to see you."

"Did you, sweetheart?"

"Of course I did," he replied, stoutly.

"I'm so glad. You've perhaps been too busy to pay any attention to women, is my guess."

"I'm trying to develop my book business. That takes up all my time."

"I'll bet. Are you out of the picture business altogether? Aren't you going to make any more?"

"I don't plan to right now."

"Well, regardless how busy you are, you may have somebody on your hands from now on, if I have my way about it."

"My, my. Sounds good to me."

"I've been thinking about you ever since that night together in New York," she called, and he could hear her getting out of costume and removing the grease paint.

"Really?" he said.

"Really, Sidney. Are you glad to hear me say that I have?"

"Sure am."

"You're so — so different from any man I ever knew."

"Is that a compliment or a — condemnation?"

"A compliment, of course."

"I like you, Edrina."

"Oh, Sidney, do you?"

"Cross my heart."

"But I can't see you," both laughed.

"I'll be patient and wait."

"I'll be ready in less than two minutes, sweetheart."

"Take your time. We won't know the difference this time next year." She laughed.

"You have a sense of humor, too," she said, coming from behind the screen, smiling and as beautiful as she was when she called on him at his office a few days before.

"I dressed so quickly until I'm not sure I did it correctly. But I didn't want to keep you waiting."

"That was awfully sweet of you, dear heart."

"Now look me over and tell me if you see anything not just right," she said, holding her arms out like a dress model, and turning from right to left, left to right. "My slip is not showing beneath my skirt, is it? Speak now or forever keep your peace," she said, at which both laughed. He looked her up and down carefully.

"Everything is hunky dory, Eddie."

"Don't kid me. If you do I won't like you."

"No, honey," he said. "I looked you over carefully as you posed and turned like a model. You look all right."

"I wanted to be sure, since I'm going out with you and I want to look nice when I do, although you haven't even asked me to."

"The fact that I was waiting backstage for you, is the best evidence that I wanted to see you, and that meant that I wanted to go out with you."

"I'm glad you do. The evening is yours and all the other evenings while we're in Washington and anywhere else the show goes, as far as I'm concerned."

"This makes me very happy, Edrina," he said, sincerely.

"Before we get too far away from the subject, I'm asking you again do I look all right?" and again she posed like a model, turning from left to right, right to left.

"You look all right, sweetheart. This is the second time I looked you over."

"Thanks," she said sweetly, and seemed to be satisfied at last. "Then we'll go." She took his hand and led him across the small room to the door and started to put a hand on the knob, then seeming to think of something she paused and looked up at him. For a moment he didn't seem to understand, then suddenly gathering her in his arms, he kissed her passionately. She quivered for a moment and trembled, too. When she could do anything, she sighed, deeply.

"Oh, my! Yours are the sweetest kisses, so warm, so soft, so passionate!" He squeezed her to him and kissed her again, as passionately as before, and again she quivered and trembled and sighed, deeply.

"Oh, dear," she managed to gasp, more than say, and swayed perceptibly, her eyes closed bewilderingly and he had to hold her. The chair upon which he had sat was near and he moved over to it, sat down and took her on his lap, where he embraced and kissed her again, and again until neither knew how many times. Then holding her close, her face against his.

"I don't know whether its just emotion, infatuation or a thing called love," he sighed, "but what ever it is, it's took me over completely."

"Call it love, Sidney," she whispered, "then tell me that you love me." She buried her face on his shoulder for a moment, and when she raised it, there were some tears which she had to find her kerchief and dry.

"If you were anywhere but on the stage, darling," said he, hesitatingly, "I would do so gladly, and without hesitation, for then I could be sure of myself, be sure of you. But Eddie, darling. I'm — I'm afraid of show girls, I — I'm almost afraid of you because you are on the stage." She sat up straight now and looked hard at him, then she got to her feet and he stood, too.

"But I'm not a show girl in the sense you mean it, Sidney, dear. Until a year ago when I went out with Mantan, I had never been on any stage. I had never even thought of going on one. So you see, darling, I can't be called a show girl in the sense you mean it."

"I hope you understand the kind I mean. The stupid kind, playing up to some cheap white man who has produced the show — not always having produced it, just hanging around it. The kind who are ready, ever to play up to such men, go out with them, to bed with them, laboring under a vain theory that he's going to 'do something' for her, and as a result she starts 'doing something' for him, first. I mean that kind, I've seen them, and I've met them. In the matter of a show, they seem to be always around, pawing over that trash. They anger me, they humiliate and lower the standard of our race and I want no part of such. That, dear Eddie, is why I've never hung around stage doors and run after show girls, as they say. I am so completely opposed to so much that goes on backstage with many of these shows until that aversion has become an obsession. I may be wrong, but if I got to liking you, as I am beginning to, and then sooner or later I came to catch or meet you pawing over some old white man, as, I said, I've seen so many of our girls do, I'd feel like killing you and myself, even for having let myself fall for you, understand?"

"I do, darling, and I don't blame you at all. If you ever caught me doing anything like that, I hope you would kill me then and there, for I'm a nice girl, Sidney. I've never done anything like that and I can assure you, I never will. Now are you satisfied?"

He nodded, but not too enthusiastically. She saw now that his convictions and his prejudices, when asserted, were deep, and any girl who won his love would have to be a serious girl, and above all, a moral girl and even Edrina knew that not all the girls who worked in shows, night clubs and cabarets were so ecstatic.

"There could be something in what you just said, dear," he was saying now. "And you wouldn't have to be — be bad just because you're in a show as so many show girls are. I know some girls on the stage who are as nice as many girls raised in the best of homes. But it is so often and so commonly said by white men who work around Negro shows, and produce them, that they can have any colored girl they want. That is what makes it hard for me to — get interested in any show girl. But now I am interested in you. I hope, from the way I am talking, dear, that you don't think I'm a nicey, nicey, boy. I simply don't want to get interested in any old loose girl, if I know what I'm doing. In fact, I won't let myself become so interested."

"I'm a kind of girl who tries to be sensible, Sidney, and no sensible girl would let herself become careless as you've just explained. I understand. No good man's going to fall for any loose, bad girl. He may run around with them, play around with them, take all they're silly enough to offer which in most cases is everything, but when he gets ready to marry, he looks right over their heads and doesn't see any of them at all."

"I believe you, Edrina. Right now I think you're a fine, intelligent and sweet kind of girl and I do like you. I could soon learn to like you much more. But if you stayed on the stage, matters might not always continue as they now are. Shows experience varying forms of fortune, often misfortune. And when they get into these bad breaks, that is when a girl might be persuaded to try save the show often at the expense of her good name. I hope that doesn't happen to you while I'm liking you. But there are angles that do not include having white men and being common. I'm thinking of the first day I met you." He seemed reflective now, thinking back those few weeks before.

"The first day?" she said, also reflectively.

"Yes, Edrina, that first day. I'm thinking of how you kept talking about the stage; kept insisting, as it were, of how you liked it. You — "

"But — but," she cut him off quickly, to argue. "That, Sidney, was before I met you, knew you — before you entered my life. Before I could know that I was going to — like you." She looked up at him so sweetly here, so appealingly that his heart for the moment went out to her, and he smiled down into her face, kissed her quickly and as he looked at her and continued to listen, she went on:

"Isn't it possible that in such a case, I might become subject to change? By which I mean that if you began to like me seriously and — didn't want me to stay on the stage, I might quit?"

"That would be provincial, and I am not provincial, and I'm still not rich."

"Not rich? I didn't say anything about—money, dear," she looked up into his face and did not understand.

"After all, Edrina, acting is an art, a very fine art. If a girl has real talent and was able by her acting, or singing or dancing, to ultimately get somewhere, it would be provincial for some man to make her give it up just to please him."

"I'm listening, Sidney, but I confess that I don't know what you're getting at," said she.

"I'll get to it in time, and then you will understand. If a girl has real talent, and is ambitious as I can see that you are, the thing to do would be to produce a show for her. That would mean financing it and managing it and so controlling it that a dear wife would not be exposed to temptation and be forced to — yes, sell her body for the benefits of some white man who'd tell her he had somebody who would, perhaps, bank-roll the show if some particular girl in the show would be nice to him."

"Oh," she breathed, and looked away, then up at him. "I see what you mean now."

"I am not rich enough to produce a show. In fact, I am not interested in stage shows, unless it would be a big broadway grosser — but show business is not on my mind. For the present I am in the book business, a publisher. The kind of a girl I would be happy to fall in love with, if such happened, would be a nice, educated and intelligent girl who would be satisfied to marry me and let me place her in a comfortable apartment in New York and just be happy to be my wife and look after me. That's the limit of my social ambition now. I've met and like you and you're in love with the stage, perhaps you expect, at least hope, to go places on it." He relaxed now and sighed. "That's why I don't know just how to feel about you. You seem to have all I want, but you're on the stage, you like it, you say you'd leave it if I wanted you to, at least that is what you imply. But if you still like the stage and had to quit just to please me, that wouldn't leave me in such a favorable light, in your estimation, now would it?"

"No, darling," she said, slowly. "It would not." He drew her to him, and squeezed her. She liked it and looked up in his face so kindly, until he was moved to say:

"But listen, Edrina, you don't know, may even never know, how hungry my heart is and has been for so long until I can hardly remember how long, for the love of a good woman. A love like that can often do so much for a man, can spur him onward, possibly before the end, to dizzy and successful heights. That is what so many men's wives have done for them and the men have been glad to say, every day, publicly and otherwise. 'Whatever success I seem to have achieved, it has been my wife who has inspired it.' How many men, and God only knows how many, have despaired, felt they could go no further and were ready to give up and quit, but their wives would not let them. They believed in their men and insisted and gave them no peace, so they tried again and maybe again and again, until in the end, complete success, security and happiness, and it is a fine thing in such a case to feel that some one near you, like a wife, made you do it.

"I guess this all sounds, to Negroes anyhow, who have failed too often as men of destiny, fantastic and foolish, and why am I saying all this now? It's not the time and place. I came here to take you out to a restaurant, where all show girls want to be taken after the show. As it is, I've given you a lecture in philosophy. So let me relax, honey, and let's get going and forgive me." As he finished, he looked down into her eyes and indulged in a big, broad smile. She smiled, too.

"Thank you, darling," she said and raised her lips. Drawing her close he kissed her with a resounding smack, and, swinging her around, opened the door, she turned when outside and locked it behind them, and together they went down the dimly lighted stage hallway, down a flight of stairs, around a corner and out into a Washington night. Getting into his car, they turned into Florida Avenue, around a corner and back into New Jersey Avenue and away to a restaurant, which he knew served good food.

CHAPTER **IX**

THE SCHULTZ'S had completed the furnishing of their apartment and were comfortably settled and Heinrich had been down to meet other Nazi spies, and had a long conversation with Hans Schiller, New York agent and was asked to keep in touch with Schiller constantly, since something sensational was expected to break at any time.

"How're you coming along with the colored picture? The one to show the colored people how the Sheeny's are taking them for a ride?"

"To be frank about it, Schiller," said Schultz, "I haven't taken the matter up with Early, my Negro contact man since I arrived."

"Ought to get right on it, Schultz. As I see it, a powerful Motion Picture showing just how they are being systematically exploited by these kykes should prove timely to stir things up in the colored sections."

"It's a sure way to start them on a campaign of destruction. The Jews run more than half of all the business in the Negro sections here, Chicago, Detroit, Philadelphia, Baltimore and Washington and other spots," said Schultz.

"A finely directed picture, filmed in the form of a good melodrama would prove about the most powerful single instrument towards inspiring some good race riots all over the country, that I can think of. How do the colored people feel about the way they're treated here in New York?" asked Schiller.

"Seem to be contented as far as I can see. My folks, you see, aren't inclined to bother much if nobody bothers them."

"That's why a good picture, the kind Early has outlined, ought to get them started into action. What about this fellow Wyeth, who's to make it. Does he hate Jews?"

"I haven't taken the matter up with Kermit, but I will. He and his lady friend are having dinner at our apartment tomorrow, and I'll take it up with him at that time," said Schultz, rising. Schiller rose and followed him to the door.

"Do that as quickly as possible, Schultz, and let me hear from you. The whole group of us are interested."

"You'll hear from me no later than next week, I promise."

"Okeh, Schultz and so long."

"So long, Hans."

Bertha, who took pride in the fact that she was both a good housekeeper and cook, had prepared a sumptous dinner to entertain Kermit Early and Mrs. Wingate. Heinrich, who was domestically inclined, was helping her and she had a chance to ask him something that had been on her mind.

"This Mrs. Wingate, Heinrich," she began. "Just who is she and what is her relations with Mr. Early?"

"She's his girl friend."

"Oh, his girl friend. M-m. A Southerner?"

"Yes. From Atlanta."

"Isn't that a bit—unusual? A white woman, and a Southerner, friendly with a—colored man?"

Heinrich shrugged his shoulders and smiled.

"Understand they've been going together for a long time," he said.

"They seem to have a perfect understanding and appear to be very fond of each other," said Bertha, as she hurried about her work.

"Something a bit strange about the whole thing. It seems they've been going together for years, many years. I have a feeling that she put him through school."

"I wouldn't be surprised," said she.

"He doesn't say much about it, and I hesitate to butt in and ask him, but I did gather from a conversation with him and other things that I've managed to piece together, that they knew each other as kids in a little town in Georgia. Of course they didn't get very far down there, but later on in Atlanta, he went to work for her."

"Is she—a married woman?"

"So I understand. Husband's a rich textile man in Atlanta—owns a string of mills all over the Southeast."

"Great goodness," exclaimed Bertha in amazement. "And he lets her come to New York to see—a Negro man, stop at the same hotel, and—"

"—live together in the same rooms."

"Whew!" cried Bertha. "This *is* a strange case." Schultz smiled and shook his head. "And as far as I can see, she's very fond of him."

"Crazy about him! It's her money, I'm sure, that has been behind him for years."

"You know," said Bertha, putting a roast into the oven, "I caught her looking at me a bit oddly the night we arrived, while we were visiting with them in the hotel."

"Jealous, I bet," Heinrich laughed.

"I don't think she need be."

"Kermit has too much sense to play around with his bread and butter."

"Have you spoken to him about Mr. Wyeth yet?"

"Haven't had time, but I plan to when they call tonight."

"Hasn't he said anything about it? How Mr. Wyeth feels about it, if he'll do the picture?"

"I've a suspicion that he hasn't consented to, otherwise, even as busy as we all have been, I think Kermit would have said something about it."

"Especially when he is so anxious about it. Who wrote the story? It is to have a story?

"By all means. Kermit wrote the story."

"It should be interesting. He's had lots of experience along the lines he is working, and with such a thorough education."

"He's a Ph.D."

"Now, Kermit, how are you coming along with the picture?" said Schultz after they had dined and retired to the parlor to smoke and talk, the night of Bertha's dinner." All eyes were turned on Early, who answered, with a bit of embarrassment.

"I have only had one short and one longer talk with Wyeth since I arrived?" said Kermit, a bit evasively.

"And?"

"He doesn't seem to share our views with regards the Jews."

"You mean, that he — is not altogether agreeable to — making the picture?"

"We really haven't gotten to the bottom of the deal yet. I saw him twice and the last time, talked at some length regarding the matter."

"What did he say?"

"Oh," said Kermit, a bit uncomfortably, "He argued that he wasn't a Red, that he didn't hate Jews; didn't go in for hating anybody and all that."

"Pardon me for making a suggestion, Mr. Early," said Bertha. "But if he isn't agreeable to doing it, couldn't you — get somebody else to direct and produce it?"

"That's the trouble," spoke up Mrs. Wingate, as if coming to Kermit's rescue. "As I understand it, this Sidney Wyeth is the only man capable of directing the picture, effectively. I've read the script and it is deep, the story, far-reaching and intense. As I see it, it would take a most intelligent director to bring it to life on the screen and make a realistic picture."

Bertha looked at her brother, who shook his head, obviously disappointed.

"It's a picture that only a Negro could direct, effectively, Bertha," said Schultz, with a look at his sister.

"I hear you, all of you, speaking about the man Wyeth. Just who is he?" inquired Bertha, looking from first one then to the other.

"He's a Negro with terrific imagination and an uncanny insight into Negro life in general," explained Kermit.

"He is also an author. Has written a fine novel which I found so very interesting."

"A writer, too," exclaimed Bertha. "I'd like to read his book. I wonder where I can get a copy?"

"At any book store, I guess," said Mrs. Wingate.

"No, Florence," said Kermit. "He hasn't pushed it through bookstores. If she wants to read it, I'll get a copy and bring it to Miss Schultz from his office. I saw a whole stack there the other day."

"Where is the office?" said Bertha.

Kermit told her.

"Then I'll go there and get a copy of it myself. Maybe I'll get to meet him and see what kind of a man this is that all of you seem so interested in."

"He's out of town," said Kermit. "I called there today and the girl said he was away."

"Then if there is somebody at the office, I could get a copy, anyhow?" inquired Bertha, looking at Early.

"Mr. Schultz," suggested Mrs. Wingate at this point. All turned to look at her. "I told Kermit the other night, that I thought it would be a good idea in the event Kermit and you were unable to persuade Mr. Wyeth to do the picture, to send Bertha to see him. Sometimes a pretty woman — "

"Why, Mrs. Wingate," exclaimed Bertha, blushing modestly. Mrs. Wingate raised a hand.

"Such a pretty girl like you, Miss Schultz — "

"Oh, Mrs. Wingate, no."

"No?" said Mrs. Wingate, turning to look at her in surprise

"Oh, I didn't mean that I wouldn't go. I'm glad and willing to try do anything my brother and Mr. Kermit asks me to. I objected to your calling me beautiful. That's what I meant."

Mrs. Wingate relaxed and smiled. Then looking around.

"I don't think we will need to argue about that. The gentlemen present, I am sure, will agree with what I said." She turned to Bertha and smiled patronizingly, while Bertha blushed, furiously.

In Washington at about this same hour, Sidney Wyeth, by arrangement with Edrina the night before, had agreed to wait for her after the show in his car around the corner from the Howard theatre. It was a pleasant night and Wyeth was glad when he recognized her footsteps and her voice as she hurried to the car.

After making her comfortable in the big, soft, cushioned seat he crawled under the wheel beside her, and turned to her.

"Now, sweetheart," he said, "instead of going to a hot, stuffy and noisy restaurant tonight, how about some good, old time barbecue, some ice-cold beer, and a ride into the country to eat and drink."

"Oh, that'll be too sweet for words," she exclaimed, clasping her hands joyfully.

A half hour later found them drawing to a stop, deep in a soft-shaded woodland, into a glade, as it were, where the moon looked down upon them with a smile. It was a night for romance, a spot for lovers.

"Isn't this spot just too beautiful for words," cried Edrina, looking around and up into the shadows of mighty oaks, through the leaves of which floated a soft breeze. Turning her eyes to him now, she placed

a hand on his arm, looked up into his eyes, softly, and cried:
"Really, Sidney, I — I believe you are really romantic after all."
"Oh, no, sweetheart," he protested. "I am not and never could be. But I can appreciate nature and beauty — and a very lovely girl" — and he kissed her quickly. "Now let's eat our barbecue and drink the beer before it gets warm."

Through, a few minutes later, he turned to Edrina.
"Edrina?"
"Yes, Sidney," she answered softly, giving him her undivided attention.
"Right now I'd like to forget the serious side of life and play at — making love."
"Why, Sidney," she exclaimed, looking up at him, her eyes wide with well-affected surprise. Then relaxed as quickly, and came closer.
"Why play at it, dear? Why not live it, feel it, say it?" Pausing, she looked up into his face expectantly. He placed an arm about her waist, whereupon she got closer and made it easier for him.
"I do want to, Edrina. I'd really like to, so much." he said, his face serious.
"Then please, Sidney," she said, grasping his hand and holding it and stroking it, "do go ahead," she breathed more than said. He drew her close and kissed her, he squeezed her, then kissed her again. She sighed deeply, passionately, her hand resting on his shoulder.
"This is heaven, Sidney, heaven. There is so much — feeling in your kisses, so much — passion!" She closed her eyes, and seemed to just dream.
"I wish I dared admit that it is love, Edrina."
"Oh, Sidney, what else can you call it?"
"I don't know, Edrina."
"You've taken life and everything that went with it so seriously all your life, dear, that you are really afraid of love when it comes to you."
"I'm not afraid of love, Edrina. I'm afraid of the stage. I've been thinking about that all day long; ever since I left you last night."
"But you do like me, don't you, Sidney? A little at least?" He looked down at her.
"If I spoke the way I feel, Edrina, I would say much more than that."

"Then why don't you, Sidney? Why do you pause and hesitate? I explained all about that last night, didn't I?"

At this he frowned, then went on:

"I — I think, or feel, we should go slower, get to understand each other better before we get too deeply into the emotional side. Don't you think so, dear."

"I do, Sidney."

"Now getting right down to facts, I must appreciate that you're on the stage and that you like it, am I right?"

"Y-yes, I guess so," she managed to say, uncertainly, and waited.

"The fact that you have spent only one season there and didn't get stranded or have to go hungry as is so often the case, is very important to remember."

"How so?"

"There's a tragedy connected with the stage that may be awaiting every one who is ambitious to become a part of it. For instance, you like the stage; you've had just a taste of it and you want more," he said, thoughtfully, gazing into space.

"What's all this got to do with us, Sidney. You and — me?"

"Plenty, Edrina. It'll explain itself in time. Please be patient."

Looking at him, she sighed a bit, impatiently.

"Howard put you on the stage and you're grateful to him for having done so. You should be. In view of the way you feel about it, that is only right and proper; the way you should feel."

Turning to him, this time more impatiently.

"Why are you saying all this, Sidney?"

"I'm coming to something. I'll arrive there presently and then you'll understand," he said. Making herself comfortable and as patient as she could, she sighed lightly again and listened.

"Go on, sweetheart."

"Getting back to Donald, you're more than grateful to him."

She is forced to turn now and look at him, a question in her eyes. He seemed to want to annoy her now; to upset her calm, as it were. Was it because he was telling a truth that didn't seem to her necessary, and that she'd rather not hear?

"Now returning to the stage and as I have said, you like it and you're hoping to go places on it."

"Well?"

"There's something more, and it is more serious, but I won't go that far now. I'll just wait and cross that bridge when I get to it. Now I'll explain about my side of it."

"Yes, Sidney."

"I don't want to go liking some girl then find out after sober consideration that she is not altogether free."

"Free?"

"That's what I mean, Edrina. You are not free as far as I'm concerned, by which I mean that it might not be wise for me to let myself get to liking you — I mean, seriously."

Turning to him again, she said.

"Won't you come right out and say what you mean, Sidney, and quit beating about the bush?"

"I mean that if I let myself go to liking you, say, a lot, in time I might want you all for myself. I might even want to marry you." She turned to him quickly, now, her eyes lit up with a glad joy. A happiness mingled with hope but restrained by fear. She said just one word then, but a word that had a world of meaning.

"Well . . . "

"If I wanted a wife, I'd want one who would be at home when I returned from a hard day's work, at the end of a day." Again she uttered just another word, the same as before.

"Well . . . "

"But in love with the stage, all ambitious to go places on it, you might not be at home when I got there. You might be here or a hundred places far away. Anyway, you might not be at home to greet and welcome me, and that, then, Edrina, would not be a home; it'd simply be a place to go." She understood what he was getting at now.

"Oh," she cried.

"That is what I mean, Edrina. I admit that it may sound a bit selfish and I'm sorry. But I've done some planning, maybe a lot of planning and in all my planning, I've pictured a wife who would be at home when I returned with open arms and passionate lips to greet me, to welcome me; with the home clean, and neat and cozy; with tasty food cooked, hot and steaming ready to serve me." And again she cried, ecstatically.

"Oh . . . "

"Now that could hardly be possible, with a wife off traipsing around with a show, and I have no interest whatever in the kind of show, yet would have to put up with it and her being with it out of consideration to her in order to get along. So now do you see, Edrina, what it can all add up to?"

"I see Sidney and I understand, but I also see and understand that you're not through yet. You have more to say, so go on while you're at it and say it all. Say everything you're thinking about — get it off your chest."

"There isn't much more, he said. "In plain words, I don't think it wise for me to go falling in love with a show girl. I want to be happy with the girl I marry. I want to just think and feel that she's everything in the world to me and while I realize that it is hardly possible for a man and woman to fully agree about everything, I do hope that my wife and I are agreeable as to the fundamentals of life together. And that first wish is for her to be home at all times and she couldn't be there and off with some old show, too. Naturally, under those circumstances, I'd expect to provide that home and supply the means to keep it comfortable so as to have it the way I wanted it. And that, Edrina, is what I mean."

"You are completely within your rights, Sidney, a man's rights. And yet, in spite of all you say, you are, I think, a bit strange about the whole thing."

"I think the word 'practical' would fit better."

"Maybe, then, I am not practical," she said, testily, "if that's what you mean."

"That is another thing I dislike about show people and show work. It fires them with fantastic illusions; makes them forget the essential things in life, and replaces it with an illusion, which so often turns out to be a delusion" he said, with a frown. She looked at him.

"As for instance?"

"We've all got to eat, provide a place to sleep, buy clothes to wear, pay rent and a thousand other things. We cannot do this on illusions."

"Well?"

"I've seen no end of actors slip out on room rent; they seem especially fond of jumping board bills. Beating people too poor to afford it, so poor most times until it is pitiful. These performers have talked, sold them an illusion about big things, big applause, forty weeks work, big pay and got them so enthused until they trust the man and look forward to some of these big things the performers are going to do, to happen—only to wake up some morning to find the actor, and all the illusions, gone with the night."

"You are certainly hard on performers," she said.

"Not hard on them; only on the things they do and that they are given to doing so much until I can seem to hear it echoing all around me. As I said, if and when I marry, the thing I would want to think of first is a place to take this wife, a place to set her down and provide for her."

"Oh, would you, Sidney," she cried, grasping his hand.

"Why of course I would, Edrina. What else would I be expected to do?"

"Then Sidney," she cried, sort of crawling upon him, "If you said you loved me, you'd — ask me to — marry you and then you'd set me up in a nice apartment — and all that?"

"I'd try to, Edrina. In fact, I would."

"Then speak, Sidney, say it now," she cried, as close to him as she could get. He smiled down at her paternally, then kissed her.

"Oh, Edrina, we can't just rush into anything so important, so serious and all that in a hurry. Without going around together for awhile, to see if we can get along, see if we are temperamentally suited to each other in many ways, otherwise, our wedding night and our honeymoon might all be broken up with quarrels; of 'well, I thought so and so and you ought to have done this, or that.' No, dear, I've lived too long to let what might be only an infatuation, turn into a tragedy."

"There it goes again," she sighed, and relaxing, slumped back into her seat. "Why can't we just love and be happy and let responsibilities wait until later. You're so serious until you incline to spoil things," she sighed, complainingly.

"And there is even more to consider than what I've said, Edrina," he said. She looked up at him, divided now between tears and anger.

"Even more than what, Sidney?"

"It's about — Howard."

She straightened in surprise, this time glared at him.

"About Howard? Well, what about him?"

"A whole lot. I — I think you're — in love with him."

"I — am — what?" she started and cried out, shocked-like. She moved away so that she could get a better look at him. "I'm — in —

love with Howard!" He reached over and patted her.

"There, there, now." He said, consolingly. "Don't get so excited. Still, and I repeat, I think you are in love with him." She sighed deeply, placed her hands on her hips, glared at him this time without restraint and exhaled:

"Well, people!"

"You're shocked because — it is possible that you didn't even know it yourself. It might not have even occurred to you that you were." Looking hard at him, she shook her head sadly, hopelessly.

"Haven't you been going around with him ever since he put you in the show?" Relaxing a bit, she is forced to think a moment, then admit.

"Well, yes, but I'm not in love with the man, never have been and never will be."

"Are you sure?" he said, looking at her so closely that she is forced to flinch and turn her eyes away, sigh deeply, and shake her head as if to say, "What more?"

"You've been quite contented while going around with him; you haven't quarreled or fought as most show people do."

"Sidney, please don't be ridiculous!" she cried, exasperatingly placing her fists on her hips.

"You're still going with him, aren't you? Not unhappy while in his company, are you?"

"But I tell you Sidney Wyeth, I do not love the man! Isn't that enough?"

"It would be — if you meant it," he argued. "Maybe you even think you do. Then maybe—" and he broke off and paused, thoughtfully.

"Maybe," she repeated, looking hard at him. Then "Maybe — what?"

"Howard has something to say about it . . . "

"Now what do you mean?" she said, frowning impatiently. He smiled amusedly, still seemed a bit hard around the corners of his mouth as he looked at her.

"I've been told that Howard is not a marrying man. He's past 35 and he's never married any woman yet. Still, he's the great lover. So sedate and agreeable, so easy for a woman to like. I call him the little prince."

She turned to glare at him, closed her mouth tight, then opened it again to cry:

"You've become not only ridiculous but utterly impossible. Please drive me back to town." He was silent now, but turned to look at her. He felt that he hadn't handled it as he ought to have. That he should have been a bit more discreet. He was a bit sorry that he had said all he did.

"I'm sorry, dear," he said, stepping on the starter. He backed the car up and turning around, started back to Washington. Glancing at her, he could see that she was angry and kept her gaze straight ahead. He sighed, increased the speed, and the huge car dashed through the night.

CHAPTER X

MARIE COLEMAN was busy, typing a letter at her desk, and had just finished when the door opened softly. She looked up and then started, perceptibly. For therein stood one of the most beautiful girls she thought she had ever seen.

It was Bertha Schultz. She paused as Marie looked at her and registered surprise, then got to her feet. Bertha took a step forward and closing the door behind her, spoke.

"Pardon me," she said, pleasantly, "but is this the office of Mr. Sidney Wyeth?"

"It is," replied Marie, courteously, pleasantly. "Won't you come in and — " paused to look around, eyes fall upon a chair, to which she pointed: "Be seated?"

"Thank you," said Bertha, and Marie thought that her voice was as beautiful as her face, as perfect as her figure.

She came close enough now for Marie to feel her presence. "I am interested in a book, whch I understand Mr. Wyeth has written. Is this the place where it is published?"

"Yes," replied Marie. "This is the place. Would you—lke a copy?"

"I would very much, thank you," replied Bertha. "The price, please?" Marie told her and went for a copy, bringing it forward and showing it to her.

"My, how beautiful," cried Bertha, as she took and began to examine it.

"Thank you." said Marie. "Everybody admires it. Shall I—wrap it?" holding her hand out for it.

"No, no, thank you. I want to sketch through it. I'm sure I'm going to enjoy reading it very much."

"I'm sure you will. Meantime, please be seated." Marie pushed a chair forward and rewarded her with a pleasant smile. Bertha sat down.

"On second thought, I think I'll take an additional copy, if you don't mind."

"We'll be delighted, thanks." Marie went for the other copy.

"And you may wrap that copy, please."

"Sure," called Marie, and proceeded to do so, returning presently with it wrapped and sealed. Bertha counted out the money for both copies.

"I want to send this one to a friend," said Bertha.

"That'll be nice, I'm sure," said Marie.

Bertha smiled, sweetly. Marie smiled back at her and sitting down, hoped that the other wouldn't hurry. Who was the girl she thought. Didn't seem like a New Yorker, nor any other girl she knew; had ever known — and so pretty, my! She found herself saying this over and over again, daring to look at her out of admiring eyes. She was speaking now, and handing her a card, which Marie gladly took.

"Here is my card. My name is Bertha Schultz. I have just returned to — America, and I'd like to talk to you, if you don't mind."

Marie looked at the card again. It was engraved, and as rich as the name written there was beautiful.

"Thank you," said Marie, rising and bowing. Bertha acknowledged by rising and bowing. They were both standing now.

"My name is Marie Coleman," and Marie reached into her desk and found her card. It was not engraved, and she felt a bit cheap. All cards should be engraved. She would have some engraved as quickly now as she had a chance. Meantime.

"I'm glad to meet you, Miss Schultz," said Marie.

"My compliments to you, Miss Coleman."

"Thank you," said Marie. They both sat down again.

"You've been — abroad, Miss Schultz?"

"I have, Miss Coleman, attending school," replied Bertha.

"Oh, that is wonderful. Do you know when you entered, I got the impression that you, well, I don't know why I felt the way I did exactly," said Marie, "but I was sure you were not a New Yorker and — for that matter, not from anywhere else that I could think of. So I was right. You've been abroad, attending school. Where, may I ask?'

"Of course. At the Sorbonne in Paris, more recently."

"At the Sorbonne in France! My, magnificent! And you attended some other school over there, before that?"

"I'm a graduate of Heidelberg."

"Heidelberg! My, my, but you *have* been attending schools, all right, such great schools." Bertha smiled. Marie looked at her with unexpressible admiration. No wonder, she thought now, she had been so greatly impressed. It seemed to stand out, such extended education, in the girl's every move, every expression. And with all that, she seemed like a nice girl, an agreeable sort of person. She knew she was going to like her.

"I'll be glad to talk to you, Miss Schultz," she said, relaxing comfortably, as she waited for the other to speak. Bertha was inspecting the book again and seemed pleased. She looked up at Marie, and reminded Marie of Schumann-Heink, dead a long time, but as Marie studied her, she kept thinking and comparing her with the great German Soprano. Held her head like Schumann-Heink had, was refined, possessed everything, she thought, that training, education and good manners could give a person. Recalling her words, Marie thought, and recalled now, that the girl had a slight German accent. She wondered if she was part German. It was obvious to Marie that one of her parents was German, and she suspected if so, it must have been her mother, she didn't look like the offspring of a colored mother by a white man, not in America. She was sure she was not.

"Looks like it might be interesting. I shall start reading it as quickly as I return home. Meanwhile," and she looked up at Marie. "I was going to inquire for it at the bookstores, some bookstore downtown, then was told that I might get a copy at the office. Since that was closer and handier I came here and am glad now that I did."

"I'm glad you did, too," smiled Marie.

"Isn't the book on sale at most of the book shops?"

"No, Miss Schultz, it is not?"

"Is not?" She looked down at the book again, turned the jacket back, admired the attractive binding with "My, how pretty. Everything about it is pretty, so well gotten up in every way, nice print, easy to read, yet not large and unsightly."

"Thank you. Mr. Wyeth, the author, has good taste about everything he does. He personally supervised the layout in addition to writing the book," said Marie.

"Indeed! Mr. Wyeth must be an interesting man."

"I think so," replied Marie.

"Is he — related to you?" inquired Bertha. Shaking her head:

"No," said Marie. "I just work for him."

"Oh." And Bertha looked down at the book again.

"I would like to know why the book is not on sale at all the shops, if you don't mind?"

"I don't mind telling you, but hope you'll understand when I do."

"I'll try to, I assure you," said Bertha, looking at her.

"First, Mr. Wyeth has not been to them and tried to get them to stock it."

"I — " Bertha started, but broke off. Then after a pause decided to go on. "I was hoping that I might meet the author, since this is his office."

"Mr. Wyeth is out of town."

"Out of town," exclaimed Bertha. Her expression showed how keenly she was disappointed. "Oh I'm so sorry."

"I am, too," said Marie. "I'm sure that he would be glad to meet you, too."

"Thank you," said Bertha, and smiled appreciatively. "Will he be gone very — long?" There was a note of anxiety in her tone.

"I really couldn't say, Miss Schultz. Mr. Wyeth is a bit unpredictable. He leaves most times suddenly and without saying anything, or where he is going, and may return the same way."

"So sorry," sighed Bertha. "This is his real name, then, is it not?"

"Yes," said Marie. "Plain Sidney Wyeth. No middle name. He's very plain and unassuming."

"Is he?"

"Yes," replied Marie. "And if I do have to say it myself, he's a very fine man. I've worked for him for many years, so I think I should know."

"You should, and I'm sure you do," said Bertha. "I'm glad to hear you say that. Now I'll know what to — expect." Marie lost her smile for a moment. Wonder overspread her face instead. Bertha looked up and saw it.

"Oh, you're wondering what my interest could be, aren't you? Well, none in particular. Mostly curiosity. I've never met a colored author."

"I guess not. We haven't very many. In fact, very few active in writing, none at all in the publishing field."

"No?" said Bertha.

Marie shook her head.

"No. I think Mr. Wyeth is about the only one, and his novel there, is the first one by a Negro author to be published in quite a long time, at least three or four years."

"Indeed?"

"I'm afraid so. Our people haven't gone in for writing so much for quite a long time. There are quite a number of new books about the Negro, a novel or two in the lot but they've all been written by white people."

"Is that so?" said Bertha, and seemed much surprised. Marie looked at her. As highly educated as she obviously was, why didn't she know.

"You didn't know?" she asked.

"I've been in Europe for so long until I am — a bit out of touch with conditions in America."

"Oh, I understand."

"Otherwise I should know some of the things you're forced to tell me," said Bertha and smiled.

"Not exactly. Having been through two great schools and all the studying it must have taken," said Marie, "you couldn't have had much time to keep acquainted with conditions in America."

"That is it," said Bertha quickly relieved. She didn't want to have to say too much about herself, and nothing about what she and her brother were in America to do, of course. Still she was curious and being by nature an ambitious, serious-minded sort of person, she was anxious to learn much — a very great deal.

"We were discussing colored authors and what they are doing in America at this time," she said.

"Exactly nothing—that is, almost nothing," said Marie.

"I'd like to know. Could you tell me, perhaps, why?"

Marie shrugged her shoulders. "That's why I'd like you to meet Mr. Wyeth. He's wonderfully well-informed. In fact, one of the most informed men in America about most anything you can think about, talk about. He could tell you anything and about everything you'd like to know, and especially as regards our group."

"That's why I wanted to meet him."

"Anything that I know and can tell you about is due to my close association with him, otherwise I might not know half as much."

"I think you're very well informed and most interesting, too," said Bertha.

Marie smiled appreciatively.

"We were talking about colored authors. You didn't finish telling me," said Bertha.

"No," said Marie. "I didn't because there is so very little to tell. We have several columnists on the colored papers. I don't go in much for column reading, so don't know much about what they write. Am sure it is interesting, however, else the newspapers wouldn't keep publishing what they write, week after week."

"How many colored men and women, would you say, are depending on what they write for their living," inquired Bertha.

"Mr. Wyeth is the only one I know," said Marie.

"It doesn't seem possible 13,000,000, and no more than one—at most two or three—receiving sufficient royalties to live on?" said Bertha in surprise.

"The word 'royalty' is Greek to Negroes. We have several music writers and recording artists who might know what the word means," said Marie. "But that would be all."

"It's really deplorable," said Bertha, shaking her head sadly. "Such amazing deficiency."

"I'm forced to agree with you. But assisting Mr. Wyeth in the selling of his book, I know much more about books and that they are writing practically nothing at all along that line."

"And again I'd like to know why?" said Bertha. And again Marie shrugged her shoulders.

" I don't know, Miss Schultz. I do know that they are not making many serious attempts, either. Mr. Wyeth and I discuss it frequently. He says that, as a whole, the Negro isn't a very interesting writer, beyond Negro history, some kind of poetry and essays, because he is too academic. Many are calling themselves anthropologists. They write a great deal about the origin and development of mankind, especially of man hundreds and thousands of years ago, which they learned in school, but seem to know little about the man in the street today, his idiosyncrasies and all that. But of how to make a dollar in a country that is strictly capitalistic, and where the possession of wealth, measured in dollars and cents is the role, and has been since the country was founded, he knows exactly nothing."

"Too academic, I can see," commented Bertha. "Entirely too academic for his own good," and she shook her head sadly.

"To write what people will buy and read, the first thing is to know people, living, breathing and moving around people; people of today," quoted Marie. "And to know people, Mr. Wyeth says, you've got to meet people, study people, find out what they are thinking, learn all about what they are doing, how they do it. He calls many of our educated Negroes, "academic Idiots," whereupon Bertha burst into laughter.

"You sure have to and that is what I mean when I quote Mr. Wyeth as explaining the Negro's failure. He doesn't study people, he's not in trade, commerce or industry. He doesn't produce much if anything worth-while, so when he attempts to write it is mostly from an academic point of view. In other words, he has acquired all he knows in school, or most of it, anyhow, and schools cannot very well teach you what to write about when people want to know about people."

"So you don't think the colored people — our people." Bertha corrected herself. She knew that it would be best in speaking of Negroes to refer to them as ours and us instead of as somebody else, "are succeeding very well as writers."

"A large share of our educated group, who depend on teaching and white collar work, have tried to educate themselves into success, by either remaining in school, or by going back and acquiring one degree after another until, loaded down with degrees, as Mr. Wyeth puts it, and starving to death, he does not, unfortunately, seem to know much of anything at all."

"That is most unfortunate," commented Bertha, and shook her head sadly. "Just what *do* they produce, anyhow?"

"Arguments, mostly," said Marie and laughed. Bertha was forced to join her.

"And trade and commerce, what do they sell; what do they have to sell?"

"Religion mostly," said Marie, humorously. "They sell Religion from every angle, retail, wholesale, in the basement, attic, on the street, everywhere. It's the biggest stock in trade with them, Heaven, Religion and Heaven."

"You possess a sense of humor, Miss Coleman," said Bertha. "It is most unfortunate as I view it, however."

"Unfortunate is the word," said Marie. "Mr. Wyeth says that because of this, we can't make any money; that the Negro doesn't know the first move of how to make a dollar, so as a writer he is as unsuccessful as in other lines, because as a writer who hopes to make money, one should know what the public will read, and write it and the public will buy it.

"He says that with nothing but academics in his mind, he isn't able to tell a story about people. Instead, he tries, if he tries, to tell a story about words, big words that he doesn't understand himself and naturally the man on the street wouldn't, so he's just not writing anything, but fortunately, they do read. They like good novels, with plenty in them about women and love and they like the book you have there and buy it and read it, every word of it and like it. For that reason, Mr. Wyeth is finding publishing profitable, and is developing many ways of reaching our group directly, for they don't frequent bookstores in volume sufficient to mean anything. Meanwhile, Mr. Wyeth is kept so busy, developing what he has already started and exploring new and other possible ways, that he hasn't had time and gotten around to sales through bookstores to a great extent. He plans and hopes to get to this by the time he publishes his next book, however."

"So very interesting. If Mr. Wyeth is any more interesting than you, he must be, as you say, a most well informed man."

"Wait until you meet him. You'll see. And he's interesting in a way that anybody can understand. Makes anything you talk about or that he talks about so simple and plain until a child can understand it."

"How remarkable," said Bertha, thrilled, but getting to her feet. She felt that she had stayed long enough, asked enough questions, but there was one more that she was careful to ask, as standing, she paused and turned back at the door, to face Marie, who had followed her.

"I suppose that if I — came again, I might — catch him in?"

"You might," replied Marie, "and if he is I shall be glad to introduce you to him."

"Thank you," said Bertha, appreciatively. "Then, will it be — all right if I — call by again?"

"By all means, Miss Schultz," exclaimed Marie, sincerely. "I want you to come by again, as often as you want to. I've enjoyed talking to you so much and am sure we have much more to talk about, now that we are acquainted. So come by any day, every day that is convenient for you to. In that way, sooner or later you'll have to catch Mr. Wyeth in."

"Thanks for the invitation, and don't be surprised and above all, annoyed, if you see me again soon — sooner if it wasn't that I am going to plunge right into this book and I'll probably have it read by this time tomorrow." Both laughed.

"I am anxious for you to come back and meet Mr. Wyeth. When he finds a person interesting, he will ask plenty of questions. I can't do that, ask people so many questions, so much about themselves, but he can. I would, however, like to know more about you."

"Then why not ask? I shall be glad to tell you."

"Oh, I will, in time; but Mr. Wyeth, if he finds you as interesting as I have, will ask you all about yourself right away and won't mind it. But to his credit, I can explain, he asks them in a way that you won't mind, maybe, at least most people answer them without seeming to mind," laughing again; they smiled at each other and Bertha finally took her leave and Marie listened as her footsteps died away down the hall.

She went back to her chair and thought about this unusual girl, and kept on thinking about her all that day while doing her work.

CHAPTER XI

WYETH'S TAKING EDRINA out and dining her each night after the show, was not lost on members of the cast. In fact, it had become the subject of much gossip, especially among the ladies of the chorus. In their dressing room two girls, not altogether fond of Edrina on general principles, were having much at the moment, to say about her.

"Have you heard about Edrina running around with Sidney Wyeth, the Motion Picture Producer," said Angel, putting on her makeup, eyes in the mirror in front of her. Angel was tall, tan and very shapely. Mantan specialized, among other things or styles, in the tall, tantalizing kind.

"I was looking out the window at Maw Williams when he drove her back last night," said Maude, not so tall, yet not too short but round and plump with attractive calves, goo, goo eyes, and kissable lips. Before she went on the stage a few years before, Maude was called the prettiest girl in Deweese Street, Lexington, Ky. On the show they called her "Cutey."

"What's the low down, anyhow? Edrina's Donald Howard gal." said Angel, wincing aloud as she pulled a long hair from her brow.

"You mean *was*," said Maude.

"I mean *is*," corrected Angel. "For she still is, regardless how much love Sidney Wyeth tries to make to her. She's crazy about that little West Indian monkey and I don't mean maybe."

"Perhaps you're right," agreed Maude.

"Anyway," observed Angel, "how come her running around with Wyeth, anyhow?"

"Maybe she's tryin' tu win a home. Sidney Wyeth has dough."

"That's the first show girl I ever saw him look at the second time. He doesn't seem to go in for us."

"Ain't it so. I've often wondered if he's 'high hat.' "

"But gettin' back to Edrina," said Angel.

"Yes, of course," from Maude.

"I tell you she's crazy about Donald Howard and it's me that knows. But as you just suggested, since Donald doesn't spend anything but his time, entertaining any girl, maybe Edrina's decided to flirt with a home and a man who can keep it up," said Angel.

"If she could land Wyeth, it would mean a home and a man who could take care of her. I imagine he's the kind of man who would take care of a girl," said Maude.

"Lucky girl if she can. I wish he'd look at me. I'd grab him and run. Anything to get out of this old show work. I'm so tired of it."

"There's no future in it at all," sighed Maude, wearily.

"It's a dog's life I tell you, and its me that knows it."

"Not you, sugar," grinned Angel, shifting to the other side of her face. "Me."

"We both know it," said Maude, with a sigh. "All we show girls know it."

"Except Edrina," corrected Angel. "She doesn't."

"Yes, she does," snapped Maude. "But she's just vain. You see she had a little luck. I mean, thus far she hasn't been stranded and forced to go out and sell her yes, yes, in order to eat or get back to New York. That's what I mean."

"And because Donald Howard's sorta sponsorin' her," said Angel. "She's fool enough to think she's goin' places."

"She is sure nuts," laughed Maude. "All Donald Howard's ever done except stage this cheap show for Mantan, was to — "

"—rehearse," assisted Angel, cutting her off and finishing her sentence.

"Rehearse is right," laughed Maude. "And how he can rehearse!"

"The rehearsenist man that ever lived."

"Remember 'Old Man Evil?'" said Angel.

"When I rehearsed from April to October in the thing? Do I remember it? You should ask me if I'd ever forget it."

"Rehearsed from April to October. Opened in November, ran two forced weeks, and — "

"—closed as usual, and—"

" — without pay. And you have the nerve to ask me if I remember it!" and she laughed a hard, bitter, laugh. "You and I and a hundred other po' niggah puhformers, or would be performers, all too hongry to be called real, standing around the stage entrance of the old Lafayette with our dispossesses, pray'n 'tu Gawd we would get some money, just a little money for all our work, not counting months of rehearsals, on account of that little slick-haird shiek."

"What a night that was, aw, what a night!" sighed Maude.

"Niggah performers was sure desperate," said Angel, retrospectively. "They'd have killed Howard if they could have gotten their hands on him."

"All of which happened before this silly Edrina got into the show business. If she'd been there with a dispossess in her hands like the most of us — "

" — all of us," corrected Maude.

"Yes, all of us. Anyway, had she been, maybe she'd have some sense by now and quit dreaming."

"It's been such a long time ago, and it was such a bitter experience, until I've tried to forget it. But since you brought it up, just what happened, anyhow?"

"The police had to come and escort him away. Three ov'm, don't you remember?" said Angel looking across at her.

After puckering her eyebrows, Maude perked up.

"Sure I do now," she exclaimed. "Three cops on motor cycles."

"Sure. They put him into a taxi. Then one got on each side of the taxi and the third one behind it and sailed away with that little niggah up Seventh avenue," they both laughed.

"And that's how he got away," said Angel, still laughing. "Now along comes this silly Edrina thinking she's going places because he's behind her," sighed Maude, shaking her head sadly.

"She will," said Angel, the meaning of which Maude didn't catch.

Turning to the other, curiously.

"Huh?"

"I said she will," from Maude humorously.

"Where?"

"To the po'house," laughed Maude. Angel laughed, too. They both laughed.

"To the po'house is right," and again both laughed.

"That's why I say," continued Maude, "that if this Sidney Wyeth is serious in the attention he's paying her, and she's got any sense at all, she'd better grab him and run—"

"—and keep on runnin' after she gets him; keep on runnin' until she gets out of sight and sound of show business."

"You're tellin me," echoed Maude.

"But she won't," said Angel, face more serious now.

"How come?" said Maude, turning again toward her.

"Because, she won't have sense enough. That's a colored woman, you know."

"Maybe you're right," said Maude. "Love and labor is our motto."

"We've been treated so bad and for so long until we just can't seem to be sensible when a good man comes along," said Angel, ruefully.

"Ain't it the truth," agreed Maude. "What makes us that way, anyhow?"

"Just born that way; born for bad luck and a hard time. My grand mammy says they were that way in her day; when she was a girl. She says that they were fightin' over yalluh men, givin' them their money and letting them make a fool ov'm, the same way as they're doing nowadays."

"I guess we just won't ever have any sense. Now take this Edrina for instance," Maude went on. "And Wyeth and Howard. Wyeth must be liking her a little, else he wouldn't be feeding her every night and asking nothing."

"Asking nothing?" inquired Angel, turning to look at her. "What do you mean?"

"I mean taking her out every night and spending money on her and not going to bed with her."

"Oh," echoed Angel. "Don't you think he's gettin' any of it?"

"I don't think so."

"How would you know?"

"Oh, I wouldn't know; but I don't think so. He drives her up to the sidewalk, kisses her good night and drives on away. That's what I see him doing, so am sure he isn't forcing her to go to bed with him."

"*Some man!* I never seen a niggah who'd spend fifty cents on a gal if he didn't demand her to go to bed with him and — "

" — spend the night," laughed Maude, "all night," and both laughed.

"Maybe he's a — "

"Naw, he ain't," cried Maude, quickly.

"How'd you know?"

"He don't act like one, don't talk like one," said Maude.

"Maybe he's savin' it until he marries her."

"There are men like that."

"What do you call them, such a man?"

"Virtuous men," and both broke into laughter.

"They say Edrina's got good stuff, too," said Angel. "They say when she puts her arms around them and begins to whine—"

"Aw, go on, gal," said Maude. "You're gettin' real dirty."

"Gettin' back to Wyeth, and Howard. If Wyeth should marry her she'd still keep Howard as a sweetie on the side, and in time, run a good man clear off. Now watch and see if I ain't right."

"She couldn't be such a fool," said Angel deprecatingly.

"But she is and it'll all be about this little old show business, I'm tellin' you. She thinks she can sing; that she's a soubrette, when all she can do is squeal right loud. But she'll fool around, tryin' to do so and by an by Wyeth'll go on about his business and let her alone."

"Ain't it too bad how some gals gets all the breaks and the rest get the boot? If ever I gets a chance to marry a good man, I wouldn't ever go running around with any no-account one, believe me." Just then somebody knocked on the door, and both started and looked around and Angel called:

"Yes?"

"Mr. Mantan," the voice called. "Are you there?"

"Sure, Mr. Mantan. Maude and I are both here, made up and ready to go on."

"All right," he called back and they heard his footsteps pass on down the hall and a moment later heard him knock on the next dressing room door.

CHAPTER XII

MEANWHILE, SIDNEY WYETH had left Washington and Donald Howard had come down from New York and now sat in a booth, in a restaurant, across the table from Edrina.

"I believe Wyeth likes you," he said, toying with a fork. He presently picked up a glass of water and took a sip. Howard was born in the West Indies, had been educated in America, had gotten away from the usual accent, but said words with such care until one wondered if he didn't have some monkey in him anyhow. Edrina smiled, looked up at him cooquettishly, while Howard went on:

"There's your big chance. You may win a movie contract — and a husband at the same time."

"Quit trying to kid me, Donald."

"I'm not trying to kid you, Edrina," he insisted, smiling laconically. Edrina didn't answer.

"Sidney Wyeth is steady, sticks to what he's doing. That's the kind of man that makes a good husband."

"But I don't think he's interested in me — at least that way," ventured Edrina. "Additionally, I'm not exactly interested in pictures, anyhow. I prefer the stage first, last and all the time."

"I've told you that it is passing, Edrina. This kind of show, especially. It's liable to break down and pass out entirely any day. The theatres we've been playing have mostly given up running stage shows. They've all gone into playing pictures exclusively." There was a frown on Howard's face as he finished. Edrina felt it a good time to express a far-fetched ambition.

"What's the matter with Broadway? Shows seem to be still popular down there."

He looked up, smiled, then frowned again.

"An illusion — a far-fetched illusion," he said and laughed deprecatingly.

"But I like illusions, Donald," smiled Edrina. "To play down there has always been my ambition, the height of my ambition, of my dreams."

"Have you got anything to sell to Broadway? They're not hot for Negro drama. Maybe something good, dirty and low down, but nothing that you'd like so well."

"I can sing," she said.

He looked at her.

"Not the kind of songs they want to hear a colored girl sing on Broadway. Then again, shows don't stay there forever, at least all of them. They close sometimes after the first night—and a bunch of bad press notices the morning after. It's too much of a gamble," he said, but she had ideas of her own.

"But I'm from Kentucky, where gambling is a virtue. I like to gamble; taking chances thrills me. Since only one horse can win, we often bet on the wrong one. We Kentuckians can take it, dear. We swallow our disappointment and wait until Derby day rolls around again," she persisted, with a fine gesture. But he was not impressed.

"All you say is fine fiction, Edrina, but in New York you have to eat, pay rent and keep going, win, lose or draw. If you lose nobody cares; but suit yourself, dearie. It's your bread, butter and future you insist on gambling with. But if you happen to throw craps, don't complain and try to say that I didn't tell you, at least try to warn you against taking chances up in the big town."

"I'm still willing to take the chance," insisted Edrina bravely.

"You can get into enough trouble with a show like this, even. There's nothing sure about it. Some morning you may wake up and find there's no place to play, which is what we may be confronted with before many weeks. The theatres don't want to be bothered with a lot of people backstage, fighting and demanding money, getting drunk and carrying on as they often do. I wish you wasn't enthusiastic about the stage, dear. It's too unpredictable, too uncertain." Then breaking off suddenly, he looked at his watch and started. "Meantime, it's near show time and I want to see what these new people I'm putting in the show looks like before the curtain rises. Let's eat this bite and get going," and he fell to eating.

Wyeth had gone down into Virginia to stage a campaign through the schools in several towns, so on the way back to New York in his car, stopped in Washington, and, of course looked in on Edrina. The show was due to close at the end of the week and move on west to Pittsburg. Donald Howard had returned to New York.

Back stage, he was waitng for Edrina to make her change. Presently coming from behind the screen where she made it, she stood before him smiling. At the sight of her his face lit up with sincere delight and he exclaimed: "My, my, but you sure look nice tonight, dear."

"Think so," she said, then turned from right to left, left to right, her arms poised like a model, displaying a dress for the benefit of a customer. He looked her up and down with care, at her skirt to see if her slip might be showing. It was not.

"Everything is okeh, honey bunch," he said, approvingly. "I think you're more beautiful than I have ever seen you look before tonight," his face beaming.

"Jive," she said, playfully. "But thank you for the words, nevertheless."

"I mean it honestly, Edrina," he insisted.

She paused thoughtfully, then raising her eyes to his.

"It's the dress you like. It's new. I bought it at a store down on F street today, and have been waiting to wear it in the hope of pleasing you. So I'm glad you like it and thanks. I wish you liked me as much as you seem to like the dress."

"I do like you, Edrina. I'm very fond of you. I've been thinking about you all the while I was away, and was anxious to get back where I could see you again and be with you before going on through to New York."

"You won't leave before I do, will you?"

"I think I'll have to."

"Please don't, but sit down sweetheart," and she adjusted the single chair which was in the room. He sat down. She moved closer but stood looking straight into his eyes.

"Let's have a serious little talk before we go out, darling," she said, and her face was serious and very sober. He looked up at her and taking her hand, pulled her down on his knee, where she nestled close to him comfortably, an arm about her waist. They exchanged a kiss, and he was emotional again, she was also, so he squeezed her.

"When you begin to like a person and you go away from them

a while, it is interesting to feel the reaction, sensational reaction," he said. "Down there in Virginia where I've been, I met so many nice girls. Teachers in the schools, many of whom were young and attractive; they made me welcome and listened to what I talked about, bought my book, many schools, the whole faculty, that is, where they were getting any money."

"What do you mean, getting any money?"

"I didn't mean *any* money, sweetheart. They all, of course get something. But in about half the schools the pay of the colored teachers has been put on a par with that of the whites, and in those schools they have money, were able to and did buy books, whereas in those where the old scale still obtains, where they were getting from about two-thirds down to about half the pay the white teachers are receiving, it was not so hot and I felt sorry for them and didn't mind if they didn't buy as well. I understood that they couldn't afford it, poor things. But what I started to say, dear, was that in spite of meeting a lot of young and pretty teachers, several times a day, just as quickly as I was out of their presence, I'd fall to thinking about you; at times with such violence until many times, I felt like turning around and coming back where I could see you."

"Oh, my," she cried, an arm about his neck but looking straight into his eyes, "but that thrills me. Old serious-minded darling like you are, to think of me and want to come back before you were through is thrilling, dear, to say the least," and she ended by giving him a big kiss, and squeezing him tight to her. "Now tell me more about what you thought about," she said. "I l'ke to hear it."

"I hardly know how to start, I just thought about you all the time, that's all. Haven't you ever did that?"

"Of course I have, silly. I've been doing the same thing about you ever since you left. Just thinking about you every day, every hour in the day, almost every minute in each hour."

"Oh, darling, no," he protested.

"But darling, yes," she cried. "Now if you thought about me all the while you were away as you say you did, then maybe it was because you've begun to like me a little, yes?"

"You mean a great deal, Edrina. Not just a little," he said and seemed to mean it. He squeezed her so close now until she could feel and faintly hear the beating of his heart against hers, hers against his. He breathed a deep sigh.

"You can feel that something, Edrina, can't you?" he whispered, hoarsely. She nodded her head, then started to complain:

"But you don't trust me, Sidney, and that — hurts. It pains and makes me sad and unhappy, so unhappy." She started crying now and began to feel for a kerchief. He came forward with one and dried her tears instead, meanwhile, stammering at something which she didn't seem to hear, or at least to understand.

"You — you don't trust me and that's why you're holding back. I — I do believe you like me some, enough to make me happy and contented, but it makes me feel bad to think that you have distrust all mixed up with your liking, and I don't like that."

"Maybe you're right, and if that is so, I'm sorry," he admitted. She sat straight now and using her kerchief, dabbed at her eyes.

"And that's what I want to talk to you about."

He looked at her, and in doing so she was forced to meet his eyes. Then suddenly with a burst of passion, he kissed her boldly, and that started it all over again.

"Oh, Sidney," she cried, tears starting, and her face torn up and slightly distorted, "When you do that, I — just lose all my composure, my control. Kiss me again, you mean old darling," and around his neck went her arms again, and the next few seconds were given up to a passionate exchange of kissing and embracing. After a time she relaxed again, and went on:

"If you trusted me," she said. "We could mean so much to each other, and it would make me so happy."

"If you could influence me into trusting you, dear heart, that would make me happy, too, very happy," said he.

"But what can I do to make you trust me, Sidney? I'm doing everything I know how to make you. I can't think of anything else that I've not already done to make you do so," she ended by looking at him appealingly. Meanwhile, he was thoughful, adjusted himself and she rose up a moment to let him do so. Then pulled her back down on his knee.

"I've trained myself all my life to accept others," he began, "as I find them. And in that respect, regardless of the fact that I think you're more deeply enamoured of Donald Howard than you like to admit, even to yourself, I am willing to take that chance."

"Then, what, dear," she asked.

He shifted uncomfortably, and a frown crossed his features. He looked at her and she met his gaze.

"It's this show business."

"The stage, Sidney," she said, quite frankly, and patiently, whereas he had expected her to explode, blow up, as it were.

"Yes, dear" he replied, looking at her. "The stage and shows. I could put up with your being with a show as long as you're single, but you see, Edrina," and he broke into a frown. She leaned forward and kissed his forehead, and then stroked his cheek kindly.

"Yes, Sidney," she said, kindly, patiently, "go ahead, get it off your chest. Tell me everything that's worrying you."

"I want a companion and the best companion for a man is a — wife. But I want my wife at home. I want to feel that that is where she is, and —" again he broke off and she understood. He didn't want to tell her that she should leave the stage if she wanted him to marry her. She squeezed him as if to reassure him. She'd try to clear up this whole misunderstanding, if she couldn't, at least she'd make a try.

"Oh, so that's what the hold back is all about, eh?" she cried, eyes dilated, with inspiration. He looked at her.

"Mostly." he said, and waited.

"Then what do you want me to do, Sidney darling?" Her question rather caught him off guard. For a moment he was puzzled, still not altogether satisfied with all he had said up to now, he frowned again, and went on:

"It is not what I want, or what I might command, Edrina. What ever you do is up to you."

"Up to me, Sidney?" she asked, slightly puzzled. "Just what is up to me, darling?"

"The stage, Edrina, your work on it. I don't want any girl for a wife, my wife, traipsing around all over the country with a show. Yet, I know that you like the show and stage show work so well until it would become a choice between the stage and me," he said, argumentatively.

"Then the choice would be you, Sidney. I'd give up the stage," she said, and by saying so, implied that that was all settled. He looked up quickly, hopefully, and a bit surprised. But not for long. He was still not convinced. After a moment of serious thought.

"I wish I could believe you," he said with something akin to a sigh.

"What do you mean, 'I wish I could believe you'," she said now, looking hard at him.

"Just what I said. I wish I could feel convinced that you mean what you say. Maybe you even think you do yourself — now." She sighed, a bit hopelessly. He patted her reassuringly.

"You see, Edrina," he went on. "That is the way you feel now. After awhile, however, you'd begin to feel different. Liking the stage as you do, you'd think about it. Then it would occur to you that you hadn't wanted to give it up, but that in order to please me, you were forced to and then at the first disagreement, you'd get mad, but always you'd be thinking that I made you give it up. Who knows that such a continued reflection, might in time become an obsession, your obsession."

"You mean Sidney," said she, "that altho' I promised to, I'd still want to continue the work, and — "

" — do like most women. Finally leave your husband, your children, if that happened, and go back to it. That has happened before and it can happen again and it is that which I'm afraid of."

"But I've said that I'm willing to give it up; I've tried to imply that you mean more to me than any stage, all the stages. Why must you continue to doubt me?"

"Because, away down in the bottom of your heart, behind all that you are insisting at this moment, you doubt yourself. Why? I can seem to see right through you and your ambitions, Edrina. You are little short of insane about it. You might promise to give it up, as you have just promised — and even intend as you feel now, to do so. Then along one day would come Mantan or Howard, or both, with a proposition.

"Supposing by that time I have become devoted to you; you have become a part of me, of my daily existence; that I love you, love you truly and am happy, you are happy, too. We have a happy home. You wouldn't really want to change it, but you'd keep thinking; you'd build castles in the air, great castles that are a part of the stage. Then you'd begin to work on me. You'd tell them to leave it to you, you'd bring me around in time. Then it would be, just for a little while, dear, only a little while. To please you, for isn't it the function of man and wife to want to, and try to, please each other? So I would try to please you, and let you go. If the show had any measure of success, that would continue into weeks, into months. Oh yes, you'd perhaps write me every day, send me telegrams, think of me and say 'my poor, darling husband. He wants me so. I must get back to him, and all that. Even as much as I wouldn't want to, I would be forced to put up with it and perhaps would. But supposing the show began to totter, to waver and threaten to fail? Then somebody connected with it might come to you. They've done it before, they'll do it again. Some old funny looking Ofay might become interested. He might not have any money, but could interest some other funny looking Ofay possibly to put up a little dough to carry on. But in order to get him to do this, inducements would have to be made. You have a soft, pretty body. I'd like to fondle that body, but I'm one of these rare idiots who exist only in the minds of a novelist. I'm willing — and even want to wait until that wedding night. I haven't asked you to — to go to bed with me, have I?"

She nodded her head in agreement.

"It doesn't mean that I am not a normal man. I am, in fact, passionately normal. But all my life I've pictured waiting until the wedding night to take all a girl can offer a husband.

"But would these 'hounds of the Baskerville's, view it that way?' The delivery of your pretty, soft round body might be the price of this Ofay keeping the show going. I know show business. If they were convinced that it would, they would keep on after you to *deliver* —and get mad and hate you in the end if you didn't. They'd advance the argument that it meant work for a whole lot of people, people that this Ofay didn't want. All this seems sordid and bitter, but a girl ambitious for the stage and hoping for success there, a colored girl under present conditions, is most likely to be forced, before it was all over, to sell her body, trade it many times, to keep the show going by pleasing some confounded Ofay, and Edrina, that's why I'm holding back; why I—oh, I'm sorry that I let myself begin to like you."

"Oh, Sidney, darling," she cried dramatically. "Please believe me when I say, when I insist, that I would do nothing of the kind. I would give you everything I have and do everything in my little heart to make you comfortable and happy. Won't you please, oh, please believe me and trust me to do what is right." She patted his cheek, kissed his lips, pawed over him, caressed his hands and kissed his forehead. Meanwhile, sighing deeply:

"I wish I could, Edrina. I don't see why I don't after all your protestations, but away in the back of it all, I can't forget that you like the stage, and it is that, more than what might happen, for it will surely happen if you stick to these shows long enough, that I can't get out of my head." He stood up after the above words, and raised her to her feet. She moved around him, however, to try to force him to look at her, into her eyes, which he avoided.

"I'm sorry I let myself like you," he said, avoiding her eyes. "I've by-passed this for years. I mean, liking show girls, which has been my environment because I didn't want to get into a squeegee as I am in now. I'm not condemning stage shows in general, but I know that the day of Tab shows like this is about at its end. So when I see you all ambitious to go places in one, I know where it may end up and I don't want any part of it."

He now walked around the small room with her following and pleading with him; insisting over and over that she was not in love with the stage and would quit any time he asked her to, but he was adamant. He had more to tell her about it, so after a few turns up and down, he paused and faced her and went on:

"I never had any confidence, patience or interest in Tab shows when they had plenty theatres to play. I know too much about them. Many performers are given to indulging in unnatural relations back stage, and if you suppose I want a wife in such an environment, then I've lost my sense of morality — and I haven't."

"I tell you Sidney, for the hundredth time, that it doesn't mean that much to me and I'll quit — I'll quit tomorrow, if you say."

"I'm not asking you to upset the man's show; I'm not asking you to quit at all. I'm only debating what might come to pass if I married you and set you up in an apartment then set out to try and be a good husband. A few weeks of happy wedded bliss, maybe, but as long as you're as fond of it as you are, it would return. The first rehearsal that you heard of going on, you'd be hanging around it. As pretty as you are, they'd sure be propositioning you. I know it.

You couldn't help feeling flattered. The fact that you'd hang around is the best evidence of your interest, otherwise you wouldn't be there. Aw, hang it," he cried abruptly and disgustingly. "Instead of being happy as I'd like to be over liking you, I'm miserable," and he started walking again.

"But why be miserable, sweetheart. I've told you that I'll devote my whole life to making you happy. Can a girl promise more?"

"No, Edrina, she cannot," he said and sighed, deeply, like he was getting tired. She looked up into his eyes.

"Still you're not convinced. I can see it in your eyes; I can feel it. Please Sidney," she went on. "You can't do this to me," and she emphasized it by breaking into tears and beating her two fists against his chest. Then turning her back to him and giving up to tears, she sobbed: "I'm due some consideration. I"—she was forced to break off because he caught her and turned her about to face him suddenly.

"I really want you, Edrina. I want you heart, body and soul. Can't you see, and can't you feel how unhappy it would be to have you go and leave me after I had become devoted to you?"

She pulled away and again turning her back on him.

"You say such fine things, and then you unsay them with so many other words that take the feeling out of the good ones you've just said. You—you just—hurt me. Treat me like—like I didn't have any heart at all." She now turned back and looked up at him, her eyes filled with sad tears. He met her gaze and seemed so miserable and unhappy. She laid her hands gently on him and let the tears go unchecked.

"How could I go away from you or do anything you didn't want me to if I loved you and loved you dearly? Doesn't loving a person mean trying to please them; trying to make them happy and contented?" she said. With a sigh as if to give up, he shuffled, and said:

"There isn't much more I can say, I guess. I've become so fond of you until it is difficult to resist your appeal much longer."

"I give up almost everything dear to a woman: modesty—almost throw myself at you, and still you won't say that you love me. What kind of a man are you anyhow, Sidney Wyeth!"

"Just a poor, unfortunate one who wants a wife to be good to him; to be home when I get there, to love and care for me, to kiss and fondle me, and to repeat it when I leave. That is all."

"Then you don't believe I'd do all that? That it would make me happy to do so?"

"I think you would do all that, Edrina, and make a beautiful job of it. I believe you'd be so good and sweet to me, I'd be the happiest man on earth; but I'm afraid that one day in the midst of this bliss, when I returned home—" he broke off and turned his face away. She didn't follow him this time, but just stood looking at him, sadly, pitifully. He turned back to her and tried again to be brave and honest.

"That is why I don't want to say that I love you, Edrina. Still, you know that I do," he said. She made no answer for she had spent herself for words to try to convince him of her fidelity. He moved toward the door now. She stood still, saying nothing, doing nothing. At the door he paused and turned back. .

"So come, dear," he called. "It's time to go. There's no use for us to argue longer. When you're convinced regarding all we've talked about, convinced yourself, then you'll come to me and say it and when you do I'll believe you. You feel that you mean it now—but you don't. And I won't say that I love you until you convince me and say so of your own volition." She still stood where he had left her, face down, but crying no longer. She had listened soberly to all that he said. Now she turned and walked slowly towards him. He looked down at her sadly, but said no further words. Then suddenly, and in a burst of emotion, pent-up emotion, she threw her arms about him and cried:

"Oh, Sidney, Sidney!" and fell to weeping all over again, this time, as though broken-hearted. It was minutes later before he had succeeded in calming her, and they were able to leave the dressing room.

Outside, he put her in the car and drove her straight to her room, and kissed her good night. As he drove away, he decided that since he was so bewildered and upset, to drive on through to New York that night, which he did.

CHAPTER **XIII**

TWO DAYS LATER in New York, he received the following Telegram:

"HOW COULD YOU LEAVE TOWN WITHOUT COMING BY AGAIN TO SEE ME? DISTRESSED. SHOW MOVING ON TO PITTSBURGH TONIGHT. PLEASE WRITE ME AT ONCE, CARE OF ELMORE THEATRE THERE, THEN CALL ME PITT 5-6783, 11 P.M. SUNDAY NIGHT. YOUR HEART-BROKEN
EDRINA

Wyeth turned his entire attention to his work at the office for the next few days to try to forget all about it, at least until Sunday night, when he would call her.

He arrived at the office while Marie was out, having reached New York around five A.M., sought a few hours sleep, then hurried to the office, feeling no worse for his night's drive from Washington.

He hurriedly penned Edrina a brief note, sealed, stamped and went into the hall and posted it, special. No sooner had he returned to his desk when Marie came back from lunch. She stopped and cried in surprise:

"Why, Mr. Wyeth, you, back!" She relaxed then and crossed to him, shaking his hand. After removing her hat and coat she brought her note book and pencil and for an hour took letters and checked accumulated matters, which needed his attention.

"Now," said he, at the end of that time, "that everything is started again, what's been happening since I've been away?"

"Plenty," replied Marie.

"Plenty?" he repeated, curiously, a bit anxiously.

"Just what I said," said Marie. "Nothing sensational, altogether. Only the usual number of murders up here, women have been killing their husbands and men, sort of reversing the order in Harlem," and both laughed.

"Well," said he, still smiling, "since we don't happen to ever be involved in any of the murders, being of the peaceful variety, what's been going on at the office that might be of interest to me?"

"Well," she said. "You've had a visitor, among other things."

"A visitor? A process server, perhaps," he said, and she laughed. "We seem to be about caught up on suits. Old film suits, the book business is too inconspicuous to attract suits, it seems."

"Nobody thinks we are making enough money to make suing us worth while," said he and they both laughed again. "But getting back to the visitor. If not a process server or the marshal, then who?"

"The prettiest girl you ever saw."

"A pretty girl?"

"I must change that. You haven't seen her. The prettiest one I ever saw, just about, at least."

"And she called here to see me? Are you sure it was not to see Thompson? That's who all the pretty girls come to the office to see."

"Not this girl. I don't think she'd take a second look at Thompson. Especially, after she looked at him once and saw there was nothing in his pretty round head, nothing on his face but a smile, that eternal and winning, or intended winning smile. No, she was here to see you, and is coming back."

"My, this is getting interesting. A pretty girl to see me, oh, no. There must be a mistake, unless it was somebody trying to get into the movies?"

"No," said Marie, with a twinkle, but quite firmly. "She wasn't trying to get into the movies."

"Then whatever could a pretty girl want to see me about, if not to try to get into the movies? Come on, 'fess up, else I'll think you are playing a joke on me."

"No," said Marie. I'm not playing any joke. The girl was here, bought a copy of the book, then decided to take another copy, and paid me for both. I invited her to be seated, which she did and we then had a long, interesting talk."

"Well, that was $5.50 worth of interest at least, and purchases are always interesting to us. Exactly, then, what did she want?"

"To be frank about it, I don't know," admitted Marie. "She didn't tell me. But she's coming back, so if you'll be patient and in the office for a few days, you will get to meet her for she will be back."

"M-m," he mused, thoughtfully

"Not only is she one of the prettiest girls I ever saw, but one of the nicest." said Marie.

"A colored girl?"

"She wouldn't mean that much to us."

"Oh, of course. I wouldn't be saying all this about—a white girl."

"Of course not," he said, understandingly.

"Added to this," said Marie, "she is one of the most intelligent."

"You mean," queried Wyeth, "Educated?"

"I mean both," replied Marie, with restrained enthusiasm.

"I found her educated, intelligent, refined and just downright nice, with all the rest."

"She seems to have impressed you, I must say, and greatly."

"And she will you, when you meet her," Marie insisted.

"Go on, I'm really interested by now. As stated, she seems to have made a great impression on you."

"And I repeat, she will on you, when you meet her, too."

"How do you know?"

"Because you like intelligent people, sensible people. People who have something interesting to talk about. And, oh, in my enthusiasm, I forgot to explain that she's read your book—took it home, sat down, so she said, and didn't get up until she finished the over 400 pages of it. She said she liked every word; said that it was magnificent, is now reading it over again and studying it this time, and wants to talk with you about it"

"I'm glad," he said, modestly.

"She said that in addition to a fine and interesting story, well told, that there is so much sound and interesting philosophy throughout the whole book. She insists, among other words of praise and delight, that it is easily the most interesting and worth-while novel of Negro life ever published, and I was sincere when I agreed with her."

"That's saying a great deal," he commented.

"Well, I don't know," she observed. "What has a Negro written during the last few years about us, at least, that could be called fine and beautiful, unless it is the story told in your book."

"Nothing so fine and beautiful," said he, "but the white people, and especially the critics, sure raved about *'Nature's Child'.*"

"*'Nature's Child'!*" she exclaimed, vehemently. "That sordid, filthy, and foul narrative, built around the adventures of a trifling, worthless, good-for-nothing, unfortunate Negro! Incidentally this girl has read it and shares the same views of most of us Negroes regarding it."

"What is there about this girl that has put you into such a state of excitement and enthusiasm? What's her name?"

"Schultz, that's her name. Bertha Schultz," said Marie, finding and showing him the card that Bertha had given her. He looked at it and seemed to admire it.

"M-m. Sounds like a German name," he mused. She looked up.

"I think she's of German extraction," said Marie. "And, come to think of it, I think I recall that she had a slight German accent."

"You're getting into deep waters. A colored girl, highly educated and intelligent, critical, and with a German accent? Now who *is* this person?"

"She's been here twice and each time I have found her so interesting, until I've been fascinated, and haven't asked her so much about herself, but now that we discuss her, there is something just a bit mysterious about her."

"Becoming mysterious now. Go on."

"Well," she said, "come to think of her, that's my impression. She appears to have all she needs, dresses tastily, but very conservative. She says that she is engaged in research, but didn't say who for."

"So you discussed *Nature's Child,* eh? Had she read *'Passion'?*"

"Yes."

"And what did she think of it?"

"She wonders why our group are so excited about it."

"A strange sort of book."

"Must be something. It's become a best-seller overnight. We are selling as many of it without trying very hard, as we are your book."

"Our people have an inferior complex," he said, thoughtfully.

"And are not aware of it. If a Negro wrote anything like that and played them down half as much as they are in this book, they'd want to have him killed—shot at sunrise," she said, shaking her head.

"I got so I couldn't express an honest opinion in my pictures. Yet those were the kind that drew. I'm finding that I like writing. I can say what I feel and not have some theatre owner jump on me and want to cut our check, or cancel my picture because some Negro came out of the theatre and said: 'How come he put something like that in a picture? We're trying to get away from that stuff.'"

"The Negro," observed Marie, "wants history, especially as far as he's concerned, obliterated. He wants the public to feel that he started right here on Seventh Avenue, with all thought of slavery and bondage rubbed out."

"But getting back to Miss Schultz."

"Yes, of course. We've digressed, as we often do," and looking up at him she smiled, tolerantly.

"It is both strange and peculiar how we Negroes and our white Americans differ so with regards to us."

"We're as far apart from the standpoint of views as two groups could be. Now with regards to *Nature's Child,* which Miss Schultz and I discussed at great length, we can see nothing but a story of the worst side of us, yet the white people called it the great 'psychological' novel, which we debated, too, and tried to understand what they meant."

"And—" he started and broke off.

"That the psychological angle was simply the psychology of a worthless, depraved Negro under favorable conditions, to commit a foul and horrible crime. It seems so easy for them to conceive us in any distorted role, and so hard to picture us as just plain Americans, living in most part, a normal, conventional life."

"They don't consider that we have or live a normal and conventional life," he said, blandly.

"It seems that way," she said with an unhappy sigh.

"Now this Miss Schultz. Did she say where she attended school. You referred to her being educated!"

"Educated—and how!" exclaimed Marie. "At Heidelberg and the Sorbonne."

"Whew!" he cried.

"Graduated from both."

"Whew!" He cried, shaking his head.

"I can see you and her talking for hours."

"I can't imagine myself being able to talk to anybody with so much education as she must have."

"But she's easy to talk to. Asks a lot of questions—like you, for instance," and she looked up at him with an amused twinkle, which made him smile. Sidney Wyeth had a reputation for asking people more questions than any other man.

"I told her," went on Marie, "that you'd ask her all about herself. I'd like to be around when you and her meet."

"Has she met Thompson?" He asked.

She looked up, amused.

"Do you know, that sap ran in one day while she was here."

"And?"

"When he saw her, he went into action quick, and then almost as quickly as he started, stopped."

"Why?"

"She began to ask him questions; questions that he could have answered readily, if traveling all over the country as he has with you had taught him anything—but of course, Thompson knows nothing but to make that silly attempt at love, which didn't get to first base with her."

"Then what happened?"

"He sneaked away after a few minutes and let her alone."

"What's he doing in Baltimore, anyhow?"

"Oh, this teacher, whom he got mixed up with down there, has put the rascal to work."

"Yes?"

"And how. You know that he could never get anything to do, being a musician, you always tried to get him to go out on a gig over the week-end, to pick up some extra money."

"He was never able to get a job during all the years he was with us. I remember, and how."

"Not a single one, not even a gig; but all that's changed since she got hold of the boop down there."

"How so?"

"She finds him jobs, and as quickly as he loses or gets fired from one, she quickly puts him on another. His hands are as hard as a laborer's." Both laughed at this.

"Good for the teacher."

"He came back to the office after he met Miss Schultz, but she had gone. Looking around, he stalled a moment, then finally said to me: 'Who was that old smart gal, and what does she think she is anyhow?'"

"And that's what I'm curious to find out. Who *is* this girl, and what's it all about anyhow?"

"You'll soon find out," she said, and smiling, plunged into her work.

Over at the Schultz apartment in the meantime, matters were just so-so. Mrs. Wingate had returned to Atlanta, leaving Early on the anxious seat, since they had decided that she should tell Mr. Wingate about her baby within three months, and at the most favorable opportunity. Early had left the hotel when she went away and took a moderate apartment in another section of Harlem and came over to the Schultz's more or less every night.

Heinrich had business most every day, staying late into the night downtown with Hans Schiller, where they were making plans to be put into immediate operation, provided America was ultimately pushed into the war on the side of England.

Bertha reported on her visits to Wyeth's office, advising that he was still out of the City. Meanwhile, Early was anxious for a showdown on getting Wyeth's consent to do the hate picture, so he was kept busy preparing for this showdown by compiling a mass of facts to try show Wyeth why he should do it.

While Bertha's calls at the office were not to spy, they naturally talked about Wyeth and the fact that he was out of the city, which kept Kermit from calling for this showdown until he could catch Wyeth.

As was generally known, America wanted none of Europe's war, but was being slowly pushed in that direction. Down at Hans Schiller's office, this fact was debated freely, and their movement to keep America out of the war had a long and popular following, and meetings and plenty of speaking every night, always found a group ready and anxious to listen. Father Coughlin came in for lots of praise. His anti-semitic leaning was daily becoming more obvious, and his picture decorated the walls of many places especially in Yorktown.

At his room the night after Wyeth returned to New York, he sat down and wrote Edrina the following letter:

Dearest Edrina:

"I decided after leaving you, and all of a sudden, to return to New York, so of course, I had no chance to communicate the fact to you since I had just left you. In addition, I am given to acting on impulses, and which I did, as explained. Also my office needed my presence, and am glad I came back as there was so much unfinished business on my desk that it was well for me to have returned for now that has all been cleaned up and I feel much better for having returned.

"Hanging around Washington would only have caused me to grow more fond of you and I am too fond of you, under the circumstances, already for my own good. In this case it seems to be more love, more pain, so what! However, I will call you at Pittsburgh Sunday night as you've asked me to, but to be frank about it, I think it best for us to end our little affair at the earliest opportunity while I still possess some self-control, leaving you to continue your stage ambitions without discouragement on my part.

"Frankly, I am sorry for both of us, and take full responsibility for letting it go this far. But it will be easier to agree to disagree now and have it over with, leaving you free to continue on the stage which you love so much, without having to listen to my objections and pointing out dire possibilities, than to prolong it.

"In conclusion, please believe me when I say that this hurts me more than it could possibly hurt you, all things considered, but I believe that in the long run, you will be glad I have taken this stand, to forget each other and remain

"Cordially and Sincerely
"SIDNEY WYETH"

When Edrina received the letter in Pittsburgh, it made her sad, for at the time she was lonely, and the letter naturally added to this feeling of melancholy.

"Oh, Sidney," she weeped. "How could you do this to me—and I've learned to love you so." She felt sure that she loved him, the cold and reserved Sidney, as she pictured him. She cried herself to sleep that night.

Came Sunday, a beautiful day. The state didn't permit stage shows on Sunday, so she managed to get through a long, boresome day, trying to read so the time would go faster. It seemed ages before eleven o'clock that night finally rolled around, with her expectantly waiting.

Promptly at the appointed hour, the call came through. However hard a time as she was having to try to convince him that she could be the kind of girl he wanted for a wife, she knew that she could depend on him to keep his word. So picking up the receiver, she called: "Yes. Miss Vinson on the phone." She had never heard his voice over the telephone before, so she was not at first sure that it was him.

"This is Sidney in New York, Edrina. How are you, dear?"

After writing her such a letter, now he was talking so nicely. In a moment she was crying, but managed to reply.

"Oh, Sidney," she sobbed. "I received and read that awful letter, and how could you send anything like that to a poor unhappy girl like me?"

"I'm sorry, dear," he replied. "It hurt me to have to write it, but I think we ought to face facts as they exist and not try to brush them by and make out like they are not there. So I was just trying to be frank and honest with you, that's all."

"Listen, Sidney," she cried, interrupting. "I understand you and please don't scold me. A girl alone in the world as I am, has to make a living, her living, and I have always tried to make an honest one. Is that right, Sidney, or wrong?"

"It's right, of course, Edrina. I—"

"You intimated from the beginning that you cared for me and I have been awfully happy about it ever since; but you won't say more, so what can I do? Well, if you won't speak, you leave no alternative, but for me to do so. To prove that I am sincere and want to please you, I've decided to quit the show here when it closes next Saturday night and go home for a while to Louisville. So it is up to you from there on. I love you, Sidney, and—goodbye." So saying, she hung up so abruptly that on the New York end, he was surprised and shocked, and thought for a moment that the phone had gone haywire.

In his room then, it was he who was both upset and annoyed. He had been thinking seriously of calling it quits. He found now that he had become more fond of Edrina than he thought, than he had planned to become. He still knew, and realized it from the outset, that he had no intention of falling in love with a show girl, any show girl.

So he rose to his feet and walked the floor for a long time, trying to make his mind up what to do. One thing he could neither overlook or forget, and that was that he had hurt her, and that was neither right or fair. Because she was stage-struck and harbored dreams as regards it, was not enough to condemn her; to injure her and make her feel as she evidently was feeling. And the fact that he had no confidence in any show girl, show girls could still have hearts, that could be hurt as well as any other girl, and he had never gone in for hurting anybody and then remain callous to the injury he had caused. So the longer he walked the floor, the more did he become convinced that he should now do something to appease her. Still, stubbornly, he refused to give in. He undressed and went to bed to sleep it off but sleep refused to come. So he sat up, got up, walked around again for a while, then ended it all by sitting down at a table to pen her the following note:

Dearest Edrina:

"You have upset me entirely and completely. I cannot stand to see you hurt and unhappy like this, because of me. I do love you, Edrina, if I must say it. I love you more than I realized. I fear that before it is all over it will be you who will be breaking my heart.

"Now, if you really mean to give up the stage, my dear I hope it is of your own volition and not just to please me, and think you can be content and happy for the rest of your life as a plain and simple housewife, then I ask you, dear Edrina, to marry me.

"I will lease a nice apartment for you here in New York and when the time comes, go with you and we can pick the furniture together to your own taste . . I am willing to do anything that I know how from now on with a view to pleasing you and making you happy . . . My only hope in doing so is that you will not, sooner or later, break it all up by slipping out and going back on the stage again. If you feel that you don't care to do this, I'll try to make you the best husband any girl ever had . . .

"My cards are on the table now, where I have laid them, face up. From now on it is up to you. Please try to understand and appreciate before you answer, that you are still free, and can refuse and reject my offer and that I will try to accept it, if to the contrary, graciously and in good spirit. If you do accept it, however, try to understand that I've always wanted a fine, dignified and intelligent lady for a wife and such a kind of woman wouldn't want to go traipsing off with some show, and the kind of show you are now in, one liable to close at the end of any engagement and without notice.

"I do not want that kind of a girl, now or ever for any wife of mine, which I hope is plain and clear.

"Now please think this all over, soberly and carefully, before you leave the show and while still in Pittsburgh, and still later on while vacationing in Louisville, and wait and then, if you care to, you can give me your answer. Please understand that I do not wish to influence you in any way; just want you to act on your own in considering my offer, altogether. As long as you are single you are free to think and do as you wish to without any regard for me. I want to feel that if you marry and come to live with me as a wife, I want it to be a good wife as I shall, in turn, try to be a good husband. It takes more in each case than mere affection and emotion for either of us to be successful in such an event. It is up to both of us to exert an effort, to make an occasional sacrifice and think of how each other might feel about a decision of importance thereafter before arriving at such a decision on our own.

"If all I've tried to say is now clear and understandable, dear, then write to me at your earliest convenience what you want me to do, and I will try, gladly, to comply with your every wish.

"Affectionately,
"S I D N E Y"

After reading it through and deciding that it was about what he wanted to say, Wyeth folded it in an envelope, sealed and stamped it and laid it on his clothes, to be posted when he got up a few hours later, for it was now long past midnight and he was relieved to feel that he could sleep at last, which he did after retiring. He went right off to sleep and didn't awaken until hours later, feeling fresh and entirely rested.

Two afternoons later in Pittsburgh where she had received the letter in the afternoon mail, Edrina was happy and was in the act of shouting for joy and reading it over again when there was a light and familiar knock on her door. "It couldn't be Donald," she thought aloud, for he was in New York, or at least was supposed to be. Anyway, after a pause, she called:

"Come in," turned and waited, eyes on the door. It was pushed open, and, stepping through, wearing a flashy fedora hat, carrying his cane, for Donald always carried a large, heavy and attractive cane, and dressed up as slick as a shiek, was no other than whom Wyeth called the little prince himself. Edrina's mouth opened, but he spoke first.

"Aw, Edrina, I'll bet that you're surprised," and laughing, closed the door as she cried, shocked like.

"Why Donald, you!" She had the letter in her hand and didn't want to let him see it, or to talk about it just then.

"I arrived about an hour ago. Got a telegram from Mantan to join him here, which I will talk about later." He was hanging up his hat and cane and turned in time to catch her trying to conceal the letter behind her.

"Au, au, au," he cried, pointing at her. "You're hiding something from me, honey bunch. You don't have to do that," he said, coming up to her. "I'm the daddy that understands all things and sympathizes freely, if sympathy is needed, you know, kid." She tried to side-step his curiosity by changing to something else.

"No need to, you know, for here I am, in the flesh," and he laughed, jauntily. "In the flesh and in person. Now come," he said, "what are you trying to hide?" He tried to see what it was but she kept on turning so that he could not.

"Why—why didn't you—let me know?"

"Sit down, Donald," she said, drawing up a chair and as she did so, he could and did see the envelope.

"Oh, a letter. Only a letter. Why were you trying to hide it from me?"

"Oh, I didn't want to talk about it—just now at least."

"I see," he said, sinking down on the chair. She continued to stand. She was dressed only in her lounging robe, and of a sudden one of her teaties poped forth and hung out. He smiled as she quickly covered it and smiled, embarrassingly.

"Bet I can guess who the letter is from," said he, ignoring the sudden exposure. She didn't answer, so he went on.

"Must have said something of importance; maybe asked you to marry him, eh?"

"Oh, Donald," she said evasively. "You mustn't ask me such questions. Such intimate questions. I told you I didn't want to talk about it just now. Now you want to know all about what he said."

"Just a friendly interest, Edrina." He paused, thought a moment, then looked up. "It is from Sidney Wyeth, isn't it?"

Her silence confirmed his words.

"I'm glad, Edrina. I've been hoping for this, and I hope he has asked you to marry him. If he has, grab him and run. He's a good man, will make you a fine husband. I'm—" and then he was suddenly cut off.

"But Donald, dear. I—" she started, her face suddenly emotional. He raised a hand, a commanding hand and kept her from saying more. He got up and walked up to her, his eyes straight into hers.

"Don't be a fool, girl. I mean that." He looked hard at her and she understood what he meant.

"If you'd—" woman-like, she began again, and again he raised a hand, his eyes flashing impatiently.

"I'm *not*, Edrina," he began sharply. "We've been over that time and time again, enough so that you ought to understand. You *do* understand, but you're still vain and full of illusions, and I've been trying to get that out of you ever since and you know it."

"Well," she said, "I just—"

"I can't do you any good. I've made it as plain as I could, over and over again that I'm not a marrying man; and that I don't want any wife. But I won't stand in a good man's way. You've got to eat, pay room rent, purchase a change of clothes now and then and all that takes money. You're liable not to be able to do any of these things, fooling around with this kind of a show. And you'd be sure to go hungry waiting on me. You've got a chance now to step into a berth of security. Don't fool around and let it get away. Grab the man I tell you and run and keep on running along with him, and forget me and show business in general. There's nothing to it any more."

He walked across the room now, his hands behind him. She looked after him and tried to weigh what he had said. It seemed hard for her to do so and she was still not satisfied. By a window, he paused and looked idly out over smoky Pittsburgh, and twiddled his thumbs behind him for a moment, then presently turning, came back across the room to her.

"If Wyeth has asked you in that letter to marry him, write him 'yes' today, then do whatever he wants you to from then on. Get what I mean?"

She nodded her head lightly, still anxious to begin what she had wanted to start, all over again. He saw it and his frown deepened.

"And again, and for the last time, give up any ideas about me, secret or otherwise, and this show, too, for that matter," he said and turned away again. She looked at him, then stepped forward and catching up with him:

"What do you mean—about the show?" she said and waited, curiously, a bit anxiously. He turned and looked at her a moment before answering

"It's closing."

"Closing?" she echoed, startled-like.

"Yes, Edrina. Closing here in Pittsburgh Saturday night, this Saturday night and not the next or the next," he said, and turned his eyes away.

"Oh," she breathed in surprise, and lowered her eyes thoughtfully, and in spite of her telling Wyeth over the telephone two nights before that she was leaving the show, she was obviously disappointed, keenly so. Meanwhile, Howard turned back and continued:

"We had only three weeks, two in Washington and this one here. We tried hard to get more, but were not successful, so we're closing Saturday night, and that is that. It's the same old story, more theatres and more theatres are giving up stage shows, preferring to take their chance on pictures. They say they don't want to be bothered with stage hands and orchestras and performers and union demands. It's too many headaches and arguments for the extra money they make, so again, that is that," and he shrugged his shoulders resignedly.

"So the show is closing," she murmured, more to herself than to him "and I don't have to quit after all." He heard her and turned to her.

"So you were going to—quit, anyhow," he said, a note of surprise in his voice. "On account of—Wyeth?"

She nodded affirmatively.

"Oh, so it's gone that far, eh?" Again she nodded, her eyes downcast. "He didn't want you in a show, did he?" She shook her head to indicate that he didn't.

"Good. And keep it that way. You should be happy."

"I'm glad you told me. I was going to give Mantan my notice tonight," she said slowly.

"Won't need to now. That's why Mantan sent for me, for me to dish out the bad news. He's gone back to New York. I've got to stay until the end of the week and face the music if there isn't enough in the till from our share to pay off Saturday night."

"I hope I get what's due me. I need it to go home on. I'd like to have a few dollars left after I get there, too."

"I'll do the best I can. Most of them will want fare back to New York, and that has to come out first."

"I'm going to Louisville," she said.

"To visit your mother and sisters? That's nice," said he.

"Mantan will perhaps organize another show in New York, don't you think," she said. The show was still on her mind. "Or, maybe, rearrange this one?"

"Perhaps. It's his living, you know."

"I was thinking," she began hesitantly.

Immediately his face lit up again with a deep frown, and he glared at her:

"Don't do it, Edrina," he exclaimed, "for if you are doing any thinking or going to do any, I know what it will be about—shows. That's on your mind so completely until its become an obsession. I can't see why you don't do a little thinking and try to be sensible."

"Now, now, Donald," she said, putting a hand on his arm, more calm than he expected. "Don't get so excited and so quickly. I'm going to take your advice and marry Wyeth and be as nice to him as I can." Again he turned upon her with impatience and suspicion.

"What do you mean by being as nice as you can?" he said, his eyes glaring at her.

"Just that. Isn't that all I can do? Be as nice to him as I can be?"

"Sounds a bit suspicious to me," he muttered, not entirely satisfied. "You'd better be sure it's good and nice and not just partly. If Wyeth was some ham actor, with a head and mind full of illusions and a hot dog only in his stomach, you'd probably be terribly concerned and worried about him. As it is—well, what's the use," he said, shrugging his shoulders in disgust.

"I'm going to marry him and be a good wife," she insisted now, a bit more positively. "Now does that sound all right?"

"Sounds better if you mean it and intend to stick to it," he agreed and seemed a bit more satisfied.

"There was something else on my mind that made me sound a bit indifferent," she said now. "That's what's worrying me at the moment."

"What is it?" he said, turning and coming closer.

"If I marry Wyeth, I've got to get a—divorce first," she said, her eyebrows knitted.

"Oh," he echoed, in another tone.

"And that's what's worrying me," she said moving around, her face clouded with annoyance. She twisted her hands and didn't seem to know what to do.

"Can you—get it? Will that little darkey you're married to out in Louisville give it to you?"

"Oh, yes," she said, reassuringly. "He wouldn't go to the trouble to contest it. Besides, we've been apart for years. He doesn't care."

"That's another reason for your going to Louisville, eh?"

"Yes."

"Then why are you—worried?" he asked, and looked at her. She looked back at him with a deep frown.

"Why?" she exclaimed. "You should know. It takes money to get a divorce and you know that I have none."

"The money," he muttered, as if to himself and thoughtfully.

"Yes, of course."

"So what am I going to do?" she said, still frowning, and looking at him, helplessly. He walked around the room, thinking deeply as he did so. Presently paused, perked up, turned and looked at her, eyes flashing with an idea.

"I have it!" he exclaimed, raising his hand and gesturing with the forefinger of same.

She turned to him with a hope that flashed suddenly across her features.

"Have what? The money?"

His smile and enthusiasm was replaced quickly by an impatient frown.

"Oh, no, of course not."

Her face fell then and she muttered in a sort of undertone.

"I thought not." She said, turning her eyes back to him. "Then what is this sudden and big idea that made you say, I have it?"

"I meant that I had an idea where you could get it."

"Oh," she said, and relaxed without enthusiasm. Then as if to see just what he was talking about, turned back to him.

"Where?" she asked.

"From Wyeth?"

"From Wyeth!" she exclaimed "What do you mean, from Wyeth?"

"Just what I say. From Wyeth," he insisted, coming closer.

"You're crazy," she said and turned away as if in disgust, then after a step or two, turned back.

"I haven't even told him that I was married. He doesn't know that I am. Then"—she said, breaking off, "Oh, they say you never had an idea that ever got anybody a dollar. Now you're proving it."

"Then tell him," said Howard, ignoring her last remark.

She turned to glare at him.

"How do you suppose he's going to feel? Haven't even told him that I was married, now to up and tell him that I am and to give me the money to get a divorce so that I can marry him is some nerve, hump!" and she turned her back on him as she finished.

"Oh, girl," he said, taking hold of her and turning her about to face him. "Quit being a child. You're a grown woman and all grown women have been married at least once, most maybe two or three times. Anyway, they've always been married once and Wyeth would understand that." She paused and her eyes took on new hope. She turned back to him.

"Do you—think I—could," she said as if she was daring.

"Think you could—what?" he didn't seem to understand.

"Tell him that—that I've been married?"

"Of course you can," he cried.

"And—an'—he wouldn't get angry?"

"Get angry! What for? Of course you can tell him. You should tell him everything. Be frank and honest for once."

"Oh, if I only could," she murmered with a sigh, more to herself than to him.

"But why can't you? Wyeth is, among other things, a practical man. That's another reason you should grab the chance to marry him. He'll be easy to live with if you could start being frank and honest and truthful with him. Then he'd trust you."

"Yes, trust me." She turned to him again. "You know, that's what's been the holdback. He hasn't been inclined to trust me."

"Why?" he said, looking straight at her. "Been reading your mind, maybe? Sees you're crazy about the stage—stage-struck, yes, that's it and he isn't going for that for the simple reason that he knows, like everybody seems to know and appreciate but you, that there's nothing to it."

"Not only that, but he's said so much about—bad morals among show girls."

"He is right."

"Says they have white men—even play up to them and run after them if they have a chance."

"They do. He was right again."

"But I don't do that, never have and I never will."

"You never have. That is true. You can't tell what you might do if you keep on fooling around with show work."

"That's what he says. That's what he's been afraid of."

"Smart man. He's looking ahead. Still, he's asked you to marry him, hasn't he?"

"Finally. That's what's in this letter." She held it up.

"Good," he cried. "That can be the end of his distrust, providing you don't do anything to bring it all up again. It's up to you, but you'd better play straight, and don't think you're going to be able to play double and fool him. He knows too much about show business, show people and Negroes all combined not to be able to see through anything."

"But getting back to the matter of a divorce," she said. "You think then, I should sit down and write him a letter."

"A nice, sweet letter," he said.

"And tell him the truth?"

"The whole truth and nothing but the truth, so help you God."

"And I—maybe I could say that I—I haven't—any—money?"

"Yes, all that, Edrina."

"—and—"

"No more. He'll understand even if you didn't say that you had no money. Being a broad and practical man, he'd know you wouldn't have any; that no Negro ever has any."

"Oh, wouldn't that be wonderful!" she exclaimed, ecstatically.

"What would be wonderful, Edrina?" he inquired.

"That I could tell him I've been married, haven't a divorce, but want one; and that I haven't any money to—"

"Stop there. You needn't say any more. He'll understand and send it to you. Besides, he'll send you extra money to take care of you while you're in Louisville, and money then to come back to New York when you're ready to marry him."

"And—and you think he'd do—all that?"

"I know he will," said Howard, stoutly. "That's what I meant when I said that he's a man, a real man. Even you have learned that most Negroes are full of nothing but jive, and promises, and—"

"—like you—never have any money," she said. "Yes, Donald, I know that. Only thing."

"Now what?"

"I wish I had told him that I'd been married."

"Oh, forget about it. As a practical man, he'd rather you had been married, at your age. Men don't go for old maids."

"I'm not old," she cried, and affected anger.

"Old enough. But getting down to business. So you'll do as I say? Sit down, write him a sweet, tender and honest letter and tell him everything?"

"I will, Donald." She said. He picked up his hat and cane now and walked toward the door. She followed. There, he turned back for a last word of counsel.

"And Edrina, from now on try to be sensible, understand?"

"Leave it to me, dear. I've got plenty sense."

"Then start right now to using it and keep it up from now on Good night."

"Good night, Donald," she said, smiling, and closed the door behind him.

CHAPTER XIV

AT HIS office in New York, late the next afternoon, Sidney Wyeth received a special delivery letter from Edrina, which read:

"Darling:

"Your sweet, sweet and loving letter is at hand, saying that you love me and asking me to be your wife, and has made me the happiest girl in all the world.

"Since I had to all but propose and beg you so hard to trust me, and to believe in me, my answer is almost unnecessary. But since it pleases and will make me so happy to say yes, I accept and will be your wife. I do love you, Sidney, however much you have argued to the contrary, and I will try to be the dearest wife to you that any man ever had. Now I am going to try to start out by being honest, frank and truthful to you.

"Because you never gave me any encouragement whatsoever, Sidney, dear, you kept me in a state of fright and of fear that I would displease and add to your distrust in me. I was honestly afraid to tell you that I have been married, and that if you want me to be your wife, I'll have to first get a divorce from the man I married when I was a mere girl, and have been away from for so long until it doesn't matter.

"To get a divorce, which I plan to secure while in Louisville, will take money, dear, money that poor Edrina does not have. So I guess you will scold and make me unhappy all over again for not having told you, but as explained above, I was afraid to.

"I am hoping, oh, so much, darling, Sidney, that you won't get angry now, but will be sweet and patient, write me a darling letter and forgive me and promise to love me forever as I plan to devote my life to loving you.

"With oodles of love and a thousand kisses, may I remain

"Affectionately,

"EDRINA"

Wyeth smiled as he finished the letter, and then raising it to his lips, kissed it. Without delay he reached for a fountain pen on his coat and wrote her.

Dearest Edrina:
"Yours of recent date, just received, and thank you. You didn't say if you were well or anything about your health, so I presume that you are well, otherwise you would have said so in your dear letter.

"Please, my dear, don't feel bad about what you didn't tell me. I surmised that you had been married, and in no way feel either discouraged or disappointed that you have been, and felt that you'd have to get a divorce if and when you consented to marry me. I also surmised that you wouldn't have any money to get it with, so am assuming this expense.

"However hard I seemed to have been, it is clear that after love, always comes responsibility and expense, both of which I expect to assume. This is one of the many reasons that girls should try to be a little sensible. Love is the sweetest thing on earth—but flies out the window quickly when there is no food around to eat.

"I will, therefore, go immediately to the post office and forward you a registered and insured letter, enclosing the cash so that you won't even have to spend a lot of time being identified so as to get an order cashed. If you will write me before leaving Pittsburg where you will be in Louisville, I'll send the money so that it will be waiting when you arrive there. I will enclose a little account book so that you can keep a record of expenditures, starting a sort of budget system before we marry even, since I am sure you will find this in the end a very satisfactory way of keeping a record of expenses. I presume that you will retain a lawyer and enter proceedings for a divorce as quickly after you arrive in Louisville as is convenient. And, of course, I shall be glad to hear from you, among other things, as to when it might be granted. Naturally, I will be anxious to know when I may expect you back in New York to become my darling wife.

"Until I hear from you, please try to think of me as
"Lovingly yours,
"SIDNEY"

When Marie arrived at the office the next morning, she found that Wyeth had been in and had gone to Jersey, by the words of a trite note, and she knew it would be to stage a sales campaign of some kind over there. She knew that Wyeth was a restless person, forever on the go, and, moreover, if he spent any unusual sum of money, the first thing he'd think of would be to get it back as quickly as possible. So since he left the office so early, she had a suspicion that he'd spent a larger sum than usual, so opened his drawer and looked at the newest stub in the check book.

It was there, as she suspected. $100.00 to "cash" for "personal." Woman like, she had stolen a peek at Edrina's messages and letters, which he left in the middle drawer of his desk, and never locked it during his absence.

No sooner had she closed the desk drawer and came out into the reception room, than in walked Bertha Schultz, dressed more beautifully than ever, smiling and peeping into Wyeth's office at Marie, in the hope that at last she was going to catch him in and meet him.

"Oh, Bertha—I mean, Miss Schultz," she began.

"You mean just what you said," Bertha exclaimed. "Don't we know each other well enough by now to drop some of the formality?"

"Why of course," cried Marie, glad that Bertha had called. She was pretty well caught up with her work, would have to stay at the office and was glad that somebody had come in for her to talk to.

"Then it is agreed. We're going to call each other by our first names from now on," said Bertha.

"O.K." said Marie extending her hand which the other grasped and held, then both broke into laughter. Bertha again glanced into Wyeth's office and Marie shook her head, sadly.

"Oh, no," cried Bertha, her tone tense with disappointment. "Please don't say that I have—missed him again?"

"I'm sorry, but I just came in a few minutes ago and *I* missed him even."

"Oh, I'm so sorry," cried Bertha and looked it. She sighed and Marie got a new idea.

"Well, let's get comfortable. He's gone for the day, and I haven't much to do, so let's take seats in his office and just talk." She led the way, and pointed to a large comfortable leather chair to one side, or in the corner of the room, while she sat down in Wyeth's chair behind the desk, which was leather, large, roomy and comfortable.

"My," cried Bertha from the large leather one in the corner, "but this is a comfortable chair."

Marie smiled across at her.

"So is this one," and she swung backward and around to face Bertha. "I'm the executive lady in charge, Miss Schultz. I'll hear your complaint now," she said in a deep, bass voice.

"By all means," replied Bertha, affecting her role with humor. "Well, your honor. It is like this. I've been to this office no end of times to meet and talk to a certain gentleman called Sidney Wyeth. He seems to absolutely refuse to be here when I call. What can I do about it?"

"Well," said Marie, then placed her chin in her hand and pretended to think deeply, which brought forth a laugh from both.

"Maybe—Mr. Wyeth doesn't care to—meet me," suggested Bertha timidly.

"Oh, no, Bertha. That's a mistake. The fact is, he is anxious to meet you." Marie paused. "Guess we can't do very good at play, so let's stay serious."

"All right, darling," said Bertha sweetly.

"Confidentially, Bertha," Marie went on, "Mr. Wyeth has got himself mixed up with a girl."

"Oh, a girl," repeated Bertha.

"Yes," replied Marie. In a mood to gossip. "A show girl, and that was not his intention."

"No?"

"Absolutely not. My boss in all the years I've worked for him, and as many girls as he has worked during all that time in the many pictures he made, has always been careful not to let himself become entangled with any. Now, when we have suspended making pictures for over two years, he should fool around and let a show girl hook him is more than I can get used to."

"But, my dear Marie, I understand that Mr. Wyeth is a man of decision, quite old enough to—"

"Do what he wants to, yes. But Mr. Wyeth has not wanted to let himself become involved with any show girl, and this escapade is something that just slipped up on him."

"Well, it doesn't seem like any of our business, but I can't blame myself if you want to talk about it. I know it'll be interesting to listen to."

"I brought it up for the reason that if he hadn't done so and hadn't sent her a hundred dollars just this morning, he'd have been here in the office and you'd have met him."

"But—" objected Bertha. Marie raised her hand.

"I just wanted to explain that when he puts out that much money for something he has no business doing, it makes him feel guilty and to get it off his chest, he jumps out early and he won't stop now until he's made it back—and perhaps that much more before he stops—and I mean he'll have it back by tomorrow night."

"From the way you put it, he must be a good salesman," commented Bertha.

"That isn't half of it," cried Marie. "He's a master salesman—and doesn't seem to be selling at all."

"How's that?"

"Just goes along in an easy, unassuming way, plain and simple, but gets into people's confidence and they fall in line and do what he wants them to, without seeming to be aware of what they are doing."

"Remarkable."

"He's a most remarkable person, that's why I hate to see him all worked up and perhaps engaged to any show girl."

"Aren't show girls nice?"

"Some of them."

"Only some?"

"Only some, Bertha. Ever been around them much?"

Bertha shook her head in the negative.

"Well, I have. Lots of experience with them from helping Mr. Wyeth make pictures."

"You, helped him?" said Bertha, anxiously, curiously.

"Oh, yes. For years, his general assistant. That's where I got acquainted with show girls—and their ways, from chorus girls up."

Bertha was listening to Marie closely, Marie continued, not understanding of course that Bertha hoped to find out something about Wyeth's intention and inclination. Having failed to meet him, she had been unable to tell her brother and Early anything they were anxious to know. Now as Marie was in the mood to talk, maybe to gossip only, it was a chance to find out just how Wyeth reacted to various angles which might help her to know more about him without Marie suspecting just why she was so interested.

"Many of the show girls are bad," went on Marie. "Most when

they start—at least, are young and vain, subject to flattery, which they get lots of, and that perhaps gets them started—and how so many do perform!" exclaimed Marie and shook her head woefully. "I hardly know anything they wouldn't do. I suppose white show girls are just as vain and carry on the same as do our girls, but they can do so without being noticed, because the men they play with are men of their own race. But our colored men, except Mr. Wyeth and Mr. Mantan, rarely run their shows. So the girls are at the mercy of the men who promote the shows, run the night clubs and hire our girls. As a result, and feeling that if they are 'nice' to these Italians and Jews who operate the night clubs, they'll get to go places, it seems logical for them then to play up to these men, understand?"

"Of course," said Bertha. "I follow you. Please go on."

"Well, as a result, their conduct as a whole is just rotten. Most men operating night clubs, grills and cabarets, are sporting life characters, gamblers, and ofttimes, former pimps and racketeers, so playing around with the women forced to work for them is their specialty. In fact, directly or indirectly, they *keep* most of them, the owner or his managers, and nobody has complained more about this than Mr. Wyeth. So you can see why I am provoked that he should go and let himself become all enamoured with one, send her money and I'm afraid, plans to marry her."

"Really?"

"Well, I think so. He wouldn't be sending her $100.00 if he hadn't planned something like that. He isn't a man that runs around or keeps women like most show men."

"No?"

"Oh, no. In all the years I've worked for him, I don't think he has ever kept a woman."

"He's not married, as I understand it?"

"No, he isn't married," replied Marie.

"Ever been?"

"Yes. A long time ago. Had trouble, something sad and which ended with a tragedy and it was that which caused him to start writing."

"I see. What are his inclinations?"

"A domesticated man, entirely; a marrying man, and would make the right kind of girl a good husband for he is home loving and wants a home. But he's off on the wrong trail and I know it, and I'm annoyed."

"I don't wonder. Just who is the girl? Did you ever meet her?"

"Yes, I met her. She seemed to be all right."

"Is she—pretty?"

"Quite pretty," replied Marie, "but she's stage struck and I've a feeling that no good is going to become of it and before it's all over, he's going to be sorry he let himself get mixed up with her."

"This is interesting," said Bertha.

"Mr. Wyeth is an interesting man and a good man, and has no business getting himself mixed up with any actress."

"You know, as you talk about him, I begin to associate him with the man in his book."

"It is, in a measure, his own story," said Marie. "His life of hell."

"I knew it!" exclaimed Bertha, rising to her feet and coming over to Marie and sitting down on the desk to face her. "From the moment that story began, there was something about it that made it read, in most part, anyhow, like the events had actually happened."

"Yes, they happened," said Marie, "and the tragic part about it, is that it happened to him, to Sidney Wyeth himself."

"This is *so* interesting. And the girl he wrote at such length about?"

"That was his wife."

"Oh, my!" exclaimed Bertha, her eyes opening wide. "Just think of it. According to the story, she seemed like a good girl?"

"She was."

"Is that so?" exclaimed Bertha again, all interest. "But she was weak."

"Yes," said Marie. "That, if you studied the book, was the cause of all the trouble."

"The book is a fine study of human psychology."

"A wonderful study," said Marie.

"And now he's in love with a—show girl," said Bertha, looking down.

"Thinks he is," said Marie.

"But you don't think it is genuine, real?"

"It could be, if she'd do right by him."

"What do you mean?"

"As I view this girl before she went out again with Mantan's show, she has stage ambitions, is stage-struck."

"Oh," echoed Bertha.

"Knowing Mr. Wyeth as I do, his engagement to her is with the understanding that she's to leave the stage."

"And you don't think she will want to."

"When a girl is stage-struck, nothing but to stride across the stage before the footlights will ever satisfy her."

"Then you think that she may have agreed to give it up just to please him?"

"That's it exactly," said Marie.

"And as quickly as she's married to him, she'll find a way to go back on the stage and being closer to him then than she could ever get before marrying him, she plans to then persuade him to let her?"

"My, how plain you make it," exclaimed Marie, smiling up at Bertha. "But that's just the way she has it all planned."

"To fool him," suggested Bertha.

"It would amount to that," observed Marie.

"Isn't a very good way to hold a husband."

"You nor I would do it, but this Edrina, that's her name, is a show girl. And as I've said, I don't know anything they wouldn't do. So inveigling Mr. Wyeth into marrying her, knowing all the time that she doesn't intend to keep any promises she's making before he marries her, is small besides what she's liable to put over on him after."

"If Mr. Wyeth is—as you've described him, a sensible man, he should see what he's letting himself in for."

"He hasn't let himself love, or fall in love with any girl for so long until she's sort of swept him off his feet—for the time being at least."

"Maybe only for the time being."

"I hope so."

"She'll probably overstep herself somewhere."

"That's what I'm expecting to happen. Still, he might just rush blindly and desperately into it and up and marry her before he gets wise to the snare."

"Does this Edrina, as you call her," suggested Bertha. "Go with any other man?"

"With a music writer by the name of Howard."

"Oh."

"I know him and know that she has not only been crazy about him but still is, another reason why I'm provoked at Mr. Wyeth's action.

"I know that I *must* meet Mr. Wyeth now," said Bertha.

Marie looked at her.

"Do you know, Bertha. You're the type of girl I'd like to see Mr. Wyeth fall in love with."

"Me?" exclaimed Bertha, pointing to herself, and laughing.

"I didn't mean exactly you, Bertha," explained Marie. "I meant the kind of girl you are."

"But why," said Bertha, "why, like me?"

"Because you are the kind of girl he's always admired. A refined, highly intelligent girl. A girl whose refinement and intelligence wouldn't let her stoop to and do horrid things like many of our girls in America would stoop to."

"Oh, but you flatter me, Marie. Flatter me too much," and Bertha sought to laugh it off.

"Please don't get me wrong, dear," Marie insisted. "I know nothing about your personal affairs. You even might be already married, as far as I know. I am, you understand."

"I know it," said Bertha.

Marie paused and looked up at her, a question in her eyes.

"A friend of yours told me. We talked about you and it was she who told me that you were married.

"And happily so. Meanwhile, I was about to explain—"

"—about me," said Bertha, cutting her off. "Well, darling, I am not married, not engaged, have no fellow, though I did go with a boy in Germany before leaving there, but he's in the army and I'm in America. So you know now that I am free, single, disengaged and the only man I'm interested in, other than my brother, is Mr. Sidney Wyeth, who, as you know, I am most anxious to meet."

"Well, that makes it mutual."

"Mutual?"

"Yes. I want you to meet Mr. Wyeth, and I promise to get hold of him and keep him here until you do. I may need your help to keep him from making a fool of himself."

"I'm sure I'll be glad to help you in any way I can."

"You may be able to, in a way that you don't know. I don't know how now, myself. But getting back to Mr. Wyeth, when I finally corner him in the office, I'm going to slip across the hall to another telephone and call you."

"Oh, will you, darling," cried Bertha, slipping off the desk and standing.

Marie rose to her feet, too.

"I will, Bertha, with the understanding that you dress and come right down."

"Will I? And I can dress quick, dear. Oh, you've made me so happy until I must—" and breaking off, she bent forward and kissed Marie impulsively.

They put arms about each other now and walked out into the reception room.

In Louisville, Kentucky, in the meantime, Edrina's sister had just signed for a telegram. Another sister, followed by her mother came up. The mother's face showed anxiety.

"Telegrams always frighten me," said the mother, waiting anxiously for it to be read. "I hope nobody has died."

"Nobody has died, mother," said Carrie, unfolding the telegram. "I'll bet it's from Edrina."

"It is," said Alice, behind her, reading it over Carrie's shoulder.

"So glad," said the mother, with a sigh of relief. "Read it out loud, please."

"It's from Pittsburg," said Carrie. "Am going to be married to Sidney Wyeth, the Motion Picture Producer and Writer. Quitting show Saturday and coming home from here to get a divorce from Arthur. Love
    "EDRINA"

"There, Lord. I knew something was happening," cried the mother. "I felt it."

"Going to marry Mr. Wyeth, eh?" mused Carrie, thoughtfully. "That's fine."

"And who, pray, is Sidney Wyeth?" cried their mother, perking up, curiously.

"He's the man who makes most of the colored pictures we take you to see, mother. Don't you remember seeing his name on the screen?"

"Yes, now that you mention it. I do remember seeing that name on most of the colored pictures I've seen. My, he should have money," she said, and seemed cheered.

"He'd have to have, to make pictures," said Carrie.

"It takes lots of money to make them," said Alice. They turned and walked back through the front room to the kitchen, from where they had been called when the messenger came with the telegram.

"I hope she treats him right and doesn't go to playing around," said Mrs. Graham.

Edrina arrived late the next day and was greeted by all, including her old mother, who cried between sobs, as she embraced her:

"Edrina, my darling. We're so glad to see you."

An hour or so later the three sisters were together in the kitchen, while Alice and Carrie prepared the dinner. Naturally the news that she was engaged to be married to Sidney Wyeth, the Negro race's only motion picture director and producer, was considered little short of a triumph.

"How'd you happen to meet Mr. Wyeth, anyhow," inquired Alice.

"Oh, just ran into him one day on the street," answered Edrina, a bit breezily.

"And you think he fell in love with you—"

"—at sight," replied Edrina, easily, smiling as she cut her sister off. "I saw it while he was being introduced. Saw it in the way he looked at me."

"Isn't that interesting." cried Alice, exchanging expressions with sister Carrie. Both turned admiring eyes now to Edrina, who smiled and seemed to be pleased.

"Who introduced you to him, Edrina?" inquired Alice curiously.

"Donald," replied Edrina, and smiled as both sisters started, obviously surprised.

"Donald!" both exclaimed in chorus.

"Oh, it just happened," said Edrina. "Donald and I were coming up Seventh Avenue; Mr. Wyeth was crossing at 135th Street and we met at the corner, so Donald, naturally, introduced us. Donald and he have known each other for years."

"I see," mused Carrie, then turning to her: "I thought it *was* Donald," she ventured.

"So did I," said Alice joining Carrie.

"It was Donald who you've been telling us about," said Alice. "Ever since you went on the stage."

"Donald in all your letters," said Carrie.

"Well," said Edrina, and hesitated.

"I'm sure you must have liked Donald very much," said Alice.

"Much more, perhaps, than you do Mr. Wyeth," said Carrie. "You've never written us anything about him, so from where did he appear so quickly?"

"Well," began Edrina again.

"Mr. Wyeth, perhaps, has money? Isn't he a man of—means?" from Carrie, and she glanced across from Edrina to Alice, whose eyes were on Edrina.

"Why, Carrie!" exclaimed Edrina, affectaciously.

"That could make some difference," suggested Alice.

"Yes," from Carrie, "a very great deal of difference," and she looked across at Alice, who seemed to be thinking just about as she was.

"On the other hand," said Alice, after a brief but thoughtful pause. "It is possible, after all Edrina has been writing us about Donald, for more than a year, a whole year, that Donald might not be a marrying man."

All of which vexed Edrina very much, but she was trying hard not to show it.

"Are you really in love with Mr. Wyeth, Edrina," inquired Carrie, "or, are you—"

"—just marrying him to get a home?" suggested Alice, cutting Carrie off, who was about to ask the self same thing. By this time, Edrina's control which she had lost for a moment, returned and came quickly to her assistance.

"Now is it just right to ask me such questions?"

"You're still in love with Donald, Edrina," cried Alice, looking at her closely, and speaking very boldly.

"And knowing, perhaps, that Donald is not a marrying man," ventured Carrie, daringly, "you're marrying Mr. Wyeth for money and for money only."

"Shame on you, Edrina," said Alice, and shook her head and made a "twt, twt, twt," sound with her lips. Cornered, caught unprepared for this chiding, Edrina was near tears, while Carrie tried to modify it by a forced laugh. Yet with more to say, went on:

"Meanwhile, she'll keep on going with Donald, and—"

"—having him just the same. Oh, Edrina, Edrina," and both she and sister Alice laughed.

"But that's New York for you," said Carrie. "You've caught on up there, Edrina, bravo, bravo!"

"Oh, hush, hush," cried Edrina, withdrawing a kerchief and dabbing her nose and her eyes. "How can you talk to me like that, both of you." Turning now, she hurried away, across the dining and reception room and up the stairway, just as their mother walked in, and turned to see Edrina, kerchief to her face disappear up the stairway. Now she turned to her other two daughters and with a frown on her face, began:

"I overheard the last of your conversation. Why did you want to embarrass your sister like that?"

Alice and Carrie turned back to their work now and were silent.

"It was a mistake to draw her out the way you did," complained Mrs. Graham, severely, looking from first one to the other.

"We didn't start out to do so, mother," said Carrie, defensively.

"No such thought was in our minds," said Alice.

"We got started talking, and it just happened, that's all," said Carrie, and seemed to feel badly because they had embarrassed Edrina.

"I'm sorry that it had to be," said Mrs. Graham. "To be frank about it, I was afraid it was that way, but you shouldn't have gone as far as you did."

"I'm sorry, mother," said Carrie penitently.

"And I am, too," chirped Alice.

"Well," sighed Mrs. Graham, with finality. "There's nothing that can be done about it now. It'll make her feel bad, with her here, I'm sure, on Mr. Wyeth's money, for how could she pay for a divorce unless some man is putting up the money?"

"And it sure isn't Donald," said Carrie.

"Lord, no," confirmed Alice.

"I heard her reading a long telegram to Mr. Wyeth over the phone just before she came into the kitchen, and in the end, I heard her say 'send it—collect'."

"I was hopeful when she first returned. Hoped that she liked Mr. Wyeth and planned to make him a good wife," said Mrs. Graham.

"Right after sending Mr. Wyeth the telegram collect, she called off another to Donald—and paid for it," said Carrie, whereupon Mrs. Graham shook her head, sadly.

"Now I'm going to be worried. No good can come of a woman trying to play two men. I'm afraid, before it is all over, that Edrina's liable to make a mess of it all."

"Still," observed Carrie, "if Mr. Wyeth is the man I'd imagine him to be, he ought to understand."

"Maybe he does and maybe he doesn't," broke in Mrs. Graham. "It's Edrina. She has no right saying a lot of honey words to one man and all the while, in love with another."

"Why hasn't she married Donald," said Carrie. "She's talked and written enough about him to have been married to him a long time ago."

"Maybe Mr. Howard has something to say about it. He hasn't, I'd bet, asked her to marry him," said Mrs. Graham, her face still serious.

"She's skating on mighty thin ice, if you ask me," said Alice, at which all three sighed and continued to think about Edrina, who was now upstairs.

"I'm sorry, if she doesn't really care for Mr. Wyeth. From the way she described him to me, and from other things I gather, he seems like a good man and might make her a fine husband."

"And he seems to want to badly, too," said Alice.

"It's been going on, it seems, ever since woman was woman and man is a man," said Mrs. Graham. "The same old thing. In love with some man who either doesn't care, is not worth the feeling, and at the same time, ready to make a fool of another, possibly a good one." As she finished she turned to leave the room, mentally very much disturbed. Pausing, she turned back for a last word.

"It isn't going to work, it isn't going to work at all," and with that she dragged herself out of the kitchen.

Late that night Edrina, in her kimono and alone in her bedroom with her hair down and feeling comfortable, finished penning the following note to Sidney Wyeth in New York:

"Arrived home safely and have told my mother and sisters all about you, and they are pleased and in love with you already.

"I've engaged a lawyer to apply for my divorce and he says that he expects to secure a decree in ten days to two weeks. He is charging me $50.00 to get it and I have paid him half of it down as a retainer."

She paused briefly, to think of what more to say, and tipped the end of the pen between her teeth, thoughtfully, presently setting it down, started out again.

"I do nothing but think of you, dear, morning, noon and night. Every day will seem an age until it is all over and I return to New York and your arms, never to leave them again; and soon thereafter we shall be married and belong to each other for good.

"My folks, in the meantime, are giving me a shower as quickly as I have secured my decree, and it is too bad that you can't be here, so that everybody could meet and fall in love with you as I have."

She paused to stretch her mouth wide and was conscious that she was becoming drowsy. Knowing that no more letters would be picked up from the mail box that night, she didn't close the letter, but laid it aside and prepared for bed.

CHAPTER XV

WYETH WAS doing so well in the sale of his book in northern Jersey, that he just drove by the office each morning for a full week, glanced through the mail, jotted down some instructions for Marie, and was gone every morning when she arrived.

In the meanwhile, after her last talk with Marie concerning the story in the book as being inspired from Wyeth's own life, told in the third person, Bertha was reading it again and studying it very closely this time as she did so.

Among the characteristics reflected in the development of the story, was, among other things, that of a man void and free of any ostentation and pretence. This was debated at some length in the story. Another angle which interested her, was his views with regards to the intermarriage of races.

Since America as a whole, was opposed to the institution, Wyeth had written of it in a most interesting way. He drew the picture of a girl, presumably white and as far as she knew, until it all came out in the end to the contrary, was a white girl. It was purely coincidental for her to fall in love with a colored man, who refused her love because he thought she was white.

Elsewhere he criticised the Negro for his failure to assume more responsibility, and his tendency to blame the white man for his condition, claiming it to be due to the under-privileged life he was forced to live and to race prejudice. He referred to that as the easiest way out. He pointed out very forcibly, that while that excuse, worn threadbare by this time, might be easy to hold up in place of success and possession, that in the end, however, it got the Negro nothing.

She compared Wyeth with Kermit Early, with so much academic training until, as she viewed him, he was largely unfit for real success and had not achieved it, had found the white man's prejudice to be such a stumbling block that he was making a supreme issue of its results. She also thought of and brought his relation with Mrs. Wingate into her mind's picture. Mrs. Wingate, a wealthy and aristocratic white woman, who was really in love with this colored man.

She had inquired of the whereabouts of the author of *Nature's Child,* having planned, in her research and the information she was turning over to her brother, to ascertain in detail any information that might later be of value to the Reich. She could not find out much about the author of *Nature's Child* other than that he lived on Long Island, was married to a white woman, and seemed to have gone into retirement after the success of his book, which although shortlived, was phenominal while it lasted.

She had also investigated another Negro author, who had written a book of research, which she found very interesting and exhaustive, and had sent copies of it back to Germany. Like the author of *Nature's Child,* this one had also married a white woman and she wondered at all this; was it customary for Negroes, after achieving some measure of success, to marry white women? Was it because women of their own race did not quite come up to their ideas, socially and otherwise? She didn't think Wyeth would marry a white woman.

Truly the Negro in America, she found, presented the most unusual situation. He seemed to be the most interesting when he was in some way involved with the white man, the women often only as a concubine, which was the subject and background of the novel, by a southern white woman called *Passion,* and which she found the Negroes buying in greater numbers than they had ever bought any book, so she was told by local booksellers in Harlem. The story was filled with the words "nigger" and "darkies" and of the term "darkies in their place," and all through, was repeated "they knew their place and stayed in it" to which they were violently opposed, and would become very angry if such terms were expressed about them by Negroes. Yet, here was the case of a white woman, a Southern white woman who put them in the "dog house" at the beginning of her story—and kept them there throughout and didn't let them out in the end—and they were buying and reading the book as they had never bought any book, including the bible. It was baffling and she couldn't understand it at all.

Surely there was much for her to study and find out, and this added to her anxiety to meet Sidney Wyeth and to have a long talk with him, and to meet him again and have more talks, for, according to Marie, he was a Negro from whom she could find out things she wanted to know, things and matters of current interest. This, she soon found out, Negroes in general did not possess and seemed to take little interest in. If they were educated they were invariably academic, academic to the point that he was more ignorant of current events, especially those concerned or related to trade, industry and commerce than he was with historical facts. She recalled that Marie had told her about their inclination and love for anthropology, and how so many aspired to become one and even dared call themselves an Anthropoligist. Something that not one person in a thousand in everyday life would understand, and who wouldn't care if they did not.

"When you talk with Mr. Wyeth," Marie had said. "If you have occasion to know what banking in Wall Street and all over America is all about, he can tell you. If you went South and would like to know what you would meet on the way down there, he could tell you all you wanted to know about Philadelphia, how the streets run even. On then toward Washington, he would tell you about the great Dupont family in Wilmington, Del., home of the greatest chemical corporations in America which Bertha would have appreciated knowing, being aware that Germany was the home of the greatest chemical products the world over. Yet in Wilmington, the Duponts were the greatest runner-ups. "But few Negroes would even know what that was all about. It wouldn't concern 'anthropology', so they would be as dense regarding it as of the forests you would encounter in the heart of Canada.

"The Negro could talk to you about Washington, because there our group hold more white collar jobs than anywhere in America, and many would be aspiring to get a better one. He could tell you about the color line there among Negroes, and that there is where they want to be regarded as aristocrats. Because in Washington there live a thousand well paid colored school teachers, aristocrats of the Negro race, aristocrats without money, and where nobody wants to see anybody get ahead of anybody else, themselves especially.

Where selfishness reigns among each other supreme, and where no Negro is appreciated unless white America has placed their stamp of approval on him, first. "Then," Marie had told her, "they get in the honored ones way, until they can't move around, wine, dine and flatter them almost to death. That is Washington and our people could tell you all about that.

"Going on South then through Virginia and the Carolina's, you meet endless colored people, but few of the intelligensia could tell you that there is the dynasty of 'LS-MFT' Lucky Strike, the world's best tobacco, or of Camels and Chesterfields which they are fond of smoking, but it is of little interest to them where the tobacco is grown that goes into them. No, he wouldn't know that and is not interested in finding out.

"He would know that other than from California, oranges and grapefruit and lemons come in large numbers from Florida, about the only commodity and fruit that he would know where grown; but continuing across Georgia, Alabama and Miss., he would also know that there is the home of King Cotton, but he hates those states and that section so badly, due to the way he is treated, and 'kept in his place' until he wouldn't want to talk much about them.

"Jumping from the Mississippi River to the Pacific coast, about the only thing in that section that he wanted and could talk to you about would be of Negroes who had inherited oil lands in Oklahoma; but Mr. Wyeth could and would tell you that there were more wealthy Negroes in the Cane River Country in Louisiana, where many Negroes, born of a white father before the civil war, were slave owners, Negroes, a hundred years ago who owned each other, and whose descendants still live on the feudal estates that they inherited. He would tell you of a strip of sandy and hilly land along the eastern edge of Texas, a strip of country, 66 miles long by 16 miles wide, which Negroes owned almost entirely up until 15 years ago.

" But why and how, you might ask, did this come to happen? And Mr. Wyeth would tell you then of how hardy old Negroes from the plantations of Louisiana and Arkansas right after the civil war, with their families treked westward in covered wagons into Texas and settled in what is now the richest valleys there. He would tell you about how the whites frightened them with the first Ku

Klux Klan hoods and fiery crosses and virtually forced them off these rich, black lands. Compelled them to flee eastward, back in the direction from whence they had come, but not as far back. For when they reached the sand hill country on the eastern edge of Texas, land that every settler had rode across and ignored, and feeling that they would not be bothered or molested, they settled there where they lived in peace for fifty or more years until one morning in 1930 when the news ran down through the Gut, that oil had been discovered. Then back to the hills came the white man, and for ten years he turned it into a land of litigation, persuasion and coercion. But at least half the Negroes stuck by their guns. They held on and in time, because it came under Federal observation and supervision, managed to retain his rich oil lands, and that today is where the richest Negroes in all America live."

"And why would Mr. Wyeth know so much about all this, and all these others, with so much education and so many degrees, know so little?"

"Not little, Bertha," cautioned Marie. "Nothing."

"Well?"

"Because they teach nothing about Negroes in our schools but the history of slavery and the war that ended it. They teach nothing about the Negro's part in our great country since then or of today. Our educated Negroes know mostly, only what they learned in schools. They try to find out little about themselves thereafter. The Negroes chief interest and great concern is to find the best possible job, and the jobs they give and grant to Negroes are not the best jobs, understand?"

"I can," said Bertha, "but still you haven't explained why Mr. Wyeth should know so much about all the things you've told me."

"Because, dear Bertha, Sydney Wyeth is an observing man, living down to earth and concerned with the things, like white men, that make, and has made America great. Even before he started making pictures, but especially afterward, he had occasion to travel all over the country to book his pictures in the Negro theatres, scattered all over creation, and on these long trips, seated in his car, he saw things and he asked about them. They interested him and he found out from day to day, week to week, month to month on these long trips, what they were all about, and so—"

"— he knows and that is why he can—"

"— talk about anything you or anybody else might want to know," said Marie, "except, of course," and Marie smiled, "Anthropology and the origin of man," and they both laughed.

"Mr. Wyeth can tell you only of what man is doing today, not a thousand years ago, at least, not very much about it," and again they laughed.

"So, Marie, dear, you have made me more anxious to meet your boss, but never, no never, is he in. Always," Bertha complained, "he is out—gone before I reach the office, so what? Will I *ever* meet him? Ever?"

Marie sighed and shook her head.

And then the very next morning, Bertha, while cooking her breakfast, had a telephone call, which, of course she answered. It was from Marie, at the office.

"Oh, Bertha, he's here; he's in," she cried, almost frantic.

"You mean, Mr. Wyeth?" Bertha cried.

"Nobody else. So, darling, eat your breakfast, for I can hear it cooking, eat it and hurry down here—run!"

"I'll run," said Bertha, and ate so quickly until she didn't realize it. A few minutes later she walked into the office of the Wyeth Pictures Corporation, to see the object of her desire, sitting at his desk, busy talking over the telephone, and a few minutes later she had been introduced to him by Marie, who left them alone to talk—and they talked!

CHAPTER XVI

"SO YOU'RE MISS BERTHA SCHULTZ," Wyeth began, after being introduced and having invited her to become seated. He looked at her, seemed to be pleased and smiled amiably. She returned the greeting.

"Yes, Mr. Wyeth," she said, prettily. "I'm Miss Schultz," and they both laughed, for they were thinking how many times she had been to the office to see him.

"I'm inclined to feel that I know you, Miss Schultz, since my assistant has said so much about you and seems to admire you very much. I want to apologize at the outset, however, for being absent so often from my office, where I am supposed to do business and meet people," he said.

"Oh, that is all right, Mr. Wyeth," replied Bertha, so pleasant he thought and so perfectly agreeable. "You're a very busy man and I can appreciate your being absent, busy developing your sales in the field which is the best place I am sure, to do so."

He glanced at her with new interest. She had just made an expression of intelligence. He could see by that one remark alone the kind of girl Marie had described, an intelligent and understanding sort of girl.

"Thank you, Miss Schultz. You summed up the case in a few words. I don't know whether you understand much about business from the Negro viewpoint, but my experience for a long time has been, that if we are to succeed in only a small way, it is necessary for those of us desirous of success to lead in the effort."

"Thank you so much, Mr. Wyeth. I am interested in finding out as nearly as I can, exactly what the Negro is doing, and from all I've been able to learn, you are about the most informed man in a broad and general way that the race possesses."

Looking at her, Wyeth thought of what Marie had said; that the girl was of German extraction, of fine intelligence and possessed self-confidence. He was interested in her, and was curious to know more about her, to talk with her, perhaps, about the things she knew. He couldn't know, of course, the many reasons why she wanted to talk with him, and of the things that might be of interest to Adolf Hitler that she was to find out.

"No one could read your book, either from the standpoint of entertainment or psychology, and not appreciate your intelligence and mass of information, Mr. Wyeth," she said sincerely.

"Then you have read it?" he said, a bit anxious to feel her out; see just what were the reactions of this girl who had spent so much time in Europe. Her reaction could be different than one so close to the things he had attempted to write about.

"Twice, Mr. Wyeth."

"Twice?" he said this in such a way that she had to explain it was not necessary to do so in order to understand it. All the comments he had heard had been to the effect that it was very simple, easy to read and understand. She read what he was thinking and quickly said:

"I didn't read it the second time because I did not fully understand it the first time."

"Thank you," he replied and smiled, a bit relieved.

"I fully understood it the first time, and that," said she, "is why I read it the second time," and she smiled sweetly, hopefully. He now understood and liked her. She was making it easy.

"You're a very interesting person, Miss Schultz."

"Please don't flatter me, Mr. Wyeth," she said and blushed, and he thought, as Bertha had told him, of the great Schumann-Heink.

"I enjoyed reading it, Mr. Wyeth. It was not merely enjoyable and interesting, but it left you feeling something."

He was thoughtful for a moment, then turned to her:

"Digressing for a moment, there have been two books published during this decade of especial and peculiar interest to our group. I'll take first the last one only recently published."

"You are referring to *Passion*, I suppose," she offered.

"Exactly. Just what was your reaction to it?"

She shrugged her shoulders lightly.

"You found," he said, "it interesting?"

"Yes, I found it interesting," she admitted.

"But you didn't find in it a book which you would say that you—liked?"

"Oh, no," she exclaimed, quickly

"And yet our people, we Negroes I mean, are buying that book in greater numbers than any current book ever published."

"You don't say so!" she exclaimed, somewhat surprised.

"They are doing just that."

"And it—oh, it has so many words, situations and so much that I imagine they would dislike; that they would complain about."

"Yes, it has all that, and there is no escape in the end from the bastardy the book puts them in—yet they are buying it as they have never bought any book that I ever heard of before."

"It's amazing!"

"It shows, among other things, that tragic realism interests them. While it is a terrible book, a dirty and very much soiled sort of book, from a moral point of view, I'm glad the woman wrote it. It has helped me."

She looked at him, not quite understanding.

"I have enjoyed picturizing the Negro in his true state in such books as I have written, and in the many pictures that I have made."

"Yes, pictures," she said, sitting up. She hoped he was going to say more about pictures.

"But they won't let me!"

Her eyebrows wrinkled.

"I don't—quite understand you."

"It would take too many words to explain, then still you might not understand. But what I mean directly is that when I try to do this, film the Negro realistically, there is so much complaint on his part, and I meet so many theatre owners that refuse to play the pictures, especially in Washington and a lot of other places, too, that I don't dare picturize him as he actually is, and at no time or in any picture have I used such words and terms as this white woman uses to describe him. In short, she puts the Negro in the dog house at the start of the book and she keeps him there throughout the entire story, and locks him up there to stay for good in the end and still they buy the book, and nobody says: 'Oh, I liked it,' still they buy it. We handle it and are selling as many copies through our mail order department as we are of mine. Why I like writing is that you can express your opinion, use words that fit best, and nobody annoys you with squawks and kicks and so much of that which dogged me all through the years that I made pictures."

"Indeed!" she exclaimed and was anxious for him to go on.

"Oh, yes. It was amazing. Now the truer my pictures are to Negro life as we Negroes experience and know it, the better they draw and the better they liked them; but there was always somebody complaining to the manager that he or she didn't like the picture and questioning why that man was doing and saying the things he did. We're trying to get away from all that stuff you hear them say. They have no regard for history. They would have history obliterated, wherever they can exert any pressure or influence, especially if it showed him in the roles we all know he played, prior to the civil war. He would have the world feel that he began right out there on Seventh avenue, from the beginning. In fact, it is so hard for one Negro to please another that one becomes despaired."

"Amazing."

"Amazing but true. To begin with, he refuses to take any of us seriously unless the white man puts his stamp of approval on us first. The very thing he would have you crucified for doing, saying or portraying, the minute the white man says something fine about it, immediately it becomes classic with them and we are then praised and lauded to the skies."

"Why?" she asked.

"Really, Miss Schultz, I don't know," he said shaking his head. "Nothing leaves you so baffled as the novel *Passion*, which if a Negro had written and the white people were not buying as they are, too, he'd demand the author, if he were a Negro to be shot at sunrise—and this runs right down through those of the intelligensia, including the many organizations, conceived and operating for the benefit of a higher millenium as regards us. This Southern woman has been invited to speak to endless groups of Negroes and they are falling over each other to hear her, because she has written a book, picturing the Negro in the lowest strata of society that he could possibly be. Nowhere in the book has she honored him. She puts words in a colored Doctor's mouth in the story, expressing a wish and a desire to marry a girl who has been the concubine of a no-good white man."

"I agree with you that in this respect," she said, "they are— baffling."

"I once heard a speaker, a colored orator of renown say that no Negro has ever achieved great success with the help of one another, and it is true. White America, we all agree and admit, seems to view us, especially the contemporary Negro, through a distorted vision. He seems to want to keep us in the dog house, as it were, talking, when he puts words in our mouths, always in dialect, rolling our eyes, being funny at all times, or if he is forced to accept us from another viewpoint, he will readily do so but as criminals, morons, degenerates—anything but what the most of us aspire to be, good Americans living a moderate and conventional American life. In fact, he seems to want to feel that we have no contemporary life. And yet, any Negro, who aspires to rise above the common masses, has got to please that white man and in some way, conform the Negro to his point of view, otherwise he is ignored and crucified. And so by this kind of silence, we are crucified by the leaders of our own race, who refuse to take us seriously because the white man has neglected to do so."

"Very interesting, Mr. Wyeth," she said. "In just what way, if any, has this affected you, and especially your book?"

"That is a long story."

"Is it?" she said. "Why have you made no effort to get your book on sale at most of the book shops?"

"I have, and am, Miss Schultz, sort of feeling my way into the depth of what I consider a rather intricate situation."

She nodded understandingly, and listened closely.

"Meanwhile, I am finding out by going slowly, yet persistently, no end of ways that might ultimately get me somewhere. By that, I mean, that I am able, by concerted effort, to make a good living and keep my assistant steadily and profitably employed, by building up the sale of the book, and perhaps other books, directly to the masses."

"I follow you," she said.

"It was the same way in the production of pictures. The Negro on the street is with you when you make an honest but worthy effort, and he will buy what you produce. Just get it to him and he will do the rest. It is the so-called or would-be leader who, in the end, fortunately, is not very effective, who lambasts you, tries to ridicule you, hold you up to contempt and tries to keep you stalemated."

"How can you explain such a—a peculiar phenomenon?" Bertha queried, her brow wrinkled.

"Yes, how can you?" Wyeth repeated. "It would take so many words to explain it that I might be here until noon trying to do so. I brought it up because I don't want you to feel that the white man holds us back as much as this very group I refer to would have you think. Through such philosophy as he practices, he helps to hold himself back. He refuses even more, I fear, than the white man to recognize and appreciate merit and ability, constructive ability, within our group and by his activity and conduct makes our lot harder. Most of this, in a word, is due to nothing but pure selfishness."

"I understand, but—I—hardly know how to—accept it."

"You could hardly," he said, understandingly.

"You see," she went on, as if to clarify her lack of knowledge of the things he was talking about. "I've spent the last ten years, most of it at least, in school in Germany and France, and—"

"—which has left you a bit ignorant of conditions here in America," he interrupted her and smiled, nodding his head.

"But now that I am—back, you see, I am anxious to learn all about us—and any condition or circumstances that involve us. I might tell you that learning these things is to be my future work. Naturally I am axious to start finding out all I can and as quickly as I can. That is why, among other reasons, that I have been so very anxious to meet you."

"Thank you, Miss Schultz," he said pleasantly. "I admit knowing a great deal about our group here in America, but I hope I don't sound boastful or egotistic in making such an admission. For so many years I made motion pictures, and I had to find places to play them all over America, any place where there were enough of our group to make it profitable."

"I am especially anxious to have you tell me more about—making pictures," she said, raising her pretty hand. "But there's something I would like you to tell me right now, and I will ask you to tell me before we get too far away from it."

"Of course," he said, and waited.

As she poised for the question he watched her closely, and again was reminded of her extremely Germanic extraction; and again he thought of the great Madame Schumann-Heink. To him as he studied her, she was the strangest colored girl he had ever met. She did not have the usual Negro inclination, accent, composure; she was anything but a colored girl in the way he knew them. And yet, she *was* colored, this was obvious in the brownishness in her otherwise bluish eyes, the wave of her hair, the darker color of her skin, which should have been, according to her mannerisms, real white.

"Before I went—to Europe," she began again. She was still having difficulty in representing herself as an American. Speaking of it so often confused her. "I heard so much of how the Negro had made such wonderful progress in the years since the Civil War. I don't hear nearly so much about this—progress now. Why?"

"We don't say nearly as much about our progress since the great depression swept the country during the past fifteen years, but which has been over long enough to forget most of it. Until the depression, which was when there was so much said about progress, we thought we had made much."

"Had we?"

"In a way, yes, but it was mostly academic. Decidedly academic."

"Not material, industrial, commercial or economic?"

"No, it was not," he said. "It was mostly academic, but unfortunately, was confused with the material, if you didn't go very deep, or investigate very far. Still, we seemed to have had more economic success before the depression than we are enjoying since, but I insist on the statement that before the depression our so-called progress was still more academic than material, but a greater value was placed on that academic success before the depression than we have since valued it."

Bertha listened carefully to his every word.

"I recall the statistical reports back in those days which were in effect that we had so many people who had graduated from college, so many from high school, so many doctors, so many lawyers, so many teachers, so many preachers, so many churches, and so many this and so many that. When the depression swept over the country, and thousands of these various grades of graduates were forced on relief, and to grab and take any kind of job that could be created, for our government went into the creation of jobs, such as through the medium of the WPA and other works administrations, much of what we had reckoned as assets, lost value completely.

When it moved on and left them stranded, destitute, what had before been considered an asset, was a pitiful liability and it was the depression that perhaps made us realize we hadn't made so much progress after all as we were inclined to boast of; that much of this so-called progress was merely potential. It most assuredly was not material, and we found we couldn't buy food, clothing or pay rent with it. Just before the great depression, there had been an orgy of buying, purchasing homes in which to live, to rent and exploit. On most of these purchases only a small payment was made, but through and during this period of inflation, it was enough to transfer the property, mostly only by contract, to the purchaser. Within a few years then, the purchaser was considered the owner of much property, as it were. It looked like we were going places, only to have the depression destroy and wipe out these potential values so quickly that it left the previous and temporary holders dizzy. Had you lived here during the worst of that period, you would have been forced to agree with the rest of us, that we were finished—that the end for the Negro had come, because we educated ones and all, in plain words, were just nothing.

"That, then, Miss Schultz," he finished, "is why you don't hear so much about our progress and achievement at this time."

"You have made it so clear. Well, what about now?"

"Now? Yes, now. Well, Miss Schultz, that is hard to say. We've had a wave of prosperity for several years. It would seem that after having survived such a calamity as the depression, that most of us would be sensitive about it and try to avoid going through such another condition by conserving our earnings, but we are not."

"Oh, no?"

"There's always some conservative people, and this applies to many of our group, who didn't go on relief during the depression; didn't go on it because they had managed their earnings carefully and though terribly restricted, didn't sink that low. The same situation applies now. In the sale of the book it is our privilege to meet many people and come to understand this condition very well. There are some people who have money all the time, subscribe for the book and pay for it whenever it is offered for delivery, but there are others who, if you don't get it to them between Friday, their pay day, and Monday morning, won't have anything left to pay with after that date. They are just careless, wasteful and extravagant, that's all."

"With regard to the church and the colored preachers, what influence do they wield?"

"Enough to live quite comfortably, regardless, and by such influence as he has, makes those who belong to the church the most conservative. Their promise is better, and they strive to keep it far more than the ones who do not belong to or are not active in some church."

"You think so?"

"I know so. If it wasn't for those who are associated with some of the many churches, I don't know what would become of us. I'm inclined to feel that we would almost disappear as a worthwhile group. Those women who are the pillars of the colored church, do more to hold us together and make us as responsible as we are, than any other influence, which is still not sufficient."

Bertha glanced at her watch.

"I know that I must not continue to keep you away from your work at such a time of day, Mr. Wyeth," she said, rising to her feet. "So I will get out of your way, but it is my wish to talk with you again, a great many times, if this can be arranged."

"I am sure we have interests in common, Miss Schultz, and will be able to meet again many times and talk about what seems to interest you, and most assuredly does me—the condition of our group here, which is a stupendous problem."

"A tremendous problem is putting it mildly," she said as he followed her into the reception room. Marie paused in her typing to get up and smile at them, and put her arm about Bertha's waist.

"I know that you both have found common interests," she said, "and you haven't got started yet."

"But we will and I hope soon," said Wyeth, smiling down on the two girls. "Miss Schultz here," he said, looking at her, "is going to prove a very interesting person to talk to, I can see that now."

"He likes that kind of person, Bertha," said Marie. "His complaint is that he cannot talk to many of us, that we don't take matters that seriously."

"Mr. Wyeth is a wonderful man," said Bertha, smiling up at him. "I could listen to him talk forever!" All broke into merry laughter at this, then with a bow and another smile, Wyeth turned and went back into his office, closing the door behind him.

CHAPTER XVII

IN LOUISVILLE, EDRINA'S shower turned out to be quite an affair. Her mother and father and their mothers and fathers before them were all born in Louisville and as youngsters had all been educated. Her mother, as a girl, was both beautiful and refined. Her father was tall and handsome. Her grandfather was a half-breed Indian, her grandmother a beautiful mulatto. So Endrina was descended from the best colored people in the town of 'Marse Henry W. Watterson.' They therefore went all out to make Edrina's engagement to Sidney Wyeth a popular event by inviting all the best Negroes of Louisville, which included most of the colored doctors, lawyers, school teachers, especially the principals of the many Negro schools, the undertakers, insurance men, two bankers, headwaiters from the leading hotels, all combined to make the affair a popular event.

With a large portion of the 100 dollars that Wyeth had sent her, which was enlarged by gifts from her brothers, Edrina had purchased and dressed for the occasion as few colored girls had ever dressed for anything in Louisville. At the moment, the party was at its height. A local orchestra had been engaged, two girls with the best voices had also been retained and rendered solos that gave the party zest and entertainment. After much insistence, Edrina consented to give a rendition which she had sung with Mantan's show, knew how to "sell" it and having just finished the song, was surrounded at the moment by many admirers. She was presently taken in charge and questioned regarding her engagement to Wyeth, whom everybody knew to be the race's only Negro motion picture director and producer.

"Will you continue on the stage after you marry," she was asked, "or retire to the life of a house-wife?"

"Oh, I could hardly give up the stage," Edrina replied, with her most gracious smile. "My public would hardly let me. I expect to open in a new play shortly after my return to New York," she informed all who heard, and was pleased with the animation the remark created.

"Will Mr. Wyeth approve?" she was next asked, whereupon Edrina answered with her sweetest and most attractive smile.

"He may not want to, but—" and she brought her large and beautiful ostrich feather fan down in a large and illustrious sweep, "I shall attend to that," and she smiled her best and bowed, again pleased with the flattery.

After a dance with Professor Jones, principal of the Central High School, and a drink of punch with Dr. Maxwell Andrews, Louisville's leading Negro surgeon, she permitted the Headwaiter of the great Brown Hotel to sit out a dance and then danced with Charles Weston, president of the Monmouth, leading Negro insurance company of Kentucky.

She brought her stage training into effect that night—and Donald Howard knew how to train a girl in the art of etiquette, and Edrina was at her best for the occasion, carrying off all honors. When the guests departed shortly after midnight, everybody was talking about Edrina; how she had improved since going to New York, and in the heart of every girl who attended, she was the secret subject of much envy.

Everybody was pleased with the success of the party, but her mother, who had overheard her speech regarding the stage, and was, as usual, worried and took her in tow when they sat down for a moment's relaxation after the last guest departed.

"I'm awfully worried about you, Edrina," she began and shook her head. "It's bad enough to marry Mr. Wyeth, who seems like such a good man and not be in love with him."

"Who said I wasn't, mother?" she lied, glibly.

The success of the party had added to her ego and self-confidence, also to her ability to lie and fool even herself. Actually she had the feeling that she *was* in love with Wyeth. "Not me, I'm sure," she finished, her head high.

"No, not you, of course, Edrina," said her mother. "But don't try to fool a mother who raised you, and even if you have been to New York and are able by your bizarre and vivacity to fool the guests as

I saw and heard you fool them tonight, you cannot fool me. You're in love with this Donald Howard and no other. You are *not* in love with Mr. Wyeth."

Getting dramatically to her feet and sweeping around the room with stage-like precision, Edrina faced her mother.

"Oh, mother, don't say that—please don't say it! I can't understand why you, Carrie and Alice keep on intimating that I'm not in love with the man I'm going to marry, and that, instead, I'm in love with Donald Howard. Positively and absolutely, I am *not* in love with Donald Howard, and would not marry him if he was the last man on earth!"

"Hush, my child, please," her mother replied, and waved her down with a motion of her hand. "Sit down and quit acting. You're not on a stage and I'm not one of an audience. I'm your mother and what I want to talk about is for your own good. So please quit acting, dear, and sit down and listen to me."

"Well," sighed Edrina, petulantly, but sat down as requested.

"Now, dear," Mrs. Graham began. "As I said, I'm awfully worried about you and I wouldn't be feeling as I do if there wasn't a good sound reason for it."

"But what reason, mother? What have I done or said to leave you worried as you insist?"

"Tonight you told everybody within hearing distance that you could not afford to quit the stage; and that you expected to open in a new play immediately upon your return to New York."

"Oh, well," said Edrina, deprecatingly.

"That was only for show; to make you appear big in the eyes and ears of those who heard you. Still, it is truthfully what you would like to do, now isn't it?" her mother insisted, pointedly.

Edrina shifted uncomfortably, but made no immediate reply, so Mrs. Graham went on:

"You said it all as a grand gesture, but behind the gesture was ambition, and you plan to persuade Mr. Wyeth to consent—after you marry him, to let you remain on the stage, now isn't that true?"

Edrina shifted more uncomfortably, and turned and tried to change the subject.

"I've promised to be a good wife to Mr. Wyeth; the best wife I know how to be. Now isn't that enough?"

"Of course—if you mean it."

"Oh, mother," cried Edrina, springing to her feet, and starting all over, but her mother caught her by the arm and pulled her back down again.

"Sit down and be patient. You don't want to listen to me because the truth hurts and you want to supplant truth with camouflage, dramatic gestures."

"Everybody who I talked with tonight said such fine things," said Edrina. "But alone with you and my sisters, you start insisting that I don't mean Mr. Wyeth any good; that I'm marrying him for security only; and that I'm planning to fool him, and—"

"—you're not going to succeed, dear. That is what I want to caution you about; that in planning as you are, in the end you'll find out that you are only fooling yourself."

"I'll be glad when it is all over; when the lawyer calls or writes me and tells me the decree has been granted, and that I'm free to return to New York. I thought you were going to be glad to see me and—"

"We are all glad to see you, Edrina, and if we could feel that you intended to do right by the man you've agreed to marry, we'd all be with you, but I'm your mother and Carrie and Alice are your sisters. We know you and we can see right through all that you are fooling everybody else with."

"So what?" cried Edrina, as if deciding to face the music and have it over with.

"Just quit playing around and try to be true to yourself if you are unable at present to be true and faithful to the man you're about to marry. You send him a telegram collect every day, and you call him by telephone almost every night, in each case, collect, and you say so many sweet words to him, assuring him in almost every breath of your fidelity, of your anxiety to please him and make his life the happiest he has ever known. And you send Donald Howard telegrams and pay for each one out of the money Mr. Wyeth is sending you. You call Donald after you talk to Wyeth, and you charge the calls on our telephone, I—"

"—I'll pay for all of them before I leave, mother."

"I'm not talking about that. You'll pay for them, I know—out of more money Mr. Wyeth sends you, not out of anything Donald sends or has ever sent, and you try to make me believe that you're not in love with this Donald. Edrina, how can you!" Edrina began to cry. Then breaking suddenly off, she faced her mother bravely and boldly.

"Please, mother, believe me. I won't let you down. Just store that in the back of your head and think and charge me with anything you like, but believe me when I say that in the end I won't let you down." She crossed over to her mother, bent over, kissed her, and patted her cheek. Mrs. Graham sighed deeply.

"Your promise to me is just as good as all those you are making to Sidney Wyeth and will be broken as promptly when and if the time comes," and Mrs. Graham, sighed again, more deeply, more hopelessly.

"I don't care how you feel—now, or what you say, mother dear. All I ask is that you leave Mr. Wyeth to me. I know how to handle him, so just leave him to me, dear mami, and watch what happens." She bent over and kissed the elder woman again and again patted her cheek and then turning, crossed the room and went upstairs to her room.

Two days later the lawyer called her and told her that her decree had been granted, and to call at the office to sign the papers and etc. The etc. meant of course to bring the rest of the money.

She called Western Union immediately and wired Wyeth the news; and that she would be ready to leave for New York as quickly as she heard from him.

When Wyeth got her telegram, he understood, and understood, also, what she didn't say. By now she knew that she didn't have to always ask for what she wanted.

Two hours later a telegraph messenger walked across the porch of Edrina's home in Louisville, and when he crossed it on the way out, Edrina held a Western Union check for a hundred dollars, which she kissed, and two days later, she started back to New York where she was met at the Penna. Station by Sidney Wyeth, who kissed her, took her bags and hat box in charge, carried them to his car, followed by her. He helped her into the front seat, smiled down at her, then went around the car and got into the driver's seat. He looked at her, smiled again, squeezed her hand, then drove her uptown to Harlem, and to a restaurant where they used to go when it all started, retired to a booth they used to sit in, and gave their order to the waiter.

A half hour later they were in a heated argument. It started over some remark he made about what happened to some show people recently, and having decided to change him over on her way from Louisville, she chose it to begin her campaign. It brought immediate response.

"But why do you dislike show people so, dear?" she began, innocently enough. "I ask you, Sidney, is that just right and fair? Why are you so against them?" He looked up quickly and in great surprise.

"Against show people? What do you mean, Edrina?" he wanted to know.

"Well," she said, slowly, carefully. "You're always ready to play them down."

"I merely related how, after rehearsing six weeks here while you were away, some fifty or more were taken to Philadelphia, where they had been promised work all winter, but actually played just one flop week. That half of them were stranded over there, unable to get back. In Philadelphia, think of it, only ninety miles away, and can't get back."

"But they can't help it. A man like you should feel sorry for them," she said, seemingly anxious to provoke his impatience.

"I do feel sorry for them, but that won't get them back to New York, nor will it compensate them for rehearsing the entire fall. I merely criticised their taking such chances. The Actors Equity Association would not have permitted such a—travesty, but they waived Equity, and did it on their own. That is all that I criticised. They shouldn't have allowed themselves to take such chances on a turkey show."

"People have got to get along somehow, is how I see it," she argued.

"There's a war going on in Europe. It may involve America before it is over. There's plenty of work and good pay. Nobody needs sympathy who ignores these conditions and permits themselves to be inveigled into a turkey show that's stranded half of them in Philadelphia, $2.50 worth of railroad fare away from New York."

"Still I feel sorry for them and you ought to feel the same way," she said.

"Do you call that being sensible or practical?" he argued, wondering why she had chosen to make an issue of an incident, foreign to both. "They weren't paid for the flop week they played, even."

"And because of their misfortune, you're against show people," she insisted. He turned to look at her more closely.

"Listen, dear, I don't understand why you brought this up and chose to argue about it, unless there is some ulterior motive behind it. Well, what is it all about? Speak up, dear, get it off your chest."

"How can I reason with you when you're so prejudiced against show people?" she argued. "They've never done anything to you, have they? Then why do you dislike them so?" She looked at him, and the very expression with which she did so seemed to him most unreasonable.

"I tell you for the dozenth time, Edrina, that I'm not against anybody nor do I dislike show people. You're not so concerned with that as you pretend to be. There's something on your mind, honey. I can smell it. You've been doing some thinking and planning. So don't sit there, beating around the bush, trying to make a mountain out of a mole hill. Just come on out with what it is."

Edrina was momentarily cornered. She *had* been planning, a single track planning, that didn't include what he might think about it or anybody else. She hadn't been very clever in starting it. Was it because she was overly anxious? Too anxious to get on the subject, and to have him agree with her, then she was going to be very sweet and persuade him that he was all wrong about shows, and that she was right. Up against a brick wall—in a blind alley, as it were, she reverted again to the same thing which by this time had become monotonous.

"I still say that you're against show people," she began all over again.

"Is this a round-about way to see if I have changed in regards to your work on the stage? It sounds like it," he said, looking straight at her.

She didn't look at him, but kept her eyes on her plate instead.

"If it is, for your information, I haven't changed at all. If the recent debacle in Philadelphia has meant anything as far as I'm concerned, I'm more set against it now than ever. We've just had a very good demonstration of what badly financed, careless show production can come to. I'm most emphatically set against it and don't want nor will I have any wife of mine, messing around with any kind of a show. It's all a gamble at best, and why should I permit a cheap gamble in which the stakes are lowest at best to interfere with my home and comfort and happiness? As I used to tell you, I know too much about the whole cheap effort to get enthusiastic and have never been enthusiastic about them since I went into the show business, years and years ago, so that is that." His tone was hard and firm as he tried to eat a mouth full of food, and there was a severe frown on his face at the same time.

"See," she cried, pointing a finger at him, accusingly. "I told you that you were against show people, and just then you admitted it."

He looked up a moment, and frowned more deeply, but wishing to avoid a further argument, lowered his eyes and said nothing. "You just hate show people—hate them," she cried, and looked hard at him and was still looking hard at him when he raised his eyes again and met hers.

"Mantan's getting up a new show. You haven't been here long enough to have been told about it, so somebody must have written you at Louisville that he was."

She couldn't answer, but it was Donald who had written her that he was. He had merely said that Mantan was getting a new show together as a matter of news and not with any thought of putting ideas in her head. Wyeth was still looking at her and now went on:

"Is that what this is all about?"

She made no answer and lowered her eyes to her plate and said nothing. He knew that it was this that was on her mind, and that she would not be happy until she had called on Mantan—to find if he had any part in it for her. He grunted. He was angry now and wanted her to know just how he felt. He was additionally angry because she had assured him over the telephone, at his expense, night after night that she had given up all such ideas and ambitions and was ready, as quickly as she returned to New York, to be all his own and make him happy. Now hardly before she arrived, she had staged an unreasonable argument, in the hope, as he could see, of getting his consent to resume show work.

"I'm still standing where I have stood all along. I want my wife in my home. I want a fine, dignified and intelligent woman for a wife and you can't maintain any such position surrounded by a lot of swearing, immoral and blackguarding vandals as these shows, most of them at least, are made up of and I won't stand for it. In short, I won't have it." She didn't answer because she didn't know how, so he went on, in a muttering tone now, more to himself than to her,

"Drinking, smoking weeds, swearing and running around backstage almost naked, and nobody caring, hunh! Pawing over stage hands and cheap white men, thinking they can do something for them when the man is hardly making enough to take care of himself. But they think that being a white man he can do something for them so start out to 'be nice' and persuade him to do so by pawing over them, inviting them to their homes, going to bed with them—crazy nuts."

Edrina glanced up, was glad that his eyes were down and that he didn't see her. She was a bit frightened now and realized that she had chosen a bad time to win him over and was sorry she had started out to, so soon. She was in a quandary as to what to do, how to turn. Presently she tried a new angle, which turned out to be just as bad.

"Mayl e you don't feel that I am good enough for you," she suggested. She said this with her eyes down on her plate but could see him raise his and look at her, felt it.

"You have everything I want in a wife, Edrina. You come of good people back there in Louisville. A friend of mine told me all about them; a friend who used to know you in Louisville. Said that you were considered a nice girl out there, that you had been raised well, and that you had fine intelligence. But since getting a little taste of the stage, you're stage-struck. You think you have something that the public wants. Maybe you have, but it's too long a gamble to find out through the medium of a turkey show. I said all along that I wanted your consent of your own volition, with the understanding that you'd be satisfied to be a housewife only. And that's what you promised of your own free will. Say what you may, feel as you may, but I didn't demand it; was careful not to. I'm sure you understood my sentiments, that any demand on my part might influence you, contrary to your wishes."

"I'm willing to be a good wife, Sidney. But I've got to tell you that I hate to see you so set against show people, that's all. They've never done anything to you, so—"

"All right, Edrina, all right," he said, cutting her off. "Since you feel as you do about it, supposing that we postpone our wedding awhile? Until you've made up your mind, definitely, just what you want to do. Let's wait. What do you say to that?" Before she could answer, for she had no answer then to make, he glanced at his watch and started.

"Good gracious," he cried. "We've been here, arguing for an hour and a half. I called your landlady and told her to wait, that I'd have you there an hour ago. She said that she was due to go out and we're imposing on her by being late." He called the waiter, paid their bill.

"Now let's go," he said, and without further words, rose to his feet, and together they left the place.

The next morning, around noon, at the hall where Mantan was rehearsing, assisted by Howard, Edrina put in her appearance. After greeting them and listening to compliments and kind words about her coming marriage, Edrina broached the question regarding a part for her. Howard didn't seem to understand what she was talking about and dismissed the question and proceeded to talk about something else. She resumed her question, this time insistently.

"I tell you, Edrina," said Donald, complainingly, "I didn't write any part in the show for you."

"But you can," she replied, insistently. "It's not too late yet."

Turning impatiently, he looked sharply at her.

"What about Wyeth? Aren't you supposed to be getting married to him very shortly? He doesn't want you in this show—any show. What about him?" She tried to ignore his question.

"Hasn't he bought you a divorce? The divorce you've been talking about getting for more than a year, but never had money enough to get?" Still Edrina made no answer. He went on, laying aside his other work and looking straight and hard at her.

"Hasn't he been sending you money, taking care of you all the while you were in Louisville? You wrote me that you bought a swell dress for your party with money he sent you? Who sent you money to come back to New York on? As I've told you, I didn't write any part in this little show for you, for I wasn't thinking about you in that regard. I thought I was giving you a chance to get a good man and a good home and security, and now, no sooner have you hit New York than here you come running, wanting to know about a part in this cheap show we're rehearsing. What kind of a game are you trying to play, anyhow?" he wanted to know, still looking hard at her. Turning to him at last and affecting tears with a dramatic gesture to fit, she held out her hands toward him:

"I love you, Donald. I've always loved you. I want to be in the show so that I can be near you, close to you."

Glaring at her with unbounded impatience, he swore:

"Well I'll be Goddammed!" and then sprang to his feet, boiling all over with anger. "I've doubted your honesty and sincerity all along, but I did think, at least hope, that you had a little sense."

She had risen, and now held her arms out to him appealingly.

"I love you, Donald. That is all I know. Please listen to me, dear. I want to be in the show so as to be near you all the time."

"Shut up!" he all but screamed, glaring at her, and brushed aside the hand she tried to lay on his arm. "You little fool, you Goddammed little fool! After all I've said, after all my pleadings, you turn out just as I feared all along. You Goddammed little fool," he cried and stamped his foot—he was that angry.

Shoving his hands deep into his pockets, he turned and walked away from her, across the room and stood by a window, looking outside at nothing, while he patted his toe on the floor impatiently. He stood there a moment, his back to her. Then as suddenly, he turned and walked back to where she now sat, and standing over her, he glared down at her and went on:

"So you've been playing Wyeth for a sucker, eh?"

"Oh, I'll marry him if you say so," she said, glancing up and shrugging her shoulders.

"Trying to make a fool of the man, hunh? But you're not fooling him, oh no! If he hasn't seen it already, he will quickly enough. He'll see right through your cheap little scheme to play him for a sucker. And when he understands what its all about, he'll throw you over—and hate you!" He paused a moment as if to let his words soak in, take effect. "Throw you right out on your can!"

"And remember that when he does, and the things that are going to result, happen, they're going to happen, not to him or anybody else, Edrina. They're going to happen to you, you God dammed little fool!" He turned his back on her and trembled with anger, as his foot played a tatoo on the floor. She was weeping now, pitifully.

"I'm not making a fool of myself, Donald, regardless of all you say. It's only that I love you, just love you, that's all." She finished and gave up to her tears now. He looked down at her without sympathy or feeling.

"Do I have to tell you again, after all the many times I've told you before, that I am not in love with you or any other woman? When a man loves a woman, the first thing he thinks about is to marry her. I've never asked you to marry me for the simple reason that I've never been in love with you, and for the second reason that I'm not a marrying man. So please, oh, please cut this 'I love you, Donald,' out, and never say it to me again. Even if I cared enough for you to consider marrying you and was a marrying sort of man, I wouldn't have you when I see what a cheap game you've been playing with one of the best men in show business. If you haven't any better sense than to play around with your bread and butter as you have in this case, what a dumbbell any man would be to trust and believe you. So go your little way from now on. I'm out of it and hope I'll see you so hungry that your tongue will be hanging out. A gal as crazy as you deserves nobody's sympathy and won't be getting it. If I run into Wyeth I'll tell him to quit fooling around with you; you haven't sense enough to treat anybody right, including yourself, you Goddammed fool." With this and another hard look at her, weeping now with face down, he turned and left the office, slamming the door behind him.

CHAPTER XVIII

IN SPITE OF DONALD HOWARD'S anger and swearing, Edrina continued to hang around the rehearsal hall, and finally caught Mantan in a charitable mood one day, and feeling agreeable toward all mankind, as well as obliging, he agreed to give her a part.

"Just a small part—in fact, a bit," he said, "But if you just must be on the stage, you can have it." After her thanks and tears, she wanted to know what kind of a part.

"A singing part, Edrina. I think it will be clever to have a nice girl in a cute dress, come out during the run of the show and sing a couple of nice, clean, popular songs."

"Oh, thank you, Mr. Mantan," she cried, gratefully, "thank you. I am sure it will be just what the show needs." She clasped her hands in an ecstasy of delight and joy and when she went to her room, was so happy until she decided to call on Sidney Wyeth at his room as quickly as the show opened, which was the following week. She hoped he'd go to see the show. It would be like him, she conjectured, to look in on it and when he saw her come quietly out on the stage in a nice, pretty dress and sing a nice, cute and pretty little song, maybe he wouldn't be so hard on her; maybe he would repent, take her in his arms, and set a date, or ask her when she was ready to marry him.

She waited until after the show had been running three nights before making the call, which she did one night after the finale.

He had retired and lay trying to read some of the manuscript he was at work on. She knocked so lightly, he was not certain if anybody was there. She repeated it and hearing him move, called: "Oh, Sidney. May I—come in?"

He recognized her voice, so got into his slippers and robe and crossing the room, opened the door. She was standing there, dressed in the suit and hat she had worn when she called on him at his office in the beginning; and when he had liked her so much. Maybe he might again, at least she hoped he would.

"Hello, dear," she cried, softly, and dared smile at him, sweetly.

"Hello, Edrina," he said, carelessly.

"Sorry to wake you up," she said, apologetically.

"I wasn't asleep," he said. "Come on in," and swung the door wider so that she could enter. She did and pausing, turned to face him after he closed the door.

"Now go right back to bed, you old farmer," she said, smiling up at him, so sweetly until for a fleeting moment, she reminded him of the time when he was most fond of her. He merely grunted, and turning, went on back to the bed and got into it, after stepping out of his slippers, and sat there to face her, his back propped against the pillows, with his robe still on. She sat down on the side of the bed to face him.

"They say you almost never stay up late."

For answer he grunted again.

"They say," she went on, "that you go to bed with the chickens."

He grunted a bit again for an answer.

"I'm not going to keep you up late, my farmer," and she laughed lightly, a little, forced laugh.

"Yes," he said, a bit grudgingly, she thought. "The farm is still with me. I guess it will never leave me. I still think of those days out west there on the Southwest of 29, dream of those old days, long for them, too. Yes, the farm is still in me, I guess it will never leave me."

"Especially when you won't let it," she said, chidingly. She had planned before calling, however, that she wouldn't argue with him about show people tonight, and accuse him of being against them. She had planned to steer entirely clear of this angle.

"I've quit trying," he was saying. "I guess it's because I like farming. I hated to give it up, but four dry years and four crop failures forced me to. I couldn't help it." Then turning to her in a changed tone. "Well, how do you like the new show?" she started, pretending to be surprised.

"How did you know that I was in it?"

"I saw it," he replied calmly.

"Oh, you did," she exclaimed, guardedly. Now was the great moment. Did he like it? What was he going to say about her part?

"Well, how'd you like it?"

"Oh, it seemd all right—I guess."

"You guess!" she repeated. "What do you mean by you guess? Is it because you—don't like shows?" There it was again. It just slipped out. She realized that in her eyes he stood convicted of hating show people. She was relieved when he didn't get angry or become impatient. All he did was to turn to her slightly and inquire:

"Who said I didn't like shows? I go to them right along."

"I'm surprised," she said, a bit sarcastically, but which seemed to be lost on him.

"You seem to have a distorted opinion when it comes to me and shows," he said.

"I don't altogether understand you at times, I admit," she replied.

"I'm all right," he said. "I thought you were very good in the little part you have."

That pleased her and she was encouraged to go on.

"Thank you, dear. Didn't you think the little part was nice and clean?"

"Oh, yes, but—" and he broke off, as if deciding after starting to say nothing further, not to finish it.

"But," she spoke up. "But, what, my dear?"

"Oh, nothing," he said and shrugged his shoulders to indicate that what he started to say had best be left unsaid.

"But you must have had something on your mind, then decided not to finish saying it. I'm curious to know what it is. Won't you finish it, please?"

Again he shrugged his shoulders and glanced at his manuscript.

"You admit the part is nice and clean."

"Yes, now."

"You're the strangest sort of person," she said complainingly. "What did you mean by now, anyhow?"

"That they often make changes in shows, quick changes. It all depends."

"You're baffling. I haven't the least idea what you're hinting at

What do you mean by quick changes?"

"That tomorrow you may be called on to do something else, something different, entirely different," he said.

She sighed.

"I'm stymied. This something else, you mention. Well, what, for instance?"

He glanced at her, then let his eyes run up and down her. She followed his gaze, then looked straight at him.

"What are you thinking?"

"That you have a nice form, attractive limbs, nice rounded breasts, Mantan might decide to make you one of his models, take your clothes off and display that body, most of it, anyhow. All of it, in fact, that the law will allow him to, and the law doesn't pay much attention to what the Negroes do in Harlem, so long as it isn't murder, and they don't take that over seriously, especially when the murder is confined to one Negro killing another."

"You're a crepe hanger. Why are you so hard to please?"

"There's nothing to please involved," he answered, matter-of-factly.

She was getting angry, and felt like saying something sharp.

"What I mean is that he's liable to change your nice little part to something not so nice, see?"

"Never!" she exclaimed, stoutly, sitting straight and fast.

"Let's hope not, but still he may, who knows?"

"He'll never take my clothes off," she said, indignantly, rising to her feet, posing, then turning, walked away a few steps and turning again, came back and resumed her seat on the side of the bed.

"He took his wife's off a long time ago. Why shouldn't he yours—if he thinks it'll help the show?"

"The next thing you'll say is that he'll be turning me over to a white man to play around with, to get the Fay man to put some money behind the show."

"No, I won't say that, because as long as I've known him, and I know he's been plenty hard up at times during those years, I've never heard of him selling any colored girl down the river to a white man. I'm not afraid that he'll do that."

"I still say he'll never take my clothes off and show my body. He's always going to keep me in nice, clean parts. I'm a nice girl with plenty of modesty and he knows it."

"They all had the same thing—until he decided to sweeeten up the show, pep it a bit, and nothing peps up a Negro show as much as naked girls. He has to play lots of midnight shows in white houses, and midnight shows mean hot shows, red hot and the more naked the show, the hotter, and better they like it."

"Nevertheless, he won't change my part. The people like nice songs sung by nice girls like me. All the people haven't filthy minds like you imply, so what if he does have the chorus girls display their bodies? I'm not a chorus girl."

"They won't care anything about those nice little songs you're singing. They'll want to look at something, and you have, under your clothes, what they might want to see."

"You're impossible."

"Think so?" he said and looked straight at her.

"What are you trying to get at, anyhow?" she said, her voice raised. He waved at her with his hand.

"You don't have to shout. I hear everything you say clearly."

"I'm sorry," she said, her voice lowered, "but you just seem to want to rub it in. And this to the girl you've promised to marry."

"You're a sweet child," he said, turning to look at her, pitifully, frankly. "And I'm sorry you're stage-struck. We might have been able to make a go of it, if it wasn't for that—in spite of the fact that you don't love me but do our boy, Donald."

"Leave him out of it, and say what's on your mind," she snapped complainingly.

"Okay, sister. It shall be as you wish. But I haven't anything particular on my mind. I was saying that people who go to midnight shows, and a very great many who go to see them regularly and right at the theatre you're playing in, want their stage entertainment, when it comes to a colored show, hot; as hot as Harlem is supposed to be. And if this idea pops into Mantan's head, or into Levine's, who operates the house, he'll strip-tease you. Before it's all over they're liable to take that nice little dress you're wearing clear off, with the slip under it along with it, and send you out there stripped clean, as naked as a jay bird's baby."

Jumping to her feet indignantly, as he finished, both angry and impatient, she glared at him, leaning over him a bit as she did.

"Sidney Wyeth," she cried out loudly, "how can you think such things much less express them in the way you're doing? I didn't think it of you. I'm surprised. You're just narrow-minded. To think that I'd stand for anything of the kind. You must be crazy!" And she posed over him impatiently, tapping her toe on the floor.

"Wait and see. I saw the show from the audience, not from in front of the footlights," he said, calmly, shrugging his shoulders and smiling tolerantly.

"Now what do you mean?"

"Sitting through it and forced to feel the reaction around me, I have the feeling there's going to be some changes made—and they might not be long in the making."

"You're utterly impossible!" she cried, stamping her little foot, and turned to walk up and down a few times, and then came back.

"And besides, would you stand for such a thing?"

He looked up at her quickly.

"Me?" he cried, pointing to himself. "What do you mean about what I'd stand for?"

"Why, as my husband do you mean to say that you'd let Irvin C. Mantan take my clothes off and parade me back and forth across that stage and display my body?"

"I wouldn't want him to, if I were your husband," he said.

"What do you mean now by you wouldn't want him to?" She sat down again and got as close as she could, leaned toward him a bit temptingly, and in a lower voice: "As your wife, Sidney, dear, my body would belong to you, only you, and not to the show or Irvin Mantan to parade for the benefit of those loud and noisy Negroes who attend the theatre." She leaned forward and before he could do anything, kissed him, tempting him almost beyond control, but he sat up quickly and coldly went on:

"But I'm not your husband, Edrina."

"But you're going to be, aren't you, Sidney?" she insisted, laying a hand on him gently, and looking up into his face appealingly. He took her hand and laid it gently aside.

She frowned at this, as if to say: "Why did you do that?" Instead she said, very soft and very low: "That's what I mean, Sidney."

His reply was prompt. He didn't hesitate.

"I'm sorry, Edrina. I was going to be your husband and wanted to badly. But you walked out on me, broke your promise and thereby our engagement. So the engagement is off. I release you from your promise." He finished coldy and formally. This chilled her, hurt her to the quick. Still she decided to keep on trying. So she reached again for his hand.

"But Sidney," she began, with great effort. She seemed to realize that it was now or never. For a fleeting moment he was again tempted. She looked so sweet and appealing; it would be so easy to reach out and take her in his arms, crush her to him and hold her there, hold her there and keep her there—all night! In the end, self-control came to his assistance, and he decided to pass it up, all of it, and go on being as he had been all his life.

"You broke the agreement, Edrina, not me. You threw me over and went back into the show. You're free from now on as far as I'm concerned. So it's up to you to manage matters your way and take the consequences."

'But Sidney," she cried, squeezing his hand and fondling it. "You love me. I can see it in your eyes and you want me, I can see that in your eyes, too. Why struggle against fate as you are; you've fought against it all along, and why? I'm yours for the asking— more, for the taking . . . Why don't you—take me, Sidney." She tried to get him into a position so she could kiss him, but he kept away from her.

"If you were in love with me when I—went back into the show, you're still in love with me now. You couldn't put me out of your heart that quickly. Going back into the show and into a nice little part like they've given me, couldn't change your love to hate, now could it, Sidney?"

"I don't hate you, Edrina, on the contrary, I feel sorry for you, and you're going to feel sorry for yourself before it's all over."

"Why do you say that? Sidney."

"I don't know right now, but I feel it; I feel something, something that's going to happen real soon, and when it happens, it's going to happen to you." She sat erect, the words bearing down on her. Donald *had said those same words.* "When it happens, it's going to happen to you." Angered suddenly, she sprang to her feet.

"*It isn't going to happen*—not to me, anyhow." She now turned and walked the floor. He looked at her sadly, as though he pitied her and that made her more angry.

"It won't happen to me, because I won't let it happen to me, that's what! I won't let it happen to me. Donald said those same words to me when I called on him to put me back in the show. He was angry and swore at me because I came back. He said I should have stayed away and married you, been nice to you, and—"

"—what else did he say to you, Edrina?" he inquired, looking straight at her. "What did you say to him to make him angry, so angry that he swore at you?"

She paused, suddenly taken aback, caught off guard and couldn't answer, or didn't dare answer. But he read the answer in her face, in the way she hesitated.

"You went to him and told him that you loved him, didn't you, Edrina, which meant that you didn't love me, now isn't that so? You told him that you loved him and wanted to be in the show so that you could be near him, close to him all the time, but he didn't see it the same way. To be near him would be to be on him when things got tough, and he didn't want that; he wouldn't stand for that. He knew you didn't love me and I knew it, too, but was willing to marry you in spite of that and take a chance. I was going to marry you and take the chance and hope for the best. But you kicked that over and rushed to Howard, who didn't want you on him and chastised you for the way you were acting, and in the end I bet he walked out on you, now didn't he?"

She made no answer and turned her face away. He put his feet on the floor now, got into his slippers and stood up. Walked over to her and being much taller, towered over her as he went on.

"Then you went over his head. You saw Mantan and caught him in a good mood. Mantan has more heart than Howard. He felt sorry for you and he created a little part and put you in it. The kind of part you wanted, a nice little part in which you're allowed to wear a cute little dress, look cute and sing two nice little songs. That done, you waited until you were sure I'd seen it, then you came here and felt that I wouldn't be so hard; that I'd changed my mind about your being in a show in general, and you've played your cards carefully. Offered me everything, more than I asked for, yes, I know. All very tempting, Edrina, and if I wasn't the kind of fool I am, God help me, I couldn't have resisted you. Unfortunately, you're a poor judge of men, real men, Edrina, for real men stand for something. Even if I had accepted you, took your clothes off and kept you here all night, it wouldn't have lasted. Real men have principle, they stand for something, and what they stand for cannot be appeased by a woman throwing herself at them. I could have had you from the beginning, and maybe I've been a fool for not taking you. But I wanted a wife to love and respect and live with until I die, and to do that I had to choose a woman that I could respect and trust. You've proved in the final analysis that I couldn't trust you. Just as you've tried to tempt me by offering me your body just now, and before, for that matter. Sometime, some place and somewhere, you'd give it to somebody else to tempt and if you'd been my wife, it wouldn't have made any difference. That's what I mean, Edrina. I guess you'll hate me from now on, but your ideas of life and men, my kind of a man, anyhow, has been all wrong, and you might as well know it now as to find it out later, after we got married for if we had, it wouldn't have lasted. We're just not suited to each other, and that, Edrina, is that. I'm sorry." So saying, he sat down on the side of the bed and lowered his eyes.

She stood there for a time. Presently she turned to look at him and sighed. Then she walked slowly toward the door. He got to his feet and followed her. At the door she paused and turned to look up into his face. There were tears in her eyes and again he felt sorry for her.

"And this—this means that—it is all—over between us, Sidney?" she said. He sadly nodded his head.

"I'm afraid that it does," he replied in a low voice.

"And—an—you—don't love me any more, Sidney?"

"It isn't a question of love, Edrina."

"Then what is it, Sidney?"

"A question of policy."

"Policy?"

"Yes, Edrina. Policy and—principle."

"Principle?"

"Yes, Edrina, as I've said over and over again. A man has to stand for something, and a woman ought to, also. You see, before you went on the stage you would have understood all this and you would have appreciated it and agreed with it. But your stage ambitions have warped your viewpoint. In a way, being on the stage would not matter all that. But the way you are, does. And you can't see any other way. It is possible that somebody might cast a big show, a big Broadway production and they might want you for a real part, and in which you might get somewhere by playing. And then again you might be left in the kind of show you are in indefinitely, subject to all the influences that go with it, and I don't want any girl I marry in any such environment, subject to temptations, and that is why it is best, much for the best, that we end it here and now and go our own ways."

"And you—you're not going to—be sorry, Sidney?"

"More than sorry, Edrina. It would be easier to go along with you, for you have so much that could mean lots to me, but in the end you'd drag both of us down and neither would be successful or happy. I'm not going to be sorry, I'm already sorry. It isn't easy for me to send you away, but I've got lots that I want to try to do before I die. In the end I must try to do these things, otherwise I'd feel that I've lived in vain. I'm sorry, Edrina. This is going to make me most unhappy, but there is no other way. Good night."

"Good night, Sidney." He opened the door and she took a step, then turned to look again up into his eyes and again he was sorry for her. He leaned over and kissed her, and she grasped and held on to him until he repeated it three times, then with a sob she rushed out into the night, and he closed the door behind her.

CHAPTER XIX

MANTAN'S NEW SHOW did a satisfactory business the first week, although nothing sensational, and, since there was nothing around to replace it with, Levine, the theatre manager and operator, decided to hold it a second week. The second week got off to a bad start, however, and threatened to slump so badly after the first day, that Levine, becoming anxious, called Mantan into his small office back stage for an urgent conference.

"The show is dying on its feet, Mantan," he declared, "and unless you can find some way to pep it up, and have it hot by Sunday, otherwise we'll be so dead by Monday, that we might as well close until we can get a new show, which I can't bring in before Thursday." Mantan was expecting Levine to squawk; he was an old showman and knew that it was a mistake to try to hold it over for a second week, but a second week meant he wouldn't have to move his people, and that was something worth gambling a second week for.

"Well, what's on your mind, Mr. Levine?" He knew that Levine had been thinking up and planning changes.

"Changes, Irvin."

"Changes?" he repeated, not letting on that he had been expecting such a demand.

"Yes, Irvin, some changes, quick and radical changes."

"I see," mused Irvin, thoughtfully. Then turning to Levine, "what changes do you suggest, Mr. Levine?"

"Well," began Levine slowly, eyes on his desk a moment, but as if he had watched the show and noting its weaker spots, had checked them and made pencil notes and was now looking at them. "That Edrina girl's act is one. Those two little songs she's singing, don't mean a thing," There it was! What Mantan was expecting. He'd been afraid for Edrina all along, and now with her checked as the first change, he was visibly annoyed. He had tried to please her, and because he had a reputation for being big-hearted, created the bit and which had pleased her to do so much until he was happy to think that he had made an ambitious, stage-struck girl happy, too. Yet, as a showman, he knew as well as Levine that for the theatre's kind of audiences, the bit didn't mean a thing. Levine was talking again and Mantan, of course, was forced to listen.

"No, her entire part in the show doesn't mean a thing."

"You don't think so?"

"I know it doesn't," argued Levine emphatically. Then, as if possessed by a sudden thought, he turned to Irvin and looked hard at him through the large rimmed glasses he was wearing.

"Can she dance?"

Irvin hesitated, then lied:

"A little."

"M-m. I notice that she has a nice body."

Irvin wondered what he was thinking. He didn't have to wait long for he turned to him in his quick and abrupt way.

"Then take off her clothes and have her do a jungle romp."

Irvin started. That was not only a radical but an abrupt change. He wondered if it was not an impossible change. Through Irvin's mind there quickly ran the recollection that no girl ever worked at this theatre who possessed a nice body, that Levine didn't, before the end of the engagement, suggest displaying that body, unless hers was an act so sensational otherwise that merely displaying her body wouldn't mean as much. Inwardly, therefore, he sighed. Edrina's body, stripped, therefore, was to Levine's mind more attractive than the little songs she was singing.

"Hasn't she a pretty body?" said Levine, turning to him. "Don't you think so?" Irvin had to admit that she had.

"Then let's sell it," cried Levine, and that, Irvin knew, was final.

It was curtains for Edrina's little act; the end of leisurely strolling across the stage, holding her hands and squeaking the two songs which she thought were getting over in a big way. As we see, Levine didn't think so.

"You can teach her the routine in a day and a night," said Levine. "Then have her ready to open Sunday in the change. That's the deadline. If we give them a good hot show Sunday, it might enable us to do some business after that, including Sunday, for the rest of the week."

Levine ran down the list and told him about the other changes, at the end of which time, he turned again to Irvin, who spoke first.

"How many shows have you planned for Sunday?" he asked Levine.

"If you're able to whip her into the act as I have it in mind and it is good and hot, six." Levine answered thoughtfully, as he rechecked the whole thing in his mind.

"Whew!"

"It's because the show is dying—in fact dead already. If you've whipped this girl's change into a hot, wiggly and twisty rhumba, with a jungle background and music in keeping with the performance until they like it, it will take two shows to sell it. You know as well as I do that if they like it, they can sell the last four, and will, as they leave the theatre."

"Guess you're right, Mr. Levine," sighed Irvin.

"I know I'm right, so it's up to you. You won't have enough coming as your share to give them a token payment at the end of the week, much less a full payment, unless you do something to bring them in this theatre, starting Sunday."

Irvin left the office and strolled to where he encountered Howard, looking glum and unhappy. Howard knew the show was dying, too, and always short of money, he knew that he wouldn't get much or anything at the end of the engagement, and that was why he was looking glum and feeling more glum than he looked. He looked at Irvin and read the annoyance in his face.

"Well?"

"Levine's squawking."

"I was afraid he would be. Been waiting for it."

"Yeh, howling his head off so has ordered changes."

"Been expecting it. Go on," said Howard, listening.

"Call rehearsals after the show."

"Okeh, Irv."

"We'll rehearse all night tonight."

"Okeh, boss." Irvin turned then and left Howard, went to look for Edrina, to tell her the bad news. He knew it would break her heart, and he hated to have to do it. Then consoling himself with the words "show business," shrugged his shoulders, braced himself for the ordeal. Added to this, he could tell her that it was Levine's orders, and Levine was the payoff. It had to be done. So with a deep sigh, he sought Edrina and found her happy and serene in her dressing room. Performers like her, could never see that a show was dying. If the three front rows were filled, they'd say "we're knocking them dead" and all the empty seats behind the first rows wouldn't mean a thing to them. He knocked lightly on her door. He didn't have the heart to do so briskly or loudly.

"Come in," she called in a sweet voice, and turned to greet him with a smile as he pushed the door open and entered, eyes downcast, but she didn't notice that.

"Oh, Mr. Mantan," she cried, on seeing that it was he. "You!" and she was glad to see him. She guessed that his visit was about herself right quick. It was to tell her that the songs were getting over big; that the audience were raving about her. That would sound nice to her pretty ears, so she turned to welcome him and the message he was bringing.

"Yes, me, Edrina," he said in a tired voice and sank onto the chair she offered. She stood near and waited, wearing her best smile as she did so. He glanced up at her, and she was looking so innocent and happy that he groaned, inwardly. "How could he do it," then decided to prolong telling her as long as possible—a few minutes anyway.

"You wanted to see me, Mr. Mantan," she ventured, after he failed to explode the news she was expecting; that she was waiting for. In that moment he realized that he could prolong it a few minutes longer. She looked so comfortable and happy with the two dresses she was wearing in her act, spread out and perfumed, making everything seem so sweet and pleasant.

"Yes, Edrina," he dodged. "In my office." The office where he had just left Levine was a general sort of office for the stage manager, the show manager, and Levine when he was back stage. He sighed. So Irvin called it for this occasion, 'his office.' He supposed he could, perhaps be a little more official telling her there than in her cozy little dressing room, where she could burst more easily into tears when she heard what he had to say, than in the little, cold, manager's office.

"Thank you, Mr. Mantan," she said sweetly. She was wondering now. Maybe he was calling her there to tell her that her act was going over so big that he felt it warranted a raise in pay.

"Soon?" she asked. He had risen to his feet and opened the door. He turned back to her now, and replied:

"Yes, soon, Edrina," and then left before she could see that his eyes were deeply troubled. He heard her say, "Thank you, Mr. Mantan," as he hurried away to the little office.

After primping herself, powdering her nose and making her face look a bit prettier, Edrina called at the little office and knocked on the door. Another girl in the show was coming toward the office and as Edrina knocked on the door, she looked up and saw her, and smiled when she realized she'd beat the other girl to Mr. Mantan. She was still smiling as she opened the door and entered Mantan's office.

Knowing that it was her, he pretended to be busy, didn't look up, but called over his shoulder for her to come in and kept at what he was pretending to do without looking up.

"Sit down, please," he said, taking on his most serious and business-like expression, "I'll be with you in a couple of minutes."

"Thank you," she said, and obeyed him, sitting down in the only other chair in the room, which happened to face him when he dared look up, which, of course, he had to after a few seconds. Presently he raised his eyes and faced her.

"Levine's kicking," he said, abruptly. She started, not understanding at first, what he meant. She only knew by his expression that it was not to raise her salary. She swallowed a moment, then managed to say:

"Kicking?" breathed deep and looked surprised.

"Yes, kicking—and how!"

"I—I—don't understand," she said.

"The show's dying, if you understand what that means." Still, she was confused, so repeated after him:

"Dying?"

"Dying dead. So, he demands changes" . . . . . and lowered his eyes to the piece of paper on which he had been figuring.

"Changes?" she said, and met his eyes when he raised them from the desk.

"Yes," said Mantan coldly. He had complete control now and was ready to dish out the bad news, regardless of what effect it had on her. "Yes, changes, and your act is the first change he's suggested."

Her heart fell. Quickly she recalled Wyeth's words at his room a night or so before. "They make quick changes in those kind of shows. You're doing something today. They might ask you to do something entirely different tomorrow," he had said, among other things. She had decried the idea, insisted that they would not change her act. She was sure the people liked it, so how dare they even suggest changing it? She heard herself faintly.

"My act," she managed to say with an effort.

"He didn't mean mine," said Mantan. "I'm not a pretty girl like you." He looked her up and down now, and she followed his eyes and wondered what he was thinking, what he was planning.

"Yes," Irvin was saying, without looking into her eyes. "You have a fine, rounded and attractive form, Edrina. Can't say as I had ever noticed it as closely before," and he continued to study the lines of it as he watched her.

"You said something about my act," she reminded him and he came back to himself, and looked up, smiled, then quickly got serious again.

"Yes, so I did," he now said hastily. "Well, he wants you to take your clothes off and do a jungle romp."

She started, violently, all her pride and ego gone completely.

"A what?" she cried, looking hard at him. She refused to believe at the moment that he meant what he said. "A jungle romp, and I'm to take my clothes off? Oh, Mr. Mantan, you're joking, surely."

He answered by shaking his head to indicate that he wasn't.

"I—I don't understand," she said, chokingly.

"It's Levine's orders. He's the payoff, you know," he said coldly.

"What—what is a jungle romp, anyhow?" she asked.

He smiled tolerantly.

"Well, it's a creation, or a creative dance," he started to explain.

"But I'm not a dancer, Mr. Mantan, you know that," she said insistently.

"He asked me to make you one."

"Make me one?" she exclaimed. "How can you or anybody else make a dancer overnight. I—"

"It isn't exactly an interpretive dance. That is, it is a combination dig-a-dig-a-do, a shake dance and rhumba."

"Oh, Mr. Mantan, no!" she cried, near panic now.

For answer he only shrugged his shoulders resignedly.

"It's Levine's orders. And, I repeat, he's the payoff, you know," and he shrugged his shoulders again.

"But he surely couldn't have meant me, Mr. Mantan. I—I thought what I am doing was—all right; I thought it was getting over fine."

"That's what *you* thought, Edrina. I'm sorry, but it wasn't. These Harlem Negroes don't care anything about nice, clean songs."

"But you know I can't dance, Mr. Mantan, never tried to dance a lick in my life."

"As I started to explain," he said, leaning forward. "You don't have to exactly know how to dance for you do not exactly dance. I can teach you what he wants you to do. The main thing is to keep moving and to wear as few clothes as is possible. In fact, you will not have on anything but a sort of—a little something down there," and he pointed to her midsection.

"Oh, My God!" she exclaimed, and again she thought about what Sidney Wyeth had warned her that they might do. There were tears in her eyes now, and, looking at her, Mantan felt sorry.

Back in Nashville where he was born and attended school, his father, long since dead, had been a preacher and a school teacher, while his mother, still living, had been the principal of a large Negro grade school. They were, he could never forget, stickers as regards morality, and although the show business had forced him to strip many ambitious girls of their modesty, he had never gotten fully used to it. So it pained him to see Edrina sitting there with tears running down her cheeks.

"What do you mean by 'I won't have to exactly dance,'" she wanted to know now, looking so pitiful and distressed.

Again he shrugged his shoulders.

"Mostly shaking," he said and shook his shoulders. At last she understood. She was to strip virtually naked, get out there and wiggle and shake and do the hootchi ma kooch.

"Oh," she cried in horror, and covered her eyes with her kerchief and cried bitterly.

"A shake dance," she sobbed, without even the benefit of a skirt. "A shake dance," she got up and tried to look at him through tear-filled eyes. "Oh, Mr. Mantan, how can you, how can you!" and she lowered her face and covered her eyes.

"Now, now, Edrina," he said kindly. "Don't take it so hard, and above all, don't put it on me.

"Then on whom?" she looked at him sobbingly.

"Levine. I told you that it was Levine's orders."

"A shake dance, oh, Mr. Mantan, no. Please say that I don't have to—to get out there and try to please all those Negroes, by wiggling and twisting like a kooch dancer."

Mantan was annoyed.

"I can't defy Levine, and neither can you or any of us." If you disobey him, he'll swear not to use any of us on the stage of his theatre again. It is the only spot where we can work in Harlem, almost the only place where we can work in New York, short of Broadway, and Broadway is a long way from us. You know I can't afford to have him say that to me." Seeming to realize further crying was useless, she sat up, dried her tears, and after a moment's thought, again turned to him.

"And if I refuse," she dared ask.

He shrugged his shoulders and replied promptly.

"Well, that would be one way out, the only way. But you'd just be out of the show, that's all."

She again lowered her eyes and again began to cry.

"I can, of course, and as you know full well, get a gang of girls to do it, but he suggested you, so if you want to stay in the show, there is no other alternative."

Edrina knew that Harlem was overrun with girls specializing in the 'shake'.

"I'm sorry for you, Edrina," he said, sincerely. "I heard you were engaged to marry Sidney Wyeth, and I was hoping that you would do so, and quit fooling around with these shows. There's nothing to them any more. Wyeth would have made you a good husband, for he is steady, is a good business man and would have stood between you and that old wolf that howls outside. But he wouldn't have you as long as you insisted on messing around with the stage. On the other hand, if you just *had* to be seen, he would have considered you, I'm sure, for a role in pictures. That would have been much better. Then when you were not working in pictures, you could have been in a nice apartment with no worry about pay days and skip-pay days. If we can't bring more **people into the** theatre right quick to see this show, we won't be able to pay off when we close. So he figures as to how with you doing this jungle romp and the other changes that he's suggested, that that will pep things up and bring the darkies in, starting Sunday, and if it does, we'll all get some money when we close. So what do you say?" and he slapped his thigh in a gesture of finality.

She sighed deeply, then nodded her head sadly, in assent. He started to get up, then thinking of something, sat down again.

"What has happened with your engagement to him, anyhow? I mean to Wyeth?"

"Nothing," she said quietly.

"Nothing?" he repeated, and looked closely at her. "Aw come now. Something did happen. I'd bet. What was it? You can tell me."

"There's nothing to tell," she repeated, evenly, her eyes away. "I saw Sidney last night."

"You did?" he cried, and seemed surprised. "He didn't want you in this show, did he?"

She admitted with a shake of her head.

"I was hoping by having the nice little part I've been playing that—"

"—yes, yes, I understand," he said, cutting her off. "You were hoping by doing a nice, mild little part that he'd relax and everything would be all right. Well, it didn't work and I know Wyeth. He has never had any confidence in these shows even when they had places to play, plenty of places. He used to tell me that they would play out. Then, when talking pictures came along, he said they were through, completely; but there would still be Broadway shows, big, gorgeous and expensive productions and some times dirty shows, too filthy to be allowed on the screen, but little shows like this, they were through. Now he's quit you. Being a woman, you won't admit this, but I can see that that is what happened. I was afraid it would happen when you started to hang around the rehearsal hall. You like the stage and are wedded to the idea, but he knows too much about it to want you in it, or any other show of the kind. So he gave you your choice, the show or him. You cut the hog by choosing the stage, but hoped to win him back, maybe and that's why you went to see him last night, not knowing that this was going to happen today."

He was through now and stood up. She remained seated and he

knew that she would stay in the show and try to do the part. Again he was sorry for her. It was now or never, and he gave her one last chance.

"Well, I'm sorry. If you think Wyeth might still relent and marry you, don't take this part. Quit the show and go and tell him. If he still says no, just hang around, be nice and in time he'll get sorry and take you back. If, on the other hand, you take the part, get ready to rehearse all night tonight and all night tomorrow night, then count it over, for when he hears about and sees you out there, almost naked, shaking and twisting your body, he will be through and put you out of his life forever." He paused and looked down at her as if to give her time to decide. Then, after a time.

"Well?"

"I'll be at rehearsal tonight," she said, without looking at him, but rising to her feet, walked by him on the way out.

He shrugged his shoulders, stepped outside, turned and closed the office door and went the other way. As he did so the girl who came up as Edrina entered, bit her lip, stamped her foot, and swore in an undertone. She wanted to talk with Mantan, but he was so worried about Edrina that he forgot and ignored her. She had heard the conversation between Edrina and him.

She was thinking about what they had said as she turned and walked away.

CHAPTER **XX**

BERTHA SCHULTZ stopped by the office next morning, observed that Wyeth's office door was open and knew by this time that he was out and gone. If and when he was in, it was always closed, so she greeted Marie, with a kiss, they had become that intimate and friendly.

"I've got hundreds of books to ship, dear," said Marie, flashing a sheaf of orders under Bertha's eyes. "Since *Passion* was published, the Negroes, anxious to read it, were told they could get it at bookstores, and when they went there, our book suggested itself to them and they've been placing orders, which come in small lots through stores, but still more directly from the customers themselves. So we're simply swamped with demands for it."

"That's fine," said Bertha. "And—"

"I have to wrap all these books, make out C.O.D.'s on a large share, which means a lot of work to get them in the mail. So that—"

"—is why you are swamped with work, eh?"

"Exactly," said Marie and sighed.

"Then, dear, let me help you," she said and proceeded to take off her coat preparatory to doing so.

"Oh, really, Bertha," cried Marie. "I didn't mean that when I complained."

"I'm going to help you, dear," insisted Bertha. "And I'll be glad to. You know, Marie, in Germany the women work, all Germans work and they don't dislike it. Everybody is raised and taught from childhood to work. That is why German people are so—aggressive, I think they call it. I'll be glad to help you. This kind of work is letting me get soft, and I'm glad to do some real work. So tell me what you want me to do," with which she made a gesture of impatience, and Marie could see that she meant to help.

"But the pay, I—"

"Who said anything about pay?" said Bertha. "I'll perhaps learn something about the book business which will be beneficial. So come on, say what I am to do," and she impatiently snapped her fingers.

"Well," said Marie, "if you just must."

"Just must is the word," said Bertha with decision. "Just must and I must, so let's go on from here," Marie laughed and patted her kindly.

"Oh, Bertha, you're a darling girl and I love you," and Marie placed her arm about her and embraced her. "I'm sure everybody must like you."

"And I like you, too, Marie. I think you're the finest girl I ever met; that I ever knew," cried Bertha, squeezing her. "In the meantime, when Mr. Wyeth comes back, he'll be cheered if all the orders have been filled, so let's get busy."

"He will that," said Marie. "Now, since you insist on helping, we'd best go back in the stock room where we keep the books and start from there."

"Then," said Bertha, "It is to the stock room we go," and she turned in that direction. Marie placed an arm about her and they went back to the stock room where they worked without pause until noon. They went downstairs then to a restaurant, chose a booth and sat across from each other.

"Now I guess we can do some talking," said Bertha.

"About what, for instance"

"Mr. Wyeth, the boss," said Bertha.

"Oh," cried Marie, and smiled. "Well, what do you think of him by now, since you've met and talked with him?"

"Oh, fine," said Bertha, smiling and looking the part.

"He is a nice fellow, isn't he?" said Marie.

"More than a nice fellow," said Bertha, enthusiastically. "A fine fellow."

"It's me that knows." Then she paused and frowned.

"What's the matter?" said Bertha, looking at her concernedly.

"I'm worried about him," said Marie, and her frown deepened.

"And why?"

"That girl?"

"Oh, the girl. How do they seem to be getting along?" said Bertha.

"I'm not sure. She's back in town—and in the show on 125th St."

"So what?"

"It isn't what he should have done. Getting mixed up with a show girl, getting himself engaged to one. It isn't going to work out."

"Now, now, Marie," said Bertha, "you shouldn't take it that way. I'm sure Mr. Wyeth must know what he is doing. I think you should trust him and leave it to him to do the sensible thing."

"Maybe all of us have to make some kind of a mistake sooner or later, but for Mr. Wyeth to make the one he seems about to make, is more than I can stand and just not say anything about it."

"I'm so sorry," said Bertha sympathetically. "Tell me more about it."

"There isn't much for me to tell," said Marie. "It is of course his affair and in everything since I've known him he's been so level-headed and has made so few mistakes—never one like this, that I don't know what to do, what to say." and she frowned and took a sip of water as if to drown it.

"Where is the girl now?"

"In that show on 125th Street."

"Oh, I thought she was in Louisville," said Bertha.

"She returned a few days ago, and is doing a turn in the show down there this week."

"I'd like to see her."

"I'm planning to take you to see the show. There's something I want to find out about her first."

"Oh?"

"Mr. Wyeth is not the kind of a man that a show girl would be falling overly much in love with."

"What do you mean?" inquired Bertha.

"That girls like her usually go all overboard on some good-looker like Thompson, you remember, and who used to work for us."

"Yes? Of course I remember the fellow Thompson. Seemed very much in love with himself. So that's the kind they usually fall for, as you put it?"

"That kind or a musician. Just one thing is sure about the kind of men they fall in love with. He must be no good," she finished and Bertha laughed.

"I mean it," insisted Marie seriously. "It is hardly within their capacity to love a good man, for a good man would not indulge them in a lot of illusions."

"Illusions, eh?" and Bertha laughed again.

"Illusions are right. They'd want somebody, when they are stage crazy, to tell them that they were going to put them on Broadway, or book them for 40 weeks over one of the big vaudeville circuits. Mr. Wyeth, you see, would not tell her anything like that. He never has told any of the girls he used to work in pictures any tales about going places.

"Most of them want to be fooled; they want somebody to tell them that after they've appeared in this picture, or that picture, and do just as they tell them to, they'll get a seven year contract in Hollywood and be flown out there in due time. I've heard him tell them repeatedly. 'Listen. This is just a colored picture, to be shown in a few hundred theatres, mostly to colored people. We are giving you so much and so much to work in it, but please don't get the idea that it's going to be shown on Broadway, or that a big fat contract to go to Hollywood is going to follow. They don't know anything about us in Hollywood, and would not care if they did. So if you're satisfied to work for the sum we agree to pay you, do your work well and should you happen to stand out in the scenes when we screen the rushes, we'll play you up in the trailer and on the posters as best we can, which in the end isn't much.' All of which, wouldn't make him appeal so much to her. Besides, he's just a plain man, and stage girls don't go overboard for plain men, either."

"She's probably calculated that he has money, and that, as you see, could interest her," suggested Bertha.

"It could and should, although Mr. Wyeth has no big money. But if that's what she's playing for, she'll fall down on the job. Our women don't know how to treat or play up to a man who could and might be willing to help them. They set out to play that kind for a sucker and give the money they get to men like Thompson."

"I'm learning things," smiled Bertha.

Marie laughed.

"What's become of this fellow, Thompson, anyhow?"

"Oh, cried Marie, suddenly. "I knew there was something I wanted to tell you. Well, old tall, dark and handsome got hooked."

"Hooked?" inquired Bertha, and Marie laughed as she saw

Bertha didn't understand.

"I shouldn't use so much slang, especially when talking to you. They didn't teach you American slang in Heidelberg or at the Sorbonne. But getting back to Thompson. The teacher took him to Richmond and married him."

"Oh, really," cried Bertha.

"She did exactly that."

"Tell me all about it," cried Bertha, anxiously, smiling.

"Well, it started when he met her in Baltimore, when he drove Mr. Wyeth down there and around to the schools where Mr. Wyeth reviewed his book and would then sell it. He developed it into a nice business, and took Thompson along to assist him."

"Assist him, eh?" said Bertha. "Did he make a good assistant?"

"Naw," cried Marie disgustedly.

"No?"

"Positively not. Mr. Wyeth couldn't interest him in learning or trying to learn anything about it. But since most schools are filled with young lady teachers, and Thompson was tall, dark and handsome, with pretty, slick black hair, all he needed to do was to make a play for the teachers, many of whom would make a play back for his benefit and that was how it all started."

"In Baltimore?"

"In Baltimore," said Marie. "He met this particular teacher one afternoon while Mr. Wyeth was reviewing his book at a school, made goo goo eyes at her, and she goo-gooed back at him. He met her that night and it got started.

"After Mr. Wyeth finished his campaign in Baltimore, he sent Thompson back to complete deliveries, and while there he ran into this teacher again. She was about ten years older than he, had been married three times, and was seasoned in the art of inveigling men, so he told me."

"But, ten years older than he, why would he—"

"—I'm coming to that. Why would he play around with a woman ten years older than himself, is what you were going to say. Well, you see, Thompson had a habit of getting a few dollars from girls when matters could be so organized."

"Oh, I see," said Bertha. "He was one of *those* kind of men."

"Not altogether so. Wasn't smart enough. Thompson didn't have a lot of brains, and the kind of men you're thinking about have to have a lot of sense—of a kind, do you understand?"

"Yes, I understand," agreed Bertha.

"Thompson, as I explained, didn't have that much sense; but since Mr. Wyeth couldn't get him interested in what he was doing, and he was around with him meeting these teachers, and being admired by them, and being in the love making business and needing more money, he had long since made a practice of giving them a long pitiful story about his boyhood."

"His boyhood?"

"He was a timid sort of boy, he'd tell them and would cry easily, and while young, as many children do, with a weak bladder until they grow older, would wet the bed and his father, a hard-up farmer in the dust bowl section of the West, where farmers more or less had a hard time, would punish him for it."

"Oh, that was unkind and thoughtless," cried Bertha.

Marie smiled and pointed at her. Bertha didn't seem to understand.

"That was how it worked," said Marie. "You see, when I told you about it, you felt sorry for him."

Bertha laughed.

"And that was how and why these girls would feel sorry for him, want to sort of mother him and take on over him and when he saw they were *taken,* he'd *take* them for a few dollars through some bad luck tale. He did it so much and for so long that it possessed him; he wasn't happy or satisfied unless he was at least trying to work it. Well, he got acquainted with this teacher. Thompson, I know, had about despaired of making good on his own, so had a vision of marrying some rich woman and in that way, getting along. But he had no realization of what wealth was exactly or what it meant. This teacher's mother, however, was buying a home, and they lived in it, and her grandmother owned another, at least was supposed to and after going out with Thompson and getting his number, this teacher, as stated, ten years older, and vain and liking young men, especially good looking ones, decided to take him for a husband, and started out to play her cards accordingly. When Mr. Wyeth sent Thompson back to Baltimore to complete these deliveries, she had a chance to play her cards, for when he got back here, he told me what he did. He told her he was a bit hard up and looked sad. She stroked his pretty dark hair over his round head, and handed him $5.00."

"Five dollars."

"Yes, five dollars."

"And finally got him for a husband?"

"For a five dollar bill," said Marie.

Bertha burst into laughter.

"Yes," said Marie, "she ultimately got him for a five dollar bill. She had married three times before in Baltimore and the fact was the subject of much gossip. One of the three men, a very bright one, she married twice. So when she got ready to marry Thompson, she took him off to Richmond, over to a little river town nearby and there married him."

"And that is why I haven't been seeing him around the office of late," said Bertha.

"She put him to work, real, hard work, out at Sparrow Point, Maryland, that's what she did, and he hasn't been up here but once since, which was the time you met him."

"Meanwhile, you've gotten entirely away from Mr. Wyeth's romance. I'm interested in hearing more about him and this—show girl, you were talking about," said Bertha.

"Of course," said Marie. "I guess you think I'm such a gossip."

"You're a woman," said Bertha and smiled understandingly.

Both laughed then.

"As regards Mr. Wyeth and this show girl," and Marie let escape a sort of hopeless sigh. "I don't know how to feel. I've always hoped Mr. Wyeth would meet the right kind of girl and make a sensible and happy marriage, but I can't see this tie-up, can't see it at all. I've hoped he'd get a good wife for several reasons."

"Among which, for instance?"

"That he's on the road to real success at last. As simple and as insignificant as it may seem, his publishing business is the most promising thing he has ever done."

"Is that so?" said Bertha seriously.

"It is. His friends think he's all through because he has suspended making pictures, but he's doing far better, for himself, in the present business than he ever did in making pictures."

"Seriously?" said Bertha, thoughtfully.

"Seriously, and I know."

"You should," said Bertha.

"I've been closer to him in both lines than any other person, and I'm in a position to see and know what's going on, and he's on the road to go places, writing and publishing his own books and selling those by others, the kind that best appeal to our group, at the same time.

"By which, you see, if he had a nice, sensible girl, like—like you, Bertha, for instance."

"Oh, not me, Marie," and Bertha blushed beautifully.

"I know, I said something like that before, but I didn't mean you exactly, Bertha. I did, however, mean a girl like you. Why, with a smart wife by his side, if no more than to let him keep his mind on what he's trying to do, nothing but death or serious illness could stop him."

"I do hope he'll get the right kind of wife," said Bertha sincerely.

"That is why I'm so annoyed by his taking up with this show girl. I get mad almost every time I think about it." Bertha had become suddenly and strangely silent, and Marie looked at her.

Seeing that she was preoccupied, Marie said nothing. But Bertha was thinking. Thinking of her brother, of Adolf Hitler, and what she had come to this country, promising to do; of how she had sworn to first serve the Third Reich; that even now she was supposed to be at work on Sidney Wyeth, helping to interest and ultimately persuade him into making the hate picture, the first schedule on their program. And, instead, she was seated in a common restaurant high up in black Harlem, talking about nothing, as it would be viewed by those to whom she had to report.

All this went through her mind in a flash, whereupon she came back to herself and to Marie's presence across the table, and relaxing, smiled at Marie and took a sip of water.

"Please pardon me, dear," she said, apologetically, and reaching across the table, laid a hand on Marie's as if to reassure her. "I just happened to think of something; something back in Germany."

"You—you have a—deep interest in Germany, Bertha," ventured Marie, guardedly. She didn't want to seem too inquisitive. By now she was aware that there was something a bit peculiar and mysterious about Bertha. It was not altogether clear exactly what she was doing, yet she was sure it was nothing to be ashamed of. But as friendly as they had become and were, she was sure that there was something, perhaps a very great deal, that Bertha had not told her about her work. Beyond a certain point she seemed vague and indefinite and secretive.

She had wondered about her unusual interest in Wyeth, more than just common interest. Was there something that she wanted to have Wyeth do, and if so, what? Yet she knew she couldn't ask her and wouldn't. It might embarrass her, and she liked her too much to risk that. Still she wished she could find out more.

"You were speaking about Mr. Wyeth," she heard Bertha saying, and became conscious almost for the first time, that Bertha was holding her hand. Holding it, she was sure, to reassure her. She smiled across at her and caught her hand and squeezed it as if to reassure Bertha.

"I think we should talk about something else, Bertha," she said. "Besides, here comes our order, and eating it will keep us busy for the next twenty minutes."

CHAPTER XXI

MARIE AND BERTHA had agreed before Bertha left the office the day before, to go shopping downtown together on Saturday afternoon, and Bertha was to meet Marie at the office and go on from there. Accordingly, Bertha called and we find them in the office before leaving, talking about the thing nearest to them.

"I met and had a long talk with one of the girls in Mantan's show on 125th Street last night," Marie was saying. "And she told me the show did fairly well the first week, but got off to a bad start on the hold over and that Levine was in a panic, and ordered changes, some quick and radical changes."

Bertha, who was fast learning much about the Negro by her association and talks with Marie, listened with close interest.

"She said that Mantan then called in Edrina, that's the girl Mr Wyeth has been engaged to."

"Has been?" said Bertha. "You mean, is, don't you?"

"I mean what I just said," said Marie.

"All right, dear. Please go on. Then what?"

"I'm coming to that, all that," she said.

Meanwhile, Bertha glanced over her shoulder towards Wyeth's office.

"He was in early this morning, but drove away shortly after I arrived. I think he's gone up to New Rochelle, for the day," said Marie, following Bertha's glance at his office.

"He seems so industrious, so full of energy, always up and going."

"He is that. Up and going most times, gone," said Marie. "That's why I'm on the anxious seat about him; to get this crazy show girl out of his system, if I can."

Bertha smiled patiently.

"And I think," said Marie, "at least hope, strongly, that's about what's happened." Marie paused, and Bertha patted her shoulder gently, as she waited for her to go on.

"This girl in the show, who happens to be a friend of mine, told me that Mantan called Edrina to his office after the order went out that they were going to change the show, and that she went into the office, all smiles and high-hat. But when she came out, she could have been bought for thirty cents, the way she looked, and that she was crying. Then, according to this girl, they were all called into rehearsal and kept hard at it until about two-thirty A. M., when everybody was told to knock off and go home, but Edrina and the piano player.

"Then what?"

"She didn't know, but that she thought Mantan was teaching Edrina some new routine, which was supposed to be sensational."

"But what has this to do with her engagement to Mr. Wyeth?"

"Oh, yes," cried Marie. "I forgot that part of the story. The girl said that while Edrina was in the office she went there and while waiting outside to see Mr. Mantan, overheard them talking; and that from what she could gather, Mr. Wyeth had walked out on Edrina after she went back into the show."

"Walked out on her, eh?"

"I'm not sure, but the girl said, from what she could gather, that Mr. Wyeth had become engaged to Edrina only after she promised to quit fooling around shows. So the fact that she went back into this, was contrary to what he wanted, so he quit her."

"The plot thickens," said Bertha and laughed.

"And becomes more interesting," said Marie. "Well, I wasn't through. The girl said that she thought Mantan was teaching Edrina to shake."

"Shake?" cried Bertha.

Marie had a good laugh.

"I guess you don't understand what all these Harlem terms mean."

"I surely don't understand what you mean by shake. What does it mean, anyhow, Marie?" said Bertha, all curious.

Having seen it done often, Marie proceeded to give her a slight demonstration.

"Good gracious, you mean, that—that she's going to do something like—that?" Bertha's expression indicated how she viewed it.

"Oh, a whole lot more than that. That was just a counter sample.

"No wonder they say such—such terrible things," said Bertha, wearing an amazed expression, "about Harlem. Shaking, whew! So indecent."

"I agree with you, and so does about every decent person. Still they come up here and thrill and cheer to the indecency. They call themselves 'slumming'."

Bertha shook her head, sadly and sighed.

"Not only does a girl have to shake herself almost to pieces to do it, but she must strip almost naked, into the bargain."

"Naked? Oh, Marie, no!"

"Oh, Bertha, yes," said Marie.

"Naked," Bertha repeated, and again shook her head.

"I said, almost, Bertha, dear."

"Oh, almost? How almost?"

"I want to take you down there to see the show tomorrow night, dear, then you'll see how 'almost'."

"Me, to see a show like that, and you, oh, no, Marie! I'm still decent, even if I am living in Harlem," argued Bertha. "We haven't sunk that low, really, have we?"

Marie embraced her.

"It's not as bad as all that, although this girl friend of mine says that they are grooming it to be 'hot, red hot'."

Bertha looked at her again and shook her head.

"But why—why do they permit so much indecency up here?" Bertha wanted to know. "Is it be—because it is a colored section, and the white people don't care what they do?"

"In a way, yes, but not altogether so. They feel that a show has got to give them something they can't see downtown in order to bring them up here, and no doubt the management of this theatre intends to bring them up at whatever the cost."

"Poor Harlem," sighed Bertha and again shook her head.

"But getting back to what I started to tell you, the girl said that they plan to start Edrina doing her new act Sunday."

"Sunday, too."

"Oh they start and do the most bold things on Sunday. Not so unusual at that. Hitler started this war, which is liable to grow into an awful war, on Sunday."

Bertha looked at her quickly, sharply, then as suddenly relaxed and made no answer.

"Well, I intend to see it and I won't like you as much as I do if you don't meet me and go with me."

"Oh, Marie, must I?"

"I heard you tell Mr. Wyeth that you wanted to find out all you could about Negroes."

"But I didn't mean going to—to an—indecent show."

"I guarantee that you won't be overly embarrassed or harmed, dear, so just make up your mind, for I'm going to take you with me," said Marie.

Bertha gave her consent by a sigh.

"Another reason I have for going, and taking you with me," said Marie, going on.

Bertha looked at her, a question in her eyes.

"Mr. Wyeth will be there."

Bertha started, and turned to look at Marie with a new interest.

"Oh, he's—"

"No," corrected Marie, cutting her off. "He's not going with us."

"But—"

"—when he goes there he goes on Sunday, and when he hears that they have changed the show, he'll surely be there."

"Oh, I see. I guess I understand better now."

"He'll want to see what they have her doing."

"Of course."

"And when he goes there, he's usually alone, and generally goes along between seven and eight o'clock." Again Bertha looked at her, a question in her eyes.

"Yes, usually alone. Other than this old crazy girl whom he's allowed himself to get mixed up with, he's never had many, if any girl friends."

"Are you sure?"

"Of course. It isn't that he doesn't care for women, but he seems to find more interest with his thoughts than with the most of them."

"If you weren't married and I know happy with your husband, I'd suspect you of having a deeper interest in Mr. Wyeth," said

Bertha, and winked, playfully. "Go on," she said.

"I've worked for him so long until he seems like a brother and a father to me, all in one," said Marie, smiling.

"I can understand that."

"And you'd want to see somebody like that, if they were getting married, to marry the kind of woman they needed; a woman who would place his interest first and look after him, wouldn't you?"

"Of course," agreed Bertha.

"Getting back to Mr. Wyeth," resumed Marie. "As I started to explain, he usually goes to the show between seven and seven thirty and sits in the section furthest over. I've been to the show and always see him seated in that section. Now we must be there, waiting when he comes in."

Again Bertha looked at her quickly, curiously, a question in her eyes.

"Because I intend before the show is over, if possible, before this girl comes out to do her new act, to be seated behind him, as close as I can get, or we can get, and watch his reaction."

"Oh, I follow you now," cried Bertha, and she seemed to understand at last.

"When we leave the show, I'll know if he still intends to marry her. Now do you understand what I am getting at?"

"I sure do, dear. What time shall I meet you and where?"

"In the lobby of the theatre at about six-thirty."

"I'll be there."

"Wait until I arrive, if I am not there. I'll buy the tickets."

"But—"

"I'll buy the tickets. Now let's get on downtown to do our shopping," so saying, she put Bertha ahead of her and went through the door, closed and locked it behind her, then arm in arm they left the building.

Edrina sighed as she took her dresses off the hangers late that night after the finale, kissed them, wept over them for a moment, and sighed again as she folded and placed them gently in her suitcase to carry home. She knew she would need them no more as long as she stayed in the show, and it had suddenly become necessary for her to stay in the show, for it was now her only means of earning a livelihood.

Sidney Wyeth had quit, walked out on her, as it were, and she was not feeling good about it. No girl feels good when a man quits her. If there's to be any quitting, the girl is supposed to do it. In her case she had been given no chance, no choice. She knew when he led her to the door and kissed her goodnight it was goodby, too. He had kissed her just to keep her from feeling so bad, but he was through. That he had been steeling his heart against her for some time, ever since she had developed the argument in the restaurant on returning from Louisville, that he knew he had enough of her. He had said it was principle and seemed to put a firm emphasis on it. And now as she folded her nice little dresses and gathered her two songs and put them in the suitcase with the dresses, she realized that when she left the theatre the next night she would be considered by all those who saw her, and by those who knew her, as another kind of a girl.

She thought of the matron, and of the girls at the YWCA which place she had been working, and had quit to go in the show, of their modesty and ideas, what they would think of her when somebody told them that she was doing a naked dance down at the theatre. It was a dismal outlook.

"Oh, well," she said to herself with a deep and tired sigh, "I asked for it, and now I've got to take it," and she sighed and was a very unhappy girl when she left the theatre, alone.

She had mastered whatever it was that she was to do to Mr. Mantan's satisfaction, although he had almost killed her, teaching her how and she was tired, dead tired. She went directly to her room and to bed. Mantan told her he'd wake her up the next morning, and continue to put her through the routine until the show opened. It was not a difficult routine but an intricate one. In it, she did about everything a theatrical producer's mind could conceive. To remember all that she was to do, would be the harder. Being an intelligent girl with a good memory, however, she was not afraid of forgetting which followed which. She only knew that she hated to do it, but realized now that she had to or else.

When she opened the door of her room, the first thing to greet her eyes was a special delivery letter which had come that night from her mother in Louisville. While from her mother, she knew that her sisters had written it, so after she removed her clothes, got into her kimono and relaxed, she turned on the bed light and opened and read it.

It was a long letter with a whole lot about her coming marriage to Wyeth. They complained that she had not written when the affair was to take place; that they had been waiting to hear from her, saying when. Then to climax it and make it worse, they said they had bought the last issue of the Pittsburgh Courier, and saw in it about the new show, and that she was in it and wanted to know what it meant. Hadn't she promised to give up the stage to marry Wyeth, then what was she doing back in the show? Had Mr. Wyeth consented? He must have, for she wouldn't throw over a good man to go back in a show. They ended by urging her to write them special and tell them all about what had happened so that they would know and wouldn't keep on worrying.

"If they could only be in the audience tomorrow and see what I've got to do, then they'd know what happened," she said with a deep sigh, reached up, turned off the light and relaxed. A few minutes later she was sound asleep.

CHAPTER XXII

BERTHA SCHULTZ did not rise early the next morning, which was Sunday. Back in Germany she lived with her mother and half brothers and sisters on a small farm outside of Berlin. And although the past six years had been spent in school, in Paris and Heidelberg, she managed to spend two months in the middle of the summer at home and loved the little farm, where they had raised many of the things that helped to feed Berlin. Marie had told her that Wyeth was born on a farm, and that just before starting to make pictures, had spent eight years as a master farmer in the Dakotas where the fields were wide and the farms large.

She intended to talk with Wyeth about it as soon as they could get around to it, so she thought about her home and the folks back in Germany. Germany had overrun Denmark, Norway, Belgium, the low countries and France and was charging like mad into Russia since she came away and everything seemed to be over, the end of the war was near. But in reading the papers and keeping herself informed regarding events, she knew the war wasn't over; that Germany, obviously a winner, was still not a winner, but from the tone of her mother's letters, she realized that the people of Germany were under the impression that they had won, and were only waiting for England and Russia to capitulate. She dared wish it could get over quickly. Germany winning, of course, but she was too close to what was going on in America, the bitter resentment, the intensely pro-English sentiment, especially on the part of the President, to indulge long in this vain hope.

She thought about Wyeth, and that she was to help pursuade him to make the hate picture, and wondered, soberly, just how she would go about it. She liked Mr. Wyeth, and she couldn't at this distance, visualize very clearly just how she was going to persuade him to do something she had a feeling that he didn't want to do.

Besides, she didn't hate Jews as Hitler had been training Germans to do. She disliked many of their mercenary ways, and was meeting lots of things here and finding that they were more mercenary in America than in Germany where there were not nearly so many. From what she understood and saw going on all over Harlem, it would be easy to stir Negroes against Jews into action, and by such could understand what the hate picture that Kermit Early had written and planned to have Wyeth film, could do to throw them into a siege of hatred and destruction. Yet, she wasn't enthusiastic over the idea. It was something, she fully realized, in the position she had accepted and assumed, that had to be done if only as a matter of policy.

After tossing about for half an hour, she fell asleep again and was surprised on awakening to find that it was nearly noon, so rose, took her bath, prepared breakfast for herself and brother, and after he left the apartment, sat down and wrote her mother a long letter.

Promptly at the appointed time, late that afternoon, she found herself in the lobby of the theatre, attractively dressed, and looking more beautiful Marie thought, than she ever seen her. A crowd was pouring into the theatre; a few were leaving. She hadn't been there long when she felt some one touch her, and turning, looked into the smiling face of Marie. After greeting each other they entered the theatre lobby where they had to wait in line. Standing, waiting, therefore, they could not help hearing the comment by those leaving the theatre. Some men who chose to linger a few minutes on the way out, were very definite about what they had just seen.

"What did you think of the show, anyhow?" said the first one, turning to the other.

"Oh, so, so," observed the other. "It wouldn't be worf a quatah if it wasn't fo' dat gal."

"You mean the gal doin' the naked dance?"

"Sho."

"Youse right. I wonduhs was she naked, sho nuff."

"Seemed lak she was."

"And man, she's sho got some purty teaties."

"You tellin' me!" and they laughed. "Dey wuz bouncin' round on her breas lak li'l rubber bubles. I'd sho lak tu hold dem bubbies in mah hand fo jes' a minet."

"Gwan, man, hush yo mouf." and again they laughed and left the lobby. Bertha and Marie exchanged expressions.

Another couple coming slowly out with the crowd, paused to comment.

"And when she'd stop, stomp her foot, den shake dem hips, aw man!"

By the loud music from inside, the show had broken, and a large crowd came out now, filling the lobby as they did so. When the lines grew thinner, they were permitted to enter. Marie decided to stand in the rear where she could watch the door, and see Wyeth when he entered, but seated Bertha in an empty seat and told her to watch the picture, while she waited for Wyeth to appear.

Bertha became interested in the picture, but found it hard to watch and listen to it, and keep looking up at Marie. About seven-thirty, however, she nudged Bertha and whispered in an undertone:

"There he goes." Bertha rose to her feet and together they watched him, followed him with their eyes until he found a seat in the section Marie had said he would find one. They crossed and found two near the aisle, a few rows back.

"As quickly as the picture is over," said Marie, in a whisper, We'll be able to get seats right behind him."

"Supposing he should look back." whispered Bertha.

"He won't look back, unless somebody starts a fight—and we'll take a chance on that at least." They both laughed, turned their eyes toward the screen and picked up the story and watched the picture to the end. As Marie suggested, at the end of the picture, half the people rose to their feet and left the theatre and before the crowd standing and waiting could pour down the aisles, they stole forward and got two seats almost directly behind Wyeth.

It was fully an hour later before the theatre became suddenly quiet, the lights dimmed and the house was almost dark, when the curtain rose and the orchestra began playing the famous diga-digado, which was followed by a sensational chorus performance. This was presently blended into an African native dance, in which drums supplanted almost every other instrument. Then came some fast dancing, a lot of wiggling and twisting, and finally Edrina put in her appearance. The house came down with applause. It was obvious then what the crowd was waiting for.

Watching it quietly from his seat, Wyeth wondered, after the shock of seeing the girl he had been about to marry, dash from the wings, to all appearances, entirely naked. There was an expression from every auditor in the theatre, an expression of "oh," and "ah's." The orchestra then played loudly, giving her a chance to dash back and forth, in an assumed dance, which, by a close observer, could be seen to be no dance at all, but a well-faked camouflage, staged by the ingenious Mantan with careful and well-ordered precision, to seem like a sensational dance.

Bertha and Marie clasped hands after an "oh," as she made her entry, and continued to hold hands, while Edrina put on her act. They watched and studied her, and associated her as the future wife of the man sitting before them whom both admired.

They could hear whispered expressions all about them, debating if she was wearing any clothes at all.

"That gal's naked, or I'm a liar," one argued.

"Naw she ain't," said another.

"How come? Where are her clothes?"

"Well, she ain't got on much, but she has something over her—"

"Ain't it a shame. That gal doin' a naked dance. Yuh know who she is?"

"Naw. Who?"

"She's the gal who used to wait table at the Y. Remember, she used to wait on us."

"Sho, I remembuhs now. Her name's—"

"Edrina Vinson."

"Sho, sho, I remembuhs her now, sho nuf. And now, Edrina Vinson doin' a naked dance."

"She sho can do hit—now look at heh."

Edrina was now doing an imitation of the hootch, which in the words of colored America, *stopped the show*. Mantan had taught her how to stamp one foot hard on the floor, then follow it up by an abrupt twist of her hips, followed by a wiggle, more twisting, how to go as low to the floor as possible, then bring her midsection up and hit at some invisible object in front of her. All the while, her rounded teaties were putting on an act of their own, due to her continued twisting and wriggling. Although bronzed, they attracted as much attention as if they were bare and looking at it, and listening to the reaction of the thrill-packed theatre, Bertha and

Marie were sure they heard Wyeth emit a slight groan on more than one occasion and sadly lower his eyes. At such times, Marie would squeeze Bertha's hand and nod her head towards him.

The act was prolonged for several minutes and they wondered at her ability to hold out so long. Finally the dance was brought to a climax when the music, mounting higher and higher until it reached a crescendo by a terrific and deafening roar, and Edrina dashing from right to left, left to right for what seemed an interminable time, fell in a dramatic sprawl on the floor. The curtain came down and the house broke into deafening applause. They kept her, wearing a robe, coming forward at least half a dozen times for encores, and Wyeth, watching it all quietly, and knowing how anxious she had been to catch the spotlight, wondered if she was pleased, now that she had it.

After what seemed an age, however, the house lit up and Marie and Bertha let him leave before they rose and followed him, keeping him in sight as they did so.

On the sidewalk he paused wearily, to look around and hesitate a while, during which Marie came up behind and touched him. He did not start, but turned and when he saw who it was, seemed relieved.

"Oh, Marie," he cried. Then his eyes fell on Bertha. "And Miss Schultz! Well, I declare!"

"And we declare, Mr. Wyeth," said Marie.

"Were you in the—show?" and he turned and nodded his head toward the theatre.

"Yes," said Marie. "You were, too. How'd you like it?"

He shrugged his shoulders, and they caught his complete reaction.

"It was interesting, I guess."

"Especially the girl," said Marie. Both girls watched him closely. He frowned, and they knew he couldn't take it and was through.

"Where are you going from here?"

"Where?" he repeated absently. "Oh, I don't know. To Heaven, maybe, or—"

"Don't say it," cried Marie. "Are you driving?" He pointed to his car, standing at the curb.

"Why not drive a couple of lonely girls around the block?"

"Why not," he said, apparently anxious for company against his thoughts which were pounding the walls of his brain like a trip hammer.

"Then what are we waiting for," said Marie, glibly. She pushed Bertha beside him where she took his arm. He seemed surprised and turned to look at her. Marie rushed around and took his other arm, smiled up into his face.

"Now, what have I fallen into," he cried, and for the moment forgot the tragedy of what he had just looked at. "Two pretty girls taking an old man in charge, my!"

"You're not old," said Bertha, softly as they crossed to the car. He looked down at her and their eyes met. Knowing that he must be tired and awfully lonely, Bertha felt it her role to comfort him, so squeezed his arm and again he looked at her out of his sad eyes and she felt sorry for him.

When they reached the car, Marie opened the door and taking hold of Bertha, helped her into it.

"In the middle, beauty," she said. Wyeth started around the car, but she laid a hand on him. "Supposing you let me, this time, yes?"

"Sure, baby. Glad to have you," he said and seemed relieved.

"Okay. Meantime, crawl in, beast, and take a seat on the right side of beauty." All laughed. He smiled a bit awkwardly at Bertha when he found himself that close to her, while she blushed, beautifully.

Marie slammed the heavy door, and went around to the driver's side, opened the door and crawled under the wheel, reached her hand across Bertha after an "excuse me," and said to him, "The key, please."

"Of course," he said, found it quickly and handed it over. She inserted it and stepped on the starter.

"Where do you want to go?" Marie asked, looking across at him. He made a gesture.

"You're the driver and the boss. Go where you want to."

"Fine," she cried. He turned to Bertha. "You heard him give me permission. Well, I'm going to show Bertha what great highways we have out of and into New York."

"I'll be so glad," cried Bertha enthusiastically. Marie pushed her over, and, of course so close to Wyeth that she found herself squeezed a bit against him.

"Put your arm around her shoulder, Mr. Wyeth, then we'll have more room."

Wyeth did so, and Bertha was thrilled.

"Incidentally, Miss Schultz, there's plenty room for three in this seat."

"Not with me driving," said Marie, and winked at Bertha. They were sailing up St. Nicholas Avenue now, to 150th street where she turned into St. Nicholas Place and at the end of it, at 155th St., they entered the Speedway and coasted along it more than a mile to the street that would carry them to the Saw Mill River Road.

The moon was shining bright, lighting up the road into an almost silvery daylight, and Bertha, her eyes on the scenery, was all excitement.

"So beautiful!"

"Never been out this way?" inquired Wyeth.

"No, Mr. Wyeth. I haven't been out of New York since I've been here," she told him. They were close enough to feel each other's flesh and both were strangely thrilled by the touch.

"Then you've been missing a great deal," he said.

"I'm sure I have by the sight of all this," and she nodded to the passing landscape.

"It is beautiful for miles out this way," he said. "All the way up into New England, and still beautiful after you get there."

"Wonderful," commented Bertha, and was conscious that being so close to him, with his arm behind her, touching her a bit, was peculiarly satisfying.

"Before you go to sleep, Mr. Wyeth," called Marie, eyes on the road ahead.

"Before I go to sleep?" he echoed, looking at her.

"He always goes to sleep when anybody else drives the car, Bertha," Marie said, the remark directed to Bertha. "So you can count on him losing consciousness completely before we reach the Merrick road."

"The Merrick road," he exclaimed, surprised like.

"Why not?" said Marie. "Why shouldn't we go for a real ride, now that I have charge of this big, fine car, with a pretty girl between you and me," and she giggled. "I know you're too much of a gentleman to fight with me across such a sweet girl as Bertha."

"Bertha is a sweet and pretty girl," he said, smiling down into her eyes.

"Marie is given to flattery," said Bertha, but was blushing nevertheless.

"She couldn't flatter you, Miss Schultz. You *are* a pretty girl, and more beautiful because you are so nice to everybody, with it."

"And now you team with her against me," complained Bertha. All laughed at this and paused while Wyeth dug into his pocket for a dime to pay the toll across the Henry Hudson Bridge. By the time they reached it and crossed it and started for the Merrick road, he stretched his mouth wide in a sigh. Marie nudged Bertha, who was afraid to look at him, but understood what Marie meant. Before they reached the Merrick road, as Marie had predicted, Wyeth was fast asleep, and they dared look at him, then at each other.

"I was hoping he would stay awake until we reached the first toll gate, but he beat us to it."

"Poor fellow," said Bertha kindly, and looked down at him where he was by now, snoring lightly.

"The reaction has set in. She's behind him now and the trouble she would have made him, with it, and I'm happy," and Marie sighed like she was satisfied.

"I don't see how any girl could disregard him."

"They wouldn't if they understood him," said Marie. "The trouble with her is, that she didn't understand him and never would have learned to."

"I can understand it better now."

"He didn't deserve such a fate, such a misfortune to interfere with the realization of a great ambition," said Marie.

"You mean writing."

"I mean writing, yes."

"I wonder how she feels by now," said Bertha.

"Perhaps bad—for awhile. But being stage-struck, she'll get over it."

"I wouldn't be surprised."

"We'll drive to New Haven, to a place I know on Dixwell Avenue, have some refreshments, then return to New York?"

"How far is New Haven from New York?"

"About seventy-two miles."

"That is the home of—"

"—Yale University."

"Yale, of course. That's one of America's great schools."

"Yep. With Harvard it is one of the oldest and the greatest."

"I'd like to see it in the day time."

"Some day if all turns out well, we'll make Mr. Wyeth drive us up here again, only this time we'll go all the way to Boston, where on the way we can see both Yale and then later, Harvard, too."

"Harvard?"

"Harvard University. That's where Mr. Early got his Doctorate."

"So I was told. I shall be thrilled to see it."

"I know you will. So will I. I've never been there, but have always wanted to visit it, as well as Boston and much of New England."

"I imagine it is very much like old England."

"It is, so I've been told," said Marie. They glanced again at Wyeth. who was completely lost in a deep and peaceful sleep by now.

"He needs it," said Bertha, looking at him kindly.

"And how," said Marie.

"And you think he's completely through with the girl back there?"

"Completely."

"It might be for the best."

"It is. Decidedly for the best."

"I'm glad if it is."

"So am I. Now my worries are over. Meanwhile . . ."

"Meanwhile?"

"If some nice girl should take an interest in him, it would help him to forget her without so much effort." Bertha didn't answer, but she understood what Marie was hinting at.

Back in New York in the meantime, the show was out and Edrina, wearing a heavy, quilted robe, was relaxing in her dressing room, after the most strenuous day she had ever had. Mantan had brought her the robe, to "keep you from catching cold after your act," he said. "Don't neglect to put it on immediately after you quit dancing, after the first curtain. You can't afford to catch an awful cold."

So Edrina sat there alone in her dressing room after the day's performance. Six times she did the act that day and had been rewarded by more applause than she ever thought she would get. The house had roared with applause all day over an act she had not dreamed one week before that she would be doing. But what would the reaction be? She knew that she would be considered a 'shake' and hootch dancer from then on, and nobody but a cold, bold and indifferent sort of girl would want that, regardless of how much applause she received.

During the moments she was thinking about all this, at the front of the house, Henry Levine, manager of the theatre, was talking with Irvin C. Mantan. He was smiling and rubbing his hands because he was happy. From the jaws of almost complete failure, the show had been snatched back into a howling success, all because of him, for hadn't it been he who thought of having Edrina Vinson do the naked dance?

"Well, Mantan, she saved the show."

"Yes, Mr. Levine," said Mantan. "It seems that way."

"Our receipts are three times as much as they would have been, had we tried to drag the old show through the day." Mantan said nothing. Levine had the floor. "So I think we should do something for Edrina as a gesture of appreciation."

"That's right. I think we should," agreed Mantan.

"So we'll go back stage and tell her and present her with—say, $25.00 as an expression of our appreciation." Mantan agreed with him, knowing, however, that Levine would take all of it out of his share at the end of the week. But he said nothing. At least, Levine's suggestion, put into operation, *had* saved the show, and in a way he was glad, for now he would be able to completely pay off at the end of the week. Furthermore, he knew and Levine knew, that there would be a line waiting on the sidewalk at the box office the next morning to get in the theatre; and that when he wired the managers at Philadelphia, Baltimore and Washington to come to New York and see what he had to offer, and when they came and saw how the show was drawing, it would repeat in all those places, whereas he knew that he wouldn't have secured a single date but for the wiggle he had taught and got Edrina to do.

Taking Irvin's arm and smiling down the barrel of his long nose, Levine led him from the office and to Edrina's dressing room, backstage, at the rear of the large theatre.

In response to their knock on her door, Edrina wearily called, "Come in."

Smiling all over and followed by Mantan, Levine entered.

"Ah, Edrina," he began, in his perfect English. He was born in this country, educated in the best of schools, and as a result, spoke the most perfect English, with no kind of accent to indicate that he was a Jew. But he looked so completely Jewish that one was reminded on looking at him, that he must have been descended directly from Israel himself.

"You were wonderful, my dear," he said, crossing to her and daring to gently pat her on the shoulder.

"Thank you, Mr. Levine," she said. She did not raise her eyes to meet his. They were, however, on the wall across the little dressing room, where in an elongated shadow, silhouetted there, his nose stretched clear across it and reminded her in her befuddled and aggravated condition of a shadowy apparition. He ran his hand into his pocket and withdrew a large roll of bills that she could see without looking up.

"And now, Edrina," he began again, turning to smile at Mantan, standing near. "I told Irvin that since your new act has practically saved this show, that we ought to do something for you as an act of our appreciation for what you've done." He paused now long enough to count out the amount. Then looking down at her, and smiling, while she glanced again at the wall across the room, where his shadow and the large glasses he wore and his long nose, were so distorted that they were comical. She thought about Snow White and the Seven Dwarfs, especially about the old hag in it who was so evil.

Levine was talking again.

"So, Edrina," he said, carefully, and laid the bills on the table before her. "We are making you a present of $25.00 as a token of that appreciation." He finished, stepped back, smiling and rubbing his hands.

"Thank you, Mr. Levine," she said, picking up the bank notes and for the first time, taking her eyes off the silhouette of his shadow on the wall across the room. Levine was very careful to use terms "we" and "us" and Mantan knew full well why. Regardless of the fact that Edrina's new act had changed a dismal box office outlook, Mantan knew that when they went to settle at the end of the engagement, it would be "you" and "yours," which meant that the extra $25.00 would come out of his share entirely.

With a fine bow, a few more kind words, Levine turned around and left the office, with Mantan following, leaving her alone. Gone, she looked at the money which she needed. Since Wyeth walked out on her, she was brought quickly to realize how helpful he had been at all times. She never had to ask for anything; he seemed to understand when she needed money and it was always forthcoming. She sighed as she folded and put the bills in her purse.

"Well," she sighed again. "Twenty-five dollars is twenty-five dollars, especially when you need it—and do I need it!" Consciously she knew it was time to put him out of her mind, but she kept seeing his tired, sad face; his deep frown, and recalled their affair.

"It's all over," she said half aloud, and felt sorry for herself. "How could he, or any other sensitive man, be happy seeing his future wife out there before 2,500 people, cavorting as I was compelled to, shaking and twisting my body—six times in one day—and with hardly any clothes on at all. I don't blame him," and again she sighed, this time, hopelessly. She thought about the wedding night that he had waited for and planned. Donald and other men did not talk about wedding nights. They talked about *that* night, but Sidney Wyeth had waited and planned a wedding night; a wedding night that never came. No, she thought aloud and to herself, there would be no wedding night for her and Sidney Wyeth. He was gone out of her life, she knew now, forever.

In the midst of these reflections, there was a light knock on her door. She was so absorbed in her thoughts that she wasn't sure about it, so waited for it to be repeated. It wasn't. The door was pushed open and when she looked quickly around, it was into the face of Donald Howard. He rarely knocked the second time. He just came on in. Donald hadn't visualized any wedding night. Before leaving New York to go out with the show the first time, but after he had sold her on going on the stage, he'd had his wedding nights. And they had thrilled to many wedding nights during the entire first tour, all over the country. As far west as Kansas City; North to Chicago, South to New Orleans. So Donald had missed nothing. Only Sidney Wyeth had. He missed everything she had to give him.

By this time, and for a long time since, Donald's entering her dressing room without invitation or a second knock, was like a husband, entering his wife's bedroom after ten years of wedded life.

"Oh, Donald," she heard herself say. "You."

"Yes, me, Edrina." He crossed the room, found a stool that was near, drew it up, sat down and smiled at her somewhat oddly. Was it, she wondered as he did so, a smile or a smirk. "Well, kid," he said, looking at her in whatever way she wondered it was. "You put it over. Yes. You put the show over big, and you're in for the season now."

"Thank you, Donald," she replied quietly, and wondered if he was thinking about how she felt; how she must be feeling after her daring performances; wondered how he would feel now, regarding her as a kooch and shake dancer, instead of the nice, pretty girl from Louisville, singing a darling little song. She seemed to catch some inference from his words "in for the season now."

Then he must know, or did he know? No, he didn't know, but he understood. He understood and meant when he said "you're in for the season now" that Sidney Wyeth had walked out; that he was not going to marry her. And after the bold performances, of course he understood and he was taunting her, not complimenting. He also meant that since she had been put into such a role, she would have to stay in it. Never again could she be permitted to go back to playing current roles.

"I heard Washington calling Levine as I came by the office, about the show, so we're booked for Washington, as soon as we can get there. That means that Sam Steinbeck'll set us in the Quay in Philadelphia, and then the Dunbar in Baltimore, then back to Pittsburgh, on to Cleveland, then Detroit and into Chicago. So, kid," he said, rising to his feet, "You've put it over, and you won't have to worry about engagements for the next ten weeks, maybe longer, and that, you know, is something. A whole lot if you're asking me."

He moved across to the door and opened it, then seemed to think of something, or had he saved it to tell her at this particular moment, when he was about to leave her?

"Oh, by the way," he said, pausing, and turning back to her. "Guess who I saw leaving the theatre a few minutes ago?"

Without looking up or at him, or making any effort to guess, she said:

"I give up, Donald. Who?"

"Sidney Wyeth," he said calmly, but watched her carefully as he said it.

She started, perceptibly, then glanced at him, to catch him smiling across at her with that smirk, written all over his face. She looked at him for only a second, then lowered her eyes back to the table before her, with what he said, beating against the walls of her brain until she could almost hear out loud, "Sidney Wyeth!" the words seemed to echo, over and over again. Then Wyeth *had* seen her; *had seen her out there before throngs, all but naked!* She realized now that he came to see her in her humiliation, but to be told that he had been there, which meant that he had seen it, seemed to shock her almost insensible. Howard was talking again, his voice seemed to come from far off, but she understood what he was saying; and she understood still more clearly what he meant.

"Yeh. Sidney Wyeth, with a couple of pretty girls." Again she was shocked. She sat up straight, and looked at him vaguely. And there it was again, on his face, not a smile but a tantalizing smirk. It seemed to please him to taunt her; to remind her what her career had come to. Sidney Wyeth, at the theatre with two pretty girls—after walking out on her less than three days before. Sidney Wyeth, who had not gone with any girl for years, so she had been told. Yet, to watch her humiliation, he had come to the theatre, bringing two pretty girls.

Donald happened to come into the theatre just as Bertha and Marie came up to Wyeth and didn't know that until then, he had been alone. It would seem at the time he saw them, that Wyeth had brought them to the show. Donald had stood for a moment and watched them, then strolled by, nonchalantly, hoping that Wyeth would see, call and introduce him to the girls. But as we know, Wyeth was suffering so from the shock of seeing the girl he had been engaged to marry a few days before, that he did not notice Howard pass by, go a few steps, then turn and retrace his steps. So from the front of the theatre, Howard had watched them until they drove away, then timed his call to tell Edrina and make her, already feeling bad, feel worse.

He knew that Marie was Wyeth's stenographer, but who was the other girl? Such a pretty and apparently high-class girl! That was the impression Bertha gave everyone who saw her. And that was the kind of girl Donald liked and would have given anything to meet. Watching them until they turned and disappeared, he had wondered who the girl was. He asked somebody about her, somebody who didn't know any more about her than he did, but who professed, when asked, to know.

"That was one of the Walden girls," he told Donald.

"Walden girls, eh?"

"Yes, one of the Walden girls of Westchester."

So with this in mind, and strangely anxious to see Edrina hurt, more than being forced to do the disgraceful act had hurt her, he kept thinking about it and planned to tell her when the show was over, so that she could have it to think about all night.

"One of them," he was saying now, "was sure a pretty thing; as pretty as a picture, and she was hanging on to Wyeth like she liked it."

"As pretty as a picture and hanging on to Wyeth's arm like she liked it," echoed and reechoed through Edrina's mind. She was not looking at Donald, but she was gazing wide-eyed into space before her. She was wondering now if Wyeth had not been playing her— and yet! If he had been playing her, then why hadn't he gone *the limit*, at least as far as he could have? Surely a man playing a girl as this would seem, would have taken what she had to give him, would have partaken of it—unless he was a *fairy*.

"Oh, no," she cried to herself. "He isn't a *fairy*." No, he hadn't done anything or said anything to give such an impression. He was just one of those rare persons called 'virtuous' men.

"I've been hearing of her," Donald was saying now. He guessed again and as we shall see, was strangely right.

"Hear she's just returned from Europe. Been in school in France, and from all appearances, she looked it—some girl!"

Edrina now found herself suddenly afire with jealously. He *had* been playing her. While professing so many words about love, he had, all the while, been seeing this pretty girl, perhaps making love to her, and all the while, making a fool of *her*."

"I understand," Donald continued, "That she is one of the Walden girls, of Westchester."

"Westchester, eh," Edrina was saying to herself now. "Westchester, rich and aristocratic, Westchester." She was conscious of suppressed rage. She hadn't been good enough for him. No girls in Harlem had been good enough. Going with a girl from Westchester; Westchester where only the 'dicty' Negroes dared to reside.

So *she* had been played for a sucker, *not him*. He had deliberately gone to Westchester and brought her to Harlem on a slumming party, brought her to the theatre to show her the girl he had been playing around with; and they had sat together in the theatre and looked at her cavort all over the stage, virtually nude for the benefit of thousands of noisy Negroes. Sat there and saw her humiliated as no modest woman could be so completely humiliated. And when it was all over, they had left the theatre, perhaps laughing about it and feeling sorry for a girl who would condescend to attempt such a dance. Now that *pretty girl* that Donald has described so aptly; that *highly refined girl* who had been to school in Europe, had just returned and was living in aristocratic Westchester, could *think about and remember her with contempt;* think of her as a *common woman* who had been engaged to marry an author and a motion picture producer; who could have the satisfaction of feeling that she had saved a good man from making a grievous mistake. Thinking of her, Edrina, as a *mistake*.

She became so angry that she rose to her feet, locked the door so that Donald could not walk back in and see her like she was. She didn't want him to have the satisfaction of seeing her angry; seeing her suffer for the mistake that she had made so he could say "I told you so." Yet she was so angry that she walked the floor for half an hour, angry as an enraged tigress, trying to hate Sidney Wyeth; hating, without much effort, the girl that Donald said he saw him with. And yet, with all her anger and accusations, she couldn't seem to get much satisfaction out of hating, or trying to hate the man she had been engaged to. The more she thought of him after becoming calm again and her anger had subsided somewhat, the less she could hate him. For in all her thinking, she could not recall any time, instance or place where he had been guilty of doing anything but trying to show her that her ambitions would in time spell her downfall. She sat down and through her mind ran his words;

"They'll strip tease you if they think making you as naked as a jay-bird's baby will help the show." How this did echo and reecho now in her memory.

"They make quick changes in these shows." Quick changes—and *what a quick* change! Just when she thought she was doing well and was going to be able to prove to him that she could stay on the stage and be nice and clean and as dignified, perhaps, as that pretty girl from Westchester, she was suddenly called and forced to learn a routine, take off all her clothes, as he said they might do, and go out there and do a dance that in one day had, perhaps, made her the most notoriously talked about woman in Harlem. She could picture the people, and the women especially, as thinking of her, and pointing to her, as the woman who did that *naked dance* on 125th St. Being so pointed out and looked at, they could hardly think of, or ever recall her as anything but a notorious woman. In her spell of rage during which time she walked the floor, trying to hate him as much as she had told him, only a few days before, that she loved him, but in which she could never feel entirely satisfied, she was in the end forced to admit, at least to herself, that it was all her fault. In her stage ambitions she certainly had never pictured being a kooch and shake dancer. Indeed no. If she had been told, and anybody had, or could have shown her, that was what it would come to, end up as, she would, as she recalled it now, most surely have quit the stage and run—run as far away from it as she could get. Which would have been into the arms of Sidney Wyeth, ultimately to become his wife.

But as she sighed deeply now and realized that she couldn't stay in that dressing room all night and would have to leave it and go home, she took the blame for it all. She would, she realized and admitted to herself, with regret, have to keep on kooching and shaking, as that was the only way left open for her to make a living. Then she thought of Alice and Carrie and her mother and the Doctors and the "big" Negroes back in Louisville, all of whom knew Sidney Wyeth by reputation, and would be watching the Colored papers to see when she was marrying him; be calling up her sisters and inquiring when it would be taking place. What could she now tell them to pass on to the folks, the best people, back there in Louisville? And then she recalled, suddenly, something that took place in the theatre while she was doing her act. She had seen a light flash and it now came to her that it was, perhaps, a reporter, and he had taken a picture of her. As she continued to think about it, it occurred to her now that it might be reproduced and used on the theatrical pages of the next issues of the Negro weeklies, all of which circulated in Louisville. As her people bought those weeklies, and they would see her just as she was cavorting all but nude—and all would conclude right quick, that it was over; and that Sidney Wyeth would not be marrying her after all; after all her display and boasting while in Louisville!

She lowered her eyes and cried, cried like her heart would break. Never could Wyeth or anyone else have showed her, much less prove to her, that she would come to this—and so quickly!

An hour later Edrina dragged herself into her room, sat down, looked hopelessly and sadly into space, with not a friend, she felt, in the world to turn to and admit that she had been vain and mistaken. With an effort she rose, removed her clothes, and went to bed at last.

CHAPTER XXIII

FLORENCE WINGATE had returned to Atlanta, and on arriving there, she entered her home on Peachtreee Street with determination to at last tell her husband the truth; tell him that she was in family way by a colored man and *proud of it!*

He was away, as he so often was, in New York, in New York at the same time she was, but neither knew of the other's presence, and of course she would not have contacted him, if she had. It was an ugly situation. She had made up her mind on the way from New York to tell him the whole truth, and have it over with. Before doing so, however, she decided to visit Wakefield—perhaps for the last time, for she knew that when word went around down there of what she had done, one of the finest flowers of the old South, married to a *colored man,* old Barber Early's son, she would never dare show her face there again. If she went now, before it all happened, she would be welcomed, treated as only the wife of one of the richest men in the South would be treated, and which she knew, would be her farewell.

Her mother had been suspicious of something; had a feeling that she had a lover on the side for a great many years, and had hinted at and tried on several occasions to find out more. Yet, as far as she had been able to learn, nobody suspected that *other man* to be a Negro. It was perhaps about the last thing anybody there would have suspected. Nobody in Wakefield would even dare associate such an idea with the former Florence Adair, scion of one of the South's oldest and proudest families.

She did appreciate her people's position in the matter, however, even though she had made the sacrifice for their benefit. Still, the South and southern people are sentimental, with their pride. The thing then to do, as she conceived it, was to drive down to Wakefield, accept all the hospitality as of old, and while there, force herself, if she could, to forget Kermit Early—as if she could! The very thought of it made her smile. For the further she got away from him, the more she found herself thinking of him.

Ever since she discovered that she was going to be a mother, he had become more dear to her, and more beloved. The South could never understand a love like hers for a Negro. They would not because they would never even consider such a possibility. The whole idea of a white woman in love with, and married to, a Negro, was too far from their minds! Yet Florence Wingate knew Kermit Early as no other woman could know a man. She was closer to him than a wife could be to a husband. During all their years of association, which had been of the forbidden type, and because of the thought ever present that it was forbidden, they had found each other's companionship more compassionate, had indulged each other sexually more than any man and woman would ordinarily indulge— and now with a child on the way, she found herself turning to him more than could otherwise have been the case. Because she could not tell anybody the great joy of becoming a mother, the greatest desire of her life, she had to keep it a deep secret from all but Kermit, so it is obvious how much at such a time, he meant to her.

But as we have seen, Florence Wingate was a resolute woman, accustomed to responsibility. She had put Kermit Early through school, all the way up to a Doctor of Philosophy, the highest degree to be secured, and from the greatest school in America. From the days when she, as a young girl, used to stick her tongue out at him and frighten him back there in Wakefield, hers had been a career of initiative and responsibility. So now, as she checked over what she was to do there in the confines of her home in Atlanta, she was prepared for her greatest task, her greatest responsibility.

As we know, she couldn't, in going to Wakefield, tell anybody— not even her mother, that at last she was going to become a mother. They had hoped and looked for it during the first five years of her marriage to Mr. Wingate. Then, when it failed to happen, it had, in their minds, dwindled to a hope, but long since that spark had died and nobody expected her to have a baby any longer. What a pleasure, therefore, and what a triumph it would be to now tell them there would be a "blessed event" after all.

Without letting herself think any more about it, which would have been to confuse her mind with no end of thoughts and plans and new plans all of which would only annoy her the more, two days after she arrived in Atlanta, she was in her huge limousine, rolling South to Wakefield where she arrived just before noon, to the surprise of all.

"Why, darling," her mother cried. "Why didn't you write to me—even wire me as early as this morning when you left Atlanta, that you were coming so that I could have made some preparations?"

"I'm sorry, mother," she said, blandly, "but I just got back from New York, decided of a sudden to come down here, pay everybody a visit and return to Atlanta—and perhaps to New York very shortly."

"You haven't been here for so long," her mother said, shedding a tear as she assisted her with such baggage as she had, "we thought when you did come you'd stay a long time. We would be glad to have you do so."

"I'd like to, dear, but when I plan anything that way, it never happens at all. So I took a notion last night to drive down. I didn't want to write or wire—didn't want to do anything but just come on down and see you and Wakefield, all right quick, and get on back to Atlanta before anybody knew entirely what happened."

"Of course we're glad to see you if only to look out the window and see you pass through the town, since its been so long. How is Mr. Wingate?"

"Fine. I haven't seen him for a few weeks, but he's expected back from the North this weekend and we—we'll be together then, thank you."

"I'm glad. Well, dear, make yourself comfortable while I go out and see if we can get you a good dinner." So saying her mother left her, and she was relieved.

No sooner had she, than she went back to the car and drove around and called on a few of the many friends of the family. Conscious that this would be her last trip, no doubt, to Wakefield, she wanted to see, meet and talk with all the people she had known all her life. It was a peculiar feeling to meet them now, kiss the wives and daughters and embrace the old men and play with the children, and feel all the while that she was saying farewell to them all; and that never would she see them again; never again to face any of them; never to dare to do so.

She sighed when she got back to the house and sat down to one of the last meals she would ever eat at her mother's table.

Back in New York in the meantime, Kermit Early had been doing some planning and some preparing, too, to get Sidney Wyeth to produce the hate picture which he had taken so long to prepare. This fact had kept him on the payroll of the subversive organizations in Milwaukee and Chicago for such a long time. So Kermit Early was ready at last to go to the bat for a complete show down with Wyeth.

He had talked with Heinrich about it at much length, and had Schultz more enthusiastic than ever about it.

"When you've had two or three long talks with Wyeth, showed him all the angles, and how the Jews, if anything, are not only not a friend of the Negro, but indirectly their enemies, I'm sure he'll see the logic of it all and ultimately come in with us."

"I'm prepared to show him all that and go the limit. There's so much I want to tell him; so much that he ought to know; so much that the Negro race in America should know, and who will go into action quickly if they can be shown."

"And it's the best way to show them and the world what a louse the Jew is; that he is the most selfish of all people, caring nothing for anybody, any place, anywhere; caring nothing for anything but the almighty dollar. Wyeth's got to be shown and convinced that in making this picture he is doing what Adolf Hitler has so ably started, and which will, in the end, reduce the influence of the greatest group of parasites the world ever knew—the thieving, stealing, lying and cheating Jew. Damn him!" and Heinrich rose to his feet and walked the floor of the apartment, while he and Early went deeper into their plan.

As we have already debated, and perhaps will have occasion to debate more and more in the development of our story, the Negro, to a large degree is seriously mis-educated. In some manner the impression went forth, that what was needed to help solve their great problem, was education. So right after the Civil War when the Negro was given the right to vote, and because he had not been trained in how to keep and hold it. He had lost, as all America knows, that right in the South, but the theory of more education as a solution of his grave problem, still existed. So in many families, with honest, hard working and diligent Negro mothers and fathers, who have been making sacrifices so long to give their offspring an education, the idea is an obsession. Plainly the theory is still in effect, to a large degree, that he can be educated into success.

Kermit Early was a victim of that widespread misconception. As we know, he managed to acquire all the education the greatest schools in America could give him, assisted by Florence Wingate's money, which had made it easy and convenient for him to acquire. Yet now after all the education, the love and assistance of an aristocratic white woman, Kermit Early was in effect, a failure, in the sense we measure success in America. But Kermit Early, if he was aware of it, was not admitting it. It is a question if he had thought of it in that sense.

In America, regardless of how much the Negro might say to the contrary, he has never been put into a position of great responsibility beyond managing schools for Negroes and supervising civic organizations for his own welfare. During the days of slavery, they were afraid to entrust too much to the Negro, not because they feared he would fail, but because they feared it would set him to thinking. They didn't want that. If he began to think, about the first thing he would concentrate on and ask, would be why he was a slave and the white man free. To put him in a position of responsibility during such times would have inspired him to think and perhaps, keep on thinking. So thinking on the part of the Negro was discouraged in as many ways as could be managed. He was given the unrestricted right to worship God, for in that respect since nobody has ever returned to either prove or disprove the theory of the hereafter, getting religion and worshipping was encouraged during the entire period of slavery. So when he was freed, worshipping and looking for his great day after death had become a fixed idea with Negroes. But shunting and avoiding responsibility had also become a part of him. He was not keenly anxious to assume it and that, with few exceptions, prevails today.

As stated, the belief that education would fit him better for life, and would ultimately do more than anything else to solve the problem that his existence in America presented. This theory still exists, and many Negroes struggle for years to get through school with only a vague idea and feeling as to what they are going to do after they secure so much education. In the case of Kermit Early, he hadn't exactly planned at the outset to acquire all the degrees he later found himself in possession of. It was his plan and ambition to go to Atlanta University and to continue there until he had graduated. He had not even planned to secure a master, beyond that, and it never entered his mind to acquire a Ph.D.

It was due to his intimate association with Mrs. Florence Wingate, who was more responsible for his going all the way in Education. Mrs. Wingate having taken up with him, as has been explained, and from then on provided the means that made it easy for him to continue in school.

He started, as we also know, to do big things, even before securing his doctorate, but with Mrs. Wingate at his elbow, not only asking but insisting on providing the means an educated man should have, he was not forced to earn a living out of it. It was assumed by both he and Mrs. Wingate, whose wealth was so convenient to his needs, that he needed time to put his plans into action.

So it turned out that nothing Kermit attempted actually paid his expenses. He understood commerce and trade only in a general way. There was nobody to hire a colored man for what he was able to do. There was nothing left, he soon found out, but to go down South and teach school. This he could have gotten, but nothing short of a deanship of a real school would have even been considered. Then, there was a distinct disadvantage of being associated with any school. That disadvantage was Mrs. Wingate's and their affair. To get all they secured from their relations, it was necessary that they first be independent. The next was secrecy. Never given to much talking as has been shown above, his relations with Mrs. Wingate made him more secretive. Any position he might have taken in the South, in any school, would have necessitated Mrs. Wingate's coming there to see him. This couldn't even be thought of, much less considered. So to make what could be a very long story very short, it was not until Kermit became associated with the subversive group in Milwaukee and Chicago, that he began to secure enough income to take care of himself. Naturally this attracted Mrs. Wingate's attention. At last, as she viewed it, Kermit was coming into his own, and she was cheered. Not that she minded carrying the burden, for she didn't, and would have gone on doing so indefinitely without complaining or perhaps thinking of it over-seriously. But she was cheered when Kermit started receiving an income in keeping with his long schooling. Since Kermit had to sell them something for their money, and with them knowing little or nothing at all about the Negro as a group, he was not questioned and the one hundred dollars a week that they paid him was considered by them, in view of their plans, a good investment.

America was now alive and flooded with German agents, and the Jew and his position in America as compared to the position Hitler had reduced them to in Germany, was a splendid issue for debate. Kermit's plan to expose and start reducing his freedom and opportunity by the production of a hate picture was so logical, and in keeping with their plans, that they were all enthused. By now he knew they were waiting to hear what was happening, how it was coming along. So Kermit was on the spot and was most anxious to show some kind of results at an early date to keep them satisfied.

We have forgotten thus far in our story to explain that in race prejudice, segregation and many restrictions that hold the Negro back, many have found this to be the best alibi that could be conceived as an excuse for failure, and have preferred to give up making a real and sincere effort on the excuse that they were not given a chance to get ahead. No man was more fully acquainted with this than Sidney Wyeth. He knew it and regarded it as a major Negro excuse and was impatient with it. He felt that it was time they were offering something better. But Sidney Wyeth knew that nothing delighted many of the educated ones of his race more than to be able to blame somebody or some condition for their failure.

In the various propaganda combinations against the Jews both in America and abroad, one of the outstanding ones was that the Jew had too much! that he had far more than his share, and that he was continually seizing more avenues and arteries of commerce, thereby depriving somebody else of their opportunity. This was one of Kermit's excuses and he sincerely believed it to be true. This justified, as he saw it, something radical, if necessary, to crush Jewish power and influence. Naturally with Heinrich Schultz, a disciple, follower and ardent believer in the philosophy of Adolf Hitler, he subscribed to this idea, and had talked it over time and again with Early.

It was decided to pay Wyeth a visit, several visits if necessary and to go to bat with him until convinced one way or the other.

"I've never been around where they were making a picture," said Kermit, "otherwise, I'd attempt the direction and production of it myself. But I know enough about it to realize I'd probably make a mess of it."

"We'll see Wyeth," said Heinrich. "I'll go along with you. I'd like to meet him anyhow."

"Meantime, what does your sister say about him?"

"Plenty. She talks about him all the time, thinks he's a great fellow."

"Fine. But has she said anything about feeling him out?" said Kermit.

"No, she hasn't. Feels that she has not known him long enough and hasn't got matters around to that point yet."

"Of course," agreed Kermit. "Meantime, *we'll* call on him."

"Maybe you'd better call him up and—make an appointment?" suggested Schultz.

"No," said Early, and shook his head.

"Why?"

"He's a plain sort of person. Doesn't appreciate much ceremony and putting on on the part of Negroes. Says we're all too poor to be officious. So the thing to do is to just walk in on him, sit down and talk," explained Kermit.

"Okay by me," smiled Heinrich. "When?"

"Now," said Early, promptly rising to his feet.

"Then what are we waiting for?" said Schultz following Kermit.

A half hour later they were sitting in Wyeth's office waiting for him to come upstairs from the restaurant, where he had gone for his lunch.

"Well, Kermit," he cried, on his return, grasping the other's hand, heartily. "It's been a long time since I've seen you. I've been thinking about you. Don't know just why?"

"And it's been a long time since I've seen you, too, Mr. Wyeth." He then introduced Schultz.

"Miss Schultz' brother?"

"That's how they are related," said Kermit, looking him over.

"Well, I hope you're as bright and intelligent a man as Miss Schultz is a girl," said Wyeth, cheerfully. "I admire Miss Schultz very much."

"Thank you," said Schultz.

Kermit smiled.

"Meantime, be seated, gentlemen, and tell me what I can do for you."

All became seated, the door was closed, Wyeth looked from one to the other, a question in his eyes.

"It's what I called to see you about, shortly after I came to New York, Wyeth," Kermit began.

"You mean—a—picture?"

"Exactly."

"I see. You still intend to make it?"

"And I'm still interested in having you direct and produce it."

"I don't like the idea of hate pictures, Mr. Early."

"It is not exactly a hate picture, if I may be excused for interrupting," interposed Schultz, leaning forward.

Both looked at him.

"When you consider how the Jew neglects to do even little things for the Negro that he could just as well as not do, but looks upon us as too insignificant and not worth that much, it riles you," said Early.

"Possibly," said Wyeth, and waited.

"In the matter of the motion picture, for instance," suggested Schultz.

"We would get a far better play, perhaps, if he wasn't controlling the industry as he is. The South's hatred for us keeps us from being cast in better parts on the screen than is given us. It also keeps us off the radio," said Early.

"I've been hearing a great deal about that," interrupted Schultz at this point. "That we can't get on any of the big commercials with an all-colored show on account of the South. Just how do they manage to keep colored people off?"

"Easily and simply," replied Wyeth, calmly. "A company producing a standard brand article, for instance, deciding to feature an all Negro show, signs a contract to broadcast the show over a national network, including a chain of stations, a large number of which lay south of the Mason and Dixon line. All may seem well until the broadcast starts, whereupon most of the Southern stations 'button' the program, put on records or have a local program ready and put it on during the time the Negro program is supposed to be on all over the country, until the program time, usually a half hour, has expired, then they go back to the network. In that way we are deprived of making any of the big money that the white people receive for entertaining over the air. As a result, except as an occasional guest artist, we are confined to 'sustaining' programs, the pay for which is mostly very small, or for which we receive nothing at all, just the advertising it might give us."

"Of what good is such advertising?" Schultz wanted to know.

Wyeth shrugged his shoulders, then went on to explain.

"If it is a quartette or a choir, singing mostly spirituals and hymns, it results in somebody, somewhere, wishing to have these singers come to their town for a program in person, for which they pay something, often a net sum and in that way the few Negroes that belong to the quartette get a break."

"So we are ruled off the big air programs, eh?" said Schultz, frowning.

"And confined to singing spirituals and hymns, just before noon on Sundays, with the usual old time darkey sermon, plenty of moaning and shouting, and that, except on rare occasions and as a guest artist, now and then, are the roles we are confined to, on the radio in America."

"Now getting back to our role on the screen, controlled almost completely by Jews in this country. He is not certain about his position in the public eye, understands that the South wants the Negro *kept in his place* in any story filmed," said Early. "So instead of giving us a play in an outright Negro picture, nationally released and exploited, the Jew hesitates to make it on the ground that many Southern theatres might not book it and show it, so he keeps away from any stories that show the Negro in any intelligent or favorable light, writers write the Negro out, if the part is not so important and if this cannot be done, he substitutes some other nationality, if this is possible. Any way it goes, the Jew makes little or no effort to give our group an intelligent and dignified role on the screen when he could just as well do so. He uses the South's objection to Negroes when the South hasn't perhaps thought of it and might not object at all."

"That's a dirty Jew for you," cried Heinrich, "the selfish sons of bitches just don't care. Yet by his money he's able to purchase plenty of propaganda and make the world think, especially America, that he's being unmercifully persecuted by Hitler," Schultz went on, angrily.

"We'll soon be in this war," cried Early, vehemently, "and it'll be nobody but the Goddamned Jews who got us in it!"

"That is what Germany is afraid of," said Schultz now, walking the floor. Pausing in front of Wyeth, he pointed his finger at him, as he went on: "Germany has never wanted a quarrel, much less a fight or to go to war with America. Above all else, Germany would like to stay at peace with this country. I know that.

"But rich Jews and their great International bankers hate Hitler, they feel that if they can get the United States into the war, that the combined Nations can lick Germany and overthrow Hitler, so by propaganda galore, created, built up and exploited by Jewish trickery, they are pushing America as straight into the war as she can be pushed."

"Don't forget our President," said Early and laughed.

"I'm not," said Schultz, "for it is through him that they are working."

"Possibly not. Yet he's given and is still giving a lot of money to help Negroes. More than Negroes are giving to help themselves," said Wyeth. "But go on. I'm listening."

"In the meantime, we are interested and are here to talk about what the Jew is doing to keep the Negro down," said Early, looking at Wyeth. "While posing and having us believe that because he is persecuted, too, that he has an interest in common with us, that he is the Negro's friend. Do you believe that?" said Schultz.

"Of course Mr. Wyeth doesn't believe it. I can't understand, after the way he's been treated by the Jew sons a bitches, why he seems to insist on standing up for them as he does," said Early, a bit angrily, frowning.

"You've been making pictures for a long time, you're the only Negro who has ever made and released more than one motion picture. You know that they butted into your little end of the business two or three years ago, made a mess of it, then quit, left it and went on seeking a better way to make money, didn't they?"

"Well, they had a right to," said Wyeth. "This is supposed to be a free country, you know."

"But the fact is they did just what I said they did, didn't they?"

"Not to force me out, exactly. They had no personal interest in messing up the little independent production business I had built up. They thought there was money to be made in it. They thought that being Jewish with plenty of money to work with and the usual Jewish self-confidence they could make a reasonably profitable business out of it. So with this bigger money, they took a flyer at it, found it wasn't all it was cracked up to be by Negroes, please understand, who hoped to profit by it, so they withdrew and refused to put any more money in it, and went about their business."

"But not until they had put you out of business," said Schultz, pointedly.

Wyeth shrugged his shoulders.

"I've never been able to understand Mr. Wyeth's complacency regarding it," said Early, turning to Schultz. Both looked closely at Wyeth.

"If they put more money into it and made better pictures—" began Schultz.

"—not better pictures, Mr. Schultz," said Wyeth, cutting him short. "Smoother pictures, a little more expensive from the standpoint of sets and detail, but not nearly as interesting from the standpoint of entertainment. In short, as Mr. Early implied. The Jew does not take us seriously. He takes us only as he sees us. We are not in trade, commerce or industry seriously. We can't borrow money from the banks as he is able to do, to promote or exploit anything. We're just Negroes as he sees us, looking for a job, or some other way to make a living. So when he was sold the idea of making Negro pictures, nobody told him that he should get Negroes to write the stories."

"More contempt. If he was going to make a Jewish picture, the first thing he'd think of was a good Jewish writer to prepare the story," said Early.

"But he has many seasoned Jewish writers to write anything he might want to film," said Wyeth.

"You mean that we don't have plenty of Negro writers?"

"No, we do not. We have a few, yes."

"Then," Early went on.

"Why did he get white men to write the Negro stories they ultimately filmed, that was what you were going to say," said Wyeth.

"Exactly," said Early.

"Nobody said anything about Negro writers, none came around to sell them any idea of writing the story to be filmed—but white writers came around seeking the assignment."

"Naturally."

"Naturally, Early," said Wyeth. "Yes, naturally the white man came around and showed and convinced them that he could write the kind of story they wanted; that he knew a great deal about Negroes. Almost every white person thinks he does, so in lieu of no Negro putting in an appearance and selling them himself, which he could have done and if he had the kind of story that was filmable, they wouldn't have been hard to persuade to buy the Negro story instead of the hackneyed effort of the white man. But since no Negroes showed up, as we never show up for anything but a cheap job at so much per, nobody ever thought that the story ought to be written by a Negro who understood Negro thought and the Negro angle as well."

"Well?" said Early and paused.

"That is why, with all the Jew's faults and his apparent neglect as regards our group, when he could do something for us, since he is in the money, when you analyze it, you'll find that it is our neglect and indifference more than anything else that keeps us out of the bigger and better things. If we have anything to say about it, it is usually impractical and unworkable. If there had been intelligent Negroes doing any writing for the screen at the time they started out to make those pictures, the pictures would have been more successful because they would have been down the street the Negroes travel, in the language that is familiar to all us Negroes. In the story the white man attempted this was not true. The writers put a lot of words into the Negro actor's mouth that he never would say. The pictures looked good, like a meal might, but when you ate it or attempted to eat it you didn't find it palatable, didn't have the taste you looked for or expected. Result, you get up from the meal disgruntled and dissatisfied, not always knowing just what was the matter with the meal. That was the effect their pictures left on the Negroes who went to the theatres to see them. Pictures that did a lot of talking but said nothing. Result, the Jews who made them couldn't and never did understand what the matter was, and the Negroes who went in at first to look at them and stopped going, didn't know. He knew that something was wrong; that they were not interesting, but he didn't understand why. Being given, long since to charging his race with failure, he now blamed the Negroes for the uninteresting pictures turned out. Negroes who had nothing to do with it. But in keeping with our hatred for each other, the Negro charged the colored actor with the failure. Said he didn't know how to act. The fact is, we Negroes have so little confidence in each other, that it seems to give most of us a peculiar satisfaction when we can charge failures to ourselves, and then go out and most shamefully run each other down."

"Still this doesn't, as I see it, absolve the Jew," declared Kermit, a deep frown on his face. "He cheats and exploits the Negro by rent gouging, and in a hundred other ways. He should be exposed!"

"Maybe so," said Wyeth, soberly. "But I find so much at fault within us and ours that it keeps me so busy thinking and trying to improve the Negro's condition that I have no time or enthusiasm for trying to show the Jew up when at least the Jew is getting along all right for himself."

"What do you mean?" said Kermit.

"Just what I say," said Wyeth. "The Jew has successfuly built himself in this country and he knows the art and business of making money."

"But he's a cheater."

"Maybe so, but he hasn't chosen the Negro as the only one to cheat. If he is a cheater as you insist, he'll cheat a white man as quickly as he does a Negro."

"But he does cheat Negroes and exploits them more than he does the white people, gentiles, I mean."

"If he does," said Wyeth, "that is because the Negroes think less and are easier to cheat than anybody else."

"And you think that's all right?" said Kermit.

"Of course it is not all right, but as long as the Negro isn't complaining, why jump on the Jew and try to make trouble?"

"I don't agree with you."

"It comes right back to what I've said already. The Negro is shiftless, thoughtless, wasteful, lazy and extravagant and doesn't give a damn if he is. Now you feel that something ought to be done to reveal how the Jew is taking advantage of all this."

"I do," said Early.

"Well, since we are the victims, wouldn't it seem appropriate for the Negro to be awakened to his own perils?" said Schultz.

"That is the object of the picture, to wake him up, let him see in vivid and unforgettable scenes and convincing dialogue just what the Jew is doing to him," insisted Early.

Wyeth sighed, but still wasn't convinced.

"Shouldn't that be enough to convince you of the logic of making such a picture, Wyeth?" said Schultz, leaning forward.

"I agree with you that something ought to be done to wake the Negro up. But I do not agree that a hate picture, which, when shown would cause the Negro to revolt, cause him to go out and break up things, destroy property, for that is too often his reaction. This would be plain suicide and I do not want to be a party to it." The men looked at each other.

"We ought to accept it and say nothing about it," said Kermit.

"I'll put it another way," said Wyeth. "I'll make a comparison."

"All right," agreed Kermit and waited.

"Everybody knows the Negro is deficient in the many ways I've just related; he's lazy, irresponsible, shiftless, with so many faults that he should, if he could be persuaded as a group, get serious and try harder to improve his condition."

"Yes?"

"Still he doesn't, and all America, especially the South, has grown accustomed to accepting him with his faults."

"Why the South?"

"Because they accept and bear with him more down there with all these faults than the North does."

"I don't understand you," said Schultz.

"I'll explain. Down South they don't want Negroes voting, they avoid any form of social equality as they call it."

"I understand that."

"But if you are of good character, have a reputation for honesty and hard work, they will help you far more readily than they will up in the free North."

"Just how?" from Schultz.

"In all kinds of ways."

"Just what kind of ways, for instance?"

"The banks for one thing, will lend a Negro money down there."

"Won't they do so up North, with the same security, with the same rating?"

"They positively will not. The Negro has no standing or rating that will enable him to borrow money in the current sense, North or South. But the South puts your character first, lends a limited amount on the assumption of character and extends them credit in many other ways that helps the Negro from an economic standpoint. In other words, the South accepts the Negro along with his faults, and feels that with all his faults, the Negro has to be taken care of and does take care of him."

"What has that got to do with the Jews cheating and exploiting him?"

"You've preached that philosophy in your pictures," said Early, "leading the Negro to a mirror and forcing him to look in that mirror and have implied that the creature who looked back at him was us, nobody but us."

Wyeth laughed, so did Schultz. Early was forced to smile even.

"But I have never preached destruction in any picture as a way to improve our lot, for it distinctly is not the proper way."

"Our picture does not preach destruction."

"But if shown, it might create destruction, which is another point of debate."

"How so?" from Schultz.

"That the Negro is given to destruction; that he for some peculiar reason seems to delight in breaking up things. He does it everywhere, but seemingly more in the larger cities North than in the South, for instance. It is a well-known fact that he is given to breaking up and destroying any neighborhood he moves into and takes over."

The other men were silent. They knew Wyeth was speaking the truth. With their own eyes, they saw it going on in Harlem, in Chicago, everywhere Negroes move into and live. Only the constant watching by policemen could seem to restrain them from destruction. Even Sidney Wyeth couldn't explain this tendency, no Negro can. Yet it goes on more currently in the free North than in the oppressed South. Always destruction on the part of the smallest boy, girls even, never construction. The strangest failing America knows. No doubt environment has much to do with the tendency but that the tendency to destruction seems to be everywhere is a fact no Negro can or will deny.

"We are almost a half million strong here in New York," went on Wyeth, "but there is hardly an example of construction on our part going on anywhere in New York other than churches. Somebody else builds a section sometimes for us and when they put men in uniforms to watch it, and by so doing, they manage to keep it fairly decent, otherwise our children and our grownups proceed to destroy it as if it was put there for them to mutilate and destroy. But the towering misfortune among all the other unfortunate situations in which we live and are involved, is our failure to catch on and learn how to produce anything. That's what I mean. The Negro has not, after eighty years of freedom and billions of dollars spent to educate him, learned anything about producing as a means of making money, and improving our lot, and helping us to be free. The Jew knows how."

"He already knew how—"

"That is no discredit to him. Knowing how to make money and making it and having it has long since made him sensitive to the responsibility of his community. Everywhere in New York and other cities where Jews live, you need only look around you to see something that he has built, from his own synagogues, Young Men's and Young Women's Hebrew Associations, and hospitals to no end of other structures."

"Well, he has the money—has made it to do it with."

"Shouldn't we do the same things?"

"We've been free only eighty years," said Early.

"That's longer than the Jew has been in this country. There were only 250,000 Jews in America in 1880. That was fifteen years after we had been freed."

"You're forgetting that the Jew was in trade and commerce before anybody else," said Early.

"Well, he is a builder and by his thrift and industriousness, is able to provide employment for thousands of his own people and more employment for thousands of others," said Wyeth. "Do we? No. Have we built anything—even for ourselves in Harlem, Brooklyn, or anywhere else, except a few churches—and most of the ones we worship in were built by white men; built by them for white people. Yes, I know, the white people became frightened when we appeared and at the sight of us, turned and ran, and we simply moved in and took over. We have a fine YWCA and a still finer and larger YMCA in New York, both built by white people for us, but not by ourselves.

"Those, gentlemen, are some of the reasons why I can't see going out and making pictures designed to stir up strife and hatred by one group against another. I admit the Jew has his faults, plenty of them, but we have far more; faults that could be corrected by us for our own benefit. Personally, I don't mean much, and making the Negro pictures I have made didn't mean much. All I can do now is a little preaching through the pages of an occasional novel for a more sensible effort on the part of our group, of whose responsibility or irresponsibility, I am a part. If you can conceive some way in which I can be of assistance in a broader and more helpful sense, I'd be glad to join and go along with you. But this is not your plan, however much you might say to the contrary.

"I don't know just who is behind this plan of yours, to produce a picture to make Negroes hate Jews and stir up trouble, but I can guess it to be some subversive group or groups, inspired from Berlin, for Adolf Hitler, and is not for the benefit of the Negro, but more to bring about chaos and trouble here in America. I wouldn't be interested in anything like that, regardless of the way we are browbeaten and held back in our own country. As bad as this is and as much as I dislike it, I realize that it might be worse," said Wyeth.

"I'm sorry but I'm afraid, gentlemen, that you'll have to count me out."

By this time it was plainly obvious to both men that Sidney Wyeth was not going to be persuaded by them, at least, to direct and produce their picture. Still resolute and determined by disposition, however, Schultz went on:

"I'm sorry, since we're in position to get the finances for you to resume the production of pictures, that you do not agree with us."

"I'm sorry," said Wyeth, simply.

"The people who are advancing the money to make our picture, stand ready to advance an even larger sum to finance the production of those that you want to make. I'm told there hasn't been any colored pictures made, except a few insignificant productions, since you suspended; and that our people are anxious to see some good ones, so by helping us, and us helping you, we all benefit. Don't you think that is very reasonable?"

"Yes, fair enough."

"Then supposing you take it under advisement. It doesn't have to be made right away, and we'll see you and talk about it again, later on." With these words, Schultz rose to his feet, followed by Early and Wyeth. There was nothing further for Wyeth to say, so when they left all were as agreeable as when they arrived. On the way downstairs and up the street, the two men talked it over however, between themselves.

"In spite of his objections, I still feel that we can ultimately get him at least to direct it," said Schultz.

"I hope so," said Early gloomily, "but how?"

"I don't know just now and can't say," Schultz replied. "This much I do know, that we won't succeed in getting him to do it as we had planned it."

"I agree with you," said Early.

"Bertha," Schultz went on to say, "seems very much interested in him. I'm wondering what her interest is."

"I'd say personal," suggested Early.

"Maybe so," said Schultz. "Well, she's a girl."

"A pretty girl and an unmarried girl," said Early.

Schultz glanced at him.

"She knows what she wants to do, even if it is personal."

"But if we ever succeed in getting Wyeth to direct and produce this picture, it'll have to be your sister who gets him to do so."

"That's what I am afraid of."

"So deciding, supposing that we count ourselves out and leave it to her to do whatever she can to persuade him to," said Early.

"I guess that is about all that's left for us to do," said Schultz.

Both men lapsed into silence, then, increasing their pace, disappeared up the street toward Sugar Hill.

CHAPTER **XXIV**

MARIE AND BERTHA had not seen each other since they drove Wyeth, still sleeping, to New Haven, where he awoke and accompanied them into a tavern where they had refreshments. Wide awake and refreshed he drove them back to New York. When he awoke in New Haven, he didn't know that he had been asleep, so all had a good laugh over it, and enjoyed their ride back to New York, during which time both the girls went to sleep, and then he had the laugh on them. It was the roar of an elevated train overhead that awakened both with a start—and they weren't aware they had been asleep until awakened by the heavy elevated cars rumbling southward overhead the way Wyeth was driving.

Naturally, Bertha was anxious to see Marie a few days later and talk about Wyeth, and while at the office, Wyeth entered and invited her into his private office. Seated, he smiled across at her and it pleased her to smile back at him.

"I've been thinking about something which I'd like to ask you, Mr. Wyeth," began Bertha.

"Fire away, Miss Schultz. Will try to answer anything you ask."

"Why don't you put your book on sale at the bookshops? Surely there are a great many people who would be glad to purchase it, if it were where they could see it?"

"No doubt, but I have just neglected to do so. But before one makes any concerted effort along such lines, it is customary to send the book out to the newspapers for review."

"Well, haven't you done that?" she inquired. He was thoughtful a moment. Then looked at her.

"Shortly after the book came out, I went to Chicago where I had planned to start to do this. We were still in the picture business and at the time far more active than now. I happened to be in Chicago when *Nature's Child* was published, and read one of the greatest reviews that was ever written in one of the leading dailies out there. The writer was a woman, the literary editor of the paper. I knew the book had won the Book-Of-The-Month award, which would naturally inspire every reviewer to read it when they received their copy. Incidentally, I would like to say at this point, that I did not submit my book to that Club, nor to any of the other book clubs. While I liked the simple story I had tried to tell, and everybody who reads it seems to like it, also their friends who borrow and read it, and our sales continue to increase and mount steadily, and the only way I can account for this is, that it is getting mouth to mouth advertising from the people who are buying and reading it. At the time I didn't consider it sensational enough to send out in the hope of awards, and I still feel the same way."

"Of course," said Bertha, listening closely and attentively to what he was saying.

"I read her lengthy review of the book, in which she commented on what had been said by other reviewers. One reviewer in particular, thought it was the greatest Negro book ever published, It is a good crime story. Naturally I was anxious to read the book, but before I had finally succeeded in doing so, it had become a best seller, but had, after a few weeks, dropped out of the list and eventually seemed to have been forgotten by those who buy books. All of which aroused my curiosity.

"At one of the theatres, where I used to play my pictures in Chicago, I met one of the men who ran it, and who turned out to be one of the best informed men on literature I ever met. It was he who first referred to it as a psychological novel, and told me that it had had an immense sale, for a short time but that it passed by the boards so quickly that it had surprised everybody. Anyway, I decided to investigate, since I was slowly getting into stride as a publisher, but not on a clear-cut scale for I was still planning to continue making pictures, so my interest in the sale of my book was not as complete at the time as it became later. Anyway, I took a couple of copies and went to call on two leading dailies.

"The first one I called on was the lady who had raved so about *Nature's Child,* She was on the big morning daily. She had written, at alternate intervals, more about *Nature's Child*. In fact, she seemed to have fallen in love with the book, and took a delight, every time she had a chance, of saying something about it in her column. So I called at her office. While waiting, I saw some one open the inner door and peep out, and imagined later that it was she; but her secretary finally came forward and asked me what I wished. I displayed my book, which she took and went into the office where she stayed a few minutes then returned with the report that the lady didn't feel it prudent or good policy to meet the authors of books she was expected to review, since it might influence her opinion regarding the book. But that if I cared to leave it she would give me her reaction within the next two or three weeks in her column. Frankly I was disappointed, since I knew that few authors ever call on reviewers; that the books are mailed to the literary department of the various newspapers and the authors would have no occasion to be calling on the newspapers as I was doing in Chicago."

"Naturally," said Bertha, wonderingly, but waited for him to go on with his story.

"There was nothing I could do, of course, but leave the book as I had gone there to do. I would liked to have spoken with the lady, but since she had decreed otherwise, I left the book and went on across town a few blocks to the literary department of another paper. The literary editor there was not in, so I left the book and watched both papers for their reaction.

"That was in September. I followed the literary pages of both papers until the following January—and I've never, even to this day, seen or heard any comment or review."

"You don't mean it!" exclaimed Bertha, in great surprise.

"While in Chicago I arranged with a large school that was located near the Negro section of one of the suburban towns there to show one of my pictures, at which showing I planned to review the book and solicit some sales, which I have since developed very successfully. I was referred to the principal, a very fine white lady, a least they said she was, and I found her congenial. I showed her the book and she was very much interested—until she examined it."

"Just what do you mean by that?" inquired Bertha.

"What I have just said. She was very much interested in the book until she sketched through it."

"I still do not understand you," said Bertha, curiously.

"I think the lady was looking for something, seeing that I was a Negro and the author of the book, that I didn't have in the book." Bertha shook her head again to indicate that she still did not understand what he was talking about.

"She inquired regarding the dialect."

"The dialect?"

"Yes, Miss Schultz. She wanted to know about the dialect; she said she didn't see any; and wanted to know about how I had treated it."

Looking at Bertha, he could see that she still did not understand.

"When I told her there wasn't any dialect, she seemed the most surprised woman on earth."

"'No dialect,' she cried, amazed. 'I don't understand,' she went on." Bertha was folloiwng him closely, keenly interested.

"No madam," I said. "There is no dialect for it is not that kind of a story."

"I see," said the lady, and waited for me to explain which I promptly did and without hesitation. "It is the story of a young colored fellow from this state, which was Illinois, of course, who went into the Dakota wilderness where he found that he alone was black. In the years that followed this young man built an agricultural empire in that wilderness, during all that time, the only other colored people, and they were not many, that came were either related to or in whom he was interested, so the story, laid far off in the great Northwest, could not have featured any mammies or uncles or any colored people who would be talking in dialect and which explained the absence of any in the book, even if it was a Negro story."

"The lady understood, but I could see that she was disappointed, and not a bit enthused. Since the papers had been so cold regarding the book, and with this lady's reaction being anything but favorable, I was forced to the conclusion, which I have stuck to since, that the white people in general were not interested in the modern, intelligent and aggressive type of Negro whom I had written about in my book, and that it wasn't worthwhile to try to force the issue. I decided then not to seek any more reviews."

"I understand you better now. But surely they must have read the book," said Bertha, her face drawn into a serious frown.

"I'm in no position to know if they did or did not."

"If they read it, they would have been almost forced to say something about it, and it couldn't have been anything but favorable," she now said insistently.

"That is why I am forced to feel that they did not. I doubt very seriously if either of the literary departments of these two great papers ever read the book or had anybody read it. It is my opinion, when they sketched through it as this principal of the school did, looking for dialect and comedy, crime or degeneration, all of which seems to interest them about Negroes more than conventional Negro life, and I'm not forgetting the crime angle which made *Nature's Child* so popular with them, and they found none of this which they were looking for, I don't think they read the book or went to the trouble of getting anybody else to read it. Anyway, nothing was said about it, and that is what happened to me. As a result, I decided to say nothing further to white people about it and, as stated, sent no more copies for review, deciding since our group liked the book so well, better, from all that I could hear, than any Negro book they ever read, that I would just go ahead and sell it in such ways as I could learn and develop, and be satisfied. And that is why it is not on sale in the shops."

"I'm surprised," said Bertha, "for it is such a splendid story, so interesting from beginning to end, and has so much human appeal that I can't understand anybody reading the book and not being impressed."

"I don't know if I have explained it, but white America, a long time ago, set us Negroes in a sort of groove. By that I mean that they developed the view that the Negro was first a clown, a comedian and an idiot, conceived and born into the world to amuse white people. And in spite of the fact that we have been free eighty years; that billions of dollars have been spent to educate and make us apparently like any other American, we still remain in his picture eye, just the same as we were supposed to be before we were freed. Funny, in a measure, but pathetic. So he seems to insist on us being one way or the other. First, and preferably, funny, so as to make them laugh. But if he can't get a laugh at the thought and sight of us, then he can and does associate us in any other way, except in a contemporary way. It seems that to change this we'll have to get them in a corner and almost, at the point of a gun, literally say: 'now, white man, I've been educated by and in the same course of study that you have. About the only difference between us is that you are white and I am black, or brown or at least a Negro. Anyway, I eat the same kind of food that you do, prepared as you have yours. I breathe like you, walk like you and in most ways, talk like you. You have, as a group, far more money than I have, and you have the preference of jobs. I must accept what I can get, but for three generations a portion of us only have talked in dialect, fewer as the years go by. All of us do not roll our eyes, show our teeth and act in all the fool ways you think we ought to.'

"It seems we've almost got to go that far to make him understand that we are not essentially a different people. For instance, a few months after these other incidents, I made an adaptation of my book to a play. I've read plenty of plays and, of course, been to see many on the stage, so I know that the manuscript of the play I made from my book was well done and an interesting script. I sent a copy to each of fifteen leading American stage critics all over for comment with a letter advising that I knew this was a rather unusual procedure but that I was planning to produce it on Broadway in the near future and would like to hear what they thought of the idea—what they would think of a play of modern, intelligent Negro life. Not a single one answered or wrote a line about it. They reacted the same way the papers had to my book. Which left me in a quandary. What was I to do, what was I to think? Their lack of interest in both cases was the same. White America, as I've said, has the Negro typed, They have us set in a groove that she has chiseled according to her own idea and style, and there we are supposed to stay and be satisfied.

"That is one of the reasons I feel that Negroes are not trying to write anything. He doesn't know how to write according to the white man's philosophy regarding us, and if he writes according to his own, he can't get it published, because the white publishers just can't see it. As a race, we've never been called on to write anything for the screen, very little for the radio, and from the standpoint of books and magazine articles, well, we're just out. And, unfortunately, we seem to accept the spot they have set us in, and for the present seem to have given up making any serious attempt to change it."

"That is deplorable," said Bertha, shaking her head, sadly. "Deplorable to say the least."

"Deplorable is the word. It all boils down to what I have felt necessary for a long time. That it is up to the Negro, and the Negro alone to work out his own salvation in the arts, the sciences, the motion picture, and to some extent, the radio. Unless we are willing to do this, we are just sunk."

"It surely seems that way from what you say," she said, then paused to look at him a bit oddly.

"Would you believe me when I explain, Mr. Wyeth," she said, sudden-like, "That you're the only one that I've talked to, I mean, in our race, who seems to take it that way; that seriously."

"I'm not surprised. Most of us don't take anything seriously. Everybody has money now and we don't give a tinker's damn about tomorrow. That is Negro America."

"But—they—they can't go on this way forever. Surely something is going to be done about it, something will be done to change it," she went on earnestly, seriously.

"Don't let it trouble you too much, Miss Schultz," smiled Wyeth. "Don't let it trouble you more than it is seeming to trouble them, for if you do, you might be unhappy. They are not. We are given to taking things so easy until you can't but wonder that most white people fail to take us seriously, why they are so inclined to look upon us as clowns, comedians and idiots, and are so unwilling to accept us in the ordinary American way."

"But they are not all that way, are they?"

"Of course not. In fact, most of us are different, but they do not consider those as a majority. Their contact is confined to a small minority, mostly to the servants who work for them, the girls, who take care of their children, the women, who cook for them, the men, who clean up after them, shine their shoes and look after them, more or less in a menial way."

"What about the teachers, the doctors, the white collar workers?"

"They don't meet them. Most white people do not know that they exist. And with regards to this class, with many exceptions, of course, they present another side of our complex problem."

"In just what way, please?"

"A very great many of them are selfish. Downright selfish and when they have a good job themselves, they don't waste many tears about the others not so fortunate."

"This is a new angle. I haven't been told about them."

"You wouldn't be, because that is the kind a girl like you would meet, become associated with and be so close to that you might not be able to see just how selfish and—often despicable they are."

"You seem to have gone deeply into the problem of the Negro in America," she said. "You know more about his conditions than anybody I've met."

"I hope you will become better acquainted with them."

"I do want to," she said eagerly.

"I don't know just how you will go about finding out. I could help you, to some degree, but it is not convenient at this time."

"What do you mean? Would you mind explaining?"

He looked at her, then he thought for a moment and looked at her again.

"I've been contemplating going on an extended sales tour into the South. I have covered some of it but this is the best time of year to go further. My errand, of course, will be in the sale of my book. I am building up a very successful business, and I like the work. It pleases me and brings me closer to the Negro than I have ever been and I have boasted of having been closer to the masses in the production and distribution of pictures, than anybody else. But the sale of my book brings me face to face with not only the masses but also the classes."

"Oh, Mr. Wyeth," she cried, shifting anxiously. I am *so* interested in what you are talking about. I would be glad to—to share in some of all this contact you speak about. Won't you please tell me all about it—everything?" She moved her chair a little nearer his as she finished, and looked so anxious that he was forced to smile.

"This trip," she went on. "Just how are you going to manage it, where will you be going?"

"All the way, if I have my way about it, from here to—Brownsville, Texas."

"All the way from here to Brownsville, Texas? That is—"

"Away Southwest, nearly 2,000 miles, on the Texas and Mexican border."

"Oh, how wonderful! Please go on. On this trip you will—exploit your book?"

"That is the purpose. It amounts to simply getting in my car right here in New York, and going on from here, stopping at all the schools that I can conveniently contact, and when I have gotten as far South as Philadelphia, I will review it to as many groups as I conveniently can. I shall carry a substantial supply of books with me, but all the orders that I cannot fill as I go along, Marie will take care of from the office. So I just drive on and on and meet people, as I said, in schools and from Philadelphia South, most of those I visit, of course, will have colored teachers. So I can make a dozen or so of these institutions a day, five days a week. I try to get to a key city to spend the night, and there I meet more groups who seem to like to hear me talk, and all my talk in the end brings out the matter of the book, so I sell many and learn lots of things of interest to go into other books."

"How wonderful! No wonder you are so well-informed," she cried enthusiastically. "Now, who will go with you on this—trip?"

He shook his head. "Nobody, just me and myself and—come to think of it, I'll probably carry my gun."

"By yourself and only your gun?"

"It will be in the autumn. Back where I was raised in Southern Illinois I used to hunt in the fall. I learned to be a very good marksman. So on this trip, too, I'll carry my shot gun, possibly a rifle, but assuredly the shot gun. Here and there, when I see something to shoot, I stop the car, get out and take a shot at it and often bring down what I shoot at."

"This is too wonderful for words and how I envy you. I would give—half of my life to go on a trip like that."

"It would enlarge your education wonderfully," he said.

"But I would not know how to go—by myself," she said, and looked at him, a question in her eyes. "I don't know much about shooting except what I was taught at school, shooting at clay pigeons, at marks and the like. I haven't fired a shot gun since."

"That is why I stated that it is unfortunate that you can't make such a trip."

"With you, maybe?"

Again he looked at her, and seemed embarrassed.

"With me? That wouldn't be quite in keeping with—with, society, I don't think," he said a bit hesitantly.

"I am not in society," she said readily. "I am not on a job to study and learn anything about society in particular. I—could go with you."

"Oh, Miss Schultz. Not with me."

"I'm sorry," she said, apologetically. "I—I guess I spoke too hastily. I guess you—you wouldn't want a woman with you. I'd perhaps be—in your way."

"I wouldn't say that," he said, his face reddening in spite of the brown of his skin. "And you wouldn't be in my way. It is only that I—I hadn't thought of anything like that."

"I'm sorry," she said and was then silent. He didn't know exactly what to say, so said nothing. After a smile, which was as if to reassure him, she rose and left, he thought, a bit abruptly.

Outside, she spoke to Marie.

"I'm going home now," she said, pausing to glance over her shoulder in the direction of Wyeth. Then in an undertone. "When Mr. Wyeth leaves the office, do you think he will be gone all day?"

"He's getting ready to leave now. When he goes, he won't be back any more today," replied Marie, looking at her curiously and wondering what she was thinking, maybe planning.

"When he leaves, I want you to call me."

"Of course," said Marie, wondering more at her strange actions, what she had on her mind.

"Then please do that, won't you? I'll be waiting right there by the phone for your call. I'm going now," She reached and quickly kissed Marie on the cheek, and turning, left the office without further words.

Marie looked after her, more curious than ever over her actions. A few minutes later, Wyeth came out of his office with his large case, in which he usually carried about two dozen books so as to have them if he might need them. He paused to consult his watch, then advising her that he was going North to White Plains for the day, left. She was going to ask him something about Bertha, but he seemed in a hurry; he was always in a hurry, so she didn't get a chance to do so before he was gone. She sat silent for a few seconds, wondering what is was all about. Then picking up the telephone, she called Bertha.

The answer was immediate for Bertha immediately picked up the receiver at the other end.

"It's Marie, Bertha."

"Has Mr. Wyeth left the office?"

"Yes. That's what I called to tell you."

"Thank you, dear. Now—will he be back soon?"

"He won't be back at all—that is, not today," replied Marie.

"Oh, I'm so glad," cried Bertha.

"So glad?" called Marie. "I don't understand you. What's this all about, anyhow?"

"I'll catch a taxi and come right down. I'll tell you when I get there," and without another word, hung up.

A few minutes later Bertha rushed into the office, breathing a bit heavily from running up the stairs.

"Bertha!" Marie exclaimed, and rose to her feet. Bertha came closer and embraced her. She turned to look in Wyeth's office.

"He is—gone?" she asked. Marie nodded her head.

"Then, we can—sit in his office?"

"Of course, Bertha."

"Meanwhile, I can wait until you—have caught up with your work."

"I am caught up. We've made the shipments for the day. Anything else can wait." They both went into Wyeth's office, where Marie took his chair, Bertha in the one she had sat in half an hour or so before.

"Tell me now, Bertha," Marie began, "What is all the excitement about? Why are you all of a sudden, so strange, so excited?"

Bertha looked at her for a moment.

"Didn't you overhear us talking?"

"Of course I overheard you, in a general way," explained Marie. "But I didn't listen to what you were talking about in particular."

"Then you didn't hear him, that is, understand his saying that he was going on a trip, a long trip South?"

"Oh, something, but of course I knew that he had planned it for some time. What has that got to do with your being so excited?"

"I want to go with him."

"Bertha!"

"I want to go with him, Marie," Bertha cried excitedly, almost in tears.

"But—Bertha, Mr. Wyeth is a man, and you—a girl."

"That is why I am so excited. But I want to go with Mr. Wyeth on this trip."

"Are you losing your mind? A nice girl like you, riding all over the country with a—man?"

"I want to go. I know it may not look just right, yet here is a chance, my chance to find out something it is most important that I learn. To be with Mr. Wyeth for days, would give me the opportunity to learn it. I want to go with him."

"But—but—Mr. Wyeth would not take you. Mr. Wyeth is a gentleman, and not that kind of a man—"

"I know, Marie, and I understand how he would feel about it."

During the night, she had been kept awake, thinking about such a trip; of the long days and nights when they would be so close together, closer than they could possibly be elsewhere or under any other conditions. She did not say that she had some strange desire to go with him. All she knew was that she wanted to go; that she wanted to be with him on this trip.

"I want you to help me find a way, to plan a way," she cried and grasped Marie's hand which she had reached and picked up.

Marie looked at her closely.

"I don't understand you," said Marie.

Bertha looked at her, sighed and shook her head.

"Maybe I don't understand myself. I only know that I want to go with Mr. Wyeth on this trip, and because I also know that it doesn't look just right that Mr. Wyeth, being the kind of man he is, might not want to take me, I'm appealing to you. It is only you who can persuade him to take me. I—"

"Furthermore, Bertha, it is a business trip with him. He has been on them before. He did well. He will know this time how to do better. He will be working, reviewing his book a dozen times a day, everywhere, to endless groups, including preachers and teachers, insurance agents—no end of people. He is well prepared for what he is going to do."

"I understand all that, Marie, dear."

"You might be in his way. Trying to be nice to you might slow him up. He is a restless, energetic sort of person. He wouldn't like to be slowed up. He—"

"I wouldn't slow him up, Marie, darling. Furthermore, instead of being in his way, I could—help him."

"Help him?" cried Marie. "Help him how?"

"Why, in many ways," Bertha replied, readily, rising to her feet, too excited to remain seated longer. She moved a few steps, back and forth, twisting her hands. Presently she stood over Marie, who looked up at her. She paused.

"I'd like to help you, dear Bertha," said Marie, kindly, taking her hand now and fondling it. "You know I am your friend, your best friend."

"And I am your best friend, too, Marie, dear. You know that. I love you better than anybody else I know. I want to go with Mr. Wyeth. You are smart, you are intelligent. You can think of some way." She paused to sit down on the desk before Marie, and facing her went on:

"Now, darling, you must help me. You must find a way to persuade Mr. Wyeth to let me go with him."

Marie looked at her a moment, bit her lip and frowned, lowered her eyes to think, looked up at her again.

"Another thing, being a single man, with you near him, might . . . It would be hard on any man that close to a girl like you, to resist becoming interested."

She looked into Bertha's eyes and Bertha blushed and turned her's away.

"Mr. Wyeth, as you know, has just escaped from the clutches of a woman who didn't mean him any good."

"But Marie, I'm not that kind of woman. I would not . . . could not injure Mr. Wyeth as she might have injured him."

"No, you would not and you could not, because you are a nice girl, the kind of girl as I have hinted before who would be—nice for

Mr. Wyeth to—like. I wish you and he learned to like each other."

"Oh, Marie," cried Bertha, sweetly, modestly, daring to take a quick look into her eyes. Then lowering her eyes again she played with the finger nails on the hand that was free.

"Of course, Mr. Wyeth is his own boss. I have nothing to do with what he thinks or does," said Marie.

"But you *are* interested in him," said Bertha.

"I am, Bertha, like a big sister. I enjoy looking after his interests and he likes me doing so. The point is, just how could anything like this be arranged?" and she lowered her eyes. Bertha, quick-witted by nature, training and disposition, was doing some thinking, too. She turned to Marie with a sudden idea.

"I could hire myself to him, be his secretary, for instance," Bertha said suddenly, and was more anxious.

Marie looked up, then smiled.

"Why smile, Marie? Couldn't that be arranged?"

"But you are already employed, you already have a job," Bertha shrugged her shoulders.

"My job is and always has been, to find out things about Negroes, to become acquainted with their condition, their position in American life in general, and to compile that information. It is obvious to you and to me, Marie, that instead of this trip being a hindrance, it could be of great help; it would mean more information the acquisition of which I desire, more than anything else. I could learn more on this trip than I could otherwise find out in years. Mr. Wyeth is a practical encyclopedia of information. I could go with him as his secretary, helping in many ways."

"To sell books, that would be the way you could help him; the way you could possibly help him lots and not be in the way, by helping him to sell his book. You wouldn't want to do that; nobody ever wants to help do that—and it is so simple, so easy."

"Why wouldn't I? In fact, I'm sure I would enjoy helping him that way."

Marie looked up with a new interest.

"You mean, Bertha, that you—wouldn't mind helping him sell the book?"

"Of course not, and why not?" Marie looked at her seriously for the first time. Drummed the fingers of her hand on the desk before her. Then looked up at Bertha again.

"If you feel that you would like to help him that way, it might be arranged, at least considered, but only after you think it over. Are you sure that you would like to help him that way?"

"I tell you, darling Marie, I would like to help him in any way. The more I think about it the more I know I want to, and I would. I've told you that I would like to be more active. That would give me a chance, and I wouldn't be any old stick-in-the-mud; I'd throw myself into the work. I bet I'd help to increase the sales immeasurably. I can operate a typewriter; I know shorthand. I could be a wonderful secretary, a secretary who'd try to help and cooperate. Oh, please, Marie, say that you'll try to persuade him to—to let me go with him."

"Let me think it over, by myself," said Marie, rising to her feet. As if to get Bertha for the moment out of the way so that she could think, clearly and without interruption. Then she took her and pushed her down in the chair.

"You sit there, and stay seated while I think it over."

Bertha smiled up at her like an obedient child. Marie walked away, then up and down a few times then finally turned to Bertha.

"Mr. Wyeth is my boss, and he's a good boss. Been a good one for years and years. I was unhappy for only a short while, because I saw he was about to get into trouble, and he didn't deserve it. I'm not going to let anybody else get in his way and mess him up." Bertha started to protest, but Marie hushed her, by laying a finger over her lips, and pointing at her.

"You wouldn't do that, and I' not afraid about that. The only thing I'm uncertain about is—something else. Something about—you."

"About me?" cried Bertha, starting to rise.

Marie pushed her back and reassured her by smiling.

"Take it easy, Bertha, sweetheart. What worries me about you is that you are so pretty and so nice and congenial and in so many other ways so good, that—that—well, supposing Mr. Wyeth, after being so close to you for days, closer than two people could be otherwise than as man and wife. Supposing that he should begin to like you." Bertha had been listening to her tensely, hanging onto Marie's every word. Now she slumped back, with an, "Oh, Marie."

"If I was a man like Mr. Wyeth, lonely, with nobody in love with me, me in love with nobody, and I found a fine girl like you right at my side, ready to assist me in a thousand ways, as I know you would be ready, willing and glad to help in any way—every way, am I so strong-willed that I could resist such a presence and—not become, possibly, interested?"

"But Mr. Wyeth would not be interested that way in me, Marie."

"Why couldn't he?"

"Be—because. Oh, he just wouldn't, that's all," and Bertha, her eyes lowered, blushed furiously. Marie stood up and looked down at her, and then it suddenly occurred to her, why she was on the anxious seat. It was because there was something about Bertha, as much as she liked her, that was secretive; something that Bertha had not and did not tell. What was it? Looking down at her she went on seriously.

"You see, Bertha, there is something a—bit mysterious about you which you have not told me. I don't know what it is, and I decided when it occurred to me shortly after I met you, that I wouldn't ask you. I do not believe it is my part to ask you. I am not asking you now. I believe, however, that it is something to do with this war, in some strange and peculiar way. Oh, hang it, I can't seem to make my meaning clear," and Marie stamped her foot, to indicate her agitation.

Bertha, in the meanwhile, knowing that Marie was speaking the truth, of course, knew why. She also knew that what she hadn't told Marie nor anybody else; knew that it was something she would never tell, remained silent, terribly embarrassed, for she was sorry that it was that way. Finally she took Marie's hand, still without looking up, and went on to say, to admit.

"There *is* something, and I know it is that something that has worried you, yet it is something confidential and I don't want to talk about it. If you are my good friend, you will just understand that there is something and won't say anything about it again. I can only tell you that it is nothing—that is against you, or our race, or anybody in particular. It is just something that I can't talk about. Now do you understand?" She dared look up at Marie now and there were sincere tears in her eyes, and Marie understood and was as she should have been, sorry for Bertha.

"Darling," she cried, and standing, moved closer to Bertha. "I understand enough to trust you, to want to help you because I know you need kindness and sympathy."

Bertha was weeping now.

"I—I like Mr. Wyeth, Marie," she said between her sobs.

Marie looked long at her.

"Oh, I don't mean that I am—in love with him. I am in love with no man—at least I don't think so. So you don't have to worry about that. I do mean when I say, however, that if there is any man that I am particularly interested in, it is Mr. Wyeth."

"You mean, Bertha," Marie was saying now, "that—that if on this trip, if Mr. Wyeth should begin to—like you, I mean, seriously, that it would—be all right?"

Without raising her eyes, Bertha nodded her head slowly in the affirmative.

"But this something that I cannot talk about, I—I'm not free. I won't be free until—until this war is over." She now rose to her feet and walked away, and with her back still to Marie. "And before the war is—over, something might happen," she continued. "It might happen to me, and if it did, I would—*never be free.*"

As we know, Bertha meant her allegiance to Adolf Hitler, of what she had sworn, before leaving Germany to do, or try to do; but whatever the case, her life, her efforts and her duty were first to the Third Reich, to Germany, her fatherland—and Adolf Hitler. That is what she meant and could not say.

"It is all so strange and—so fatal," said Marie, standing close behind her. "This subtle something—but I won't say any more about it. I am satisfied. In the meanwhile, if Mr. Wyeth should begin to like you before this trip is over, he would not embarrass you. It would have to be you who made the overtures, and by what you say, I can see that you are not free to do that, not now. But if all or any of it should come to pass, it would have to be you who would take the initiative. Mr. Wyeth might grow to like you, but he would keep it to himself. He would never force it on you. He would not believe that you would or could ever fall in love with a plain man like him."

Bertha was emotional again and turning, threw herself into

Marie's arms and cried like her heart would break. After a time, she relaxed, dried her eyes and looked frankly at Marie.

"I can only tell you that I like Mr. Wyeth, and if he should in turn, begin to like me, other than this something that I can't tell, it would be all right. I am interested in him and if you help me or help persuade him to take me with him, I can assure you that I will look after him—like you would, and you need have no fear that—that everything won't be all right."

She turned now and walked into the outer office. Marie followed her. Out there, she paused. "I—think I will go home now," she said simply, and turning, she left and Marie did not try to stop her, for she, too, wanted to be alone with her thoughts.

We pause at this point and digress to explain why Bertha was so excited and why she wanted to go away from New York, on this long and extended trip with Sidney Wyeth, so badly.

She had been called downtown on several occasions, recently, to consult with leaders of the various subversive groups that she and Heinrich were associated with, including Hans Schiller, who was so friendly with her brother.

Plans were on foot to begin to sabotage as much of America's war efforts as was possible. The leaders were very much concerned over the active preparation going on everywhere, and especially as regards New Jersey and Connecticut, both of which could be reached from New York, and their underground headquarters, quite easily.

Bertha knew that conference after conference had been held, and more were scheduled to be held with a view to blowing up and destroying as much of these works as might be managed.

Her brother was one of the most active leaders in this development, and was at that very moment, the busiest man in all New York in this connection. For days she knew he had been planning one act of sabotage after another.

For some reason, especially after meeting Wyeth and coming to admire him so much, Bertha was beginning to sour on the whole plot. Hating Jews and all the propaganda making connected with it, she was not only beginning to dislike, but it was becoming repulsive to her. Yet she realized that she was expected to take an active part in it.

She heard it suggested that she be sent to Bridgeport, New Haven,

Waterbury and Hartford to take jobs. She was to stay on each job only as long as it was necessary to get the lay of things. They had hinted that being so pretty, she might be able to inveigle bosses and foremen into "talking" and in which way get closer to the guarded departments. Possibly be able to plant an incendiary or time bomb here and there where it could do the most damage.

She had heard them debate the idea and plan to plant these bombs, if unable to in the precision departments and works, then in the lunch rooms and recreation departments, with the bombs timed to go off during lunch and recreation periods when the explosions would kill and maim more people. All of which she viewed with horror and as nothing short of plain murder. The more she heard it debated and planned, the more repulsive the whole scheme became to her.

Sooner or later, however, she was able to see, she would be called on to go into action and attempt some of these plans they were devising. The fact that to do this would kill and injure scores of innocent and defenseless people didn't seem to matter at all—in fact, recalling a remark of Hans Schiller, to the effect that the more it killed, the merrier, and the more the effort would be considered as a long step towards success.

After learning of Wyeth's proposed trip, she was quick to appreciate that if she could slip quietly away with him, she would be unavailable to engage in or commit any of the dastarded acts.

She had been sent to America at the outset to investigate conditions pertaining to the Negro; of his treatment and of his reaction to that treatment. Plain and simple research, the kind of work that she had prepared herself at both Heidelberg and the Sorbonne to do, and not to commit sabotage, destruction and plain murder.

There were plenty men—and even women, among those sent here, however, who were perfectly agreeable to doing anything they were asked by the leaders to do, in so long as it could be considered for the "dear Fuehrer."

She had even tried to bring herself around to their way of thinking, since they were all supposed to be united in a common cause. But she had failed in the effort miserably. She just couldn't accustom herself to such ideas and sleep good.

Immediately—even as Wyeth related his plans to her, she decided to by pass all the subversive efforts, if she could, that was going on downtown and go away with Sidney Wyeth. During the night that followed her conversation with him, she found herself picturing herself on such a journey. It would not only make her unavailable, when it came to carrying out, or attempting to carry out their nefarious tenets, which she knew that in due time she would be called on to try perform, but the trip itself would provide the opportunity to gather so much widespread information, even if only in a general way.

Then there would be the pleasant association with a man she liked, to go with it. In meeting Wyeth and what conversation she had exchanged with him, it was her wish to get into a position where she could, if possible, be closer to talk with him still further. So the more she thought about the trip, the more the desire to go possessed her.

CHAPTER XXV

FLORENCE WINGATE stayed two days in Wakefield, was careful of what she said, even to her mother, dropping no hint about her plans, then returned to her home on Peachtree Street in Atlanta, where she found a message from her husband. It was from Charlotte, where he wrote her on hotel stationery, that he had his chauffeur meet him and would make the rest of the journey to Atlanta by motor, stopping over in a few places enroute, but that he would, however, endeavor to reach Atlanta by Saturday night.

Seated by a window, she counted the days, only a few away. She sighed. Close to it, she was conscious now that she dreaded it, yet realized that it had to be done and the sooner the better. Yet, as she contemplated leaving Mr. Wingate, who had never been a real husband to her, she was strangely sorry. For more than ten years she had tried to endure him. She had even permitted him to satisfy himself in his own way. As she stood there thinking about him and about Kermit and about her people, she decided that before she left him she would let him satisfy himself again, as revolting as it always was to her. She moved across to a comfortable chair and thought about her baby. This seemed always to compensate for any sacrifice, for everything. It made her brave and resolute. A child was what she had done it all for. Now, since the child was on the way, she felt equal to any task, any burden that might be forced upon her, for the great privilege.

As she sat there, looking out into the street, it became dark, slowly, very dark, so dark that she got to her feet and going to the window, looked out at the sky, which was overcast. A wind was blowing, a soft wind, but a wind that felt like it was preceding a storm. It had been hot and sultry for two days, and everybody was looking for the heat to be broken by showers, but as she looked up at the heavily overcast sky, then heard the rumble of distant thunder, with a flash of lightning that frightened her, she realized that it might be more than a shower. A storm was approaching Atlanta, coming down from the northwest.

Mammy was busy lowering windows upstairs. She could hear her and Florence now hurried to lower the windows downstairs. A few minutes later the storm broke. Daring to look out at the row of trees that lined the wide street, she could hear and see limbs being torn by the wind from them and fall crashing into the street. Lightning, great flashes of it, lit the dark outside up into a silvery like shimmer. The rain came down in torrents and it continued to storm all through the afternoon and into the early hours of the night.

She had just finished her dinner and mammy was clearing away the dishes when the telephone rang. She went to it and when she answered, some one asked if she lived there. She answered in the affirmative. The operator said it was long distance calling from somewhere in South Carolina. She became anxious. She tried to think who would be calling her from South Carolina. After a time, she could hear voices from the other end, then a man's voice said: "I am trying to get Mrs. Wingate, are you Mrs. Wingate?"

"I am," she replied, and was very curious by now. There was more talking on the other end, which she could pick up in bits, through the receiver. Then the man who had been talking to her began again.

"I would like to talk to Mrs. Florence Wingate."

"I am Mrs. Florence Wingate," she said, and waited, while the person seemed to turn and exchange more words with others, apparently in the room. She heard another voice, talking evidently to the man on the phone.

"That's the name on the identification card. Mrs. Florence Wingate," and he called the street number, "Atlanta, Georgia."

"All right," said the voice on the phone, but to her. "All right, I'll tell her. You've put it on me, so I'll tell her."

"What could it mean?" she asked herself, now very anxious.

"Hello," called the voice.

"Hello," she replied.

"Are you Mrs. Wingate?"

"I am Mrs. Wingate."

"Mrs. Florence Wingate, and you reside on Peachtree Street, in Atlanta?"

"I am Mrs. Florence Wingate and I live on Peachtree Street in Atlanta, thank you. Now what do you want; what is this all about?"

"This is Sergeant Winslow, of the highway patrol, at Florence, South Carolina, Mrs. Wingate."

"Yes, I hear you, and I understand. What has happened? Why are you calling me?"

"To tell you that a Mr. Wingate, residing at that address in Atlanta has been—" somebody interrupted again, but only for a moment while she held her breath, "—has been killed."

"Been killed!" she exclaimed. "I don't understand. You say Mr. Harold Wingate, has been—"

"—killed, Madam. I'm awfully sorry, but somebody had to give you the sad news."

"Do you mean to tell me that—"

"—Mr. Harold Wingate, the textile merchant and mill owner has been killed in an accident."

She was near to fainting now, but as we have described her before, Mrs. Wingate was not a weak woman as women go, but strong and resolute. A woman, because of the unusual manner in which her life had been diverted, and because of having to assume responsibilities that few wealthy women, or women of wealthy husbands, have had to shoulder, had become used to many things. Now she was steeling her nerves to a —tragedy. Her husband had been killed! She could hear the Sergeant's voice again.

"Yes, madam, he was killed while crossing the Southern Railway tracks, north bound tracks, during a blinding storm. He evidently, or the driver evidently, didn't hear it, the car seemed to have stalled. It is our opinion that they didn't hear the approach of the train. The driver jumped out and escaped and Mr. Wingate, from all appearances, started to, but failed to get clear of the tracks, when the train crashed into his car, killing him instantly and wrecking the car, which we found half a mile down the track, after the storm had subsided. Sorry madam. Are there any instructions you wish to give us?"

"Yes," she said, faintly. "Hold the—body until I arrive. I will leave by train as quickly as possible."

"Thank you. Kindly call the police station at Florence, South Carolina, when you arrive."

"I will," she said faintly, and hanging up the receiver, sat there, bewildered, like—trying to fathom what it all meant. She couldn't, for a long time, get used to it. Meanwhile, mammy coming down the hall, paused on seeing her looking so pale, came forward.

"Whassa matter, Mi's Wingate? Has you had—bad news?"

She looked at mammy oddly, out of eyes that were bewildered and strange looking. She nodded her head and mammy came closer, looking at her anxiously.

"Mr. Wingate, mammy, has been—killed."

"Killed!" exclaimed mammy, recoiling violently.

She looked at mammy but was not conscious that she was there, but still knew she was. Everything seemed to be in a whirl. She was conscious that she was about to faint, and then thought about what Kermit had once told her. That if at any time one feared fainting, to lean forward. So Florence Wingate leaned slowly forward. In a moment it had passed and she sat straight, and realized that it was not all a dream as she had been about to conjecture, but all too true.

"Yes, mammy, that was the police, calling me from South Carolina, to tell me that Mr. Wingate's car stalled while crossing the railroad tracks in a blinding storm. A part of that storm which just passed here, no doubt—and he was —killed."

"Great God almighty, forgive us," cried Mammy, and rushing to the kitchen, returned a moment later with a pitcher of cold water. Mrs. Wingate took a drink. Mammy was saying a lot, but she silenced her with a wave of her hand, and then motioned her away. She wanted to be alone to think. The first thing she thought of doing was to call Wakefield, tell her people what had happened. She then wondered if it wouldn't be better to wire them, then she wouldn't have to be bothered by the condolences they would insist on forcing on her. Mr. Wingate was dead, had been killed and her first duty was to get ready and leave Atlanta and go to him, or where they were holding his body. On the way there, she would have time to recover from the shock and think of other things to do. So steeling herself as she had long since become used to doing, she drew up a pad, found a pencil and calmly wrote two messages. One to her mother in Wakefield, advising what had happened, the other to New York, advising Kermit Early of the same thing. This done she took hold of herself and prepared to leave Atlanta before the wire she had called over the phone could reach and be delivered in Wakefield and her mother could call her.

The first train North from the Terminal Station, therefore, carried Mrs. Wingate northward to Florence, and to the body of her husband.

CHAPTER **XXVI**

MARIE COLEMAN did a lot of thinking regarding her conversation with Bertha Schultz after Bertha left. And at home, Bertha did a great deal more. Bertha saw in such a trip, the greatest opportunity she would ever have to study and learn the Negro, and the conditions that controlled and influenced him. She could buy a car, and she could cover in it the Negro section of the country all over—but without Sidney Wyeth, and his wealth of general information regarding every place and every condition that would be brought under her observation and discussed as only he was able to discuss it, made thinking of going alone seem vain, useless. She thought of it and continued to think of it all over again and the more she did so, the more convinced she became, that she'd just have to go with him. In the meantime, Marie in her home, was talking with her mother whom she was always glad to turn to for counsel.

"Why don't you take it up directly with Mr. Wyeth, dear," her mother was saying.

"I am planning to, but it has me on the anxious seat," said Marie. "I am wondering what he is going to think of the idea. I'm wondering how having a pretty girl, sitting beside him and going with him everywhere, staying in the same hotels and all that, is going to appeal to him?"

"Well, all I can see is for you to talk with him about it. He's always been very broad-minded."

"Yes, I know," replied Marie. "That's what's making me hesitate. I don't know just how to approach him on it. He's a very scrupulous person, you know."

"Choose a time and place to bring it up, then talk about it."

"I was so glad he got out of that other mess without me having to say anything about it."

"That was most fortunate. What about that girl now?"

"Oh, I don't know. I haven't thought much about her after that night when she pranced around on the stage as naked almost as the day she was born."

Her mother laughed.

"I guess it was seeing her that way, exposed to everybody's gaze, that finished her with Mr. Wyeth."

"I think he had finished with her before she did the dance. He went there and looked on to feel sure that he didn't want her," said Marie, and again her mother laughed.

"What about Bertha? Maybe that will turn out to be a match?"

"I don't know, I wish it would, but there is something Bertha hasn't told me."

"Why?"

"She can't."

"You mean she won't?"

"No, mother, I don't mean any such thing. I think that she would like to, but she simply cannot."

"What is it?"

"That's what I don't know; what I can't understand."

"Have you talked with Mr. Wyeth about it?"

"No, but I want to."

"Then why don't you?"

"Do you feel that I should?"

"By all means."

"Then I will. At the first opportunity."

"Meanwhile, does she seem to—like Mr. Wyeth?"

"I think so."

"You think so. Very much?"

"She seems to a great deal. I don't know if it is that kind of interest. Bertha is so highly trained. She is so far above and beyond foolish people; so far away from doing foolish things."

"I'm glad to hear it. That, I should think, is the kind of girl Mr. Wyeth needs, the kind it seems that he would want."

"It is, and he would like a girl like her."

"Then what is he waiting for?"

"Oh, he'd never make any passes at her."

"Why not?"

"She's too pretty. It would be hard for her, even, to convince him that she would care for a plain man like himself. He'd expect her to fall in love with the kind of man most of our girls fall for."

"Good looking, full of a lot of wind and hot air."

"Exactly."

"Like Thompson," suggested her mother.

Marie laughed.

"Bertha would never fall in love with anybody like Thompson. Five minutes talk with him and she was convinced that he was hopeless. Attractive, but dumb, nothing in his head."

"Oh, yes he has."

"What?" inquired Marie, turning to her.

"Frog eggs and rain water," said her mother. Both laughed.

"Getting back to Mr. Wyeth and Bertha Schultz. You say she's highly educated?"

"A Doctor of Philosophy from The Sorbonne, Paris."

"Whew!"

"Just about as high as one can go."

"I'll say."

"And so nice with it, lovable, tender and sweet."

"Why haven't you brought her to see me?"

"We've been so absorbed in each other, and so interested as regards Mr. Wyeth, when we meet that I haven't got around to it."

"Well, get around to it. I want to meet her, see her for myself and draw my own conclusions."

"You'll have the same reaction as I had. I'm sorry for her."

"Why?"

"Something's troubling her."

"That something she cannot tell you?"

"Exactly."

"The more reason you should take it up with Mr. Wyeth. I'll bet he'll understand it."

"You think so?"

"Try him and find out."

"I've said I would."

"When?"

"As quickly as I can have him alone without anything to interfere."

"Perhaps tomorrow, then?"

"Maybe tomorrow. I'll try to get to it tomorrow."

And the next day Marie did. Wyeth gave her the chance.

"How is Miss Schultz?" he inquired of Marie, after they got through the letters and he had signed and was handing them back to her.

"Fine," replied Marie.

"Glad to hear it."

"Yes?"

"She left rather abruptly the other day. I had something I wanted to talk to her about."

"What, for instance?"

"My trip."

"Oh, your trip. What could you have wanted to talk with her about?"

"Oh, nothing in particular. Just tell her about it, I guess. She seems so interested in the serious side of life, and I think I'd have enjoyed telling her more about it."

"By the way, Mr. Wyeth," she said carefully, evenly. "Had you thought about taking anybody with you on this trip?"

"Not exactly. Why?"

"Oh, I don't know."

"You're not thinking about digging up Thompson, perhaps?"

"Lord, no!"

"Then why did you ask me if I was thinking about taking anybody?" He paused and looked at her, a question in his eyes.

"I was thinking about—Bertha."

"Bertha! You mean Miss Schultz?"

"Miss Schultz."

"What ever made anything like that suggest itself to you?"

"Oh, I don't know. Maybe I had a reason."

"This is getting a bit deep. Why would you associate Miss Schultz with going on a trip like this with me?"

"Maybe Miss Schultz."

"Come, Marie, you're talking in riddles. Miss Schultz, I am sure, hasn't thought of anything of the kind."

"Hasn't she?"

"What do you mean, anyhow?"

"Have you thought much about Miss Schultz, Mr. Wyeth?"

"Well," he said, slowly, thoughtfully, "no further I guess than that she's a nice girl, an intelligent girl, the kind of a girl I admire, the kind of a girl I could like without much effort."

"I see."

"You see—what?"

"Have you observed that in some respects, she is—a bit secretive?"

"Explain yourself."

"That there is something she hasn't perhaps told us, told me, at least?"

"Oh, yes." Marie turned to him abruptly, and looked hard at him. He was very calm, unexcited.

"I'm asking what you mean?" said Marie.

"Just what you suggested; that there is something she has not divulged. Incidentally, I understand what that is," said Wyeth, slowly.

"What is it?" Marie asked.

She rose to her feet, stood over him. He looked up at her, still calm, quiet.

"That she's German," he said

"A German, yes, I know that."

"That she's also a German secret agent," he said.

"A—what?" she cried.

"A spy."

"Oh, Mr. Wyeth, no!"

"But, Mrs. Coleman, yes."

Marie dropped into a chair, out of breath.

"Well, people!'

"Didn't you understand—that—that she was?"

"Of course not," she cried.

"I have all along," he said with a smile.

"And haven't said anything about it?"

"Perhaps I thought you knew. You should have."

"Why should I?" she wanted to know.

"You're an intelligent girl, at least that's what I've been taking you to be all these years."

"But Bertha, a spy, I can't believe it."

"A Nazi spy," he said.

"Great God!"

"Sent to this country along with others, by the German foreign office to check on American activity."

"Are you joking?" said Marie, bewildered.

"Of course I am not. America is literally swarming with Nazi agents, checking on everything that's going on in this country."

"But Bertha, and her brother?" she cried. "I can't believe it."

"They are both spies; he's the chief one."

"I'm astounded," said Marie.

"I'm not.'

"You can buy me for a nickel. And you've been talking with her, just as though being a Nazi spy didn't mean anything."

"Why should it?"

"Now you are getting worse," she exclaimed. "Why shouldn't it?"

"Because it shouldn't. They're colored, interested in the welfare of the Negro as well as we are."

"But Nazi spies. Aren't you going to report them to the FBI?"

"Of course not."

"But—but why not?"

"Because I don't want to."

"But they will be reported," she said.

"Not unless you or I do it."

"I'm dumbfounded," she said, excitedly.

"Take it easy, Marie."

"What am I to do?" she blurted out, looking at him oddly.

"Just what you've been doing," said he.

"You mean, be—nice to her, and—all that?"

"Of course," said he.

"But how can I now, knowing what—you've just told me. What are you going to do?"

"Go on just as I have been."

"Admiring her and being interested in her," said Marie.

"Sure," he smiled.

She shook her head and didn't for a moment know what to do, or say.

"You see, Marie, Hitler is smart. All Germans are smart, as smart, almost as Americans, who think they're smart, are dumb and badly informed, which is the reason they're in trouble; why they're going to be in greater trouble. Some of these mornings we're going to awaken a shocked nation; so shocked that we won't know what has happened until it *has* happened—and then it will be too late!"

"What are you talking about?"

"That the Germans have got our number. Hitler is wise in many ways. I don't know fully what it is all about. In fact, I admit I don't know anything about it at all. Just a feeling, but after talking with Bertha the first time, I could see what had been done. They were born in Germany, of a Negro father, whose father before him was a German. He was lost on the Emden, a notorious raider during the first World War. The Emden sank lots of ships before a British man-o-war finally caught up with her and sank her off the coast of South America. I was a young fellow at that time but remember it well. Nobody was saved. So that was when and how they lost their father.

"Their mother brought her and Heinrich to this country, after she married another colored man, a soldier this time, stationed after the last war in the Rhineland, and who brought her and these two kids to this country where they lived some eight or ten years, long enough, as it were, to become very thoroughly Americanized. Then he died and she took Bertha and Heinrich, youngsters, but old enough to know a lot, back to Germany and put them through schoool. If the truth was known, I bet that they had assistance from their government. Anyway, they were thoroughly educated in Germany, and later, in France."

"At the Sorbonne."

"The Harvard of France."

"They are both Doctors of Philosophy."

"German thoroughness."

"Evidently,"

"Now, grown up, as wise in the ways of the world as training can make them, they are sent back to this country to—"

"——spy."

"Well, don't condemn them for that. Only smart, intelligent and well-trained people make good spies. People willing to put their country ahead of everything else—all else.

"In a way, I respect their position, and the way Germany has honored them. Compare it with the way we are treated here in our own country. Played down, kicked around, ignored, all because the South insists on keeping us in 'our place'. Heinrich knows that as

Negroes, living up here in Harlem among us, that they won't be watched; that they can operate freely, get valuable information regarding the movement of ships, dispatching of convoys, and relay it on to Germany, nobody the wiser. Hitler knows it, so they have his complete cooperation with plenty of money at their command to work with, see?"

"That's why she wants to go on this trip with you," Marie said. He started, paused, looked at her. "I can see through all her anxiety now. Cunning anxiety," said Marie to herself.

"What did you say?"

"She wants to go on this trip with you."

"She does?"

"To spy on what you are doing, what the Negro is thinking—everything."

"That's interesting," he said, and lowered his eyes, thoughtfully.

"You puzzle me. Meanwhile, what about this man Early. Is he a Nazi spy, too?" she said calmly.

"No," he replied, shaking his head.

"Why not? If the others are?"

"Kermit is working with them, rather, with some subversive group, but he isn't a Nazi spy, for he's an American Negro."

"What about that white woman he's going with; that rich white woman, from down South?"

Wyeth smiled.

"Lucky Negro."

"Now what do you mean?"

"Just what I say. Kermit is one of these highly educated Negroes, educated beyond his scope. He's been mixed up with some subversive group for quite a while. He was mixed up with them while I was writing my book in Chicago, two years ago."

"And you knew?"

"Of course I did, Marie. But what if I did? He's a Negro just like us, trying to get along. He's too highly educated to get anything to do, so if somebody chooses to pay him something for—"

"—doing nothing."

"Oh, no, you're mistaken. He's a very busy man."

"Doing what?"

"Trying to get me to make a hate picture, for one thing."

"A picture to make Negroes hate Jews?"
"Something like that."
"Are you going to? You hate Jews, don't you?"
"No," he said.
She looked at him.
"After all they've done to you?" He ignored the remark.
"After all that some of them have done to you, at least," she corrected, "I think you'd hate them."
"I don't hate anybody. It's bad philosophy. Besides, some Jews have helped me."
"I know."
"Of the $2,200 it cost to get my book out, over $2,000 was advanced by Jews."
"I know that, too."
"So shouldn't I be grateful?"
"I guess you should."
"I am, but even if this hadn't been done, I'd still feel as I do."
"I thought you hated Jews. You curse them often enough."
"I curse Negroes still more."
"And how!"
They both laughed at this.
"They say you're hard on Negroes."
"I'm not. They're hard on themselves, but don't know it."
"I guess you're right. But getting back to Miss Schultz and this trip."
"That's what we were talking about."
"Knowing as you do now, that she's a Nazi spy, you won't consider taking her now."
"I'm favorable to the idea."
Again she looked hard at him.
"You mean that you'd consider taking that girl on this trip with you, knowing that she is spying on our country and sending the information back to Germany?"
"She isn't doing it exactly that way."
"Then what way?"
"Hitler has sent her and her brother here to gather information for Germany, about the way the Negro is being treated, to counteract the complaint about how they are treating the Jews. Some-

body higher up among their agents has perhaps asked Heinrich to have me make this hate picture to stir up trouble."

"Well, isn't that enough to stop everything right here; to expose them. Wouldn't that be our duty, our patriotic duty?"

"Yes, and no."

"Now what do you mean?"

"In sending them to a far country to find out something about our condition for whatever value it might ultimately be to Germany, is showing, in a way, a greater interest in Negroes than our own country is doing without great pressure being brought to bear, and so far as I'm concerned, I'm glad of it. Hitler has been able, away off there in Germany to realize that 13,000,000 Negroes can mean something, regardless of the fact that our own country is unwilling, or seems so anyhow, to take us that seriously."

"I agree with you there."

"I am not sure about her brother, for he is shrewd and cunning and would go as far in the interest of Germany as the most ruthless Nazi. But his sister is simply trying to help him. She isn't so sure about herself, but behind all this, she is not a Mata Hari. She's just a nice, sweet and intelligent girl and I am sure she has no ulterior or sadistic purpose in wishing to go with me on this trip."

"What else could she want to go for?"

"Well," he said, thoughtfully, "she's had a lot of education forced into her head. Like most German people, she is not afraid of work, and sees in such a trip an opportunity to broaden her viewpoint."

"She seems to be fond of you. What does that mean?"

"I wouldn't know. I can't imagine, much less picture, any pretty girl like her becoming interested in me, further than for the information I could give her."

"How do you feel about her?"

"I've already said that I admired her. I even like her," he said.

Marie sighed.

"Then?"

"I'm willing to take her along if she wants to go."

"Wants to go?"

"Yes. Do you think she would really like to go?" He asked, a bit anxiously

Marie laughed, kept on laughing.

"Why are you laughing?" he asked.

"About you asking if she wants to go when she is all but insane to do so."

"Really?"

"Oh, Mr. Wyeth, you should have heard her pleading with me to get you to let her."

He smiled now, all over his face.

"You mean to say that you would take her," she said, surprised.

"Listen, Marie, what are you interested in?"

By her expression, he could see that she didn't understand.

"You would like to see us sell a lot of books, wouldn't you?"

"Of course. You know how much I want to see this go over."

"Then, take it from me, Marie, as energetic, intelligent, pretty, willing and glad as she is to work, she can help sell so many books that you'll have to hire three or four extra people to help you ship them."

"You think so?" she said, looking at him in surprise.

"Think so?" he echoed. "I *know* so. I've always needed somebody like that to help me. I never hoped that I'd meet anybody who wanted to and could."

"She wants to—badly."

"You mean, to help me sell the book?" he asked, anxiously.

"Exactly that. She said she would be glad to act as your secretary, do anything you asked and wanted her to do, and that she would be happy to help sell the book above all else."

"Then it's a deal, Marie, and you can tell her whenever you are ready that I accept her offer. Why, when I introduce her to the teachers in all the schools I plan to call on; in the churches on Sunday; to groups of Negro insurance agents—to all kinds of Negroes, everywhere, as Miss Schultz, Doctor of Philosophy from Heidelberg and The Sorbonne, they'll go crazy."

"I can see them falling for that."

"And how! Why, she'll have the children running home to get money from their parents to buy the book. They will be glad to do that, in the hope of a smile, in the hope of being remembered by her. In fact, every teacher will be afraid not to buy if she just smiles and acknowledges an acquaintance with them for fear she might forget them."

"I can see that happening. As crazy as they are about highly educated people, they won't want to let you take her away."

"They sure won't. So let me take her along. You can take care of shipping all the books we'll need, but I'm telling you that with her assistance, I'll never again have half the chance to sell as many books as I will on this trip.'

"I'm relieved," sighed Marie. "I was afraid you wouldn't even consider it. You don't have much patience with women, you know."

"No, I do not. Not when they are forever holding me up, fixing at themselves, then nagging me about what I ought and ought not to do."

"She won't do that."

"I know it, and that is why I am agreeable to taking her along."

"Maybe you'll be falling in love with her."

"Don't be a fool, dear. A pretty girl like her wouldn't think of falling in love with a plain somebody like me."

"Don't be too sure about that," said Marie.

"I wouldn't want her, after I misunderstood a fine friendship to say, 'I don't like you that way.' No, don't think I'm going to make a fool of myself.'

"You came near doing so not long ago," said Marie, with a knowing glance. Then smiling, a twinkle in her eye, she adjusted her clothes and sat down

"Oh, you mean my show girl."

"Nobody else.'

"I slipped out of the nozzle before it tightened. She didn't care anything about me.'

"She was playing you for a sucker.'

"That's what I discovered."

"In time. I was praying for you," said Marie, happy and relieved, now. She went back to her work, smiling over her shoulder at him as she did so.

CHAPTER XXVII

BERTHA SCHULTZ had a restless night. To go with Wyeth on his long and extended sales tour, had become an obsession. The more she thought about it, the more anxious she was to go. All the while the fear that neither Marie nor Wyeth would be agreeable to it, kept her awake with anxiety all night, and it was not until the small hours of the morning that she fell into a fitful and troubled sleep.

She could hardly wait until ten the next morning to call Marie to see what had happened.

Wyeth had been forced to do a great deal to persuade Marie to continue to be as nice to Bertha as she had been. Being a woman, with deeper prejudices, and having been told what Wyeth told her, it was hard for her to continue to feel toward Bertha as she had. It was hard to drive out the feeling that Bertha had deceived her.

"If you must blame somebody and feel that you have been deceived, then blame her brother, Heinrich. It is all his idea, not Bertha's exactly," Wyeth insisted, when she brought it up again.

"But she could have told me—"

"—what?"

"Well, hinted at something anyhow."

"Didn't she? At least you said she did."

"Yes, but—"

"Oh, be broad, Marie. Give the girl a chance," Wyeth went on, insistently. "Try, please, to understand first, that the girl had been kept in school all her life. To secure a Ph.D at her age, not a month could have been lost or wasted."

"I can understand that."

"In fact, she must have made somewhere along the line, two years in one, in order to secure her final degree at her obvious age."

"I agree with you," said Marie.

"Then getting through, acquiring almost all the education schools can give a person, and being German with their usual and customary thoroughness in doing anything, it must have made her happy to so quickly find work; the kind of work she had prepared herself to do; work like they've been sent here to do."

"Yes, of course."

"She didn't know that she was going to meet anybody like you when she left Berlin to come here."

"Nor like you, either," replied Marie, slowly. "Meeting me wouldn't have been very important. It was meeting you and being able to see that you offered her the opportunity she wanted. Don't think that she hasn't been able to compare you with all the other Negroes—and whites, too, that she's met. It is you she is so interested in and can see that by taking this trip with you, sitting there by your side, day after day, night after night, that in a matter of three or four months she will know more about Negroes and America in general than she could possibly learn by talking to half the educated ones in the United States."

"Oh, I wouldn't say that," he argued modestly.

"I say it. Why, I can't forget what Woodruff, the Negro historian on his return from Europe, the first time he was over there, said when he met you in Philadelphia, and rode with you to New York,"

"Yes," said Wyeth, "I remember the time."

"He told me in this office one day shortly after, when he came by to see you and you were, as usual, out. He said to me, 'Mrs. Coleman, I've never been examined so exhaustively in my life. Why, before we were half way to New York, Mr. Wyeth had asked me a thousand questions about Europe in general; asked me more questions than all the Negroes I have met since I returned, put together. The fact is, he went on to say, about the only questions the rest have asked me, the men especially, was, what's the Negroes' chance to have a white woman over there'."

"Our people go to the bottom of nothing very seriously, and Bertha has discovered that already. Schools and getting more education would be about all they could talk to her about, and she isn't particularly interested in any more academic contact. She wants person to person contact and information. She wants to learn something that she doesn't already know. She wants to know more about what the

Negro is thinking and doing, if he is thinking and doing anything really worth while. She wants to know what the white man thinks about all this, too, and if he is considering what the Negro thinks and is doing, very seriously."

"She likes your plain, simple and down-to-the-earth philosophy. She said she could listen to you talk forever; listen to every word for in everything you say you reveal something; something she wants to know."

He smiled modestly.

"Take Kermit Early, for instance, with all his education, all the way from high school in a small town in Georgia, through Atlanta University, the University of Chicago, with a Ph.D from Harvard, and the best he's, able to do is to try to get you to make a picture to cause Negroes to hate Jews."

"Speaking of him, I understand the white woman who put him through school and paid for most of the education he has, lost her husband."

"Is that so?" said Marie

"I ran into Schultz at a newsstand downtown the other day and he showed me an account about Mr. Wingate having been killed while crossing the railroad tracks during a blinding storm and I remarked to Schultz that he had the same name as Kermit's girl friend. He smiled and told me that it was Kermit's girl friend's husband."

"Well, that should mean a break for Kermit," said Marie.

"I said something about it to that effect to Schultz and he said Kermit didn't talk much, but that he thought it would be, too; and that she might marry him soon, now that her husband was out of the way."

"What do you think of Early," said Marie, looking at him.

Wyeth shrugged his shoulders.

"Oh, I don't know."

"You've known him a long time?"

"Yes. Several years."

"Yet you don't know much about him?"

"No more than I have just said."

"Umph!"

"What do you mean by that, Marie?"

"Oh, nothing in particular."

"Nobody knows much about Kermit Early. Years ago he and Phillip Merivale edited a weekly, and threatened for a while a new era in Negro journalism. But before, or at least while they were, everybody was talking about how highly educated both were. During that period, Negroes were reckoning the success of each other largely on how much education one had. So Early and Merivale were on most everybody's tongue, especially the tongues of the intelligentsia," said Wyeth.

"Then what happened?" She asked.

Again he shrugged his shoulders.

"What happens to most Negro efforts, and has been happening ever since I can remember. The publication needed dough. They didn't have any, of course, but nobody expected them to, being only a pair of young fellows, with lots of training, academic training. Anyway, the publication needed money, and they didn't have it, didn't know how to get it, and were, perhaps, too impatient to just stick and make the paper pay, so they disbanded and the paper ceased to exist. Merivale, later on, went out and started the organization which has made him one of the leading Negroes in our race today. He's a real success."

"He is sure that. About the only leading Negro that the masses trust, believe in and follow."

"He has a good income from the organization he founded and has built to success. When a Negro has money, is actually successful, he isn't inclined to be penurious and little like a great many of our would-be and so-called leaders are. It is poverty that so often warps and twists the Negro all out of proportion, due to a lack of the wherewithal. It is because he has no money and worse, because he does not know how to make any, that makes him like he is more than anything else.'

"Are these the kind that Booker T. Washington referred to as 'just educated'," suggested Marie, and smiled.

"They thought, while getting it, that the education would make money for them. As they viewed it while in school, all they had to do was just finish, get their degree, and all would be well."

"Maybe that is what Kermit Early thought?"

"Perhaps. But I wouldn't know. He has always, as far as I can learn, been a sort of man of mystery."

"Maybe it's that wealthy white woman he goes with. Maybe she's been providing the money to help make him this 'man of mystery'."

"I wouldn't be surprised, and that may be another reason for his keeping so much to himself. I've seen them together in Chicago. I wouldn't be surprised that going with her has had lots to do with his silence and seeming mystery."

"If you go on this trip, you won't get to make this hate picture he seems so anxious for you to direct," said Marie.

"I wouldn't direct it if I wasn't to go on the trip. I haven't anything against Jews, even though some of them are often, it seems, rather mercenary."

Marie laughed, and moved over to her desk.

"What shall I tell Bertha when she calls or comes around?"

"Well," he said, moving across to the door, preparatory to leaving. "Maybe I'd better leave that to you. Only this, I do want you to be nice to her, Marie."

"Are you falling in—love with Bertha, Mr. Wyeth?"

"Why, Marie!"

"Oh, you'll never tell her that you are, but you do like her, don't you?"

"I do like her, yes. And I want you to keep on liking her, too."

"Just like I have been?"

"Just like you have been, Marie."

"All right, Mr. Wyeth. I will. About her brother, excuse me for holding you up, but I've wanted to talk with you about him for some time. What do you think of him?"

"He's a 100 per cent Nazi, out and out, and in a way, I'm—well, afraid of him."

She looked up, quickly.

"I mean," said Wyeth, eyebrows wrinkling, "that he is, or could be, and might turn out to be—well, dangerous, before it is all over."

"This is interesting. If he is likely to be dangerous, and I suppose you mean, to American welfare, mightn't he—involve his—sister?"

"He might."

"She would be expected to follow his lead; do whatever he wanted her to?"

"Yes."

"Then is it—prudent to continue this interest in—Bertha?"

"If I take her on this trip, yes."

"Now, perhaps you're putting yourself in for something."

"I don't think so.'

"Getting back to her brother. So you fear he may be—dangerous to the country's welfare—in time?"

"I feel sure that he will."

"Aren't you going to do anything about it, say anything about it?"

"I don't know."

"Don't you feel that you—should?"

"I—I don't know."

"You're rather vague and—indefinite. Is it because of his—sister?"

"Oh, no."

"Then why?"

"Maybe it's because of America's attitude toward us. We've been over this before. Naturally none of us Negroes like the way we are treated."

"None of us," said Bertha.

"And I repeat. We don't like the way they play us down, keep us down, and think we should be satisfied; that we should be happy about it."

"It is really funny the way they feel about us, compared to the way we feel about ourselves."

"We are as far apart as heaven and earth."

"So you don't feel that you ought to say anything or do anything about Heinrich?"

"No. Besides there's nothing I can say, nothing I could do now. He hasn't done any of the things he is likely to do—when the time comes —yet, so there would be nothing for me to do or say now, even if I wanted to. Maybe I wouldn't do or say anything when I know that he's stirring up trouble."

"You think maybe, then, that finding out should be the duty of—"

"—America herself. As I see it, he's going to have an easy time of it when the time does come."

"Why so?"

"Because nobody will be watching him. Nobody is expecting Negroes to do anything but cry about the way they are treated. They won't ever be checking to see what we are doing—until after it is done, at least. Heinrich will be able to work without being suspected or molested."

"Just what do you think he's likely to do, as a starter, for instance? Now that you are definitely decided not to make this hate picture. They won't have that to start trouble with."

"I look for them to find some other way, providing they don't get somebody else to make the picture."

"It'll have to be some other way. For if you don't direct the picture, it won't be made. I overheard them while waiting for you, say that. In the way they talked, I'm convinced that if you don't direct it, it might not be made."

"Then it won't be made."

"You feel sure then, that you won't make it?"

"I've never guessed that I would or would not. I simply never intended to."

"I believe they sent Bertha in to try to persuade you."

"Perhaps."

"But after meeting you, she's become so interested otherwise until I don't think making the picture is that important to her, any more."

"I hope not. She couldn't persuade me to, either."

"I'm sure she couldn't, but I don't think she will try to persuade you to do so very hard."

"Heinrich wants it made as part of what he is up to; but it's Kermit Early's big idea. I think he's sold somebody the idea that he will get me to make it, and he doesn't want to be let down on it."

"Now about what you think they might do to start some kind of trouble between Negroes and Jews. What?"

"Race riots."

"Race riots?"

"Of course."

"But how will they go about developing a race riot?"

"Easily."

"But how?" she insisted.

"Oh, there are many ways. A few hired agitators, perched on a step-ladder, facing the sidewalk in a Negro section. On Seventh and Lenox Avenues here in New York, for instance."

"I've seen them on ladders up and down those streets and have been seeing them on ladders like that for years."

"And they pitched a disastrous riot a few years back, too."

"And how! I'll never forget that night," said Marie, and sighed.

"But that riot didn't have a Heinrich Schultz and Kermit Early behind it, either," said Wyeth.

"No?"

"Of course not. Heinrich was in school in either Paris or Heidelberg at the time, and Early was in Chicago. I saw him out there."

"But now?"

"It'll be Heinrich directly, who'll pull it. Kermit isn't just the aggressive and ruthless type. That's Heinrich. He possesses everything Hitler wants in him to start things—and when he does, they'll begin to happen."

"I think you ought to do something, feeling as you do about him."

"He'll develop his own undoing in time. It is not my responsibility."

"Yet you are—fond of Bertha?"

"I am fond of Bertha. If I do anything, it will be with a view to saving Bertha from the disaster that will ultimately befall her brother."

"How?"

"Well, taking her on this trip, for one thing."

"Just how will you, then? Talk to her about it?"

"By no means. Never will I say a word against her brother, or for him, to her, for that matter."

"Then how?"

"Oh, Marie," he said, rising. "I hadn't thought into it that far. As to Bertha, I believe that in an environment which her brother doesn't dominate, where he is not around to influence her, that she will be more rational. As I view Bertha, she is a good girl, who hasn't gone in for any of Hitler's hatred of Jews, or has become imbued with his 'master race' dream or anything like that yet, although being close to her brother and his philosophy might in time envelop her."

"So you feel that on a trip like this, she might get entirely from under such influences?"

"It is not with any such idea that I am agreeable to taking her with me. I am interested in taking her for two very clear and definite reasons."

"And those reasons?"

"First, she'll help me sell more books than I can otherwise sell, with all the plans for doing so that I have in mind."

"I follow you."

"The next, by the time we leave, and if she goes, of course, I'll have completed the voluminous manuscript of my new novel that I've been working on these many months. With her complete education, and being so close to me, she can help put it into the shape I want it, understand?"

"Of course. You always have your manuscripts thoroughly edited by some highly educated person, before sending them to the typesetter. Having such a complete and thorough education, she can check it intelligently without interfering with or interrupting your work, and, being close to you—"

"—can go through it, sentence by sentence, putting it into such perfect rhetoric and grammar until by the time you get back and turn it over to the printer, it will be as you want it, letter perfect."

"Exactly, Marie. I should have a finer script than I've ever had a chance to have, before."

"I agree with you."

"I knew you would. Maybe this time I might have a novel that white reviewers will read."

"Let's hope they will."

"Also the would-be Negro reviewers, who borrow the book, as they did in the case of the review the woman gave it in the Courier," and Wyeth laughed.

"She didn't review the book, even after borrowing somebody's copy and writing her impression. It was a ridicule."

"That's it," laughed Wyeth. "Not a review, but a ridicule," and they both laughed.

"They'll give us a review if the white papers speak well of it but with the white people viewing us, either as a bunch of clowns, comedians and idiots on the one hand—"

"—or a criminal, moron or degenerate on the other, what can we look forward to?" she said.

"Our people are a mess. It's amazing when you think of it. Why do we hate each other so?"

"The most unfortunate part about it is, that so few seem to be conscious or aware of the contempt we hold each other in," said Wyeth.

"The fact that the Negro race hasn't produced a novel in almost five years, hasn't seemed to have occurred to them at all."

"They don't do that kind of thinking," said Wyeth.

"Not a day passes that we don't get from one to a dozen letters—often more, from people who buy your book and read it, praising it to the skies. Yet when our so-called reviewers say anything about it, it's a knock, a ridicule."

"Meanwhile, getting back to the white press."

"We've gotten entirely away from what we were talking about."

"It was about the white people whose work is to review books," said Marie

"I've tried to write it so they will. They keep me so angry and out of patience by seeming to deliberately say: 'Write that story in dialect, Negro, with plenty of clowning, comedy—or create some distorted characters like in *Nature's Child,* and to a degree, like in *Passion,* where the Negro is 'kept in his place' or may frighten somebody, especially the reviewers."

"I'm glad you thought of all that before you started writing."

"I have written the story the same as I have all the stories I've ever attempted. According to my philosophy of life, and to please myself. I have simply tried to conform, and include such startling situations which I believe, at least strongly hope, may inveigle them into reading the first hundred pages, anyhow. If they'd read even the first 25 pages of my present book, they would have to read it all and—"

"—like it," said Marie, interrupting him.

"But when they open it, looking for Dinah and old Sambo, or a dice game or some old darkies moaning a lot of spirituals and hymns, at least don't find some dialect, they close it and lay it down and give it away, perhaps, to the colored porter or maid and the book never has a chance."

"They may not read this one, either, but let's hope they will."

"I have put the most I know, anyhow, into it. Beyond that I've got to gamble, so we'll wait and see what happens. Meanwhile, hope for the best."

"One advantage that you have over any other writer, black or white, is the fact that you publish and sell your own books. They can never keep you out of some measure of circulation. However, the whites receive this new book, if they decide after it is published to read and accept it at all, or do not do so, we know in advance that our group are going to."

"I believe they will like it, too," he said hopefully

"They'll rave about it, and buy enough to continue to make our little company prosperous," said Marie

"That's something to be thankful for; that we can always count on a good living from the sale of any book I write, and that I like." He was at the door now and she got to her feet.

"So it will be all right to tell Bertha you'll take her with you?" she said.

"I'm leaving it to you, Marie," he replied, opening the door.

"I plan to draw her out before I tell her that you will. There's more to find out about Bertha before I will be satisfied to again like her after what I've learned."

"Well, be good to her whatever you do," he said, and turning, went down to the hall on the way to the stairs and his car.

CHAPTER XXVIII

A FEW MINUTES after Wyeth left the office, Bertha Schultz rushed in, almost out of breath with anxiety and excitement. Marie smiled easily as she heard her footsteps, rushing toward the office door. Bertha's steps were ever firm, and direct. Bertha, the Nazi spy girl, knew what she wanted to do, who she wanted to see. As she opened the door and looked in, her eyes seemed more blue today than they had before. Marie looked at her out of different eyes. She was not looking at Bertha, the girl she had begun to admire and to love from the day she met her. She was looking at another woman, yet the same person in the flesh. She was looking now at Bertha Schultz, an international spy. It gave her a peculiar feeling. She had read of women spies; of Mata Hari, and her cunning adventures. Now she was face to face with Bertha Schultz, in the service of Adolf Hitler—Bertha Schultz, a Nazi spy.

"Oh. Marie," cried Bertha, evenly, but with restrained excitement, as she walked stealthily-like into the office, glanced toward Wyeth's office, saw the door was open and knew by that that he was out. She breathed a sigh of relief, then crossed to Marie, not having noticed that Marie had been looking at her closely, studying her, weighing her in the balance, as it were.

"Bertha," Marie exclaimed, this time deceitfully, rising to her feet.

Bertha crossed over to her and smiled.

"I'm so glad to see you today," Bertha said, and relaxing, smiled again at her and Marie couldn't help but feel she *was* a sweet girl, kind and tender, just like the girl she always thought her to be.

"If Mr. Wyeth has gone for the day, may we—" and she pointed toward the office which had a fine desk, a leather sofa, and two comfortable chairs which they had become accustomed to talking from, until sitting in them while doing so had become a habit.

"Of course, dear," said Marie, and reaching out her arm, let it encircle Bertha's slender waist. Together they entered the private office and took the seats they had become used to sitting in.

"This is such a comfortable chair," sighed Bertha.

"It *is* comfortable, Bertha."

"And now, what did Mr. Wyeth say?" she asked, suddenly leaning forward. Marie turned and looked at her a moment before answering and in doing so, studied her and thought of her connections again. She wondered if she would ever be able to look at her and think of her without a lot of ugly thoughts intruded.

"Well," began Marie, thoughtfully. "We talked about it," so saying she looked at Bertha who met her eyes directly. Bertha did not flinch or turn away. In that moment Marie began to admire her again. She was not a weakling nor a coward. Bertha Schultz was still a brave and resolute person, ready to squarely face whatever she had to face.

"You talked with him?"

"I talked with him, Bertha, rather, we talked about it."

"I see," said Bertha, thoughtfully. Then looked squarely at Marie. "And what did you decide?"

Marie did not reply immediately, but lowered her eyes momentarily, then raised them to Bertha.

"As I told you, dear. Mr. Wyeth has planned this trip with a view to selling his book, only."

"I understand that, Marie."

"When he goes out to do that, he doesn't like to be interfered with in any way.

"I both understand and appreciate that also."

"Shortly after the book appeared, he took Carter Thompson with him to help sell it."

"And?"

"After trying in every way he knew how, and failing to get Thompson to do anything but make love to the younger teachers, he gave up in disgust and said that he would never try to get anybody to help him again. Nobody." Bertha started, her jaw dropped. She looked discouraged.

"Then, he—he doesn't want me?" she said, slowly.

"I didn't say that," said Marie.

Immediately Bertha's eyes flashed with a new hope.

"But, he doesn't intend to make the same mistake again."

"You know I wouldn't deter him, Marie."

"He hadn't planned, as stated, to take anybody with him. You must appreciate Bertha, that for a man as serious-minded as Mr. Wyeth is, and going on a trip which has been planned as long as he has planned this—ever since he got the book out and found that this kind of trip would pay, that to consider changing anything so important at such a late date, isn't quite in keeping with his way of doing things."

"I've thought of all that, too, dear Marie, and I am willing, as I told you, to do anything Mr. Wyeth might wish me to, if he will only take me."

"You know that he is very plain, doesn't like a lot of show and ceremony, and doesn't like to have his time taken up with any such things. He has a way of jumping into his car when he is ready to go somewhere, and going. Has no patience with women who insist on him waiting while they do a lot of primping, powdering and putting on."

"I have never primped or put on, Marie. I don't even use lipstick; I rarely use powder."

"He always gets up early. In making these schools and insurance offices, it is often necessary for him to be at a school or an office around eight o'clock. Maybe he has to drive some miles to get there by that time, so he can speak to the teachers before they begin their classes, to the agents before they leave their office. If he is by himself, he doesn't have to worry. Just jumps up, gets into his clothes, steps on the gas and within a half hour or less, is where he wants to go. Nobody to wait for and make him angry or get him impatient. Nobody to complain about what he does, or doesn't do. Are you sure you'd be willing to put up with all that?"

"It is exactly what I would like to do. Why, on our little farm on the outskirts of Berlin, Marie, we rise with the chickens, get a lot of work done this time of year before the sun rises. German people raise their children to work hard, and work all the time—and not mind it. That is what I'm used to doing; what I'd like to do. I could be of so much help to Mr. Wyeth. He'd find me waiting to go whenever he was ready. He'd find me ready to help sell his book, lots of his books. I could take and type his letters, and after I had done so awhile, all he'd have to do would be to tell me whom he wanted to write to and something about what he wanted to say, including you, and he wouldn't have to dictate it, and fret over proofreading it. I would do all that and do it right. Please believe that I would Marie, darling."

Marie looked at Bertha while she talked to assure herself of Bertha's sincerity. She kept back a smile, also words that she would like to say, but she grew more convinced that Mr. Wyeth's desire to take her was a sound and sensible one. Of all the girls in the world, there was perhaps no other who could and would be so helpful to him as she. Just the kind of a girl any man in his position needed and could use. She knew that Bertha would not hold him up and delay him; be quarrelsome in the mornings and try his patience as Thompson had. Wyeth complained that he could not get Thompson to go to bed, because he'd always get himself invited to some affair every night, where some silly teachers would paw over and keep him until often the wee hours, making love to him—some even proposing. In Thompson's case, the women did the proposing and Wyeth told her that he was sure that Thompson had more offers and proposals of marriage than any other man. Almost every day during the while he drove Wyeth around, some teacher or girl or both met and was sure that Thompson was the angel from heaven that they had been waiting for all their lives.

Bertha would be admired. She could picture many men and principals of schools and others, including the best men the race afforded, making overtures to her. It is obvious that they would, a beautiful, refined and so highly intelligent sort of girl. But that was why she could be depended on to go on about her business and Mr. Wyeth's, and because she was too intelligent to let meeting a lot of people interfere with what she was doing. She wanted to rush across to Bertha, gather her in her arms and tell her that Mr. Wyeth wanted to take her, would be glad to, but Marie was a conservative girl. She had long since caught on to the responsibility of what they were trying to do and liked it. She knew better than any other woman how hard Mr. Wyeth had struggled to try to succeed; she knew all about the many and almost endless handicaps that had been in his way, of how he had been forced to surmount all those obstacles and go on. She knew that in all the years she had worked for him that he had been at all times on his own; that he had never had any encouragement from his race who never understood nor even tried to understand just what he was doing or was trying to do. She knew that whenever the Negro newspapers had a chance to knock and injure him, they had seemed to delight in doing so, although professing great admiration for him and saying a lot of fine words, but which for some peculiar reason, they never printed. She knew that Wyeth had long since given up hoping they would and was succeeding, not by their help or cooperation, but in spite of it. She knew that although they had sent the book to only some three white newspapers for review, because in failing to get any notice of any kind from them, that he had ceased to send out more books for that purpose. He had gone on and learned to sell the book in numbers large enough to make their little company independent and prosperous, a fact that few knew and none believed. She knew that many colored papers asked for copies; which he sent until he found that somebody on the paper merely wanted it, none made any effort to review it, which Wyeth knew was due to the fact that the white papers had not done so. Wyeth hadn't expected them to and had found that he didn't altogether need it, if making more sales was why. She knew and he knew that their people, thousands of Negroes all over the country, liked the book, praised it to the skies, told of how good and interesting it was to each other, and kept their mail filled with a stream of orders, as the result of their mouth to mouth advertising. So many people, unbiased and unprejudiced could not be wrong. They were told by letter and otherwise how much they liked the book. She knew, and had read, and so had Wyeth, about every novel for the past ten years that Negroes had written, which were not many. The publishers had them on their lists and sent all books by Negroes to them for examination and had done so for many years, in the hope that Wyeth might find it possible to film them. Mr. Wyeth had been anxious to do so, and was ever hoping that he might find something good and had paid about the only money any Negro ever received for the screen rights to a book, whenever Wyeth thought that he could do anything with it at all.

She knew, also, that if Wyeth hadn't been a writer, given to conceiving a plot about Negroes whenever one was needed to film, after reading it, that he wouldn't have been able to make the great number of motion pictures that he had filmed, for there would have been no stories to make them from.

In the very short while the Jewish promoters attempted to make Negro photoplays, the Colored papers had given them miles of space and publicity. She presumed that they had gotten some money for it, but during all that time, Wyeth, who had made the first Negro feature length picture, and since more than all the others put together, was ignored by the Negro newspapers just as if he had never filmed a single one. And yet, although he had suspended producing pictures because he was finding that publishing his own books was more profitable for his own efforts, the great amount of printer's ink that had been given by the Colored papers to the white people's efforts, had been unable to save those producers and keep them going. All had failed and quit within two years and left the field in disgust after losing all the way from many thousands to one hundred thousand dollars for their efforts.

Now in his early forties, Sidney Wyeth had reached sound maturity and knew what he was doing. Given to the art of characterization, he had had twenty years of practice in writing and making pictures, and knew pretty well what it was all about and was about to finish a novel, to interest both races with enough sound sensationalism, to compel the indifferent reviewers on white newspapers to possibly read it. Marie felt that if they did, they would give it a good review, and if they read this one, they would, no doubt, send for their present book which they would then read and like and give a favorable review. She was glad they had not sent it out for general reviews when it was published, at which time it might not have been read by many, the same as the few who did get it and had failed to read it.

Now what Sidney Wyeth needed more than anything else, Marie knew, was intelligent assistance. In all the entire Negro race, with as many educated ones in proportion, as there were in the white race, it was the hardest job of all to hire anybody that could do anything. The war was on and the demand for stenographers had about absorbed all the colored girls the same as the white girls who could operate a typewriter. She knew that the Negro race had few persons with any sort of executive ability to help build a small corporation with splendid possibilities into a larger and more substantial one. Besides, the Negro mind didn't seem to run that way. They made fair clerks for white people when white people wanted to hire them, but when it came to salesmen, they knew little or nothing and cared less. So she was Sidney Wyeth's sole support. She managed so that with only a little assistance, she could take care of the work of several people. It was necessary. Wyeth had long since given up hoping to get any man to help at all. Now they were offered the help of a brilliant girl, a girl who could be of tremendous assistance and who was begging for the chance; a girl who would never go off on another job, but a girl who could only be used in the capacity she was applying for while Wyeth was out of town, which would be, happily, for several months.

Being satisfied by now that Bertha would help Wyeth as no other person would be capable of, yet feeling that to make it seem that he was not sure if he wanted her or not, would permit her to impose certain conditions that might be necessary. So Marie frowned, looked wise and serious, and continued to keep Bertha on the anxious seat.

"We're both so afraid that—that it might not be just the proper thing," she was saying.

"Please trust me to do the proper thing, Marie. Please believe that I will," pleaded Bertha. Marie looked at her, cold and businesslike.

"There is another important thing. I said something about it before."

"Yes?"

"Is it just the proper thing for a girl, a pretty girl like you, Bertha, to be riding around alone with a single man?"

"I know that is something that has to be—adjusted," said Bertha, and the frown on her face was evidence that she had considered how it might look.

"People might be inclined to—talk."

"That is possible, but between a lady and a gentleman, this shouldn't be overly difficult. Mr. Wyeth is a gentleman."

"Mr. Wyeth is a gentleman," said Marie.

"And I—am a—lady," said Bertha.

"You are a lady, Bertha, a fine and beautiful lady."

"And I am not afraid to—go out with Mr. Wyeth; to travel all over the country, sitting there by his side."

"Have you consulted your—brother, about doing so?"

"I have," replied Bertha. "He—trusts me."

"Will he—trust Mr. Wyeth?"

"If I trust Mr. Wyeth, my brother will trust me with him."

"I see. Well, Bertha.'

"Yes, Marie," replied Bertha, and rose to her feet and crossing, paused, and stood over Marie, so anxious until Marie was forced to reach out and lay a hand on her, whereat Bertha relaxed a bit and sat down on the desk before Marie and made herself patient.

"If you promise not to—make Mr. Wyeth fall in—love with you."

"Oh, Marie. Mr. Wyeth is not going to fall in love with me," cried Bertha, blushing in spite of the seriousness of the situation.

"Any man would fall in love with you, Bertha, as pretty as you are and as nice and agreeable, Any man would, so however you might talk, insist and feel, any man would under the circumstances, fall in love with you."

"I don't altogether agree with you, Marie," she said, still blushing. "But if Mr. Wyeth should, I—wouldn't be angry." She turned her eyes away now.

"Now, Bertha," cried Marie, pointing a finger at her. "If you play around with my boss and then let him down, I'll be angry and never like you again," and looked at Bertha, tantalizingly.

"Oh, Marie," cried Bertha, throwing her arms about her and crying just a little. "I would always treat Mr. Wyeth right—regardless what—what happens to me." She was quiet and then turned away, and Marie knew why. Bertha was thinking of her commitment; her pledge to the Third Reich, whereby it came first and she didn't know what the subversive organizations spying on American activities might demand of her, what sacrifice. Bertha's freedom did not belong to her, not even her own life. If it were not for those solemn commitments, Bertha would be free and if Bertha was free, she believed she would like Sidney Wyeth, that in time she might even marry him. With a wife like Bertha Schultz, no heights would be impossible for him to reach.

But, and she sighed to herself. Bertha was first committed to the service of Germany, and Germany might become ruthless in its demands on her. Who knew. She didn't, and she knew that

Bertha didn't. So she decided to make it as easy for the poor girl; as easy as she could. If Wyeth took her away on a long trip and kept her, she would be at least free until she returned. Furthermore, she would be where her brother, whom Wyeth did not trust, could not easily reach or influence her. And thinking of this, it occurred to her that before telling her that Mr. Wyeth would accept and take her with him, she could demand that Bertha agree, and have her brother agree, that in consideration for taking her, she would have to agree to continue with him for the entire trip, and have her get her brother to agree to let her, so that he could not suddenly recall her from some far-off point, to leave Wyeth stranded, as it were. So she called Bertha.

"Now, Bertha, I'm contemplating asking Mr. Wyeth to consider your offer."

"Oh, darling, you make me so happy," cried Bertha, turning, too happy for words.

"Just a minute, dear, before you take it for granted. There is a condition involved, if I do."

"Yes, Marie?"

"If Mr. Wyeth condescends to take you, it will be only after you agree to certain things."

"I'll agree to anything if he will just take me."

"Very well, Bertha." Marie moved up to the desk, found a pad and pencil. Bertha stood beside her and waited.

"Note number one," said Marie, putting it down on the pad. "You agree, if Mr. Wyeth consents to take you, to do anything he asks you to, considering that he's a gentleman and that he wouldn't expect or ask a lady to do anything not in keeping with her duties."

"Of course," agreed Bertha.

"Second, if Mr. Wyeth agrees to take you and he finds your assistance helpful, he would naturally like to feel that he could expect you to continue to assist him as long as—he was on the trip, for the period of the trip."

"Of course, and I agree, cheerfully," said Bertha.

"About your brother. Supposing that he should decide to call you in to help—help in what he is doing, and what you have, no doubt agreed to assist him in doing. You must bring a letter to Mr. Wyeth from your brother, agreeing to let you continue with Mr. Wyeth during this entire trip."

"I'll do that," said Bertha. "My brother will agree." Marie paused now and thought of how she would get Wyeth to cover as much of the country as he could and take as long as he could so that Heinrich could not have Bertha do some sabotage work or something else as mean and contemptible.

"I shall be glad to continue with Mr. Wyeth as long as he desires me to," said Bertha.

"He often stays away a long time. He might decide when he got to Texas to go all the way to—California, for instance."

"I wish he would. I'd like that even better."

"Well," said Marie, pausing, "I'll check through all the conditions and make a record of them and have them ready tomorrow for you to read. Meanwhile I'll talk with Mr. Wyeth again about you, and if he is agreeable, and you are agreeable, maybe we can get together."

"Please do, darling," cried Bertha as Marie rose to her feet. "As I've said, I can learn so much about what I want to know on a trip like this, and from Mr. Wyeth that I shall be agreeable to any terms or conditions that he might impose. I'll help him and he will be glad that he took me with him, I assure you of that."

Marie believed her and was glad, even though she didn't intend to let Bertha know how glad she was.

Marie came to the office earlier the next morning than usual as she wanted to be sure to catch Wyeth before he went out.

"So," she said, smiling after opening the door. He was sitting at his desk, hard at work and she knew, would be going in thirty minutes. "I beat you to it today."

"Beat me to it, Marie? What do you mean, beat me to it?"

She came into his office before removing her hat and coat, paused to face him.

"I mean, Mr. Wyeth, I got here before you got away this time, see?"

"Oh," he said, smiling and relaxing. "That is nothing. Maybe I was going to stay in the office all day today."

"With that case of books," she said, pointing to it, "and the car half full? I could see them when I came in," and she laughed. She turned now and removed her coat and hat and coming into his office, sat down. He turned to face her.

"I had to see you today because I've got to give Bertha her reply, and wanted to talk with you again before I did so."

"I see," he replied. "And what did she say? How does she feel about it?"

"Oh, she's crazy to go, but after talking about her brother yesterday and that you didn't trust him, it occurred to me that we'd better tie her up as best we can, before agreeing to take her."

"That was very thoughtful of you Marie, and, timely."

"That's how I felt about it. Since they are both spies, and as you say, with him liable to call her in, maybe, to pull some sensational act of sabotage if he takes a notion, and get her mixed up in it, I thought we'd better take such precautions as we could now, when we have a chance."

"I'm glad you thought about that, too. I positively do not trust Heinrich. I don't believe there is anything he wouldn't do if he thought it might please Hitler. And in that respect I mean as much as murder."

"I think you ought to report him."

"If I did they would jail Bertha as a suspect and keep her jailed for the duration. Would you want that done?"

"Oh, no," she cried, hastily. "I hadn't thought of that."

"Then until Heinrich has planned a murder, don't think or say any more about reporting him. If our America were half as considerate of Negroes as they ought to be, they'd put some smart Negroes on the FBI and they'd sooner or later, catch up with the subversive activities of Heinrich Schultz—and Kermit Early, for that matter, and put them both out of circulation. Since, however, they refuse to take Negroes seriously enough to watch them and their activities, then let them take the consequences. This much I will promise you, however, and that is when they begin to inveigle Bertha to the extent that her life and freedom is in danger, then I may do something. Until then my lips are sealed. Now what," he said, changing the conversation.

"I believe that since you have made everything so clear, that Bertha can be of great help to you."

"I know she can."

"Not only a lot of help, but a great deal of comfort. I think she will look after you personally and if you're going to be gone so long and travel so far, that is something worth considering."

"Thank you, Marie."

"So I haven't told her that you would take her. I've just let her feel that you might, and will keep her on the anxious seat for a while longer yet. Meantime, I am making everything so exacting, until she'll be willing to do everything she can think of to make the trip convenient and successful."

"I think she would do that anyhow, but there is no harm in making the conditions seem severe. One thing I like about it, and will prolong the trip as long as it may be necessary, is that it will take her from under Heinrich's influence and be sure to keep her out of trouble that much longer, anyhow."

"That's how I feel about it. I even went so far as to demand that she bring a letter from her brother, agreeing to let her stay with you during the entire trip, or no go."

"Good! Bertha is a good girl. I don't think she would ever do anything she'd ought not to unless somebody like her brother, to whom she is greatly devoted, would make her."

"That's how I feel about her. So now that that is understood, when I see you tomorrow I'll have everything ready and sealed, as it were." She rose to her feet, thought of something else, turned to him. "When do you think you will get away?"

"Within the next few weeks."

"Then I'll reckon that way." Started toward the door, Marie thought of something else and turned back to him.

"In the meantime, I don't see why you wouldn't take a couple of girls to a show and a night club, maybe, before you go away." She smiled and he laughed.

"Of course I will. When, dear one?" She shrugged her shoulders, perked up, looked rather cute.

"I'm giving you a chance to be with Bertha," she smiled again mischievously at him. "I know that's what you want to do, but I'll help you get used to each other by going along one time. Well, we'll let you know," and she went back to her desk and to work.

"Now Heinrich," said Bertha, at their apartment a few hours later. "Mr. Wyeth is going on a very long trip in connection with the sale of his book and I've asked his stenographer to let me go with him."

"Why, Bertha, go on a long trip like this with a—man and alone?" He frowned a moment. She patted his shoulder and sat him down. She had more influence in some ways over him than he over her, contrary to what Marie and Wyeth were thinking. Yet, when he asked her to do something, she always did it without questioning the logic of doing so, most times. She sat down across the table to face him.

"I wouldn't have considered it if I hadn't seen in going on it, the biggest opportunity I could ever get to study conditions all over the country."

"And maybe on the trip persuade him to make our picture," he added, with some enthusiasm. She did not react immediately to the suggestion but replied off-handedly:

"Perhaps. The main thing is to accompany him on the trip, be close to him. He will talk, I will talk. He likes people to ask him intelligent questions. I like to ask those kind of questions."

"And how!"

"So from such a trip, I should return about the wisest person among the secret agents of our country."

"You should that."

"His stenographer in the meantime, is smart."

"How so?"

"She wants a letter from you stating that you won't recall me before the trip is over."

"How long will the trip take—but that's all right. Type the letter," he said, rising. "I've got to meet a Doctor Gustave Von Barwig, from Stettin, due in this noon via Argentina."

"Who is he?"

"One of Hitler's closest advisers, being sent to America to take complete charge of activities in and around New York."

"What about Hans Schiller?"

"He's never been in complete charge. Meanwhile, he'll act as one of Von Barwig's advisors."

"What is going on, anything in particular?"

"Confidentially, they're expecting Japan to pick a quarrel with America and England and while Hitler's armies are crushing Russia,

Japan will declare war on America and England and draw much of their force off to defend their interests in the Pacific," said Heinrich.

"Big doings."

"I'll say. I hope Wyeth doesn't keep you too long. I might be needing you most any time if these things happen."

"I hope it won't force me to run around with those silly women I've been meeting in Yorktown."

"Who knows," Heinrich laughed.

"If I go on this trip, I won't be here for them to annoy me."

"Easy, sister, they're of great help to us."

"I guess so, that is why I have tried to be nice to them, and will continue to be, but I don't like them."

"You seem to like the girl Marie, and are especially fond of Sidney Wyeth."

"Mr. Wyeth is a lovely man."

"What is this, Sis? Are you—falling for Mr. Wyeth?" He looked at her quickly, curiously.

"Why, Heinrich! As if I dared like anybody that way. My life, like yours, and my first duty is to the cause of the Third Reich."

"Of course, but that doesn't keep you from liking somebody, and you do like Mr. Wyeth?"

"I do, Heinrich," she said, with lowered eyes.

"M-m. I thought so. How much?"

"I don't know, Heinrich."

He smiled and shrugged his shoulders.

"Write out that letter so that I can sign it. I must get down to Schiller's office to meet the Herr Doctor."

Bertha typed the letter carefully. Heinrich signed it and rushed out to join Hans Schiller and others, to go meet the Herr Doctor, coming in from Germany via the Argentine. Bertha was getting dressed preparatory to going out when the telephone rang. She answered promptly.

"Bertha," said Marie from the other end, recognizing her voice.

"Oh, Marie, darling."

"Come down."

"Of course. Right away?"

"Right away, precious."

"That's a darling," said Bertha, her hopes high. She hung up the receiver, finished her dressing, and in half an hour was seated in the comfortable chair in Wyeth's office.

"Did you get the letter?" inquired Marie.

"From my brother, you mean?"

"From your brother, Bertha." Bertha handed it over.

"Well, that part is settled," said Marie after reading it, "and Mr. Wyeth has agreed to take you with him."

"Oh, Marie," cried Bertha, rising from her seat, rushing across to Marie, and throwing her arms about her. "I'm so happy, darling, so pleased," she cried, between kisses on Marie's cheek. "I won't ever get through thanking you," she now all but cried.

"I'm glad. I hope it works out."

"It *will* work out, Marie, dear. I'll see that it does."

"You have a great deal of self-confidence, Bertha."

For answer, Bertha smiled and shrugged her shoulders. She sat down and Marie was pleased to see her so happy and so greatly relieved.

"Now when does Mr. Wyeth plan to leave?"

"In a few weeks."

"Fine. That'll give me time to have you both up to dinner."

"Really?"

"Yes. Meantime, Mr. Early's girl friend from Atlanta is back in town. Would it be all right to invite them?"

"Of course."

"Well I wanted to know how you and Mr. Wyeth felt about it before inviting her."

"It will be all right with Mr. Wyeth. I'm speaking for him, too."

"Then I'll invite them," said Bertha.

"Please do. I'd like to meet this Mrs. Wingate. A white woman, you say?"

"A very pretty white woman, rich, dignified and refined."

"Indeed. Rather unusual."

"It is. Very unusual, I've thought."

"What do you think of Mr. Early?" Marie wanted to know, casually.

"I don't know much about him," said Bertha, shrugging her shoulders. "He and my brother seem to have a great deal in common."

Marie would have liked to ask her more about her brother; she would have liked to talk with her at length about Heinrich. Bertha was talking again.

"In view of the—race relations in this country, Mr. Early and this Mrs. Wingate have aroused my curiosity. In Germany or in France, nothing would be thought about it."

"So I understand," said Marie.

By her expression, Bertha saw that she was deeply interested and decided to talk a lttle more.

"No. Nobody thinks or pays any attention to a white man with a colored woman or a colored man with a white woman."

"Not if they marry?"

"Oh, no. The only way it would be noticed, if the colored one was very dark. Then they would just look or glance at them. There are very few colored people ever seen, except, in Paris, for instance, and only in certain quarters there. So the look or glance at one would be confined to curiosity," said Bertha.

"Negroes and whites go together and marry frequently here in New York and all over the North, but they will sure look at you, that is, at a colored man with a white woman here in New York and everywhere else, especially if the woman is pretty."

"Really?"

"Break their necks, almost, especially the white people."

"They do?"

"And how! Look at them so that it must make the couples uncomfortable. Many of the white people, men especially, look at you so hard; like they'd like to do something about it; ask you some questions. I imagine they often do. On the other hand, most have become accustomed to the fact that there are a great many colored people who are so nearly white until it might be a colored person they'd be talking to."

"In regards to Mr. Early and this Mrs. Wingate, for instance."

"I understand they have been going together for a long time," said Marie.

"A very long time," said Bertha. "I think, from what my brother has told me, that she put him through school; financed his education."

"That's what I've been told," said Marie.

"He's a graduate of Harvard, you know."

"So I understand," said Marie. "A Ph.D."

"That's right. A Doctor of Philosophy."

"And you are a Doctor of Philosophy? From the Sorbonne or Heidelberg?"

"The Sorbonne. Both my brother and me."

"Whew," cried Marie. "Makes me feel like I'm a dumbbell."

"Oh, Marie, no. How far did you go in school, anyhow?"

"High School, teacher's course, then two years during which I majored in business administration."

"You have as much practical education then, as a Doctorate could give you. Beyond what you know is a whole lot that one rarely needs; that one rarely has occasion to use. How far did Mr. Wyeth go in school?" said Bertha.

"Not very far."

"He's a graduate in the philosophy of life; of common sense and knowing what to do, what to think, how to think, the greatest education a body can possess."

"I agree with you. Meantime, we were talking about this Mrs. Wingate."

"Talked right away from her," laughed Bertha. "Well, she's a widow now and I'm wondering if she and Kermit are going to get married."

"Has he said anything about it?" inquired Marie.

"No," replied Bertha. "He doesn't talk so much."

"Let's try to draw her out at the dinner," suggested Marie.

"All right. I'm with you. We'll try to do so. She seems quite talkative."

"Is that so?"

"Seems to want to."

"Do you think Kermit would object?" said Marie.

"I don't think so. In a way, she seems to wear the pants."

"She should, if she's paid for all the education he's got," said Marie and laughed. "And she's from Georgia?"

"Atlanta," replied Bertha.

"Next to Mississippi, they tell me that's the worst state in the Union," said Marie.

"How so?" from Bertha.

"How so?" and Marie looked at her,

"Yes," replied Bertha, innocently, curiously.

"Of course you wouldn't know as much about that as somebody who's lived here."

"I'd still like to," said Bertha.

"Georgia is the home of Judge Lynch."

"Judge Lynch?" asked Bertha. "Who is he?" Marie looked at her, then smiled.

"You need to go on this trip with Mr. Wyeth."

"You know how anxious I am to go."

"It will be your larger education. You'll learn a whole lot about America, the South, and the Negro," said Marie.

"I shall be glad to learn all about it. Do you know," and Bertha paused briefly as if to pick her way. "You don't hear as much about —lynching right here where it is supposed to go on as you do— in Germany." Marie looked hard at her.

"What do you mean?"

"What I say. Why, in Germany, since the war broke out, especially, they print the most terrible things about how the Negro is treated in America, also feature some of the worst pictures."

"Oh, no," cried Marie, amazed.

"Oh, yes. Pictures of a grove of trees, for instance, with Negroes hanging from all the limbs by their necks."

"Oh, my God!" exclaimed Marie.

"They play it up so, and more, my mother writes me, as the war goes on. When you come to the house, I'm going to show you some of the clippings. Shows fifteen or twenty Negroes, men and women, hanging from trees with captions under the picture: 'American Democracy'."

"Great goodness!" exclaimed Marie.

"Is it as—as bad as that down there where we are going?" said Bertha, a bit timidly, hesitantly

"Oh, no," cried Marie. "The fact is, there are very few lynchings any more."

"Is that so?"

"Of course not," said Marie.

"But, Marie, isn't it possible that there are many, maybe, and— they don't publish it?"

Marie shook her head,

"Lynching is always news and the papers say lots about it. So when one takes place, it is in all the papers."

"It is?"

"Positively. The north and the better people in the South, I mean better white people South, don't condone lynching. It gives them and the states where it takes place, a bad name. They are against it and are consistently trying to stop it."

"But how can they when the—the leaders," said Bertha, a bit insistently, "say so much in the papers about 'White Supremacy,' and all that?"

"They fear the Negro in the South, so try to keep him down, 'in his place', they call it. They fear that if he is given complete freedom, they'll run the country."

"Is it so?" said Bertha. Marie shook her head.

"No, it isn't and the politicians are making a fool of themselves by saying so much about it."

"Yet they keep talking about it, evidently, from what one reads in the papers, hears over the radio?"

"I agree with you and it would seem sensible on their part if they'd quit talking so much about it. But the war has something to do with it now. You see, if we are forced into this war, it'll mean an equal proportion of the colored men will be drafted into service, along with a proportionate number of whites. And while they will do all they can to keep the colored soldier down, there will be a great many petty officers—corporals, sergeants, second lieutenants and a few higher officers, and the South can't stand that. It makes the politicians and leaders down there fighting mad. They hate the idea of the Negro being honored in the smallest way. They keep us out of so many things, the Motion Pictures, other than as stupid menials; they confine us to singing spirituals and hymns, praying and shouting on our way to 'heaven' over the radio, but when a war pops up, it is awful hard work to restrain all that it will develop. They don't want the Negro to get big notions in his head; they do everything they know how to discourage him."

"Then how can they preach, as America does, about so much democracy? Is that which you've just explained, democracy?" Bertha had grown insistent. Marie relaxed and smiled.

"You've talked me into deep waters. I cannot debate all that so well. You need to talk that way with Mr. Wyeth." Marie looked at the clock on the wall, and started.

"It's after five, time to go home." She jumped to her feet, followed by Bertha.

"Please call and tell me what time you're going to have this dinner so that I can come early and help you prepare it. I'm anxious to meet Mrs. Wingate."

"That's so sweet of you. Mr. Early will perhaps come by to see Heinrich tonight. I'll phone you more about it tomorrow."

"Thanks," said Marie, as Bertha helped her into her coat. A few minutes later they left the office.

CHAPTER XXIX

"NOW KERMIT, dear," said Mrs. Wingate, settling into a comfortable seat beside him on the sofa of their apartment in Harlem. "Can we talk about something very important for a few minutes?"

"Why, of course, Florence. I shall be glad to."

"Thank you, dear," she replied. Her face took on a serious expression now. She paused briefly as if trying to decide just how to start and where to start. "It's about the estate." Kermit was listening, attentively. She saw she had his undivided attention, so went on.

"The will was duly probated, and thanks to Mr. Wingate's sagacity, he left a will that was easy to probate. One half of the estate to me, largely in trust with one of the banks in Atlanta, the balance to his relations, so nobody will have to go to court and spend a lot of money on lawyers. I'm glad it is that way, as I'd dislike so much to go through a lot of court proceedings." Mrs. Wingate didn't say, since it was not necessary, that if she had to go into court in Georgia later on, after marrying a colored man, that it would be most embarrassing. She knew better than anyone just how the white people of the south, all of those she had met and knew through all the years of her life, would regard what she was about to do—marry a colored man. All would be strangers to her from then on. It was a choice between the man she loved and had been a companion to these many years, and the white people of the south, on the other hand, and she had long since made her choice.

"I announced that I was moving to New York, and got everything settled in such a way that I won't have to go south again for a long time, if ever."

"You could, by yourself, dear."

She shrugged her shoulders. Laid her hand on her stomach and sighed.

"In a few months now we'll have our baby. That is all I'm interested in. I can forget everything that is behind me without much effort, while we look to the future."

"To the future, Florence," he said, and smiling, reached out, placed an arm about her waist and drew her closer and kissed her. She relaxed a bit, tired like, laid her head on his shoulder. After a time, she lifted it, thought for a moment, then turned to him.

"When shall we get married?" He turned to her.

"Whenever you say, dear." After a brief thought, he turned to her: "Now that you are—free, do you really want to marry me, darling," She looked at him in surprise.

"Why, of course, Kermit. That is what I have wanted to do all these years. Why do you ask such a question?" For answer, he squeezed her. Then looking into her eyes.

"I just wanted to hear you say it, darling," he said. "Now that you are free to see if that could make any difference."

"Oh, darling," she cried, throwing her arms about him and hugging him. "Nothing could make a difference with me about you. I'm so happy now that it is all over and we are free to marry, until it bewilders me." She relaxed her embrace, looked at him a bit oddly, then shook her head.

"I can't seem to realize that we are free; free to become man and wife at last. It makes me—sort of—dizzy, dear." She looked into his eyes again and again he kissed her, patted her cheek.

"Then everything is all right, sweetheart. We'll be married just as quickly as you say."

"Where?" she asked. He paused, thought a moment, turned back to her.

"Oh, down at the city hall, perhaps?" She frowned.

"No. I want to be married by a—preacher, a minister of the gospel." He thought again and looked at her.

"There's a church downtown, called 'the little church around the corner'. Lots of people get married there." Again she frowned, then stuck her mouth out and pouted.

"I want to be married up here in Harlem; by a—colored preacher."

He smiled, patted her cheek, relaxed happily.

"That'll be so much easier. I'll get any kind of preacher you want. I mean, any denomination, and, we'll be—married right here." She clasped her hands, then relaxed again and thought for a moment, turned to him

"I have it," she cried, her eyes lighting up with delight.

"All right, honey. What do you have?" said Kermit.

"Let's arrange to be married at the Schultz's!"

"Okeh, dear." then after a pause. "But I'll have to speak to Heinrich and his sister about it first."

"Naturally."

"But it'll be all right. They've invited us to dinner. Maybe we can arrange to be married at this—dinner?"

"Oh, that would be too delightful for words, darling." Cupping his cheeks with her hands, she kissed him with a loud smack and then stood up. He followed her

"I'll take it up with them today."

"Who have they invited to dinner, other than us? Do they know many people?" Kermit was thoughtful for a moment, shook his head.

"I wouldn't think so."

"Maybe they're going to invite this man Wyeth?"

"Wouldn't be surprised. And the girl who works in his office. She and Bertha seem to be very friendly."

"Speaking of Mr. Wyeth." Mrs. Wingate walked over by the window, adjusted the light, turned to face him. "What's happened to your deal? Is he going to direct the picture?" Kermit's face fell, his smile died.

"I'm so sorry, dear. You have such an interesting story, have worked on it so long and so hard. Why won't he?"

Kermit shrugged his shoulders. "The same old thing."

"Don't like the 'hate the Jew' angle?"

"That's it."

"I don't understand.. The Jews ruined his picture business, messed it, as you say, all up. Still he won't go in for exposing them for what they are, a bunch of chisling Sheneys?"

"Both Schultz and I went to him while you were away, argued it out pro and con. We didn't get anywhere. Still refuses to make it."

She looked at him, at a loss for a moment what to say.

"What about his sister, I mean, Bertha Schultz? Has she tried to do anything?"

"Yes. She's been working on him, in a way."

"In a way? What kind of way?"

"He's about to take a long sales trip. She's persuaded him to let her go with him."

"Oh!" she exclaimed. "That ought to do it."

"I hope so," said Kermit. Mrs. Wingate was thoughtful again.

"Is this Mr. Wyeth a—single man?" Kermit nodded.

"Yes. He's single." Mrs. Wingate smiled.

"If he takes her on this trip, he's almost sure to fall in love with her, a pretty girl like she is."

"That shouldn't be hard to do."

"I'll say. I would if I was him. I hope you don't go to doing so before I marry you," she smiled and pinched his cheek, chidingly.

"She's a pretty girl and a smart girl."

"Keen as a razor's edge."

"You say she seems to like Mr. Wyeth?"

"Appears to."

"That way?"

"I don't know. Maybe."

"Well," she said and shifted so that the light was in her face. "If he takes her on a trip like this, she ought to be able to get him to do whatever she wants him to, before it's over."

"I hope so," said Kermit.

"Meanwhile, please find out from Miss Schultz, if she is inviting him to dinner. I'd like to meet him myself," said Mrs. Wingate.

"I will. He's interesting."

"Is he—good looking?"

"Plain," said Kermit.

"Plain," she said, "but that wouldn't make much difference with Bertha. It's brains that count with her." "And he has the brains, you think?"

"Too much. If he wasn't so smart he'd have accepted our offer; be working on the picture by now."

"I still believe she can get him to direct it—if she tries hard enough."

"That's it," said Kermit.

"Do you think she's really interested in trying to get him to do so?"

"Heinrich is. She'd do anything to please him."

"Then the thing for you to do, as I see it, is to put plenty pressure on Heinrich," Mrs. Wingate said.

"I'll do that."

"We'll have a chance to study them all very closely at the dinner. Meanwhile, suppose I go on a shopping trip downtown? I want to select something to get married in."

"I'm due to meet Heinrich downtown today."

"Downtown, eh? Where?"

"At Hans Schiller's office, to meet Doctor Von Barwig."

"More Germans. This country seems to be swarming with Germans lately."

"It is."

"Trying to keep America out of the war?"

"That's it. Trying to keep America out of the war," said Kermit.

"Think they'll succeed?"

"I don't think so."

"Why?"

"The Jews are closer to Roosevelt. They want it and Roosevelt is itching to get into it. That's what the Jew influence is doing to him. Nobody in America wants to get in the war but Roosevelt, the Jews, and the British."

"They carry a lot of influence, I mean, the British."

"And how. For instance,"

"What?"

"Have you noticed that a very large number of the screen actors lately are English?" said he.

"Most all of the best ones, the highest paid ones," she said.

"The Jews are behind that. All this is indirectly pushing us closer to the war. It may be necessary in order to save the British Empire."

"This country is terribly pro-English. Always has been."

"Especially the South," he suggested.

"They adore Royalty."

"Don't leave out the president and his wife."

"Just take the whole country, and you won't miss anybody," said Kermit and laughed.

They turned now and went into the dining room.

CHAPTER XXX

THE TELEPHONE rang in Wyeth's office and Marie picked up the receiver and called, "hello," and then recognized Bertha Schultz's voice from the other end, apparently very much excited.

"What is it, Bertha?" Marie now called back, sitting up and taking notice.

"If you're going to be at the office another half hour," she cried, "I'll tell you. I am coming right down." She hung up without saying another word.

As Marie hung up and looked around, she found Wyeth looking at her from his office. He had left the door open and couldn't help hearing some of the conversation.

"What's going on? A new murder in Harlem? That shouldn't excite anybody."

Marie smiled, got to her feet, came into his office and sat down.

"It was Bertha," she said.

"Bertha!"

"Yes," she replied, "she was all excited about something."

"I wonder what it could be?" he said curiously.

"Didn't take time to tell me, but said she would be right down," Marie said.

"In the meantime, how did you two come out regarding the trip yesterday?" he now said, looking at her with some interest.

"Oh, all right. She's ready and raring to go whenever you are."

"Good! I can see a lot of books moving out of our stock room very soon now."

"You seem to have lots of confidence in Bertha's ability to help you," said Marie.

"Bertha's got what it takes to do just that. But best of all is her willingness to do it."

"'I guess that can mean a great deal. She's planning to have us up to dinner soon."

"Really?"

"Yes. She's to let me know today when she is going to give it. She's inviting Kermit Early and that white woman he goes with."

"Yes?"

"She asked me if I thought she should include her."

"Is that so. Why?"

"Well, she said that she didn't know if it would be proper to do so. Mrs. Wingate is a Southerner, you know."

"From Georgia, where they eat Negroes."

"What do you mean?" She seemed curious.

"I mean, they are hard on Negroes," he laughed.

"We talked about that yesterday," said Marie. "I told Bertha that Georgia was the home of Judge Lynch."

"And what did she say?" He began to laugh.

"She thought he was some man. I had a hard time making her understand that he was only a figure of speech; that the term meant lynching."

"Then what? How did she react?"

"One thing she said during the conversation that surprised me," said Marie, "was that they play up America's lynching of Negroes in Germany something terrible."

"Good!" he cried. She looked at him in surprise. "That's good propaganda for us. I knew they did, not only in Germany but all over Europe, even a great deal in England."

"Is that so?" cried Marie, in surprise.

"They do just that. That is why America is not so highly respected, even in South America, where they play it up, too."

"I didn't know that."

"Well, it's so, and that is what the South with all its prejudices and everlastingly playing us down, and—"

"—white supremacy up—"

"—is doing for our America. We are making the whole world into a lot of hypocrites. To get our money, which Roosevelt and his New Dealers seem anxious to give away to everybody who'll just pretend to be friendly to us, they must smile in our faces and tell the Administration that we are the World's great democracy, which—"

"—doesn't include Negroes, of course."

"Of course not. That's the South. They never get tired trying to keep us in our places. As a result, they give the whole country a bad name. Actually, America isn't really popular anywhere, and the way the South insists on treating us is the cause of a share of it."

"And with the South running the administration at Washington, politically—"

"—there's nothing that can be done about it. But getting back to Bertha and what she talked about yesterday."

"Well, she said that Germany regards America as a great big joke, implied that they consider us stupid, but being rich and having so much money we are able to force our opinion and ideas on many people who kowtow to us to get some of it. But she didn't say anything about South America."

"She might not know so much about it. Her brother would, however. You can bet he'd know all about it. I really think they hate us more in South America than they do in Germany."

"Oh, sure. The fact is Germans, not even Hitler, hate us. They're annoyed, of course, for the help we are giving England whom they really do hate, but Germany, even if soon at war with us, does not hate us. After the last war there was a greater friendship when it was all over between the Americans and the Germans than between England and the United States."

"Why so?"

"The Germans are in a way, a better people than the English. The English, including the Negro West Indians here in this country, tend to be egotistic and arrogant. Out west where I come from, there were so many Germans and they were, along with the Scandinavian people, the best people I've ever met in all America. Big-hearted, honest, splendid farmers, the best kind of neighbors—just good people and personnally, I'm sorry Hitler invaded Poland and Russia and started this terrible war. If he had just been patient he'd have finally gotten the fifteen mile corridor through Poland, for Poland would have ultimately given in to him. But he'd had too much success in getting Austria and Czechoslovakia. It made him over-confident, so he started a war that is going to all but ruin the whole world before it is over. In the end it will be his end, whereas, had he been patient, he would have come out on top completely and been looked upon and admired as the greatest man in the world."

"Do you think so?" questioned Marie.

"I know so," said Wyeth, firmly. "Why, at the outbreak of the other war, the Kaiser was considered the greatest man in the world of that day, which you can't understand very well at this time, but he was and so was Hitler—in fact, so *is* Hitler at this hour."

"But they hate him."

"Naturally, but if he wins this war, he'll be lord of the world."

"What about the way he's treating the Jews?" she said.

Wyeth shrugged his shoulders.

"If Germany loses the war, that'll help the Jews some, but not as much as the people might think. Unfortunately, nobody likes the Jews anywhere in the world. They put up with and tolerate him actually here and in England, but nobody loves him, nobody trusts him. It has been that way since civilization began; it will be that way as long as civilization lasts and most of the people worship God."

"You seem to like them."

"It isn't a matter of liking, as far as I am personally concerned. I have always believed in tolerance, and most people are the same way. But in time of war, and more so, after wars when we get back to the work of readjustment, it doesn't work so well, that is when the forces of evil within men begin to assert itself; when hatred begins to break forth into flame and assert itself. That is when you see how men feel—but I don't want to get into a long discourse on the troubles of the world. I'm just a poor author, trying to sell his own books, and am satisfied with the good success I'm having. Besides, if I recall correctly, we were talking about Bertha Schultz, who—"

"Is due here any moment," said Marie, getting to her feet and then pausing to listen.

Both heard a pair of footsteps coming down the hall rather hurriedly, and looking at Wyeth, Marie nodded her head and said in a low tone, "that's her right now," and she crossed into the reception room just as the door was pushed open and Bertha entered.

"Oh, Marie," she cried. "I just had to see you. I—" then she broke off for Wyeth's office door was open and her eyes fell upon him sitting there. He smiled, and bowed when their eyes met.

"Good morning, Miss Schultz," he said, pleasantly, amiably.

"Good morning, Mr. Wyeth," she replied, agreeably, leaving Marie to cross to him, her hand outstretched. He rose to meet her. "May I shake your hand this morning?" she said as he held out his and grasped hers.

"It is a pleasure, Miss Schultz," and then he looked down. She looked down, too. He was still holding her hand and she was wondering what the matter was.

"Such a small, but soft and beautiful hand," and he took his other hand and laid it over hers.

"Oh, Mr. Wyeth, you will insist on flattering me," she cried, blushing. Meantime Wyeth held onto her small hand, raised it and cried:

"I ask you, Mrs. Coleman, is this or is this not a small hand, and is it or is it not a beautiful hand?"

It had now become a joke and Bertha, snatching it away, blushing all over, turned to Marie.

"Mr. Wyeth must be happy this morning, and in a mood for joking."

"You're here, dear, to see me about something very important," said Marie. "So we will close Mr. Wyeth's door; shut him in, as it were," she began and moved a step to do so, when Bertha, after a moment of quick thought, caught and stopped her.

"Oh, no," she cried. "What I have to tell you, I'd just as soon Mr. Wyeth hear, too. In fact, I'd like him to hear it, providing he has the time to—"

"—I have the time, Miss Schultz. What there is to be done can wait, so sit down," he said, waving at the chair in which she usually sat, and toward the sofa, to Marie. The girls looked at each other, then smiling, obeyed. Wyeth sat down, and looking at Bertha.

"Now, Miss Schultz, if it's agreeable with all concerned, and it is with me, you may—proceed." And he made a gesture which reflected direction. Pointing a finger at him, Bertha cried:

"I'll bet you are a splendid director."

"And a still better actor," said Marie, joining in the spirit of the moment. Turning to Bertha. "He is a splendid director, Bertha. It is too bad that one who has learned the art so well and the only one in our race, had to give it up in the prime of his career," and Marie sighed, turned to look at Wyeth kindly, sympathetically. Bertha looked at him also. She turned to Marie and Wyeth with a sudden impulse.

"Mr. Early and my brother have a picture they want him to direct; they say, or at least Mr. Early says, that he is the only one in all America who can bring it to the screen like he wants it brought—but I am not here to talk about directing pictures," she broke off to say. "I'm here to tell you and Mr. Wyeth," she said, turning from Marie to Sidney, "that Mr. Early called on my brother last night and told him that he and Mrs. Wingate were going to be married, and wondered if we'd mind if they did so the night of my dinner."

"O-o-h!" cried Marie and Wyeth together.

"Yes," said Bertha. "They're going to be married, and I'm here to talk to both of you about it. Heinrich told Early that it was O. K. by him, but that he'd like to speak to me first, and then when I came in from a picture show, Heinrich told me about it and I told him I'd like to come and see what you thought about it?" She turned from one to the other now, and Marie turned to Wyeth.

"Why not?" said Wyeth, throwing his hands out.

"Yes," rejoined Marie, "why not?"

"Then you think it will be all right?" said Bertha, turning eyes from one to the other again.

"Of course. Give Kermit and his—Southern white girl, a break," exclaimed Wyeth, showing interest. Bertha nodded.

"Then I'll tell my brother to tell him that it will be all right?"

"Now the next thing," said Bertha. "Will it be all right to tie their wedding up with—my dinner?"

"Why, of course," cried Marie.

Again she paused and looked at Marie, who, in turn, looked at Wyeth again, who promptly noddded approval.

"That'll give us a chance to witness it," said Wyeth.

"A white woman marrying a colored man.. I've never seen it done, so I'll be tickled pink to look on," said Marie.

"Me, too," cried Wyeth. "A Negro getting married not merely to a white woman, but a rich one—and topping it all, a Southern woman."

"Oh," cried Marie, grasping her hands. "It will be a thrill."

Bertha seemed a bit confused.

"It is all a bit confusing to me. My mother, a white woman, married two colored men. In Germany, it wouldn't mean any more than one white person marrying another, but in this country, it's—"

"—very different, Miss Schultz," said Wyeth. "So different that if they wanted to get married in Georgia, where the lady hails from, they could not."

"What—do you—mean?" Bertha exclaimed.

"Just what he says, Bertha, dear," chimed in Marie. "The laws of the state of Georgia and all the other states down there—"

"—and several states up here, in the north and in the west, have laws against the same thing," interposed Wyeth.

"But don't let that concern you. The state of New York permits intermarriage, and that's all that matters in this case. Kermit Early and this Mrs. Wingate have a perfect right to marry each other in New York and most northern states, so just forget about it. Mrs. Coleman and I are animated because of certain phases of it. We both wonder how it came about. Mrs. Wingate, a wealthy and aristocratic Southern woman, whose husband, a millionaire, just killed recently. Yet, they seem, Mr. Early and Mrs. Wingate to have been sweethearts for a long time, which was while her husband still lived. None of our business, of course, but the circumstances are so unusual—"

"—extraordinary would be a better word, Mr. Wyeth," said Marie. Bertha looked on, still a bit bewildered.

"Extraordinary *is* the word, Miss Schultz. It just isn't done here in America, as far as I can recall. So naturally, Mrs. Coleman and I are both curious and anxious about it."

"And now that we are invited to see it take place it will be the biggest thrill I've ever had a chance to experience," cried Marie, gleefully.

"Well," said Bertha, emitting something of a sigh. "We'll all get to see it, so it'll be more interesting to me than would have otherwise been the case. I'll be anxious to witness it now myself."

"What sort of looking woman is this Mrs. Wingate?" said Wyeth.

"Oh, she's pretty," said Bertha, promptly.

"Is that so?" mused Wyeth. "And about how old? Older or younger than Mr. Early, would you say?"

"I'd say about two years younger. Of course I wouldn't know."

"Of course not. Doesn't matter."

"We'll all get to meet her and talk with her," said Marie, then pointing at Wyeth, "and you—dance with her," then laughed, Bertha laughed, Wyeth looked embarrassed

"My boss, dancing with a pretty white woman—oh, my," cried Marie, teasingly

"I can't recall," said Wyeth, "if I have ever danced with one. Not a Southern one, at least. In fact, I'm sure that I've never danced with a white woman at all." Both the girls looked at him and pointed their fingers at him, teasingly.

"It'll be a big night for Mr. Wyeth," Marie kept on, tantalizingly, "dancing with a rich, Southern white lady."

Bertha smiled and looked at Wyeth with new concern.

"He'll get to dance with you, too," said Marie, chidingly. Bertha blushed, furiously.

"Oh, Marie," she cried, and lowered her eyes.

"As big a thrill as it may give him to dance with Mrs. Wingate, it will give him a still bigger one to dance with you." Bertha blushed more, and when she raised her eyes to look at Wyeth, she saw that he seemed highly elated, and that made her blush the more.

"Oh, Marie, please hush! Mr. Wyeth will get to dance with me lots, maybe, when we go on the trip," and she raised her eyes to look at Wyeth, and in that moment Bertha Schultz got a feeling that she was beginning to like Sidney Wyeth. As he looked at her, he felt a strange and peculiar reaction. He din't dare let himself think what it was, but Bertha did. For the moment she forgot that she was a Nazi spy, in this country to gather information and send it back to Hitler; she forgot everything for the moment but the fact that she was a woman, and Sidney Wyeth a man. That Sidney Wyeth was a lovely man, and a lonely man and that she could be not only a great help to him in his honest and sincere efforts towards success, but that she could be of comfort to him. Had they been alone at the moment and closer together, he might have said something and her reply would have been soft, tender and agreeable to whatever he said. And then as suddenly she forced all of this out of her mind, and returned to the commonplace.

"Well," she said, getting to her feet. "May I consider everything settled?"

"As far as we are concerned, Bertha," said Marie, "Yes." She turned to Wyeth, who was standing. "Is it all right by you, boss?"

"All right by me, ladies," he said, agreeably.

"Then we'll consider it settled," said Bertha, moving toward the door. "I'll leave you now," she said, pausing and turning back to Wyeth in the doorway. "I'll find out from my brother just what day Mr. Early and Mrs. Wingate would like to be married, then I'll set the date for the dinner and let Mrs. Coleman here know. Will that be all right, Mr. Wyeth?"

"Perfectly all right, Miss Schultz."

"Then I'll bid you good morning," she said, sweetly, bowing a bit, and smiling happily. She moved into the reception room then, followed by Marie, who closed Wyeth's office door behind them and followed Bertha across the reception room and bid her goodbye at the outer door. She turned and coming back, knocked on Wyeth's door and entered.

"Well," she said, pausing, "What do you think of it?"

"It'll give us something to look forward to; something to think about."

"I agree with you. I'm already thinking about it, this Mrs. Wingate and Mr. Early."

"A rather strange case."

"Stranger than fiction, if you ask me. How did it all start, and where?"

"Schultz and I talked about it the day we met downtown and he told me that her husband had been killed. He didn't know so much about it, but more, of course, than I did, as he met this Mrs. Wingate in Chicago when he was out there and I suppose Kermit had said something about it to him."

"Where did he meet her, and how?"

"Down in a little town in Georgia where they both came from, it seems."

"In Georgia. But how could two people, so far apart socially, meet and start to like each other in a little town in Georgia, a beautiful white woman and a Negro?" said Marie. He shrugged his shoulders.

"You've heard me say that Kermit Early doesn't talk, and I don't know. All I know, or have found out is that she put him through school and has been friendly and intimate with him for years, over ten, so I understand."

"And now she's going to marry him."

"Yes, marry him."

"He'd better not go back to Georgia with her afterwards," she said.

Wyeth laughed.

"If he does, he'll never leave Georgia," and they both laughed.

"Of course," said Wyeth, "both of them know all about that and when and if she goes to Georgia from now on, it will be alone."

"I'll sure be glad to see her, meet her and talk with her. This is one time I'm going to look into somebody's business and study them."

"It should prove interesting."

"Ought to give you something to write about."

"There is plenty to fire the imagination. If I knew their whole story, I bet it would make interesting reading."

"If you'll agree to make Kermit's hate picture, bet he would agree to tell it to you," she said, and smiled. Wyeth joined her.

"That is *one way* I could get it."

"But you won't," suggested Marie.

"I won't."

"Bertha managed to get in a word about it, if you noticed."

"And swerved right away from it so quickly that I couldn't express an opinion much less an answer," he said, smiling.

"Bertha's a smart girl,"

"And shrewd with it into the bargain."

"I'll say."

"Yet there is something about her, so sweet and feminine, that she—"

"—gets you. That's what you mean. And she's got you," said Marie, pointedly.

"Now there you go," he said, chidingly.

"But she likes you. I saw it awhile ago. So if you like her, it is mutual."

"I don't know," he said and sighed a bit.

"It's her work, her mission to America that restrains any more expression. If the war ended tomorrow, she'd be an entirely different girl. Then she could be herself. Now when she is about to, she thinks about what she was sent here to do and holds back."

"That's it, I understand."

CHAPTER XXXI

KERMIT EARLY came back into the bedroom after having been called to the telephone by Heinrich Schultz, who told him that Bertha and he would be glad to have he and Mrs. Wingate get married at their apartment, and to decide with Mrs. Wingate just what night they wished to, so that they could tie the wedding up with the dinner Bertha had planned.

He found Mrs. Wingate sitting up in bed waiting for him when he returned, so sitting down on the side of the bed, he told her and she was relieved.

"Thanks, dear," she said. "Now get back in bed and let's talk. There's something I've wanted to discuss with you for some time and this morning, since you won't be going downtown before noon, should be a good time to discuss it."

Seated, a moment later, propped up against pillows, Mrs. Wingate proceeded to get that *something* that had been on her chest, off.

"Now, Kermit, we haven't been out socially in all the years we've been together, but now that we're about to get married, and in a few months the child will be here, I think it is appropriate for us to look into the future, don't you think?"

"Just as you say, Florence. Anything that will please you will be O. K. with me," he said.

"You've never been so strong for going around, I know. I've learned that people don't know much about you, which has been all right. In view of the way we've had to get along, socially, maybe it's just as well, since we haven't had to do much explaining. But after we get married it is obvious that my friends, or at least your friends may be my friends, and we will desire at least a few."

"Of course."

"I am not, nor will I complain—nor even regret ending the association that has been mine. I have had you, and it has been you who has given me all the happiness I've ever had, so you come first, in my life. In the past, of course, I've had to live a sort of—double life; a dual existence, as it were, but from now on that must be changed." She paused and he took her hand to comfort her. He saw that what she wished to say was a bit hard, as close to each other as they were. What Florence Wingate was trying to make clear was that now that she was marrying a colored man, she could and would have few if any white friends from that day on. Such as she might have would be new friends, mostly in New York. These old friends and acquaintances in Atlanta and Wakefield, when they heard what she had done, would be through with her forever. She had thought of and considered all that, years before, so she was prepared to change over when the time came—and the time is now.

"One thing Schultz asked," he was saying, "was if we would like anybody present; if Bertha should invite anybody?"

"Whom, in particular, did they have in mind. Did he say?"

"I don't think anybody but Mr. Wyeth and his secretary. As I told you, Bertha is very friendly with this Mrs. Coleman and had invited them to dinner before thinking about inviting us. Then when we decided to get married, and they suggested tying it up with the dinner, Mr. Wyeth and Mrs. Coleman were naturally included, see."

"Of course, dear, and I will be glad to have them witness our little affair."

"Then it will be all right for them to come?"

"I want them to. I don't know anything about Mrs. Coleman, of course, and I haven't met Mr. Wyeth, but you know that I am anxious to. So when you see Mr. Schultz, please tell him that I am anxious to meet their friends."

"Would you like them to invite anybody else?"

"Not unless they want to and you want to. Maybe some of your old friends?"

"Oh, I don't care to dig up any. It's been so long ago, and I'm interested in only a few at present. I don't think the Schultz' have many friends, except the white people they are associated with downtown. I think Bertha planned to only have Mr. Wyeth and his secretary and us, so if they haven't planned to invite anybody else, it'll be all right with me to just confine the party to those already invited and let it go at that."

"Then let it remain as is. And now, dear, I'll return to what I started to talk about and I think we should be perfectly frank with each other and face our new life in harmony."

"You mean, Florence, that in—in marrying me, ours will be a new life—especially yours?"

"I guess we can call it that."

"It will be that," said Kermit. "From the day you marry me you—you're a white woman in a social sense no longer. It is a sacrifice you will have to make when you marry me."

"I'm prepared to do so, Kermit. In fact, I'm anxious to get started at doing so."

"When the child comes, you also understand, that it will be considered a—"

"—colored child. Yes, I understand. Majority will not obtain in a matter of this kind. You're at least one-fourth white, but our child will be considered a colored child, so I am satisfied to be a *colored woman* from now on."

"You'll still be a white woman; a white woman married to a colored man, unwelcome, however, on the white side, your lot will be with Negroes from then, on, and—"

"—that is what I resigned myself to a long time ago and am ready and anxious to get started at it. I want you to direct me in this change as you call it," and she smiled. "I want you to help me make myself agreeable to this new order. I suppose, after all, however, that I'm not the first white woman to marry a colored man?"

"No, dear. There are plenty of others. In Chicago, there is a circle that includes only mixed couples. I was to an affair they gave out there once."

"Was it—interesting?" she asked, curiously.

"Oh, nothing unusual. Because of Mr. Wingate's wealth, yours will be different, I fear. If the papers find it out—and they will, we may get a lot of notorious publicity. Reporters from many papers may call to see us, take our pictures, and print them."

For a moment she seemed a bit frightened, then steeled her nerves to the coming ordeal as she had been doing since she fell in love with Kermit Early.

"You—you think they will—do all that, Kermit?"

"They won't miss doing it."

"Then—then, if they do, and, I have a baby so much sooner than I would be—due to, that—that wouldn't sound so good, would it?"

"I guess not, dear," he said.

She was silent, thinking deeply a moment, then went on:

"I—I don't like—scandalous notoriety. If what you say happens, I think we ought to—to go away for awhile. To—to, oh, where could we go for about six months; where they wouldn't know just when —the baby came? All Europe is at war. We can't go there?" Kermit was thoughtful. She was holding onto him like she was dependent on him—she *was* dependent on him. He could feel her trembling slightly.

"We could go to—South America, dear. We could find a haven down there to sort of hide away, then go to some big place a couple of months after your delivery, then return here."

"But that would interfere with your work, dear; with your making the picture?"

He shrugged his shoulders.

"You come first, Florence. Unless I can get to the picture before we leave, it'll have to wait until we come back."

"Oh, I dislike so much to—"

He stopped her. "That's all right, Florence. I won't mind. Our baby is the important thing now. If we go to South America, take ourselves into the Andes Mountains or off to Patagonia, there will be no newspaper reporters around to expose our family life and use it for headlines. So about two months before it is due, we'll sail quietly away from here."

"Perhaps go by plane. I'm expecting America to be drawn into the war any time. If we are, Germany'll fill the Gulf of Mexico and the Carribean with submarines. We might be torpedoed. We'll go there by plane."

"Meanwhile, let's not let that worry us any more right now."

"No, dear. Let's think about the wedding."

"By the way, Florence," he said, and his mind seemed to be on something.

"Yes, dear?"

"About your—your folks back in Wakefield?" She sighed.

"They'll just have to—take it," she said.

"But you must be thinking, at least must have thought, just how it would—react on them?"

"I have thought of it, Kermit, been thinking of it for years. When I went down there last, I planned it as my final visit. I saw them again, later, of course, when they came to Atlanta to Mr. Wingate's funeral."

"Will you write, maybe, and tell your mother that—you are going to get—married?"

"I've thought of that, too. It will be best that I not do so."

He turned to look at her. She read what he was thinking.

"You see, if I write and tell them that I'm going to get married again, they'll tell everybody in Wakefield. Tell all our old friends. Then, if, as you say, the papers got hold of it and published our pictures, it—"

"—would put them on the spot," he said, interrupting.

"So if I say nothing about it and they read it in the papers, the shock will be all at once—oh, Kermit, I don't care," she said and began to cry. He took her in his arms to comfort her.

"I'm so sorry, sweetheart," he said, patting her shoulder while she continued to cry. "I'm so sorry. After all they are your parents. And there are your brothers and sisters to think of. I've thought of all that, and that is why I asked you the other day—" And he stopped.

"There, there, dear. We have been happy together. We'll soon enjoy a greater happiness. We're going to be married. There is no law in heaven against two people marrying that love each other. Because of the customs of this country, however, it will be considered in Georgia, anyhow, wrong and a crime against society. So we must just forget Wakefield and Georgia—and my people. That's all."

He tried to smile, but she could see that he was conscious of the sacrifice she would be making; could see that it pained him to have her do so, and Florence Wingate knew that it would take him a little while to get over it. At that moment she felt a quick, sharp pain in her stomach and started. He turned quickly to her. She laid a hand on it.

"Dear," he cried, and placed an arm about her.

"Just a little pain. I think women begin to have them when a child is on the way. I'll go see a Doctor."

"I will take you—" he said, then hesitated when it occurred to him that she had best go alone. There would be nobody to do any thinking if she did. After they were married,—he would take her to a colored doctor in Harlem, but—it was best for her to go to see one now, downtown and alone.

"I'll find out if it is my pregnancy that's causing it. I'll go this afternoon. Now I'd better let you go. Shall I—get up and—fix you some breakfast?"

"No, honey. I'll get up and go meet Schultz and get a bite downtown while there. Now be sure to go downtown and see a Doctor and find out about those pains."

"I'm sure they are due to pregnancy," she said; "but I'll find out if they are."

"Please do. Go to a good Doctor, have him examine you thoroughly."

"I'll do so and tell you all about it when you come to dinner tonight."

He kissed her then and she lay back to rest, feeling strangely tired.

Bertha and Marie had a great deal to talk about, at her apartment, where they had come to from the office.

"Well," said Bertha. "My party is all set. I had my brother call Mr. Early and tell him that it was all right this morning, then they arranged the date."

"When?" from Marie.

"Next Thursday at 5 P. M. Is the date okeh with you?"

"Sure. I'll tell Mr. Wyeth about it in the morning."

"I do hope he can arrange to come," said Bertha, a bit anxiously.

"He will."

"Sure?"

"I'll make it sure," said Marie, and Bertha seemed satisfied.

"We're not inviting anybody but Mr. Wyeth and you, Mr. Early and Mrs. Wingate, but if you and Mr. Wyeth want to—"

"—we won't want to, dear. We're both too anxious to meet Mrs. Wingate and—sorta study her. Another thing, and Mr. Wyeth told me to warn you."

"Warn me, Marie? Warn me about what?"

"That as quickly as the newspapers find out that the wealthy Mrs. Wingate is going to marry a Negro, they'll storm this apartment for a story."

"You think so?" she said, looking up at Marie anxiously.

"I'm sure they will. 'Wealthy white widow, marries a Negro', is news and this lady's husband was a millionaire textile manufacturer, and a Southerner. With his widow getting married to a Negro will be news, big news. So Mr. Wyeth says if you don't want this news to break and spoil your dinner party, to have Mr. Early and Mrs. Wingate keep very quiet about it. After they marry, it will have to break; but if nobody knows about it before it happens, it will not interfere with the party. Otherwise a lot of reporters will be ringing your bell and spoiling our party."

"I'll tell Heinrich about it as quickly as I can get hold of him. I'm sure he wouldn't want a lot of reporters coming here."

"They'll sure be here. As quickly as they hear about it."

"I'm glad you told me. I'll call Heinrich—no, he'll be home shortly, then I'll tell him."

"Then see that everything is kept strictly quiet," said Marie.

"Thank you, dear," said Bertha.

"Meantime, I'm going to get here between two and three next Thursday to help you get ready."

"Maybe I can hire somebody."

"Why do that when I can help do a better job, Bertha. So everything is set. I'll be seeing and hearing from you, no doubt, before next Thursday."

"Since you insist on helping, I'll call you and have you help me do the marketing. I'm a bit out of practice. Then again, you'll know what they might like to eat, better than I do."

"I know all about what they like, Mr. Wyeth especially. When he goes to a dinner, he goes to eat. Throws formality and ostentation out the window, eats his fill and enjoys it."

"Then do help with the shopping. It will please me so much to feel that Mr. Wyeth enjoys his dinner."

"After he eats, I'll see that he does some dancing, otherwise he'll sure fall off to sleep." Bertha laughed.

"He will. I know him. Whenever he eats well he goes right off to sleep."

Again both laughed.

"I hope he won't do that at my party," said Bertha.

"He can't help it, unless he does something to keep himself occupied. He won't want to at your party. He will be too anxious to talk with Mrs. Wingate and we both want to be present when he does so. We must not miss that," said Marie.

"Yes?"

"By all means. He'll ask her a thousand questions and bring out all we'd like to find out about her."

"You think he will—do that?" said Bertha, anxiously.

"I know he will. He's just itching to do so." Bertha laughed. "Ordinarily I would object to it. But at this party I'll want him to," said Marie.

"But you said he will go to sleep."

"Not the way I have it planned. You see, immediately we have dined, I intend to have him dance with Mrs. Wingate.'

"I see."

"That will interest him, not that he will care so much about it, but it will interest him and put him in a talking mood. Now as I plan it, I want him to dance with her first, then you, then me, then back to her, by the end of which time he will be wide awake and ready to start talking to Mrs. Wingate."

"Heinrich says that she is anxious to meet Mr. Wyeth."

"Yes?" from Marie.

"Very anxious to. I think, among other things, she wants to feel him out regarding Mr. Early's story, the one he wants Mr. Wyeth to direct."

"Then that's enough. If she is anxious to meet and talk with him, and I tell him that she is, we can leave everything then to him. In two hours we'll know more about Mrs. Wingate than we could learn if we saw her every day for a year."

"I could listen to him talk, it seems, forever," said Bertha enthusiastically.

"It will be Mrs. Wingate who is going to do the talking—answering his questions. He won't do much. She will do it all."

"Oh, won't that be fine. I met her the first night we arrived and as I recall, she was rather curious about me, and has been every time I've met her since," said Bertha. "Now she is anxious to meet and talk with Mr. Wyeth."

"And he is anxious to meet and talk with and study a wealthy white woman about to marry a Negro. Before we leave this place that night, he will have brought out everything of real importance in her life. Now watch and see if he doesn't," and again they both smiled, and Marie took her leave.

CHAPTER XXXII

AS THE TIME APPROACHED for their wedding and dinner at the Schultz's, Mrs. Wingate kept thinking about Sidney Wyeth, so much so that meeting and talking with him had become almost an obsession. She was seriously concerned about Kermit's story for the hate picture. He had been so wrapped up in getting it made and for so long, that she had become sold on the idea almost as completely as he and she visioned that if they could persuade Wyeth to just drop his book efforts and put in a month or two directing and assembling it, she could then go away and have her baby without the public knowing that she had become pregnant so long before her marriage.

She didn't say anything about what was on her mind to Kermit, but she was conscious of his agitation and disappointment. Getting the picture made was his chief concern, the thing he had sold all his associates on and who were looking forward to it to start a disturbance on the part of the Negro, and while he did not openly complain to Mrs. Wingate about Wyeth's refusal to direct it, she knew and could feel how anxious he was about it.

During all the years since she and Kermit had become intimate, and because of his inclination to quiet, keeping to himself and taking only a few people into his confidence; and also because their love was something between just themselves, she had taken the initiative in almost everything to the point now that it was a part of her. For that reason she wanted to meet and talk with Sidney Wyeth herself about it. She was tempted to call on him at his office alone, but since it was now arranged to meet him at the party and their wedding, she restrained this impulse, deciding that after the dinner, however, she would do so to exert such influence as she might bring to bear on him. As she visualized it, if he could be persuaded to do it, she could stay in New York or go to Hollywood and be around while it was being made. Then, as stated, go far away to South America as they had decided.

The next thing that entered her mind and persisted in occupying a great deal of her thoughts, was her future as the wife of a colored man. Looking forward to becoming a mother had inspired her to develop some associations. She and Kermit had been entirely alone, hadn't developed a single friendship in all the years they had been together. She had many associates in Atlanta, but owing to her husband's peculiar deficiency, she had never grown very enthusiastic about the friendship down there, seeming to keep thinking about him and conscious of a fear that many of his friends might be the same way. Her chief happiness, therefore, had been Kermit.

Now that her husband was dead, thereby removing the task of having to tell him the truth as she was about to when it happened, and she was at last free, she was happy to know that she was soon to be married, to a man she loved, and was now looking forward to the life she was to live afterward. She knew that if she made new friends and developed any sort of association, it would be up to her. Kermit, as we know, by disposition was quiet and not given to doing so, was growing more fond of keeping to himself and not making friends as she could readily see.

If she was to live the life of a white woman married to a colored man, she realized that most of these new friends would be colored people. She would, in order to make friends and have friends when her child arrived, have to find and select these friends, so having to do it, she was anxious to get started, and the first start would be the night of their marriage at the Schultz'. She didn't want to see many present that night—just those few who would be there, would be enough. She wanted to feel her way, and from what she had heard about Sidney Wyeth, that would be the best person, of all others, whom she would best want to meet.

They procured their license at the City Hall, the afternoon of the wedding and were stared at by the clerk and by others who heard them apply, which curiosity they ignored and left the office as quickly as it had been secured and breathed a sigh of relief when it was over. It had kept them both on the anxious seat.

After they left the clerk's office, those employed gathered around and studied the application. One, a girl, was the first to speak.

"Florence Wingate, born in Wakefield, Jasper County, Georgia. Last residence, Atlanta, Georgia." Raising her eyes a bit excitedly, "I'll bet that's the Mrs. Wingate whose husband was killed crossing the railroad tracks in South Carolina not long ago."

"Oh, no," said another. "I read about that. He was a very rich man. Several times a millionaire. That couldn't have been his widow, going to marry a—Negro."

"It wouldn't seem so, but that's the same name. He lived in Atlanta, and I'd bet that she's his widow."

"She was pretty and refined; you could see that."

"And was wearing the finest diamond on her engagement finger I ever saw."

"That's the widow of the Wingate who was killed, I tell you," insisted the girl who had suggested it in the beginning.

"Well," said the clerk, who had issued the certificate. "There's one way we can find out—and quick."

"How's that?"

"By telling the reporters when they come around this afternoon about it; describing the couple."

"That'll be news. 'Rich white widow to marry a Negro'."

All laughed and returned to their work. When the reporters called just before the office closed, they told them about it. The reporters evidently considered it news, the way they dashed away to their offices where most of them aired their suspicions to the editor and were sent out to find out more about it, and get their pictures for publication. They didn't succeed in locating the couple at once, thanks to Kermit Early's tendency to stay in the background. We turn now to the party, with Kermit and Mrs. Wingate arriving at the Schultz apartment, dressed appropriately for the occasion. Mrs. Wingate was wearing a rich, light blue afternoon dress with a corsage of white orchids, while Kermit wore a dinner jacket, also made up especially for the occasion. They were admitted by Heinrich who also wore a dinner jacket.

A moment later, they were being introduced to Wyeth and Marie, and as they already knew Bertha, who came from the kitchen to greet and make them welcome, they were seated and Marie and Bertha returned to the kitchen to continue preparing the dinner they would serve before the ceremony which had been arranged for ten P. M.

after the meal and perhaps after they had danced and become better acquainted.

Wyeth was also dressed for the occasion at the insistence of Marie, who prevailed on him to go dressed correctly, otherwise he might have gone in a plain business suit.

"And you are Mr. Sidney Wyeth," said Mrs. Wingate after she was seated comfortably, by her own choosing, near him, and she looked him up and down curiously. He did the same thing as regards her.

"That's what they've been calling me for quite a long time," he said, smiling agreeably. "And you are Mrs. Florence Wingate from Georgia," he said, coming directly to the point without delay. Bertha and Marie in the kitchen heard them and immediately became alert and listened.

"From dear old Georgia," she said, smiling back at him. "I understand that you've traveled America up and down. Ever been in Georgia?"

"And how," he cried and laughed. Kermit and Heinrich looked up, smiled and listened. Mrs. Wingate and Wyeth had the floor it was easy to see, so all others made themselves content and decided just to listen.

"I've been all over Georgia—just about every town in the state, I think," he continued. "You're from Atlanta?"

"Yes," she smiled, "Atlanta."

"Atlanta's a fine town. I have lots of friends there and like it. Were you born in Atlanta?"

"No," she said. "I was born in Wakefield, Georgia. A small town near—"

"—Lagrange," he said, as if to assist her. She started, perked up.

"Yes. Have you been to Lagrange, too?"

"To Lagrange and Wakefield, also," he said, smiling. Then proceeded to describe Wakefield in some detail.

"Well, I declare! You've been there. It's just a small place. I wouldn't have thought you had."

"They have a colored theatre there, open three or four nights a week, which of course, you wouldn't know much about."

"I know where it is," she said, after looking at Kermit and Heinrich and smiling, then back to him. "Yes, I've seen it."

"That's what took me there."

"For what?"

"Oh, to book my pictures. They're always glad to get them. Played every one I've made."

"Is that so?"

"Yes, Mrs. Wingate. That, of course, as stated, is what took me to Wakefield."

"I understand that you—you're the only—colored man who has ever directed pictures. Is that true?"

"I guess so. I'm the only one who was that crazy," whereupon he laughed and was joined by the others present.

"I think that is wonderful," she said, appreciatively. "In fact, I consider it an achievement."

"Oh, I managed to make a living doing so for almost twenty years," and he smiled again.

"For nearly twenty years!" she exclaimed. "Now isn't that remarkable," and turned to the others. "Don't you think so?" They nodded and agreed it was but Wyeth didn't.

"Oh, there is nothing remarkable about it. I started out by writing a novel, then somebody sold me the idea of making a picture from it. I hired a stage director to help me do so. He didn't know anything about motion picture direction, but learned enough while we were making it to see what it was all about, after which I directed them myself, and that is all."

"All! What more?" she wanted to know. "What more? And in addition to being a motion picture director, you are also a writer." He smiled. She went on. "I've read your latest book."

"Oh," he exclaimed, modestly. "You did or just sketched through it?"

"Sketched it? By no means. I read it, word by word from the beginning to the end. Read it in Chicago shortly after it was published. I liked it."

"Really, or are you just saying that to make me feel good?"

"Oh, Mr. Wyeth, no. I don't like your saying that. I read your book and I liked it, enjoyed reading every word of it and have been reading part of it again, only recently."

"I thank you. Glad you liked it. If I don't like a book it's hard for me to read it."

"Well, I think everybody likes it that reads it. I'd like to see some of your pictures. Sorry I missed them in Wakefield and Atlanta."

"They weren't shown where you go."

"How is that?" She looked at him quickly.

"Well, in Atlanta you'd go to The Fox, Loew's Grand, The Paramount, Capitol and such theatres as those."

"Yes. I've been to all of them."

"My pictures were shown only in the Colored theatres, down on Auburn Avenue, Decatur Street, Ashby, West Mitchell and in the colored neighborhoods only. That is why you never had a chance to see them, even if you had wanted to at the time."

"I'm sorry. Are there any of them being shown in New York now? Up here in Harlem? If so, I'll go to see the first one that will be shown."

He shook his head. "They've all been played out. I haven't made any for over two years."

"You haven't. Why not?"

"Oh, for one reason and another," he said, with a bit of a sigh and a shrug of his shoulders.

"Just for what reason, do you mind saying?" she asked now, solicitiously.

"Oh, for lack of money to make them with for one thing."

"Lack of money? Can't you—get the money?" She was getting close to what she wanted to talk about now. She was watching him anxiously, weighing every move, every gesture, every word.

"Oh, I suppose so; but it wasn't so profitable when I laid off. To get back into it, I'd have to give up my present work, books, in which I am doing very well, so wouldn't like to give up to go out and get money from somebody to make them with."

"Maybe it wouldn't be so hard," she ventured, suggestively and glanced at Kermit and Heinrich. They were interested, were becoming anxious. He saw it and understood why. He didn't want to get into an argument or bring up the hate picture at this time. So tried to change the subject.

"Oh, you know when you give up something and get started doing something else and have some success, it's rather hard to go back to something you've quit."

"I understand making pictures is—fascinating. I'd think you'd want to keep at it," she said suggestively.

"I liked it. Didn't think I would ever quit during all the years I made them." He paused and sighed, perceptibly:

"You should not have to quit, Mr. Wyeth. Why, you're the only man of your race to ever direct and produce pictures. I think it is a grave and serious mistake for you to quit. I think that deprives—even your race of an achievement. Of course you are a man of decision. You perhaps know better than anybody else what you want to do."

"I'm afraid I must agree with you. I may, of course, return to making pictures, but not until after I have put what I am doing on a solid and satisfactory basis."

"And how long do you think that will take?" she asked, eyes still on him. He smiled and again shrugged his shoulders.

"Who knows. It might never."

"Oh, Mr. Wyeth, not that, I'm sure. If it is for lack of money, I am sure that can be solved." She paused briefly to look around at Kermit and Heinrich, both interested, she could see by their anxious expressions. Their eyes told her to go on. She turned to Wyeth, with an idea that had just at that moment popped into her head.

As we know, she knew all about Kermit and Heinrich's offer to finance the cost of producing other pictures, with the understanding that he would direct and produce their hate picture first. It hadn't worked. Now she had a new idea and decided to execute it—at least advance the idea at once.

"I am interested in your—genius, Mr. Wyeth. I've been told so much about your, shall I call it, uncanny insight into human nature; the reaction of human emotions, until I would be willing to consider —assisting you, if it is agreeable."

He looked at her. What did she mean? She had caught him for the moment, off guard, unprepared.

'I mean, Mr. Wyeth, that a man of your ability in the production of pictures, shouldn't just quit as you say you've done. I can appreciate what you are doing and since writing and making pictures are related, it would seem that you could—could do both, no need to give up one for the other."

"Well, no. Making pictures would not mean that I would have to give up my literary efforts, but in the past, I don't think I—"

"Now, Mr. Wyeth, pardon me for cutting you off. But in the past, as I understand it, it rather strained you to—finance your pictures, did it not?"

"Strained me? It all but ruined me," and he laughed, ironically.

She nodded her head in understanding.

"Naturally, under such a strain, you couldn't think of anything else, much less do anything else. Now is that correct?"

"Absolutely."

"Then, Mr. Wyeth," she went on, surprisingly intelligent, he thought. "If you were relieved of the—financial worry and responsibility; if somebody, for instance, should take that over, leaving you free, absolutely free to concentrate all your energy, your genius and effort on just making the picture, directing and doing whatever was necessary to turning out a first-class product, wouldn't that interest you?" She paused and waited for him to reply.

He glanced at Kermit and Heinrich, who said nothing, but Mrs. Wingate understood what he was thinking about and raising a pretty hand, went on quickly.

"I mean, Mr. Wyeth, if somebody wanted to help you do something for which you are so capably fitted, and I am sure you would like to do, and that somebody would be willing to do this without attaching any kind of string or condition whatever, to having you do so, wouldn't you be willing to reconsider?"

"Well, I'm afraid I would seem stubborn if I didn't. That doesn't mean of course, that—"

"—you are consenting to do anything that is not agreeable to you. What I want to make clear, Mr. Wyeth, is that whatever might be advanced would not put you under any obligation to do anything not agreeable to you. All this is just a suggestion, possibly just an idea of mine. What I would like to do would be to call you up, say, very soon, at your office and make an appointment to—come and see you and air what is on my mind. Would you be agreeable to—seeing me, and hearing what I have to say?"

"Why, of course I would. In fact, I would be glad to welcome you and listen to anything you have to say."

"Thank you, Mr. Wyeth," she said, smiling so sweetly at him that he was flattered. "Then you may look for me to call at your office very soon, and again let me thank you." He bowed in reply to her smile and wondered what new angle she had in mind to help Kermit out. Just then the phone rang and Bertha came from the kitchen to answer it. After a word, she looked at Mr. Wyeth and told him that it was for him. He got up and went to it. He was expecting to hear from a bookseller in Philadelphia and it was he who was on the other end. He had left a note on his door where he would be and where to call.

The Jew who spoke very broken English advised that he had come for the hundred copies of the book, and would he mind coming to the office and giving them to him. Wyeth consulted his watch, called Miss Schultz and asked her if he was gone for half an hour, would she mind. Marie came up and Wyeth explained to her what is was for. They agreed that he could go, but to be sure and come right back.

He went into the reception room and explained that he had to go, but would return very shortly, and a few minutes later was in his car on his way to the office. Bertha and Marie returned to the kitchen, and to talk. With Wyeth gone, both Heinrich and Kermit turned anxiously to Mrs. Wingate. She proceeded to explain.

"It occured to me all of a sudden," said she, "that I could offer to finance Wyeth's own pictures, let him make them first, then, while he was doing so, to work on and perhaps persuade him to do ours after he finished his own."

The men looked at each other, then turned back to her, a big smile on their faces.

"What an idea," exclaimed Heinrich enthusiastically, turning from Mrs. Wingate to Kermit, who was beaming.

"It seems the Madam has outsmarted us," cried Kermit, turning to Florence. "Why didn't you suggest that angle to me long ago, darling?"

"It's a brilliant angle," cried Heinrich. "By saying nothing about our picture, but advancing him the money to make his, we put him under a moral obligation to make ours. What an idea!" He turned back to Mrs. Wingate, who had suddenly become thoughtful.

"I'm not sure if he would go in for it if he thought it was this other money he was using," she said, her face serious. Then looked in the direction of the kitchen, she motioned them to keep quiet.

"I don't want his stenographer to overhear us. Let's move—" She looked around the room. "Over there by the window." They rose now and crossed the room.

"I will think it over, and you both do some thinking, too; but my idea is to call on him alone, as I suggested. Since I could finance his pictures if he will let me, then I think it would be better for me to advance the money, don't you think?" She turned to Kermit.

"If you think it best and care to, dear," he said.

"I think he would accept it and be more likely to let me than he would if he thought it was this other money. I have a feeling that if we work it this way, he can be persuaded to ultimately do it."

"I agree with Mrs. Wingate, Early," said Heinrich, both turning now to Kermit, whose face was highly animated with the hope that Wyeth might be persuaded.

"From the little conversation I've had with him thus far, I'm sure he won't make it the way you've been trying to get him to. But once back into the swing, with no worry about money and able to concentrate as he has perhaps never had a chance to before, I think it will soften him and then, with a little persuasion, we will get him to make ours."

"Again I agree with Mrs. Wingate, Kermit," said Heinrich.

"Then, Heinrich," said Kermit. "It looks like we'd better turn it over to the Mrs. and let her do whatever she can with Wyeth."

"He's a man, I venture to say, of deep convictions," said Mrs. Wingate; "a man who wouldn't go back on an obligation." She looked at Kermit, and Kermit understoood when she continued:

"It will be necessary for me to see Mr. Wyeth, and to get together with him at the earliest possible moment, so I plan to see him tomorrow, no later than the day after. When he returns, therefore, I will suggest that I see him tomorrow afternoon, and arrange an appointment accordingly."

The men agreed with her. They returned to their former seats now to wait for Wyeth to return.

Meantime, while this was going on, the reporters from all the big dailies, had been and were still very busy. Long distance calls had been made to Atlanta, and all had ascertained that the Mrs. Florence Wingate who had called at the license bureau with one Kermit Early, colored, was the one and the same Mrs. Florence Wingate of Peachtree Road, Atlanta, and were now all combing Harlem to try to find out more about it; to locate the couple, photograph them and have their stories and photographs ready for the morning and early afternoon editions of their papers.

Word had got around to the reporters of the Associated Press, International News and the United Press, and they had men on the job to seek and find the couple that were due to be married,

CHAPTER XXXIII

WHEN WYETH RETURNED from the office, Heinrich put a dance record on the combination Radio and Phonograph, a fox trot, which was very entertaining; made all present feel like dancing. Mrs. Wingate looked at him and smiled.

"Do you dance, Mr. Wyeth?" she said. He smiled a bit awkwardly.

"I used to—when I was young," he replied and laughed.

"Young," she cried, and stood up. "Why, you're not old." She made a step toward him and he stood up. "Would you mind dancing with—me?" she said and held up her arms. He was embarrassed and flushed, but he realized that he couldn't refuse a lady, so put his arms about her and did the best he could. It wasn't bad, and looking up into his face with a pleasant smile, she chided him.

"Why, you're a good dancer," she said, and relaxed comfortably into his arms. He was embarrassed and wondered if the two men saw how flushed his face was. He was doing his best. It was the first time, he could recall, ever dancing with a white woman. She was a splendid dancer, light on her feet and before he was aware of it, was enjoying it. Again she raised her eyes and looked at him. And again he flushed. He had plenty of imagination, which was now on fire. Her body was soft and seemed to fit into his arms as if she had been made for them. Terribly excited, he exerted himself to avoid missing a step and embarrassing both.

"You have a good sense of humor, Mr. Wyeth," she said, smiling up at him. Afraid he would blunder or make a mistake, he managed to inquire.

"A sense of humor, Mrs. Wingate?"

"Yes, Mr. Wyeth. A splendid sense of humor."

"I don't understand you."

"Why, Mr. Wyeth," she said, somewhat surprised. "I mean that you are a wonderful dancer. I'll bet you've won prizes."

"I haven't danced," he laughed, "for years. I was afraid I'd forgotten how."

"Indeed!" she exclaimed, "but you haven't. As well as you do, you'll never forget. You say you haven't danced much in recent years?"

"Hardly at all."

"I'm surprised."

"Why so, Mrs. Wingate?"

"Because it is so—pleasant to dance with you, I'd think you danced a great deal." He smiled at this.

"I was fond of it many years ago. When I was much younger."

"To hear you talk one would think you were really old."

"I'm not so young any more."

"And you are—not married, Mr. Wyeth?"

"Not so fortunate, Mrs. Wingate."

"Why not?"

"Oh, I don't know. Because nobody will have me, I guess."

"That sense of humor again. I said you had a good one," she said chidingly. The music stopped and they relaxed. She took his arm and led him toward the window.

"Why don't you marry Bertha? She's a nice girl, intelligent, and so very pretty."

"Oh, Mrs. Wingate," he cried, abashed. "Miss Schultz couldn't be expected to like anybody like me."

"And why not? I think she would. Have you tried making love to her?"

"Out of the question," he said, flushing in spite of himself. "I haven't tried making love to any woman." He experienced a feeling of guilt, as he recalled Edrina.

"But a man like you should be married, Mr. Wyeth. I bet you'll make some nice girl a fine husband." He looked at her, and was surprised to find himself able to talk so freely with her. She was interesting; she was entertaining. She was talking again.

"You must pay attention to Miss Schultz. She's the kind of girl for you. You need a fine, highly intelligent and dignified girl for a wife. She's that kind of a girl, don't you think?"

"I do, and I am rather fond of Miss Schultz. But I wouldn't make the mistake of trying to—make love to her."

"I'll bet she wouldn't discourage you. Just try and see how she reacts." Again he looked at her. She met his eyes and smiled back, He was growing to like Mrs. Wingate, but he wondered at her amiability. He did not know and he could not understand what Mrs. Wingate had planned. She wanted to know colored people, interesting and worthwhile ones. She was finding him all they had declared him to be. She decided to list him among those friends of the future that she planned to make.

Meanwhile, Heinrich had turned the record over and was playing the number on the other side. Wyeth looked across the room and saw Early standing alone. He turned to Mrs. Wingate:

"I'm sure you wish to dance with the lucky man now," he said. Taking her hand then, he led her across to Kermit who insisted that he continue to dance with her, but he would not hear of it. So with his arms about her, they danced away, with Mrs. Wingate smiling back at him and making him feel more abashed. He wanted a drink and crossed the parlor then into the dining room where he found Bertha and Marie setting the table. With the music shutting out their being overheard by Kermit and Mrs. Wingate, they now turned to tease him.

"Did you see him, Bertha," cried Marie, pointing at him.

Bertha looked at him teasingly.

"Oh, how. Dancing with the gorgeous and beautiful bride-to-be."

"And was he dancing, dearie!" cried Marie and laughed.

"I'm jealous," said Bertha, pouting a little.

"Jealous?" said Wyeth, wonderingly.

"Shouldn't I be? You haven't danced with me. You haven't even said anything about dancing with me."

"But I—I would be glad to, Miss Schultz," he said, quickly.

"Then take her and proceed at once," said Marie, coming forward and taking Bertha by the arm and leading her up to him. Wyeth was flushing all over with embarrassment. "The music is going, go on into the parlor, boss, and do your *stuff*."

All but pushing them together, she ushered them into the parlor with: "I'll finish setting the table, dear, now go on."

A moment later Wyeth found himself going around and around with Bertha in his arms, his face burning with the blood that had rushed to it. He looked down at Bertha, who was as soft to hold and as good a dancer as Mrs. Wingate. She looked up to meet his eyes, blushed, lowered hers, but tightened her hold on him which pleased him, and, as he had with Mrs. Wingate, tried to do his best. During the short time the dance continued, he caught Mrs. Wingate looking at them and smiling meaningly, which he didn't know how to take. Bertha seemed pleased and to be enjoying the dance, which ran out a minute or two after they started, and Bertha, with a pleasant bow of thanks, excused herself to rush away to the kitchen, where she began to get the meal ready to serve.

A half hour later, all were seated, with Kermit and Mrs. Wingate beside each other, and Wyeth at the head of the table, where he could look at and converse with Mrs. Wingate without any effort.

"So you've been all over my home state, Mr. Wyeth," she said, as they were being served.

"I like to be in Georgia at least twice a year."

"Why only twice, Mr. Wyeth?"

"Twice in particular. In the summer when the peaches are in full bloom around Columbus and Fort Valley, then again in the fall during pecan picking time. I have enjoyed going from Atlanta, via motor, to Jacksonville, Florida, which takes you right down through the heart of the pecan and cotton territory."

"Doesn't it thrill you?" said Mrs. Wingate.

"Nothing like it."

"Wakefield is in the heart of the same kind of territory. In fact, we have fine soil around Wakefield."

"Deep, red and rich," said he.

"Red and rich is the way to describe it," she said, and sighed a moment. "Dear old Georgia, in spite of all the mean things they often say up north about it, is a great old state and I love it, but Kermit doesn't," ventured Mrs. Wingate, looking at him, with an affected frown, whereupon Kermit paused to look at her kindly.

"It's a great state, all right—to stay away from," said Kermit. Other than Wyeth and Mrs. Wingate, the others didn't understand just what he meant, although Bertha and Heinrich, looked up and tried to be agreeable.

"Did you ever hunt any in Georgia, Mr. Wyeth?"

"I sure did. One fall, down around Albany."

"At Albany? You've been there, too," exclaimed Mrs. Wingate

enthusiastically.

"Hunted squirrel and quail, shot a few rabbits, too, down there."

"Wonderful! It is a great place for game shooting."

"Plenty to shoot."

"I'll say. Ever been to Augusta?"

"On the Chattahoochee? Lots of times. They have two theatres there and they played my pictures and I've been going to Augusta ever since I started to make pictures."

"If you keep talking about pictures, you'll have to let me see you make the next one."

"It's interesting work, but not so interesting to look at."

"Why not?"

"Oh, most of the time is taken up getting ready to shoot. Then you shoot a minute or two, then go back and lose another half hour fixing, rehearsing and then you shoot again, maybe, for two minutes. So to look on soon bores you."

"Nevertheless, I'd like to see you make one. And speaking of pictures, while it's on my mind, will it be all right for me to call at your office about say, three, tomorrow afternoon?"

"Why, yes, Mrs. Wingate. I'll make it a point to be there." Bertha and Marie exchanged a meaning glance, then turned their eyes to the others, who went on.

"You say that you—like Atlanta?"

"Oh, fine. I've always liked it. I've spent lots of time in Atlanta. In fact, I lived there for six months several years ago—right after the Leo M. Frank trial."

"You did!" she exclaimed, pausing and looking quickly at him. Kermit looked at him, too. The others wondered what it was all about.

"The trial had just closed when I arrived there to spend six months early that year. The trial was on everybody's tongue."

"And how," she cried. She looked at Kermit. "He was down there at that time, too."

"Oh, you knew Mr. Early then?"

"Sure. We've known each other since we were kids. Were you in Wakefield around that time?"

"I went through there about that time, which was while I was not much more than a kid myself."

"Kermit's father ran a barber shop on the main street of the town. He still lives there, but doesn't do any work in the shop any more."

"And your people, what did they do there?"

"Until he was retired two years ago, my father was cashier of the First National Bank."

"Oh, a banker, eh? Then you come of rich folks?"

"No, Mr. Wyeth," said Mrs. Wingate. "Not rich. My great-grand parents were, a long, long time ago. They owned more than a hundred slaves, and thousands of acres of land, before the Civil War, but the war broke them and while my people have always stood well in Georgia, they were not rich."

"Mr. Wingate was, however," said Wyeth. She shrugged her shoulders.

"I've seen his name on mills all down through the South—the Wingate Mills is how the signs read over the top of them," he said, then looked at Kermit, who was living up to his reputation, saying little. Mrs. Wingate looked at him, and smiled. She turned to Wyeth.

"Will you be going to Georgia again soon?"

"I'd like to go there this fall, during the open season, to shoot partridges," said Wyeth.

"Why don't you," said Mrs. Wingate. "It would be a splendid diversion. I'm sure you'd enjoy it."

Wyeth laughed. She looked surprised, frowned a bit.

"Why do you laugh Mr. Wyeth?" she inquired, looking straight at him. He paused, respectfully.

"I must apologize," he said now, a bit meekly.

"Why an apology?"

"For not explaining that I couldn't give up what I am trying to do long enough to run down to Atlantic City over a week end, much less take the time to go all the way to Georgia to shoot quail. That's for people with more money and more leisure time than I can afford. That is why I should have explained before breaking into laughter, which you could hardly, under the circumstances, have understood. I'm sorry."

"I believe you're being overmodest, Mr. Wyeth," said Mrs. Wingate. "I believe that you have adopted modesty as a mode of conduct to the extent that it has, perhaps, become an obsession. With a little planning I'm sure you could find the time to run down to Georgia, shoot quail and rabbits and go opossum hunting at night—just have a grand time. With all the good food you could get to eat. I'm sure you wouldn't regret such a trip—even if you had to make just a wee bit of a sacrifice to do so," she said, insistently.

"You'll make me very unhappy if you keep on talking about it. It would be a throw back to my youth. I use to hunt every fall when I was a boy—until I left home."

"And where is your home, Mr. Wyeth? Where were you born, and where did this—genius begin to sprout?"

"Please, Mrs. Wingate. You'll make me think I'm somebody, if you keep on."

"Well!" she exclaimed, elevating her eyebrows. Looked around at the others, who agreed with her by the expression on their faces.

"But I was born in Illinois, down in the lower end of Illinois, near the town of Cairo, if you ever heard of it," he said.

"I certainly have. In fact, who hasn't heard of Cairo? Down in Egypt, they call it," and she laughed. All of those present exchanged expressions, turned to look at Wyeth and Mrs. Wingate who were easily the center of interest.

"And that is where you attended school?"

"Yes, Mrs. Wingate."

"There's a state school about fifty miles north of Cairo. Is that where you got your college training?" Marie laughed. Those present turned to look at her.

"Please pardon me," she said, lowering her eyes.

"What for?" from Heinrich. Marie looked up at Wyeth, who smiled, turned to the others.

"She was compelled to laugh when Mrs. Wingate inquired about my college training." Turned to Mrs. Wingate. "I didn't get any college training, Mrs. Wingate. I know where the school is that you refer to. That's the Southern Illinois State Normal, and the town is Carbondale. I've been there often, but not to attend the school."

"Do you mean to tell us, Mr. Wyeth, that you—never went to college; that you didn't actually graduate from any college?"

"He never *went* to any college, Mrs. Wingate—not even to high school. He did reach the eighth grade in a country school down where he came from," said Marie, speaking for him. She turned to look at him, as all the others were doing.

"Would you believe it!" exclaimed Mrs. Wingate, looking at him now out of different eyes.

"I can understand your surprise, Mrs. Wingate, and you'll all please excuse me for speaking for Mr. Wyeth. I think he'd want me to," Marie said. She turned to look at Kermit Early now, who was also looking at Wyeth in surprise and so was Heinrich.

"I suppose it's time for me to quit talking," said Wyeth and shrugged his shoulders, resignedly.

"Why so?" said Mrs. Wingate.

"With all of you so highly educated, I must look like a—dunce, perhaps."

"With less school training, perhaps, as you admit, than any of us, I venture that every one present will vote that you—are the most thoroughly educated."

"I vote in the affirmative," said Bertha, promptly speaking for the first time.

"And I vote the same way," said Kermit. All followed in the same order.

"Which gets none of us anywhere. I vote that we talk about something else. Mrs. Wingate was saying something about my going to Georgia to shoot quail."

"And you were insisting that you couldn't take the time off to go, so I want to say that it's too bad and I'm sorry. You're entitled to a vacation and it might be to your advantage, I was saying, to take one in spite of the urge of your business."

"And when I got back, I'd perhaps not have any business to attend to," he said and laughed ironically.

"You're so interesting to talk to, Mr. Wyeth," said Mrs. Wingate now, looking at him kindly, sincerely.

"Are you trying to flatter me, Mrs. Wingate?" he said, smiling across at her.

"Why no, Mr. Wyeth. Why do you say that?"

"Because of what you just said. I am, perhaps, more of a—curiosity." She shook her head now, and pouted just a little.

"That was an—unkind remark and I—won't like you unless you apologize this time, sure enough."

"Then I apologize," he said, readily.

"I forgive you on condition that you agree to believe me from now on, even if I do seem to flatter you."

He laughed, turned to the others. "Mrs. Wingate and I seem to have the floor, talking about exactly nothing. We are wonderfully well represented here tonight, with so few of us. We certainly ought to find something to talk about that would interest us all." He turned his eyes to Bertha and Heinrich now.

"We have Mr. Schultz, and his delightful sister, Bertha, from Berlin—all the way from Berlin, Germany. I could talk a great deal about Berlin—rather, I could ask a lot of questions about Berlin."

"You can talk about Berlin: ask Miss Schultz those many questions which you claim you'd like to ask, some other time" interposed Mrs. Wingate, "Right now I want to talk about you." She paused to look at the others, a question in her eyes which all present seemed, by their expressions, to answer in chorus.

"Go ahead, Mrs. Wingate," said Heinrich. "I'm certainly enjoying listening to you and Mrs. Wyeth. I can keep on listening."

"By all means," joined Bertha. "Please do go on."

"Now, Mr. Wyeth," cried Mrs. Wingate, triumphantly. "It's been moved and seconded that we continue, you and I, to talk. So, will you—proceed?"

"All right. But where, and about what?"

"Your book."

"My book?"

"Your book."

"Which one?"

"Which one?" she asked.

"Yes," he replied. "Which one? I've written a new one."

"Oh, a new one," echoed Mrs. Wingate, surprised. "I didn't know about that one. I'm talking about the one we've all read."

"Oh, that one. You see, when I finish a book, I soon forget about that one. All my thoughts are about the one I'm either going to write or am writing. Meanwhile, what is it about the one you've read that you want to talk about?"

"The girl in it, Mr. Wyeth."

"The girl?" He paused and his eyebrows contracted. Turned to her. "Which girl? There were two girls and I think I said a great deal about both."

"I agree with you. In fact, I want to ask you about both. But I'd like to talk about the one you had your hero to—quit; walk out on. Because—"

"—what?"

"Be—because he thought she was a —white girl."

"Oh," he exclaimed, and smiled.

"You weren't altogether kind—to her." She said this a bit softly, seemed momentarily embarrassed, looked around at the others. All who had read the book were thinking. They glanced unconsciously at Kermit. They were putting two and two together. They understood that Mrs. Wingate was associating herself with the story now; associating Kermit with it, too.

Kermit hadn't walked out on her because she was a white girl. Of course, she was thinking of herself, also. There was no parallel in the two cases. She hadn't let Kermit Early walk out on her.

"You'd—rather not talk about it, perhaps?" she said now, glancing across at Wyeth, hesitantly.

"Oh, I don't mind," said Wyeth, readily. Then turning to her in a changed expression. "Do you think you'd—like to—talk about it?" As he finished, he glanced unconsciously around at the others. They were all thinking about the same thing. Mrs. Wingate and Kermit Early. All wondered why she brought the subject up; wondered why she wanted to talk about it.

"Why did you have the hero leave her when she told him with so much feeling, so much pathos, that she loved him?"

"That was my inspiration."

"But you put it into words. He admitted that he loved her—more than any person in the world, and she cried so. I felt sorry for her. I even cried with her, when I read that part."

Everybody's eyes were on Mrs. Wingate now. The situation had grown strangely tense. Not only were they looking at Mrs. Wingate, about to marry a colored man, and associated her naturally with the white girl in the story whom Wyeth had his hero to quit.

"You can, of course, understand my reaction to the situation in your story, because—I'm about to marry a—colored man," and she looked at Kermit, who was embarrassed and didn't know how to feel.

"You've considered, of course, everything. . . ." said Wyeth.

"Everything, Mr. Wyeth."

"And are satisfied?"

"I'm satisfied. Now after what you showed in your story, what is your—opinion?"

"I don't wish to express any."

"But you do have an opinion?"

"Perhaps."

"After what you said in the story, I'd like to hear it."

"I think we should talk about something else," he said.

"I'll change the subject," she said and forced herself by an effort to seem cheerful.

"Thank you," said Wyeth, and seemed relieved.

"But I'm still going to talk about the story in your book," she said, somewhat defiantly.

"I'm glad that it interested you that much," said Wyeth, agreeably.

"You painted a beautiful picture of the other girl. I mean, the colored girl."

"You think so?"

"You most assuredly did. Seems like it was actually taking place."

"Thank you."

"But behind it all, I could still see the picture of the other girl."

"I suppose so," said Wyeth.

"That was because he loved her, wasn't it?"

"Yes, he loved her." Mrs. Wingate seemed more satisfied now.

"Those other people: her father and her sister, who were so awfully mean. About the meanest people a writer could create. Were they—real people?"

"Real people, Mrs. Wingate," he admitted.

"I thought so," said she. "In fact they were all real people, weren't they?"

"Oh, Mrs. Wingate, please."

"And one of them—was you," she said and laughed now, somewhat brazenly, or was it desperately. She had wanted to marry Kermit for ten years. Why was it playing on her emotions so now, Wyeth wondered. She was talking again.

"And did they, Mr. Wyeth, do all the terrible things you had them doing?"

"Most of it."

"It doesn't seem possible, as I think about them, for two people to be so—mean, so heartless."

"There are lots of such people, maybe," he said.

"I agree with you," she said, and thought about how the white people, friends of hers and of the family for generations, were going to think—and act, when they heard about what she was about to do. Then she forced it out of her mind.

Bertha rose, followed by Marie, and served drinks. Mrs. Wingate took a strong drink. She was not a drinking woman, had never drunk anything very strong. She had never been drunk. Felt like getting drunk all of a sudden. Then decided it wouldn't look nice. But she did take a large drink and Kermit looked at her a bit anxiously.

Feeling better, she turned again to Wyeth. She wished it was possible for her to meet him again, to talk with him at great length.

"You built the last hundred pages of the book up to a tremendous climax. It fairly thundered with action—and drama!"

"Thank you," he said and smiled, modestly.

"Your ending was so beautiful. I read and reread it and cried again."

He smiled. He was interested. She went on.

"Of course that was purely fictional, the end, I mean. Wasn't it?"

"Why?" and he looked straight into her eyes.

"Because the girl didn't have any Negro blood in her as you showed, which made it possible in the end for him to marry her without—transgressing tradition. She was actually a white girl and when he left her to go to Chicago and become engaged to the colored girl, he went out of her life altogether. Wasn't that the way that part ended?"

"So inquisitive, Mrs. Wingate. So exacting," he said and forced a laugh.

"Because, Mr. Wyeth," she said rather boldly and defiant, glancing at the watch on her wrist. "Within an hour you're going to witness the transgression of a tradition. I'm not afraid. I defy it." Paused to look across at Kermit now, then turned back to Wyeth, with more defiance in her eyes and tone than ever. "I'm a white woman. I love a colored man and have been in love with him for ten years, ten years, understand? And I'm going to marry him. Yes, marry him right here tonight, and I don't care anything about what the white people are going to think about it!" She paused now and looked at the others, a bit helplessly.

"Maybe, after a while you will write a story about us—Kermit and me. A white woman who loved a colored man—and was proud of it!" She laughed now, a bit hysterically. "Proud of it!" Laughed again, then lifting her partly filled glass, emptied it.

The situation had grown more tense, more embarrassing. Nobody said anything, nobody dared say anything.

"I want to ask you, Mr. Wyeth. I'm asking you because you are, I'm sure, broad minded and liberal in your views. The question may seem rather—difficult to answer, but I want you to answer it." She paused now and looked him straight in his eyes, bravely, even though defiantly.

"What do you *honestly* think about the—*intermarriage of races?*"

The question *was* a difficult one, a bold one, an embarrassing one. Every one present knew that Wyeth didn't dare to answer it honestly, frankly. They were anxious to hear what his answer to her question would be, however, since she had asked it, and expected an answer. Wyeth answered more promptly than they expected.

"I consider it every man and woman's privilege to marry whom they choose. I have no other opinion as regards it."

"Thank you. Now I'm going to be more bold than I have already been tonight, then I'm going to hush. Quit talking. I've said too much already, and Kermit, here, is burning up, I know. But I've just got to get this off my chest."

"What is it that you want to ask, Mrs. Wingate?" said Wyeth, calmly, evenly. She turned and looked straight at him before going on.

"Would you—*marry a white girl* if you were in love with her?"

He started, looked around at the others, who were all looking at him.

"If I was in love with her and she with me,—"

"—what?" said Mrs. Wingate, pointedly.

"I would."

"But you'd be careful not to let yourself fall in love with one, to begin with, I'd bet," and Mrs. Wingate laughed, a strange mocking laugh. "That is all, folks," and she bowed to those present, who smiled and was glad it was over.

Just then the doorbell rang, and Bertha excused herself and hurried away to the door, returning a few seconds later to advise that the minister had arrived.

"And now the minister," said Wyeth, looking from Mrs. Wingate to Kermit. They exchanged expressions for a moment.

"To marry us. Oh. Kermit," she cried, and blushed.

Wyeth decided not to delay the ceremony by prolonging the conversation and in due time they had finished a fine dinner and retired to the parlor, where promptly at the appointed hour, Mrs. Wingate and Kermit stood before the minister and those present heard them pronounced husband and wife.

They exchanged a kiss, and blushing, Mrs. Wingate turned and those present proceeded to kiss her, including Wyeth, whom it thrilled. It all seemed a bit strange, odd and unusual, he reflected. This wealthy and aristocratic woman of the old South, being married to a Negro in an apartment in the Negro section of New York.

After the ceremony, Kermit led the minister, over to the door, paid him and he left.

When the Reverend Doctor left the building he saw some white men led by a Negro, as he crossed the street and was about to take the subway to his home.

"Pardon me, Reverend Doctor," said the Negro, stopping him. "But we are looking for a couple that are due to be married, tonight. Would you mind giving us information, if you have any?"

"Just what kind of information?" inquired the minister.

"Oh, no kind in particular. A Mr. Kermit Early and Mrs. Florence Wingate applied for and secured a license to be married at the City Hall late today, so we are reporters and would like to find them and get a story about it."

"Well," said the minister, "If that's what you're looking for you'll find them at Apartment 76-M in that building," pointing back to where he had just left. "I just married them a few moments ago."

"Oh, thank you," all cried, almost in a chorus, gratefully, and made a dive for the building, leaving the preacher standing looking after them and wondering if he had acted wisely.

Heinrich had put another dance record on the phonograph and they were dancing when the reporters arrived and rang the bell. Kermit had just danced with Mrs. Early and turned her over to Wyeth, who was enjoying a dance with her, Kermit with Bertha, Heinrich with Marie, a happy group, having a dandy little party, all enjoying themselves, when the group of reporters suddenly burst into the room the moment the door was opened.

"Pardon us, folks, but we're from the press. Just heard about the marriage. We wonder if you'd mind, giving us a story and posing for some pictures?" They turned to Wyeth, immediately identifying Mrs. Wingate because she was the only white person present. They had to guess which was the bridegroom, however.

"Do you mind?" said one, coming up to Wyeth, "posing with the lady for a photograph?"

"But I am not the lucky man," corrected Wyeth, turning to Kermit, upon whom he laid a hand. "Here is your man."

"Oh, pardon me," Immediately they posed the couple, who were taken so completely by surprise that they didn't have time to protest. Flash after flash followed, then single poses, profiles, straight on, sitting, standing, just about every pose they could think of. By the time this was over, they sat the couple down, and plied them with a number of questions, and before either could object, they had their entire history, from birth to the present time. As quickly as they had burst in on them, just as quickly did they leave, leaving everybody and especially the couple, confused and bewildered.

"What's it all about?" cried Mrs. Early. "What do they want with all they have asked; with all the pictures they took?"

"You'll see by tomorrow morning's papers," said Wyeth.

"You mean," cried Mrs. Early, "That—that they will—publish our pictures in—the papers?"

"Every paper from here to San Francisco, Mrs. Early, allow me to compliment you. From Canada to the Gulf of Mexico," said Wyeth.

"Oh, no!" she cried, brought to a sudden realization of what it was all about; that *every paper* would include the Atlanta papers; her picture, standing now beside Kermit Early, her husband, a Negro. Publish it all conspicuously for them to read in Atlanta, in Wakefield. When she got to Wakefield, in her mind, she closed her eyes as if to try to shut out the sight. This had to be. Kermit Early was now her husband, had been her sweetheart since she was little more than a girl but nobody knew anything about it until tonight. Now everybody would know about it before the sun went down the next day.

"Oh," she sort of choked. "I—I didn't understand what it was all about."

"Don't you like to see your picture in the papers? Most people would be glad to, Mrs. Early," ventured Marie. "You have to be an important person to get your picture in all the papers."

"But—but," she stammered, nervously. "We are not important, Kermit and I, are we Kermit?" He laid a comforting hand on her.

"They won't do this, will they? They won't dare do it. We didn't give them permission to do so, did we?"

"When they were allowed to enter the place and we permitted them to photograph us, that was our consent. They'll do whatever they want to with the pictures, dear," he told her calmly.

"You—you mean, Kermit," she said, excitedly, "That, that we can't do—anything about it?"

He shook his head, while she raised a jeweled hand to her face, looked around her bewilderingly. She didn't know what to do. Everybody's eyes were on her.

"Let's—let's go home, Kermit," she cried suddenly. Her face, all could see, was torn with worry, anxiety, for she was thinking of Wakefield; she was seeing a picture of her mother reading the papers, about what she had done; she was seeing a picture of all her mother's neighbors and friends after *they read it.* They could not look hard at her, snub or avoid her; but they *could her mother,* her poor, helpless mother. Strange, but she hadn't thought of that until this moment. She had been able to keep her association with Kermit Early secret and from her mother for so long, that it hadn't occurred to her that it would reach her mother this way. Her poor mother, down there in Wakefield, alone, to be pointed at and snubbed. This was too cruel for her to stand, for her to think of, even. She could stand all their snobbery, their contempt, for it was she and she only who had married a Negro.

But she was in New York, deep in the heart of Harlem, where she didn't have to see them, hear them—but what about her poor, helpless mother?

As they rode to their apartment a few minutes later, she was so distressed with the thought of it that she hid her eyes and cried. Kermit tried to comfort her by placing his arm about her, but he could not shut out the picture she was seeing, the words she was hearing them say to her poor mother. Never since it all started so many years ago had she been brought to realize so vividly what she had done. She had a picture of her mother when she read the papers next day, and the next day and all the other days as long as her mother had to stay in Wakefield. She could seem to hear, too, these far away, cries on the streets of Wakefield.

"Ole' Mrs. Adair's daughter married a nigger, married a nigger, married a nigger!" Yes, that was what they would be saying, the children, the old folks, the young folks. Nothing about it would they be able to appreciate, much less forgive. All they would think of and cry, pointing a finger at this helpless old soul, her mother, would be:

"Old Mrs. Adair's daughter, married a nigger, married a nigger, married a nigger."

She was hardly conscious when they reached their apartment and Kermit helped her upstairs, to undress and put her to bed. She was distressed beyond words. She just wanted to be alone for the time being, to think, think and to think.

She was still shut in when Kermit got up the next morning, dressed and went to a newsstand where he purchased all the morning editions of the papers and dared when he got a few steps away, to look in them. He didn't have to look far to see himself and his wife, both looking fine and convincing. But there they were, their pictures, with headlines about their marriage.

WEALTHY WIDOW OF SOUTHERN ARISTOCRAT MARRIES A NEGRO !

Every paper carried the account in screaming headlines, along with one or more of the pictures they had posed for; before either had a thought that they would see them again, reflected back into their faces from the papers. He was rather pleased at the way they were featured, but sighed as he thought of his wife, as he went back to her.

As he entered the door, he heard her voice from her bedroom.

"Kermit?"

"Yes, dear."

"Oh, I'm so glad you're back. What did you go out for?"

"The papers, dear."

"Oh, yes. Do they have anything about us?" By now he had reached the bedroom, so opened the door, crossed to where she was sitting up in bed and laid the papers before her. She hurried through each, and started, as she saw their pictures and headlines about the marriage in every one. She sighed, hopelessly. He sat down beside her. Paused a moment, then spoke:

"I'm so sorry, dear," he said consolingly. She looked up at him, then smiled, tired-like.

"I'm all right, sweetheart, and I don't mind all this publicity. What has me worried is my mother. Poor mama. She won't be able to stay in Wakefield. We'll have to do something about it."

"Yes, dear. What can we do? What shall we do?"

"I don't know, yet, sweetheart. I only know that when they read all this stuff in the Atlanta and Macon papers down there, she simply won't be able to stay there. She'll be so ostracized, that she will hardly dare go to the grocery to buy food. I know the people there."

"They could forgive almost anything but this."

"But this, Kermit," she said, and sighed.

"It's the price I'm costing you, Florence."

Quickly she looked up. She beckoned for him to come closer. When he did, she embraced him.

"Don't let it worry, you, darling. You are my husband now. Nothing can ever come between us but death, death. This matter about my mother I will adjust in due time. That will mean to get her out of Wakefield."

"Out of Georgia. She won't be able to stay near anybody that knows her, so why not send for her to come to New York? You can rent an apartment somewhere downtown where she won't have to face—what she will soon be facing in Wakefield." Florence was silent, while she did some thinking. Looking up at him, then.

"Since the baby will be coming along before it could possibly arrive ordinarily, and we are going to have to go away for a few months as planned, when I hear from mother, and she is agreeable, why not have her come here and stay in our apartment while we are away?" she said. He nodded in agreement.

"I'll call mother tonight, long distance, but if she hasn't read about it in the papers, I guess I'll have to tell her. I'd rather that she read about it in the papers first, and then I won't have to experience the shock that telling her will give."

"She'll have read all about it by nightfall. Both the Atlanta and Macon morning and evening papers circulate in Wakefield. So if you don't call until after nine tonight, she'll know all about it."

"Very well, then. I'll call her after nine tonight, and see what we can do."

CHAPTER XXXIV

THE FORMER MRS. WINGATE didn't get to Sidney Wyeth's office at three P. M. the next day after the wedding and party, because she was in too much trouble. It was fortunate for them, she and her husband, Kermit Early, that the apartment they had rented had an observer through which they could look and see who was outside, and those looking through the observer from the inside, couldn't be seen well enough to be recognized. For from nine A. M. of the morning after, until late the same night, a stream of reporters beat a path to their door. After a time they disconnected the bell, and a few minutes later, reconnected it, because, while the bell did not ring, they pounded on the door, which was more annoying than listening to the bell ringing. Neither dared venture out, due to the annoyance of curious people who insisted on bothering them until around noon, when Kermit called the Police Department about their predicament, and officers were sent to keep people from bothering them further.

In the meantime, the afternoon papers had featured their marriage with stories, and their pictures as conspicuously as had the morning papers, and every newspaper in the country published it and had a story about it, along with their photographs. So before the sun went down the day after their wedding, Mr. and Mrs. Kermit Early were the talk of the entire country.

But it was the Southern papers, that carried more than a story. Many of them devoted their entire editorial section to it. Under sensational captions, they published editorials that were read by all the subscribers and purchasers of their papers, as few editorials were ever read.

SOCIAL EQUALITY IS HERE! NEGRO'S MARRIAGE TO WEALTHY SOUTHERN WHITE WOMAN MOST SENSATIONAL EVENT IN YEARS !

So began an editorial in the Memphis Gazette:

For years the South has been warning America regarding social equality; that Negroes, if given an opportunity, would intrude themselves into white society. The South, for generations has preached the necessity of white supremacy. For generations the South has also tried to show that it was necessary to keep the Negro in his place. But the vain and selfish North, always delighted to laugh at and decry such ideas, and pander to the Negro vote, has always played down such insistence on the part of the South.

Well, in an apartment in the Negro Section of New York, known far and wide as Harlem, it happened last night. Social equality with all its threat to white society is here. Mrs. Florence Wingate, a wealthy aristocratic and refined white lady, product of one of the oldest and proudest families in all the Southland, took unto herself a Negro, one Kermit Early, for a husband.

Occasionally a white woman marries a Negro. But until last night, such marriages have not been taken seriously for several reasons. First, if the white woman who participated in it was wealthy, the marriage on her part has most often been inspired by sexual desire. Such marriages, mostly to a Negro butler, or a chauffeur, rarely lasted long because, after such women's passions have been satisfied over a period, they have found that living with somebody so far beneath them socially soon became boresome, tiresome and ultimately impossible, and they usually left such Negro husbands and went their way.

On the other hand, marriages between white women and colored men have been and are, the result of being thrown together via employment or other contact, and have represented at best, only white women of the middle class, but most of all such marriages have been between white women of the lower classes, many of the underworld, who have lost all social responsibility, have become prostitutes and would marry anything called a man. Such marriages, therefore, have not been taken seriously as they do not threaten society.

But the marriage of Mrs. Florence Wingate, widowed only a few weeks go by the death of her many times a millionaire, mill owning white husband, to Kermit Early, a highly educated Negro, a Doctor of Philosophy from Harvard University, entirely changes the social picture. While the marriage on the part of this wealthy, Southern white widow, was no doubt inspired in the main, as most all such marriages, regardless of class, by sexual desire, Kermit Early was not a butler, a chauffeur or a Negro pimp, whom Mrs. Wingate would tire of shortly, but an intensely thoughtful Negro. From the standpoint of intellect, Mrs. Wingate's equal, if not superior. A Negro, no doubt, who has been far-sighted enough to see and understand that he could and would profit immensely by such a marriage. While this has not been discussed or debated to any great length, it is the highly educated Negro who threatens our social existence—and the marriage of Kermit Early, Negro, to a scion of great wealth and the finest blood, of the South, is not to be dismissed and forgotten, and unless the North sits up and takes notice, and passes laws, perhaps, as every Southern state has on its statute books, prohibiting marriage between whites and Negroes, and joins with the South in every way it can, to keep the Negro in his place, they will soon rue the day they granted the Negro so much freedom.

The Macon, Georgia Chronicle, in its editorial column, which paper is widely circulated in Wakefield, went on to declare:

YANKEE NORTH, WHAT NOW?

It has happened as the South has so long predicted; and at last is here. Social Equality. A rich and beautiful white woman, a Southern white woman, mind you, has taken herself a Negro husband. Not an ordinary Negro, but a highly educated and no doubt, interesting Negro. A man that she can look up to, respect and admire, for only such could inspire a Southern white woman to so disgrace herself, and her family—and the South in general, knowing that, of all things she could do, this would be the most unforgivable.

It took a generation of political manoeuvering to get the Negro out of politics in the South where carpet-baggers from the North put him, as a tool to exploit the South, helpless and poor after the disastrous Civil War. But through persistent bravery and patience, the South finally recovered, has managed the race situation so well that lynching has declined until it has almost disappeared. The white people and the Negro who lives here get along fine together, due to the fact that the Negro knows and keeps in his place, and is no longer a threat to our society and white supremacy, if it were not for the North, which persists in meddling into our way of life. The travesty of a wealthy and aristocratic Southern white woman marrying a Negro, a highly educated Negro, previously from the South, could not have happened here, nor anywhere else in the South, because our laws, put on the statute books by far-seeing white statesmen, a long time ago, would not have permitted it. But the Yankee North, with its pampering and playing the Negro against their own interest for political gain and power, does, in a great measure, serve to defeat what the South has done. This couple could not have become man and wife anywhere south of the Mason-Dixon Line, but they could, and did, slip off into the free North, and there stand side by side before a Negro minister and hear themselves pronounced husband and wife—to the eternal disgrace of American Society!

The Birmingham Scimitar went on to say:

. . . the only thing missing at this wedding, was the wife of the President. She should have been on hand to give the bride away. We feel sure that she would have been glad to do so, and, perhaps, invite them to the White House for their wedding reception! This, people of the South, is what, due to the North, and their ideas about Negro Freedom is beginning to happen. Social Equality is the word for it. The South has said much over a long period of years, and warned persistently and repeatedly that this is what would happen if restraint was relaxed as regards the Negro.

The South has done everything they could think of to keep the Negro in his place, and as far as his actions in the South are concerned, the problem is settled and has been for a long time. But as long as the North persists in their so-called idea of freedom for everybody just that long will the highly educated and scheming Negroes like Kermit Early, try to do what happened in New York last night!

Every Negro who reads about this wedding, will be thrilled. Even in our Southland, where he will not publicly say anything about it, but before the sun goes down on another day, it will be debated among them quietly and secretly, and how many others, of this highly educated class, will plan, if he or she can, to repeat what Kermit Early did last night. If and when Kermit Early and this white woman have a child or children, who will benefit by this white woman's great wealth? They won't want to be like other Negroes. They will remember that their mother is a wealthy white woman; that their father is a Doctor of Philosophy from the greatest University in the Western World, and that they will be too good to marry one of their own race, so will seek to marry a white person. If they fail here, or to find such association agreeable, there will be plenty of poverty-stricken white people in Europe who will be glad to trade a royal name for an American fortune, even though the possessor of the wealth be a Negro. That is the only thing that you can call it: Social Equality. And the marriage that took place in New York last night will do more to foment unrest and inspire social climbing on the part of the Negro than anything that has happened since the Civil War!

The Atlanta morning and evening papers, known to be the most liberal in the South, published only the facts in the case, but did not run any editorials on it. But those and the Macon papers, one of which went the limit editorially, reached Wakefield and soon the sleepy little town was ablaze with gossip, much of which soon reached the ears of Mrs. Adair, Mrs. Early's mother—and as was to be expected, shocked and mortified her. She shut herself in and didn't go out the entire day. Neighbors and friends of old, kept adroitly out of sight, but curiosity seekers passed before the house and lingered for a while during the day. Children gathered and pointed to the house, and cried, cries which she could hear, although the shades were drawn.

"Old Mrs. Adair's daughter, married a nigger, married a nigger, married a nigger."

The poor soul wept and prayed. The only consolation or comfort she had during the day, was in phone calls from her other children from other towns where all were married and lived, and who were able to escape a large share of the ostracism now raging in Wakefield. They were all sorry for her, begged her to be brave; that it wasn't she who had committed such an act; and they couldn't understand why Florence did it. Was she crazy? She must have been . . . Any woman must be crazy, a white woman who would marry a Negro, regardless of how highly educated he was, or how good and kind he might be. He was a Negro and that was more than enough to keep Florence from bringing such a disgrace on them. They asked her to come and stay with them, get out of Wakefield where they knew she didn't dare to show her face on the street. Florence had done something that could never be forgiven; something so brash that the whole family would be forever disgraced. They told her to call a doctor, but she was afraid to do so! Along towards nightfall she had suffered so much that calling a doctor was really necessary.

She went to the phone, picked up the receiver. Then she put it down. Their family physician was an old man. He had brought all her children into the world. But he was a *white* man. She was afraid that even he might ostracize her. It was more than she could stand. She lay down on a cot, she felt just like giving up—dying. She fell into a troubled sleep, and did not wake up until the phone awakened her at nine that night. She opened her eyes and tried to listen. It rang again and she sat up. Must be one of the children calling again, so she went to it, called back, "hello," in a weak voice, very quietly. Florence, in New York, on the other end, recognized her and called back, softly, kindly, sympathetically.

"Mother?"

Mrs. Adair recoiled, caught her breath.

"Florence?"

"Yes, mother. This is Florence, in New York."

"Oh, Florence," she began, sinking on a chair. "How could you,

Florence, how could you?" Again she fell to crying. Florence heard her and realized that this was a moment to be brave and strong. She knew more than even the people of Wakefield, what her marriage had done. But this was her mother, old, mortified and helpless.

"Then you've heard about it?"

"It's in all the papers, all over town. People on the sidewalk pointing to your picture standing and sitting, then standing again beside this—nigger,"

"Mother!" Florence cried, sharply.

"Pointing to the house, saying terrible things, looking at the house as though they wanted to set fire to it, burn it up, burn me up in it. Maybe it would be just as well. Oh, Florence, my darling, my child, how could you do it, *how could you?"* and she fell to weeping again.

"Listen, mother, it is too long a story to go into and talk about over the telephone. I know just how you feel; I know how the town feels about me, about you even. You did not do it, but since I'm not there for them to point at me, they will at you. I was only waiting for you to read it in the papers, for it is in all the papers everywhere, so that I wouldn't have to tell you." Her mother crying was the only answer, still she knew that she heard her, and was listening, so went on:

"Now, mother, I can't stand having you suffer any more than you must naturally suffer because of what I've done, I'm calling with a view to getting you away from Wakefield."

"The children have been calling and asking me to come to them. I—"

"You will have to leave Georgia, at least for awhile. Go far away where nobody knows you or what I have done. I've thought of all that, hours ago, before I did it even. Meanwhile, I want you to come to New York."

"To New York? Darling, I've never been in New York."

"Which doesn't mean that you cannot come. There are plenty of trains to bring you."

"But—but—what will I do in New York?"

"See me. I will send you money to come, meet you when you arrive, take care of you and get you out of Wakefield where you can have peace, do you understand?"

"But, Florence, daughter. You are still my daughter, even if you have done such a terrible thing, married a nigger."

"Please mother, don't let's talk about that now. We'll talk about it after you arrive in New York. We'll have a long talk. Maybe then you'll understand, but I won't go into that now."

"But—but—darling, I—I don't know if I can get to New York. I'm sick now. I need the doctor, but I' afraid to call Doctor Ware. I'm afraid . . . "

"Mother, listen, please."

"Yes, dear."

"I've thought even of all that; that Doctor Ware might act so that you would feel bad if you called him. But there is a doctor who will come to see you."

"What doctor, dear? We've never had any but Doctor Ware. What doctor?"

Florence was silent for a moment. Her mother listened, anxiously.

"Mother?"

"Yes, Florence?"

"Call Doctor Johnson."

"Doctor Johnson? Who is he?"

"He's the colored Doctor. His office is down on Railroad Avenue."

"A nigger Doctor? Oh, Florence!"

"Please mother. Take it easy. Don't continue to abuse yourself. Doctor Johnson is a young man and a good doctor. A better doctor than old Doctor Ware. But you won't need to call him. I'll call him. I'll tell him to come and see you. I'll ask him to take care of you; to drive you to Macon and put you on the first train, in a drawing room and send you on to me in New York."

"But Florence."

"Please, mother, do what I ask? If you keep fretting you'll get worse; maybe die. So just be quiet and lay down until Dr. Johnson arrives. I think he keeps a nurse. I'll ask him to bring the nurse and take care of you until you reach Macon. If he thinks it advisable, to send the nurse on with you to New York. Now do you hear, mother?"

"Yes, I hear, darling."

"Then sit down and take it easy until the Doctor arrives. I'll call him from here and if he can't get there for awhile, I'll call you back and tell you when he will arrive. Now is that all right, dear?"

"I—I guess it will have to be. I'm here all alone, and all this trouble has upset me. I'll do what you say."

"All right, then, mother. I'll talk to the Doctor now. Please be quiet, take it easy and be patient."

After a few more words she hung up and immediately asked long distance to call Dr. Johnson, the Negro physician, down on Railroad Avenue.

Dr. Johnson had closed his office for the night, but was still in it, checking his accounts when the phone rang. Picking up the receiver, he said:

"Hello, Dr. Johnson talking."

"Dr. Johnson, this is Mrs. Kermit Early, in New York. I'm the former Mrs. Wingate of Atlanta."

At the mention of her name, Dr. Johnson got a shock, recoiled so violently that he almost fell from the chair. Before him were all the daily papers that were sent to Wakefield, and all of which he had read and was glad to close the office so that he could read them over again.

He knew Florence as Negroes know white people, prominent white people and although he was only a small boy when Kermit Early left Wakefield to go north, he also knew Early. And now a call all the way from New York from a woman whose picture was in all the papers before him, was a distinction, and he stammered a bit before he got himself, on hearing her voice, under control. However, he did very quickly and called back:

"You mean, that you are—"

"Mrs. Kermit Early, nee Mrs. Florence Wingate, and I am calling you on urgent business from New York, Doctor Johnson."

"Yes, Mrs. Early, Thank you. I think I understand. I will be glad to serve you in any way I can."

"Very well, Doctor Johnson. You know my mother, Mrs. Adair?"

"Yes, Mrs. Early. I've seen your mother. I know where she lives."

"Well, Dr. Johnson, I've just talked to her, and the—events which you may have heard about have so shocked her that she is ill. You have heard about it, have you not, Dr. Johnson?"

"I have, Mrs. Early. I have read about it. It is in all the papers."

"Then you understand, Dr. Johnson?"

"I understand, Mrs. Early, and I repeat, I will be glad to serve you in any way I can. Just say what you want done."

"Go and see my mother. If you have a nurse, take her with you. Have you a nurse?"

"I have, Mrs. Early. She is off duty now, but I can call her. I will pick her up and take her with me to Mrs. Adair."

"And leave her there, Dr. Johnson."

"I will leave her there, Mrs. Early. I will take good care of your mother, see that she has everything she needs."

"Thank you, Dr. Johnson, but that is not all."

"Yes, Mrs. Early?"

"I want you to send her to me in New York."

"Send her to you in New York? I understand, that, too. When, Mrs. Early?"

"Just as quickly as you feel that it is safe for her to travel. I want you in the meantime, however, to go to her, take care of her and call me back, say, at noon tomorrow and I will make any arrangements that you advise."

"Thank you, Mrs. Early. I'll get my car, pick up the nurse and go at once to your mother and make it a point to be here at the telephone when you call me tomorrow at noon. Now is that all you wish at this time, Mrs. Early?"

"That is all. As I understand it you're going to see her at once, and if so, I won't need to call her again tonight?"

"You won't need to Mrs. Early. I'll go at once. Be there in half an hour or less."

"Thank you, Dr. Johnson. That is all. Good night."

"Good night, Mrs. Early," replied the Doctor and hung up the receiver. He immediately called his nurse and told her to be ready so that he could pick her up and would be by her house forthwith.

The nurse was flattered to attend a white woman although most she attended were white people, she was flattered and glad to attend Mrs. Adair, for she, too, had read all about the marriage in New York. Meanwhile, Dr. Johnson took just a moment to reflect. Then, he, too, swelled with pride. It is always a distinction for a Negro physician to be called to attend white people. And while the Adairs were no longer wealthy, they were still regarded as among the best people in town. But to be called all the way from New York, by a woman, wealthy he knew, and whose picture was in every paper the country over, was more than a distinction, it was a thrill that Dr.

Johnson had to pause a moment to enjoy. The next moment he put his feet hard on the floor and twenty minutes later was ringing the bell at the Adair home.

Old, but still healthy, destined to live a great many years, Mrs. Adair was suffering only from shock and fear. Not a single white person, other than her children had called to offer a word of condolence, not a single one had rung the door bell to give her a word of kindness, and she was not surprised. She knew that what Florence had done was the one thing no white person in the South would or could either condone or forgive. So when Doctor Johnson called, was admitted and showered her, along with the nurse, with kindness, it was more than the poor soul could stand. And after a few minutes of being treated, again like she had a heart and soul, she fell to weeping and the doctor had the nurse put her to bed and prepare her hot food which she ate and enjoyed, for she had been too upset by it all to even eat.

He left the nurse with her, with instructions to administer to her every need, left the house, but called early the next morning to see how she was faring, to find her up and well and ready to leave for New York as quickly as arrangements could be made to that effect, which she wanted made as quickly as the doctor could effect it.

After a long talk over the telephone to Mrs. Early in New York, the doctor agreed to look after the home, which she would close, but which Mrs. Adair, wanted to feel was being looked after. The doctor had an old colored woman whom he knew would be glad to stay there, keep it up and be happy in doing so, and so advised Mrs. Early accordingly.

"Very well, Dr.," Mrs. Early said. "I will go to the bank and wire you $600.00 at once. $500.00 please give to my mother, for expenses for her and the nurse to New York, the balance as a retainer to you on account of service. So you attend to everything and look after the home. I will send you funds regularly for the upkeep and pay for the woman you put there. Now please wire me from Macon collect just what train you put them on in Macon and what time it will arrive in New York."

The doctor was flattered to do everything he could, and did it well, and two days later wired Florence Early in New York that her mother was on the way and what time she was due in New York.

CHAPTER XXXV

SIDNEY WYETH UNDERSTOOD why Mrs. Wingate failed to keep her appointment at his office the day after the wedding.

She called him the next day, however, to apologize for failing to keep it, which he graciously accepted. In fact, he was relieved that she did not. He had suddenly decided to finish and get his new novel out before going on the proposed trip, so called Bertha and explained to her that he would not go as soon as at first planned; that he would like to finish the new book and publish it before going, and which would delay the trip into the autumn. She was agreeable, although, was obviously, by her tone, disappointed.

"In the meantime, I have the manuscript almost completed and I wonder if you'd mind going through it for me, making it English perfect and improving it in other ways, or wherever it needs it in general?" Wyeth asked Bertha.

"I will be glad to help you," she said, "if you feel that I am capable of doing so, Mr. Wyeth."

"I can't think of anyone whom I have more confidence in to do it, Miss Schultz."

"Thank you, Mr. Wyeth. I appreciate the confidence you have in me. Now when would you like me to call and begin to check it? Or would you prefer bringing the script to our apartment and we could start to check it here?"

"Why, since we might be bothered here, and it is no trouble for me to call at your apartment, if agreeable to you."

"That will be fine, and I shall look forward to seeing you. Now when?"

"I am not engaged tonight, so can bring it up there around eight o'clock?"

"Then please do so, Mr. Wyeth. I'll be waiting for you."

"I'll be there, Miss Schultz," he said and hung up. He paused to stretch himself, then went out and had his dinner. Promptly at eight, he rang the bell at the Schultz apartment and was admitted by a smiling and neatly dressed Bertha, who welcomed him pleasantly.

"I want to thank you for a wonderful dinner night before last, Miss Schultz."

"Oh, thank you, Mr. Wyeth," she said, "but you are due to thank Mrs. Coleman more than me. She supervised its preparation."

"Then I want to thank you both. It was a fine dinner, and I enjoyed it and really had a good time up until—"

"The reporters came," she said, finishing the sentence for him.

"Have you seen the papers?" she said, and then before he could answer, she went on. "But of course you have."

"Who hasn't? What a write-up they got!" he said, shaking his head.

"In every paper in New York," she said.

"In the United States," he corrected.

"I suppose so. My brother bought several out-of-town papers and they all had a big story about it, along with their pictures."

"You ought to read the editorials about it in some of the Southern papers," and so saying, he took some from his pocket. She moved over close to him to examine them, which pleased him strangely and seemed to please her. She then read two of the editorials out loud at his request.

"My, what emphasis they put on it. I don't understand," she said, lowering the paper and looking at him, inquiringly. "Is all they say, possible?"

"Nothing to it," he smiled and shook his head. "Just two people, one white, the other colored, in love with each other, have long since found an interest in common, and have sealed it by getting married, and that is the beginning and end of it."

"Do you think so?" she said, looking at him closely.

"Of course, the South would make much ado about it because of the fact that a wealthy white woman married a Negro which alone is enough to throw their social ideas all out of kelter."

"And—you don't think it will have any such results as they imply; that they even say?"

"None whatever."

"You don't think it will inspire other Negroes to—want to emulate them?"

"It may not happen again in ten years. As to our race trying to emulate them, that is silly. In the first place, few Negroes are even thrown into any association with the whites, and almost never with white people as wealthy as Mrs. Wingate happens to be."

"I suppose not."

"Negroes and whites, especially whites of the upper and wealthier classes never meet socially, north, south, east, or west. We Negroes really have little to interest any white people, much less a wealthy one."

"One of the papers," she said, looking around as if to find it. She could not without rising, so sighed a bit and went on, giving finding the paper up, perhaps as not worth while, "gave a very good story of how it started. Back in that little town in Georgia, and said something about her financing his education."

"We all knew that, at least I did."

"My brother did also. In the meantime, she seemed very much interested in you." Wyeth looked at her and smiled a little.

"It made me a—a bit—jealous," she dared to say, and when he turned to look at her quickly, she lowered her eyes and blushed.

"Looks like you are developing a sense of humor," said he, looking at her shyly. She raised a pair of beautiful eyes to him.

"A sense of humor?"

"A sense of humor. Meaning, jealous of the lady." She laughed, blushed, went on.

"But I was."

"Oh, Miss Schultz."

"I felt it very much when I looked out and saw her dancing with you. She seemed so pleased, and you seemed the same way."

"Miss Schultz!"

"I felt better after you—danced with me."

"Thank you."

"You don't believe me?"

"I refuse to."

"I'm sorry. I wish you would. In the meantime, maybe we'd better get to work on your story?"

"I think we should, too." She lowered her eyes in a way that he always liked to see her do. He pulled the heavy manuscript out of his portfolio and handed it to her. Her eyes opened in surprise, as she took and examined it a moment.

"Gracious, what a manuscript!" she exclaimed, looking at it as though it frightened her.

"That is only a part of it," he said, calmly. "Happily, the greater part."

"Such a thinker," she said, looking up at him in admiration. "A prolific thinker."

"Oh, I wouldn't say all that," he protested, modestly. She was now examining the script.

"Seems to be very well written. I don't think it'll require so much changing, much improving," she said, glanced back up at him again, and smiled with admiration. "You're a born writer. I hadn't any idea you had written all this—and doing all the other work you've been engaged in at the same time. How can you do it—how do you do it?" and again she looked up at him, out of her eager, blue eyes. He shrugged his shoulders to indicate that it meant nothing.

"A little every morning, a chapter mostly. Then now and then a chapter when I get the time and feel inspired. On Sunday I try to write more."

"So interesting. You grow more interesting with time. The better I become acquainted with you, the more interesting you seem to become. I think this is longer than your present book."

"It is. Will run between 500 and 600 crowded pages."

"A big book. You will—charge more for it?"

"Twenty-five cents more, I plan to," he said. She nodded her head in agreement and continued to examine it. "Plenty of novels are as long as that, however."

"A few. Not so many."

"Some are even longer, even twice as long."

"Yes, but not by Negroes. They've never written a book as large as this manuscript is going to make." She looked up at him. "Have they?" He was thoughtful. "You know they haven't," she said, and smiled, placing her small hand on his arm. "You're so modest about it all, too. So modest about everything. You just work hard and long and persistently—and say nothing. Don't even seem to think." She paused to look up into his eyes now, smiled sweetly and in that moment he knew he liked her. What a girl she was, he thought. "You're a wondeful man, Mr. Wyeth. A splendid person to know. A fine person to assist, and I'll be so glad to help you put this mass of work," looking down at the script, "into as good a condition as I know how."

"I'm glad to feel that you know how," he said. Her eyes had been lowered to the script, she raised them back up into his, and smiled at him again, sweetly. Her hand was still on his arm. She seemed to have forgotten it, but he hadn't. He looked down at it, she followed his gaze, blushed, furiously, drew it away, looked up at him, blushed again.

"I think you are due some compliments yourself," he now said, in a low voice. She looked up quickly in surprise.

"Me? For what?" He smiled down into her eyes. He hadn't intended to but in the moment he couldn't seem to help it.

"For being such a lovely person, such an agreeable assistant, so nice about—everything."

"Oh," she said. "That is nothing." Kept her eyes downcast, but the blood was in her face.

"I think it is," he heard himself saying. "I think you are." She looked up at him again now. His face was afire with what he felt. She saw it and her heart in the moment, went out to him.

"Do you think I am, Mr. Wyeth? Really?"

"Really, Miss Schultz. I do think so. I think you're about the most wonderful girl, about the nicest girl—the loveliest girl I ever met, and I—" and then he broke off. Hesitated. She looked quickly up, her face aflame with a feeling she didn't quite understand, herself.

"—what, Mr.—Wyeth?"

"I—I—oh, I'm afraid to say it," and he lowered his eyes. Again her small hand went forward quickly. Placed it on his arm. Looked up into his eyes frankly, honestly.

"Please do, Mr. Wyeth," she said. He raised his eyes and theirs met. What was in hers was in his. Was it affection?

"I—I don't think I—ought to, Bertha—that is, Miss Schultz." Her hand on his arm tightened, the fingers around his wrist, trembled even.

"Please call me Bertha—that is, if you want to."

"Do you want me to?" he asked.

"I do," she said, and lowered her eyes, but kept her grip on his wrist.

"Then I have a first name. Maybe you might try calling me—by it," he said. She looked up at him.

"Sidney," she said and lowered her eyes again. "It's a pretty name."

"I'm glad you think so."

"I've always thought so. There is something, in the meantime, on your mind, Sidney," she was saying now, eyes lowered, but daring to glance up, only to lower them again, as she went on. "Why don't you—get it off? Say what it is; what it is that you're feeling."

He was silent and she noted it, looked up, a question in her eyes.

"I'm afraid to," he said, calmly but frankly.

"Must—I say it for you?" she asked, eyes downcast.

"I would like you to," he said.

"You want me to say that—that you—like me, Sidney?"

"I do like you, Bertha. At the same time, I'm afraid that you—that you are not free. That is why I—I don't want to say so much—now, at least." Raising her eyes to his now, into which had gone suddenly a softness.

"You're—so wonderful about everything, Sidney. So understanding, and—I trust you, and—like you, too. I like you a whole lot. But you are right about what you said; that I am—not free. I *am* not free, Sidney, and because I am not, I am sorry. Sorry for myself, sorry for you."

"That is the way I feared it was. It is because of that that I don't want to say much more—just now."

"You're a darling," she said, eyes down, tears flowing; she was using a kerchief. He moved closer. He placed an arm about her waist and she made it easy for him to do so.

"I—I understand everything, Bertha, and I want to—help you."

She was weeping now and laid her head on his shoulder. He placed a hand beneath her chin, tilted her head back slightly and kissed her lips. She did not draw away but returned the kiss, and wept harder. He didn't kiss her again. He was sorry for her. He squeezed her hand and she did not resist. He knew at last that he loved Bertha Schultz and that she loved him. He knew and appreciated that Bertha was a German agent, a Nazi spy, sent to America by no less a person than Adolf Hitler on a mission; with a task to perform. He knew that this mission might call upon her to do many things subversive, and he was sorry that such a sweet and beautiful, tender and lovable girl was shouldered by such a nefarious task. Yet he understood that she could not be free as long as it lasted; that she couldn't stop it and feel that she was doing her duty.

He decided then and there, however, to keep Bertha from doing anything that would make it impossible for her some day to *be free*. America was on the brink of war, but still wasn't in it yet. Because of that, Heinrich, the ruthless, the scheming and designing, might not call her to do something that would endanger that freedom, before he could get her away on their trip. Once away he would keep her away as long as he could; keep her away and out of danger.

He had read about German women, often good housewives, embroiled in subversive activity. Had seen their pictures in the papers. Angry women, their arrest and jailing made them resentful. It would make Bertha the same way. Beautiful and kind and sweet Bertha, in jail, hatred in her eyes, in her soul. He squeezed her to him tighter.

"I am thinking Bertha; thinking what this task you are shouldered with might lead to. It's dangerous; it is fraught with terrible risks. Once you become enmeshed in the throes of the law, it will change you Bertha, harden you. I—I hope your brother doesn't send you to—do anything before we get away on this trip, to risk that happening. You're too fine a girl to be arrested and thrown into jail." He felt her quiver at the words. "I'm so afraid for you." She was still crying and her grip on his arm tightened, signifying that she understood and would dislike to have to do anything that would risk all this.

"But I understand the position you're in. You can't quit. I know that you've got to—see it through."

"I'll work hard on the script, Sidney, night and day so that you can have the book printed as quickly as possible, so that we can get away. I'll be glad to be away—and with you, Sidney, for as I said, I trust you and I—love you, Sidney, dear. I love you very much."

Again she was weeping and grasping his arm tighter as she thought of his warning; of the danger connected with it. She didn't want to do it but couldn't refuse. That was the law of Nazism; of Hitlerism. The Third Reich first, personal danger forgotten, shoved aside, not to even be considered. And now these two people loved each other.

So withdrawing his arm from about her waist while she dried her tears, he rose to his feet and she stood up beside him, tried to look into his eyes. He took her in his arms, and then kissed her, several times. She trembled with the love for him that was in her heart. He said no words, but presently turned and walked to the door and paused, turned to face her. Again he embraced and kissed her and she trembled in his arms. After a time he turned and without another word, left the house.

CHAPTER **XXXVI**

MRS. EARLY WAS WAITING at the Pennsylvania Station for the train that was bringing her mother from Georgia to New York, to arrive. It was late as most trains were at the time, so she found a seat, purchased a magazine and made herself comfortable, and patient. Meanwhile, Mrs. Adair, aboard the train which had just left North Philadelphia, was relaxing comfortably, and was enjoying the ride.

Dr. Johnson had been able to secure a drawing room for her and the nurse. The papers were still publishing something about her daughter's marriage to a Negro, so Mrs. Adair decided since everybody knew about it and were talking about it, to talk to the nurse, whose name was Betty, about it. She began to do this before the train had gotten out of South Carolina. When she heard Florence called, she recalled that it was while crossing those same tracks that Mr. Wingate had been killed, so turned to Betty abruptly.

"Did they say Florence, Betty?"

"Yes, Mrs. Adair. This is Florence, South Carolina."

"Florence, South Carolina," she repeated more to herself than to the girl. "This is where Mr. Wingate was killed."

"Were you—speaking to me, Mrs. Adair?" said Betty who had been sitting, but had risen quickly and now stood by the old lady who looked up at her quickly, a bit surprised.

"No, Betty. I was talking to myself, but sit down there," pointing to the seat facing her. "Maybe I might talk to you. I want to talk to somebody."

Betty sat down. The old lady looked at her closely.

"You look like an intelligent girl, Betty."

Betty flushed, didn't know just how to answer.

After a pause, during which she framed a simple reply, she spoke:

"Thank you, Mrs. Adair. I try to be."

"Well," Mrs. Adair went on. "You are an intelligent girl and a nice girl. Too bad you're not a white girl."

"I'm satisfied to be just what I am, Mrs. Adair."

Mrs. Adair looked at her again.

"Have you read that new novel, *Passion*, Betty?"

"Yes, Mrs. Adair. I've read it."

"What did you think of it?"

"It was interesting," she replied.

"But did you like it?"

"It wasn't a story that one would, I think, exactly like, Mrs. Adair. Not the way I see it, anyhow."

"I'd think that the colored people would dislike it. That educated colored girl in it, in love and pregnant by a scalawag white man who couldn't marry her. Who didn't want to marry her."

"Colored and white people don't usually marry each other," said Betty. "Nobody expected the man to marry the girl."

"Yes, but he got her in family way. According to the law of God and all that is holy, he was due to protect her."

"He tried to, in a way," said Betty, simply.

"Sure he did. Gave a big, black, buck of a nigger money to marry her."

Betty laughed.

"I read the book but I didn't like it. Didn't like anything about it, but it had lots of truth—too much truth, maybe. And maybe that's why lots of us people in the South don't like it. Yet we're all reading it. That will make the book, or help make it, at least, a financial success."

"I'd think so," said Betty.

"This race question, strange thing, isn't it, Betty?"

"I'm afraid so," said Betty.

After some hesitation, like as though she wanted to say something and didn't know just how to start, Mrs. Adair finally picked up a paper, turned to Mr. and Mrs. Early's pictures and held them up to Betty's gaze.

"Been reading about them, Betty?"

"Yes, Mrs. Adair. I've been reading about them."

"The woman's my daughter."

"So I understand, Mrs. Adair," said Betty.

"A sort of Passion in reverse, Betty."

Betty smiled, said nothing, waited respectfully, her hands folded in her lap. Betty was raised in Wakefield. Had been trained to listen to white people when they talked and answer when spoken to.

"Naturally it's got me all upset. I've had to leave my home. Born in Wakefield, lived there all my life. Then this had to happen—and I was afraid to meet anybody I've known. I'm running away now, like a criminal, in a way. Nobody has said a word to me, not a word in a town where I'd lived until nigh onto seventy years. Isn't that something, Betty?"

"I'm afraid so, Mrs. Adair. I'm sorry."

"I'm sorry for myself, Betty. Yet what can I do? The woman who did this, and whose picture you see in that paper is my daughter. A beautiful woman, Betty, a rich woman."

Betty looked at the pictures. "She *is* beautiful, Mrs. Adair."

"Ten years ago she was considered the prettiest girl in Wakefield, belle of the town." She picked up the paper, looked at the pictures, shook her head, hopelessly.

"The man. He used to live there, too, was born there. Went from this town about the same time my daughter married Mr. Wingate, a rich mill owner, in Atlanta. I know his father, knew his father's father. Fine niggers. Ran a barber shop there for generations for white trade. Fine niggers, I tell you, respected by everybody in Wakefield—and now he shows up in New York, head full of fine education—and marries my daughter, a white woman." She lowered her eyes to cry.

Betty came over on the seat beside her, placed an arm about her and comforted her. After a good hearty cry, with Betty comforting her the best she could, she sat up, pointed to the seat facing her, whereupon Betty moved over and sat down again to face her.

"My own daughter, to break her mother's heart. Do something like this when she knew that they would never, never as long as there is a speck of blood in their veins, stand for or forgive. Why, even the dogs in Wakefield like me; they bark at and play with me when I pass along the street. And, over night, I lose every friend I have—almost every soul in Wakefield. I think even the dogs, are mad about it. I can picture them running away when they see me now, howling with their tails between their hind legs. I don't see why she did it. I'm on the way to her. For if everybody in Wakefield has turned and run from me, Florence is still my daughter, my own flesh and blood, and I can't go back on her—even if she did have to disgrace us all and the whole state of Georgia by doing what she did—marrying a nigger. I don't see why she did it," and again Mrs. Adair had to cry about it, and again Betty comforted her.

"Florence is rich. Husband was many times a millionaire—and left her half of it. Has plenty. Will never have to worry about anything and could have married half the single men and widowers in Atlanta, if she wanted to. But she must up and kick over everything by marrying a nigger." By now she was about exhausted from crying so she could only sadly shake her head.

"Enough to set me crazy. I was just about to go crazy with fear when that doctor came to see me and brought you. I'm sure I'd a died if you hadn't come. Now I guess I got to go on living. It's like living through a perpetual nightmare. I got no objection to colored people, in their place. Wakefield's full of niggers. I love them. Was raised by a black mammy, loved her better than I did my own—but who'd a thought at this stage, in the late afternoon of a long life, that it would come to this? My favorite daughter marrying a nigger." Again she paused to shake her head.

"Better take it easy, Mrs. Adair. You'll make yourself sick. Please don't get excited any more and take it easy," warned Betty, kindly.

"All right, Betty. You're right. I got to take it easy, I know, and be patient, at least, until I reach New York and meet that child of mine, look at her, examine her head and let her try to tell me why she did such a terrible thing. Marrying a nigger. Lord, Lord, Lord."

"I think you should lay down awhile, Mrs. Adair," said Betty, rising and pointing to the sofa. "I'll adjust this so that you can stretch out awhile on this sofa, and try to forget what you're talking about. Remember that the doctor warned you not to think so much about it."

"I'm trying not to, Betty," she said, letting Betty lift her and help her across to the sofa, where she sat down and the nurse swung her around and onto the couch, adjusted her head on the pillow, made her feet comfortable and sat down presently.

"If I could just forget about it for awhile, it wouldn't be so bad. But my confounded head just keeps throbbing from thinking about it. I wish somebody could knock me out and I wouldn't come to until I got to New York. Then I could quit thinking about it and have some peace." She sighed deeply, and closed her eyes. Before either she or Betty were aware of it, she had fallen off to sleep and when she awakened, it was time to go into the diner for dinner, where Betty took her.

As the train neared New York, Mrs. Adair was composed, was able to forget for the time being so much about what Florence had done, and found herself anxiously waiting to see her.

Florence was standing just outside the gate as Betty, led by a Red Cap came through, leading her mother. She didn't see Florence until she heard her name called, and turned to meet her eyes as she cried:

"Mother!" A moment later Mrs. Adair felt her arms about her and hot kisses planted all over her face. Betty and the Red Cap stood aside, respectfully, until the greeting was over, and Florence turned to say:

"Take us to a taxi, porter," and followed him, as, with the luggage he started in that direction, with Betty beside him.

An hour later, high up on Sugar Hill, in their apartment in Harlem, when everything had been adjusted and Betty sent to a hotel where Florence had engaged a room for her, she turned to her mother and began:

"Now mother, you won't need to start telling me what I already know is on your mind. All you've been thinking about and talking to yourself about ever since you read about it in the papers." Florence always dominated her mother by sheer force of will. So her mother nodded and said, meekly:

"Yes, Florence, dear."

"It all started a long time ago."

"What do you mean, Florence?"

"When I was in school in Virginia."

"In school in Virginia?" said Mrs. Adair. Florence turned to look at her and she trembled slightly.

"You haven't forgotten what the Dean wrote you, Mother? You haven't forgotten your sisters, Aunt Harriet and Aunt Jennie?" Mrs. Adair lowered her eyes. The aunts Mrs. Early spoke of had escaped prostitution only by being married off right quick, after both had become pregnant before her mother's sister had succeeded in frightening the men into marrying them, and saving both from disgrace. In short, Mrs. Adair knew that extreme sexual desire ran in the family.

She understood and Florence knew she understood, what she was talking about.

"I had the hardest time keeping nice while still too young to think of getting married. It was then it started. I was sensible enough to realize that I couldn't play around with white boys back there in Wakefield, so I turned and tried to make Kermit satisfy my desires."

Her mother's eyes opened wider. "But he refused. He wouldn't let me, I tried to *make* him. I kept on trying to make him until I virtually ran him out of Wakefield. He had to leave his home because I kept after him so."Again Mrs. Adair opened her eyes wide.

"So all this Kermit is being charged with, is not his fault. It was not his doing. It was me. Me, Mother; please get that straight in your mind at the outset. Not Kermit. Me, Mother, Me!

"You know all about how I met Mr. Wingate; you knew that he was old; that I did not love him, but consented to marry him and finally did to help you, my brothers and my sisters; to give them their chance in life."

" Yes, I remember and understand all that, daughter," said Mrs. Adair, with lowered eyes.

"It turned out to be a greater sacrifice than any of you thought; than any of you ever knew."

Mrs. Adair looked up. She found her daughter looking straight at her, with eyes that seemed to burn holes through her.

"What do you mean, Florence?"

"As badly as I needed to be married, needed to have a husband to satisfy all that nature had put into me, the night following the afternoon that we got married in Wakefield, and went to Atlanta, where we stopped over that night on our honeymoon to Europe, Mr. Wingate broke down in our bedroom and made a *shocking confession.*"

Mrs. Adair started.

"Florence, *what do you mean?*"

"He told me that he was not a normal man, mother."

"What!" cried Mrs. Adair.

Florence, still looking straight and hard at her, nodded her head.

"He told me there on our wedding night, that he was *not a normal man,* mother."

"You mean?"

"That he was like—like—Leo M. Frank. You remember the Frank

case?" Her mother was gazing across at her, stupefied.

"Oh, my God!" cried Mrs. Adair, and covered her face with her hands.

"Just like Leo M. Frank, mother," Florence repeated. Her mother was weeping now, weeping so until Mrs. Early had to move over by her and put an arm about her. The old lady grasped her, trembling. She had followed the Frank case day by day and knew all about what caused him to kill little Mary Phagan, those many years ago. She knew that Frank was a sexual pervert!

"Why didn't you tell me, daughter? Why did you stay with him, oh, why didn't you leave him that awful night and come back to me?"

"I had made a bargain, mother. My body and my soul to help put Frank and Arthur and Magdalene through school. That is what I thought about. By staying with Mr. Wingate I could do that—and you need never know. So I didn't tell you, I didn't tell anybody, until— I met Kermit in Atlanta a year after I was married. I told him and I made him then do what I had tried to make him do in Wakefield. Yes, I made him, and I'm not ashamed of it. I never have been sorry since. Now you know.

"And that, mother, was how it started. Me again, me as it had been, trying to persuade him in Wakefield, two years before. After all I was a pretty girl. I wanted Kermit, and I made Kermit want me. I finally persuaded him to take me. I continued to persuade him and in time I came to love him. I've loved him ever since, I still love him more now than ever. And so I married him. That is all, and still it isn't all," she said and paused. Mrs. Adair looked at her, a question in her eyes.

"You know that I always wanted children, mother."

"I know you did, dear, and in spite of Mr. Wingate being rather old when you married him, we were hoping that there would be a blessed event sooner or later. We lived on, hoping and looking for it for several years after you married. Now, of course, I can understand why there wasn't; why there never could be. I'm so sorry for you, darling."

"Don't be sorry for me any longer, mother," said Florence with a glorious smile on her face. Again her mother looked at her oddly.

"I'm going to have a—baby, dear."

The old lady recoiled, her mouth open. Florence raised a hand.

"I know what you're going to ask. How could I when I just married hardly a week ago. Kermit and I have been friendly for over ten years, mother. Ever since one year after I married." Her mother looked distressed, and again Florence raised a hand.

"Please, mother. I understand and appreciate all about how you must feel, and in that respect I'm sorry for you. But, after all, mother, my life has always been my own. I've explained how it all started. It grew into love and for more than ten years now I've loved the man I seem to have shocked everybody by marrying. But my life has been my own. It is still my own. I'd have married Kermit years and years ago had it not been for Mr. Wingate. In spite of his deficiency, I tried to be good to him, I even tried to satisfy him and I did. He must have felt that there was somebody else, but knowing that he was deficient like he was, he never complained. He was good to me and I was just as good to him as I could be. I felt sorry for him, I knew that he could help it. So I didn't marry the man I had long since learned to love, but proceeded from then on to live a dual life. Then I discovered four months ago that I was pregnant, and knew then that something would have to be done.

"When I visited Wakefield the last time, I left there with plans to tell Mr. Wingate the whole story, and ask him to divorce me. It was the Lord's will that I didn't have to. There was no longer any reason why I should not marry the man I loved. And so, mother, that is the story. You'll say and feel that I could have married a white man; that I could have chosen from among many white men. With Mr. Wingate's money, I could have picked just about whom I wanted. But I wasn't in love with any white man, mother. Fate had decreed that I loved Kermit Early. He is the father of my unborn child, and I am happy, mother. Just as happy as I can be, and have been happy, in spite of the way we've had to share our love for years. So you will just have to resign yourself to this fact, mother, and make the best of it.

"I know how Wakefield and about every white person feels about it. I know that it just drove you away from Wakefield. They'd refuse to ever forgive even you, who had nothing to do with it. I thought of and weighed all these consequences long before I did it. So when I did so, I had reckoned every phase of my life, your life. After father died I wanted to take you up to Atlanta to stay with me, I could have even knowing that I was in love with a—colored man, and was determined to marry him just as quickly as I could. Why, I've wanted to divorce Mr. Wingate for years, but he, Kermit, wouldn't let me. And that is why I didn't have you come to live with me in Atlanta after father died.

"Now, since you didn't care to risk ostracism by trying to stay on in Wakefield longer, I planned that just as quickly as you had read about it in the papers, to send for you and bring you here where nobody would look at you with contempt, and make your life unpleasant.

"I want you to understand that I love you as much as I have always loved you, and I want your declining years to be as comfortable as I can make them. I don't want to force my husband on you; I will not, if you don't think you can stand it, but my husband and my child come first in my life, mother. Because the child is due here in four to five months, we've planned to go away and stay away several months; until the child is at least two months old, for reasons that you can understand." Mrs. Adair nodded her head that she did.

"If we do, we might as well give up the apartment; but since you have nowhere to go, I'd like to keep it and leave you here in it until we come back. By that time you will have had time to adjust yourself to this new life, and then we can adjust matters as best you see fit."

"You are so kind, Florence," said her mother. "So considerate and while I know it's going to be hard for me to—to get used to—what you've done, you've made your position clear, and there's nothing to do but abide by it." She paused a moment to look around the room.

"It's a nice place, dear, a splendid place to live in, and you will be perfectly comfortable here," suggested Florence.

"It *is* a beautiful place—but must be very expensive."

"Not nearly as much as the part of the city that the white people live in, but that doesn't matter. All that matters is, do you think that you'd like to live here for the next six or seven months, anyhow, or would you prefer living downtown among—the white people? I'll rent a place down there and keep you there if you wish." Her mother looked at her and there were tears in her eyes. Florence got up. She came over and put her arm around her mother, who again started to cry.

"I'll stay here and look after the place for you, dear," she said with finality.

"I'm glad, mother. I had hoped that you would. Kermit and I will be leaving in a week or ten days."

"Just one thing, darling," said her mother. "The girl I brought with me from Wakefield. I would like to ask her to stay with me, if she wants to. Being from Wakefield, she understands me better, I would feel that—"

"I'll ask her to. If she's agreeable, I'll call Dr. Johnson and ask him to release her."

"Oh, then I will soon get used to it. Being from Wakefield, I won't be afraid of her as I might be of some of these northern darkies—"

"Now, mother, that is one thing you must not do; **that you must** get used to not doing."

Mrs. Adair was bewildered, turned to **Florence.**

"Did I—make a mistake, dear?"

"Yes, mother, you did. You musn't call colored people 'darkies' and 'niggers' up here. They don't like it. They don't like it in Wakefield, but they have to take it down there, so just shrug their shoulders and pretend it doesn't matter. It does, and you must get used to using the word 'colored' and 'Negroes' and then you won't make anybody angry."

"Of course not. I'll be careful, darling. We shouldn't call them such names in Wakefield, and I will be glad to quit calling them by those ugly names."

"Now the next thing, mother. In marrying a colored man, I knew that my future association would be mostly with them. While you don't have to, it will be well if you just try to get used to that, too. You won't have to associate with anybody that you don't want to. New York is where nobody pays any attention to anybody else, unless it is mutual. You can live right in this apartment for ten years and they wouldn't try find out who you were from next door. So you can live right here, in the way you want to live. The town is filled with churches and you can go to any one of them that you want to, come on home and do what you want without being bothered by anybody. I hope the girl who came along to attend you will want to stay in New York for awhile at least, for she will make a better companion for you than anybody up here."

"That's what I want, honey. **Somebody for a companion and Betty** is a lovely girl. She will look after an old woman and be patient and kind to me. I do hope she will want to stay."

"She will if Dr. Johnson tells her to, and I will call Doctor Johnson and have him tell her to. In that way you can feel pretty sure that she will."

"Oh, Florence, thank you. I'm beginning to get used to it already."

"I'm glad, mother. And now the final but most important thing."

"Yes, dear?"

"My husband."

Mrs. Adair was silent. She didn't know just what to say, so said nothing.

"He will be home shortly, and I am going to prepare his dinner now."

Her mother looked at her, wonder in her eyes.

"We haven't any servants, dear. We've preferred to live a quiet and simple life together. I like to cook and keep house, so I cook for him. I know what he likes and how he likes it. But if you stay here, and that is understood, you'll have to meet him; and you'll have to get used to him."

"Yes, dear," said her mother, trying to be agreeable.

"I want you to try your best to treat him just like you would have treated—any white man that I might have married, do you understand what I mean, mother?"

"I understand, Florence, and I'll do my best."

"You—you musn't—embarrass him, mother. Please try to remember always, that he is my husband, that I love, honor and respect him, and that if anybody insulted him, I wouldn't like it. I would take his side against the world—against my own mother."

Mrs. Adair sank down on the seat now and tried to hold back the tears. Florence sat down beside her and comforted her. She knew her mother. She had looked for her to take it just that way. She knew, too, that after she had cried, she would be stronger and would agree to meet Kermit and treat him as she wanted her to. After a time, Mrs. Adair relaxed, forced a smile, and turned to Florence.

"Trust me, daughter. I'll act as you want me to."

Florence kissed her then, and stood up. Mrs. Adair stood up, too

Florence knew it was all settled; that her mother would be nice to Kermit and before long he would be fond of her, for she was a good mother.

"Now, I must go and start the dinner," said Florence, with finality.

"Can I help you, dear?" said Mrs. Adair, solicitously. Florence drew her close and replied:

"Of course you can, you old darling."

Then arm in arm they went to the kitchen where an hour and a half later they had prepared a sumptuous dinner for Florence's Negro husband.

Kermit Early had been busy all day with the New York end of the subversive group with whom he was affiliated, and had had little time to think about the notoriety that marrying Mrs. Wingate had aroused. He had been told by his wife, however, that she had sent for her mother who was due to arrive some time that day. Now as he clung to a strap aboard an Independent Subway express, homeward bound that afternoon, around six o'clock, it came back to him and he wondered if she had arrived, and then recalling that she was coming from Wakefield, remembering and recalling her, he wondered just how she would greet him. Then he thought of Florence and relaxed. She would have that all taken care of, as she always had taken care of everything, regardless how delicate, how difficult, how intricate. He smiled to himself. Being her husband now made him feel different than just being her sweetheart, as he had been these many years. She was proving a capable wife, and he sighed with happiness. He knew he didn't have to worry as to how he would be welcomed.

Mrs. Early had everything ready when he reached the apartment. Everything neat, in order, the table set, food cooked and ready to serve when he walked in. When he entered the door she came forward, smiling, placed her arms about him and kissed him fondly. Mrs. Adair was standing near and saw it. It shocked her in spite of having made herself get used to what she would see, but she swallowed her feeling and when Florence turned and held out her hand and her mother came forward, took it and acknowledged the introduction. She was surprised, however, and relieved when Mrs. Adair greeted him by his first name and stepping forward, kissed him.

CHAPTER XXXVII

AFTER HAVING declared their love, Bertha and Wyeth found it easier to greet and welcome each other and to work together. They both seemed happier after that, and started going together regularly. He began to take her to shows and to moving pictures, dining together frequently and going for long rides in his car, growing more devoted to each other as time went by. Meanwhile she was assisting him with his completed manuscript and was improving the reading of it tremendously, without adding, as she admitted, a single thing to the story that he had told. Her assistance was simply making the story easier to read, and more beautiful in its general construction. Bertha enjoyed the work and Wyeth and Marie were pleased to have her so near. All three had much in common.

He provided a desk for her near Marie's in his office and she spent considerable time there and neatly retyped the manuscript after going through it carefully. It was a voluminous mass—when he finally wrote finis at the end of it. Before retyping, as stated, she went through it, sentence by sentence with the most infinite care, and both were greatly satisfied with it as they turned it over to the typesetter.

"I want you, Bertha," he said, as they sat in his car in a glade of a forest in Tarrytown, where they had driven for a Sunday's outing, and from which spot they could look down on the lazy waters of the Hudson as they floated south to meet the salt waters of Long Island Sound, "to read the proofs with as much care as you have checked the manuscript."

"'You know how glad I will be to do so, sweetheart," she said, her little hand in his, his arm about her waist.

"You have changed my whole life, Bertha. In spite of the fact that you cannot marry me until this awful war is over, and I am not asking or expecting you to, you have brought more happiness and contentment into my life than I have ever known," he said with a happy sigh as he squeezed her.

"I'm so glad to hear you say that, Sidney, dear. Words are inadequate to express how much you have brought into my life. I'm *so* happy, in spite of that which you spoke of, until I want to sing a little prayer every night when I retire; every morning when I arise, to thank God for it. I love you so much that nothing else matters. It just thrills my heart to think that I have you; that we have each other," and she laid her lovely head against his and just sighed with contentment.

"In the meantime, Kermit and his wife just suddenly disappeared. Disappeared as if into nowhere. I wonder why?"

She was silent a moment, and he turned to look at her.

"She told me before she left, dear, but in confidence, why."

"Oh," he cried, then broke off and didn't ask her to tell him. She sat up straight, looked at him, then patted his cheek.

"I'll tell you, dear, because I know you won't repeat it to anybody."

"You don't have to tell me if you don't wish to, darling," he said.

"But I wish to, Sidney. Mrs. Wingate is going to have a baby in a short while."

"Oh," he cried, understandingly. "That's why they went away so suddenly, eh?"

"Yes. If they stayed here and she had it, long before it would be due according to the date they married, it would—"

"—look bad—and might get into the papers," he said understandingly.

"That's it, and is why they decided to go away where no one here would know anything about the time when the child was born."

"Very sensible on their part."

"That's what I thought," said Bertha, "since their marriage created such a furore, the birth of a baby so soon after they married might get a whole lot more unfavorable publicity at this time, so they are trying to avoid that."

"I'm rather glad they had to go away when they did, however," he said. She looked at him, inquiringly.

"He had been after me for a long time to direct and produce a picture from a story he had written and was most anxious to bring out. A hate picture designed to make Negroes hate Jews and put them into action as far as they were able to go, against them, and I didn't want to do it."

"I know you didn't, Sidney, and I, too, am glad he went away since I know that you didn't want to make it."

"That was what she was going to come and see me about, after making the appointment the night of their wedding."

"But when the newspapers came out and threw them all out of balance," said Bertha, "added to which, she had to send for her mother down in Georgia, where they had ostracized her so, that she couldn't stay there longer, all on account of her marrying a colored man; and then having to go away to keep from being talked about again, so she had to give up seeing you."

Wyeth smiled. "I knew it, and am relieved. I suppose he had sold her on the idea and she had plans to try to persuade me to do so, but in another way."

"A way that they didn't get to. Meantime, just about when do you think we'll get away on our trip?" she wanted to know.

"In October."

"October? I will be glad when the time comes, dear," she said. He looked at her.

Her face was serious and she did not turn to meet his eyes. She was thinking about her brother. He had been busier than ever lately. Ever since Von Barwig arrived, meeting after meeting had been the order of the day. Her brother told her that Japan was planning on attacking America very shortly; and that in view of the fact that America was considered by Germany to be practically in the war on the side of England, and that if and when Japan attacked America, would be the signal for Germany and Italy to declare war on America. He told her that when this happened the long delayed plans that had been formulated, and were still being whipped into shape, downtown would go into effect, and that he hoped Wyeth would not take her away, as he was sure they would be needing her very soon.

She had to pretend that she would be ready to do whatever they wanted her to, but she wasn't enthusiastic about it any longer. Ever since she had met Sidney Wyeth and become impressed with his philosophy, she was conscious that the purpose they might assign her to carry out, would be very distasteful. She had not told her brother that she was in love with Sidney, although she found him looking at her often a bit oddly as if with a feeling that she was, but he was too deeply enmeshed in what he was doing to talk about it, and she was glad that he did not. She had become, in fact, far more interested in Sidney Wyeth and what he was doing than she was in carrying out the wishes of Adolf Hitler. Since she and Wyeth had declared their love for each other, she found herself thinking more about her future life in America, as the wife of the man she loved, than of the glory of Adolf Hitler, who at this time was rolling across Russia, well on the way to the Volga, and who, at the time, was expected to capture Moscow, an expectation that was shared in by the entire world.

What Bertha was thinking most about at the present, however, was to get away where her brother could not reach her very easily to send her on any subversive mission. She was still going downtown, meeting a lot of women that she did not care about and never had, but who were the busiest people she ever met, "keeping America out of the war," they called it, while all the while, America, she knew, was headed as straight for it as she could go, and according to her brother, would be in it by the first of the coming year.

She relaxed after a time and sat back in her seat.

"Will we be going anywhere near this place where you used to live in South Dakota, Sidney?"

"No, dear, not very near." He looked at her quickly and smiled.

"Oh, I'm sorry. You talk so much about it; of how you settled there and lived in a sod house all by yourself, and seemed to have been so happy and hopeful; regarding the future, until you've got me thinking about it, too. Thinking about it and hoping some day I will see it and, perhaps live with you those years again which you've said that if you could have had—me, then, that you would never have left there."

"Had it been possible for me to have known you then Bertha, and to have had your love and help as you are giving it to me now, I would still be there, with, no doubt, a large and fine family by this time."

"Oh, Sidney, no," she cried and hid her face on his shoulder.

"We're going to have that family yet, Bertha, dear, even if we can't go back to that farm I developed off there in South Dakota." For answer she squeezed him and both wished then that they could drive to a magistrate or a minister and be married and start to having the family both dared dream about. Then the thought of war with it's millions of young men dying, with other millions now living and happy and hopeful who would die before it was all over, came to them and they dismissed all ideas of any immediate happiness in marriage—and decided to be content just to love each other until they could do better.

October came as it has been coming once a year since the beginning of time, and Wyeth's new book was ready. They had busied themselves, compiling a list of thousands of names and addresses of people who had bought the other book, copy for newspaper advertisements and about everything needed for Marie to work with, while with a goodly supply of both books, Bertha and Wyeth left early one morning, heading Southward on their long planned trip.

PEARL HARBOR!

On the morning of December the Seventh, which was Sunday, they awakened to hear over their portable radios, somewhere in the Southland, that Japan had launched her sneak attack on America at Pearl Harbor. America was at last in the war, but from a direction nobody had been expecting her to enter it, are to be drawn into the conflagration!

CHAPTER XXXVIII

"WELL, DEAR BERTHA," said Wyeth, when they sa٠ down to breakfast together just before noon that fatal Sunday. "It is here. America is at war."

"Isn't it terrible, darling," she said, shaking her head sadly. He shook his head helplessly.

"I knew it would come. I've been afraid it would for a long time," he said.

"My brother told me that it was brewing, and that the Japanese Ambassador would call on Secretary Hull during the hours of attack as a gesture."

"With all due respect to our Secretary of State, I thought his answer to Japan was most stupid," said Wyeth. Bertha looked at him. "Japan has no doubt planned this move for a long time, and now when it seems that Russia is completely licked and may be broken up as a result of the war, who knows. Still, I was flabbergasted when I read his reply to Japan, ordering her to do all those things when it should have been obvious to anybody that since Japan had gone as far as she had and at such cost she wasn't going to turn back completely just because our Secretary of State asked her to."

"My brother said that America would find Japan a more bitter and ruthless enemy than Germany."

"I've never trusted Japan, and I agree with your brother. It sure looks bad for us. I'm afraid it's going to be a long war and a hard and bitter one," he said, with a sigh.

"Will it make any difference in your immediate plans, dear?" she asked, her eyes on him anxiously.

"None, Bertha. I'm too old for the army, and I cannot help my country in any way by changing my plans," he said. Bertha seemed relieved when he said that, and turned to eating her breakfast with a greater relish.

In the meantime, back in New York, Heinrich had been called by order of Dr. Herr Von Barwig to the office of Hans Schiller to meet with most of the other German agents operating in the Eastern area. Activities were in full force. The call, as stated, had been sent out by the Herr Doctor, who knew well in advance of Japan's carefully planned sneak attack on Pearl Harbor; and who knew also that it would be followed by a declaration of war on America by Germany and Italy. All of which had been planned by Hitler and Mussolini to coincide and follow Japan's sneak attack.

Von Barwig also reckoned, and well, that promptly after all this happened, a nation-wide dragnet would be thrown all over America to uncover and stop as quickly as they could be found, all subversive activities which had spread and were operating in no end of places under the guise of "America First," and other "patriotic" organizations. This activity had become so general that it was going on to a small degree in the streets of most towns. Solicitors were everywhere, contacting and soliciting joiners right in the streets, and in broad daylight, all directed from one central point under the supervision of Dr. Von Barwig.

Knowing that all such activities would fall immediately under suspicion, and would be promptly investigated by agents of the FBI, Von Barwig had called this meeting for the purpose of, among other things, disbanding insofar as further meetings at that particular address were concerned.

"The FBI," he said, addressing the agents assembled, "will go into action on a scale far more sweeping than ever before. It has started already and it is only a question of a few days, possibly only a few hours, before we will be investigated. So it would be foolhardy for us to attempt to continue meeting in this hall."

He then advised all present to wait for a call from him, designating where to meet in the future.

"In the meantime," he went on further to advise, "Secure some kind of a job. The best you can find, and fitted to your likes and what you can best do, but get a job so that when and if you happen to be questioned, you can answer satisfactorily and avoid being taken to police headquarters and investigated. Every man and woman of German extraction and with German sympathies will fall under suspicion and immediately after the Fuehrer declares war on this country there will be wholesale arrests. Many will be jailed, mostly on suspicion. So now while all is still free and clear, get busy; get your story straight; let it be a logical one, and stick to it when and if you are hauled in. We have a long list of good lawyers in our ranks, so do your part and we'll see that you are properly defended in the event of arrest and attempted prosecution."

After the meeting Heinrich met Hans Schiller in a tavern, where, over their beer, they had a long talk.

"What kind of a job do you plan, Heinrich?" said Scihller after he had drunk deeply from his stein, which he now set down before him, and waited.

"I'm already employed—in a way," said Heinrich, toying with his stein, his eyes on it and a smile on his face. Schiller looked at him in some surprise.

"I doped this thing out," Schultz went on to explain, "a long time ago, when I had a feeling it might come to this."

"So," said Schiller. "How? Come on and let me in on something."

His eyes still on his fingers as he toyed with the stein, Heinrich raised them to Hans now, and became a bit serious. "I'm sorta tied up with a little, struggling Negro newspaper in Harlem. I'm their star reporter—and part owner of it, into the bargain," and then he smiled again, as if to himself.

"What's this?" said Hans. "Sort of a joke?"

"No," replied Heinrich. "Strictly on the level."

"Is that so?" said Schiller, a touch of doubt still in his tone. "Well, let a fellow in on it. Tell me about it."

"I don't mind," said Heinrich. He took a swallow from his stein, then went on.

"To know colored people, you've got to be one. In spite of having been thoroughly schooled in Nazism, I lived for ten years before that in America. Those were my adolescent and tender years when certain things become a part of you. Those ten years gave me a certain outlook on life in keeping with the way the Negro is treated in this country, and the sympathies I developed in his cause during those ten years still linger with me, so I am able to alternate into his philosophies as readily as I want to. I am at war, along with the Reich, against America, but I am in sympathy with the Negro in his fight here for a greater freedom and am out to help when and however I can."

"What's all this to do with this—paper, you started to tell me you are associated with?" said Hans.

"Just that. Now with regards to this paper, I am in sympathy with what it stands for. But enough philosophy. I'll tell you how it happened.

"One of the first things you learn when you live around colored men is that few ever have any money."

"I can understand that," said Hans. "They don't make so much."

"Not exactly that," corrected Heinrich. "They do not, on the whole, of course, make as much as white people. But when they earn as much, and most of them are making a lot of money now, they don't seem to manage as well and have nearly as much. Just don't know how I guess. Still they won't have as much, regardless how much they make. They are forever on the hustle. That's the way you find them in Harlem and every other place I've been—and now getting down to how and why I happened to tie up with this newspaper.

"I became acquainted with a group of young fellows in Harlem, who were trying to run it—and having one hell of a time, especially when it came to the printer. In fact, the printer was forever giving them hell about his pay and threatening to refuse to print their paper every week, just before it was due at press."

"You met them through a—girl, I'd bet," interjected Hans, smiling across at him. Heinrich laughed.

"I met and became acquainted with them. It is of no interest at this time just how."

"Go on. I'm interested and I'm listening."

"I dropped by their little office one day and found the group in a near panic. I paused when inside the door to hear the printer declare: 'It's the same old story, almost every week and I'm dead tired of hearing it. I've heard it so often that I've grown to expect it. I hear it in my sleep; hear it while I'm awake; hear it so much until I imagine that I see it all the time. You ain't got the money now, but you'll have it. Always you'll have it—but you never have. How do you expect a man to run a printing press with paper to buy, men to pay off, rent to pay, a family to take care of on mere promises which you never keep.

"'Well', he paused with finality written all over his face. 'I've gone as far as I can. If you can't raise $175.00 to apply on all the printing you owe me for, I can't print your paper tonight, and that's final. I'll have to pie all the type and give up printing it altogether. I'm sorry, but that's the way it stands!'

"Those poor devils pleaded so long and so hard until their throats were dry; they couldn't do much more now than make gestures with their hands, but I could see that this was one time the printer was going to stick to what he said. They had to give him some money, and as I've told you, being colored, they didn't have any but were 'going to' have some—soon, of course. Meantime, they had to have the paper on the street the next morning, or else they were a pair of cooked geese.

"The printer, as if convinced that he wouldn't get any, started to leave the place and came toward the door. Just as he reached me, I raised my hand and he stopped. 'I couldn't help overhearing the—controversy,' I said. 'May I ask what is the trouble?' Just as if I didn't know. He went on to tell me, while they cut in with this alibi and that alibi. He would wave them down and start all over again, and they in turn would start all over again with more and new alibis. I listened for a couple of minutes while he tried to tell me, but could never finish for their butting in. Finally I raised my hand and, stopping them from trying to tell their side, I said:

"'These fellows are friends of mine. Why don't you give them a break?'"

"'A break!' he shouted loudly, throwing up his hands. 'That's what I've been giving them. Breaks, nothing but breaks. Now *I* must have a break—$175.00 or else!'

"He was in a new rage and started past me out the door, when I laid a hand on his arm and said, reaching for my wallet with the other hand. 'All right, my friend.' I counted out $125.00 and looked at him. He looked at the money hungrily. 'I haven't $175.00, but here's $125.00 that belongs to somebody else, but I'll take a chance and give it to you on their account, providing you print the paper as you are due to tonight. Is it a deal?'"

"Then what did he do?" asked Schiller, curiously.

"He took it, of course."

"And printed their paper. Then what?" from Schiller.

"I became part owner."

Schiller laughed.

"Part owner for I've had to advance dough twice since. They're into me now for $225.00, and I am not only, part owner, but star reporter. By which you can see I stand all right if Mr. FBI choses to check on me and ask some questions."

"Smart boy," said Schiller, enthusiastically.

"Not only that, but I have a press card, so am privileged to go anywhere, call on anybody and ask plenty of questions myself—and that's exactly what I've been doing—and am going to do more of as quickly as Hitler declares war on these United States."

"Meaning—what?"

Heinrich looked around carefully, then on seeing that there was nobody listening, leaned a bit closer and went on:

"I'm finding out as nearly as I can, just when ships will be sailing down to the West Indies and S. A. You see, most everything sailing down that way carries Negro mess boys, cooks, some seamen—a lot of colored help on almost every ship."

Hans looked at him closely, eyes narrowed with subtle interest.

"It will be my business—in fact, I've been doing some preliminary work already, to get acquainted with the wives, sisters and daughters of these men, their friends and their friends' friends."

"I follow," said Hans.

"You see, colored people talk freely to each other. They all understand that they are not to talk; but that means, to them, not to talk to white people. To another Negro, all I've got to do is to get acquainted. If we're in a tavern or restaurant, I treat. To treat is to get acquainted; to be acquainted is to ask questions. I know that even the crews are not advised as to the hour of sailing, but are told to be on shipboard at a certain time and I've found out that means sailing in twenty-four hours.

"So I mill around as a cub reporter, getting news, asking questions, getting acquainted. I'll be able to find out a whole lot about when every ship with colored people employed is leaving out. So I'll advise the Doctor and you and—"

"—we do the rest. Meantime, it was a smart move on the Doctor's part to arrange connections in Argentina while there."

"Argentina is friendly to the Axis and is going to remain so."

"Roosevelt's good neighbor policy hasn't turned them against us."

"On the contrary," said Schiller, "they hate the U.S.A."

"Hate them like poison. They tried to play along to get American dollars, but they simply will not go all out as many of the other S. A. states have done, regardless," said Heinrich.

"The Doctor is all set with communications. You get the lowdown on when the ships will sail, turn the information over to us, and old Doc will shoot it on in code to the Argentine, and they'll relay it to the commanders of the U-Boat wolf packs as they are called, and—bingo, another ship goes to the bottom."

"As easy and as simple as taking candy from a baby—in a great big and supposedly smart country like America," and Heinrich smirked.

"It doesn't seem possible."

"It wouldn't be possible and so simple in my case if it wasn't because they play the Negro down so. A few smart Negro dicks on the FBI milling around Harlem and they'd soon catch on to my racket and throw me in jail."

"Maybe they'll be sending some up there if they get suspicious as to where the leak is coming from."

"Never," said Heinrich, shaking his head.

"Why not?" Schiller wanted to know.

Turning to him, then taking a big drink of beer, Heinrich set the glass down and went on, his face dark with resentment.

"It's the South."

"The South?" echoed Schiller, not understanding.

"That's what I said. The hand of the South, reaching out to cow the Negro, discourage him and keep him as they put it 'in his place'."

"You're talking Greek now."

"I'm talking German, a language that we both understand. And I tell you that it is southern influence and control that keeps the Department of Investigation from even hiring any Negro for secret service, much less training any in the art. Although practically one third of the people south of the Mason-Dixon line are Negroes, only a few towns down there have Negro police, and when they do have they are supposed to confine most of their arrests to Negroes."

"You don't say," exclaimed Schiller, amazed.

"You, a German, wouldn't know that, of course, and I wouldn't if I wasn't a Negro, living with and putting up with all that is forced on them. But I know that always during a Democratic Administration, the South is ever in the saddle and the white people from that section are united in keeping the Negro as far back as they can place him. They don't want America to get into this war because they know it will mean drafting Negroes for service in the same proportion of numbers as whites. If they uniform a Negro, make one an officer here and there—not any more than the North will force them to accept, they fear it will change the Negro's viewpoint. He'll begin to consider himself an American, then, just like them. And then he'd want to come in the front door and eat at a table, where now they force him to go around to the kitchen and eat off a shelf as has been done for so long that most Negroes accept it and think little about it any more. But war will start them to thinking. Oh, yes."

"And this in a so-called Democracy—huh!" sneered Hans.

"In a democracy that keeps most Negroes angry half the time when they think of it and when they hear it preached."

"I think we should get the Negroes to do a lot of sabotaging for us," suggested Schiller.

"No," said Heinrich, shaking his head. "He won't go in for that. He's as loyal as any white American and loves his country. He just hates a lot of people in it, including most white Southerners."

"Then you don't think he'll go in for sabotage?"

"Not by a long shot. Whatever we get out of him or get him to do, he will do it unconsciously."

"Meaning that he won't know that he is doing it?"

"That's it, and the only way."

"Well, I was sure I had thought of something, but I guess I hadn't. Go on with your story."

"I was explaining why they won't be sending any Negro undercover men to Harlem or any other section of the country."

"Yes, that was what you were talking about."

"He's a job man, but as far as I can learn, he hasn't applied much for service in the Federal Bureau of Investigation. If he did, he'd be discouraged. I don't know whether Hoover, the head of it, is a Southerner, but I do know that there is enough Southern influence near to give it the cold shoulder and as long as the Negro hasn't done much applying for jobs in it nor hasn't tried much to get into it, where they'd most likely crucify him at the source by making the examinations so hard that he would never get out.

"So he'll not get far enough into it to be in my way. That's the way they do it at the Naval Academy at Annapolis. They've made it so hard for a Negro to even enter the Academy, and they've been careful to see that not even one has ever gotten through. Not a single one has ever graduated from the Academy in all its more than 100 years of existence."

"Great goodness—and again I say, they call this a democracy!" exclaimed Schiller. "What a joke."

"That's what I call it. But when it comes to a Negro's advancing beyond a menial job and a few white collar ones, teaching school and managing something relating strictly to Negroes, the South never relaxes. And they pour this sentiment into northern white people who in the beginning might, and still have a tendency to be favorably inclined toward the Negro. The Southerners are, too, and claim it very loudly—but that is according to their idea, their philosophy, and their idea is not to honor any Negro as a secret service agent, getting big money for being wise and uncovering any efforts of sabotage in Negro sections of New York or anywhere else. According to Southern philosophy, that's a white man's job and they've got white men milling around up there, trying to check up on activity."

"Yes?"

"Sure. Plenty of them. I see them; I've even met and talked with them and—"

"—and didn't arouse their suspicion?"

"Why should I? I'm only a Negro, a 'pretty' Negro, the women up there call me. A pretty yaller man with the softest and prettiest hair. Anyway, few Negroes arouse any white man's suspicion when it comes to anything like I'm doing. That would be the last thing they'd think of. So I'm safe from suspicion. It is my business to get other people to talk, not to talk myself."

"I get you," said Schiller.

"It's when white men come around and ask questions that the Negro shuts up. He has never 'seen anything' nor ever, knows 'anything.' The very sight of two well dressed white men, browsing around in a Negro section, is the best signal for silence, so they would never find out anything—even when it is going on under their eyes."

"Will you confine your information gathering to New York?" said

Schiller. "Just around New York City, I mean."

"Hell, no!" exclaimed Heinrich. "I plan to scout the whole coast from Boston to the Virginia capes. I can get a lot of information in Norfolk and Newport News where many of the ships put in port for coal. But mainly, the cargo ships sailing down through the Caribbean and the Gulf of Mexico will go right out through Sandy Hook, so I will gather most of my information right here."

At this point Schiller called the bartender and ordered two more steins of beer. After drinking about half of it, he seemed to think of something, and turned to Heinrich.

"By the way, what's become of Early? Haven't seen much of him since he married that pretty and rich white widow that the papers made so much noise about. What's happened to him, anyhow? Did they have to leave the country?"

"No, they didn't have to do anything, but they did leave the country."

Schiller looked at him quickly, a question in his eyes.

"Early had been friendly with this woman for over ten years. You see, he knew her as a kid in some little town down in Georgia where they were both born. Later she married this millionaire mill owner and went up to live with him in Atlanta. The guy turned out to be a sexual pervert which left her stranded, as it were." He paused Schiller laughed.

"She ran into Early, who was there going to school and persuaded him to come and work for them. And that was how it started. It continued and she put him through school, clear up and through Harvard and the guy is loaded with education. Has so much education, as our friend Wyeth, the motion picture producer, puts it, that he doesn't know anything at all."

Again Schiller laughed, then his face became serious. "I don't know. I thought he seemed to be a very smart fellow. He wrote a great story for the Jew picture. I read it. I'm telling you he had something."

"I agree with you, and I also agree that Early is smart and will by and by be of great help to us. However, for the present he is sort of incommunicado, due to the fact that he had gotten this woman in family way before he married her. Marrying her stirred up so much publicity, that they decided it wouldn't look so good for her to come up with a baby a few months later, so they went off to South America where they plan to stay until nobody can very well guess how old the kid is when they get back. And that is what happened to him."

"So for the present the picture he was to make is out, eh?"

"It is out."

"And what about your sister? Haven't seen her for quite awhile."

"She's away down South with this fellow Wyeth, getting information. In the meantime helping him with his book."

"That's good. I'm sorry you let her go, though. The old man and I were talking about her no longer ago than yesterday when we had something that she would have been better able to do for us than any of the women we know. When'll she be back?"

"I really don't know. She doesn't tell me, but seems very well pleased with what she's doing and has sent me considerable information regarding the lay of the country and what's going on over the sections she has traveled. Then, there's another thing."

"What other thing?" said Hans, looking at him.

"I think she's in love."

"Oh, in love. Has she told you?"

"Oh, no. It isn't like her to do that."

"Sorta close-mouthed."

"It's in keeping with her training. I like her to be that way."

"Of course, Heinrich. Meantime, who is she in love with?"

"The man she's working for."

"Wyeth?"

"Sidney Wyeth."

"Aren't you afraid that he might—influence her against us?"

Heinrich shook his head, negatively. "No. She isn't easily influenced and nobody could influence her against our Fuehrer or against me," said Heinrich, reassuringly. Hans nodded but there was a frown on his face and Heinrich saw that he was not satisfied.

"But I'll get her back on the job as quickly as I can if the Doc and you feel that you might wish to use her."

"Then do that, Heinrich. The fact is, the Doc and I have been counting on using her for some time. We haven't anything in mind for her to do just now, but who knows when we might, what with this declaration of war expected any day now."

"All right, Hans. I'll get in touch with her soon."

"Just one more thing before we go. What's your alibi as to where you are from, where you were born, who are your parents, and where you get so much money to spend?"

Heinrich looked at him oddly, a smile on his face.

"That's another thing I thought of even before I came back to this country a long time ago. I knew I couldn't tell the truth, so I made up this story.

"My mother, who was a Negress, is dead. My father is a retired, wealthy Southern white man, who 'played around' when he was young and 'got me'." He smiled and Schiller burst into laughter. He drank the rest of his beer.

"So I'm a yaller bastard, who shakes the old man down, because of the sins of his youth, for plenty of dough when I want it. I've told this lie so often that I'm almost beginning to believe it myself," and both burst into laughter, rose to their feet still laughing, and left the place.

CHAPTER **XXXIX**

AS WAS EXPECTED, on December 11th, 1941, Germany and Italy declared war on America, and within a few weeks, Japan drove the United States out of the Philippines, Guam, and Midway, and having declared war on England at the same time, captured and drove the English out of Hong Kong, and headed for Malaya where in due time she captured the great English naval base of Singapore, considered the most powerful fortress in the Pacific. Those were the darkest days for England and America in all their history. Meanwhile, Hitler's fascist armies were at the gates of Moscow and the world was expecting both it and Leningrad to fall any day.

Truly it was Hitler's and Japan's greatest day, and the thousands of German agents hidden away all over America were gleeful.

Somewhere in the Southland, Sidney Wyeth and Bertha Schultz were busy in the sale of Wyeth's two books, but were happy and successful. They found each other's company most agreeable, and had developed a fine companionship. If Bertha was thrilled by the success of the armies of Hitler, she did not in any way express it in words or action to Wyeth. Accordingly, therefore, Wyeth avoided discussion of the war and its events in her presence as best he could. Occasionally, however, it intruded itself into their conversation as it did one morning while they were driving along a stretch of good road en route to a city where they planned to review the books in several schools and other places. Wyeth was reading the paper and Bertha was driving along, leisurely, her eyes on the road before her. Wyeth paused and chanced to remark:

"Regardless of how much is said to the contrary, I will always consider our Secretary of State's answer to the Nipponese, relating to policy, the most stupid thing imaginable. Wendell Willkie criticised Roosevelt during the 1940 Presidential campaign about doing so much big talk with few guns and not nearly enough ships to back it up."

"Politics," said Bertha, quietly, her eyes still on the road ahead.

"Politics is right," said Wyeth. "Our president, as I view him, is such a politician, unfortunately, that every move he makes and every word he utters, seems to be inspired from a political point of view. Now returning to Japan, for instance.

"Until a few months before the sneak attack on Pearl Harbor, we were selling Japan millions of tons of scrap iron which she quietly stored and is using it now to shoot at and make a fool of us."

"Heinrich wrote me from Chicago, that Japan will take and control almost everything in the western Pacific before many months," Bertha said.

"It doesn't seem possible, but I'm afraid he's right. But it's hard to even visualize, much less believe. I still feel that she went too far in attacking the two greatest powers with the greatest navies in the world. Yet, I'm forced to admire her nerve."

"What do you think of our—of—Adolf Hitler, by this time?" she dared, after a pause, to ask. This was the first time, that he could recall of her ever referring to the Fuehrer directly. After a quick glance of surprise at her, he replied:

"I think he will soon conquer Europe in toto, and be lord of the continent—for a while."

She glanced at him, then turned her eyes back on the road ahead.

"Then, when the day of reckoning sets in, he'll not want to admit defeat but will fight on to the bitter end, until he is conquered in his own Germany. This is sure to mean the death of millions of healthy and hopeful young men. But in the end, he will be conquered, although that may not be for a long, long time."

He turned again to checking through and reading more headlines, and an account of ships, and how fast they were being sunk off America's east coast. This attracted his attention and he immediately thought of her brother. He turned to glance at her as if to compare her with him. In some strange way which Wyeth was unable to understand, he pictured Heinrich as being associated with and responsible for many of the sinkings. He had a mental picture of Heinrich at that very hour, perhaps, gathering information regarding sailing dates and sending the information in some way to the commanders of the U-boat wolf packs lurking off our eastern shores.

Not only once, but many times, rescued seamen from sunken merchant ships, told the same story: that after they had been torpedoed, many of the commanders would surface their craft and call across to such of the crews as had survived the explosion and sinking, to inform them that they knew just when they had sailed, and knew when they would be coming along and that all they had to do was just be patient and wait, which they had done, and that they would then laugh and order their craft to submerge.

Meanwhile, at the Schultz apartment on Sugar Hill in Harlem, Heinrich had a visitor. It was Schiller, with whom he was in heated debate with at the moment regarding the war.

"Well," said Hans, cheerfully, a big smile of satisfaction lighting his face. "It looks like everything is all over but the shouting," and felt greatly cheered. "As I see it, it'll be impossible for this country to replace enough of the ships that our U-boats are sinking, in time to defeat Hitler. It just can't be done," he cried, convinced in his own estimation that it could not be and rose to his feet and walked up and down for a few minutes. This was Schiller's way. A restless and determined person, he was estimating the progress of the war and felt sure that Hitler would win it.

"Perhaps not," said Heinrich, "but they're sure going to try like hell. I've been looking in on all their efforts from the state of Maine to the Virginia capes, and I have never seen such feverish activity. If the Fuehrer beats them, he'll have to start doing it in a mighty big hurry, and go like hell before those thousands of ships they have set to building, go sliding down the ways."

This annoyed Schiller, and he started walking again, back and forth, up and down, presently paused.

"You mean, ship building?"

"I didn't mean skiffs. Also every other kind of building that will produce goods with which to shoot at Hitler."

"Well, that's what you think. Germany's won the war and all that's left to do is for the United Nations to sue for peace and stop the slaughter and the losses while there's still something left for them to start over again with." He started to walking the floor again impatiently, then pausing, turned and pointing a finger at Heinrich, cried:

"Getting back to what we were talking about, Heinrich—sinking ships off the east coast here. At the rate they are being sunk, how in hell are they ever going to catch up? Build as many as we are sinking?"

"At the rate our U-boats are sending them to the bottom, they'll finally develop a better measure of protection. They'll have to. This high rate of sinkings can't continue."

"Understand that they've decided to withdraw all oil tankers already. That'll burden the railroads which already are overloaded."

"The Herr Doctor was telling me," smiled Heinrich, "of how the commanders, contacting him via short wave, were laughing about how easy the tankers were to hit. They said that they could release a torpedo as far as three to five miles away—release them if they wanted to while still submerged, and hit one of those quarter-of-a-mile long fellows, with perfect ease. They say that it's like taking candy from a baby," and both laughed.

"Now there you are. What are they going to do about it?"

"You mean the shipping, the coastwise shipping?"

"That's what I mean. All their destroyers are tied up, convoying the ships going to England."

"That is why we have such a free hand on this side of the Atlantic. They haven't any destroyers to protect convoys, South—but they'll get some by and by and my little racket will play out. Besides, when I see this begin to happen. I've sense enough to turn to something else to mess matters up and make it hard for them."

"What do you have in mind?"

"I could manage to wreck a few trains. I've made a careful study of how. And by the time I've gotten around to it, I'll know better how," and Heinrich winked at Schiller and poured another glass of beer.

The former Mrs. Wingate, now Mrs. Kermit Early, living with her colored husband at a hacienda, far to the south of Buenos Aires in Patagonia, had been taken to the nearest hospital in that far off country and had given birth to a pair of twins, babies, a boy and a girl, and both she and Kermit were delighted.

As we return to them again in our story, she had left the hospital with a Spanish nurse to take care of the little ones, returned to the hacienda where they stayed another three months, then moved into Buenos Aires, where they had taken an apartment. At this time, with the children able to crawl around the floor, they were contemplating returning to America in a few months.

Meanwhile, Kermit was still determined to make his hate picture in some way and to begin to show it as quickly as this could be managed.

During his idle time in Buenos Aires, he hung around a motion picture studio, and met one, Werner Stoll, a German film director who at one time had been very popular in America and had directed several massive productions along with Ernst Lubitsch, and other German directors of that period. He recalled that at that time the Germans were considered the ace and most outstanding motion picture directors, and had turned out pictures that showed great genius.

He and Stoll became friends and he got around to telling Stoll his troubles and finally showed him his script, which Stoll read, liked and was enthusiastic about it. Incidentally, Stoll was a believer in Hitler's philosophy which included hating Jews. He even hated them more at the time he met Kermit because, controlling the great film industry in America, they had gradually pushed all the German film directors out of it with the single exception of Ernest Lubitsch. So what Early wanted to do, and implied that there were ample funds to do it with, interested Stoll and he came forward with a suggestion that proved interesting to Early.

"Now, Early," said Stoll, "you understand Negro psychology, don't you?"

"As well as any man in America. I've done nothing but study Negroes all my life. I sure know Negro psychology."

"Then you should go ahead and make this picture."

"But what about a director?"

"I'll direct it," said Stoll, and met Early's eyes squarely when he looked at him quickly, doubtfully.

"I can direct the picture—but *you* will direct me, understand?"

Early was quickly thoughtful. Of great intelligence, he began to see and understand what Stoll meant.

"You mean, that I—would act as a sort of—supervisor?"

"Exactly."

"That *is* an idea," replied Early, thoughtfully.

"If you followed pictures before talkies came, you can recall, and will agree, also, that the German directors were the best. Remember 'Metropolis', 'The Cabinet of Dr. Callagari', and some of the great pictures that starred Emil Jannings and others?"

"I sure do, and with few exceptions, they were tops. I was especially fond of going to see them."

"Those were the days, the days of great motion picture art and entertainment." He paused to sigh. "But the Jews felt they could direct. They pushed themselves into it. Commercial minded to the point that genius from the standpoint of art soon disappeared and the industry became so commercialized that it is sickening to think about it. Meantime, once a director, always one, and I'd like to do a picture. One with a lot of feeling as you have written into your script. If you are serious about making it, think it over."

"I'll do that, Stoll," cried Early, enthusiastically. "I'll talk it over with my wife right away and let you know."

Mrs. Early was not only agreeable, but enthusiastic. She still believed in Kermit. She was anxious to help him find his star.

"Your man Wyeth," said Stoll, the next time they talked together, would know what both you and I know, and wouldn't slow up the picture while you tried to make clear what you wanted. He'd know better than both of us exactly how to handle it, but give us a week or two longer and we can make the picture. Perhaps, just as good as Wyeth might have."

"I'm not so sure about that; but we'll do our best," said Early.

Six months later Early and Stoll had finished their picture in Hollywood at considerable cost, and Early, with his family at their apartment in New York, left Hollywood with prints and started to show it. Soon, race riots began to break out wherever it was shown.

CHAPTER **XL**

SIDNEY WYETH AND BERTHA SCHULTZ had completed their trip, which had been prolonged by Wyeth, not merely to keep Bertha from being returned any sooner than possible to where she would again come directly under the influence of her brother, but because they had developed such a complete measure of success, that staying out paid and paid well.

Wyeth's new book had become, to an appreciable degree, a best seller, and the demands from bookstores and other sources, required their attention and service in New York and, immediately following their return, they were compelled to enlarge their office space. Bertha, who by now knew as much about it as did Wyeth and Marie, became an executive and was given her own office and a stenographer.

Meanwhile, the war had been going its destructive way, but England and America, after meeting no end of disaster, defeats and loss of territory in the Pacific, which Japan had seized so quickly that it didn't seem possible, were at last beginning to see the light in the clearing.

Montgomery had stopped the "desert fox" at El Alamein. Not only had he stopped him when the whole world had expected the early fall of Alexandria and the capture of the Suez Canal, which Benito Mussolini had thrown Italy into the war to secure, but were expecting in due time, Cairo, further down the Nile, to capitulate.

Instead, after turning Rommel back at El Alamein, Montgomery's 8th army had fell upon the far flung legions of Adolf Hitler's African Corps, and chased them clear across North Africa, finally catching up with them and cornering them at Bizerte, where the entire army was forced to surrender. But Rommel escaped by plane to Italy, where Americans joined with the famous 8th army, to drive the Axis from Sicily, onto the famous boot, where after stalling them for months at Cassino, finally broke through, drove on north through

Rome, Florence and to the Po valley, and ultimately out of Italy to the never-to-be-forgotten Brenner Pass, where, once upon a time, two great dictators use to meet and make world history—until America got into the war, forced Italy to fire Mussolini, and then capitulate.

Meantime, Hitler's armies, which had swept across Russia, capturing the historic Ukraine where two great crops had been harvested and the grain sent back to the Reich to feed Germans, had been finally stalled at the gates of Stalingrad; Stalingrad on the Volga, where blood of men flowed like water, but where Adolf Hitler, after verging southward to the Caucasus Mountains and the rich oil fields of Southern Russia which he needed and wanted so badly, had stalled. After a prolonged stalemate, the tables were turned and what had been considered the greatest armies the world ever knew, were forced to retreat, a retreat that had not ended before the end of our story. But a retreat that drove Hitler back over the lands he had overrun, including the mighty steppes, the Cremea, the Ukraine, into Poland, over Bessarabia, into Roumania, which capitulated, reorganized under red control, and along with Bulgaria and Finland, turned to fight their former allies.

Meanwhile, D-day had come and gone. Led by Eisenhower, America and England had stormed across the channel, crawled upon the banks of France, and after a long stalemate in the Cherbourg peninsular, finally broke through, came in behind the mighty Atlantic Wall, from where Hitler with his secret weapon, was sending bats out of hell to kill and maim thousands of innocent women and children in Southern England. In a time so short that it must have shocked and surprised even Hitler himself, Paris had been liberated, most of France, Belgium, Luxembourg, a part of Holland and as our story is being written, the "holy" soil of Germany had been invaded, the first time in more than 100 years, when Napoleon had stormed across it to be turned back in Russia, where Hitler's retreat begun.

We have, however, drifted entirely away from the story we have set out to tell, which at this point concerned two characters, at work inside black America, which we will return to now and go on with the story.

Kermit Early and Heinrich Schultz had inspired, by the exhibition of their hate picture, one of the bloodiest and most vicious race riots in the history of America at Detroit where Americans fought Americans and many bled and died. Soldiers were rushed in from all over Michigan, to the humiliation of all loyal Americans, both black and white, who deplored the disgraceful outbreak. But hardly anybody, including the investigating committee, afterward, ever found out or how and where it all started, and what started it.

While all America was wondering about it, Early and Heinrich slipped quietly back into New York, where, after secretly and quietly exhibiting the films in halls and other spots in Harlem, on a quiet Sunday night, while all merchants were resting quietly at home over the weekend, stores locked and their merchandise obviously secure, a riot burst suddenly forth into flame and before enough policemen could be brought to the section to halt it, millions of dollars worth of merchandise, mostly Jewish owned was stolen and destroyed. Almost every plate glass window in Harlem was broken, streets and sidewalks were littered with what an hour or two before, had been merchandise, with what was left.

For some peculiar reason, thousands of apparently peaceful and law abiding Negroes had turned to vandalism, and wrecked the whole section so completely until it was hardly recognizable. Yet, nobody to this day can say truthfully why it happened. But Kermit Early and Heinrich Schultz knew why, however.

There was another person who also knew, and that person was Mrs. Kermit Early. She had been growing apathetic as regards her husband's activities for some time, and noted with alarm that the results being achieved from exhibition of his hate picture, while highly satisfactory to the subversive elements with whom Kermit was allied and had been working with for a long time, was not to the best interest of America itself, as she saw it. She considered that she was still an American, even if she had married a Negro.

She got into her car and drove through Lenox, Seventh, Eighth Avenues and 145th, 125th and 116th Streets after the outbreak and when she returned to her apartment, she decided that what she had seen was not Americanism as she had visualized it all her life.

A few weeks later Kermit Early took charge of a struggling Negro magazine, became its editor and publisher and retired from subversive activities, and so his wife and he pass out of the picture and our story. Mrs. Early had "taken over" completely.

After losing the cooperation of his ace assistant, Heinrich drifted westward, turning his evil genius very successfully to wrecking trains, ending up in Chicago, which he made his headquarters while he worked out more plans to sabotage the war effort. It was in Chicago that he met and became friendly later, with a private car porter by the name of James Watson.

Tall and handsome, with pretty hair, a well met disposition, a part of his procedure, and with ample Nazi funds in his pocket, Heinrich soon became a favorite in the Negro sections of the Southside. Soon band leaders at every night club put on specials when told that Schultz was in the audience. He decided that that would be the best spot from which to gather information to specialize in wrecking trains, and was soon in the confidence of no end of porters and waiters, and from the porters, especially, he was able to gather information regarding movements of important persons connected with the war effort, and it was through and from Watson, that he learned that the Secretary of War, of the Navy, the Chief of Staff and other important officials were due in Chicago at an early date, and would go west from Chicago on Porter Watson's car, attached to the Pacific Coast Limited on their way to San Francisco. So Heinrich immediately set out to court Watson's confidence, and unconscious cooperation.

Watson had a very pretty girl friend. And, like most colored girls when a tall, handsome man with good hair, enters a picture, she began to make a cunning play for Heinrich. Unfortunately for her, however, a still more beautiful friend of hers, who shared her apartment, felt the same way about Heinrich, and didn't hesitate to start making passes at the handsome Lochinvar.

Both knew lots of porters, and since Heinrich for no reason that they understood, and made no effort to understand, seemed very fond of porters, mostly, of course, Pullman Car Porters, they proceeded to introduce him around. All the porters running to the Pacific coast, would alternate into and out of Chicago about once a week, then they would have several days' lay over and during such times, Heinrich was able to meet many, and find out even more about who they were hauling.

Watson was a very cheerful fellow with a big mouth, much bigger he was to find out in due time, than it should have been, for his own safety—and that of his country. Watson was sociable—and talked, freely; told everything he knew. Heinrich listened with keen interest, to everything he said, interposing a question now and then. So in the language and slang of Negroes, Watson spilled his "guts".

Soon, Heinrich knew more about the war officers' trip westward than Watson himself. At a point, Heinrich raised his hand and said:

"While passing through Iowa, on the way from the Pacific coast a long time ago, I recall crossing one of the highest bridges I ever saw."

"That's on the Northwestern," cried Watson. "Sho. We cross it on the way to Omaha, just west of Boone, Iowa, over the Coon River."

"Over the Coon River, eh?"

"Sho. About ten miles West of Boone."

"It is sure one high bridge," said Heinrich reminiscently.

"Said to be the highest in the world." replied Watson. "Over 100 feet from the bridge to the river. So high that all trains slow to twenty miles an hour when they cross it."

"It that so?"

"Sho is, brother. I'm the one who knows. You'll find me a man who is informed. I can tell you about every Railroad in America, especially west and South.

"So these high officials will be passing over that bridge if they go west to the coast?"

"Sho. But I haven't told you the whole story," said Watson, swelling with pride.

"No, Watson?"

"Naw, man. Dey asked fo' me through the office. Dey told old Giltzow to hold me in reserve or dey would go over another railroad. So old A. W. sends fo' me and told dem not to sign me out on any other car, but to hold me in reserve for this special party of nuthin' but big men."

"They know a good man, Watson," said Heinrich, patting his shoulder. "In the meantime, I'm due to go to Omaha soon and I'll plan the trip so that I can go on the same train that hauls your car."

"Why not do that, boy? We'll have a good time all the way to

Omaha. Plenty good food, good whiskey, nothing but Scotch. Wish you was going all the way to the coast."

"Sorry I won't be."

Heinrich decided then and there to go to Omaha, beforehand, stop off at Boone, go out to the high bridge, and study for his own benefit, the best way to handle a delicate situation.

The next day he took an earlier train to Boone where all trains except the Streamliners change engines and crews. Most trains remain there for ten to twenty minutes, but the streamliners from only five to ten.

He carefully checked the Pacific Coast Limited into Boone, and out of Boone to the high bridge, which took exactly eleven minutes. It was one minute later when the train reached the center of the structure, where you looked straight down into the Coon river, which seemed like a small rivulet, it was that far away from the bridge.

He made a pencil note of everything and observed that after the train reached the west end of the bridge, the engineer pushed the speed forward and after it hit the level country west of the river, went up to near a hundred miles an hour, retaining that rate of speed right into Council Bluffs, on the Iowa side of the Missouri, directly across from Omaha.

He took a day train the next morning back from Omaha, and viewed the bridge more carefully, noting that there was a high grade on either side at the approach of the bridge.

In Boone he hired a Taxi to take him to a small town just across the river, to view the bridge from the highway and while they were passing through the valley of the river, a train passed over the bridge. It looked like a toy, it was so high above him.

Returning to Boone by the same taxi, he double checked on it, mentally, and when he took the next train from Boone back to Chicago, he had all the information that he needed, and decided to wreck the Pacific Coast Limited the night it passed over that bridge with the Chief of Staff and other high officials of the government, including both the Secretary of War and of the Navy.

His plan was a simple one, depending for success on everything working out according to plans.

As a precaution, he decided to reserve a seat to Omaha on the

Pacific Coast Limited for three consecutive nights. The night before the scheduled night of destruction, the night of and the night after. So in case a quick change was made and the party went one night sooner, or one night later than scheduled, he would be in position to put over his act, nevertheless.

He planned to get off at the first stop, if the car was not picked up the first night. Since the movement of these high officials was an army secret, Watson explained, they would board the car at the Austin Avenue passenger yards, and the Limited would pick the car up as it passed through the yards after leaving the Northwestern Station downtown. So all Heinrich had to do was to check on the activity of the train when it passed through those yards. If it stopped and he heard a car bump the train from the rear, he'd know to shape his plans to wreck it after it left Boone, three hundred and fifty miles westward.

If it failed to stop at the yards as it passed the first night, then he could and would leave the train at Oak Park and return via the elevated railroad to Chicago, and would not have to be bored with a journey westward without any purpose.

Checking into his scheme further, he conceived a plan for placing the time bomb, in Watson's car, concealed if he had a chance, or left under a table or a seat, or anywhere he could secrete it.

He observed that all trains, as Watson said they would, slowed to twenty miles an hour while crossing over the bridge, which seemed like walking after racing up to it from 50 to 80 miles an hour.

His plans were to visit with Watson in the private car until after reaching Boone, set the clock to explode 12 minutes after leaving the town, which should set it off near the center of the bridge. He would try to secrete the bomb over the trucks of the car, and depend on the concussion to bounce the trucks off the track, thereby wrecking the entire train and not just blowing up a single car.

The fact that it might kill more than one hundred innocent persons, made planning it more interesting to Heinrich. That was a part of the philosophy Adolf Hitler had taught him during his youth training. So the more people killed, the more successful would his efforts be regarded by the subversive groups and the many agents, engaged in all kinds of sabotage efforts in America.

He had checked the embankment leading to the bridge and saw

that when the train slowed before reaching the bridge, all he had to do was to open a vestibule door, jump off and roll down the embankment to safety, then get to his feet and wait for the explosion.

He then set out to play Watson and his two girl friends to the limit by putting on a big party, making the popular night spots, and finding out anything else he wanted to know from Watson.

In all the maneuvering to gather information that Heinrich had engaged in, during which he was perhaps responsible for sending more than one hundred American merchantmen to the bottom, on the east coast, he found it popular to be free with funds. The National Socialist party had seen to that before he left Germany, so money was no object.

Anybody but Negroes would have, in time perhaps, grown suspicious at such cheerful spending, and begin to ask where he got so much to spend. But Negroes rarely, if ever, concern themselves with where anybody gets money, or how. All they concern themselves about is, if they have it—and spend it. If you spend it you're a good fellow and you have the key to their homes and hearts. So Heinrich had it and Heinrich spent it; and Heinrich was popular.

He was handsome into the bargain, with soft, pretty slightly blond hair, which in itself was unusual. There are few Negro blonds. Instead, they refer to all such Negroes as "marinny" darkies.

Not only did Heinrich blow them to a big party one week before Watson was to play host aboard the private car to the highest officials in the United States Army, but when they arrived at the apartment, he made each girl a present of a crisp, new $50.00 bill—and that finished it. The girl he stayed with almost wore him out that night trying to demonstrate her gratitude.

He insisted the next morning, that since he might not be around Chicago much longer, that they put on another big party the night before he and Watson left to go west, to which, of course, agreement was unanimous. To be sure that nothing would interfere with his plans, he suggested taking the girls downtown the afternoon before to do "a little shopping", to dinner afterward, and then to the Regal Theatre where one of the big colored bands would be playing, then to the Club De Lysia for a final party.

While Heinrich, as we have shown, was busy preparing to wreck the great Pacific Coast Limited, with more than a hundred human beings aboard, for the cause of their Fuehrer, let us now turn again to his sister, Bertha, sent to America at the same time her brother arrived, but who had been almost won over to a new philosophy as inspired by the man to whom she was now engaged, and prayed that the war could get over with, and leave her free, whereupon she would marry Sidney Wyeth and continue on in America indefinitely.

In the movement of events, she had almost become lost in the shuffle and had not been called on to engage in any subversive activity for so long that she hoped she was forgotten. She was happy in the work she was doing, and still happier as the sweetheart of Sidney Wyeth, who took her frequently to shows, the best pictures, to dinner, and in long drives out on Long Island, or north to the Catskills and now and then up into the Adirondacks.

As to the war, as she now viewed it, with Hitler's retreat from Stalingrad, bloody Stalingrad, back through the Ukraine, into Poland and with the Red armies pouring into Silesia and Eastern Germany, while the Allied armies, having freed France, Belgium, the Netherlands and Luxembourg, and now charging across the Siegfried line into Western Germany, she could picture nothing but ultimate defeat; possibly, unconditional surrender.

But freedom for Bertha Schultz was not to come so easily. For as Germany drew nearer and nearer to collapse, with the armies of the allies converging on them from all sides, the Fuehrer and his cohorts grew more ruthless and seemed bent on destroying as much of the world as they could reach before the inevitable collapse overtook them.

They had conceived and were sending daily and almost nightly, bats out of hell over Southern England and London, killing and maiming thousands of helpless and innocent non-combatants, and were, as they neared the bitter end of their folly, planning more methods of ruthless and terrible destruction to European mankind.

In complete sympathy with their efforts, and planning to add to the orgy of death and destruction wherever they could, his agents were planning schemes to upset and shake America to its foundations.

In charge of these plans, advancing and concocting more, was, of course, none other then Doctor Gustave Von Barwig and Hans Schiller, Heinrich's good friend.

Seated across from each other in the Herr Doctor's suite, high up on the top floor of a large downtown hotel, about this time, the Doctor scanned a number of Negro papers that Schiller had brought in, having purchased them during a trip to Harlem where Heinrich had written him from Chicago to go and check on something of interest to the group.

"The president's wife," observed Von Barwig, raising his eyes to Schiller, "seems to be very fond of traveling around the country, speaking to colored people."

"I'm told that she is very fair to them," said Schiller, drawing away at a cigarette and glancing at one of the papers he had brought in.

"So I see," said the Herr Doctor, with a strange cunningness developing around his eyes. "I see by this paper, where's she's to meet and speak to them very shortly at the Golden Gate Ball Room in Harlem."

"Yah," said Schiller, in German. In fact, when alone, they always talked in German.

"So I observe," said Von Barwig. "Now, if something should happen to the president's wife during one of her trips to speak to colored people, for instance, it would give the people of America, and in England, something to talk about."

"And something to think about, also," suggested Schiller, cunningly.

"Yah," Von Barwig went on, thoughtfully. "With the papers full of news about colored people, strikes in plants when they dare to up a few, or try to advance a few into better positions. Now if the president's wife should—be assassinated during one of these trips to speak to colored people, it would make sensational news."

"Both here and in England. She is, as you know, Herr Doctor, a very good friend of the queen of England."

"A *very* good friend, and also of the king. So if something should happen to her, as stated, and she should suddenly—quit breathing, blown to atoms by one of our bombs, it would be—most sensational news, eh, Hans?"

"They'd feel like killing a lot of Negroes if it should happen."

"I see by this paper," said Von Barwig, looking at a news headline, "that the Southern white people are demanding the continuance of 'White Supremacy', during the war, and after. If, as stated, something should happen to the president's wife while speaking to a hall filled with Negroes—" and he broke off and raised his eyes to smile, cunningly. Hans greeted his smile with another fully as cunning.

"Just how could something *be made* to happen, Herr Doctor?" inquired Schiller, naively.

"If one of our adherents should venture to 'turn the trick,' some one who hasn't done anything for the cause for a long time."

"Like Heinrich's sister, Bertha, for instance."

"Yah, Bertha hasn't done anything for the cause for a long, long time, if I remember correctly."

"She has never done anything."

"Most regrettable, most regrettable, indeed, Hans. Why have you permitted such neglect; such gross neglect?"

"Well, I've sort of left that to Heinrich."

"Heinrich has done well—enough for both, perhaps, but his sister took the same oath to our Fuehrer, at the same time as did Heinrich. Now since she has been so neglectful, why not put her on *this* job?"

"Why not?" agreed Hans.

"She ought to be able, without attracting any suspicion, to get close enough to the president's wife when she comes to this Golden Gate Ball Room to speak, to—"

"—toss a little pineapple, maybe . . ." and Hans laughed, a cold, hard and diabolical laugh. Von Barwig smiled naively.

"Just *what is* the girl doing, that she hasn't been around for some time to help the cause along?"

"Understand she works in a Negro publishing house up in Harlem."

"Works in a publishing house, eh? Well, she's a very thoroughly educated girl. She should be well fitted to work in a publishing house. Who runs the business?"

"Belongs to a fellow by the name of Wyeth."

"Wyeth?" the Herr Doctor repeated, thoughfully. "Where have I heard that name before?"

"From Heinrich and me. He was the fellow whom Heinrich and Early tried so hard to get to direct Early's picture." Von Barwig struck the table so hard and loud that the glasses trembled.

"That's it! Thought it sounded familar. So he's the guy whom they tried to get to direct the picture—and he ran out on them, eh? Must be a Jew lover."

"He insisted that he didn't hate **Jews**, and repeatedly refused to make the picture."

"So he loves Jews, eh?'

"I didn't say that, Herr Doctor," corrected Schiller. "I said he didn't hate Jews."

"Why doesn't he? He should. Everybody should hate Jews."

"Getting back to Bertha. If you want to contact her, that's where you'll find her. At Wyeth's office."

"The way matters are going," and Von Barwig frowned as he said it, "our cause needs some headlines."

"If we get somebody to assassinate the president's wife, that'll mean headlines, plenty of headlines," smiled Schiller. Von Barwig grunted, and then laughed deep down in his fat belly like it rather hurt him to laugh.

"Headlines all over the world—and what headlines!" and Von Barwig laughed some more, deep now and loudly, and then as suddenly he calmed, eyes narrowed, turned to Schiller.

"A nice little bomb, with even more explosive power than the one they planted to try to blow our Fuehrer into hades, but missed, which will make the results more sure. Just tossed very lightly to fall at her feet. If it falls within many feet of her, it'll be all the same, of course," and Von Barwig held back his laugh this time by laying a hand on his belly.

"The Junkers mis-planned our Fuehrer's demise. That was it, mis-planning," said Schiller.

"We don't intend to mis-plan this one. Somebody must be present in the hall and toss it. That's the sure way. No mis-planning, oh, no."

"Because the Junkers mis-planned, our Fuehrer has lived to do some planning of his own for another day."

"It happens to be very—fortunate that Bertha is a—colored girl. That makes it much better."

"If we sent a white person, they might get—suspicious," said Hans.

"They might, Hans. That was the first thing I thought of when the idea popped into my fat head."

"A nice looking colored girl like Bertha, would attract attention only because she is so pretty."

"She *is* a pretty girl, isn't she," said Von Barwig, thoughtfully. "Lucky for us. Nobody would expect a pretty girl like her to go tossing bombs."

"Nobody would expect *any* colored person to toss a bomb. In all the history of America, no Negro has ever done anything—rational, or shouldn't irrational fit better," and again both laughed.

"I suppose we can count on this girl? I mean, she is —loyal? Even though she has been—out of circulation, as it were, for some time. She wouldn't dare refuse, run out on us, is what I mean."

"I'm sure she's loyal. Our Fuehrer taught all the subjects to be loyal. To them, 'death, their is no sting', when it is for the cause."

"Good, Hans," said Von Barwig. "That is very good. If she is duly loyal, and the—explosion does not—'rub' her out, as they put it in America, she might live on; she might even escape, with our assistance, for we must have a sufficient number of the faithful, scattered about the hall to help, or at least try to help the poor child escape. Of course, should Bertha, after permitting herself to become so inveigled with this man, Wyeth, refuse or try to run out, one of our boys will have to—you understand," and he smiled blandly.

"I understand full well, Herr Doctor. In the meantime, I remember that Heinrich told me the last time he was here, that he thought his sister had fallen in love with this man Wyeth. Think he said that they even planned to—get married after the war."

"Oh, she is taking liberties! Falling in love with an—American pig. A black pig. The nerve of her. Planning to marry him—after the war, eh?"

"I'm sure that's what Heinrich told me."

"The fact that she's put it off until after the war, sounds like she has considered her pledge; the pledge we all took before leaving the fatherland. I hope she is still faithful. We all dedicated our service—and our lives, if that be necessary to give up, for the cause, first last and until death to the Fuehrer and the Third Reich, God being our helper." He paused to shove his right hand forward now.

"Heil Hitler!"

"Heil Hitler!"

This over, both then drank deeply of their beer and, turning to Hans, Von Barwig ordered:

"Well, Hans locate this girl, and when you have, tell her to get right down here and see me. I've got something for her to do, and I don't mean maybe."

He got up then, and picking up the papers, crossed the room and put them in a locker, turned and came back to where Hans had stood up and was waiting for him.

"Heinrich told me that since the white people refuse to take the Negro seriously, nobody is expecting anything to happen to anybody when they come to Harlem to speak."

"That makes it easy, so I'm going to sit down and work this thing out carefully, and plan just how to put it over—big. We've got to figure every movement out in the most minute detail. When she is due at the hall, have the girl, if possible, sitting right on one of the front seats where she has only to take one or two steps forward, toss the pineapple—and that should be the end of America's First Lady," he ended, sneeringly. Then both laughed and, turning, Von Barwig crossed the room with Schiller. At the door, he paused for a last word.

"You need not, of course, tell the girl what I want to see her about."

"I understand."

"Just saunter into the office nonchalantly, and when alone with her, tell her that I want to see her and let it go at that."

Schiller left the room then and Von Barwig went to a table, sat down and began to check deeper into his plans for the assassination of America's First Lady.

CHAPTER **XLI**

BERTHA AND WYETH had tickets to go see a big musical show on Broadway on the Monday night following Von Barwig's instructions and it was late that afternoon that Marie Coleman looked up, on hearing the door open, to see a white man, whom she had seen once before enter the office and glance around. For some reason that she could not immediately understand, she had not liked the man's looks when she saw him the first time, when he came to the office with Heinrich Schultz and Kermit Early. For some peculiar reason, which she was less able to understand at this time, she still didn't like his looks.

He greeted her, raised his hat, and inquired regarding Miss Schultz.

"Be seated," she said, pointing to a chair, "I'll call her." He obeyed with a "Thank you," and sat down, looked around, and then lighted a cigarette.

Near Bertha's office door, Marie paused and turning back, walked over to him and said: "The name, please?"

"Oh, sure," cried Schiller, rising quickly to his feet, started to reach in his pocket, then smiling regretfully. "Sorry that I don't happen to have a card, but the name is Schiller. Mr. Hans Schiller. She'll understand."

Marie thanked him and started across the room to Bertha's door again, recalling as she did so that she had heard Schultz call him Hans and Schiller both when he was in the office before.

She knocked lightly on Bertha's door. She could hear Bertha dictating a letter to the stenographer, and just before she knocked, she heard her close it. She followed her knock by entering and met the stenographer on the way out with her note book and pencil. Closing the door behind the typist, she turned to Bertha, who was standing now, looking at her curiously.

"Yes, dear?" said Bertha as she came up.

"A Mr. Hans Schiller to see you," she said, waving in his direction with her right hand. Bertha started, and frowned visibly. Crossing to the door, cracked it and peeped out at Hans, waiting for her. She closed the door and paused to think a moment while Marie waited. Presently she crossed to leave Bertha's office and that brought Bertha back to her presence. She started, and then smiled. She had, in that second, thought so much about Schiller, and what he was calling to see her about, that she had forgotten Marie's presence.

As Marie came up, she stepped aside and thanking her, said:

"Send him in, please." Marie bowed and opened the door. Bertha crossed back to her desk and sitting down, was facing the door when Hans entered a moment later.

Recalling that he and her brother were closely associated and had known each other back in Germany, and while she was very annoyed at having him call, she realized that he had perhaps been sent, so she decided to do her best to be agreeable and courteous. Rising up after he entered her office, and coming forward to meet him, she stretched out her hand and cried, in her best German:

"Ach, Herr Schiller, I am glad to see you again," and grasped the hand that he extended. After exchanging greetings, she invited him to be seated, and moved a chair near to hers, waved him to it, then sat down herself and turned to face him with a forced smile and a forced cheerfulness.

They exchanged some more formalities, and talked about her brother. She told him, which of course they already knew, that he was in Chicago. In fact, they knew much more than Bertha did about Heinrich and what he was doing in Chicago, and were in telephonic conversation with him almost daily. In fact, Heinrich had long since quit talking to or telling Bertha anything regarding his sabotage activities, and in truth Bertha really knew little if anything about what he was doing.

Looking around the office presently, Hans turned to her and smiling. "You seem to be fixed up very comfortably," he said, and looked at her large, new desk; at the comfortable office chair she was sitting in.

"Thank you," replied Bertha, pleasantly. "I like it."

"You should. I'm inclined to envy you," at which Bertha smiled, deprecatingly, and wished he would tell her what he was there to see her about. She was on the anxious seat, so anxious, in fact, that she was nervous.

"Do you just—work here," he went on. "Or do you—have an interest in the—business?"

"Oh, just work here, Hans. That's all. Helping them out for the present," she said, causually.

"I see," said Hans, carelessly, but watching him, she was sure that she caught a slightly evil glint in his eye. "In the meantime, I won't take up much more of your time."

"Oh, that is all right, Hans. Glad to see you again."

"And I am to see you, Bertha. Haven't seen you downtown or heard anything from you for so long that we've been wondering what happened."

"Nothing in particular, as you see," she said, apologetically, and made a little gesture with her hand. "I want to apologize for my neglect to drop by or run in more often, however. But I am all right, as you see."

"Still ready for—any service in the cause, I suppose," he said, as if feeling her out. She hesitated very briefly before replying, during which delay his face clouded visibly.

"Of course, Hans. Always ready to serve our Fuehrer; always glad to be of any service to the Reich."

"Good," cried Schiller, promptly and seemed relieved.

"Have you—something in mind, Hans?" she asked, testily.

"Me, oh, not me, but the boss has."

"Oh," echoed Bertha, and her heart fell. She had a sudden and peculiar premonition. She had an ugly vision. "Well," to herself, "What is it?" He was talking.

"The Herr Doctor has some plans, so he sent me up to see you and tell you to come down and see him—real soon, if possible."

"I see," said Bertha, evenly, steeling her nerves for the worst. "When?"

"Well, if it isn't too much trouble, he'd like to see you—tonight, maybe." He was looking hard at her now and his eyes were as cold as steel through the pretended smile and ease on his face. He did not take them off her, so she was afraid to frown, to even think. The Bertha that Wyeth knew and loved, suddenly faded from view, and the Nazi Bertha took its place and her face became hard and cold to meet the situation she knew she was in now. While she was still the human Bertha, she started to tell him that she had an engagement that night. She knew, however, that if she said that, it would make it bad for her. The Fuehrer came first.

"Very well. Where?"

"The same place. His hotel."

"What time, I mean, at what hour?"

"Nine o'clock. There will be others there when you arrive."

"Very well, Hans." She stood up now and if they had been where nobody could hear them, they would have exchanged the salute: "Heil Hitler!" As it was, they exchanged a silent one with the raising and stretching out of hands in the usual way, then turning, both in a goose-step like way, they crossed to the door, where Bertha put her hand on the knob, but before opening the door, she repeated:

"The hotel, at nine o'clock. I'll be there. Good day."

"Good day, Miss Schultz," he said in English, and stepped outside. She followed and opened the reception room door leading into the hall, and bowing to each other again, he left. Bertha closed the door behind him. Marie was listening to his footsteps go down the hall outside. Bertha turned from the door and paused thoughtfully, seemingly unaware of Marie's presence until she looked up and upon seeing her, forced a sweet smile, and turning went back to her office, closing the door behind her.

Her action was not lost on Marie, however, who knew without being told, for, of course, there was nobody to tell her anything, that Schiller's visit meant Bertha no good.

She heard no sound in Bertha's office after she went back in there, and she had a vision of Bertha in the throes of sudden unhappiness. She knew that she had restrained much happiness out of deference to what she had been sent to America to do. She had never gone in for a good time completely, and she was ever sorry for her, for she knew that Bertha wanted to.

Now, after feeling that she might be let alone for the duration, after which she would be free, she is suddenly the recipient of a visit and certain instructions, which she knew would not add to the girl's happiness.

This was confirmed a few moments late when Bertha came out of her office with her coat and hat on, dressed to leave. She crossed to Marie and talked.

"Mr. Wyeth and I were to attend a stage show downtown tonight, but I've just been called to meet somebody that I cannot refuse to meet or put off. So will you please tell him that I cannot, and that I will see him—you both, tomorrow morning," and she forced a smile with much effort. "Please get word to him about this, for I fear that he has purchased the tickets already. If you can reach him in time, he might be able to use the tickets. Maybe he'll—take you," and she tried to force another little smile, behind which Marie saw misery, deep and serious. When she spoke, it was with an effort to cheer Bertha.

"Mr. Wyeth wouldn't be interested in taking anybody but you, dear. However, I'll see that the tickets are not wasted. I'll take my mother, thank you," and she smiled, got up, saw Bertha to the door, and after closing it behind her, listened to her footsteps disappear down the hallway.

Promptly at nine o'clock that night, Bertha was waiting in the lobby of the hotel to see Von Barwig, and a few minutes later followed a bell boy along the hallway upstairs to Von Barwig suite.

Von Barwig himself admitted her and was very profuse as he welcomed her on entering.

"I'm very glad to see you, Miss Schultz," he said, extending his fat hand which she took, pretending to be glad to see him, also.

"I'll thank you to follow me into the next room," and took her arm, graciously and led her across the heavily carpeted reception room, opened another door and before her eyes, seated around a large table was a group of other agents, some of whom she had met, others that she had seen.

All stood and bowed graciously to her as Von Barwig proceeded to introduce each one. While he talked to her in English in the reception room, he was now talking in German and she answered in the same. All the conversation that followed while she was there was in German, and after the smiles that were exchanged during the time he was introducing her, all became serious now and looked very solemn while Von Barwig, after seating her, proceeded with the business of the meeting.

He made a very lengthy and eloquent speech leading up to the mission they had selected for her to go on, and he went to considerable length to explain and show their justification. Then after a "Heil Hitler" with all shoving their hands forward, he turned to Bertha.

"We were compelled to select you, Miss Schultz, because you are the only one of us who could get close enough to her up there in Harlem and not arouse suspicion."

Bertha was naturally shocked when she heard what they had selected her to do and was too dazed afterwards to do anything but listen, stupified, but still understood full well what it was all about.

"The time is here when the enemies of the Reich need to be shocked to their foundations. I realize that we have imposed a great responsibility on you; an effort that may imprison you if you are caught, for the rest of your life—you may even be electrocuted. But when you consider how much blood has been spilt by our brave country, hundreds of thousands of the best young men in our land dead, on account of our enemies, you will appreciate that no sacrifice on the part of any of us, even if it costs us our lives, is too great to make to injure and destroy our enemies when it can be done. This war, as you know, and the world knows, but, of course, refuses to admit, was forced on us. This is therefore a fight to preserve our very existence. It will be said, 'In what way will assassinating a woman help your cause?' But we feel otherwise. Our enemies, through traitors in our own country, tried to assassinate our dear Fuehrer, didn't they? And had they surceeded, the whole world, outside of our associates, would have rejoiced, especially in England and America, wouldn't they? Had this attempt been successful, it would have called for the greatest holiday on their parts of all times.

"Now we will give them something to feel unhappy about, something to shock and humiliate them, something for them to think about. And it will be up to you, Miss Schultz, to do this deed for the everlasting benefit of your fatherland, and our brave and beloved Fuehrer." So saying he pushed forth his heavy hand and led off:

"Heil Hitler," which was followed by all those around the table, including poor Bertha.

"Heil Hitler, Heil Hitler, Heil Hitler!"

It was near midnight, when dazed and bewildered, with everything seeming vague and far away, that Bertha left the hotel and tried to find her way back to Harlem and home. She took the wrong train and found herself away out on Long Island instead of Sugar Hill, and had to get out at Forest Hills, come back to 7th avenue and 52nd street, where with much effort, for she was so depressed, downcast, frightened and hopeless that she felt she would be better off if she could just die.

A brave girl, she forced the unhappy mission imposed on her out of her mind as best she could, in which she was not successful at all, but finally retired, to roll and toss until daylight when she fell into a deep and troubled sleep.

While at Von Barwig's suite in the hotel, she had been shown and given the local colored papers, and the New York editions of the out of town ones, all of which headlined the fact that the President's wife would speak at the Golden Gate Ballroom the following Tuesday, and gave much space to the occasion. Before retiring, she had spread them on the table and then forgot about them.

All she could think of was the proposed assassination. "Seven more nights to live," ran through her mind, over and over again, all through the long night that followed. "Seven nights to live—and then." She was in a blind alley, and all around her were high walls through which and over which she could see nothing.

For the first time since it all started and she had started for Genoa, Italy, to take passage for America, she frowned when she thought of Adolf Hitler. And yet, she could do nothing but acquiesce, which she had done without objection or hesitation. When she thought about the person she had been selected to assassinate, she cried out loud.

The First Lady had been severely criticised all over the South because of her views regarding the Negro. She had shown the Negro more appreciation and encouragement than all the other presidents' wives combined. And of all the women and men in America, they had chosen to assassinate her, just because such a tragedy would shock the allied nations, and condemn the Negro in the eyes of America, which they had not thought of and would not have cared about if they had thought of it.

Before she finally fell off to sleep, she found herself debating suicide. She would rather die, she knew, than commit such an act—but she was committed to perform the nefarious task. As an individual, she did not count or matter, so to commit suicide was no way out according to Nazi philosophy. At daylight, in this troubled and mortified state of mind, and as stated, she had fallen into a deep and troubled sleep.

When Bertha failed to show up by ten thirty the next morning, Wyeth called Marie into his office.

"I didn't like the looks of that old white man when he came into the office," she said, in answer to the question he asked her, and frowned.

"You say," said Wyeth, "that he was an—old man?"

"Oh, no, I didn't mean that he was actually old. Fact is, he wasn't old at all, but I had a feeling when I saw him that it meant trouble for Bertha—and it did. In years he was a young man."

Wyeth sighed, and drummed on the desk with the knuckles of his hand. Presently he looked up. She was still standing.

"Sit down, Marie," he cried, impatiently, and then sighed. He was very much upset.

"Don't jump to conclusions, but take it easy."

"I'm worried," she said, obeying. "It isn't like Bertha to stay away, unless something has happened. She's always on time, here before I arrive, you and—in fact, she's the first one to arrive every morning. And now," she went on, glancing at her watch, "it's after eleven and not a word."

"Did you happen to—overhear them talking while he was here, while he was in her office? Maybe if you can recall what they talked about, that might give us some idea what took place."

"I overheard them talking all the while he was in there—but they talked in German. Naturally—"

"—you didn't know what it was all about. I understand."

"Supposing that I call her up," suggested Marie, starting to rise, but Wyeth waved her down.

"Not right now. Let me think about it for a while. Meanwhile, I've met this Schiller once or twice and seen him around with Heinrich several times. Like you, I didn't like his eye—but I guess that's because of what he's doing. It isn't Schiller who's done this—whatever it is, however. It's somebody higher up. That somebody possibly sent Schiller here to ask Bertha to come down and see or meet with some of them. The fact that she had to cancel our theatre engagement makes it evident that she had to go meet them last night.

Beyond that, it is all a mystery. A mystery that we've got to solve if we can, in order to save Bertha.

"It is my opinion that they have planned something," he said, pausing briefly, then went on: "Something sensational which doesn't mean this country, or Bertha, any good. Sabotage is perhaps the word for it."

"Sabotage!" exclaimed Marie, and jumped to her feet. Again he waved her down and she sat down again, but very much disturbed.

"Take it easy, Marie."

"But sabotage. You mean—to—blow up something, maybe?"

"Maybe something, or somebody, even."

"Maybe the president."

Wyeth shook his head. "Not him. They couldn't get that close to him. Somebody else or something of value. I can't guess which, but something I'd be willing to bet."

"I still think you ought to let me call her up. She might have been taken ill, even."

"Bertha is not ill. My conviction is that she is home and so upset that she doesn't know what to do and I'm thinking about going to her." He stood up then, and went on.

"In fact, that's exactly what I'm going to do—and right away," and he started toward the door. She rose up and met him while he was coming around from behind the desk.

"Just a minute, Mr. Wyeth." He paused and looked down on her, his face impatient.

"Even if you find her when you get there, she'll never tell you."

"I suppose not, but I'm going to do the best I can," and he turned and crossed the reception room. Marie followed him. He paused and turned as she came up.

"Whatever it is, it must have thrown her all out of sort—upset her so that she must be sick. She's got lots of will power. In fact, she's a brave girl, but I'll not soon forget the expression on her face when I went in there yesterday and told her who it was that wanted to see her."

"She has always declared that she was not free and would not be until the war was over—and maybe not then, but I've hoped for the best," said Wyeth.

"If you don't come back very soon and have a chance to phone, please do so," said Marie. "I won't be happy until I've heard something. I've got a nasty feeling, away down in the bottom of my stomach. Until I hear something I'll continue to expect the worst."

"If I'm not back in an hour, I'll try to call you," said Wyeth, and left the office.

After Wyeth left the office, Marie, in her anxiety regarding Bertha, walked over by the window and looked down into the street. She saw him cross the sidewalk, get into the car and drive away in the direction of Sugar Hill where Bertha lived. She could see that he was greatly troubled.

CHAPTER XLII

BERTHA WAS WALKING the floor of her apartment in a state of distracted bewilderment when Wyeth arrived and rang the bell. She stopped nervously and trembling, turned to look in that direction. She imagined all kinds of things. With the arrival of daylight the thought of what she was to do had become more realistic, and her nerves were at the breaking point. With a suspicion that it was Schiller, perhaps, bringing the bomb she was to toss at the president's wife, she turned presently and nervously crossed to the door and peeped out through the observer. She breathed a sigh of relief when she saw that it was her lover.

She opened the door softly and cried as she did so, her eyes bloodshot and swollen, a fact he noticed the moment she opened the door, which confirmed his suspicion that she was in trouble.

"Oh, Sidney, you," she cried. "Come right in, darling."

"Marie and I had a feeling that you—were in trouble, sweetheart." he said, as she turned to face him. She tried bravely to force a smile through all her unhappiness, but succeeded badly and closing her eyes, swayed a bit. He reached out quickly and caught her and drew her to him and embraced her, whereupon her pent up emotions broke and she began to cry. He led her into the sitting room and placed her on the sofa, then sat down beside her.

"Oh, Sidney, darling," she cried, more emotional than he had ever seen her before. "I'm glad you came, so glad." He placed an arm about her waist and drawing her close, kissed her twice. Turning her face away, she went on.

"Oh, dear, I'm—I'm in trouble, and I'm—so unhappy."

She fell to weeping now, all restraint gone, out of control. He waited until it had spent its force at least temporarily before speaking.

"I was afraid you were, Bertha. When you didn't come to the office I was sure of it. The time has come now, dear, when you need me, and I am here to help you, to comfort you."

For answer she leaned on him and tried to still the misery in her heart.

"I'm in trouble, Sidney, great trouble."

"I know you are, Bertha, and I'm here to help you," he repeated.

"Thank you, darling, but you can't. Nobody can help me."

"As long as there is life there is hope, darling. I'll find a way, for there is a way, in spite of how hopeless it may all seem—now."

"There is no hope for me, Sidney. I've been condemned and soon I—may die. I wish I could die now. I would even—kill myself, but I don't dare to. It is just that—terrible, this what I have been selected to do." She shook her head, hopelessly, her heavy hair down over her shoulders.

"I understand something about what you mean, dear," he said. "I know also, that you don't dare talk; but maybe, Bertha, if you could—just give me some kind of a hint."

"I don't dare do even that, Sidney. I can only say that it has reached its climax. I know that you've known all along that I—I am a—spy, sent here in the beginning to find out all I could and report it. Both my brother and I. But—be—fore I got started actively, I met you. I liked you from the beginning. You were—so understanding, so constructive, and I became interested, more interested in what you were doing than what I had been sent here to try to do. So I was drawn to you by some strange and irresistible force. Then I began to—love you, darling. I grew to love you more and more as the months went by. I prayed in my heart for this terrible war to end so that I could be free and have you, be your dear wife and help you carry on your fine work without feeling that subtle restraint, which has always lurked like an evil spectre in the background. I even permitted myself to become vain and hope that I would escape, and dared build castles in the air about the future with you, darling. And then suddenly, yesterday, at if from out of nowhere came a command. I have been ordered to commit a terrible act. I don't want to, but you understand that I can't refuse. I must attempt it, and that is almost as sure to be my end as it is hoped to be the end of the person I must do it unto. Oh, Sidney, darling, I wish I could die, now, here, in your arms."

She fell into another fit of weeping and rising to her feet walked the floor while he sat there and just looked at her for a time, presently rising to his feet and going over by her. As he paused by her side where she was standing with eyes down and shaking her head slowly and hopelessly, he chanced to glance at the Negro papers, spread out on the table and started as he read about the president's wife coming to the Golden Gate Ball Room.

Like a shot had struck him, he got an idea then and there what it was all about. *Bertha had been ordered to assassinate the president's wife* when she came there. That was what it was all about. She could not, he knew, tell him or admit that that was what she was so upset about—but *he knew now!*

The headlines about it in the papers gave it all away, and the fact that Bertha had the papers, every one of them that carried a headline account announcing the event. Otherwise, he asked himself, why did she have them? She had become suddenly calm. He raised his eyes to see why, and found her glaring with a wild and seemingly faraway hope in her eyes. Slowly she turned those strange eyes to meet his, and whispered.

"There is but one way to save me, Sidney, just one way to—*save me from myself.*"

"What way, Bertha?" he asked.

She reached and laid a hand on him, looked in his direction but saw nothing, her eyes being wild-like and opened so wide until they seemed unnatural.

"You've known all along, from the very beginning that I was a spy. Yet you at no time thought of reporting me as you had every right to do in the interest of your country. I knew all along that you knew too, and I learned to love you more because I knew I could trust you. I've been commanded by the forces who control my destiny, to commit a diabolical deed. I must at least try to do so. It has been so well planned that it might succeed, and I—I don't want it to, Sidney."

She was back to herself again now and tears were again in her eyes.

He placed an arm about her now and drew her close. While she wept on his shoulder, he said:

"What is it, Bertha? What do you want me to do?"

"Report me, Sidney. *Tell your country that I am a Nazi spy and* order my arrest. Have them throw me in jail where they will keep me until this terrible war is over. That is the one way that you can keep me from doing this terrible thing, Sidney."

She wept so now that her distress forced tears to his eyes. He squeezed her to him, and patted her convulsing shoulders.

"Listen, Bertha, and try to control yourself for a little while. I said at the outset that as long as there is life there is hope. You've been ordered to do some terrible act that you can't tell me about. I am not going to report you to the FBI, and I am not going to ask you to try to keep from doing this terrible thing."

She paused to look up at him, strangely. He met her eyes squarely.

"I didn't report you in the beginning because I hoped that right would win out in the end over this wrong mission they had sent you on, but it would have to run its course so that in the end you would have your own self-respect."

"My—my self-respect, what do you mean, Sidney?"

"I mean that if you are permitted to let it run its course and it then failed, you could feel that you had done your best, even though it failed. But if you became weak for your own desires, selfish and a quitter, you would hate yourself all the days of your life ever after."

She lowered her eyes away to think, turned them back and looked at him in a strange and vague sort of way.

"I could play sure and save you by doing as you suggested, and if anything went wrong before this is all over, that would be the better way. But if I did that those secret agents who have commanded you to do this, would know that you had squealed and asked me to do it to save your own skin—and they would rightfully hate you, consider you a quitter—and I don't want these murderers to feel that my darling is a quitter."

"Oh, Sidney, you are so brave," she cried, enthusiastically.

"You've got to see it through, Bertha, and I don't want you to tell me any more than you have, which is nothing, except that you have been commanded to commit a foul deed."

"But Sidney, this all seems—vague and peculiar."

"I intend to prevent you from doing this deed, darling. Prevent you from doing it when the time comes. If you fail, you can feel thereafter that it was not your fault, and will have the satisfaction of knowing that you tried to do your duty, and was prevented. They will be forced to see and feel the same way. Then, after it is over and if I am successful in keeping you from doing this terrible thing, I may turn them in so that they can't go ordering you to do anything else that will risk your dear life and your freedom."

"Oh, Sidney, you are wonderful," she cried and embraced and kissed him tenderly of her own volition. A moment later, however, a frown overspread her face, and she turned her eyes again up to him.

"But Sidney, supposing that—"

"—I should fail?"

"Yes, Sidney. Fail?"

"But I will not fail, Bertha. I have not asked you to tell me what this thing is. I feel that I know and from now until then I will do nothing but try to think your way out of it—and I'll succeed. I've *got* to succeeed, Bertha, can't you understand?"

"You've—*got to* Sidney, because you—love me?"

"Because I love you, Bertha. You mean more to me than all the world put together. I have lived all these years waiting and hoping to meet you somewhere, and then out of the strangest direction you came and since you entered my life, it has all changed and I am happy. I intend to share this happiness on a larger scale and I can only do so if I save you, darling. Now is that not worth doing a great deal for?"

"Oh, darling, I believe you."

"And I want you to forget as much as you can from now until that fatal hour, all about it. But if it does persist in annoying and upsetting you as it has, you're just to think of me and that I am not going *to let you do it!* And I mean that. So the time has come when you have to place your freedom and your future life in my care and trust and leave everything to me."

"Oh, Sidney, my brave and resolute hero. I believe you, I trust you, and now I feel—so much better, sweetheart. It is all strange and I can't understand how, but I will believe as you say and—".

"—go wash that terrible face you're wearing and let me take you to a restaurant and buy you the best steak they will sell. After that, I'll take you to the office where you will resume your work just as though you have not been commanded to do anything—right up until within a few hours of when you are to do it. Now will you believe me and do just that, my own?"

"I will, sweetheart. And now I will go and—take a bath and make myself look again like a human being. Will you kiss this awful face just once, my own, and then sit down and be patient? I shall not keep you waiting long."

"You have never kept me waiting long, Bertha." He kissed her then and she went cheerfully to the bath room and a few moments later he could hear the shower.

Out west in Chicago, in the meantime, Heinrich had completed all arrangements, preparatory to wrecking the Pacific Coast Limited while it crossed the high bridge over the Coon river, with its cargo of high officials of the war department and other innocent travelers, and was quite pleased with the way he had it all planned.

His story about having business in Omaha, and just taking the train to which Watson's car would be attached to be with Watson that far and to bid him good luck when they reached Omaha had gone well with Watson, who was perhaps incapable of even suspicioning what it was all about.

"My cah will be attached to de end ob thu streamliner. So, jes' come on back anytime and I'll take ceh ov yuh," he replied, cheerfully.

Having reserved a seat on the same train for three consecutive nights, starting one night earlier and another one night after the car was to be picked up, when the time came, he took the train the first night with a ticket through to Omaha, with everything in readiness, "just in case."

When the train roared on through the Austin Avenue yards without even slackening speed, he breathed a sigh of relief, slipped off it when it stopped to take on some Pacific coast passengers at Oak Park, and returned to Chicago via the West Side elevated train.

When he got back to Chicago, he called Watson's girl's apartment and confirmed the date to take the party to dinner, to the Regal theatre after, and then to the Club Delysia, for a final and grand good time. He could hear the girl he'd been playing around with, insisting impatiently on talking to him over Watson's shoulder, but he managed his conversation in such a way that he hung up before slow-thinking Watson could get to put her on. He was making a play for high stakes, according to his Fuehrer, so didn't want to begin to act until the time came and it was necessary. He naturally had no interest in the girl beyond his play, so didn't want to be bothered until the show started.

It was the gayest party he had ever staged, everything going off just as he planned and engineered it. Seeming to be drinking as much as they, he was careful not to drink much of anything and when they retired that night, with the rest pretty well stewed, he was as sober as the lord, and woke up early the next morning, looked at the girl sleeping soundly and snoring beside him and heard the alarm go off that Watson had set to awaken him.

Watson awoke when it went off all right, raised up, looked at it sleepily, then turned on his side and went promptly back to sleep. Fifteen minutes later Heinrich got up and going into Watson's bedroom, awakened him.

"Great goodness," cried Watson, sitting up and fully awake. "And me gotta take de biggest white fo'ks in de noo nited States wes' dis mawning'!"

He started to scramble into his clothes when he paused and looked up to see Heinrich standing smiling down on him, chidingly.

"Brother, but how you can sleep," said Heinrich. Watson grinned.

"Tankey, pal. Yuh saved mah life."

"Oh, you'd have awakened in time," said Heinrich, turning to go back to his room, then paused to turn back as Watson called:

"Yeh. When dem white fo'kes called me fum de ya'd's, maybe. Den ole man Giltzow, de sup'ntendent 'ud come out to de ya'd, all de way fum downtown tu gib me 'ell."

Heinrich laughed good naturedly, and waved at him.

"All right, Watson. I have to make the same train myself, so forget about old man Giltzow and catching hell, and chase on over there and be ready to receive your passengers when they arrive."

"I'd bettah be. And since you woke this fool niggah up, I'll be Johnny on de spot."

"Well," said Heinrich, "I'll be up ahead and will be seeing you later."

"Sho, fellah. Sho, sho." cried Watson, cheerfully. "Be sho' tu cum back. I'll be lookin' fo' yuh."

With a smile Heinrich again started for his room, when he was again stopped by Watson's voice:

"And by de way."

Heinrich went back and stuck his head through the door.

"Yes, pal?"

"Don't go to de diner. Try tu git along ontil one thu'ty, den cum back aftuh we leaves Clinton. They'll mostly be thu' den, and we'll have dat end of de cah all to ouhselves, get me?"

"I've got you, Jimmy," said Heinrich, with a big smile. "I'll remember."

"The cah's loaded wid du bes' food, and I mean de bes'."

"I'll bet."

"De bes' drinks."

"You're tempting me, Watson."

"And you and me's gwine eat and drink ob nuthin' but de bes'."

"Solid, boy, solid!"

Both laughed then, and proceeded with their dressing.

At 11:30 A.M. the Pacific Coast Limited pulled out of the Northwestern Station with nobody, perhaps, but Heinrich Schultz, with a time bomb concealed carefully in a small case, within a larger case, aware of his nefarious plot. He planned to take the bomb at the proper time and deposit it in the proper place, somewhere in Watson's car.

The passengers relaxed after the train pulled out of the Station, and those who had traveled on it before, didn't expect it to stop until it reached Clinton, Iowa, on the west bank of the Mississippi, across from Illinois in Iowa. So when Heinrich, expecting and listening anxiously for it to do so, heard the breaks applied and the train slow down when it reached the Austin Avenue yards, he was relieved. People sat up in their seats and wondered what was the matter.

Heinrich smiled and relaxed his nervous tension and anxiety shortly after the train, slowing down to a stop, heard the private car bump the rear of the streamliner, easily, a few moments later, and knew that everything was set. He closed his eyes and visualized an explosion when it reached the center of the high bridge across the Coon River that night, and perhaps the entire train falling and landing in the green waters of the Coon River, one hundred and more feet below.

Such was the state of mind of this student of Adolf Hitler, who had been schooled in ruthlessness and disregard of life, liberty and property, as well as the rights of others, a few years before in Germany.

He made himself patient and shortly after the train crossed into Iowa and pulled out of Clinton, first passenger and freight division on the North-Western, west to Omaha from Chicago, he looked at the little case containing the high explosive time bomb in the larger case. With his story all ready made up to explain to Watson, if and when he looked at it, or inquired why he had brought that back, that it contained great valuables which he was taking in person to one of the big banks in Omaha—and show Watson that it did contain such.

The fact is, he did not place the bomb in the small case before he rose up and strolled back to the car. Instead, he placed certain valuable securities and a substantial amount of currency of large denominations in it and spread them carefully over the top of a false bottom, to make the amount it contained appear much larger than it really was.

His explanation then would be logical; that because of its great value it was obvious that he keep it with him at all times. By taking it back with him at this time, he would be expected to bring it back when he came back again, just before the train reached Boone, and he planned to remain back there until the train left Boone, set the time clock connecting the bomb, and find some way to secrete the missile then go back forward and leave it behind him.

Everything worked out according to plan. As stupid as Watson was, he looked at the case, and Heinrich after a wink and a glance around to see that they were all alone, called him to one side, explained in an undertone and in confidence, regarding the valuables, then showed it to Watson, whose eyes opened in shocked surprise. Thereupon he agreed with enthusiasm that he was doing the proper thing to bring them with him and offered to lock them up for him while he was back there. Heinrich shook his head and declined to let him, whereupon Watson stepped to one side and opened a locker and pointed to the inside. With a view to perhaps secreting the missile that night in such a place, Heinrich looked in, agreed that it was a good place, but that his instructions from the big Chicago bank was to keep them in his sight and never let it out, so he hoped that Watson would understand.

Watson said he did, assuring him, at the same time, however, that nobody had keys to the locker but himself, and displayed the key from among a large ring of keys. All of which Heinrich noted with ulterior purposes, and was more than usually cheerful during the big meal Watson had prepared, and the fine drinks he served afterwards.

When Heinrich went forward about two thirty, promising at Watson's insistence to get back around seven thirty that night and remain as long as he wanted to, Heinrich was satisfied and visualized success when the time came.

Heinrich checked the time table carefully as the train streaked through the late afternoon like a long gray phantom, west from Ames, through Marshalltown and Dennison and neared Boone. With the small case, containing the bomb this time and the small clock, with the valuables in a long fat wallet in his inside coat pocket which pocket was deeper than the usual such pocket, permitting the wallet to rest securely, without protruding much or slipping out when he bent over too much.

He played his cards during the evening meal with extreme care, urged Watson to drink freely, which Watson did, and was almost "high" when somebody called him to the front of the car to perform some service. They ordered some drinks and while Watson was up there, Heinrich saw his chance and secreted the bomb in the locker which Watson had showed him so profusely. Some soiled towels were visible, laying on the floor, so Heinrich spread these over it, managed to close it, return to his seat, and was reading at something when Watson came back, excused himself, prepared the drinks and went forward to serve them.

By this time the train had reached Boone and when Watson came back and went into the pantry to prepare another order, Heinrich saw his chance. He went around and sticking his head into the pantry told Watson that he had gotten friendly with an *Ofay gal* up front who was getting off at Omaha, and that he was about to *make her* and planned to have her spend the night with him in Omaha, so was going to go up front, kid her along for a few minutes, and come back—after a while.

Women were always a language that Watson understood, and "getting next" to them was something he understood still better, so he laughed and agreed for Heinrich to go up there and *stall* her, but to be sure and come back soon.

Heinrich could see that it would take a couple of minutes to complete the order, so pretending to leave, he dared stop at the closet, lift the infernal machine from its hiding place, set the clock, replace it and hurried forward just as the train was getting underway.

According to the calculation he had made when checking on it out of Boone before, the train should reach somewhere near the center of the bridge in exactly twelve minutes. And he had set the clock accordingly, so when he left the private car, everything was arranged and in exactly twelve fatal minutes the bomb would explode—and God help all those in the car, and possibly on the entire train. For Heinrich had also observed that the locker in which the missile of destruction was hidden, was directly over the rear trucks of the car, and the concussion should throw the trucks from the tracks, and if so, wrecking the train would be inevitable.

He sat down in his seat, but kept his eyes on his wrist watch, his ears alert. His escape all depended on the train slowing down when it approached the bridge, which he was sure that it would do, for he had been told repeatedly, while discussing the high bridge, that no trains ever crossed it at top speed. The railroad company considered it dangerous, so he counted on the train slowing down and was relieved when he heard the brakes being applied, so got up out of his seat as if he was going to the men's room. He passed one of the attendants as he was leaving, who glanced at him carelessly, and Heinrich slipped around the bends in the car, into the vestibule, over by the glass door and looked through it out into the gray night. A full moon was shining and he could discern that they had reached the long graded stretch that led up to the eastern end of the bridge, and that he would have to jump off within one or two minutes, otherwise, after they reached the bridge it would be dangerous. He might even lose his life, or be injured severely. He looked at his watch. In three minutes the bomb would go off. So opening the vestibule door, he looked down, swung his body outward, maneuvered so that he closed the door as he went out and tumbled on the soft dirt grade and rolled safely to the bottom of it, perhaps twenty to thirty feet below and got to his feet, with only a few bruises for his trouble. The train, disappearing in the night like a grey ghost, was rolling toward the bridge and he was able to keep it in sight until he had crawled back to the tracks, and even then he could see it faintly and heard it when it hit the bridge.

We now return to Watson, who was preparing an order as Heinrich left. No sooner had Heinrich closed the door of the car on the way out than that Watson spilled something on the floor and annoyed, thought of something to dry it, and the soiled towels in the locker promptly suggested themselves to him. He left the pantry, and going to the locker, reached down and picked up a hand full of towels—and exposed the case which he knew, on seeing it, belonged to Heinrich. He paused in surprise, looked at it, then picked it up and wondered at its weight.

"Wonduh what this thing is doin' heah?" he said to himself, and turned to look in the direction Heinrich had gone. Then he attempted to open it and found it was locked and became more curious still. He shook it and could seem to feel a vibration. Became more curious. Raised it to his ear and could hear the faint ticking of the clock. He lowered it and started, and began to use his imagination.

A thousand things went through his mind then in a few fleeting seconds.

"*Who was Heinrich Schultz!*" he asked himself, wonderingly. "*Where did he come from?*" He grew excited now, suspicious. "Where did he, a Negro, get all the money he had been spending, *where!*" In all his life he had never met a Negro who seemed to have as much sense as Heinrich Schultz, and that *ever had any money!* Money to spend like water, to give away until in the short time he had run around with him in Chicago, he had spoiled the girls and made them feel that life was a fairy land and Heinrich was a man from heaven and they would have to do nothing any more, but eat, drink, buy clothes with the money he gave them and be merry!

Such a procedure was not for Negroes and never had been.

"Now he comes back heah and leaves this *case of valuables,* and instead of a lot of money in it, it's locked and ah heahs a clock tickin' inside."

Then, of a sudden, through his thick skull it occurred to him that it might be attached to a bomb, a bomb to blow him and that car and that train and everybody on it to hell a comin'!

"Great goodness alive," he cried, half aloud. "It's a bumb. It's a bumb and Schultz uz a spy, maybe a Natsi spy, and he lef dat thing heah to blow us up!"

He thought of the train conductor. The thing to do was to call him, cry out loud, tell the people on the train, on the car — tell everybody! Then as quickly as all that suggested itself to him, as quickly as he realized that any such thing would be imprudent. Meantime, that clock was going, ticking on and on and soon, maybe any second, it would explode that "bumb" and —

"Lemme git rida dis ting," he now cried more soberly. He started towards a window, but realized as quickly that the car was air conditioned and he couldn't raise windows. He'd have to break it and throw it out the window and he drew the case back—and decided very quickly, that when it struck the window it *would sure* explode. He was in a terrible quandary. *What would he do?* He looked around him in a panic, all the while he could seem to hear that clock, tick, tock, tick tock, ticking on to destruction! Of a sudden he remembered that the car was attached to the end of the train and that all he had to do was to open the rear door, walk onto the vestibule, up to the steel, latticed gate and heave that thing overboard—then hear it go off, but far away from the car and him!

He went into action that split second. He stole through the back door, crossed to the gate and looked over it. Found himself looking down into Coon River Valley, a mile below it seemed to him, in his intense excitement, for they had reached the bridge and were nearly half way across by this time.

With a swing and a heave, ho, he swung it clear and watched it hurtle through space toward the river below and was still able to see it, although it was just a mere speck, when it suddenly went off with a deafening roar, so loud and so powerful that it seemed to shake the heavy train and almost blinded and deafened him, as it did so.

Hurrying down the track toward the bridge, with his ears wide open, for he knew the time was near, Heinrich paused suddenly and looked at his wrist watch, saw its hand reach the fatal second, and registered great satisfaction as he heard the bomb go off and shook his head with evil satisfaction when he could feel that everything had gone *according to plan!* Yet, but had it?

Listening, his ears keen, he did not hear any after effect; that roaring and tearing and grinding that should have followed as the train fell, car by car from the bridge and tumbled into the waters of the river below. Why?

He was puzzled, then started with a new realization. He heard the explosion all right, but now as he recalled it, it hadn't seem to come exactly from the direction he was expecting it; as it should have, straight down those tracks. It had come from below the tracks, far below. But why?

To satisfy his curiosity, which was tensely aroused by now, he ran down the tracks to the foot of the long, high bridge and pausing, could see clear across it, and saw the rails all the way across — and there was nothing amiss anywhere.

"Well I'll be damned," cried Heinrich. "I'll be God damned!"

The Pacific Coast Limited had hit the long, level stretch on the other side of the Coon River bridge now, the stretch that led into Council Bluffs across the Missouri River, just east of Omaha, and the Diesel Engineer had pushed the throttle forward and the Streamliner was doing fully 100 miles an hour and would keep it up until within ten miles of Council Bluffs, after which the train would have to cross another bridge before rolling into the Union Station at Omaha.

The explosion had naturally caused a world of excitement. Everybody was asking everybody else, what had happened, how it happened, where it came from, and who was responsible. Conjecture, followed conjecture. The consensus of opinion was that a Nazi spy had tried to wreck the train as it crossed the high Coon River Bridge but had failed somehow.

Nobody as we know, knew the truth but Watson. Even a stupid Negro can become very sensible and *close-mouthed* when it might be necessary for his own safety and salvation. Watson knew that if he talked this time, he would have to say more. He would most surely be relieved of his duties at Omaha, taken up town, thrown into jail and, questioned, and cross questioned by about everybody, including a gang of newspaper reporters, and in the course of this all, most likely be struck, maybe beat up, because he couldn't tell any more than what he knew, which they might not choose to believe. If he didn't talk, say anything, nobody would suspect him. For nobody had. He didn't know that he would be about the last person that suspicion would be directed to.

All Watson did was to think. He was surprised at himself. He hadn't realized before that he was capable of doing so much thinking, deep thinking, and then he talked with himself. And his conversation to himself ran about like this:

"I ain't never met no niggah, come tu think ob it, lak Henry." They had given up trying to call him Heinrich shortly after meeting him in Chicago, as it was too hard for them to say. "Nevah as long as I've libed. Yet I nevuh taught nuthin' 'bout hit ontil I seed dat bumb. Lawdy mussy, I ain't nevuh been so close to bein' killed, all because ah mus' open mah big mouf an' talk lak a fool.

"An' Henry comes back heah, eats mah food, drinks mah liquah, kids me long—den' leabes dat ting tu blow eveh body up, whew!

"Dat's whut day's been callin' sabotage, and Henry was sabotaging. Henry was a spy, all right, nuthin' but a Natsi spy, and I done tell 'im eveting. Open mah big mouf when eve' whah dey has signs, 'don't talk,' keep yuh mouf shet tight, don't talk.' And dis niggah talked! Umph! I tell Henry eve'ting and dat's how Henry come tu know and planned accawdingly, umph! Ah'm jest a big mouf niggah, wid no sense a tall.

"But when dey says 'don't talk,' I taught dey meant don't talk tu white fo'kes, not tu niggahs, and taught Henry was jes' a putty niggah, jes annudder niggah lak mah se'f. I taught, puhaps, dat he'd done stole a lotta money and got away wid hit.

"'Cose, in a way, it's de white fo'kes fault. Dey play us niggahs down so dat we don't have a chance to eber be smaht. We'se always got tu act a fool to please dem an' try tu make dem laf. We'se acted a fool so long, mos' ob us, anyhow, ontil we ain't got much sense no mo—'specially when it comes tu sumpin' lak Henry was out to pull.

"Well, dey say de bigges' fool is de one dat keeps on bein' one. Don't ceh ef ah has been actin' lak one, and openin' mah big mouf and tellin' mah guts. I got sense enough when tu quit; tu keep it shet and stay free, 'cause I sho don't 'tend to be thrown into no jail and mauled around and git a whole lotta publicity. So ah'm *fugittin'* ebe'ting, an' tendin' tu mah own little bizness fum now on."

He stood up then and yawned and stretched, and concluded the conversation with himself, with these words, spoken softly, lowly:

"Ah ain't seen nuthin'; ah ain' hea'd nuthin'; an' ah don't know nuthin'," and so concluding, Watson went about his duties.

CHAPTER XLIII

BY KEEPING NEAR BERTHA, placating her in an almost endless number of ways, so that he was able to keep her mind off what she was scheduled to do, Wyeth managed to keep hope alive in her breast, during those days that led up to the fatal night, or the night that was to prove fatal, perhaps, to millions of people all over the world. Only at night when he was not and could not, of course, be with her, did she become discouraged and verge on panic, and often fail to get the proper sleep.

Schiller and other agents of Von Barwig came to her apartment on several occasions at night during this time to check on her, study her and see if she was likely to break under the strain of thinking of it. But as has been explained on occasion, many times before, Bertha Schultz was a brave girl, with plenty of will power and able to direct her movements at will, and so far as they were able to see, every time they called, she was standing up well, no threat of cracking under the strain and that they could count on her to be strong and ready when the time came.

During these visits they gave her little peace. Over and over again they sought to impress upon her the necessity of doing it; that it was for the cause of their dear Fuehrer, who was battling bravely to the inevitable end of the war he had imposed upon the world, which, of course, was not the way they put it, so it was the least she could do, when theirs was such a great opportunity, to commit the act.

Nobody, they told her, but stupid Americans would permit their first Lady to go around the country, exposed to such hazards, without a group of agents to surround and keep anybody from getting near enough to her to do what Bertha would be able to the night she came to Harlem.

"It's just like Heinrich told me. They don't take the Negro

seriously, and even if the President's wife was usually protected by agents, they'd probably leave them in Washington when she went to speak to Negroes, for Negroes wouldn't be smart enough to plan anything against anybody, much less the president's wife."

"So their stupidity is our opportunity, and it's all up to you, Bertha."

They succeeded in purchasing seats for the occasion which was in the interest of the Red Cross. They applied early and got her a seat, on the aisle, front row, which according to their check up, should put her close enough to the first Lady, to be able to reach her by rising to her feet and tossing the bomb twenty or thirty feet at most, and felt sure that they would be able to get it over.

For fear that his plan to keep her in sight might possibly fail at the last moment, Wyeth was inclined on more than one occasion, to report the matter to the FBI and play safe. Then he considered sending a telegram asking that they advise the First lady not to come, all of which he dismissed and finally decided to take a chance by keeping close to Bertha from the moment she left the office that Tuesday until the president's wife had both come and gone.

He observed that she was extremely nervous and agitated all that day and when he offered to drive her home at closing time, and she let him, he was relieved, for once he saw her enter her apartment, at least the building, he was sure of keeping close check on her movements from there on.

Arriving at the apartment, he simply let her out, but observed when he went around the car to open the door to do so, Schiller's large, green limousine parked a block away across the street and knew that they were waiting for her and watching him, perhaps at the same time. He bid her goodby, whereupon she looked up at him and her sad distracted eyes spoke more, and appealed to him more, than any words she could have spoken. "Just a few hours more," they seemed to say, "and it will all be over, for better, for worse," and both sighed as he left her.

He drove by the big car with eyes straight ahead but saw as he did so, that only the driver at the wheel was sitting in it, but saw him glance toward a nearby tavern and surmised correctly that the others were there waiting for the driver to advise them that Bertha had reached her apartment.

Wyeth drove around the block and coming from an opposite direction, parked in the shadows of some buildings, reaching the spot in time to see Schiller and two other agents cross the street and enter the apartment building and estimated that when they came down, they would have Bertha with them.

He guessed correctly, for about thirty minutes later one of the trio appeared and beckoned the driver in the waiting car to drive up to the entrance, which he did. Immediately the car stopped, the others, with Bertha accompanying them, left the building, crossed the sidewalk, and entered the car which drove away.

Wyeth followed at a safe distance and was glad that it had gotten dark while they were sitting so that they might not be able to see that he was following.

They drove to the ballroom in a roundabout fashion, crossing the Harlem river, driving over across Grand Concourse, then turning to the left, backtracked and came through the underpass below Grand Concourse, and crossed the 149th street bridge, then south and parked in Lenox Avenue, two blocks below the hall.

Wyeth, while this was going on, parked across the street from the ballroom, hurried across the street, presented his ticket and, entering the ball room, secreted himself as best he could and watched the main entrance. He was relieved after a time to see Bertha enter, present her ticket at the door, and heard the usher tell her where the seat was, and that another usher would meet her near there and show her to the seat. She thanked him and went that way, followed at a safe distance by Wyeth, who had purchased a dozen tickets, scattered all up near the front so that he could pick one nearest to where Bertha would be seated, so that he could get to her more quickly and easily when the time came.

She was seated almost in front of the speakers' platform, on an aisle, near where the First Lady was expected to address the Negroes from. Wyeth, after checking through his tickets hurriedly, chose the one nearest her seat which also happened to be on the same aisle on which Bertha was seated, a half dozen rows behind her, on the same side, and where he could watch her without her being able to see him, unless she turned almost around and searched for him carefully, which she would not likely do.

There was plenty of music and as the people poured into the place there were loud noises everywhere, which pleased him, for then he could watch without being noticed, and possibly move up to her when she was ready to toss the bomb, without also being noticed.

It was shortly after nine P. M., with the hall packed and people standing all around the walls and in the rear when, by the loud handclapping and whistling, he knew that the president's wife had arrived.

She appeared, presently, being brought to the stage from the rear, and the crowd went wild, whistling and clapping with enthusiasm. Before she could be seated, a lone line of people were permitted to file by her and shake her hand. She smiled continuously and greeted everybody cheerfully, looking out over the audience at intervals to bow and smile until she, a very homely woman, seemed at a distance, beautiful.

After a long list of speakers, who served to bore the audience and make them very impatient, she was finally introduced and began to speak — and the tragic moment when she would continue to live or be blown to atoms, neared. Fortunately, the audience was respectful, and gave her their undivided and uninterrupted attention, and every word could be heard distinctly. So distinctly in fact, that when Wyeth heard a cough, and another person coughed in another direction, then still another elsewhere, and Bertha glanced around, and then started to open the big hand bag, containing the missile, Wyeth knew the time had arrived for him to act promptly and expeditiously, and he did! Leaning down a bit he rose to his feet and hurried to Bertha's side and before he leaned over her to interrupt, he caught a glimpse of the round, dark object, and then laid a hand on her arm nearest him and on the aisle which was to her right. She started, and looked up at him wild eyed. Leaning over her as he grasped her right arm like it was in a vise, but not before she closed the hand bag with a snap and caught her breath.

"Pardon, Bertha, but word has been received that your brother is seriously injured, possibly killed. Please come with me."

She said no word, perhaps realizing that Wyeth had come at the psychological moment to save her from herself as he said he would. She rose to her feet and permitted him to, all the while grasping her right arm under which she carried the bag, holding the bomb, lead her all the way to the rear, through the lobby, across the street, where he placed her in his car. Going around to the driver's side, he got in the car and drove away.

They had no more than gotten started, however, when the street and seeming all Harlem, broke into a wild and roaring pandemonium of noise, with a single cry on everybody's lips:

"Armistice!"

Then, as if from every throat came forth the same word, "Armistice! Armistice! Armistice! The war is over, Armistice!"

Bertha grasped his arm and drawing close to him, cried:

"What's the matter? What has happened?"

For answer, the cries continued:

"Armistice, Armistice, the war is over, Armistice!"

"Armistice," she repeated now after them. "What do they mean, Sidney?"

"That the war is over, Bertha. There was a hint about it on the radio shortly after we left the office."

"But," she exclaimed.

"Germany has surrendered, dear. It is all over."

"Over?" she repeated, blankly. "Germany, surrendered, oh, no!"

"It was inevitable, dear. It could end no other way. The war is over, Bertha, and you are—free—at last."

"Free?" she repeated, still blankly.

"Yes, Bertha, free. . . ."

"But, my—brother. You said—"

"—had been injured, was maybe, dead. That was only a stall. I was watching you. I heard the coughs, saw you open the bag, and felt the time had come to save you, dear."

"Oh. Then that was how you planned it?"

"I was terribly frightened. Was afraid I might miss. Then see what would have happened? The president's wife assassinated and the war over. Aren't you glad I—came, Bertha?"

"Of course, Sidney. *So* glad. But I am all bewildered. My head is in a whirl. I'm wondering and asking if I'm awake, or is this just one terrible dream and that I'll awaken presently and find myself back there in that hall, with Hans Schiller and Von Barwig and all the others scattered around, waiting, watching and urging me on. Please Sidney, pinch me. Pinch me hard."

He did so, and she asked him to repeat it three times. At the end.

"Yes, I'm awake." They were beside a small park now and he drove into the shade of some trees and stopped. They were all alone except for the noise of whistles, and bells and every conceivable noise, and could still hear the shouts of, "Armistice, Armistice, the war is over, Armistice."

"It will take me a long time to recover from this night, Sidney. No one will ever know how much it cost me, those waiting hours, picturing, thinking, picturing, dreading, crying out like a soul lost in the wilderness, but always behind me those—"

"—vandals, urging you on, crying in your ear, 'Heil Hitler!' Thanks to God the use of that phrase is over."

"I wonder what's happened to him?"

"Abdicated, maybe, if he could, taking Mussolini with him. I have a picture of them fleeing to the Argentine. Maybe Goering and Goebbels and Doenitz and Himmler—all who could escape, with them, across the Atlantic to the Argentine, into the wilds of Patagonia. Or may be by submarine to Japan. Then, perhaps, they are all dead, who knows."

"Who knows, Sidney." And now she turned to him, her face lit up with a heavenly smile.

"And you and I, Sidney, by the grace of God, we still—live."

"We still live, Bertha," said he, turning and placing an arm about her soft body.

"Isn't it beautiful, Sidney, that we still live and that I am—free?"

"Free, darling, to—marry me, Bertha?"

"To marry you, Sidney. Oh, how much I want to."

"Do you, really, Bertha, now that you are free?"

"As quickly as we can, darling. If you want me, I'll marry you tomorrow, only one promise I ask you to make?"

"Anything, my sweet."

"That you will take me on our honeymoon off there to the farm you founded and had to lose because you were reduced and sad and helpless, but which you have bought back and which I know you will keep until you have died, until after, perhaps, we have both died. But now I want you to take me there, Sidney. Will, you, dear?"

"I will, precious."

"Then—kiss me, Sidney."

THE END

AFTERWORD

SINCE SO MANY PEOPLE who have read advance copies of the foregoing story have inquired as to what became of Edrina, who dropped out near the middle of the story, I have decided to tell them, as well as others who will, perhaps, be as curious.

Shortly after her sensational hit in Mantan's show, she was contacted by one Louie Epstein, who opened one of the finest night clubs in Harlem, and engaged Edrina to do the "shake" as his star attraction. Opening with a fanfare, the club got off to a great start and threatened to cut in so heavily on the business of the older night spots that the owners, gangsters mostly, called a council of war and went into action immediately, storming and breaking up Epstein's place so completely until it left him dizzy. Furthermore, they ordered him to "clear out" or be—*rubbed out*.

In Los Angeles shortly after, Epstein reopened a closed night spot on Central Avenue and billed Edrina as the sensational dancer from New York as his star attraction. He opened with a great fanfare—and closed a few nights later, the biggest flop to ever hit Los Angeles.

Somebody had beat Epstein to the punch. "Shake" dancing had already been introduced to Los Angeles, done by young and beautiful things, Hollywood style, who out shook and out twisted Edrina so completely that it made her seem antiquated and old. She met and became acquainted shortly after with Cliff Welch, struggling actor, but a wonderful Ethiopian type, tall and straight, with fine features, and whom she took up with immediately. Persuaded him to come to New York where she got Donald Howard to attempt a revival of "Old Man Evil", with Welch as the star. Welch demonstrated great acting ability, but the piece just didn't catch on and failed as completely and miserably, as it had when it opened originally.

Meanwhile, Edrina, still nursing stage ambitions, "lucked" into a good role in a new show which opened on Broadway, made a great hit for a few weeks, due it was said, with the exception of Tobacco Road, to the fact that it was the dirtiest ever offered. Too dirty to stay on 42nd Street for long, even. Was booked to play Boston who sent a reviewer—who told them, after seeing it, not to come. They jumped to Chicago instead, where after one week's run, the Mayor advised them to "take it somewhere else", so they closed.

Some time later, Welch was selected to play the greatest role ever portrayed by a Negro in a picture, an adaptation from a stage play with a colored cast, that had run five years. The producers were said to have paid the highest price for it ever paid up to that time for the screen rights to anything. Cliff Welch jumped into nation-wide notoriety overnight and was shipped off to Los Angeles in a blaze of glory, carrying Edrina, who claimed to be his wife, with him. Immediately they returned to New York, however, Welch took up with a young and more beautiful thing—and declared he never married Edrina. Beaten, Edrina returned to Louisville.

Calling on her while he and Bertha were exploiting his books in Louisville, Wyeth found her living with Arthur again and sewing for a living. She admitted to him, sadly, that she had never divorced Arthur, and that she had "worked" him for the divorce money and all the other monies that he had given her. Wyeth smiled and thought of Bertha, to whom he was engaged at the time and later married and as we write these lines, are in New York living together happily as husband and wife.

OSCAR MICHEAUX, New York City, N. Y., October 1st, 1944.